JOPLIN'S GHOST

ALSO BY TANANARIVE DUE

The Black Rose

My Soul to Keep

The Between

The Living Blood

Freedom in the Family

The Good House

TANANARIVE DUE

JOPLIN'S GHOST

ATRIA BOOKS

new york   london   toronto   sydney

ATRIA BOOKS

1230 Avenue of the Americas
New York, NY 10020

ISBN-13: 978-0-7434-4903-8
ISBN-10:   0-7434-4903-7

Library of Congress Cataloging-in-Publication Data
Due, Tananarive, 1966–
Joplin's ghost / Tananarive Due.
p. cm.
1. Joplin, Scott, 1868–1917—Fiction. 2. Composers—Fiction. 3. Musicians—Fiction. I. Title.
PS3554.U3143J66 2005
813'.54—dc22
2005048207

First Atria Books hardcover edition September 2005

10 9 8 7 6 5 4 3 2 1

ATRIA BOOKS is a trademark of Simon & Schuster, Inc.

For information regarding special discounts for bulk purchases,
please contact Simon & Schuster Special Sales at
1-800-456-6798 or business@simonandschuster.com.

Manufactured in the United States of America

To my new son,

Jason Kai Due-Barnes

and

To Jan Hamilton Douglas

1939–2002

Musician and educator—

Curator of the Scott Joplin House—

for telling me about the ghost

If at night while passin' a graveyard

You shake with fear the most,

Just step a little faster forward,

Before you see a ghost.

SCOTT JOPLIN, *Treemonisha*

"We often dream

without the least suspicion of unreality:

'Sleep hath its own world,'

and it is often as lifelike as the other."

DIARY OF LEWIS CARROLL

What we play is life.

LOUIS ARMSTRONG

JOPLIN'S GHOST

PRELUDE: A PIANO

I.

1917

The new arrival wheeled himself through the day room of Manhattan State Hospital on Ward's Island, whispering to his dead wife, who always walked beside him. The man had outlived one wife and his baby girl— *pure bad luck,* his first wife had called him. His second wife, Freddie, was the only one of the dead who still enjoyed his company.

He was talking to her, as he often did, about the stage set he was going to build as soon as he was able: murals of cloud banks, majestic live oaks and a sea of ripening cornstalks. Talking to Freddie was like walking onto the stage itself, standing in the stare of a footlight. The light filled him with wonder, and wonder was hard to come by these days.

But Freddie's voice interrupted him so loudly that he wondered why the droop-jawed attendant in the doorway didn't call for them to hush that racket near so many insane and dying.

There it is, Scott, Freddie said, quivering his ear. *There—do you see?*

Scott Joplin gazed around the room, where the streaked windows invited in an awful dead winter sun that stole more than it gave. Institutional wooden chairs circled a scuffed old table that offered two checkerboards but no checkers, beside a Graphophone with a working motor but no needle to play the cylinders. A sobbing younger man sat cross-legged on the floor, his nest of privates in plain view from a hollow in his thin, urine-stained gown. Why would Freddie wrest him away from his beautiful setting to bring him back to this lunatic's meeting hall?

Do you see it? Freddie, as always, was persistent.

Then, he did see it: An upright piano stood against the far wall. Scott's eyes had missed it before because it was in a shadowed corner, nearly invisible in the room's bland light. It was his rosewood Rosen-kranz, the piano he had found in the alleyway when he could still stand and walk. The piano he had played for Freddie during her dying days. Scott blinked, sure it was a trick of his imagination. One always must be on guard against one's imagination, he remembered. "Did you do this somehow, Freddie?" Scott said. At Bellevue, his last home, he'd been forced to live without a piano within reach for the first time in memory. But here he was in a new place—a worse place, one step closer to obliv-ion—and his own piano was waiting for him.

Another hallucination, then. It wasn't the first, and wouldn't be his last, or so his doctors said. Every day held another bizarre surprise. But this hallucination was more stubborn than most. Scott flopped his arms against the wheels of his wheelchair, making slow progress across the room, and the piano remained in place. Closer, now. And closer again.

"I'll be damned," he said, panting from his effort.

Scott reached out his trembling hand. Although his wrist dangled as if it were broken, he was able to press a single key. High G. No halluci-nation could sound so sweet.

The single, delicate note awoke the memory of being at Lessie Mae's on Main Street in Sedalia, waiting quietly in the wings while Happy Eddie or Mo the Show clowned on the piano with acrobatic fervor for the hooting crowd. Those boys played like carnival performers, drawing men's purposeful eyes away from bold cleavage and half-empty glasses of whiskey. When it was Scott's turn to play, Lessie Mae always waved at him with her damp pink handkerchief from behind the cash register, her mark of approval. *Go on, Scotty—TEACH 'em, professor!*

When he played, the carnival ended. A concert began.

"Music's swell. You play?" the sanitarium attendant said to Scott.

Scott nodded slowly. He did everything slowly now. "Used to," he said. His voice was a sick old man's, and he wasn't yet forty-nine. He couldn't always remember his age, but the sight of the burnished piano had bright-ened his mind. Brightened every part of him.

"Go on ahead and take five minutes, then. They say a lady donated it to the hospital in a patient's name. Mind you don't break it."

Break it! That was a stupid thing to say. *The woman who sent it was my wife, you fool. Don't you know who I am?* Scott thought. But that was the point, wasn't it? He was the only one who knew, and the occasional ability to forget was the only part of his illness he enjoyed. Lottie *had* said she'd have a surprise for him when she came to see him this Friday, but she'd never said she was sending the piano after him. God bless Lottie again.

But this piano would have followed you whether Lottie sent it or not, Scott thought, and such thoughts didn't disturb him the way they used to. Accepting the state of things had made his days easier. The Rosenkranz would follow him anywhere he went. He had found the Rosenkranz in the alley and wiped it clean with his own hands, and the Rosenkranz wouldn't forget.

"I think I will play," Scott said. His tongue was no longer useful, and his words had sounded like *ayethinnniwillplayyyy,* a mouthful of oatmeal.

He hadn't let anybody except Lottie hear him play a piano in two years, since that show in D.C. where they had practically pushed him on the stage. What could he have done? *Sounded like a little child.* That's what he heard Eubie Blake said.

"Yeah—I'll p-play." He was excited now.

Scott's wheelchair was too low for him to reach the keyboard comfortably, so he hoisted himself into the mismatched chair at the piano's knees, another labor that took his breath. The attendant steadied him, but Scott had moved out of his chair by himself, so he *wasn't* helpless. For a moment, Scott felt bewildered as he stared at his hands, shivering claws against the keys. His skin didn't smell right either—urine and talcum and something else buried beneath it all, something sickly that could only be Death. That smell was everywhere here.

"Do you know 'I'm in Love with the Mother of My Best Girl'?" the attendant said. "I love that one. It's a hoot."

Scott nodded, but only to silence him. Anything he played was sure to be unrecognizable. The Rosenkranz was not a forgiving piano; he'd learned that the first night they were reunited. But he would play, if only because Lottie wanted him to. Small solace was better than none at all.

Habit took Scott's hands to a natural pose, and his fingers plunged, striking the opening notes. The music plodded like old honey hugging the bottom of the jar, but he was shocked his fingers remembered how to move at his bidding at all. *Maybe I CAN play a tune or two—*

Scott's middle finger slipped, curdling the melody with a B-natural in the second measure. He cringed, playing on, but his piano didn't offer him any music—only awful, mind-rending noise.

You coldhearted trickster, Scott thought, remembering the old conjurer from the train who had celebrated the chance to curse him with his fate all those years ago. *Are you and your master happy with what you've reduced me to?*

Scott let out a soundless moan, suddenly striking his hand against the keys so hard that the ragged edge of a keytop snagged his pinky, biting into his tender flesh. Droplets of Scott's warm, runny blood marked the piano keys with red fingerprints. Scott was so consumed in pain—most of it in places people couldn't see—that he had no senses left to notice something so trifling as torn skin. *But you don't mind, do you? You know the taste of blood already, don't you, my old friend?* The Rosenkranz had been soiled with blood the day he found it in the alley. If only he had recognized a bad omen when he saw one, he thought. He had been cursed all along!

Scott's lips parted to release a moan. His head drooped, suddenly too heavy to carry, and tears splashed from the tip of his nose to the piano keys, seeping between them, turning his blood pink and dampening his useless fingers. If he could choose his time and place to die, he had found it. *Take me, whatever your price, and let my soul rest here.* He prayed to anyone who would hear him.

Something made Scott look up, interrupting his tears. His tall, lovely girl-bride stood beside him, half-shrouded in misty light. Freddie had not shown herself to him since his confinement to this wretched place. My God! Could she be an emissary from the Hereafter? Was his prayer answered so quickly?

"Freddie?" he said, peering more closely at his beloved. Freddie's face was always dreamlike to him, in the way his dreams were often spare of details. Scott felt her spirit near him, yet he could not quite see the woman he remembered hidden in the light.

"I'm here, Scott." Her voice was not in his ear, this time, but from her lips.

"T-Take me with you." He couldn't even climb to his feet to go to her. She would have to carry him wherever he was going next.

"I'm sorry, Scott. I can't," she said. After all these years, now it was

Freddie who sounded reasonable, and he had become rash. Freddie glided closer, until she stood directly over him. His nostrils longed for her scent, and he thought he smelled chrysanthemums. He tried to reach for her, but his arms failed to move, useless.

"Who're you talkin' to, Uncle?" the attendant called from across the room, where he was pushing a mop in halfhearted circles. "If you're not gonna treat that piano with respect, don't play it at all. Bang on it again like that, and you're goin' to your room."

Do you see what it's come to, Freddie? I'm treated like a child, as if I've never lived in the world. I've vanished before my eyes. How can any man endure this curse of obsolescence?

"F-Freddie . . ." he begged, struggling to be understood. "Take me."

Freddie's head shook back and forth, kind but firm. "Do you want me to help you play?"

"Yes," he said, relieved. Death was best, but playing would give him a moment's respite. "Yes, I w-want to play."

Freddie leaned over him, her gentle warmth draping his shoulder. She took one of his gnarled hands into hers, then the other, and raised them back to their berth on the piano keys. When she touched him with those light, cool hands, Scott felt an ugly premonition seize his frame, a future memory that made him pull his hands away. Freddie was visiting him from somewhere so far away that he couldn't calculate what or where it might be—but Freddie was only meant to visit. Mingling their hands on this bloodied piano would be a terrible burden on her soul, imprisoning her here. His dear girl deserved to be free.

"Freddie . . . wait," he said, the most selfless words he had ever spoken.

"*Shhhh,*" Freddie said, and her fingers slipped inside of his as if he were a hollow glove. The power of her youth coursed through him, electric. "Play, Scott. Use my hands to play."

Before Scott's amazed eyes, his fingers webbed apart, stretching. He wiggled them all, witnessing the return of an amazing limberness he had forgotten in these years of horror. Scott gasped, tears springing. "Dear heart . . . how . . . ?"

"Play, Scott. *Play.*" Her urgency told him he didn't have much time. Already, Freddie's voice was more coarse than he remembered, someone else's altogether.

Scott played.

The first piece that came to his eager fingers was the one he composed for Freddie in his worst hours of mourning, his dignified waltz in a flowing *cantabile* that captured his heart's song like no other. Her offered it to Freddie again now, with exaltation instead of grief.

"That one's my favorite, Scott," Freddie whispered, as he had hoped she would.

Scott hated to rush through the waltz's *andante* finale, but so many pieces awaited! How could he forsake his dearest and most loathsome child? Perspiration sprang to Scott's forehead as he played "Maple Leaf Rag" in the manner it deserved, crowning himself the song's master again for the first time in years. His joy made him breathless. His heart, which he thought had died, raced to the syncopated melodies cascading like fall leaves from his nimble fingers. The piece made his feet twitch, longing to dance. "Maple Leaf" erased his sorrow, even now.

He would have this played at his funeral! He would make Lottie promise.

"That's *old*. I'm tired of that one, Uncle," the attendant said.

When Scott finished "Maple Leaf," he played the Overture from *Treemonisha* next—leaping from his most overly praised creation to his most ignored. This time, the effect upon him was even greater: Scott's daydreams sprang to life in the music. Suddenly, he and Freddie were in his cornfield, beneath an infinite afternoon sky, with merry circles of dancers. So many familiar faces! Here was dear Louis, in his Parisian coat and white Stetson. And his brother Will, stepping higher than the rest. Around and around they danced.

"I'll be back soon, Scott," Freddie said.

When Scott looked toward the voice, Freddie was gone.

No, Freddie. Don't leave me yet. Not again.

Scott's right hand jerked, slapping *Treemonisha* to a halt with four noisy, uninvited tones. He was exhausted suddenly, sagging, all but paralyzed. How had he ever sat upright? The piano's last note stayed suspended in the air for a time, then floated down to silence, nothing.

"Help me, please," Scott said, the three words in the English language he most despised.

"Say, that was pretty good, fella," the attendant said. "You a jass minstrel?"

Scott shook his head. Lottie had a liking for jass music from New Orleans, but Scott had been too sick to go to a cabaret to hear a jass minstrel band. From the way Lottie described jass music, it sounded like ragtime sprinkled with blues, following its own rules.

"I'm a composer," Scott said, but he was almost sure the attendant didn't hear.

When the attendant lifted him by his armpits, helping him back to his wheelchair, Scott's anguish tore at him, a dagger of fire in his chest. He should not have played, he realized. Why should he have remembered just to lose hands again? How had Beethoven survived his deafness? Maybe heartbreak *would* kill him just as Lottie always said, because death could not feel worse.

Why did you leave me, dear girl? Why can't I be free, too?

Scott heard the sound of clapping hands, a meager audience.

He turned to look over his shoulder, blinking vision back to his eyes from the white-gray soup of his tears. He saw more than a dozen patients standing behind him, grinning while they staggered or swayed, gazing at him wide-eyed as if he were Prometheus and had just brought them fire. The men were Negro and white, equal in their suffering, and Scott had never seen a more grateful audience. To these men, at least, he would never be forgotten.

God help me, was this where my life was supposed to take me? All so I could be here today to ease the journey for a few wretched souls like me? Was this Your gift to me all along?

The patient who had been crying on the floor stood among them, a man so young he might be a teenager. His face was damp, but there were no tears in his bright, smiling eyes. He followed the wheelchair, patting Scott on the back with blows so earnest they hurt. "Say, you playing again tomorrow, mister?" he said, as if miracles could be commanded.

"I'll do my best," Scott said. *Allldooomabesssss,* his words came out.

But Scott Joplin never played again.

Scott visited his piano in the dayroom whenever he felt strong enough to return, always in a wheelchair, but he never tried to play, and by then he was too sick to be sad about it. Breathing was enough work to keep him occupied. He only came back to the piano because at a certain hour, when daylight and dusk mingled through the windowpanes, he always thought he heard Freddie's voice calling. The Rosenkranz kept her close to him. That much he knew.

The other patients, meanwhile, avoided the piano as if it had been brushed by plague. Coming within three steps of it made them feel little bursts of electricity dancing across the hairs on their arms, or made their feet itch. That piano didn't *want* to be played by anyone except Scott, so with their blessing, the piano grew a coat of dust.

When Scott Joplin died on a spring morning, he was in bed, not at his piano.

The start of the Great War buried the news of Scott's passing, even in the few circles where his passing would have been news. At his funeral, Lottie remembered her promise to her dying husband, but how would it have looked to have a song as gay as "Maple Leaf Rag" played on a burial day? Lottie would regret her decision the rest of her life, but on the day Scott was put to rest in his pauper's burial plot, no one so much as hummed her husband's most beloved song.

Lord knew she'd done right by the man in every other way.

Lottie Joplin hadn't been able to understand her husband's last words to her, so she had comforted herself by imagining tenderness in Scotty's weak murmurings. She had known his heart had private spaces the minute he told her he was a widower, but she liked to think his dying words might have been *Lottie Joplin, you're the only woman I ever truly loved.*

Or something gentle like that. Just not angry, for once. Not afraid.

Lottie was no child of God, truth be known—being in the sin trade, she'd had to let go of Jesus to make ends meet—but she prayed her dear husband's last words were happy. Scott never got what he deserved, not a single day of his life. *Lord, give him peace at last,* she had thought, imagining calm surrender in the mangled whisper Scott had breathed into her face.

Scott's last words to Lottie weren't peaceful, calm or loving, and they would have surprised her if she had understood him—because his last words were an admonition.

Find the kerosene, Lottie. Burn that piano to Hell.

I I.

Phoenix Smalls was ten years old the day she nearly died.

Years later, distant relatives and forgotten schoolteachers would claim they'd always seen a special spark in Phoenix, That Certain Something proclaiming she was going to make a deep groove in this world somehow. For the most part, these were lies. Until she nearly died, Phoenix Smalls had never done a single remarkable thing.

Phoenix got good grades, but her schooling hadn't caught afire. She'd always liked to sing, but she had what her chorus teacher called a Fourth-Place voice, never likely to place in the top three. Phoenix studied violin, but with only enough diligence to keep her lessons from sounding like catfights. She'd been playing the piano her grandparents bought her since she was six, and she'd made it a good way through the Robert Whitford course, but her recitals weren't inspired or impressive.

Phoenix's father thought she could do better. He turned practicing the piano into a military exercise, with a timer. First twenty minutes, scale drills. Second twenty minutes, practice a required classical piece from her study book. Only in the third twenty minutes did she have free time to play what she liked from the sheet music in her *E-Z Hits of the '80s* book (that had Madonna *and* Whitney Houston songs in it). Under her father's arrangement, Phoenix hated practicing the piano more than she hated anything else in life. Phoenix had called her father *Sarge* by the time she was eight, and the nickname stuck. Sarge could take the fun out of anything.

Phoenix felt cursed to have been born into a family where *both* parents loved music: Her mother was a former ballet dancer who played piano and still owned the Silver Slipper, the jazz club Phoenix's grandfather had opened on Miami Beach in the 1950s. Phoenix's father occasionally played the piano one-handed, humming to himself, or he played his trumpet to old jazz records in the garage, in sporadic bursts and peals both on-key and off. He also managed musicians and bands, which kept him on the road more than Phoenix or her mother liked.

Whenever Sarge returned from the road—sometimes after days, sometimes after weeks—he had new stories when he thought Phoenix was asleep and couldn't hear him and Mom sitting up half the night at the kitchen table. *You'd think they didn't have mamas and daddies. You should have seen the mess they left in the hotel. He was so strung out, he fell asleep at the microphone.* Phoenix loved Sarge's road stories. When she heard her parents going toward the kitchen, she climbed out of bed to hide just out of their sight, next to the china cabinet beyond the kitchen doorway. The stories were a window into a world without rules, perfect entertainment. *You don't snort it, fool,* was one of the punch lines that made Mom scream from laughing so hard. (Phoenix's cousin Gloria told her later that joke had something to do with drugs, inside knowledge Phoenix thought Gloria had no business knowing at eleven—but that was Gloria.)

Over time, though, Phoenix began to resent the performers her father worked for. It was bad enough Sarge was gone as often as he was home, but he was gone babysitting a pack of spoiled druggies who didn't deserve him. By the time Phoenix was ten, show business seemed like one of the fancy chocolate candies her grandmother served from boxes every Thanksgiving: tempting on the outside, but likely to be licorice or cherry on the inside. Downright unappetizing, when you got to the taste of it.

Phoenix's own dream was to be famous with *dignity,* chiefly by finding her way into the *Guinness Book of World Records.* Every day brought new inspiration: holding her breath (she made it up to fifty seconds), longest moonwalk (she practiced moonwalking across the kitchen floor every day after school) and longest kiss (even with Saran Wrap separating their lips, kissing Gloria was mostly gross—mostly—so she didn't have anyone to practice with). It was only a matter of time before she discovered her hidden talent, whatever it was, so it was best to get started early. She would break or create *any* record, as long is it didn't involve performances of any kind, or a stage.

Or, of course, a piano.

The Silver Slipper didn't help reduce her aversion to show business. When Aunt Liv couldn't babysit or the weekend shows went late, Phoenix was a fixture on the club's cot in the office upstairs, sleeping through the throbbing bass drums and whining trumpets from the stage beneath her. The Slipper wasn't a big or popular club, so the acts who came through usually weren't happy to be there. Some were frustrated because they wanted to be farther along, and most because they had already been farther along and were on their way back. Each night, Phoenix witnessed their neat trick of suddenly remembering to smile before they took the stage, where their restlessness and resentment were in her plain view.

Her last shard of innocence was lost the night she heard her favorite singer say that if she had to do that *fucking* song from the radio again, she would lose her *fucking* mind, she swore to *fucking* G—d, which Phoenix was sure meant (1) her favorite singer wasn't going to sing the song Phoenix had wanted to hear so badly that she'd begged her parents to stay up late on a school night, and (2) her favorite singer had blasphemed and was going straight to Hell.

At ten, Phoenix would have been very disappointed to learn that show business, and music, were in her future. Downright horrified, really.

Then came the piano. And the accident.

The old piano had sat inside 565 Alton Road since the two-story brick building first opened its doors in 1927 as an all-girls' school, before the building fell from grace as a flophouse, then found salvation as a jazz club. The piano had been collecting dust against the wall in the upstairs storage room as long as anyone knew: from when Phoenix's grandfather, Bud Rosen, sold his club to his daughter right before he was indicted for tax fraud in 1982; from when the Silver Slipper regularly drew Sinatra and Jackie Gleason to its linen-draped tables; and from the reigns of two or three owners before that who had their own stories to tell. The piano had a story, too. Anyone who gazed at its sullen, aged cabinet for more than a few seconds knew that, even if they didn't know anything about the story except that it wasn't a happy one.

Phoenix found the old piano in the storage room during a bored fit of exploration one summer day, when she discovered that the storage room wasn't locked as it usually was. The room was little more than a closet, crowded with old sound equipment, boxes stamped with Dewars labels, and stacks of ratty chairs with broad backs that looked like patio castoffs. The piano sat in the middle of the floor, facing nothing in particular, misplaced even within disorder.

The piano was so ugly it was surly. The upright piano's blond rosewood finish had rotted away, and its cabinet resembled old, cracked leather, riven with uneven checkers, like a dusty lizard's skin. The ivory keys were so brown they looked coffee-stained, and the ones with missing key tops looked worse, stripped to the bone. The golden Rosenkranz label would have brightened it, but the lettering had been swallowed by rot. The piano's twin candelabra, tarnished black, stood with defiant stateliness above the keys although no candles had burned to light this piano in lifetimes.

Phoenix loved the piano on sight.

Maybe it was the Sarge's timer and the piano lessons. Maybe it was her boredom at being forced to sing along while her mother played "My Way," "I Left My Heart in San Francisco" and "Ebb Tide" on the living room piano after dinner on Friday nights, when Phoenix was *sure* there was something good on cable. Whatever it was, Phoenix liked the look of that rotted old piano. She liked its rot best of all.

As she did with all treasures, Phoenix wanted to share her discovery with her cousin Gloria, who was also her best friend. Gloria was from the white side of the family. She lived two blocks from Phoenix in the palm- and pine-lined suburbs of southwest Dade County, a Jewish girl with curly blond hair and faint freckles on her nose.

"This is an ugly effing piano," Gloria announced when she saw it.

That stung. Gloria's words often stung. Nothing gentle came out of her.

"Well, you're wearing an ugly effing shirt. Hammer's getting played out," Phoenix said, answering her cousin's truth with an outright lie. Phoenix envied the long-sleeved M. C. Hammer concert jersey Gloria wore to school at least twice a week and usually on weekends. Aunt Liv had spent fifty dollars on that shirt. Mom would never spend fifty dollars on a concert shirt, even if it was a concert for Jesus and his Second Coming Tour.

"You're just effing jealous," Gloria said. *Effing* was Gloria's favorite new word.

"I am *not* fucking jealous," Phoenix said, feeling bold.

"Ooh, I'm telling your dad, Phee."

"Go ahead. I don't care. He knows you cuss way worse than me."

"It's only cussing if you *say* it. I said *eff*-ing. You are in *trouble*."

Durn. She would have to beg. "Don't tell, Gloria." She used her no-playing voice.

Gloria shrugged, dramatically rolling her eyes away. *Maybe I will, maybe I won't.* "Does this thing even work?" Gloria said, turning her attention back to the piano. "It looks whack. Straight-up, girl. For real, though."

Much to Phoenix's irritation, her friends often remarked that her white cousin Gloria sounded more black than *she* did. Gloria could front all she wanted, but she didn't have a real, deep-laughing black daddy like Sarge. Phoenix had cornrows and caramel-colored skin that stayed tan all year, and Gloria turned as red as a box of Cap'n Crunch if she was in the sun for five minutes. Gloria was just confused—but then again, so was Mom, since Christmas was Mom's favorite time of year, and Mom's own sister wouldn't even let Gloria have a Christmas tree.

Phoenix pressed the piano's middle-C key, and it was silent except for a muffled clicking sound. The D played, but it was soft and off-key. Phoenix's piano teacher, Mrs. Abramowicz, would hate that sound. Ugly *and* broken. Maybe Gloria was right. Maybe it was an old broke-down piece of nothing after all. "I guess it's not anything special," Phoenix said.

"Naw, it's all right, though. It's not *that* whack," Gloria said, arms linked behind her back like an archaeologist. "It's got attitude."

The piano *did* have attitude. If she had this piano instead of the respectable one Grandpa Bud and Grandma Oprah had bought her (no, not *that* Oprah; it was a Hebrew name before it became a brand name, Grandma Oprah always said), she might not mind Sarge's practice sessions so much. This piano would make a racket. It would mangle *Für Elise* and put Beethoven to shame. Sarge would *beg* her to stop practicing.

"Maybe I can take it home," Phoenix said.

Gloria looked at her like she was crazy. "Why?"

Because it's sad, Phoenix wanted to say, but she didn't, because Gloria would laugh.

And besides, that wasn't quite right, Phoenix thought as she let her hand glide across the piano's rough cabinet, halfway expecting to pick up a splinter. The piano was *mad*. That was closer to the truth. Maybe it wouldn't be mad anymore if she gave it a home. She wanted to take care of the piano more than she'd wanted to take care of her guinea pig, Grayboy, before he died last year. She loved the piano already, somehow. She had to have it for herself.

"Maybe this is the freaky piano my mom told me about," Gloria said.

"What piano?"

"My mom told me there was this piano here she thought was haunted. She saw it move by itself, or some shit like that." At first Phoenix thought her cousin was teasing her, but the half grin across Gloria's face was more thoughtful than mischievous, and she wasn't *that* good an actress.

"I don't believe you," Phoenix said.

"I don't care if you do or not. I know what she told me. She said she was scared of it, and she's still scared of pianos. And it made her feet itch."

"That last part was stupid. You should lie better," Phoenix said. "*My* mom's not scared of no durn piano. If there was a haunted piano, both of them should be scared."

Gloria shrugged. "Eff off. I know what my mom said."

"You eff off." Suddenly, Phoenix was tired of arguing. Maybe Gloria wasn't lying, and the piano really was haunted. There could be a Guinness World Record for the spookiest piano! She would have to research this. Some of the records were very unusual.

"Come on. Let's ask Mom and Sarge if I can have it," Phoenix said.

Downstairs, walking along the rear wall of the lounge behind the sea of empty red-draped tables, they passed what Sarge called the Gallery of Greats, a row of poster-sized framed photographs of the jazz artists

Phoenix's father played in the garage. It was a parade in black and white, grinning faces in old-fashioned hats and clothes. Phoenix knew their names from their faces and labels, a game she'd devised when she was eight, and she named each in a whisper as she passed: Scott Joplin. Jelly Roll Morton. Louis Armstrong. Duke Ellington. Count Basie. Billie Holiday. Coleman Hawkins. Benny Goodman. Ella Fitzgerald. Lionel Hampton. Artie Shaw. Mary Lou Williams. Charlie Parker. John Coltrane. Miles Davis. Thelonious Monk.

Phoenix could tell their personalities from their faces. Miles Davis, Billie Holiday and Scott Joplin were frowners, looking like somebody owed them money or had gotten on their last nerves. Louis Armstrong, Duke Ellington and Count Basie were ready to get on with the show, with enough smiles to make up for the rest. Especially Louis Armstrong. Louis Armstrong could smile for days. Whenever Phoenix heard the phrase *grinning from ear to ear,* she thought of Louis Armstrong in that photograph, with his forehead, horn and teeth gleaming. It was hard to imagine what one man could have to be so happy about.

Phoenix found Mom and Sarge on the stage walking from microphone to microphone, doing a sound check with Javier. Sarge's booming voice filled up the room: *checkcheckcheckonetwo.* A woman Phoenix didn't know stood by watching them. The woman had bleached-blond hair and wore a pantsuit that looked tight, bulging around her body's every lump, and Phoenix wondered how she could breathe. Her pale hair sprayed behind her as though she were standing in the middle of a private storm.

She must be tonight's singer, Valentina somebody. Latin jazz. Phoenix had seen her poster outside the front door, but the woman in the poster was younger and thinner. The woman in the poster was also smiling, and Valentina was not.

"What are you looking at?" the woman snapped at Javier, who was bending over behind her to plug a cord into an amp. "Put your eyes back where they belong, you useless starfucker."

She said it so loudly that Javier's face went red.

"Bitch," Gloria muttered under her breath, since she had a crush on Javier even though he was an old man, nearly thirty. Phoenix couldn't help giggling. She liked the sound of *starfucker;* the front half was glittery and the back half vulgar, the way the perfect cussword should be.

Sarge's head swiveled to look back at the singer. Beneath his mud-cloth African skullcap, his eyes burned bright. "We don't talk to staff like that here," Sarge said. Her father's voice was its own growling storm.

The singer shot him a look as if she was ready to unload some more inventive words, but Sarge's eyes, or maybe his voice, made her keep her lips pinned shut.

"Apologize to him for that language," Sarge said.

The woman's lips peeled back against her teeth as if she wanted to bite Sarge. To Phoenix, she looked like that vampire lady in *Def by Temptation,* the sexy horror movie she and her cousin had watched on cable at Gloria's house after her parents went to bed. But the woman said, very softly, "*Lo siento, lo siento,* let's just get finished already. *Dios mio.*"

Something she said must have been *I'm sorry* in Spanish, because Sarge's eyes left her and he went back to yanking cords. Phoenix saw Mom give him a frown. Mom had told Sarge that if he ever talked to her the way he talked to the artists, she would kick him to the curb. But Sarge saved that tone for grown people who thought they were children and didn't know how to act. He didn't even talk to Phoenix like that, except when he told her to bring him his belt.

Phoenix climbed onstage to give her mother a shameless hug. She only hugged Mom before she was about to beg her for something. Mom's bosom smelled like perspiration and Ombre Rose, her favorite perfume. She was wearing her loose purple batik pants and matching top with the mirrored, sparkly collar, like an Indian princess. Mom only wore clothes that draped over her body, hiding it. Mom was never through with her stories of the starvation and broken bodies from her days with a ballet company in Boston, but as long as Phoenix had known her, her mother had weighed more than two hundred pounds.

"What's up, Buttercup?" Mom said, blowing a strand of hair out of her face. Her dark hair was limp and straight, except when it got wet, when it turned nearly as wiry and curly as Phoenix's. Phoenix enjoyed posing in the mirror with her mother when their hair looked alike.

"I want to ask you something."

"Can it wait?" Mom said, keeping her eye toward Sarge and the singer.

"Peanut, come here," Sarge said, beckoning. He was winding a black cord around his thick arm, from his palm to his elbow.

The singer left the stage and stood watching them from a few yards away, her arms folded across her chest. She was so mad, her face looked bright pink. Hibiscus pink.

Sarge lowered his face to Phoenix's. His neck was almost as thick as his face, and he had a broad nose that flared when he was mad, or when he laughed. Phoenix couldn't see herself in her father's face either, although everybody told her she looked just like him in the eyes. She wished she had browner skin and could shave her head like Sarge, or else she wished her hair would lie down flat like Mom's and Gloria's. She had a little of each of her parents, but not enough of either.

"Did you hear Queen Isabella?" Sarge said softly. "I had to give her The Ray."

Sarge had told her Benny Goodman used to give his musicians The Ray with his eyes when he didn't like what he heard on the bandstand. Sarge did it with his eyes *and* his voice. Don't be fooled by that Sunday school teacher suit and glasses in the picture, Sarge had told her—you did *not* mess with Benny Goodman. Nobody messed with Sarge, either.

"She had it coming," Phoenix said.

"Be that as it may," Sarge said, "your mama's giving me looks. So I want you to go on over there and do that little-girl thang. You know how you do. Give her a smile, bat your eyes, and say these words exactly like this: 'You're so pretty. You look better than your picture.' "

Phoenix rolled her eyes. "That's a lie."

Phoenix heard Javier chuckle from behind the drum set. Sarge lowered his voice. "It's not a lie. It's an exaggeration. Besides, beauty is subjective."

"What does subjective mean?"

"It means she looks pretty if I tell you she looks pretty. It's a matter of *opinion*. Go on."

"Really, it's shameful," Mom said, walking past them toward the grand piano at the back of the stage. "If you teach her deception, it'll come back to you."

"One song getting airplay on public radio, and she struts in here acting like she's somebody. I'll send her ass packing right back to wherever
she's from." Sarge barely kept his voice down when he said that. His eyes
looked restless, like he might give the singer The Ray again because his
memories were making him mad. "Musicians come do their job. In and
out. But singers? Always the same shit."

Phoenix reminded herself, yet again, that she would never, ever be a
singer.

The singer pulled out her cell phone to call someone, glaring at Sarge
from her safe distance against the wall. She was about to walk out, and
that would be the end of the show. Phoenix could feel it. It had happened before.

"I'll do it, but I'll have my fingers crossed behind my back," Phoenix
said. "OK, Mom? That means it's not a lie."

"Oh, so that makes it all better. What a relief," Mom said sarcastically.
She dismissed them with a wave of her hand and disappeared behind the
backstage curtain. Phoenix heard Mom promising herself she would sell
the Silver Slipper, and she meant it this time, no matter what her father
had said about family legacy.

Suddenly, Phoenix remembered the piano. "Can I have that old
piano, Daddy?" When she wanted something, she'd learned it was better
to call him *Daddy,* not *Sarge.*

"Which old piano?"

"Upstairs. In the storeroom."

"We'll see. I'll take a look at it," Sarge said, winking. From Sarge, *We'll
see* was only a short hop to *yes.* When Mom said *We'll see,* it almost always meant *no,* another of the differences between her parents. "Now go
on and work your magic, Peanut, before I get in trouble. If we lose this
one, your mom's gonna be just about through with me."

After beckoning for Gloria to come with her ("*What,* Phee? Javier was
finally noticing me!"), Phoenix sidled up beside the woman. The singer
was punching the buttons on her cell phone as if she wanted to break
them. She put the phone to her ear, and her flurry of Spanish began.
Phoenix had heard some of the words at school: *Puta. Maricón.
Comemierda.* Angry words. Go-to-the-principal's-office or meet-me-
after-school words.

After a deep breath, Phoenix stood in front of the singer and stared up at her with admiring eyes. Following Sarge's advice, she blinked a time or two, trying to bat her lashes, but she thought she probably looked more like she had dust in her eyes.

The singer sighed, and her breath smelled like the strong Cuban coffee Mom drank from little plastic cups the size of thimbles, like motor oil with sugar. The singer put her hand over the phone's receiver. "What do you want?" she said to Phoenix.

"I'm sorry to bother you, but you are *so* beautiful," Phoenix said.

The singer's face froze, waiting.

"You're much prettier than in your picture. And you sing great, too," Phoenix went on. She remembered she'd forgotten to cross her fingers behind her back, so she did it after the fact.

An amazing transformation took place: The lines near the singer's mouth vanished as her lips became a smile, her eyes were suddenly girlish, and her face glowed like a newly lighted candle. In that instant, Phoenix realized she wasn't lying, because the woman's face on the poster outside was posed and fake, but Valentina's face had become lovely and soft and honest. She was older than the woman in the poster, but that did not make her less pretty; in fact, her beauty seemed more lasting, more precious, because most of it sat in her gentle brown eyes.

"Thank you, *gracias,*" the singer said. She blinked, and Phoenix could tell she was close to tears. Phoenix had never seen such a powerful reaction to her words. "You are a very sweet girl to say that. Not everyone thinks so. Some say I am a foolish old woman."

"They're just stupid," Phoenix said. "I hope I can be as pretty as you one day."

"For real. Can we have your autograph?" Gloria said, holding out a napkin. Gloria could be a royal pain when she wanted to, but Phoenix could count on her cousin to back her up every time. While Valentina signed the napkin, Phoenix glanced around to look at her father on the stage. He was grinning as wide as Louis Armstrong.

Phoenix would tell Sarge she hadn't even lied. She was proud of that.

"You two are best friends?" the woman said, when she'd finished signing her name in a swirl of cursive, illegible but still beautiful.

"Cousins," Phoenix said.

Valentina didn't blink or frown. Most people couldn't understand how brown skin and white skin, or black cornrows and blond hair, could be in the same family. That was tiresome.

"Ah, cousins! But friends, too?" the woman said.

Phoenix looked at Gloria, who smiled at her. They both nodded. Everybody at school knew they were best friends. Anybody who messed with Phoenix was messing with Gloria, and messing with Gloria was a bad idea. Gloria wasn't afraid of anything or anybody. In that way, Gloria was more like Sarge than Phoenix was.

Valentina put one hand on top of Phoenix's head and the other on Gloria's. "Always stay friends, not only cousins," she said. "*Siempre. ¿Comprende?* Always."

Then Valentina went back to the stage, with a regal walk like a queen. She walked straight up to Javier and gave him a tight hug, her true apology. She purred at him in Spanish.

"Bitch," Gloria muttered. "Her hand is almost touching his butt!"

"Stop looking at that old man like that. You're so gross, Gloria."

"I'm an early bloomer."

"You're a Freakazoid."

"Takes one to know one."

"I can't help it if you're my cousin."

"I can't help it if you're too much of a baby to know a cute guy when you see one. I got my period already, remember? I'm a *woman.*" *Double-gross,* Phoenix thought. She wouldn't care if she didn't get her period until she was as old as Valentina. She had seen Gloria wash out her bloody underwear in her sink at home, and stained underwear was nothing to brag about.

After hugging Javier, Valentina went to Sarge next, although she did not hug him. Sarge was not the kind of man people tried to touch without an invitation. She kept her distance, but she was smiling. And The Ray was gone from Sarge's eyes.

The show would go on. Sarge owed her now. She would get her piano.

Phoenix wanted to see her piano again, to make sure she hadn't only imagined it. She beckoned to Gloria, and they made their way back past the Gallery of Greats to the bright red EXIT sign over the rear doorway that forked right for the bathrooms and the emergency exit, left for the stairs to the second floor. The sticky floor smelled like old beer.

Halfway up the stairs, Phoenix's heart went cold in her chest.

The piano was no longer in the storage room. It was at the top of the stairs.

The piano was sideways, but there was no mistaking the weathered wood she had just run her hand across a few minutes before. The lighter wood planks underneath the piano showed because it dangled nearly halfway over the landing.

"Hey!" Gloria called up. "Who's messing with the piano? It's gonna fall!"

No one answered from behind the piano.

"Somebody thinks they're real funny!" Gloria said.

Who could have moved it? Mom and Sarge were downstairs, and so was Javier. She'd seen some musicians earlier, but they said they were going to Lincoln Road Mall for a late lunch. She hadn't seen the janitor today, and the servers and bartenders wouldn't come until later. The Bell boys, the janitor's sons, might have moved the piano, but why would they be here if their father wasn't? Besides, usually they only came upstairs to sneak cigarettes in the storeroom. The Bell boys were thirteen and fourteen, truly repulsive creatures. They made Phoenix dread the fall, when she would have to go to school with seventh and eighth graders. If the Bell boys were any indication, middle school must be like Hell.

The Bells from Hell had moved the piano, because jerks must be jerks.

Gloria had the same idea. "We know it's just you guys, and we're not scared," Gloria called. Gloria *was* a little scared—Phoenix could tell by a slight waver in her voice—but Phoenix was impressed at how well Gloria pretended she wasn't.

"We better tell Sarge," Phoenix said.

"We don't need Sarge. Let's push it back. Or else it might fall."

"What if it's not them?" Phoenix whispered. "You said there's a haunted piano here."

"It's *them*. They heard us talking, and they're being dickwads."

Before Phoenix could open her mouth again, Gloria was already bounding up the stairs. Phoenix's heart tripped with alarm, and she felt dizzy as fear flushed her body. This felt all wrong. This felt B-A-D, and not like in Michael Jackson's version.

Gloria squeezed herself past the piano. There was just enough room for her to get by. Nothing would stand between Gloria and an adventure. "I'll pull from behind, and you push from the stairs. OK, Phee? On three."

Phoenix didn't move. Her hand held the banister tight. Mom said Gloria was too much like her mother; act first, think later.

"Are you coming or not?"

"I'm gonna go get Sarge."

"Go on, then. He'll think we moved it and get pissed off at us."

No he wouldn't, Phoenix thought. Sarge knew she wasn't a liar, even if Gloria's parents didn't have the same confidence in Gloria. Gloria hadn't earned her parents' trust, Mom said. But Gloria was probably right: It was stupid to be afraid of the piano, thinking it had moved by itself and had made up its mind to fall. The Bell boys had done it, even if she hadn't seen them. Phoenix couldn't guess *why* they would do it, but it was almost impossible to guess why boys did anything. She and Gloria could move it back themselves. That would show those boys that girls weren't as weak as they thought. Stupid jerks.

"OK, I'm coming," Phoenix said. She climbed up the last eight steps and leaned against the piano with both palms.

"Wait, I said! On three," Gloria said.

"OK."

"One . . . two . . ."

There was never a *three*.

The piano scooted forward and teetered. *"Hey!"* Phoenix said. The piano's sudden weight against her hands scared her, so she drew back and stepped down a step. Above her, the piano rocked, tipping.

The piano was going to fall.

Gloria, above her, sounded frantic. *"Oh, shit, I'm sorry, I didn't—"*

The loud rumbling came next as the piano launched down the stairs. Pale splintered wood flew from underneath the piano as it crashed on the hard steps, charging from one to the next, *chunk-chunk-chunk*. It sounded like a locomotive, Phoenix thought.

Then, she stopped thinking and turned to run.

Gloria yelled out to her from above, but her cousin's words were too hurried and slurred to understand. Phoenix had never heard Gloria sound so scared.

Phoenix was scared, too, but she heard herself laughing as the rumbling sound grew louder behind her. *The little piano that could,* she thought nonsensically, just like the children's storybook about the Little Engine she'd read when she was little. Maybe there was a World Record for racing a runaway piano! Her feet tripped down the steps two and three at time, flying. The picture of herself running away from a piano seemed funnier all the time.

The stairwell twisted, surprising her with nowhere to run. When the piano's bulk nudged the small of her back, Phoenix's laugh became a scream.

Marcus Smalls had thought his life was over when he went to Raiford Maximum Security Penitentiary in Raiford, Florida. He'd been locked up in March of 1971, the same year Louis Armstrong died, so it was a sad year all around—five to ten for illegal weapons after a Florida Trooper found his two high-powered .223 rifles in his trunk while he was making an overnight run from Atlanta to St. Pete, giving a broke friend a ride. No good deed goes unpunished. Sarge hadn't even remembered his rifles were still in the car, truth be told, but no judge liked to see guns in the hands of a black man with a good recollection of history, even a black man who hadn't been forced to defend himself yet. When the judge asked him why he had the guns, Marcus told him to turn on the evening news. Fuck Vietnam. What fool couldn't see the war at home?

Marcus served eight years, just long enough to miss all three of his children's adolescent years, the ones that might just have mattered most, from what he could see. Locking a man away from his children should qualify as cruel and unusual punishment, Marcus believed, but the judge hadn't seen it that way. No pussy was bad enough, but not as bad as watching from a distance while Serena, Marcus Jr. and Malcolm grew up wrongheaded without him. Marcus had laid down his life and future at Raiford as surely as if he'd died.

He'd gone to jail for love, he always said. Love for his history. Love for his people. Love for the Panthers. Love had taken Marcus Smalls to Hell and back.

At Raiford, he had seen four men stabbed to death, and would have stabbed one himself if that racist asshole hadn't seen something in his eyes and decided he'd rather back down and live another day. Marcus also wouldn't have minded snapping the neck of a CO who routinely confiscated his books because he must have hated to see another black man reading, and *that* self-restraint still amazed him. Marcus had been so lonely for a woman, he'd gleaned the first whisper of *understanding* how lifers could see a fine-featured young man as a substitute, which was more understanding than he'd considered himself capable of in one life-time and much more than he'd wanted to know. Marcus had never seen so much despair in one place.

At Raiford, Marcus had realized that the revolution not only wouldn't be televised, it wouldn't be noticed at all. He and his cause had vanished. A petition with two hundred signatures had circulated on his behalf soon after his sentencing, but he never heard of another effort to free him. Worse, he'd realized that the very people he'd gone to prison hop-ing to motivate and liberate were sitting home laughing at Archie Bunker, Jimmie Walker and "The Jeffersons," never expending a brain cell worrying about how they were going to build a black nation and re-claim what they had lost in the blood price their forebears paid. That had hurt almost as much as being locked away from his kids.

All in all, Marcus had thought Raiford was the worst thing that could happen to a man.

But he'd been wrong. The worst thing that could happen to a man, he learned, was seeing his little girl hurt. Seeing Phoenix hurt.

His second-chance life wasn't supposed to bring new tragedies. He'd seen to it.

He'd cut his ties to the old warhorses he used to run with, those that were still out there running. After the first year, those niggers hadn't sent Swarita and his children a dime while he was locked up—and his family had been *homeless* for a time—*So fuck those niggers anyway,* he told himself, even though he knew they were busy catching much hell themselves.

God helped him most of all. Marcus felt God's arms around him in a way he never had before, an embrace that drained anger from his heart. It was a daily struggle, but one he'd been carrying on like breathing. He'd pulled some old contacts to get work managing bands on the road, making a reputation for himself he was proud of. You could ask anyone from Earth Wind & Fire to Gladys Knight, and people knew Marcus Smalls got the job done. He'd made enough money to help Serena open a beauty shop in Atlanta, he'd set aside a little something for Marcus Jr. for when he got out of the pen for dealing shit on the streets, and he'd gotten Malcolm off that same shit by sending him to rehab and helping him get that job deejaying in Savannah. His older kids weren't the Brady Bunch, but they were doing all right.

The biggest surprise of all: He'd found Leah Rosen. All these years Marcus had been bad-mouthing other niggers for their white women—it had seemed like a damn initiation rite among the nationalists to pluck a stringy-haired, wide-eyed white girl to follow them around—so God had played a practical joke on Marcus by sending him a white woman, too. The gazes he and Leah occasionally encountered from white men were nothing compared to the laser eyes of the sisters, who could sense a black man with a white woman before you turned the corner. Marcus knew what the sisters had been through, but he couldn't apologize on behalf of the brothers who'd forsaken them for forbidden fruit. It wasn't like that with Leah. They dug each other's souls, and they were the only two people who needed to understand that. Fuck anyone who couldn't take the joke, as far as Marcus was concerned.

He'd met Leah the night the Miami riots started in May of 1980, when he'd been free a little more than a year and was still having nightly dreams he was still at Raiford. He'd been in Liberty City trying to plan a gig at a community center when he heard about the Arthur McDuffie verdict on the news, the police brutality case everybody in Miami was talking about. Marcus had known that verdict would mean trouble. Outside, he'd seen a white woman waiting at a red light on Northwest Fifty-fourth Street in a black BMW with no idea that the teenagers walking in her direction with baseball bats weren't on their way to a sandlot game. If he hadn't pulled her out of that car and taken her inside, Leah would have been another statistic on the nightly news. The riots might have turned into hunting season on black folks in the days to follow, but white folks were *dying* that first night, when the verdict came down.

And there was Leah after he'd brought her inside, fresh from her near miss with death, tears shimmering in her eyes. She wasn't crying out of gratitude, or because she'd abandoned her bourgeois status symbol in the middle of the road and nearly been killed. No, Leah was sobbing because she couldn't believe the twelve cops who'd pulled Arthur McDuffie off his motorcycle and beaten him to death had been set free. *How could the jury say they're NOT guilty? How could anyone say that? They BEAT him to death and tried to make it look like his motorcycle crashed. What's not to understand?* Leah had been hysterical, like she wanted to go back outside and burn something down herself. A moment like that shows you who someone really is. That was when Marcus Smalls realized he could love a white woman.

Marcus had never expected white cops to be convicted for killing an unarmed black man, and he'd learned after Martin died that the swell of power that came with chants of *burn, baby, burn* vanished with the flames and the morning light. As for killing bystanders, that was between the rioters and God; that had nothing to do with McDuffie. But Marcus didn't go back out in the streets trying to tell those kids how to feel either. They'd be more likely to shoot him than heed him, and powerlessness was a lesson every generation of black men had to learn for itself. *Safe journey, young bloods,* Marcus had thought sadly as he watched plumes of smoke floating into the clear Miami night sky. *Safe journey.*

Marcus didn't know if he would have married Leah if she hadn't gotten pregnant within a month of their meeting, but that was a moot question as soon as he heard the news. It had been Leah's idea to name their baby Phoenix. Rising from Liberty City's ashes.

The day Phoenix was born, Marcus had held his tawny daughter in his arms and vowed to be a proper father to her. Period. Nobody was going to make him mad enough to go to prison again—not if he was an eyewitness to another Arthur McDuffie killing, not if the revolution started today and got twenty-four-hour coverage on all three networks. Marcus Smalls was going to be about his own business and God's, and no one else's.

Phoenix was his second-chance child, and this was his second-chance life.

That was why Marcus felt bewildered each day as he sat as his daughter's bedside at Miami Children's Hospital ten years after she'd been born there and tried to fathom how his little Phoenix could be in a coma. This was not supposed to happen to him now. He thought he'd sown his major tragedies behind him.

It wasn't *technically* a coma, the doctor kept telling them—she was *unconscious,* as if the distinction made a damn bit of difference to him when his daughter had not opened her eyes in a week solid. Phoenix had been lying in a twisted heap behind that piano on the stairs when he'd found her, and she hadn't moved since. Broken ribs. Broken leg. A *crack,* not a break, in her skull, thank Jesus. The gash to his daughter's head had painted the piano's keys with a stripe of blood. If he hadn't been so desperate to get help, Marcus would have curled up on the floor and cried at the sight of her. And he'd thought nothing could feel worse than Raiford.

"Phee? Can you hear me?" Marcus said daily, squeezing her hand. Marcus had more stomach for the hospital room than Leah did, so often he sat alone with her, leaning against her bed's aluminum guardrail, so much like a baby's crib. The swelling on her face was going down after a week, so she looked more serene to him, as if she really were only sleeping, after all. "It's Daddy, sugar. It's Sarge. I'm right here, Peanut. I'm just waiting on you to wake up. The people from the World Records called, and they're gonna make up a new one just for you."

Sometimes when he said that, her eyelids seemed to flutter. He was sure of it. She'd be mad as hell at his lie, but he'd make it up to her if God gave him the chance. Phoenix had such long, lovely eyelashes, they rested beneath her eyelids like the soft fur of a mink cub. Against her white pillow and sheets, Phoenix's cocoa-butter complexion looked bronze.

He blamed himself for the accident. Gloria had a lot to answer for, too—that headstrong, too-grown brat—but he and Leah knew they had to watch Phoenix when her cousin was around, because something going on in Leah's sister's house was making that girl grow up too fast. They hadn't expected a crazy stunt like trying to move a piano, but with

Gloria you never knew. That was the way it had always been. It was his own fault.

Eventually, Marcus stopped talking to Phoenix much during his hospital vigils, because he figured she was in a place words couldn't reach. Music would speak for him, he decided. He kept his cassette player on her table, playing new music each day. Only the best, though.

Miles Davis's "Kind of Blue" or Ellington in the morning, Mozart at lunchtime (*Eine kleine Nachtmusik* was still his favorite, with that timeless violin burst at the start), and the earthier stuff at night: B. B. King and Otis Redding and Marvin Gaye. Or Mahalia Jackson and Shirley Caesar, but only if he wanted to cry. Marcus Smalls played all the music he was afraid his daughter might not live to hear: He played Miriam Makeba and Jelly Roll Morton, Sly & the Family Stone and Scott Joplin, Gil Scott-Heron and Louis Armstrong (the Hot Five sessions), Dizzy Gillespie and James Brown. He played her a 1928 recording of Paul Robeson singing "Ol' Man River," and Billie Holiday singing "Strange Fruit" in 1939. He played Beethoven's *Moonlight Sonata,* John Philip Sousa's "Thunderer," and "Respect" sung the way only Aretha could. He played Earth Wind & Fire and Arturo Sandoval, Al Green and Eric Clapton, Fats Domino, George Gershwin and Ella Fitzgerald. Each day, Marcus offered Phoenix the best music he could, hoping to guide her home to him, or else home to God. She'd be humming and happy either way.

Nine days after her accident, when Phoenix finally opened her eyes with a matter-of-fact "Hi, Sarge," she affirmed what he suspected: She had heard the music in her dreams.

"Were you playing your trumpet?" she said. Her voice was unchanged, and for a moment he only blinked as he stared at her. She'd been unconscious, but now her cinnamon-colored eyes were wide open, and she'd asked him a question. A miracle in a heartbeat.

"I only wish. That was Pops." Marcus's mouth was dry. His joy and sorrow, intertwined, made his limbs gel beneath him. He felt God walk through the room, assess His work for a hot minute, and move on. "Hallelujah, Jesus," he whispered.

"Mom promised me a new doll. Any doll I want. I heard her," Phoenix said.

"She sure did." Marcus squeezed her hand so hard he startled himself, afraid he might crush her little bones.

The next thing Phoenix said was, "Is the piano all right, Daddy?"

The piano was very all right. Too damn all right. Except for the bloody keys, it looked no worse to Marcus than it had in the storeroom all these years. He and Javier and the boys had moved it next to the stinking Dumpster outside the Silver Slipper's rear exit, naked to the elements to await disposal by Miami Beach Sanitation. Many times, sitting in this very spot, Marcus had sworn to drive out to the Silver Slipper in the middle of the night and set that piano on fire, or to smash it into dust. But something in Phoenix's earnest yearning froze Marcus's tongue when he tried to tell her that.

"The piano's fine. And you're fine," Marcus said. He didn't notice his tears until then.

Phoenix smiled, seeming satisfied, but when that spark of earnestness melted away, he saw lines near her eyes that had never been there before, and the pallor of her skin, and a small, pained wince in a secret corner of her mouth that only a father would see.

Phoenix's recovery was slow, and almost as terrible as her coma. Marcus had never been able to stand seeing his baby in pain, and for a while she was in pain all the time. He couldn't tell if it was harder on Phoenix, or on him and Leah. The burden shifted back and forth. During the time Phoenix was hospitalized, Marcus saw Leah wilt. She snapped at Phoenix most of the time, mad at her for nearly dying, then she would catch herself and collapse into tears, rocking against Phoenix while she braided her hair, singing her a young child's lullabies.

"It's OK, Mom," Phoenix told her. "The world record for being in a coma is thirty-seven years, a hundred and eleven days. I wasn't anywhere close to that."

Phoenix asked about the piano so often that, after a while, Sarge felt obligated to rescue the deadly hunk of wood from the garbage pile. He couldn't muster the warm feeling toward it Phoenix still had somehow, but he'd do anything to make her happy.

He found it in the moonlight, soggy with rain. The sight of it filled Marcus with rage.

Still, he strained and groaned to wheel it back through the rear entrance, careful not to bump its underside too hard on the doorstop. That done, Marcus went to a corner market to buy some talcum powder and powdered milk to see if he could lift those bloodstains off the keys, a trick he'd learned at Raiford. After two hours of scrubbing, Phoenix's blood was gone and the keys shone as much as their age allowed. Without the blood, the sight of the piano did not piss him off nearly as much. He left it alone when his feet started itching, but not before he decided to consider granting Phoenix's wish. Maybe he *could* ask Javier or Mr. Bell and his bad-ass boys to help him take the thing home.

He never got the chance. As soon as he mentioned the idea to Leah, his wife ranted to him about how the accident with Phoenix proved that the piano was cursed. Marcus couldn't pretend he didn't understand his wife's conviction—he'd had a few brushes with things he couldn't explain when he was Phoenix's age, and he knew that everything on this Earth is not meant to be understood. He didn't like the piano any more than Leah did. But Marcus also wasn't willing to sacrifice his daughter's wishes on the basis of superstition, not when Phoenix was already suffering so much. He and Leah debated for three days, until his wife threw her hands up and told him she could live with whatever he thought was best.

The next afternoon, the piano was waiting for Marcus on their front porch.

When Leah changes her mind, she don't waste time, he thought, pushing the piano into his living room the way he'd pushed it out of the rain. But that was his wife: always a hundred percent, never fifty. The subject was still sore between them, so he didn't question Leah about what had motivated her to call the movers herself. And she never mentioned the piano to him.

So, Phoenix had saved the piano. The piano saved her in return.

When Phoenix screamed in a tantrum during physical therapy—like she almost always did, because the doctor said she might not ever walk right again if they didn't push her—Marcus used the piano to coax her through. If she just could finish her last set of leg lifts, he reminded her, if she would just finish the rest of her sessions, the piano was waiting for her. Except for the blood, he promised he would leave its sad appearance exactly as it was, because that was what his Peanut wanted.

Phoenix was in the hospital for a month. That month passed like a
dozen, and when it was over, it was as if a powerful tide had swallowed
them and stolen much of what they recognized from their lives. For a
time, everything became different.

Marcus began turning down gigs, even though money was tight, because he couldn't bear a long stretch away from home. That lasted for a
while, anyway. When he did go for a week or so, Leah had less patience
for his raunchy road stories, or any stories that didn't paint a world
where good people did good things and were rewarded for their works.
Leah still seemed to be in mourning although Phoenix was better all the
time, so Leah's mother sent her to therapy. The therapist called it post-
traumatic stress disorder, an affliction Marcus knew all too well, but he'd
always called it "the shakes." For years after he'd walked out of Raiford,
the shakes had snatched him from sleep in the middle of the night with
dreams that he was still behind bars.

After the accident, Marcus never again dreamed about being inside.
His baby girl had lived, so he'd been set free. *Truly* free, this time.

The biggest change, though, was Phoenix's.

Instead of carrying her dog-eared copy of the *Guinness Book of World
Records* with her everywhere she went, she left it on her bedroom desk,
always open to the same page. And she played with her toys, but not the
way she used to. Phoenix's imaginary tableaux were usually all over the
house: Tonka fire vehicles parked beside the fireplace awaiting their next
rescue mission; a Barbie U.N. beach party on the patio (Barbie dolls
from around the world sitting stiffly at miniature patio tables and sun-
ning themselves by the plastic pool); and a ferocious GI Joe standoff in
the Florida room, where two fallen soldiers were buried beneath a handkerchief while their three brethren crouched just beyond them, their
M16s trained on whatever giant enemy might round the corner.

One day, Marcus noticed that the fire trucks were gone, the pool party
had ended, and the soldiers had gotten leave. Curious, Marcus inched
Phoenix's bedroom door open and found her made-up bed covered in
toys. Her Tonka trucks were propped up on her pillows as if climbing a
tough terrain, manned by oversized GI Joes. The international cadre of
Barbies was huddled together in a group, in their ceremonial clothes. The
only Ken was shirtless, a casualty lying facedown on the mattress while an

African Barbie mourned over him. A GI Joe consoled a blond Barbie with one arm hooked around her thin waist while the other soldiers guarded the perimeter, guns drawn. Phoenix's *Star Wars* figurines, which Marcus had not seen in years, were scattered throughout, mismatched in size. One bearded GI Joe stood at the edge of the mattress with his arms planted on his hips, his head tilted upward so his eyes were trained toward any intruder in the doorway. Yoda stood beside him, as if in counsel.

"How long has this been like this?" Marcus asked Leah in the hallway outside of Phoenix's doorway. Their daughter's room smelled like peppermint.

"A few days. She's been sleeping on the floor in her sleeping bag so she won't muss it."

The collection of dolls and action figures on the bed meant something, he knew, but since Phoenix was spending the night at Gloria's, he didn't ask his daughter to explain the intricacies of the story line that had brought all of her toys together, a snapshot of his daughter's youth. When Phoenix came home, her toys vanished into a box in her closet. He never saw her play with them again. When he asked her about them, she mumbled about going to middle school in the fall, so she had to stop playing with dolls.

But she did play her new piano, which sat in the middle of the living room floor like an unkempt visitor. Phoenix practiced for an hour each day, sometimes two, playing the slightly sour-sounding keys while her eyes hung on the sheet music and her tiny hands struggled to stretch from one octave to the next. She began to master her assigned pieces, playing without a single mistake. The accident had matured her, Marcus thought, and he was glad. Focus would take his daughter a long way in the world.

One night after Phoenix was back at home, Marcus dreamed he saw his wife lying beside him in a white dressing gown, the kind her grandmother might have worn. Something was wrong with her. He felt the same despair as when he'd seen Phoenix at the foot of the stairs, a hurt that made him sick to his stomach. Leah's face looked younger and smoother in the dream, not like her much at all, really, but it was his wife just the same. He knew that in the dream.

And she was sick, he realized. She was dying. Marcus shook her, try-ing to wake her. "Freddie?" he whispered, as if that were his wife's name.

That was the end of it.

When Marcus awoke, he realized Leah was shaking him, not the other way around. He expected her to have the face he'd seen in his dream, but it was just her usual face, and she had her hair knotted be-hind her head in a scarf the way she always did, not hanging loose like the woman's hair in his dream. In his dream, Leah's skin had been darker, too, just a drop.

"Do you hear that?" Leah said.

"What?" Despair still flamed in Marcus's stomach, acid.

"That piano."

Then, he did hear it. He must have heard it all along, because its commanding sound filled the house. While the bass notes set a slow, confident waltzing pace, the melody repeated with a simplicity shroud-ing deep mournfulness. The piece played like a waltz, but it hadn't been born in old Europe. There was something else to it, a nagging familiar-ity. Had he dreamed this song?

The piano's next passage was louder, the melody emboldened by two octaves instead of one. Phoenix had never played so well. Her right hand must be stretched to its limits.

"It's a record," Marcus said, a realization.

"No it's not. It's that piano."

Leah was right, he realized. He'd paid a tuner, but he'd told them tun-ing would be impossible without new parts, so the old piano's notes dangled at the edge of tonality, never quite right. The effect gave the music an added plaintiveness, and Marcus remembered how it had felt to see Leah gasping for life in his dream. And thinking Phoenix was dead. The world seemed an awful and unforgiving place, the way it had been at Raiford. Marcus Smalls shivered in his bed.

"It's that piano, Marcus. I want it out of the house."

"It's not out there playing by itself."

"Go see if Phoenix is in her room." Leah drew the covers up to her chin, like a young girl. "I bet you ten dollars she's sleeping. I *told* you we shouldn't bring it here. Livvy used to say that a piano at the club was haunted, and maybe she was right. Maybe *this is that piano.*"

"Woman, you're talking crazy," Marcus said, but he couldn't ignore his heart's gathering drumbeat. That *wasn't* Phoenix on that piano. It was somebody grown, and somebody good. Better than him, and even better than Leah. Someone who'd been playing a lifetime.

"I tell you, it's the piano, Marcus. It's the piano."

Marcus had just about talked himself into believing her foolishness when he cracked Phoenix's door open and saw that she wasn't in her bed, her rumpled covers left behind. Closer to the living room, as the song's opening melody repeated, the playing was louder and sharper to his ear, too vibrant and immediate to be a recording.

Phoenix.

His daughter sat at the piano in her Snoopy nightshirt, playing with her eyes closed, without sheet music. Marcus's eyes smarted with tears as he heard the music flow from his daughter's hands. It was a beautiful piece, an old piece, and she played like an angel. The music was heartache she hadn't lived long enough to meet up close, and he hoped she never would.

"Peanut?" Marcus whispered.

Phoenix didn't hear him. Her head swayed slowly as the bittersweet melody coursed through her. Her playing only stopped when the song reached its conclusion: hopeful for a sustained note, followed by a pause, then its sad finish, as inevitable as death. Phoenix sat perfectly still, her hands frozen on the keys. Gently, Marcus rested his hands on his daughter's birdlike shoulders. She did not move to acknowledge him.

"When did you learn that?" Marcus said.

Instead of answering, Phoenix began to play again. This time, Marcus recognized the piece right away: It was a rag piece by Scott Joplin. "Weeping Willow." His grandfather had taught him to play it when he was a teenager. Marcus hadn't thought about that piece in years. Hearing it, for an instant, he thought he could glimpse his grandfather's speckled beard and round spectacles. He remembered his grandfather's cottonfield in Valdosta, a blizzard of white, and how cotton used to gather like snowdrifts along the roadside when it blew from its stalks.

Marcus sat at the piano against the wall, the one Leah's parents had bought Phoenix, a child-sized spinet. His large hands felt monstrous on the piano's small keys, the reason he almost never played it. When

Phoenix repeated the song's melody, Marcus joined in, matching his daughter's pace, if not her accuracy. When he stumbled, he tried to catch up. By the next refrain, he had twinned her playing, and their sounds mingled, inseparable.

That was how Leah found them when she followed the music to the living room, armed with her husband's golf club: Phoenix sat at one piano and Marcus at the other, their hands flinging with abandon as they communed within the joyous music. The sight of her husband and child at the pianos cast a spell that made Leah feel her life slip back into normalcy, like a fuzzy television picture rapped to clarity. Everything would be fine, she decided.

The next morning, Phoenix said she didn't remember waking up during the night.

Although she remained diligent about her practicing, the flaring brilliance she had shown that night was gone. Phoenix also lost her fascination with the old piano. More than that, she was afraid of it. The story her mother and father kept spinning about the late-night concert scared her, especially when her father bought her a Joplin songbook; one glance told her that "Weeping Willow" was years beyond her abilities. The waltz she'd played—called "Bethena," it turned out—was no picnic either. On top of that, the accident had been strange. The Bell boys insisted they hadn't moved the piano to the top of the stairs, and what if they were telling the truth?

Phoenix and her parents agreed that it was time for the old piano to go.

A collector advertising for antique pianos in the *Miami Sun-News* came to their house to inspect it. Although the man didn't seem impressed by the piano's model or condition, he paid them fifty dollars and carted it away. Before he left, Phoenix saw the collector slide a pencil inside his loafer, eraser first, to scratch his foot.

The piano was gone, and none of them missed it, not even Phoenix.

But for the rest of Phoenix's childhood, she had a recurring dream of sharing a stage with her father at the Silver Slipper, dressed in formal concert finery. They sat at two ivory-colored grand pianos arranged back to back, their delicate notes filling the room like a songbird's call as they played a slow, sad waltz in perfect synchronicity.

In the dream, the Silver Slipper's seats were jammed, and the overflow crowd stood watching from as far as the Gallery of Greats. Everyone in the audience was rapt, their teary eyes trained on the father and daughter playing as one, giving language to joys and travails no words could express. While Phoenix and her father played in the dream, an orchestra conductor always stood before them, waving his baton with manic fervor, his face hidden beyond the harsh stage lights.

Phoenix always awoke from this dream with her eyelashes caked together, her cheeks raw from crying through the night.

Part One

Muthafucka, I'm a baller—

I'll smoke you for my dolla.

Pop you 'round the corner

'Fore you get a chance to holla.

G-RONN
"Don't Fuck with What's Mine"

The hall was illuminated by electric lights;

It was certainly a sight to see.

So many colored folks without a razor fight,

'Twas a great surprise to me.

SCOTT JOPLIN
"The Rag-Time Dance"

CHAPTER ONE

Someone rapped on the hotel room door.

Gloria squealed, laughing. "He's still there, Phee."

"*Shhhhh*. It's not funny." Phoenix wasn't in the mood for fan bullshit. If this was the same boy, he'd been outside their hotel suite two solid hours, knocking softly every half hour to let them know he hadn't gone anywhere. What had been amusing at ten wasn't at midnight.

Phoenix pulled a velvet throw pillow from her cousin's bed across her eyes. Before the last knock, Gloria had been flipping through *The Source,* fantasizing about which men she'd like to hook up with when they had the chance to shop backstage at the Grammys or the MTV Music Awards—*It's a tough choice between Tyrese and 50 Cent, huh?*

Phoenix's only fantasy right then was to have the strength to walk to her master bedroom across the hall, brush her teeth and go to bed. The OutKast CD sounded tinny and awful from the cheap CD player that doubled as a clock radio, and Phoenix knew she *had* to be tired, if OutKast couldn't wake her up. She couldn't remember being this trashed on the road before, even when she still had a band hauling instruments and amps.

The knock on their door came again, bolder.

"What's your name?" Gloria called toward her open doorway, and she might as well have been calling down the street. This was the biggest room of Phoenix's tour so far, an elegant suite with two bedrooms, a living room with a dining room table for six, phones and televisions in each bathroom, and Phoenix's master bedroom, with a canopied bed so high off the ground that it came with its own steps. *Welcome to the future,* Gloria had said when they arrived last night. The room was comped, or Sarge would have put them up at the Budget Inn as usual. At least at Budget Inn, she didn't have to walk so far to go to bed. *Everything has a price,* she thought.

"Don't encourage that boy," Phoenix said, slapping Gloria's thigh. "I'm not kidding."

"I'm Kendrick," a voice came back, full of false confidence. He sounded young, a kid.

"How'd he find my room? I'm calling Sarge," Phoenix said. Sarge wasn't in for the night yet—he was surely out at one of the clubs schmoozing the radio folks and music writers—but Sarge's cell was always strapped to his belt, fully juiced.

"Don't call Sarge. Damn. Just *talk* to the man. You haven't been laid in a month."

True enough. Ronn was busy, and so was she. Ronn was in L.A. recording a CD and trying to get his film production company going, and she was in the middle of her radio tour to promote her first CD on Ronn's label, *Rising.* Three Strikes Records was better known for gangsta rap than R&B, but Ronn had put a lot of labor into *Rising,* and not just because he sometimes shared his massive four-poster bed with his new artist. With a hit-maker like D'Real producing her tracks, Ronn had told Phoenix she'd better get used to people knowing who she was, the good and the bad.

Was this stranger outside the door part of the good, or part of the bad?

"I rode the bus from New York to see you, Phoenix," said the young man's muffled voice. "I'm prelaw at NYU, not a stalker. I'm only asking for one night, and I won't be bragging to my boys in the morning. I want to be a gentleman and treat you like a lady."

"Phee, boyfriend is *smooth.* Ask him if he brought a partner," Gloria whispered, and Phoenix pinched her cousins's arm to shut her up. Gloria was crazy if she thought they were going to tag-team groupies tonight, Gloria's favorite fantasy.

But the man had come from New York to St. Louis on a *bus* just to lay this rap on her? How did he know where she'd be staying, much less where her room was? This boy better hope her father wouldn't stop by the suite and find him standing there. After a month straight on the road, Sarge would not be in the mood for a stranger who didn't understand boundaries.

Phoenix stood up. She was still wearing the tattered jeans and white T-shirt from rehearsal for Friday night's show at Le Beat, her peanut-butter-colored makeup smudging her collar and shoulders. She lifted her underarm, and her tart scent assailed her nose. Gloria was a M.A.C. girl who kept herself glam day and night—streaked hair moussed to perfection, face painted to glorify all the right angles, blouses cut low across her cleavage—and compared to her cousin, Phoenix knew she looked like one funky mess. Funky and tired.

So why was she wasting the energy she'd saved for brushing her teeth to walk to the suite's white double doors? Phoenix put her face close to the doors. She could smell cologne in the cool air through the crack, one she knew. Calvin, maybe. Not Kenzo, but not bad.

"How'd you find my room?" she said to the crack and the cologne.

"Oh, Father Jesus," she heard him say, surprised. His smoothness had evaporated.

"You know you're not supposed to be standing outside my room, right?" Gentle but firm.

His voice came closer to the crack, and she saw a blur of dark skin. "Miss Smalls, I *love* your music. I have your CD from back in the day, those cuts with the mad keyboard riffs, that first one you put out. You're a straight-up genius."

Phoenix's first CD had been born and buried four years ago, so this was a hard-core fan. Phoenix and her band in Miami had poured their souls into two CDs, and their old label hadn't sold enough copies to pay for them. That had hurt so much, she'd come within a breath of telling Sarge she was ready to quit, except that she knew how disappointed he would be. At Three Strikes, Ronn and D'Real had laid down the law: Her original music was too this, too that, not urban enough, not enough like D'Real's vibe, and D'Real is the producer and the producer is God. *Hell, D'Real's the real star, let's be real.* Sarge had warned her things would be different at a major label, and he'd been right. As different as different could be.

"One of my cousins works here, and she told me where you'd be," the boy said through the door. "Please don't try to make me say who. I promised not to get her in trouble."

This was rich. "Someone's pimping me out at the front desk?"

"It ain't like that." She heard the smile in his voice, saw the white of his teeth through the crack. Polished, peroxide teeth. "I told her I would slide up on you for an autograph. But I couldn't get this close and miss my chance to scrub your back while you take a bubble bath. And take some of this massage oil to rub down your muscles. I have strong hands, Miss Smalls."

Damn, that does sound good, she thought. Her knees and thighs were throbbing, sore.

"If you want to take it to the next level, of course I have protection," he went on. "And just to keep it safe, I brought a doctor's report you can look at. I don't play."

"Oh, no he *didn't* say that!" Gloria said, Miss Blue-Eyed Ghetto Fabulous in the flesh.

"This is a joke," Phoenix said, certain. Arturo and the dancers had nerve bothering her this late. "Who is this?"

Phoenix opened the door, and the man who stood there was a stranger. He was tall and lanky, with tree-trunk shoulders, a boyish face the complexion of Wesley Snipes, and a shadow of fuzz on the deep cleft of his chin. It wasn't a joke. Phoenix assessed the stranger's loose linen pants, bone-colored knit shirt, leather sandals, and close-cropped haircut. *Nice.* He had a leather duffel bag slung across his shoulder, probably his Booty Kit. He would be a magnificent man one day, but he was young. Very young.

"You're a baby, Kendrick," she said. "Let's see some ID."

This must be how Carlos had felt with her, she realized. Phoenix didn't think of Carlos often, but she wished it was Carlos at her door instead of a stranger. Carlos's memory might be bad luck for this boy, since Sarge had knocked one of Carlos's back teeth loose.

Gloria posted herself beside Phoenix, no longer laughing, her guardian. Phoenix couldn't pay her cousin much—a little pocket change, free travel, and free hotel rooms—but she would definitely pay Gloria more one day. *That* was a fact. One day soon.

Kendrick reached for his wallet, clumsy. It took him nearly thirty seconds to pull his license from its sleeve. Kendrick Allen Hart, Brooklyn, New York. Just turned nineteen. If he'd been seventeen or eighteen, Phoenix would have sent him back to the playground. Nineteen made him more interesting. Hell, she was only twenty-four, and her promo packets claimed she was twenty-one. There was only a two-year age difference between this boy and Phoenix singular, *The* Phoenix, no last name necessary. Sarge said if Beyoncé and Ashanti and Imani didn't need surnames, neither did she.

"Phoenix, ma'am, you're more beautiful in person," Kendrick said, smart enough to keep his distance in the hall. She saw perspiration across his forehead, but his cologne smelled fresh. His smile struggled against a twitching bottom lip, but held on.

"Thank you. Give me your bag," Phoenix said.

Quickly, Kendrick complied, ducking beneath its strap as he swallowed hard.

Phoenix gave the lightweight duffel bag to Gloria, who unzipped it behind her, stone-faced. Most days, Gloria was hardly better than no help at all, but she liked playing bodyguard. If Kendrick forgot himself, Gloria would put him on his back.

"You coming to the New York show?" Phoenix said, small talk during the inspection.

Kendrick's admiration, loosed from all restraint, leaped free. "*What?* I ain' missin' it! Front and center. I can't hang out in St. Louis and see you Friday 'cuz of my Af-Am lit final, but I *will* hear you at the Osiris. *Believe* that. History in the making. Phoenix, you are off the *hook.*"

Friday's show was a small listening party at a club called Le Beat near the University of Missouri, no big deal. But next week, Phoenix had a gig opening for the New York leg of the Hip-Hop R&B Summer Mega-Jam, joining the show at the historic Osiris Theater in Harlem. That show would be the biggest of her life, maybe seventeen hundred people. A few days later, she would begin shooting her first music video for her single on location in L.A. *The sun is about to shine on you, Peanut,* Sarge told her. *Time to open the blinds.*

"Where'd you get the nerve to come stand outside my door?" Phoenix said to the boy.

"I prayed on it. I won't get another chance after you blow up like you're gonna do."

"You know you're crazy, right?"

"Hell, yeah. Gotta be crazy in a crazy-ass world."

Gloria was grinning while she went through the duffel bag. "Ooh, he brought the good kind," she said, playfully shaking a black box of condoms. Lambskin, the brand Ronn preferred.

She was going to do this, Phoenix realized, her heart racing. She had never done this before, not with a fan on the road, but she was going to do this tonight.

"You really brought a medical report?" Phoenix said.

"Yes, ma'am. Got it from my doctor on Monday, before I left. It's in there."

"Bring your crazy ass in here, Kendrick. Don't make me sorry. And if you call me ma'am again, you're gone."

"What should I call you?"

"What do you think? Call me Phoenix."

The sound of her name lit his face afire.

*P*hoenix worked hard not to think about Ronn as she climbed out of her robe and sank into the jetted marble tub Kendrick filled to the sky with bubbles. The boy's eyes on her made her body feel clumsy—breasts too small, legs too thin, stomach pooch too big—but her uneasiness vanished in the embrace of the hot water and the blanket of bubbles. The bubbles rose up past her chin as water beat into the tub amid the whir of the jets. In Kendrick's eyes, she was a goddess.

Kendrick let his shirt fall from his shoulders, past his hips, revealing the banks of his dark chest's muscles, unburdened by body fat. His erection cast a shadow across the crotch of his pants in the candlelight. He looked like a Herb Ritts photo, except his head wasn't shaved.

He was beautiful.

Shit. She was really going to spend the night with a fan. What would Ronn say if he could see her in a candlelit bathroom with this half-naked manchild? She and Ronn had never said they were exclusive. She hadn't seen Ronn in a month. He only called her every three or four days now, not every night like he used to. It wasn't like he was going home alone every night. She'd be crazy to believe *that.* "You know who my boyfriend is, right?" Phoenix said, to cover her obligations.

"Just what I read," Kendrick said. He didn't sound concerned.

"Keep that in mind before you say anything foolish to anybody. We're straight?"

Ronn would never hurt her, and she didn't think he'd try to hunt down a groupie she'd met on the road if he heard about it, but you never knew. One of Ronn's overzealous fans might give Kendrick a beatdown if he started bragging. Anything could happen after that crazy shooting last month in New York, everybody saying G-Ronn and Three Strikes was behind it. That was bullshit—Ronn had hustled a little in the projects way back when, but he'd been more a businessman than a thug. Still, you couldn't guess what other people would do in your name.

Kendrick hooked his hands into the waistband of his linen pants. "You don't have to tell me twice. This is about me and my memories, and hopefully you and yours."

Kendrick must have put too much bubble bath in the jetted tub, she realized. The bubbles were a mountain in front of her, so Phoenix had to carve a tunnel to see through. The bathroom reeked of the bubble bath's sickly sweet strawberry scent. *He'll learn,* she thought.

"Didn't you promise to scrub my back? Better hurry, before I drown in these."

"Sorry," he said, timid. He knelt beside her, one knee against the marble floor.

He knocked away some of the bubbles, a path. "Lean over," he said in her ear.

Phoenix leaned forward, her ears drowning in the water's rush from the faucet near her face. Kendrick's fingertips traced the trail of her spine. His fingers were more steady now than when he'd been in the hall, all hesitation and boyishness forgotten. His fingertips were smooth, and the tickle she felt at the end of his fingers grew into a burn.

"Phoenix." He said her name as he rubbed soapy warm water across her back. He said it again as he encircled her with his arms, resting his palms across her breasts, gently pinching her waiting nipples with his fingertips. *Phoenix.* There was wonder in his voice.

And in his touch. Phoenix was shocked at the way his squeezing fingers locked the rest of her body in place, almost fetal, as if it were afraid to release something. Her lips parted as her body seemed to expand beneath the warm water, pleasure in a balloon.

"Does that hurt?" he said.

She shook her head. It wasn't painful, but torture all the same. "Let's go to the bed," she said, thinking about how Gloria must be eating her heart out. Gloria was probably hoping Kendrick would sashay his chocolate loveliness over to her room next. Too bad. With blond hair like a magician's wand, Gloria usually had her pick—but not tonight.

In her bedroom, Phoenix noticed her Rolex on her nightstand, a small, gleaming window to her conscience. The watch had a diamond bezel and dial, and it was the only gift she had accepted from Ronn. Her Rolex was the most expensive item she owned, more than her car and keyboards combined. She burrowed beneath the mound of covers, cool sheets swaddling her overheated skin, and felt like she was hiding. She hadn't expected to feel bad. She'd told herself when she hit twenty-one she would stop doing things she felt bad about.

Kendrick climbed under the covers beside her. His long, bonelike manhood nestled against her hip, pulsing gently whenever she inhaled and her body rose. When he leaned over to kiss her breast, his lips were so gentle that they might have been kisses, or only hot breath. She could barely feel his lips and tongue. Ronn always took her breast in the palm of his hand, making it bulge like a melon, and lathered her nipples. She always knew when Ronn was there.

Kendrick guided her hand toward where his eager body strained against her, and she grasped him the way she might hold a stick, feeling his juices beading already as she rubbed her thumb across his most sensitive spot. He moaned against her neck, waiting. *He's tripping if he thinks I'm going down on him,* Phoenix thought, and she let him go.

Kendrick pulled her thighs apart and burrowed beneath the sheet, but his tongue felt dry and lifeless on her, as if he had lost his way. He was just a kid, she remembered.

"Get the condoms, OK?" she said, because she was ready to be done with it.

Kendrick was better at intercourse, luckily. He kept his eyes on hers, watching her face as he inched his way inside of her, steadying himself with his arms locked. He didn't expel right away as she'd feared, and he no longer felt like a boy. Kendrick was so long, he seemed endless. Phoenix felt her body loosen and flood, embracing him. His measured, confident strokes felt so good, she almost had a full-blown orgasm. Almost. That would take more practice, and Kendrick wouldn't have time to learn. When he was ready, Kendrick gritted his teeth and tilted his head so far back that his Adam'a apple bulged. "Oh, shit. Oh, shit."

Then, it was over. This was the same way it had been with the Dominican guy she'd danced with at Crobar on her twenty-first birthday: The heat of a buildup realized in brief bubbles, the pleasure over too soon, and wishing she could roll away as soon as it was done. She suddenly wanted to ask Kendrick to leave. She hoped he wasn't expecting to spend the night.

But Kendrick had made himself comfortable, gazing at her from his pillow.

"Phoenix . . ." he whispered beside her, disbelieving. She could smell a trace of his last meal on his breath, something spicy. She would not kiss him. Kisses were too intimate for a man she didn't know.

"Why do you keep saying my name like that?" she said.

"Like what?"

"I don't know . . . Like it's . . ."

"Like it's the name of an ancient Egyptian goddess? It is. Like it's the name of a force of nature? It's that, too. *Pheeeee-nixxxx,*" he said. He cupped her chin in his hand. His eyes were swathed by thick lashes, and he gazed with a gravity she found unnerving. "I'm jealous, girl."

"Jealous of what?"

"I'm jealous because I knew about you first. I knew you when nobody else did. And now everybody's about to come late to my party. I have to share you." When he stroked her bare shoulder, his hand lashed fire. Her body didn't mind if he stayed a while.

"You really think I'm gonna be all that?" she said. Her voice cracked.

Kendrick laughed, his head rolling against the pillow. "Don't even front. You know it."

She smiled. "Yeah, you're right." Sarge would see to it, that was all.

"But you changed your sound. I heard a *Rising* demo, and you're different now."

Phoenix had nearly forgotten that anyone would know her old sound. "Better, right?"

"Different, not better. Maybe not as good, in some ways, not to me. Too R&B radio. I miss the rock riffs, the freaky keyboard, the worldbeat. But you're still in there. I still hear you."

Phoenix had gone so long without hearing the truth, she hadn't realized it was missing. When was the last time anybody had the nerve to say something like that to her? Not Gloria. Not even Sarge. Nobody since Carlos, who had seemed to enjoy telling her exactly what she didn't want to hear. Having a truth-teller was like having God himself in the room, so Phoenix tried to think of a question worthy of Kendrick Allen Hart. She covered her bare chest with the sheet. They were two people talking now, not a wannabe singer and her one-night stand. They could be in a junior-high schoolyard sharing a strawberry soda.

"What's the worst cut?" she said.

He shrugged. "A couple of them are weak."

The word *weak* made Phoenix's stomach cramp with gas.

Kendrick went on: "Truthfully, tracks five and seven could go. That's the producer talking, not you. He drowned you out. He was putting out that same shit two years ago."

Damn. Phoenix tried to think of what to do about the seventeen hundred people who would hear her singing behind those recycled beats at the Osiris. They would boo her off the stage. Had Sarge given her an escape clause in her contract? Sarge usually took care of that.

"But that one 'Party Patrol,' that's gonna bump all summer," Kendrick said. "Reminds me of Prince, or the Gap Band, but with your own flava mixed in, too, like that Middle Eastern vibe. It's *tight*. Nothing on your old CD was that good. It's gonna make you a star, girl."

Phoenix felt herself breathe, her heart pounding. "Party Patrol" was one of the few songs on *Rising* that had felt like a collaboration, at least pieces of it. At first, D'Real hadn't liked the sound of the Egyptian-style violin intro she'd asked him to weave inside the opening measures, but he'd relented, mixing her until she sounded like a full string section. "Party Patrol" was one of their few true moments of musical collaboration.

"But is the CD any good?" she said.

"Yeah, mostly. It's real good, Phoenix. It's *on* for you, girl. All I'm saying is, my favorite ones are when you're in there, too. Not your voice, but your *music*. The best part."

Phoenix's stomach cramped again. In today's rehearsal, she hadn't been able to get through the choreography of "Party Patrol" without sounding breathless when she sang, and on the last song her voice was smothered beneath the exploding tracks. She wished she had a voice like her sister's, because Serena could *sing*. Serena could bring it like Aretha and Patti and Whitney, from her soul-space.

But Phoenix would have to be Phoenix. Whatever she was, she was.

Phoenix wanted to ask Kendrick if people would think she could sing worth a damn, but she had heard enough truth for one night.

Me and my crew's gonna roll . . . We're on a Party Patrol . . ."

Kick-cross-step, kick-cross-step. Phoenix spun, hitting her mark a fraction behind the beat. Head cocked left, then right. And *sliiiiiide . . . two, three, four . . . sliiiiiiide . . . two, three, four. . . .* Hunched shoulders, snapping high. "We're losin' control . . . Out on this Party Patrol . . ."

The more Phoenix concentrated on her dancing, the more sluggish her energy felt. Arturo and the other two dancers seemed to follow her lead, missing cues, stumbling over steps and performing by rote, as if they were unmoved by the music blasting from the giant club's speakers. Phoenix's voice cracked on the last high note, fluttering to nothing, barely audible in the speakers from her headset microphone. She was so breathless, the recorded vocals drowned her out. Her voice was worse than yesterday. And her lower back throbbed, the old injury taunting her.

The rehearsal at Le Beat was not going well.

"OK, guys, let's take a deep breath," the choreographer said, stopping the music.

Phoenix was grateful for the break. The label hadn't paid for backup singers on this radio tour, much less dancers—but Sarge had convinced Manny to give her dancers in St. Louis and at the Osiris. *Hell, it's all coming out of your end eventually, Phee,* Sarge had reminded her. Dancers would make the concerts look better, give Phoenix more dancing practice, and give her and Sarge a chance to audition their choreographer before the video shoot began.

But the choreographer Olympia was pushing for too much too soon, trying to show off for Sarge. Phoenix had studied a little dance in high school and had always been rhythmic, but Olympia's finely regimented contortions took her mind away from her voice, and apparently her voice needed more attention. How could they perform this tomorrow night? How could they dance at the Osiris, with only a week of rehearsals left before that show?

Olympia sighed. The lithe, short-haired woman was twenty-two, but something officious in her voice made her sound like a Student Council president moonlighting as a B-girl. "Guys, was that your way of telling me it's time for lunch?"

That was the first good idea Phoenix had heard today.

Sarge was waiting for them in the club's tiny conference room, standing against the wall with his arms crossed as they filed in with their bags of lunch from Wendy's across the street. Sarge was always her watchman and taskmaster, with his shaven head, trademark skullcap, and mole-splotched face that hadn't changed since her childhood. The only part of Sarge that aged was his temper, which had gotten more brittle. Sarge gave her a look: *What's the problem?*

Phoenix shrugged. She wasn't in the mood for Sarge on an empty stomach. While she waited for the dancers to negotiate whose food was whose, Phoenix's eyes studied the room's wood-paneled walls, which were plastered with concert posters dating back a decade. Everybody had been through here, apparently. Nelly, of course. Chingy. Ginuwine. Lauryn Hill, from forever ago. Even Gloria Gaynor, still surviving on a long-ago comeback tour. This room reminded Phoenix of the Gallery of Greats in the Silver Slipper, before her mother sold the club like she'd always promised to. There was even a piano against the wall, like déjà vu.

"I have a migraine after that sorry display," Sarge told the group, as the dancers took their seats in the plastic chairs, crowding the table. "Maybe since this isn't New York or L.A., you think this show doesn't mean shit. Well, there's no such thing as a *small show*. Maybe I need to call my friend R.J., who's doing Ronn a solid even *having* you on his stage, and tell him my crew isn't *ready* for Le Beat . . ."

Sarge could go on all day.

Arturo sat sullenly beside Phoenix, stirring his chili with a plastic spoon. The other two dancers were Olympia's contacts, but Arturo was Phoenix's friend from high school, and she always hired him when she had a chance. He was a great dancer, perpetually underemployed. Arturo was six-four, a colossus who could leap over a horse.

"Maybe you need to learn to let people eat without all this noise," Arturo muttered, and Phoenix slapped his thigh under the table.

Sarge pierced Arturo full force with The Ray. "You know what? You're the first one I'm sending home. And don't think I'm gonna have you in that video or on my stage at the Osiris if this is the best you've got. I'll send you back delivering those damn pizzas, or whatever the fuck you were doing when Phoenix begged me to call you. You're not ready for this level, son."

Arturo's ego must be screaming, Phoenix thought. She'd met him at Miami's New World School of the Arts when they were both fourteen, and he was still one of the most dynamic dancers she'd ever seen, able to make his body defy physics. After studying dance on a college scholarship, he'd somehow ended up back in Miami managing a Domino's Pizza. She didn't want Arturo to blow this chance. She could take him with her, if only he'd get out of his own way. Under the table, Phoenix squeezed her friend's hand. *Chill, sweetie. It's just Sarge.*

As Sarge beckoned Olympia through the door to tell her something privately, Arturo spoke close to Phoenix's ear. "He's got it twisted if he thinks I'm a sissy queen shaking in my shoes. I *will* take him outside to throw down, whether he's your father or not," he said. Arturo had a low-pitched, satiny voice that had always made Phoenix wish he weren't gay.

"No stress," Phoenix said. "It's just trash talk, Arturo. You know Sarge."

He pecked her lips, standing. "Only for you do I tolerate this, *chica*. Believe that."

The dancers rushed their lunch, since no one wanted to wait for Sarge to come back, so Phoenix waited for her father alone. She pulled one of the plastic chairs up to the piano and tested the keys. Surprisingly, it was nearly in tune. She slid her foot to the sustaining pedal and ran her fingers through a hurried version of the largo from Dvorák's *From the New World Symphony*, which had been a recital piece her freshman year in high school. Playing felt good, a chance for her fingers to dance. She hadn't brought her red Roland AX-1 or Moog Liberation shoulder keyboards for this tour, the first time ever. But there was no substitute for a piano.

Phoenix didn't realize Sarge was behind her until she heard his chuckle. "Haven't heard that in a while," he said. "Your mama would be glad to know you can still play it."

"By heart," she said, concluding with the stately D-flat chord.

She played better than she sang, Phoenix realized, and the thought made her spirits wane. In high school, she had told Mom she would attend one of the arts colleges that had been cramming her mailbox with solicitations by the time she was a sophomore, Juilliard included. But when Phoenix was sixteen, she decided she wanted to be a star like Janet Jackson, and Juilliard didn't have classes on that.

The band Phoenix started in high school, Phoenix & the New Fire, hadn't worked out, even with Sarge's contacts and enough momentum to get bookings and a small record deal. Their two CDs got great reviews (*when* they were reviewed), but they never found an audience in R&B, pop, alternative or anywhere else. Maybe she could have stuck it out like Lenny Kravitz, waiting for the audience to find *her*, but there were plenty of bands whose music was never heard, and never was a long time. Sarge had known multiplatinum rapper G-Ronn since his first tours, so when Ronn said he was looking for an R&B singer, Sarge suggested her. Just like that. Now, Phoenix was flying solo. *And it's a long way down by myself*, she thought.

Sarge looked at her closely. "What time did you get to sleep last night?"

"Late," Phoenix said, guiltily. Her hair still smelled like strawberry bubble bath, and the scent irritated her now. She'd been in such a hurry to get to rehearsal that she'd barely said a word to that boy as she walked him to the door, much less offered him a number. She wished she could erase last night.

"You know better," Sarge said, as if he knew everything. "Your voice sounds worn-out. Where's Gloria?"

"Probably at the hotel ordering room service and watching pay-per-view."

"Tell her to stop wasting up our money, hear? Ronn isn't paying our tab, and nobody here is rich. Your advance has to last."

A hundred thousand dollars had sounded like a fortune a year ago, but no more. Phoenix had banked a chunk of her first major advance so she couldn't touch it, but she hated to think about how much of the rest she had already spent. "I've told her," Phoenix said.

"You should have left her home, Phee."

"Don't start, Sarge." Her cousin could be a pain in the ass, no doubt, but without Gloria, the road would be a cruel companion, beyond lonely. Sarge had agreed to Gloria's presence on the tour, and Phoenix had agreed to give D'Real and Ronn the creative direction of *Rising*. Most days, it hardly seemed like a fair trade.

Phoenix heard the Egyptian string tracks from "Party Patrol" squall through the open doorway as Olympia queued up the CD. Although she'd heard it two hundred times, Phoenix still felt a charge when her multitrack violin solo came on the club's speakers. Kendrick was right about this song: It was a hit-in-waiting. It didn't all belong to her, but a piece was enough.

"The show doesn't feel right yet, Sarge," Phoenix said. She almost called him *Daddy*, craving comfort, but he preferred *Sarge* when they were working.

"It isn't right. But you'll get there. Give it a couple more hours, and come back strong in the morning. We have time to tighten it up before tomorrow night." Sarge had promised never to bullshit her when it mattered, so she prayed this was one of those times.

"The radio stuff is really splitting my attention," she complained.

"There's no more radio interviews in St. Louis. You got bumped because of the blues festival. You're a free woman until the show."

Good. Canceled interviews would give her more time to rehearse, rest and watch a couple movies with Gloria, even if Ronn and the publicity department wouldn't like it. *Publicity is paper,* Ronn always said. Even though she was sure Ronn had nothing to do with the shooting that killed DJ Train's bodyguard in Brooklyn, Ronn said he'd seen a big bump in his SoundScan numbers because everybody said he was behind it. Publicity was paper, all right. If anybody knew about money in the bank, it was Ronn.

"I talked to Serena today," Sarge said. "She's coming out to join us in L.A., and she says she'll stay on through New York."

Phoenix hardly knew her two half brothers, but Serena was a true sister despite their twenty-four-year age difference. Phoenix had only seen Serena two or three times in the past few years, and she'd been begging her to come on this tour. "She said she'll sing with me?"

"We'll work on that. For now, she says she'll do your hair so you won't look so nappy."

Phoenix laughed. Serena owned a beauty shop in Atlanta, and was a virtuoso with hair. Ronn wanted Phoenix to get a more television-friendly weave, and Serena would hook her up. At the moment, Phoenix's blowout Afro was a curly brown-red crown reaching toward the sky, virtually untended. Not suitable for mass consumption. Ronn hadn't said it quite that way, but that was what he'd meant.

"What about Mom?" Phoenix said.

"Call her yourself, but she still says she's not coming until New York. Sorry, Peanut."

No surprise there. For years, on the rare holiday occasions they all stayed in the Miami house, Mom slept in the master bedroom and Sarge hibernated in the garage he'd refinished for himself. Her parents were married only in name, and probably had been longer than she'd known. Phoenix wondered how much of her parents' long, slow drift she could blame on her career.

"I'm gonna go hit that stage again," Phoenix said.

"Save your voice for tomorrow night, though. Work on your moves."

Sarge followed her through the doorway back out to the cavernous nightclub, where the bass for "Party Patrol" resounded like thunder.

Le Beat was a two-story nightclub bedecked in mirrors and shiny poles against a black dance floor and dark walls. The deejay booth lorded high over the stage like the control panel of a space shuttle. They passed the VIP section just beyond stage right, with a velvet rope partitioning off Art-Deco-style furniture, the room's only bright colors.

There might be more than five hundred people there Friday night, the club owner had told them, and the most important ones would be in the VIP section: deejays, music writers, record buyers. The airplay sentinels.

Olympia was taking Arturo and the other two dancers through the opening, which started with them lying flat on their backs, thrusting their torsos high and leaping to their feet after a B-boy-style spin. Phoenix could see that Arturo had taken Sarge's criticism to heart: His motion was energetic and crisp, the way she remembered him at New World. His body sailed through the air, and he landed solidly, cranking his shoulders into the next move, hitting his beats. The other two dancers looked like children at play beside him. She could only imagine how lame *she* must look trying to pull off Olympia's moves.

"Ronn knows I'm not Janet Jackson, right?" Phoenix said to Sarge.

"You don't have to be. But trust Olympia. She understands illusion, how to make you look like you're doing more than you are. By the way, Arturo looks good. A little discipline, and he'll shake things up when it's time to start shooting that video."

"I know," Phoenix said, smiling. Arturo's personality clashed with hers too much for a deeper friendship, but she and Arturo had lived through a storm when their friend Jay died of AIDS complications in high school. She and Arturo had shared their first tragedy in common. "Could you just ease off on him a little, Sarge? He's touchy."

"Why quit a tactic when it works?" Sarge said, winking. "I'll think about it. Listen, where are you going after rehearsal?"

"Back to the room with Gloria, I guess. Why?"

"I'm gonna make a call and set something up for you."

"Please don't, Sarge. I'm tired."

"Not an interview. I want you to go to the Scott Joplin House. It's near the hotel."

For an instant, Phoenix was sure her father was just trying to get a rise out of her, but no smile cracked his face as he gazed at the stage. It was bad enough rehearsals and interviews were driving her into the ground, but in each new city Sarge was trying to be a tour guide, too. In Atlanta, he'd dragged her to the King Center when she'd barely gotten four hours of sleep. In Memphis, the Lorraine Motel.

"Sarge, I said I'm *tired*."

"That's your own fault for staying up late. It's a state historic site. I'd go, too, but I have to work my phone. Gloria can drive you. Make her earn her damn keep for a change."

One oversight in Phoenix's quest for stardom had been learning how to drive. She'd better *hope* she could afford a driver one day. "OK, you're not hearing me. I can't be running all over the place twenty-four/seven on some kind of history lesson."

As always, her words seemed to have no effect on Sarge, as if they were a wind gust he had to tolerate before he spoke again. "Just go for an hour. You can't get where you're going until you know where you've been, Phee." His voice quieted as he locked their eyes. "Remember me telling you about how you played that Joplin in your sleep? And the two of us played a duet in the living room while your mom watched?"

It isn't fair to bring up those days, Phoenix thought.

"I wasn't asleep. I just don't remember it," she said. The skin on her forearms fluttered every time Sarge talked about that night. That year came with a slew of bad memories: a long, boring hospital stay; painful therapy; and worse, seeing for the first time how fragile her mother was, understanding what a *nervous breakdown* was. That was a bad year.

And the story of the piano at the center of it all scared the hell out of her. That damn thing had almost killed her. And she'd never *heard* the pieces Sarge told her she'd played in her sleep, much less should she have been able to play them. She could hardly remember the piano anymore. If not for her family's corroboration, she wouldn't believe it had happened. And whatever it was, Phoenix didn't want to nudge it to see what else might stir.

"You need to go over there and pay your respects," Sarge said. "That man helped open the door for every one of us in music with black or brown skin. Simple as that."

"You say that about everybody."

"And it's true about everybody I say it about."

This was her punishment for hiring a former Black Panther as her manager, Phoenix thought. Hell, this was her punishment for hiring her *father.* Why was it so hard to stand up to him? *Gloria's right. I'm too old to be such a Daddy's girl.*

Phoenix had forgotten Scott Joplin ever lived in St. Louis, and she didn't care. She'd played a little of Joplin's ragtime in high school as part of her classical piano curriculum, but the happy syncopation sounded like the soundtrack to old black-and-white movies, and she'd never even seen *The Sting,* the movie Sarge told her had made Joplin internationally famous. When it came to old music, Phoenix preferred blues. Or even jazz, Sarge's favorite. Maybe Scott Joplin had been ruined for her that night when she was ten, she thought.

What if you'll jinx yourself if you diss Scott Joplin on his home turf? The last thing she needed before this show was a jinx.

"OK, I'll go to the Joplin House. But this is the last diversion, Sarge. I mean it."

"Good girl, Peanut," Sarge said, grinning. "You won't be sorry."

I'm already sorry, Phoenix thought, suddenly so weary she couldn't imagine another two minutes of rehearsal, never mind two hours. Then, under her father's vigilant eyes, Phoenix joined her dancers on the brightly lighted, waiting stage.

CHAPTER TWO

St. Louis
1901

Scott saw the teardrop of bright blood on Louis's shirt collar before he noticed the rag wrapped around Louis's right hand, liberally stained in crimson. Despite the frigid air outside, Louis's thin overcoat hung open, buttons torn. Fresh snowflakes clung to his wind-wild hair.

"God in Heaven," Scott said.

"I'll answer to that." Louis grinned in the doorway with a prettiness that had always seemed misplaced on a man. Louis reeked of lavender and whiskey. His youthful complexion and delicate curls made the boy grievously handsome despite his dishevelment. At nineteen, he lived in a world not sampled by most men their entire lives.

"What happened?"

"This nigger on Market got mouthy, tellin' me he never did meet a Creole could fight. I told him I might be small, but I'd show him if Creoles could fight or not. Before he could blink, I took a swipe at him—" Louis took a half step and shunted to demonstrate, thrusting an invisible razor. "He got lucky and cut my hand, but he wished he hadn't after that."

This boy was a fool. An injury might destroy Louis's ability to play. No insult was worth losing his music. "You need a doctor," Scott said.

"*He's* the one better go find a doctor. Bet he won't say that no more." Louis leaned against the doorjamb. "I'm hungry. Let's get some grub. Where you been, Scotty?"

Belle was upstairs cooking supper, but Scott didn't dare invite Louis to join them. She couldn't abide liquor, and Louis smelled like a brewery. Belle tolerated Tom, Otis, Sam and Arthur fine, but Louis would confirm all of his wife's misgivings about their move to the larger city two hundred miles from Sedalia, in a flat so close to the sporting districts. Lower Morgan and Chestnut Valley were too close for Belle's comfort.

Behind Louis, a covered black Purina wagon loaded with bags of feed rumbled just ahead of a blustering horseless carriage. The day traffic of peddlers, furriers and delivery wagons on Morgan was thinning into the more languid pace of night traffic and its more dubious pursuits.

"I've been here," Scott said. "Working."

"Scribbling, you mean. Hey, you heard Mother's moved her girls to Chestnut? She's tryin' to compete with the Rosebud. Paying top dollar for professors, too—not just tips. And twelve dollars to the winner of the Friday-night contests. She can afford it, 'cause I swear Mother charges for cooze like it's plated in gold—"

"My *wife* is upstairs." Scott gave Louis's shoulder an irritated shake.

Louis clapped his good hand over his mouth. "Aw, shit," he said, but he laughed.

Scott found the money he'd folded in his pocket after his last student left, three dollars for the week's lessons. With his expensive habits, Louis spent more money than most people made, so Scott guessed he was begging for a meal. "Go to the Rosebud and eat. I'll meet you later."

"I ain't gonna eat no food at Tom Turpin's place. Something I ate there the other day tore a hole in my stomach. He's tryin' to poison me, he's so damn jealous he can't play as pretty as me," Louis said, but took the money anyway.

"Tom'll sit on you if I tell him how you're talking. You're drunk, Louis."

"Man, Scotty, just let me in out the damn cold."

"You smell like a bawdy house."

"Old man, don't make me go tell stories on you," Louis said. "Scared of your wife! Shoot, your mademoiselle's gonna like me better than you want her to." He tipped his hat and flashed a smile toward an imaginary Belle, miming a peek at where her cleavage would be.

"You're a sad excuse for a Creole, little man. A mademoiselle is unmarried," Scott said.

"They all forget they're married when I'm near, professor."

Scott heard quick footsteps on the stairs behind him. It was too late to send Louis away.

"Your hand," Scott whispered. Louis gave him a maddeningly ignorant look for several seconds, mocking him, but Louis slid his bandaged hand into his coat pocket, hiding it from sight.

"Scott? It's suppertime," Belle said, a ready chide for whoever was at the door. She was a sturdy woman, nearly as tall as he and twenty-six, with a dark, comely face beneath strands of early silver hair dotting her temples. Scott noticed an ember of intrigue in his wife's eye. Louis's beauty, again.

"I wish you hadn't come all the way down. My friend is leaving," Scott said tightly. "Have you met Louis Chauvin? Louis—this is Belle Joplin, my wife."

"Madam, sorry to bring you down all them stairs," Louis said. He not only tipped his hat; he took it off and pressed it to his breast. Louis could imitate a gentleman's behavior with an actor's ease, which made Scott all the more impatient with the boy's coarseness. "I'm one of the young men fortunate enough to look upon your husband as a great teacher and friend. I've known Mr. Joplin since I was a young Sunday school student in Sedalia. Belated congratulations on your marriage, madam. You must be very proud to be Mrs. Scott Joplin."

Liar! Scott had met the boy in St. Louis two or three years ago, when Tom pointed him out at Mother's and his ears had first thrilled to Louis's elegant musicianship. Sometimes Louis lied for the sheer pleasure of telling a story. All musicians were liars, to hear Belle's opinion, and he wasn't sure she was wrong. Scott intervened before Louis could trip himself up. "Louis only stopped by—"

"Because I wanted to congratulate my old mentor on his success. We boys back at Holy Church have always known Mr. Joplin walked a higher plane. He's no coon musician, madam, oh no. Our Mr. Joplin is an artiste. And it has been the joy of my life to see him held up beyond our small circles. It's no time before he'll be composing for the Governor's Ball and eating with royalty in Germany. He is a true credit to his entire race."

Scott nearly groaned at Louis's sarcasm. "It's a shame Louis can't stay," Scott said.

Belle looked disappointed. "Where are you going, Mr. . . . ?"

"Chauvin," Louis said, with a half bow. "Mr. Joplin says I should go to the Rosebud for supper, but my mama says St. Louis's streets are too rough for an honest boy at night."

"Tom's place?" Belle said, looking at Scott, surprised. "But I just finished cooking."

"We didn't expect a guest," Scott said.

"We have plenty." Belle's eyebrows scowled at Scott's lack of manners. "You can't send a gentle young boy to Chestnut Valley at night. After he's come such a long way!"

"He's been to St. Louis many times, Belle," Scott said. "It's like his second home."

"Scott, for goodness sakes, let's let your young friend in out of the cold."

"Yes, Mr. Joplin, for goodness sakes, let your young friend in out of the cold . . . motherfucker." Louis muttered the last word nearly inaudibly as he passed Scott in the narrow hallway. He stepped hard on Scott's toe as he walked inside, a private insult.

While Louis spun fairy tales, embellishments and fantasies about his life for Belle, Scott directed him to the upstairs washroom, where he gave Louis a washrag to clean himself. Scott did not trust the mysterious smile on his wife's face while she busied herself in the kitchen, but there would be more peace in the house that night if Belle kept smiling.

Scott found a clean white shirt in his wardrobe and knocked on the washroom door.

"We goin' to a funeral?" Louis said when he saw it.

"Change that shirt. You have someone's blood on your collar."

Louis sighed and took the shirt without further argument. Scott stood in the doorway while Louis shaved in the mirror. Louis never went anywhere without his straight razor, and not because he needed one for his fine, spare facial hair.

"Let me see your hand."

"It's already seen after, Dr. Joplin. I rinsed it clean," Louis said. "Don't worry about me, worry for your own self. Yessir, you're up here living the hincty life, scared I'll shame you. No wonder you don't want nobody stopping by. Tom told me about you, walking 'round with your nose stuck up in the air. You won't play nowhere like you used to, huh? But I understand, Scotty. Listen, you got a nice little flat up here. You'll never go hungry with a butcher shop next door. Folks say durin' the war, this was a real pretty neighborhood."

Scott lived upstairs at 2658-A Morgan, in a brick row house identical to every other building for blocks. Their five-room apartment had been improvised from a single town house, so two families now lived in the space intended for one, although the building's refinement was still apparent in the long balcony winding the length of the building from the bedroom door. Scott noticed the apartment's shortcomings most often as he climbed the mountain of steps—more than twenty!—his hand squeezing the rude pipe that had been fitted against the wall as a banister. At the upstairs landing, the pipe ended and met its regal ancestor, the shiny wooden globe that crowned the banister like a recollection.

Still, it was the finest home he had ever had, and Louis knew it. It was a long way from the packed-dirt floors of his youth, and music lived in the very walls. Scott awoke each morning with the memory of a new tune from the previous night's dreams. *Da-daa-da-daaa-da-daaa.* Even now, a worrying musical strain cried for attention in Scott's head. He would rush Louis home after dinner so he could begin capturing it.

"We're doing fine," Scott said. He'd learned never to discuss money with Louis unless he wanted his affairs made public. The first two years had been slow, but last week John had told him that John Stark & Son could barely keep pace with the orders for "Maple Leaf Rag." Already, ragtime brought out something in him like nothing else in all his years performing, and no one expected him to blacken his face. It was a small miracle, and getting bigger.

"Whatever you're doing, it ain't what Mother's paying," Louis said. "Folks are comin' from Kansas City and everywhere else to hear those cuttin' contests."

Yes, but I don't have to spend my nights in a whorehouse trying to convince myself I'm in Heaven, Scott thought. He almost uttered it aloud, but decided if he was going to say anything, he might as well say the thing that was most true. "Cutting contests aren't for me anymore," Scott said. "I don't play like I need to."

Louis half shrugged, but Louis, of all people, couldn't argue. The last time Scott had tried to compete, Mo the Show had shamed him with "Maple Leaf Rag," no less, dressing his own child with needless embellishments and turning it against him.

"I'll give you lessons cheap," Louis said.

Scott chuckled. Louis was joking, but he might need lessons if he ever hoped to play the wild piece that kept chattering in his head, one he hadn't had time to chase with his pen yet. Not that he would ever take lessons from Louis, who had been only seventeen when they met. "What you've got can't be taught, youngster."

"I gotta agree with you on that one, professor."

Louis looked like a new man by the time he'd washed, shaved, and buttoned his clean shirt. Scott handed him a spare tie to finish his transformation.

"What the hell is this?" Louis said.

"A tie. It's Sunday dinner."

Louis muttered curses as he whipped the tie around his neck. "If you got to wear a tie to eat in your own house, Scotty, then you ain't home."

But Louis was wrong: For the first time in his life, he *was* home. And it was a proper home on his own terms, not in any white man's cornfield or cotton patches, kitchen or railroad yard. He didn't play a fiddle for the pleasure of his master, like his father. And he didn't play in a whorehouse, not anymore. Scott knew musicians who played pianos by peepholes in brothels so they could improvise music to match the ardor in the bedroom!

Money wasn't enough to lure him back to that. It was bad enough that so many white men John and Nellie introduced him to raised their voices and spoke to him in simplified language, as if addressing a deaf foreigner, or a child. He couldn't have them thinking he worked in a bawdy house, too. Stupid *and* bestial, they would say. Scott Joplin did not work in a brothel. He worked in his home. A gentleman's vocation.

Scott gazed at his new bedroom, where the fireplace glowed, lighting the room. His window's view was confined to the patterns of bricks from the building next door, but he had memories enough of open fields and oak trees. The quilt from Belle's grandmother lay snugly across their mattress, as it always did, her anchor to the family she missed so much that she'd cried every day their first two weeks in St. Louis. The braided rug from the Starks, their wedding gift, covered the length of the bed-room; he and Belle had discussed using it in the parlor instead, but they agreed they didn't want to expose the handsome rug to visitors, espe-cially with so many students in and out. In the bedroom, the rug was theirs alone, a private luxury to keep their bare feet warm when they first climbed out of bed.

Scott realized he had never been happier. He was thirty-three, but he might as well be as young as Louis. He might be overshadowed as a musician, but he was a *composer* now. Music and royalties lived for years. Forever, sometimes. And Alfred Ernst, the director of the St. Louis Choral Symphony, seemed determined to take him to Germany next summer. Ernst had been kind enough to allow him to hear re-hearsals for a striking opera called *Tannhäuser* by German composer Richard Wagner, and Ernst insisted an American composer might also gain notice in Germany—even if he was a Negro. Scott would have considered Europe beyond his reach a few years ago, when bawdy houses and cakewalk contests were his mainstay, but things were dif-ferent now. Everything was different. Even Louis had to know that, whether or not he could admit it. Life as a married man was only one thing that had changed about Scott's prospects.

"Belle is sensitive, so don't be a nuisance tonight," Scott said.

"Your wife likes me fine. If I was you, I'd be worried she'll shine to me *too* much."

"I'm not worried."

They ate in the kitchen at the table barely big enough for three. Through Louis's eyes, Scott saw the absurdity of formal dress in such cramped quarters, but Belle had always dressed up for Sunday dinner as a child in Sedalia, and Scott enjoyed the ritual. Scott sat in the chair nearest the coal stove, where the persistent heat baked his back, but he didn't mind. He and his wife—soon to be the mother of his first child, if Belle's female instincts were right—were entertaining one of his friends in his home, the finest musician Scott knew. This might seem a simple pleasure to some, but not long ago, he had feared he would live his life from a trunk, counting his pennies from one gig to another, with no hope for a true home.

He would have a dining room like John Stark's at his next house, he decided. Meals warranted their own room. He and Belle would entertain composers, scholars and musicians at their table. He would teach Belle the violin, and she would amuse their guests. *Scott tutored her, of course. She had never played a note.* One day, he and the children would form a quartet. They could play the way he and his family played in Texarkana; his father on his fiddle, his mother on the banjo, Robert on cornet, Will singing strong, and him on the piano his mother had bought him when he was thirteen. And none of his children would wear burnt cork as minstrels, or dream of it. They would keep their own faces.

Belle was uncharacteristically shy in Louis's presence at dinner, answering everything with *pretty good*. She thought their flat was pretty good. She liked this neighborhood pretty good. St. Louis was pretty good, as crowded cities went. Across the table, Scott could see Louis's eyes turning muddy while he tried to engage himself in conversation with her.

"Mr. Joplin's a big man since that 'Maple Leaf Rag,'" Louis said. "He's caused such a stir the white folks put an article about him in their paper. They say he's gonna tour in Germany next year. First we got Booker T. Washington eating lunch at the White House, and then our own Scott Joplin playing ragtime over in Europe. Won't that be something?"

"Scott loves his music pretty good," Belle said.

"Enough about me, Louis," Scott said.

But Louis wasn't finished with Belle. "Won't that be something, though?" This time, oddly, Scott heard no sarcasm from Louis. Louis stared at Belle intently, waiting.

Belle shrugged, an unattractive gesture that made Scott cringe. "I'm not much for music," Belle said. "But Scott makes a pretty good living with it."

Louis's eyes went to Scott's and held them. For the first time, he looked entirely sober.

The habañera Louis was playing at the parlor piano cascaded like a melodic waterfall, and it was only a piffle to him. His fingers flounced carelessly across the keys, the way a child might play with a toy. Yet, it was breathtaking. Each time Scott heard Louis play, he cursed Louis's lack of discipline. What if Chopin had only tossed his creations to the wind? Louis had an enviable singing voice, too, like a cherub's, and his dancing was dizzying. He was a born performer. A lesser man would loathe him, Scott thought. The piano, a black Kohler & Campbell upright grand, had come with the apartment and was worth the monthly rent now that Scott had heard Louis make it sing.

Scott walked to the parlor window, staring down. Outside, gas lamps were an exhibition of bright white light, rows of full moons on poles. Wet snow fell gracelessly from the darkening sky. Even with his window closed, Scott heard a passing woman's ribald laughter below.

"Belle is Scott Hayden's sister-in-law? I can't believe it," Louis said as he played. "She's a bore. No wonder her first husband dropped over dead. She don't like *music?* Dog my cats, old man. That's like Joseph married to Mary, saying he don't much like Jesus."

"I wish you'd lower your voice."

Louis only played more loudly, changing to the key of G. Lovely. "We ain't all whisperers like you, Scotty. Why'd you have to marry such an old lady? You could have your pick of those young ones. Shit, any one of Mother's girls would make you a better wife. That new singer at the Rosebud, Leola, keeps askin' after you."

Scott felt blood rush to his face, although he tried to hold his expression fixed. A drink and conversation two weeks ago with the comely nineteen-year-old singer from Kansas City had turned into an offer to walk her home, and he'd found himself kissing her in the shadows of her doorway. She had taken his hands and guided them across her pliant bust. Despite being a widow, Belle behaved like a virgin, always expecting to be led, and she had never once guided his hands that way. Scott thought about Leola more than he wanted to. Competition at the cutting contests wasn't the only reason he had been avoiding Tom's Rosebud Café these days.

"Men don't trade wives like you trade beds," Scott said. "No more on this subject, Louis. Belle's an upright woman. She's made me a good home."

"Well, don't *that* sound like true love?"

"I'd hate to meet the fool who'd take advice on true love from Louis Chauvin."

Louis laughed. "Yeah, well, you right about that, old man. You right about that," he said, crossing his arms in a rapid arpeggio that ended sweetly on high G.

That finished, Louis stood up abruptly, sighing. He joined Scott at the window, staring at the falling snow. In the silence, Scott heard the memory of Louis's striking improvisation. He would sit this boy down and force him to learn notation even if it was at knife-point. Louis's laziness was criminal!

"So what you scribblin' on nowadays?" Louis said.

"I'm going to write an opera. I mean to call it *An Honored Guest,* or *A Guest of Honor.*"

Scott had never spoken of his aspiration, even to Belle, but the thought had been in his head for some years now. Opera was the most sublime form of music, or so Julian Weiss in Texarkana and his music teachers at George R. Smith College in Sedalia had believed. The music of *Tannhäuser* had strengthened his resolve. He had only lacked a subject from Negro life he could translate to such an epic form, until now.

A week ago, Scott had found his answer in the pages of the *St. Louis Palladium:* Booker T. Washington's lunch with President Roosevelt! Scott couldn't wait to see his father and hear what Giles Joplin thought of a Negro dining with the president. But Booker T. Washington was no ordinary man. Scott hadn't yet read Washington's new book *Up from Slavery,* but he could guess at the man's beginnings from his father's stories of bare feet and lash marks. Any man who could rise from slavery to the president of a college, then to the White House, in one lifetime was worthy of an operatic tribute, indeed.

"Say which? An *opera?*" Louis said. "Oh, you'll be an apple in the white folks' yard after that. They'll give you honorary membership, blue-black as you is. You already talk like 'em."

"You know that's not why I'm doing it."

"Ain't it?" Louis said, gazing at him askance with a crooked smile.

"How did you become such a cynic? You're not nearly old enough."

Louis shrugged. "Just seems funny, a ragtimer writing opera. Or ain't you the same Scott Joplin writing my favorite new coon song?" He sang, raising sad eyes skyward while he clutched his hat mawkishly to his breast: *"I am think-ing . . . of my pick-a-ninny days . . ."* Louis must have seen the score he was writing for the lyrics his friend Henry in Sedalia had sent him.

"There's no harm in earning a few bits," Scott said. The public's fascination with coon songs about the joys of plantation life was endless, and if Negroes didn't write them, white composers would. "I'm talking about a different style altogether, a ragtime opera. I'll write my own music and lyrics."

Scott felt his neck warming as his imagination simmered. One of the opera's pieces could underscore Negro patriotism—a lively two-step called "Patriotic Patrol," perhaps. He could open with an Emancipation Day cakewalk and end at a grand luncheon scene, with a portly, fair-skinned actor dressed like President Roosevelt; moustache, spectacles, cane and all. Scott could almost hear the production: rolling baritones, a libretto of pure poetry.

"When this opera's on the stage, no one will believe all those folks shying bricks at ragtime, saying it brings American music down low. Or else saying Negroes are too ignorant to create art," Scott said. "You can be my tenor."

Louis chuckled. "One thing about you, Scotty, your problem ain't lack of imagination."

"Tom says I never learned how to be satisfied. He's the same sort."

"He's right about that. You listen to Tom, he thinks he can be mayor of St. Louis. Between you, Tom and good ol' Booker T., I guess it won't be long 'til a Negro's voted president." Louis suddenly shook his injured hand, as if playing had aggravated it. His eyes drifted back to the window.

"Another razor fight planned for later?" Scott said.

Louis shook his head. He took a long time to speak, unusual for him; and when he did, his voice carried a weight Scott had never heard before, as if the boy had aged by many years. "I got somethin' to say to you, and after tonight we ain't gonna speak of it," Louis said.

The lack of jest startled Scott. "Agreed."

"I got the dog, Scotty." Louis didn't look at him as he said it, still staring out of the window. The room suddenly felt chilled despite the fireplace.

"Of course you don't," Scott said, although he couldn't dismiss the idea completely, with Louis's habits. "You might get sores, but it isn't always . . ."

"The sores are long gone, but it ain't just that. I heard it from the doc. Anyway, I knew 'fore he told me." He held his hands out, palms downward: Scott saw an unmistakable trembling in his fingers, more severe in his right hand than his left, but visible all the same.

The breath left Scott's mouth. "Lord Jesus," he whispered.

"I ain't told nobody but you, so leave it quiet."

"Of course." Scott blinked, and his eyes prickled, already gathering tears as he realized how trivial his earlier concern about Louis's razor fight was. Syphilis could permanently disable him! Scott moved toward Louis to hug him, but the smaller man pushed him back.

"Hey, hey, watch out," Louis said. "I ain't your candy man. And don't bury me yet."

Despite his worry, Scott chuckled. "You can't hear it in your playing," he assured him.

"Damn right. And when you do, that's the day you better shoot me as dead as Stack Lee shot Billy Lyons down at the Curtis Saloon."

"You're being treated?"

Louis sucked his teeth, which made him sound petulant, all the more boyish. "Mercury makes my breath stink, and I hear it turns your teeth black. You *know* I can't muss these pretty teeth. 'Sides, I felt sicker with that shit than without it. They say mercury don't do nothin' 'cept make you feel like you doin' something. Ain't no real doctor's cure for the dog, Scotty. I found me a hoochie-coochie man from New Orleans, though. He say somebody underworlded me with a spell, all right, but he's fixin' me up."

"For pity's sake . . . You should hear how you sound. That's silly superstition."

"You'll see your way 'round to hoodoo one day, Scotty."

"And that's the day you shoot *me*. Take my advice: Listen to your doctor."

"That doctor's tryin' to put me in the ground 'fore I'm twenty-five, by what *he* says."

Scott didn't dare ask if Louis was exaggerating. His dinner had turned to stone in his stomach. Syphilis was a horrible death, the musician's plague. And no wonder, with so many sweet-faced angels of death within such easy reach.

Louis kneaded his hands together, as if he felt the cold, too. "Anyway, I didn't tell you so you could give me that sad-eyed look . . ."

"I'm sorry," Scott said. "I only—"

"Don't you worry about me. I got bags of luck to spare, an' I'm burnin' so many candles I'll set my bed on fire. There's more to it than what I've said, and there's a reason I said it to *you*." Louis's eyes gazed at him so solemnly that Scott felt his throat constrict with dread, expecting worse news. Still, he couldn't have imagined Louis's next words: "It's Rose that gave it to me. I guess I don't know that for a fact, but she took sick. She's got it, too."

Scott's skin turned to ice. He wrapped his arms around himself, stunned silent.

Rose was a beautiful octoroon with hair hanging past her waist who'd worked for Mother when Scott first met Louis. Louis had bragged that she was the best lay in Chestnut Valley, and she'd blushed at the compliment, her gold eyes flashing like a firefly's. True to Louis's promise, she had been a gifted and imaginative lover. After their first time, Rose refused money for her company, asking to see him after her working hours were done. Scott had visited her at least four times when he was in St. Louis, entertaining fantasies of taking the lovely prize as his bride—before common sense sent him to Belle instead. Scott didn't even know the woman's real name, since "Rose" was surely a diminutive, after the rosewater fragrance she doused across her shoulders and neck. Scott hadn't thought about Rose in more than a year.

Furtively, Scott looked for a shadow in the hall that would betray Belle's approach.

"How do you know?" Scott said, once he was satisfied Belle wasn't near.

"Mother's tryin' to keep it quiet how Rose took and run, but she went home down South, and it's the dog for sure. I don't know for sure I got it from her, like I said, but . . . I'd swear to it to a judge. A damn shame for a pretty thing like that to get spoilt, ain't it?"

Scott's hands curled into fists. He *did* have some hard, open sores on his upper thigh for a time a couple years back, but after two weeks, just when he'd begun to worry, they'd vanished. And he'd had a recurring

rash on his feet a while later, but he'd assumed that was a simple foot in-
fection, the kind he'd suffered in childhood when he shared his brothers'
shoes. The discomfort had bothered him on and off for a few months,
then it had vanished, too. That was during his strenuous effort to mount
his first, short-lived ballet at the Wood's Opera House in Sedalia, *The
Ragtime Dance,* and he'd nearly fallen asleep on his feet many times. Was
fatigue a symptom?

He had seen Rose each time he visited St. Louis that year. That much
he remembered.

Jesus Almighty, Scott realized, his heart stalling. He might have it,
too. He *might.* Scott tugged his handkerchief from his pocket and
mopped his brow, which was damp with sudden perspiration. The last
traces of his meal sat sour in his mouth.

"I ain't gonna ask you what ain't my business, but I remember how
you ran with Rose awhile. The dog sleeps, Scotty," Louis said, his voice
somber. "Sometimes a long time, the doc says. It leaves you, then it
comes back to bite."

Scott could only nod, robbed of speech, and nearly robbed of
thought. He'd hardly heard Louis. The grief he had felt when Louis told
him he was sick had felt deep and genuine, but what he felt now was
deeper than he had known fear and grief could burrow. He felt impaled.

My God, he might have passed it to Belle, and Belle to their unborn
child, if indeed she was pregnant as she hoped. He had heard syphilis
killed babies in the womb, or else soon after. Belle had already lost two
children soon after they were born, with her only living son in Sedalia—
what if he caused her to lose another? *My God. My God. My God.*

How could his life have stood so grand one moment, ground to rub-
ble the next?

Louis sighed, and Scott smelled the sweet whiskey on his friend's
breath. Scott was a poor drinker, but he longed for a sip himself. Maybe
he should go to Tom's after all. But how could he, when his limbs refused to move?

"I hope you don't got it, Scotty," Louis said. "Me? Well, I ain't never
been no good. But you—it wouldn't be right, professor."

Scott blinked. "That's a backwards lie," he said, remembering the
boy's graceful melody.

Louis only shrugged with a bare smile. "Listen, I got a yen, and I ain't gonna sleep if I don't go get me a smoke. Come on with me."

Opium. Scott had suspected the boy's oft-bloodshot eyes were the result of more than spirits. "I can't see how that habit's any good for your condition."

Louis chuckled. "Shows what *you* know. That's how the doc used to give me my mercury, but I like opium better without it. The pipe's good for up *here*." He tapped his temple. "My pipe's the only thing that's ever treated me right. That and my sweet lady." He turned over his shoulder to gaze soft-eyed at Scott's piano against the wall. Louis stretched his fingers, wriggling them one by one. "I'm man enough to take dying, Scotty—hell, I should'a died five times over by now, tonight on Market, too. But I sure am gonna miss my sweet lady one day."

Scott didn't know if the tear creeping past his eyelid was for Louis or himself. Maybe it was for both of them, or *all* of them. Half of Chestnut Valley must be in a panic over the news about Rose. How could communion with that heavenly creature hasten them so surely into Hell?

With a pat on Scott's shoulder, Louis said it was time for him to go. When Scott offered to walk him downstairs, Louis refused, asking him to thank Belle for dinner and bid her good night. With Louis gone, Scott stood alone in the empty parlor for a long time.

Belle came to announce that she felt queasy and would go to bed. *I must be expecting for sure,* she said cheerfully, hugging him from behind. Scott couldn't find it in his guilty heart to kiss his wife good night.

He stood at the parlor window and stared at the falling snow, which tumbled down more quickly now, burying everything in his sight.

CHAPTER THREE

The area skirting the Scott Joplin House on Delmar Boulevard in St. Louis was so bare that Gloria and Phoenix drove past the historic site twice before they realized they'd missed it. Only an open field, maybe a park, sat across the street from the huddle of newer two-story brick buildings on a curb bordered by bricks, like a movie set amid the drabness. A wooden sign identified the building as a historic site designated by Missouri's Department of Natural Resources.

Gloria idled the rented Ford Focus at the curb, lighting up a Newport with her pearl-colored lighter. "Have fun. I'm gonna find some Chinese. See you in an hour."

Phoenix had expected a regal Victorian with trellises and a white-washed porch beneath century-old trees, not a town-house-style building. The area near their hotel in the heart of St. Louis's downtown district had struck Phoenix as desolate, too. The streets emptied out after dark, so she guessed most of the residents had fled for the suburbs long ago, or else been driven out. Downtown St. Louis, like this area, seemed incongruous with the St. Louis of legend, full of hardy businesses and Mississippi River traffic bringing fortune seekers from all over the world. What had changed so much in a hundred years?

Phoenix grabbed her cousin's wrist. "Girl, don't leave me here."

Gloria sighed, and her bloom of cigarette smoke irritated Phoenix's nose. "You're the one who thinks you've got to do everything Sarge says like when you were six. Look, we're here, we've seen it, so why don't you just get out and kiss the earth so we can go? I'm starving."

"Starving from *what*? All you do is sit on your ass."

Phoenix thought Gloria's caustic wit might give her a shot at stand-up or comedy writing, but Gloria wasn't interested in any pursuits that entailed actual work. Gloria had dropped out of the University of Miami as a junior, and she'd quit her job as paramedic only six months after finishing the fire academy, complaining about long shifts. Since then, she hadn't done much of anything except answer the telephone at her parents' health-food store in South Miami. As far as Phoenix could tell, Gloria didn't have any plans except waiting for her cousin to get rich. *A hybrid with twice Gloria's ambition and half of mine might be a normal person,* she thought.

Gloria flipped her a bird. "Eff off. Check yourself, cuz. You sound like your father."

"You eff off." Phoenix looked at her Rolex, which felt like stolen property on her knobby wrist. "It's a quarter to five. I bet this place is about to close."

"Even better. We can say we tried. Sarge has major control issues, and you *enable* it. This is some codependent shit. It's straight out of Psych 101, truly." Gloria never missed an opportunity to trumpet the two and a half years she'd spent in college.

Phoenix ended the argument by climbing out of the car. Two white men in cycling shorts emerged from the building's bone-colored door, ambling toward the mountain bicycles chained to the wrought-iron fence beside the car.

"Are they closed?" Phoenix asked the cyclists.

"Don't think so," said one, whose face was burned red from sun. He had an English accent that reminded Phoenix of Hugh Grant. "Worth popping in. Are you a music student?"

"No . . . just a fan," Phoenix said, although the word *fan* felt trite.

"Cheers," the second man said, mounting his bicycle. He was English, too, and he was unsmiling, apparently eager to cut the conversation short. Maybe he was hungry, like Gloria.

Don't stir this up, Phoenix's mind implored, but she felt trapped. Shit, if these guys from England thought it was important enough to come—

these *white* guys, her mind clarified—then she had no excuse. This was her heritage. Phoenix turned to the car to look at Gloria, one hand slung to her hip. "You're really not coming in? Are you actually *allergic* to cultural growth?"

Gloria waved her cigarette hand through her open window, and its ash flared bright orange before falling to the asphalt. "Black History Month was in February. Call my cell when you're done kissing Sarge's ass. I'll bring you curried chicken."

The cyclists set out in one direction, Gloria in the other. Alone on a street that now felt truly deserted, Phoenix stared up at the building with resignation. If she walked in and someone was playing "Weeping Willow" or "Bethena," she decided, she was gone.

Inside, there was no music playing. A black man with a shaven head, round spectacles and a V-shaped gray goatee met her at the door. He wore a uniform like a park ranger, a tan short-sleeved shirt and blue-gray slacks. He smiled warmly. "Miss Smalls?"

Phoenix nodded.

"I'm Van Milton, the curator here. I was expecting you. I hear you're a famous singer, but I'm sorry to report I don't know any of your songs."

"You and the rest of the world," Phoenix said with a smile, shaking his cool, dry hand.

"I know one!" called a sister with bleached-blond hair at the rear of the room. She wore an identical uniform, leaning against a glass display full of books presumably about Joplin and ragtime. "I heard one on the radio today—Party something. Your name is Phoenix, right?"

Phoenix nodded again, dumbstruck. She didn't know "Party Patrol" had already hit the airwaves in St. Louis! None of the songs from her first two CDs had made it beyond the underground and college radio circuits, so she'd only heard her own voice on the radio cooing background vocals on G-Ronn's "Calling Collect," which had ruled the airwaves last fall. "Whassup, Phoenix?" he'd said on the recording, so everyone would hear her name. She had appeared for thirty full seconds in his video, in a scene it had taken her all day to shoot in a pushup bra, stilettos and a black catsuit two sizes too small. "Calling Collect" was when she'd known her ascension was officially under way, nestled beneath Ronn's expansive wing.

"Do you remember which station?" Phoenix said, knowing Sarge would ask.

The woman shrugged. "All I know is, my fingers were popping. We got a celebrity here today, Van, so don't act up."

"Not a chance," the man said. "Let me give you a tour."

"You sure? If it's too late . . ."

"Nonsense," he said. "Let's go to the Rosebud first. I helped oversee its construction."

The Rosebud, it turned out, was an outside building attached to the house by a wooden walkway. Van Milton told her it was a replica of the Rosebud Bar that had been a center of the black social scene in turn-of-the-century St. Louis: part hotel, part bar, part cafe—and a hangout of all the top "professors," as ragtime players called themselves. The original was blocks away, but the replica had been built beside the Joplin House, since he had been its most famous patron.

The Rosebud replica was made up of wooden wall planks, wooden floors and wooden tables and chairs, striving for an aged appearance. An oversized antique cash register gilded with elaborate chrome flourishes sat before the large mirror that spanned the length of the bar. Behind the bar, against the far wall, sat an upright piano. A large, grainy photograph of Scott Joplin hung above it. Phoenix had seen that photograph before—it was the same one from the Gallery of Greats in the Silver Slipper. In it, Joplin looked like a college instructor, with a face slightly too broad for his tiny earlobes, full lips, close-shaved hair and dark, inscrutable eyes staring away from the photographer, as if lost in their own pursuits. His dress was formal but unremarkable: a dark suit, an old-fashioned shirt with a high collar, and a necktie. Phoenix couldn't guess his age.

"Joplin died young, didn't he?" Phoenix said. She forgot where she'd heard that.

"Maybe not by the standards of the day, but he was forty-nine when he died in 1917."

"How did he die?"

"Syphilis," Milton said grimly. "A sad waste. Let's move to the other displays."

Back across the walkway, inside the Joplin House, Milton walked her past maps of old St. Louis, original Joplin sheet music, and displays of ragtime instruments like banjos and fiddles. One small, brightly lighted room was home to two upright pianos side by side beneath a large color painting of Joplin on the wall, the omnipresent noble. Phoenix admired the large foot pumps on the player piano, then the compartment for piano rolls.

"I could put on a roll for you," Milton said. "It's not Joplin himself playing, but . . ."

Phoenix shook her head, smiling. She sat at the cushioned bench and launched into "Maple Leaf Rag" on the slightly sticking keys, startling herself with how easily the music returned to her. Her fingers romped, playing the song as deftly as she had as a senior in high school, after untold hours of practice. Images often sprang to Phoenix's mind as she played, and this time she saw a succession of women's long skirts flaring and twirling in synchronization with the bold bass notes and infectious melody. Dancing. Men in derbies lifting their partners airborne. Maybe it was her presence in Scott Joplin's house, but Phoenix had never enjoyed the sound of it so much.

Phoenix was grinning by the time she finished, in her best mood since waking beside a stranger that morning. Screw Gloria. Sarge had been right to send her here.

Milton's mouth was parted slightly, exposing the bright pink soft inside his lower lip. His salt-and-pepper eyebrows were raised in surprise. "We have an aficionado," he said.

"I play a lil' bit."

"I love to see young people play Joplin."

"He's no joke."

"If he were here, of course, he would tell you to play it more slowly."

"Him and my piano teacher both." Ms. Garcia had almost been as disappointed as her mother when Phoenix told her she wasn't going to a conservatory after high school. Phoenix and her rival Gregory Ballsley had raced "Maple Leaf Rag" to a frenzy in Ms. Garcia's class. That memory almost made her laugh aloud.

"You can grace me with a concert," Milton said.

"You must hear Joplin all day."

"I hear it and play it, and for a salary. It's the privilege of my work."

"No, that's all right, I'm good," Phoenix said. Standing, she felt weightless, buoyed by the music's vigor. She followed Milton to the next room, humming "Maple Leaf Rag" under her breath, her fingers still exhilarated from their exercise.

In the main display room, Phoenix noticed that the black woman who had been behind the counter was gone, and no one else was in sight. She checked her watch again: It was a quarter after five. A telephone rang in a back office, unanswered. After six rings, the phone went silent. They might be the last ones here, she realized.

"I feel bad keeping you after hours," Phoenix said. "You sure I'm not tying you up?"

"Not at all. My wife tells me this is where I *really* live."

Phoenix scanned the large room, trying to imagine it as a house rather than a museum. "So . . . which of these rooms did he sleep in? Do you know?"

"None of these," he said. "The actual residence is upstairs. I've saved it for last."

With a sweep of his arm, he indicated a doorway leading to a separate section of the building, where she could see the brightly painted yellow wooden floor planks reflecting like a pool of gold against the wall from the sunlight pouring through a hidden window. Phoenix thought she felt the hair at the nape of her neck sway, and she rubbed her palm there. She'd expected this pronounced response when she first set foot inside the house, but it had been absent before. Now, it was here.

Milton led her toward the doorway, pausing to flip the sign hanging in the window on the door Phoenix had used from OPEN to CLOSED. "This door is for visitors," he said. "There's another door alongside it, the one Joplin would have used, the entrance to 2658-A Morgan Street, the former address. We don't have any of the original furniture up there, but . . ."

The phone in back began its persistent ringing again.

"Listen," Milton said quickly, "we usually don't allow visitors upstairs on their own, but be my guest. I'll take care of this and join you shortly."

Before Phoenix could offer to wait, he had hurried off, weaving past the displays with agility. He silenced the phone in midring. Phoenix heard a rise of recognition in Milton's voice, and she guessed his call would not be a quick one.

The stairwell was narrow, with a door identical to the main entrance on one side—its window covered by a semisheer white curtain, the painted street numbers showing backward through the pane—and a long trail of steps on the other. The wooden wall supporting the banister was deeply scarred. When Phoenix held the banister to climb the steps, it was cold to her touch. The banister was just a pipe, she realized, maybe original to Joplin's time, too.

He touched this, she thought. That hadn't been true about the rest of the house, since nothing here had belonged to him. But she had no doubt that Scott Joplin's own hand had once rested on the banister. Phoenix's disappointment about the external appearance vanished. This was where homeboy had *lived*. Even if this had been a raggedy shack, what did it matter?

She wished Sarge hadn't been too busy to come. Sarge would have dug this.

The backs of Phoenix's thighs felt rock-hard and sore as she climbed the endless stairs. Too many dance rehearsals. "Man, I wish you'd lived downstairs, bruh," she muttered.

Upstairs, Phoenix found a piece of time frozen in the late-afternoon light.

A door stood open at the top of the stairs, welcoming her to sky-blue walls and glossy wooden floorboards covered with area rugs, a long hallway. This was a home, sprawling in three directions. She saw a bedroom doorway to the left of her (the knobs of an antique bed frame in her view, like the one from Disney's *Bedknobs and Broomsticks*), a larger parlor with a fireplace in the entryway beside it, and a long hallway directly ahead of her with a writing table nestled in a far corner, leading to a room at the end of the hall with a small table and chairs that might be a kitchen. Phoenix felt like an intruder.

"Hello?" she called.

As she would in anyone's home, Phoenix walked toward the parlor first. The room wasn't large—her parents' living room in Miami was much bigger—but its regalness and warmth put her at ease. The centerpiece was the white fireplace, which wasn't ornate, but bore enough details in its decorative grill and mantel to satisfy her appetite for Victorian-era trappings, as did the elegant matching settee and armchair propped beside it, ready to entertain teatime guests. A large photograph of Joplin preserved in an egg-shaped, gold-colored frame hung above the fireplace and its antique wooden mantel clock.

The furniture and globe-shaped lamps in the room were largely mismatched, probably scavenged from antique stores and thrift shops. The mauve Oriental rug in the center of the room retained coloring only at its edges; the bulk of it was so threadbare that the fabric had been worn nearly gray. The upright piano against the wall across from the fireplace hadn't been Joplin's, but Phoenix guessed it occupied the same space Joplin's had. The sheet music to "The Entertainer" was propped on the piano, one of the pieces Milton had mentioned Joplin probably composed while he lived here, along with, yes, "Weeping Willow."

The stillness in the room was intoxicating. Phoenix stood beside the piano, not touching anything, listening for the silent hum of the room's past. Two parlor windows against the far wall filled the room with brightness, so Phoenix went to one of them and stared down at the street. The view wasn't much more encouraging than what she'd seen outside; there was a compound of multistory redbrick buildings a couple of blocks away, but many of the rectangular windowpanes were missing, leaving a checkerboard of shadows. Beyond that, she saw the pale green steeple of a brick church that looked as if it, too, might have survived since Joplin's day. The mass of buildings depicted in the detailed maps downstairs were mostly gone, but that church was still standing.

Syphilis, Phoenix thought suddenly, saddened, as she stared outside. Napoleon, Oscar Wilde, Joplin. She'd learned about the disease's long, horrible death when Sarge told her about the Tuskegee Syphilis Study, government doctors withholding the cure from dying black men for decades after the discovery of penicillin. *Thank the Lord I was born in 1981 and not a minute sooner—can I find a witness?*

Phoenix heard a faint bumping noise beside her, which made her jump, but she realized it was only a horsefly throwing itself against the windowpane, as if it intended to break free. The fly's wings glistened purple and green, flitting in an angry blur. The fly's intrusion broke Phoenix's spell. She left the parlor, passing through to the bedroom, with its quilted bedspread, smaller fireplace, wooden wardrobe, antique sewing machine, and lacy curtains. She pulled open a half-propped door and found a turn-of-the-century version of a master bathroom, with a clawfoot tub and exposed fixtures where a toilet might once have been.

Back in the hallway beside the stairs, there was still no sign of Milton. Phoenix made her way across the long hall to the room she had correctly guessed was the kitchen. This room was especially quaint, crammed with relics: an old-fashioned icebox, an antique stove, a washboard and a slew of gadgets she didn't recognize. Still, she knew none of these items had belonged to Joplin. She barely felt his memory here.

The parlor was her favorite room.

Phoenix walked back toward the parlor to wait for Milton, deciding she would go soon. She wasn't going to find whatever she'd been afraid of here, even if a small part of her craved affirmation of her childhood connection to Joplin. Joplin's world receded, and hers came back into focus. Sarge would be glad to hear "Party Patrol" was on the radio here. And she hoped Gloria would follow through on her promise to bring her curried chicken. She couldn't take another night of bland room service.

In the parlor, a man stood staring out of the window where she had been a moment before, where the fly had interrupted her. The sight of him froze Phoenix in the entryway.

"Oh, sorry," she said, but the man didn't turn to acknowledge her. His profile told her that he was dark-skinned like Milton, but he had a smaller frame, and he wasn't bald. He wore a white dress shirt that hung over his dark slacks, his hands locked behind his back. He could be a statue. *This place is like Mecca for musicians, a place for worshippers,* she thought.

Phoenix's cell phone chirped, and in the stillness the sound was deafening. She grabbed it, quickly stepping away from the parlor entryway so she wouldn't annoy the man. "Hey, girl," Gloria's voice said. "I'm parked outside. Come on, while the food's hot."

The knowledge that food was waiting downstairs made Phoenix's stomach growl. She heard Milton's footsteps climbing up at last. "Yeah, I'll be right down. Perfect timing."

Milton was halfway up the stairs when Phoenix met him at the top landing. She took two steps down, speaking in a hushed tone. "Mr. Milton, this has been incredible, but my ride is outside, so I have to go. I got a great self-guided tour. Thank you so much."

"You're sure?" he said. "I'm so sorry about the interruption."

"No, it's fine. I've already kept you here late."

With a satisfied shrug, he turned to descend the stairs ahead of her. The stairway was too narrow for anything except single file. "Then I guess I'll lock up behind us. My wife will be shocked to see me for dinner."

"Wait, though," Phoenix said, on his heels. "There's a last guy upstairs."

Milton turned back to face her, tilting his shiny head. "Oh?"

"In the parlor."

"At the window?"

"Yeah . . ." Phoenix said, a beat before she wondered how he knew.

Milton's cheeks expanded as he grinned. He carried on his climb downstairs, jingling his keys in his hand. "You *are* the special one today," he said.

"What do you mean?"

Milton unlocked the door marked 2658-A Morgan and opened it for her. Phoenix could see the red hood of Gloria's car waiting at the curb. "Most visitors aren't lucky enough to get the full welcome," Milton said. "Miss Smalls, you've just met our resident ghost."

Phoenix felt her blood slow to a cold crawl.

I still say he's full of shit," Gloria said, scooping the last of the moo goo gai pan into her mouth from the carton with her chopsticks. They sat together on their suite's living room sofa while a *Seinfeld* rerun played on the twenty-seven-inch screen—the episode when Jerry, George, Kramer and Elaine can't find their car in the parking garage. She and Gloria never bothered with the dining room table, always eating in front of the TV the way they had when Phoenix spent the night at Gloria's house as a kid, freed from Mom's strict rules.

"I don't want to talk about it anymore," Phoenix said. Her curried chicken was too salty, and she'd lost her appetite anyway, so she'd eaten only a bite or two. After her shower, she'd put on a long nightshirt she'd bought from a tourist trap on Ocean Drive in South Beach; an aqua-colored shirt with a smiling dolphin she wore almost every night on the road to remind her of home. Her fuzzy slippers were her other familiar comfort, except that she didn't feel comforted.

"Tell me what this alleged ghost looked like," Gloria said.

Phoenix sighed, wrapping her arms around her knees, cradling them to her chest as she leaned against the supple sofa cushion. "I told you, he just looked like a guy standing there."

"But . . . did he look fuzzy or shimmery or anything like that? Was there any bright light around him? Was the room cold?"

Phoenix shook her head, exhaustion flooding her. She was getting a headache, the malady she'd inherited from Sarge. Soon, if she wasn't careful, she'd feel the telltale nausea and sensitivity to light that signaled a migraine. The only cure for that would be bed, and although it was only six-thirty and not yet dark outside, bed seemed like a good idea.

Gloria jabbed her chopstick at her in an *ah-HA* gesture. "That dude was bullshitting you. That wasn't any damn ghost, Phee. Don't let him mess with your head."

"Maybe," Phoenix said, just so Gloria would be quiet.

Phoenix had practically clung to Van Milton as he walked her through Joplin's apartment to show her that no straggler had been left behind. The spot at the window had been empty, and he'd taken her as far as the expansive, near-empty attic to prove his point. No one else was upstairs. She had been the last person to leave.

The last *living* person, anyway, she reminded herself.

He only comes out when it's quiet, Milton had explained calmly. *I see him most often in the early-morning hours, before opening. The first time, like you, I thought he was a stray visitor at the window. That day it was near closing time, as it was today, and when I came back to let him know we were locking up, he was gone. I've never been one to believe in ghosts and such, but it's different when it happens to you. Once I accepted him, I ran into him more and more often, as if he'd learned to accept me as well. Usually I see him standing at the window, or else sitting by the fireplace with his back turned to the doorway. Once after a busy day, I think he was a little irritated; and I stumbled at the top of the stairs, as if someone had pulled a string to trip me. There was no string, of course, but I felt something, and I nearly lost my balance. I think about it every time I climb down those stairs, and I'm just grateful I didn't tumble down and hurt myself. It's a long fall, as you can see.*

All that said, I don't think he means anyone any harm. He just gives you small things to notice. For instance, one morning I'd just straightened out the bedroom, and when I turned around to pass the room again, I found the lampshade swinging askew. It's little things like that. I see him exactly as you said: He's not a ghost like you see in the movies. He looks like a flesh-and-blood man, and if you walk right by him, you'd never know any different. I bet you could walk up and touch him if he'd stand still long enough.

Phoenix didn't believe Milton was lying, and she knew that if Gloria had come inside to meet him, she wouldn't think so either. Milton was an erudite man who ran a museum, not the eccentric caretaker of an amusement-park-style haunted house.

"Did you call Ronn back? He left you a message," Gloria said.

"Shit," Phoenix said. She picked her tiny white flip-phone up from the coffee table, wondering what she would say to Ronn. She should have called Ronn before now, she told herself with a ripple of guilt that lingered much longer than she wanted it to. It was amazing how easily he fell from her mind, considering how funny, sharp and gentle he was—*and RICH too*? Something was missing, and it puzzled her more all the time. She still couldn't feel relaxed about Ronn, and they had been sleeping together for six months. Hell, what was Phoenix Smalls doing trying to hang with a former crack dealer turned multimillionaire who could have his pick of any woman, from a phalanx of backstage skanks to bona fide movie stars?

She was sleeping with her boss, the mother of clichés, and Sarge had warned her, or tried to. But if it was a mistake, it was hers alone. Sarge might have chased away Carlos when she was sixteen, but he didn't have a say over her love life now. *If it were up to Sarge, he'd try to make me marry my career, just like him.*

Ronn picked up the phone on the first ring. His gravelly profundo basso voice made her stomach squirm, a reaction that hadn't changed. "Hey, baby girl," Ronn said. "I'm about to have a little sit-down, so I'ma have to get back to you. How you been doin, though?"

"Rehearsing my ass off. And I just went on a tour of the Scott Joplin

House." She almost mentioned the ghost, but thought better of it. She didn't want to sound like a flake.

"Whose house?" Ronn said, and Phoenix· heard a sudden flurry of voices and men's booming laughter, like a frat party finding its rhythm. It amazed her how often Ronn's work sounded like play; he had a gift for making it look easy, even when it wasn't. "Hey, Phoenix, hold up. Can I holla back at you in a couple hours? You gonna be up?"

"Sure," she said. "Just call me when you can."

He made a kissing sound, his voice soft. "A'ight then. Later." Then his voice rose to a booming laugh. "Hey, playa, *how you doin*—" Then the phone clicked dead.

Love across the miles, Phoenix thought ruefully, closing her phone to hang it up. She couldn't complain, though. It wasn't any better on her end.

"I don't think Ronn knows who Scott Joplin is," Phoenix said, thinking aloud.

Gloria was flipping through the menu channel to see what movies were on pay-per-view. Phoenix hadn't been to a movie theater in at least three months, so she didn't recognize any of them. "So? Lots of people don't know who Scott Joplin is. Quit being such a snob. You didn't know Ra-Kim. All you knew was M. C. Hammer."

In truth, Gloria was a much bigger fan of rap than Phoenix. Phoenix's staples on the road were Billie Holiday, Michael Jackson, Lauryn Hill, Stevie Wonder, Rubén Blades, Led Zeppelin, the Mississippi Mass Choir, Sweet Honey in the Rock and jazz piano wizard Gonzalo Rubalcaba. She could go months without her rap CDs, except for Talib Kweli and Out-Kast. She'd been embarrassed more than once at Ronn's parties, where her ignorance was obvious.

Phoenix sighed. "I'm just not sure I'm really feeling this thing with Ronn."

"You don't have to have his babies right off. Just give him a chance, Phee. And don't get silly and tell him about your extracurricular activities last night," she said, smiling.

"That's *your* fault. I'm not crazy, dang. Not that he'd care."

"Don't fool yourself. You know the double standard."

They agreed to watch Denzel's last thriller, but Phoenix only made it halfway through the movie before she fell asleep, and not because she wasn't *trying* to hang on to Denzel's every word and movement. She only realized she was sleeping when the image of Denzel and a woman in a hat riding on a dark, shaking train didn't match the movie's dialogue. That, and Denzel didn't look at all like Denzel—and the woman in the hat might be her.

A squealing, frenetic car chase woke Phoenix. She sat up, confused. She didn't see a train on the television screen, just a police car speeding after a gray older-model car. Gloria was munching on a bag of chips from the minibar. "You're paying me for those," Phoenix mumbled, half-asleep. Their last minibar bill had been nearly a hundred dollars.

Gloria gave her the finger, not looking away from the television screen. "Eat me."

"You wish," Phoenix mumbled.

"No, *you* wish," Gloria said with a sly grin. They still argued over whose idea it had been to practice kissing through plastic wrap, each insisting it was the other.

"Eff off. I'm turning in."

The room was cold suddenly, as usual. *Rule #1 of hotel life: All hotel rooms have two temperatures—too hot or too cold.* Phoenix forced herself to stand up. She could make up for her foolishness last night and get eight hours of sleep. Thank God her morning-drive radio interview had been canceled. She wouldn't have to brace for Sarge's six o'clock wake-up call.

"Love you, cuz," Gloria called softly as Phoenix shuffled toward her room.

"Love you, too, cuz."

Phoenix realized she was shivering, her molars clacking softly. *Now* she knew why this hotel, unlike Budget Inn, offered two thick terry-cloth robes hanging in the closet. Four-star hotels definitely had their charms, she thought. Phoenix pulled open the slatted doors to her large walk-in closet, hoping to find a bathrobe waiting.

With the door open, the overhead light in the sweetly scented closet flickered like a waking fluorescent bulb, then flared, bright. Phoenix's concert costume hung in a dry-cleaning bag, the only clothes in the closet. Most of her other clothes were in the bureau drawer, already unpacked. She couldn't relax anywhere until she had moved in, which drove Gloria crazy.

Phoenix saw a blue-covered ironing board hanging from hooks on the wall. Two terry-cloth robes hung beside it on plush hangers, so Phoenix tugged on the robe closest to her. As it came free, Phoenix noticed two shiny black shoes on the floor. Men's shoes, by the look of them. Had Kendrick left a pair of shoes behind?

The robe still hanging above the shoes fluttered in tiny ripples, as if it were a flag billowing in a slow breeze. That was when Phoenix realized there was a lump behind the robe. She saw the neck and chin of a black man half-hidden beyond it, not four feet from her. Her heart dove. The two black shoes shining on the floor were *on this man's feet*. A man was hiding inside her closet! At first, Phoenix only gaped at the shoes and back up to the lump and the exposed skin, feeling her rib cage bind itself around her lungs. The robe's fluttering grew so violent that Phoenix heard the hanger rattle against the wooden rack. What was he *doing*?

With a yell, Phoenix balled up the robe in her hands and threw it at the man as if it were a weapon. Then, she backed outside of the open closet door, slamming it shut behind her. The sudden motion made her lose her balance, landing squarely on her backside. Despite the carpet's padding, electric pain stabbed Phoenix's taibone.

The pain did it, as if it were a harbinger of more to come. Phoenix let out a fevered scream unlike any that had passed her lips since she was ten.

*B*y ten o'clock, the hallway outside of Phoenix's suite was so jammed with people that it looked like a concert after-party. Even in Phoenix's shaken state, a half dozen police officers seemed excessive. *They must have me confused with Beyoncé.*

Security officers had come in matching numbers, dressed like parking valets in crimson jackets with the hotel emblem sewn in golden thread across their breasts. Arturo hung protectively near the elevators, his eyes watching anyone coming or going. The other dancers—Milli and Vanilli, as Phoenix had started calling the dreadlock-wearing teens—sat cross-legged on the hallway's carpet, eating snacks as if they were watching a movie. Sarge went from person to person, overseeing as usual. Gloria had not left Phoenix's side, holding her hand.

The police hadn't found the intruder yet. Two officers were still in the suite, and Phoenix had overheard a discussion about a K-9 unit to back them up—which wouldn't be a good thing if Gloria still had the dime bag she'd scored in Houston—but so far the search had failed. The room had windows, but who would be crazy enough to try to escape from ten stories up?

This was not what she needed the night before a concert. Phoenix tried to block out the commotion so adrenaline wouldn't keep her awake and blow her gig.

Gloria's voice suddenly caught her ear: "His name was Kendrick Allen Hart, from Brooklyn, New York." She was talking to a wiry, crew-cut officer taking notes.

At first, Phoenix thought she must be hearing wrong. But Sarge had overheard Gloria, too, because he stood behind Phoenix like a towering oak. "Who's Kendrick Allen Hart?"

Gloria gave Phoenix an apologetic look over her shoulder, then she went on, "He's a fan who stalked her last night. I'm sorry, Phoenix, but it's true. He found the room last night and kept knocking on our door. Someone from the hotel told him she was here. He wouldn't leave."

"Why the hell didn't I hear about this before?" Sarge said.

Phoenix pulled her hand from Gloria's grasp, irritated by the heat of her cousin's palm. "That's my private business. The man in my closet was much shorter. It wasn't Kendrick."

"You saw his face?" Sarge said.

"No. But I *know* it wasn't Kendrick. He wouldn't do that. Gloria's exaggerating."

"How the hell do you know what a stranger would or wouldn't do? A *fan?*" Sarge said it like it was a dirty word. He'd put a few overzealous fans in the hospital, or jail, over the years.

"He's right, Phoenix," Gloria said.

Gloria had been the one trying to push her into bed with that boy, warning her to keep it quiet, and now she'd made it public record! Phoenix couldn't wait to get her cousin alone. Angry tears smarted in Phoenix's eyes. She forced herself to gaze directly at her father's face, where anger glittered from his molasses-colored irises. She recognized bright fear there, too, and she had never seen Sarge afraid of anything.

"He spent the night with me," Phoenix said softly, but not softly enough. Phoenix glanced toward Arturo down the hall, who had lowered his chin to give her a *say-WHAT?* look. The anger in Sarge's eyes melted into disbelief, then snapped to anger again. He didn't speak, but his eyes spoke volumes, The Ray times six.

"For the sake of argument," the officer said, "just tell me what you know about this Kendrick Allen Hart. He won't get in trouble if he didn't do anything wrong."

Phoenix felt her face burning, and she prayed she wasn't blushing, one more reason she wished she had more of her father's melanin in her skin. "I know it wasn't him."

"He's a student at NYU," Gloria said. "He said he came to see her on a bus."

Phoenix had to physically restrain herself from slapping Gloria's face. What was *wrong* with this girl? This wasn't an episode of *Law & Order,* this was her personal business!

As if on cue, Phoenix's phone vibrated. The phone suddenly felt like a rescue boat, and Phoenix snapped it open, turning away from both her father and the police officer. "It's probably my mother," Phoenix said, before anyone could object.

But it wasn't Mom. "Are you all right, baby girl?" Ronn's voice said. He sounded hyped up, like he could pounce through the phone.

Phoenix couldn't repress her tears. She felt moisture roll down each side of her face, racing toward her chin. "Yeah," was all she could manage.

"You don't sound like it."

I'm about to kill my cousin, that's all. "Just a little stressed."

"You want me to fly down there on the next red-eye?"

"No, don't do that. Really, it's fine. They've got half the force up in here." Phoenix glanced up at the officer, whose attention had turned back to Gloria while she gave him a physical description of Kendrick. Her cousin sounded as if she were a police officer herself, full of meticulous detail. Phoenix's anger and embarrassment cinched her stomach.

"I'm just worried 'bout you," Ronn said.

"Don't be worried. He didn't touch me. It's probably a joke or something."

"Naw, fuck that," Ronn said. "I don't like this shit, Phee. Not with this DJ Train drama. You know what I'm sayin? There's mad beef against Three Strikes these days."

"I know."

"Well, it's like I just told Sarge—this ain't no game. I was gonna pull you out, but if you wanna finish your business, I'm hooking you up with a new room at the Ritz. You go on and do that show tomorrow night if you want, but my cousins from Kansas City are on the way, and they'll be in front of your door until the sun comes up. Then I want you to fly to L.A. first chance you get. I wanna hold you and make sure my baby girl's safe. A'ight?"

Phoenix nodded, momentarily forgetting he couldn't see her. She wondered if Ronn's cousins would be armed. Her life was becoming a foreign landscape. "All right."

"Miss Smalls?" the officer said, irritated. "I need your attention. I'm filling out a report." *You spoiled-ass diva,* he was probably thinking.

"I gotta go, Ronn," Phoenix said, almost a whisper.

"A'ight, baby girl. Call me from the Ritz. I love you, Phee."

Ronn had never said that before. Kendrick never would have gotten through the door if Phoenix had suspected the words *I love you* were anywhere in Ronn's mind.

After she hung up, Phoenix told the officer no, she didn't have anything to add to her cousin's statement—*Except that Gloria can kiss my ass,* she thought—and could she please be excused? The officer gazed at her skeptically, then closed his notebook and fanned it, dismissing her, as if he figured she'd brought whatever had happened on herself.

Gloria squeezed Phoenix's shoulder, whispering in her ear. "I'm sorry, Phee. If it turned out he was the one, and something happened to you, I'd never forgive myself, cuz."

"Don't even talk to me right now," Phoenix said in a frozen voice, and Gloria let her go.

The two officers investigating the suite came out with relaxed shoulders, shrugging. "Well, whoever was in there is gone now," the heavier officer said. "It's all clear."

Phoenix brushed past Gloria to go back inside, hoping for peace, but she heard a din of voices behind her as others followed. In her bedroom, the bureau drawers were wide-open, and her clothes and underwear had been scattered on the floor, in trails. The linens were thrown from her bed, exposing a slightly stained mattress cover underneath. She recognized the black tank top that was part of her concert costume crumpled on the floor inside her closet, inside a tangle of dry-cleaning bags. Sonsof*bitches*.

"These damn cops are crazy. This is bullshit," she said.

She hadn't realized anyone was standing behind her until she heard a man's voice. "It was like this when we got here, miss." A black hotel employee stood in the doorway.

Phoenix's skin fluttered as if she were inside a swarm of insects. If the mess had been there already, then even *after* the intruder knew he'd been busted, he'd gone through her room to mess with her in little ways, taking his time. Phoenix suddenly felt violated, and the adrenaline she'd tried to keep at bay coursed through her. Who the *hell* . . . ?

"They searched the room? The *whole* room?" she said, to be sure.

The man behind her was wearing a tag identifying him as the hotel night manager. He reminded her of her half brother, Malcolm, in another life, with the same big, intelligent eyes. "Up and down. There is nobody in this room who isn't supposed to be," the man said. "Miss Smalls, let me apologize again on behalf of the hotel. If it's true someone on this staff revealed your room number, we *will* take immediate action."

"This wasn't him," Phoenix said. "It was someone else."

"Either way, it's a serious breach." He walked to her closet and peeked inside again, just to see it was empty with his own eyes.

Scared to death of a lawsuit, I'm sure. Scared your hotel will be all over BET News.

Kendrick's cousin would be fired, and Kendrick might get arrested. Gloria's wreckage was multiplying. Phoenix sighed, amazed at how silly a grown woman could be.

Phoenix felt a new pair of eyes on her from the doorway, and she whipped her head around, startled. She expected to find the strange man behind her, the taking-his-time man who had ravaged her room, watching her as cool as an autumn breeze.

Instead, she found Sarge leaning against the doorjamb with his arms crossed, gazing at his daughter as if he was amazed at how silly a grown woman could be. "You let a *fan* spend the night with you? Some strange-ass man?" he said.

Phoenix's manager had gone to bed. The man in the doorway was her father.

CHAPTER FOUR

Los Angeles

*T*hree Strikes Records was headquartered in the Leimert Park section of South Central L.A., an understated clay-colored, two-story building across the street from Tavis Smiley's new complex on Crenshaw. The label's only identification was a brass plate beside the door engraved with the script letters *TSR*. Phoenix liked the funky little neighborhood around it, which was emerging as a community power center. TSR was flanked by a black-owned restaurant and coffeehouse, the Lucy Florence Cafe, and a smattering of other small businesses taking a chance on redevelopment, including galleries, a village theater and a dance co-op. The area hummed with promise, and to Phoenix it felt like a launching pad.

The glass door to TSR was black, impossible to see beyond, and motion-activated video cameras tracked the movements of anyone who approached. The first time Phoenix had stood before this door, she'd shivered to her toenails. The multiplatinum rapper, actor and master entrepreneur G-Ronn wanted to meet with her about a possible record deal! That day, Sarge had driven her in the ancient Corolla she used in L.A., counting on friends to drive her.

Today, she and Sarge were chauffeured in Ronn's custom-armored black Lexus LX 470 by Ronn's personal driver and sometime-bodyguard, a man named Kai who looked like a Sumo wrestler, the son of an American soldier and a Japanese barmaid. As she climbed out of the SUV, Phoenix's eardrums were ringing from the vehicle's sound system. Kai was pumping out Public Enemy's "Welcome to the Terrordome" like the car was leading a street parade, but she didn't mind. At nine, when she'd been exposed, wide-eyed, to the explosive colors, music and messages in *Do the Right Thing,* Phoenix had fallen for both Spike and P.E. for life. She, Ronn and Kai had once sat discussing that film for two hours while they worked late one night. Ronn said *Do the Right Thing* inspired him to be a rapper and make his own movies.

"You be good, baby girl," the big man said, winking as he deposited her.

Phoenix leaned through his driver's window to wrap her arms around his neck. "You too, Krispy Kreme," she said, and he chuckled. Kai almost always had a box of Krispy Kremes on the passenger seat beside whatever book he was reading, ready for both guests and personal consumption. Even Kai's breath was sugary. *Kai's the sweetest nigger you never want to fuck with,* Ronn said of his childhood friend. Kai was the principal suspect in the DJ Train incident in Brooklyn, and that alone told Phoenix the charge was bullshit through and through.

"Safe journey, young blood," Sarge told Kai with a clenched-fist Panther salute.

"You know it, dawg."

Wordlessly, Sarge strode ahead of Phoenix to TSR's door. There were a series of unfinished arguments still suspended between her and her father, so she stood beside Sarge in silence, returning the blank stare of the dark door as they waited to be buzzed in. She slouched under the weight of the dread she had felt since their plane landed that morning.

Felicha's girlish eyes twinkled above her round, dark cheeks as she met them at the door, practically squealing. "I can't believe baby girl's finally come to call on little ol' us!" Felicha said, clamping her arms around her in a spirited hug. She was another of Ronn's cousins; almost everyone who worked for him was either family or a longtime friend. "Girl, it's so good to see you! You too, Sarge. But I know you can give me a better smile than that."

"Afternoon, sweetness," Sarge said, leaning to kiss Felicha's forehead beneath the spill of her glistening curls, although his smile didn't improve. Sarge's face had been like a plaster cast since St. Louis, his thick jowls frozen in place. Sarge said her behavior might have jeopardized their working relationship with Ronn, and she thought his Panthers-era paranoia was in overdrive. But now that she was at Three Strikes, she wasn't so sure.

"Ronn's beside himself, he's so excited you're coming," Felicha told Phoenix with a deep, private gaze. "He's tryin' to front for his boys, but he has *missed* you, Phee."

"I've missed him, too," Phoenix said, her mouth dry. She didn't glance toward Sarge.

As Felicha led them down the hallway, full of chatter about Ronn's new film ventures, the row of gold and platinum records garnered by G-Ronn and his Three Strikes protégés gleamed on the walls like portals to the sun, moon and stars, Phoenix thought. Her nose picked up the sharp scent of marijuana, which always lingered in the hallway, however faint, like a favorite incense. The day she'd met Ronn, there had been a mound of lush marijuana on a silver serving tray in his office, as if it were cookies and tea. Only Sarge's presence had kept Ronn from offering her any, she figured. Phoenix couldn't wait to call Gloria and tell her about it.

But Phoenix was not going to think about Gloria today, if she could help it.

". . . took me to dinner at this joint Spago last night with a cat from Universal Studios, right? Phee, this man was a *trip*. I never saw nobody kiss Ronn's ass like that in my life. I was fixin' to ask him if he wanted to get down under the table," Felicha said. She was the only one who laughed at her joke.

"That's nice Ronn took you with him," Phoenix said absently, after a pause.

"Hey, girl, when you're out of town, I get to be Ronn's date *everywhere*. I had my picture with Ronn in *Vibe* and *US Weekly* last week! I ain't mad you're back, though."

The red light was on outside of the studio door, signaling a recording session in progress. Even with the soundproofing, Phoenix could hear the tenacious thump of the bass through the door. Her heartbeat vaulted to match the music's pounding, and her palms tickled with perspiration. Phoenix didn't know if it was premonition, Sarge's fears, or only guilt amping up her nerves. All three, probably. *I hope I don't have to go in here and kiss Ronn's ass like that movie exec at Spago.*

Felicha held her finger up to her lips as she grabbed the studio door-knob to let them in.

There were three other studios at TSR, but this was Ronn's main recording studio, nicknamed The Mothership, large and lavish, deco-rated like a junior-high schoolboy's fantasy—arcade-quality videogames, Mortal Kombat and Galaga, sat on either side of the door as she walked in, and the walls were a riot of concert posters and centerfolds of women in various states of undress. The studio itself was a showroom of state-of-the-art sound equipment—knobs, boards and monitors that might as well be the control panel of the space shuttle. Phoenix could deal with the MIDI controllers and synthesizers fine—anything that helped her play what she heard in her head—but she didn't have enough gadget appreciation for the rest of Ronn's toys.

The first day she came, Ronn had toured her through The Mothership like a science geek dissecting his annual project. *This is the true shit, our Sony DMX-R100 "Baby Oxford" Digital Production Console—check it. We got an E-Mu XL-7 Command Station goin' on, and a Kurzweil K-25000 RS sampler/sound module—of COURSE—and we run all that shit through this Manley Massive Passive Parametric EQ.*

Ronn's love for his studio had been touching, but a *band* spoke to Phoenix. Her band in Miami—the late, great Phoenix & the New Fire—had Phoenix on keyboards; Jabari channeling Jaco and Bootsy like a madman on bass; La'Keitha tearing up her electric guitar; and Andres playing those drums and congas like he was sending urgent warnings across the whole of Mother Africa. Phoenix had occasionally picked up her electric violin to add shades of Cairo, Dublin, Nashville or Vienna. The Mothership had its own music, but Phoenix didn't know all its dialects. And even after hours in this studio with Ronn and D'Real—first recording, then mixing (with the magic of gadgets re-placing the sounds of her band)—she was hardly more fluent than the day Ronn unveiled it to her. Much of it was still a mystery, jabbering in blinking lights.

Phoenix saw the back of Ronn's head in his characteristic white Kangol cap in a slant across his closely shaved scalp. D'Real was here, and so were label employees Manny, Lil' Mo and Katrice—as well as two men in all-black L.A. Chic Phoenix didn't recognize. None of them had seen Phoenix and Sarge walk in because they were mesmerized by the recording booth. Ronn bounced on the balls of his feet, nodding to the rhythm of a muted dance-hall-style beat that was trademark D'Real, schizoid and unruly. A lightning storm rocked The Mothership, and all of its crew had been called to the deck to witness it.

There was a rapper in the booth. Phoenix hadn't noticed him at first, but she heard rapid-fire words from a coarse voice that sounded midway between a playground and a battleground. The boy had a crisp, stutter-step delivery.

> *All these niggas tellin' lies, sayin' cold is hot,*
> *Niggas tellin' lies bout how they ass was shot.*
> *Yo' mouth is always movin' but you ain't sayin' a lot.*
> *You spent up all yo' loot cuz you ain't savin' a lot.*
> *My flow's my gat, my gat's my flow;*
> *I'll murder yo' ass in a studio.*
> *Like the nigga say in* Amistad, *"Give us free!"*
> *Yo' time's up, BITCH—you can't flow like me.*

The boy in the booth spat the final words into the microphone, and he suddenly backed away from it, throwing his baseball cap against the glass, his flurry of bravado finished.

"Oh, *shit!*" D'Real said, whipping his wiry arm around to find Ronn's in a tight clasp. D'Real was only five-foot-four, and he was Ronn's age, but he had a face that would always look like a teenager's, almost hairless. D'Real lived in his off-center white Howard University baseball cap and white Pony jogging suits. Strangers who saw D'Real would never guess he was the mastermind behind a string of multiplatinum hits, but Phoenix had learned in the studio that D'Real was as intractable as he was unassuming. All she remembered about recording her CD was arguing with D'Real. And Ronn always taking his side.

"They on notice!" D'Real told Ronn, nearly breathless. " I *told* you all them mush-mouthed, no-rapping niggas out there is on notice." Phoenix envied the boy in the booth. He might have found a real advocate in D'Real, which was more than she could say.

The boy in the booth was slender and almost pretty, a stark contrast to his husky voice, and he looked barely old enough to shave. He reminded Phoenix of Chingy. His smooth face betrayed nothing of what he must be feeling, save for a small tugging at one corner of his pink-tinged lips. Trying to pretend he wasn't excited. *When will these young brothers feel safe to show their true hearts to the world?*

"T's our battle champ up in Oak-Town," said one of the strangers in black, who looked like a schoolteacher behind wire-frame glasses. "Can't nobody touch him."

"T, your flow is *sick*," Ronn said with a curt nod, grabbing the boy's hand. Ronn's face, too, was as unyielding as iron, with no hint of a smile. "I can work with that."

"Hell, *yeah*, we can work with that," D'Real said. "It's new-school West Coast."

"And so photogenic," Katrice murmured, half to herself, imagining his cover shot.

The boy couldn't hide the luster in his eyes. Phoenix knew that look, because that was how she'd felt when Ronn first anointed her: He couldn't wait to call his mother.

Ronn suddenly seemed to feel Phoenix's presence. He turned over his shoulder to meet her eyes. *Phee,* he said, surprised, only mouthing her name. The iron melted from his jaw.

*P*hoenix had researched Ronn Jenkins before she ever visited Three Strikes Records. Knowledge is your best weapon, Sarge always said, and she'd arrived with a full arsenal.

Ronn had been thirty-two when they met, so now he was thirty-three. He'd been raised in subsidized housing in St. Louis, until his family left Lou's and moved to L.A. when he was fourteen. He was the second of three children, the youngest of two brothers. Ronn refused to talk about his older brother, Darnell, who'd been killed in an unarmed police shooting, although there was plenty about it on internet tabloid sites. Ronn's mother was a postal clerk, still working, and his father had been a phantom from the time he was five. ("I cut off a piece of my soul and buried it when that nigga split," he'd told Touré from *Rolling Stone* in a reflective mood.) He'd been selling weed when he was fourteen, crack by sixteen.

And he was a genius. He had such a quick business mind that within three years, by nineteen, he'd been running his own crews and earned enough money to buy houses in cash for both himself *and* his sister. He was popped in a sting at twenty, but released on a technicality. Then he'd begun rapping with his best friend D'Real, and scored a record deal by fooling a record exec into believing they already had a following when all they had was a suitcase full of demos and attitude to spare. ("Music was an easier hustle than slingin'," he'd told *Vibe*.)

The rest was rap history. G-Ronn had been born.

Mom freaked out the day Phoenix told her she was dating Ronn.

Listen to the terrible messages in his music. Think of all the good he could be doing for his community, and all he talks about is getting laid, getting rich and getting even with his enemies. Phoenix was surprised Mom knew that much about G-Ronn's music, and she couldn't argue with the summary. She also couldn't defend Ronn's lyrics, because she didn't like them much herself. Hell, when Ronn was at home, he listened to Miles Davis and Stevie Wonder.

To Ronn, the violent scenarios in his lyrics were part reportage—he'd lived it, after all—and part fantasy—because he hadn't lived it in a very long time. Either way, it was all money to him. He'd put it this way: He could follow the path of a poet, or he could be a multimillionaire. To a man who remembered picking wildflowers for his mother to boil for dinner when money was tight, financial security was its own religion. Ronn might be shortsighted, but he was honest.

Mom wasn't looking at the big picture either, Phoenix thought. Instead of imagining all the things Ronn *should* be doing, why couldn't Mom let herself see how far Ronn had come? He was a child of poverty who was now the CEO of a major corporation, he'd just launched a film production company, and his two children (by two previous girlfriends) went to private schools and had college funds. Maybe Ronn wasn't Malcolm X, but he was his own miracle. The age of thirty was a milestone in Ronn's circle, a defiance of the laws of probabilities.

On some days, despite herself, Phoenix felt she *was* too good for Ronn; but on other days, she didn't feel good enough. How were her choices so different from his? Her truest expression had always been through her fingertips, on her keyboard. Three Strikes hadn't wanted a band, only a new singer to put a voice to their vision—any voice would do—and Phoenix's keyboard had been relegated to the shadows. The label had refused to consider hiring her band, and the band wouldn't have followed her if she'd asked. Not if they were playing someone else's music.

You've got to go for what you need, Phee, and nobody but you needs to understand, La'Keitha had told her when she emailed her about Three Strikes, more condolences than congratulations. By then, La'Keitha had moved to New York to tour with rock bands, and hers was the most polite response from her former band-mates. They had once assumed their music would bond them forever; but Phoenix had not heard from them, or reached out to them, in almost a year. Jabari, typically, hadn't minced his words in his last phone call: *If you're gonna sell out, sistah-girl, I'm glad you're doing it in style.*

Fuck them. What good was music nobody would hear? Maybe D'Real was right: Their two CDs had sunk to the bottom of the music world's ocean because their music wasn't radio-friendly. Their band had been too eclectic, too self-indulgent—*and you never said it plain, but let's be real, D'Real—too white.* Phoenix wasn't interested in genteel poverty. She wanted to be *heard.* She wanted people to know her name. Once she established herself, she could do whatever she wanted, like Alicia Keys. Like Prince, she could turn herself into nothing but a symbol one day. *But Kendrick heard, didn't he? He rode a bus to tell you. Who else heard?*

"You had me worried, baby girl. Come here," Ronn said, outstretching his arms to her once they were alone in his office. Ronn's voice changed, softening the way it did when he was at home, and no one but her could hear.

Ronn's face was too pitted with razor scars to be handsome, but she was a hostage to his large brown eyes, and in his ample lips, which, whenever they touched her, seemed to wrap her in a cocoon. He kept his body padded with tight muscles in his weight room at home—he got up to work out every morning at five-thirty, no exceptions—and he had shed most of the tackier hallmarks of wealth he'd been famous for years ago, when his mouth gleamed in gold and his chest was bedecked in chains. Nowadays, Ronn had his own teeth, favored tailored suits over baggy jeans, and his six-karat diamond stud earring was the only jewelry he wore. He had made the transition from child to man, as he liked to say. In the world of hip-hop, you were a seasoned statesman at thirty-three, a tribal elder, and he enjoyed dressing the part.

Phoenix hesitated slightly before she walked around Ronn's large marble desk and scooted herself up onto his lap, where he hooked his arm around her middle, a gentle giant. They were not usually this familiar at his office, an unspoken rule. She felt awkward, expecting someone to come crashing through his door and look at her like a hoochie. *One bitch in the hand, one hand in the bush,* as one of G-Ronn's most popular anthems went.

Ronn rested his chin on her shoulder from behind. "You sure you're a'ight?"

She leaned back against him, relaxing at last. His body heat was an electric blanket beneath her, and she could feel his heavy heartbeat. "Yeah."

"You wanna tell me what happened?"

Phoenix didn't know how to answer, or which *what happened* to tell him about.

"I need to show you something. Don't trip," Ronn said, and pulled open his desk drawer. He pulled out a tabloid newspaper and laid it atop his desk. "What do you see?"

In the blur of newsprint, her eye found a photo of Ronn with his arm around her, one that must have been taken when he visited her on South Beach last January, in those early days when his courtship rocked her mind. ("Girl, *he's calling me from home right now!*" she'd screeched into Gloria's ear, nearly hyperventilating when she saw Ronn Jenkins's name on her caller ID.)

Someone had snapped a photo of them eating outdoors at the News Cafe on Ocean Drive. In the photo, Ronn was wearing his sailing whites (he had a yacht docked outside his home on Fisher Island), and she looked respectably fine in her bikini and shades, her face burned bronze, her hair wet and wild from a recent swim. Not the most flattering picture, but a candid one that captured the glow on her face, all the wonder she felt.

"I never saw that picture of us," she said, smiling.

"It just came out. Now read what it says."

It took Phoenix a few seconds to find the story that accompanied the photo, and when she did, the pint-sized headline made her tongue swell in her mouth.

WHEN THE FAT CAT'S AWAY . . .

Rap mogul G-Ronn might want to keep an eye on girlfriend Phoenix Smalls (pictured left), a 21-year-old R&B princess-in-waiting on G-Ronn's Three Strikes label. Our spies in St. Louis say a male fan talked his way into Phoenix's upscale hotel suite and didn't leave until morning. Where was G-Ronn? In Los Angeles, finalizing plans for his upcoming movie *The Yard*.

Pretty gutsy move, Phoenix, since G-Ronn's biggest hit this year is "Don't F*** with What's Mine."

Strike one?

Phoenix had heard the term *speechless* with no understanding of what it meant, until that moment. Her mouth and throat felt like a wind tunnel, her brain had ceased all function, and she had only the barest memory of language. Everything vanished except the article, which she read and reread, hoping the words might be different. She read until she couldn't see past a sudden sheet of tears that fell across her eyes. She sat on Ronn's lap with her head bent over his desk, frozen.

Ronn spoke first. "What pisses *me* off, they didn't mention the name of your CD."

Phoenix felt her head shaking back and forth, a silent denial. "R-Ronn . . ."

He squeezed her from behind, his large arm locking around her middle, then letting go. "Welcome to the big-time, baby girl. If anybody says shit to you, just say it ain't true."

Phoenix blinked, and one fat droplet fell onto the newsprint, leaving a splotch across the photograph. "It is true," she whispered.

Instead of answering right away, Ronn opened another desk drawer, and Phoenix tensed. *Shit, he has a gun.* The thought made her feel guilty even before Ronn produced a Kleenex instead. Phoenix took the tissue gratefully. She no longer wanted to be in Ronn's lap, but she couldn't think of a polite way to climb down. She couldn't even look Ronn in the face.

Ronn sighed, and she felt his breath against her neck, scented with weed and clove cigarettes. "Listen, Phee, Lou's is where I came up, and people gon' talk. Somebody got paid fifty bucks for calling that shit in, maybe some maid in the hall. Maybe somebody you know. Besides, you think I wasn't all over that police report tryin' to see who was messin' with you? I had that report faxed to me *that night.*"

"It wasn't him, Ronn. I swear it wasn't." Sarge had told her a private detective in New York had questioned Kendrick, but he had an alibi. His bus ticket and other receipts proved he'd been on his way back home that night, confirming what she'd always known. "I *swear.*"

"Naw, that's what I heard. I ain't tryin to fuck with nobody. Don't cry, girl."

"I feel like such a jerk. It was just that one time. I don't even know why I did it."

Taking her shoulders, he gently turned her around. He bent close to her, probing her with his eyes, those paired brown lances. "Well, you're the best one to answer that question, but I guess you was lonely. We never said where we was at." She saw sadness in his eyes, and she hated feeling responsible for other people's sadness.

"I'm sorry, Ronn. *Shit.* Everybody's gonna read . . ."

Ronn laughed, and his laugh almost sounded genuine. "Nobody thinks that shit is true."

He was downplaying it, Phoenix thought. Everyone would know.

"Are you gonna kill the CD?" she said. The question hidden in her mind popped out.

For the first time, Ronn looked genuinely hurt. His head snapped back. "*What?* Phee, I ain't that petty. We're about to bust this shit wide open."

Phoenix's nose was leaking, so she plugged her nostrils with her Kleenex. She'd need another one soon. She had never felt this combination of horror, guilt and something else: relief. Yes, relief was buried in there. She was glad he knew. She hated secrets.

Ronn patted her knee with slow, deliberate beats. He was warming up to something.

"Look," he said, blinking. "You blow my mind, Phoenix. I learn something new every time I talk to you. Some days I run in here and look up words you said in the dictionary. You said something one day—you said I was *canny*. I realized I was a grown-ass man and didn't know what that meant. So I looked it up. It means shrewd, right? Wise."

Silently, Phoenix nodded. She didn't remember using that word with Ronn.

"You know the other day, when you said you were at Scott Joplin's house? I was like, 'Shit, who is that?' I kinda knew the name, but I couldn't remember. So I went to Katrice and asked her—Miss College girl and all that—and she told me he was that guy from *The Sting,* the one who did all that music, 'The Entertainer,' right? I remember that song when it was all over the radio when I was a little kid, back in the seventies. You couldn't go *nowhere* without hearing that song. You make me remember things I'd forgot, things I should *know*. History and shit. I love that about you. Me and school didn't get along too good when I was coming up. But see, you were lucky, Phee. Sarge brought you up in those books. I wish I'd had that. Mama couldn't make me do shit I didn't want to do."

"You're one of the smartest people I know," she said.

"Shit, I'm one of the smartest motherfuckers *out* there. Smart ain't what I'm talkin' about. You make me see what else I coulda done, that's all. I'm hangin' with you, and I get ideas for these new sounds, you know what I'm sayin'? And *Rising,* that shit's just the beginning. That kid, T, you saw rapping? I'm gonna sign him. His flow is different from my other artists, and I'm groovin' to that about now. But if he'd come in here a year ago with that *Amistad* shit, I wouldn't have been feeling that for Three Strikes. You did something to my ears, Phoenix. You got powers, baby girl."

The patting had stopped while he spoke, but it started again. Ronn sighed. "Anyway, I've had too much drama in my life to try to bring some where there don't need to be none. All you gotta know is, I respect you, and I ain't mad at you. For real. But I don't think we're in the same place when it comes to the romance part. You feel me?"

Phoenix struggled to swallow despite the new mound in her throat. Slowly, she nodded. There wasn't a damn thing she could say.

"Good." This time, he squeezed her knee, lingering before letting go. "Nothin' else is gonna change. I got a lot more shit I want to learn from you, and I think I got a couple things to teach you, too. Right?"

"Hell, yes. You're amazing." Her voice was thin, because her brain was beating in a frenzy: *Since we're being so honest and intimate, Ronn, can I tell you that* Rising *isn't half of what it could be, even though it's about to be In Stores Everywhere? Can I tell you I'll be sleepwalking because the music isn't mine? Would you hear me if I said to dump D'Real and let me get my band so I can bring myself back to life?* But Phoenix spoke none of those thoughts aloud. Most often, she did not even let those thoughts out for air.

Ronn smiled, and his face dimpled boyishly. "A'ight then. I'll take you to dinner somewhere there's lots of paparazzi this weekend, keep the buzz goin. Publicity is paper. But on the real, we're just friends."

Her face hot, Phoenix fumbled to unfasten her Rolex. "I have to give you this . . ."

"Aw, *hell* no. That's a gift, baby girl. You keep that."

Phoenix sighed. "I can't, Ronn."

"Think of it like a 'welcome to the label' gift, something like that. Strictly business."

Ronn was canny, all right. That was the only thing he could have said to convince her.

Phoenix almost walked away believing Ronn's patience and understanding were superhuman. She was halfway down the hall before she heard him slam his door.

*W*ell? How'd it go?" Sarge asked, when she met him in the TSR lobby. He could probably see bad news on her face. Phoenix had pulled herself together long enough to talk about her video and promotion with Manny and Katrice and say her good-byes, but now she wanted to curl up under a bed somewhere. Sarge was alone in the lobby beneath a giant-sized framed poster from Ronn's first feature film, *Paid in Full.* In it, Ronn loomed larger than life above the movie's title, a stone-faced monster with a 9mm resting against his jaw.

Phoenix sat beside her father and curled herself into the crook of his arm. Instead of answering, she pulled out the tabloid article she'd folded as a sad memento. She hadn't wanted to leave it with Ronn. She hoped he would never see it again.

Sarge read the article with a pained grunt, as if he'd been kicked in the gut. Then, he handed it back to her. "SOBs didn't mention the name of your damn album," he said.

Phoenix wanted to laugh, but was afraid it would be a sob. "That's what Ronn said."

Sarge kissed the top of her head, sighing. He paused a long time. "How mad is he?"

Not as mad as he has a right to be, Phoenix thought.

"He said he's not mad. He won't be inviting me over anytime soon, though." Realizing she had spent her last night in Ronn's bed, Phoenix felt a cramp above her pelvis. She was barred from his inner space. She could suddenly smell his spicy deodorant and the hairs clustered below his navel. Ronn was only her boss now.

Sarge didn't have to say he'd told her so, but she could almost hear it screaming from his mind. She was grateful for his self-restraint. "And everything else?" Sarge said.

"We'll see. He promised me everything else is straight. Meanwhile, I'm the *ho-of-the-week*. I feel like the world's biggest fool, Daddy. I want to hide."

Sarge didn't answer, but his sigh was its own language. *Been there, done that.*

"Daddy . . . did you cheat on Mom?" Phoenix said suddenly. Phoenix had never asked him, but she felt entitled. No matter how far Sarge's fall from grace might have been, he had never been dumped by an international star on the word of a tabloid magazine. A fall that steep and mighty had to have a few privileges, she decided.

Sarge's pause, this time, was longer. His silence sounded like a *yes.* "It's not that simple, Phoenix. She knew I was away a lot. As long as I kept it away from home, it was my business."

Gloria had told her long ago she thought Phoenix's parents had an open marriage, but the term had sounded so salacious from her cousin's lips that Phoenix had rejected the idea. Now, for the first time, she had confirmation. But if the marriage had been open for Sarge, had it been open for Mom, too? She didn't think so. When Sarge was away, Mom had been home with her.

"So what happened to you guys?" she said, not bothering to try to sound like an adult.

Sarge stretched out his limbs beside her, slumping until he was low enough to lean his head against hers. Phoenix suddenly remembered being a little girl again, in physical therapy, with Sarge coaxing her to do *one* more leg lift so she could walk right again. "To me, it felt like getting lost," Sarge said. "One day, I just couldn't see my way back home. And I guess she stopped feeling like she was married to me. That's all."

"And she still wants me to go to Juilliard. I'm sure that doesn't help."

"You had nothing to do with it. Relationships are hard in this business, Phoenix. You better know that before you start."

"Fine. I'm gonna quit relationships while I'm behind. You can make me a chastity belt."

"I've already got one on order," Sarge said.

At that, miraculously, Phoenix did laugh, but it was for the last time that day.

Sarge took her hand and squeezed it. "You sure this is what you want, Peanut?" He sounded weary suddenly. Maybe whatever was tiring her was catching.

"What do you mean?" Phoenix said, although she knew.

"This. Three Strikes. Tabloid stories. Pop radio."

"Don't you?" Phoenix said. She had heard Sarge tell someone at a party that signing her with G-Ronn was the most exciting moment of his career. "You've worked hard to get me here."

"Honey, I'm almost sixty-five years old. I'm not living for anyone else, and nobody else better be living for me. What *I* want is the revolution. I want to turn back the clock to the days when our neighborhoods were sanctuaries and our people were willing to die for change. What's that shit got to do with here and now? What difference does it make what I want?"

Sometimes, not often, Phoenix heard the bitter quaver in her father's voice, remnants of the militant he had slowly smothered to death in prison. She often wondered what it would have been like to know him then, but Serena reminded her that she wouldn't have had the chance to know him hardly at all.

"Answer my question. *Are you sure you want this?*"

Phoenix couldn't choose between *yes* and *no.*

Sarge's lips twitched with irritation. "This is what you've talked about since you were in pigtails at New World. You said you wanted to be Janet Jackson, and you asked me to help you make it happen. You said, 'Daddy, I have a calling just like you did.' "

"I *know* . . ." Phoenix said, covering her face with her palm, as if he'd shined a light on her.

"And instead of ramping up to make sure you don't waste this opportunity, I see you coasting. I see you making errors of judgment. There's a part of you even trying to put on your brakes to slow it down, sabotage it. Well, that don't cut it here, at *this* stage. That's why you better learn the answer to that question, Phee. Because if you *want* it . . ." —his eyes shimmered as he looked at her, his Daddy stare—"Phoenix, if you *want* it, there is nothing and no one that can stop you from having it. It's handled. But if you *don't* want it?"

Sarge shook his head, sighing again. "If you don't want it, you will fail. You hear me? *You will fail.* There are a hundred traps already set for you. And that's not even the bad part, the sad part. Let me lay it on you: Why in the world would you waste so much God-given time and energy on something you don't want? There's no sense in that. That's just a damn shame."

Phoenix blinked with new tears. "I want it, Sarge."

"What?" Sarge said, cupping his ear. *"I can't hear you."* He used to say that when she was supposed to be practicing the piano. Even if she'd only spent thirty seconds craning her ears to hear the television in the family room, or flipping through a comic book she'd hidden inside her sheet music, Sarge's voice would come booming through the house: *I can't hear you!* That was how she'd started calling him Sarge.

Phoenix smiled. "I want it," she said, more loudly, drying her eyes.

"Again."

"I want it." That time, she even believed it.

"Then you damn well better start acting like it."

When Kai arrived to drive them, Phoenix felt grateful to leave Ronn's building and be shielded beyond the Lexus's opaque windows, so no one could peek inside at her. *Ain't that the fool who cheated on G-Ronn? If I ever had a man that rich, I'd treat him like a king.*

Sarge wanted to be dropped off at a rental car company, so Phoenix asked Kai to take her to the West Hollywood one-bedroom apartment she shared with a film production assistant who was usually away, their version of a time-share. She and Nia watered the plants in the window and kept the dishes clean, but rarely saw each other as they chased dreams in different directions. It wasn't as much a home to Phoenix as Mom's house in Miami, with her room intact from high school, but it was the closest thing Phoenix had to a home of her own. Her pathetic white Corolla was waiting at the curb, the windshield buried under a fallen browned palm frond, like some junk car.

This had been the worst day of her life, except when Grandma Oprah died when she was fifteen. There had been bad days after her band's first two CDs were released—the slow, awful realization that the sales were going to be disastrous—but that had been different. Today was worse, somehow. Her bones felt crushed to powder.

Phoenix suddenly realized Kai had been idling at her curb a few seconds beneath the neat row of towering royal palms, and she'd forgotten to open her door and get out of the car. The big man leaned back to look at her, and she saw her drawn face reflected in his sunglasses.

"You ever read any of the I Ching? The book of Chinese philosophy?" Kai said.

Phoenix shook her head.

"'Pac turned me on to it. You know Tupac was a reader, right? His crib was like a library. He'd spend hours over at the Bodhi Tree, that bookstore on Melrose?"

Phoenix only nodded, feeling numb. Kai talking about Tupac and the Bodhi Tree felt like a new, deeper manifestation of the strange dream her day had become.

"Whenever I see a look on anybody's face like you got on yours, I lay my I Ching on them," Kai went on, playing with the traces of dark fuzz that grew above his top lip. "The quote goes like this: *'When the way comes to an end, then change—having changed, you pass through.'* Meditate on that, Phoenix. Take care of yourself, baby girl."

Shit, Phoenix thought. *Kai knows what happened, too.*

By the time Phoenix let herself into the shade-darkened, stuffy apartment and fell across the futon, her face hurt from the effort of tears. *What's the matter with you? You told Gloria you weren't into Ronn, and now that he's dumped you you're torn up like somebody died.* She remembered what Sarge had said about feeling lost from Mom, and that was how she felt, too; except she was lost from herself, the worst kind of lost.

Phoenix wanted to call Mom and Gloria, but once she lay down, she couldn't move. Tired of feeling sad and awful, Phoenix forced herself to go to sleep, trying so hard it felt like she was shoving her consciousness into a hole in the earth.

As soon as Phoenix's mind started playing, letting go of the day, she heard footsteps striding across the apartment's tiled floors, walking toward her. *Nia?* She'd thought Nia was on a shoot up in Vancouver. She tried to say her roommate's name and open her eyes, but her lips wouldn't obey, and her eyes refused to acknowledge the daylight glowing in fuchsia through the shade from the window above her.

Cool breath played across Phoenix's earlobe, making her skin squirm. Raising her hand, she flicked at her ear to deflect the current, which skated to the nape of her neck.

"Freddie?" a man's voice breathed urgently in her ear, on top of her.

The strange man's voice made Phoenix sit upright, flung from sleep with a gasp. She raised her hands, ready to fight somebody if she had to.

But except for the wilting plants propped bravely in the windowsill, there was no living creature in sight.

CHAPTER FIVE

*S*cott stood outside of the limestone facade of the Stark Music Company publishing house and printing facility on the corner of Fifteenth and Locust, hunching his shoulders against the gnawing February cold that was too harsh for snow. Scott stared up at the lines for electric streetcars strung like twine up and down the cobblestone street, then he closed his eyes and breathed in a mouthful of the frigid air. It had been a mistake to come back here before his trip home to Texarkana, but it was done, so he would say hello to Nell and make a quick departure.

Scott had left his gloves behind in the room his former student Arthur Marshall and his wife had offered him for the night, and now he wished he had stayed inside. Or, better, he wished he had ignored his itch to visit St. Louis and gone straight to Texarkana from Sedalia like he had planned. St. Louis held bad memories now, and he hadn't vanquished them as well as he'd thought. Last fall, he *had* been touched by the parade in his honor down Market Street, but he didn't want his friends putting themselves to that trouble to raise his spirits again. Besides, for all its good intentions, the parade had made him feel like a fraud. So much for the much-ballyhooed tour of the Scott Joplin Ragtime Opera Company.

As a wind gusted down the tunnel of buildings, Scott looked at Stark's tempting doorknob. But cold or not, he couldn't make himself go in.

Scott noticed that Stark's building was a marked improvement over the meager shop Stark had had in Sedalia the day Scott walked in and handed him the pages for "Maple Leaf Rag." Back then, John Stark's best prospects had been as a piano peddler, and a middling one. Now, his business looked prosperous. Scott noted the replicas of the cover sheets in the window for "Maple Leaf," "The Entertainer," "Sun-Flower Slow Drag" and "Elite Syncopations" beneath a banner proclaiming *"Home of the King of Rag-Time, Scott Joplin. Only true classic rags!"*

John was nothing if not a salesman. John's *King of Ragtime* invention grated on Scott's nerves nowadays. Besides, he did not have a home here. To say so was a lie. *Here I am, like those freed slaves after the war without the heart to leave their masters.* The bitter thought brought an almost physical pain with it, as if wrested from another man's mind. Many of Scott's thoughts had become foreign to him, unsuited to his temperament. Heartbreak had remade him.

Scott heard the jangling of bells, and John suddenly stood in the doorway as if he'd been summoned. Someone was playing a rudimentary version of "Something Doing," inside, either a student or an employee in dire need of lessons.

John was the rarest of white men, one who never seemed to age. He had been fifty-eight when Scott met him five years ago, and he didn't look a day older now, his hair preserving its youthful swarthiness despite his ivory beard. Blue eyes glittered from behind John's round-frame spectacles as he smiled. "Well, well, the prodigal son returns," John said. "I thought that was you lurking. I didn't hear a celebration in the streets this time. Come inside, Scott."

Scott didn't return his smile. "I'm looking for Nell."

"So am I. I don't expect you're planning to wait outside."

"I'm fine."

An impatient grimace replaced John's smile. "Come on in, Scott. Don't be an ass."

"Don't be an ass yourself." Again, the words sounded like another man's, spoken harshly. Scott's voice caught the ear of a passing white man in a trench coat and derby, and the hot look he gave Scott could have melted the ice beneath his soles. The man paused his step, as if he could walk no farther after bearing witness to the spectacle of a nigger mouthing off to a white man.

Looking quickly away from the stranger's eyes, Scott removed his hat and walked toward the warmth and safety of John's building. Forgetting himself that way in any of the towns he had toured in the past few months would have resulted in disaster. For all John's faults, at least he wouldn't have him lynched. Inside, Scott felt palpable relief settle over him.

A white man playing the upright piano near the door glanced up at Scott for an instant, then took his eyes back to the keys, not recognizing the composer of the piece he was mauling.

"I'll take that," John said, snatching Scott's hat. "Your coat, too."

John's showroom was impressive, an array of pianos that filled the room with the pleasant scent of rosewood and mahogany. Racks of sheet music lined the walls, with pianos on hand so visitors could test the piece themselves. Scott had never seen the printing facility, but he knew it must be a sizeable one, to need so much space.

"You're living well on my royalties," Scott said, shrugging out of his overcoat.

"No better than you should be," John said. He gestured toward the rear, where he kept his office. "What happened on your opera tour?"

Scott chuffed bitterly. John had nerve, all right, bringing up the *Guest of Honor* tour.

"It's a polite inquiry," John said, when Scott didn't answer. "I've heard it didn't go well. If that's true, I'm sorry."

"That's charitable." Sarcasm was another of Scott's new gifts.

"Hogwash. Just because I didn't publish it doesn't mean I wished you ill. Have a seat. You look tired."

Suddenly, Scott *felt* tired. He sat in the straight-backed wooden chair beside John's desk and its meticulous stacks of sheet music. John had never given *A Guest of Honor* a chance even after the St. Louis show with thirty performers to prove with every note and step that Negroes *could* stage an opera using themes and music from their own traditions. Dr. Booker T. Washington and President Roosevelt would have lauded it themselves, had the opera had a chance to live. But it had been destined to die. John had only a partial hand in sealing its fate.

The tour sat in Scott's memory like a bleeding wound. He had resigned himself to the indignities of travel—the name-calling, malevolent stares and presumption of servility that followed Negro performers wherever they went—but he couldn't have imagined that a member of his own company would steal their meager proceeds, leaving them without pay. Or that every copy of his masterwork would be confiscated in a trunk in Pittsburg, Kansas, because he couldn't afford to have it released to him.

There were a half dozen people he could beg to help him retrieve his trunk, and John was no doubt one of them. But the opera, clearly, had been cursed. Not the sort of curse Louis believed in—at the hand of a hoochie-coochie man—but a strange kind of curse all the same. A curse of foolishness. A curse of vanity. Booker T. Washington had dined at the White House, so had he believed *all* of the confines of his race had been shattered?

The truth was, no one cared to see niggers singing opera, or a rag king composing one.

"This might cheer you . . ." John said. "I have an associate from New Orleans, and he told me he saw a little boy on the street corner outside his store hawking watermelons to the tune of 'The Enter-tainer.' He sings it like this: 'Water-me-lons, they're wet, they're cold!' And he always rouses a big crowd, that boy." John chuckled

Scott's throat was suddenly so dry that it hurt. "Maybe I'll collect a penny royalty for every watermelon he sells. That'll be high living. I've had the wrong intentions all along."

Annoyed, John swallowed his chuckles. "All these years you've said nary a peep, and now you're chock-full of nonsense. Any other composer would be tickled by that story. You haven't got a lick of humor, Scott."

That was true enough these days. "Where's Nell? I can't stay."

"Will you hold your horses? She'll be here. We meet every Friday for lunch."

Scott had first visited Nellie's studio on Lucas Avenue, hoping to see her without having to run into her father. He had just missed her, he was told. "How is she?" Scott said, deciding that John's daughter, mutually loved, was their safest topic.

"A busy young lady. She's performing, of course. She's finally even courting a bit. The fella's a bit young, but I'm just glad someone's caught her fancy at last."

Even Nellie's good news felt discouraging. Scott had never entertained a union with John's daughter Eleanor, nor she with him, but she had always served as his unfailing advocate. Nellie had convinced her father to publish at least an excerpt of *Rag-Time Dance* after his initial refusal, and then argued passionately on behalf of *A Guest of Honor,* ranting to Scott in tears when her arguments failed. She played his music as well as he did, like a Negro at heart, and she first introduced him to Alfred Ernst, helping Scott imagine himself accepted in white circles he had dared not dream of. Such a softhearted, talented and lovely girl! Could he ever hope to meet a woman like Nellie who was also a Negro?

John's voice grew soft. "You've had a run of bad luck, Scott. I'm sorry for it."

"Bad luck." Scott repeated the words, assessing the phrase. *Pure bad luck,* Belle had called him before she left. Maybe their infant daughter's death two years ago could be blamed on bad luck, and Belle leaving him after that. Perhaps his brother Will's death that same year was only bad luck again. But whatever he was up against felt worse than bad luck.

"You've got to keep your chin up, Scott. Take hold of your life. Give me a new piece, and I'd love to put some money in your pocket. Hell, maybe if you'd agree to expand the book for *Guest of Honor* like I told you all along, tinker with those lyrics—"

"That's the past."

"If that's true, then why are you so ornery about it? 'Palm Leaf Rag' is grand work, sure, but you should have let me publish it. It's a slap to my face, going to that Chicago house."

"Keep the darkie in his place, is that it?" This time, the intruder who had taken control of Scott's tongue appalled even him.

John's face tightened as if he'd been struck. His pores blushed crimson. He raised his pipe to Scott like a gnarled, pointing finger. "How *dare* you give me that guff, Joplin. I wasn't drafted in the war, I *enlisted*. I didn't have to, but I did it, and there's hardly a night I don't dream about those graveyards they called battlefields. Lots of times I asked myself what the hell a Kentucky-born boy was doing in a blue uniform, but I did it because I gave a damn what happened to those slaves—people like *your parents*—so don't talk to me about keeping darkies in their place. If you were anyone else, I'd sock you."

John had been a bugler more than a soldier in the Civil War, from what Nellie said, but it was true he had been willing to die for the cause of abolition. Scott looked away, toward John's window. "I had no call to say it. I apologize."

John's face relaxed again. "Well, at least now I see for myself the state you're in."

"A poor one, I'm afraid," Scott said reluctantly.

"You're earning steady. 'Maple Leaf' is selling close to three thousand a year, and it's still climbing. It's a *classic* rag, Scott. Those penny royalties add up, trust me."

That was typical John: He knew the business of a matter, not its heart. Writing the opera had helped Scott endure his losses after his baby died and his brother followed. He and Belle hadn't dared give their baby a name, she'd been born so sickly; the three months she'd lived had been a miracle. Losing Will, the spitting image of their father, had cut something deeper out of him. By the time Belle left, her departure seemed almost trite, a predictable turn in his life.

A Guest of Honor had rescued Scott's heart, then it had seduced him with its promise. With proper backing, he could have taken his opera to Hamburg and Vienna and Paris, and once he was embraced in Europe, American scholars would have had no *choice* but to see beyond his skin color. Nellie had told him Negroes were treated as ordinary men in Europe. In Europe, he would find credibility he could spend two lifetimes seeking at home. But two years after Ernst's promise to take him to Europe, Scott had given up hope of it. Ernst hadn't even replied to his letter two months ago. Ernst was busy, of course, but it smarted.

"Alfred Ernst will be musical director for the World's Fair. That's the rumor," John said, as if he knew Scott's mind.

"Will he?" Scott didn't bother to brighten his voice.

"I tell you, a musician who got a proper introduction there would be heard by the whole country, by and by. That's a real sendoff."

" 'Ah, yes, Joplin, you're a genius, young man. I'll dedicate an evening to the music of Scott Joplin, *und* naturally have you on our grandest concert stage,' " Scott said with a sweep of his arm, imitating Ernst's German accent. "And then he won't remember saying it."

"He means well." John looked defensive, lowering his eyes. Ernst was a family friend.

"Meaning isn't doing."

"There are politics at the fair," John said quietly.

"You mean I'm a Negro. Say it plain." Scott remembered how the Negro musicians had been shunted to alleyways and saloons at the Chicago Fair in 1893, while white musicians enjoyed the large venues where everyone could hear them. He couldn't expect this one to be different.

John made a sour face. He had no patience for Scott's complaints about the traps of his skin color. "You don't need Ernst. Write me a piece in time for the fair, and we'll have it playing all over town, in the places fairgoers go at *night*. And there'll be a breezeway at the fair. It won't be the same as a concert stage, but it's a place to play. We can't have the World's Fair in St. Louis without the King of Ragtime."

Scott saw the light in John's eyes when he'd said that, a quicksilver reminder of John's awe of him. But John reserved his awe for the familiar, what was expected. John was a stubborn sonofabitch, so tight with a nickel that he didn't trust Scott's talents to elevate him beyond rags. And this was the one person who should know he had already proven himself! Scott remembered the *Indianapolis Freeman* newspaper notice about him last year, which had sounded like a chide as much as encouragement: *The day is fast approaching when a great colored composer will be recognized in this country, especially if he advances from being a ragtime idol.*

"I don't feel any new rags coming," Scott said.

"Sometimes you don't need to feel 'em 'til they're done, Scott. You know that. Write something fast. I don't mean to pry in what isn't my concern, but if the tour bled you dry—"

Scott laughed, a dry chuckle from deep in his throat. That was an understatement. He was as close to penniless as he'd been since he was a teenager, and he'd lost his dream in the transaction. "That tour bled me every way it could," Scott said. "The money's the smallest part."

"Well, you're a composer, Scotty—*compose*. Climb on down out of the clouds and try to get along with us earthbound folks. Leave the clouds to those Wright brothers."

Scott stood suddenly, buttoning his coat. He couldn't stomach another of John's lectures on the necessary union of art and commerce. "I can't wait for Nellie. I have to go."

John pretended he hadn't heard, talking on. "I'll tell you one thing, Scott, and it may be the only good advice I'm capable of giving you anymore: You've got the idea somehow that everyone is supposed to recognize what you are on sight. Well, you need to shake that idea out of your head. A composer who can't work because he's convinced he ought to be revered is a composer who seals his own fate. Swallow your damn disappointments like the rest of us."

John's tongue was as coarse as Louis's, only less profane. Despite a few enthusiastic audiences starved for entertainment, *A Guest of Honor* had never shown itself to be anything but a failure. Why had God given him the inspiration and teased him with promises that were lofty only in their delusion? How had he believed he could use his music to carry his brethren on his back when he couldn't find his own footing? There wasn't enough time in one lifetime to climb to those heights from the low place he had started.

"No one will know me until fifty years after I'm dead," Scott said, half to himself.

John laughed. "You'd still be luckier than most, fella."

Back out in the cold, Scott realized John was right about one thing: He needed money. He wasn't a pampered artisan in a European noble's court. When he came back from visiting his family in Texarkana, he'd need to start booking concerts in Sedialia, St. Louis and Chicago—no costumes or dancers or choruses, and no one to share the earnings with. *Plenty of folks will pay top dollar for a private concert by Scott Joplin, the Rag Time King.*

With his bad luck, that title would follow him to his tombstone.

But better the king of the ragtimers, he thought, than a pauper with no place to call home.

*H*ey, folks, lookie who we have in our midst here tonight! It's *Scott Joplin!*"

Tom Turpin, that great bear of a man, brought a hush to the room when he made the announcement from the piano. Scott had slipped into the Rosebud unnoticed from Eugenia Street in the rear, hoping to avoid Market's nighttime bustle, but Tom's announcement ended his anonymity as he made his way to an empty table. Tom had been playing the hell out of the upright the moment before, but now gasps replaced the hypnotic currents of the "Blue Danube." Dancers stopped their synchronized twirling, ladies' skirts deflating. Scott heard necks crack as people craned backward. Next, a swell of applause and rowdy hoots, a room of grins. There were many familiar faces, but more unfamiliar ones. These were admirers, not friends.

Scott had never seen so many people gathered here, shoulder to shoulder, and his face flared with embarrassment. Their attire wasn't overly ostentatious, but the customers had come to preen. The women wore their celebration clothes—fur wraps, satin bows and evening hats—and their escorts nearly outdid them in their silk hats, pearl gray derbies and canes with silver heads. There were more whites than usual at the Rosebud tonight, a sign that word had spread, but most of the patrons were Negroes with high expectations in their gazes.

Scott tipped his hat to Tom and took his seat.

Good for Tom. His gentleman's club was exactly what he'd planned it to be, a showcase for the best ragtime players, and Scott was proud of his friend. Lighted with electricity and with rooms enough for drinking, dancing, dining, gambling and the company of willing women in the hotel upstairs, the Rosebud was nearly as big as a city block. It was truly a world unto itself, much bigger than the Maple Leaf Club in Sedalia. He should write a piece to honor the Rosebud. That would be effortless enough. Already, Scott could hear a six-eight march tempo in his head.

Three young men at the table beside Scott's whipped off their brown caps, leaning close to him with hands outstretched. They each had a mug, although Scott suspected they were barely out of short pants, much less old enough for beer. "Hey, sir, we didn't know you was *Scott Joplin*. I taught myself piano from hearin' "Maple Leaf Rag"! I can't believe I'm sittin' next to *you*! I'm here for the contest," said the tallest boy, shaking Scott's hand with vigor.

"I'm a professor, too, Mr. Joplin," said an even younger boy, this one probably not yet fourteen. "All you gotta remember is Lightning Jack from Carthage!"

"No, Billy the Kid from East St. Louis!" the third boy said. "Those fools can't play."

A restless scuffle followed, with the boys jostling.

"Learn to read music, boys. And *write* it, so you'll have something on paper. Paper lives forever," Scott said, but he wondered if they had heard him over the room's din. Belle had complained that he spoke so softly, he might as well be talking to no one but himself.

"All you need is a robe, and you could be a preacher. Leave those kids be," a familiar voice behind Scott said. The voice had changed since he'd last heard it, more man than boy now, but he couldn't mistake Louis.

"Louis!" Scott said, rising to his feet. He hugged his friend.

"You sound surprised. Where else am I gonna be tonight?" Louis wore his oversized white Stetson, an immaculate suit of clothes—Parisian, no doubt—and a bright purple ascot. Louis only dressed up when he was working.

"Is that Chauvin?" Scott heard one of the boys whisper. "Ain't nobody gon' beat *him*."

"Damn right you ain't. And all three of your mamas is outside waitin' with a switch to whip you for losing," Louis told the boys, winking. The crowd growing around them laughed, and Scott saw three young faces turn mournful. Louis had been that young when Scott met him, he realized. Neither of them seemed young anymore.

"*You* gonna play, Mr. Joplin?" the youngest boy asked, an anxious afterthought.

"No," Scott said, his eyes darting to Louis's. These boys weren't the only ones who wouldn't relish competing against Louis Chauvin. "Just a visit to see friends."

Tom made his way back to Scott's table, clasping Scott's hand with a meaty palm. Perspiration shone from Tom's forehead, the effort of his exertions at the piano and the heat generated by the excited Friday-night contest crowd. A group of eager men stood ringing the table, but none had the nerve to step forward. Tom Turpin, Scott Joplin and Louis Chauvin were the closest thing they knew to royalty, and no one dared disturb their circle.

"St. Louis ain't the same without you, Scotty," Tom said.

"Looks the same to me."

Tom, unlike John, had the delicacy not to bring up *A Guest of Honor*. Scott was sure the story of his opera's grand failure had wound its way through town, but Tom wasn't one to pry. Even after Scott moved in with Tom for a time after Belle left him, Tom never brought up personal questions without an invitation even if they sat up talking about music for hours.

"How long you back?" Tom said. "I'm having my Third Annual Ball and Piano Contest on the twenty-second, and it'll be a sight to see. We're doin' it up big, at the New Douglass Hall on Beaumont. You don't wanna miss that, no sir. Folks who swear they've never set foot in Chestnut Valley will show for that one, and in high dress."

"Me and the big man are goin' toe-to-toe," Louis said.

"I'll have to miss it. I'm on a train for Little Rock tomorrow," Scott said. He could stay longer if he chose, but he wouldn't want to. He had hoped to feel happier here.

"Well, come on back for the fair, hear?" Tom said, taking a seat beside Scott. He motioned to a bartender behind the long, mirrored counter, signaling for drinks. "We're gonna do a ragtime contest like nobody's ever seen."

"It'll be the biggest one I've ever won," Louis said, slapping Tom's back.

"Why do I feel some fool's dainty little hand on me, Chauvin?" Tom said, eyeing Louis over his shoulder. He did not like to be touched, especially by Louis. When Louis wasn't intoxicated, Scott wasn't sure any living man could beat him, and Tom knew it, too. Luckily for Tom, Louis was just as likely to show up drunk as not. Tonight, so far, it was hard to tell.

"There's somethin' so regal about a big man in a suit," Louis said. "Ain't there, Scotty?"

"I *know* your hand ain't still on me."

Louis dropped his hand as the barkeep dropped three whiskey glasses on the table. "Go on and drink up," Tom said, rising. "It's time."

Louis laughed, watching Tom lumber off as the crowd parted to let him pass. "You see him runnin' scared?" Louis said. "He didn't touch his whiskey, and he knows you can't drink worth shit. That big ol' nigger thinks he's clever, but he ain't." Nonetheless, Louis downed the first shot and took the second glass in his hand.

At a stage in front of the room, Tom whistled to command quiet, and the bustling bar became a funeral parlor in an instant, except for the sound of silverware and conversation in the adjacent dining room. Tom's voice rose like a riverboat's foghorn on the Mississippi. "Ladies and gentlemen, it's time for the Friday-night contest at the Rosebud Bar, and we've got fourteen professors here to compete for title of best rag player in Chestnut Valley—which means the best in the *world*. Anybody who aims to win has to get past yours truly first. Let's draw places!"

Tom drew from the hat first—proprietor's privilege—and also claimed the first spot in the contest, the least coveted. In the wine room, Tom's favorite piano was elevated on blocks so he didn't have to sit on a stool with his three-hundred-pound bulk, but in a contest he had to take his seat like everyone else.

To Scott, Tom looked like a bullfrog perched on a toadstool. When he started playing, Scott knew after only a few measures that even with three drinks in him, Louis would beat Tom with ease. Tom was a solid composer and performer, but Louis's assessment was probably best: Tom attacked the piano like a tasty meal, beating the keys into submission.

When Louis's turn came, he stood over the piano and shook his hands melodramatically before he sat. Then, he paused on the stool, as if deep in thought. Word of Louis's upcoming performance had reached the girls working upstairs, who stood watching from the wooden staircase with grins as large as the bosoms showing through their sheer, colorful costumes. The crowd stirred restlessly, sending up calls and whistles. Then, Louis began.

Louis launched into an homage to "Maple Leaf," the famous B section rendered at a dizzying pace, then he teased in a little of Tom's

"Harlem Rag," playing in a purposely stodgy style. Louis's fingers flew, making the melody its own surprising, electrifying creature. His music was wizardry; Scott's heart pounded as his friend played tenths with his left hand even while his right-hand harmonics demanded more skill. Louis sounded like two men playing at once. Shouts rose from the crowd midway through, and by the time Louis finished, the shouts were a roar. Scott came to his feet, joining the tumult.

The boys Scott had met from the next table performed admirably, and Joe Jordan always made his competitors sweat, but the night belonged to Louis Chauvin. He would likely win Tom's contest on Beaumont, too. Louis was still a marvel.

While young men and women flocked to Louis's side after the contest, hoping to breathe in some of his talent for themselves, Scott sat in the dining room jotting notes for a "Rosebud March" on a napkin for a half hour while he waited for the late supper he'd been promised. The music wasn't much yet, just something to occupy his mind. If not for tomorrow's train, Scott would have left long ago and planned to see Louis another time, but he didn't want to miss him. Louis had offered to treat him to prime rib, a Rosebud specialty, and Scott was glad to be treated.

"God in Heaven, you've improved," Scott told Louis when he finally joined him. Louis's face was flushed from the praise of admirers, his collar colorfully stained with ladies' promises.

"Some of us don't got sense enough to be satisfied, do we?" Louis said, fanning out his winnings on the tabletop, fifteen dollars. Scott wondered how much of the money he had already spent and how much would be left by dawn. Usually, Louis spent most of his winnings on the girls upstairs. Scott didn't mind relieving his friend of a couple of his dollars, since the food here was magnificent. Tom took as much pride in his kitchen as he did in his playing.

"When are you gonna come back to St. Louis, where you belong, Scotty?"

"I don't know," Scott said. "My father needs to see me, after Will. Then I might come back, or I might not. I'm afraid I'll be an old man sitting at this same table."

"I got news: You're *already* an old man sittin' at this table, old man."

Scott smiled wanly. "I'd go plumb crazy, Louis. I'm halfway there now."

"Well, your soul's here in St. Louis. See how the place lit up when Tom called your name? They were all lookin' at you sayin', 'Damn, that nigger over there sold copies of a song he wrote to thousands and thousands of folks who ain't his mama, white folks to boot, and he's one of us.' Tom would cut off his hands to be Scott Joplin, and you know it. Your soul is here, and *that* ain't goin' nowhere. That's a fact." Louis raised his wineglass, and Scott clinked his against it, toasting. He had never heard Louis speak about the soul. He noticed that his friend's eyes seemed red and glassy from something that wasn't liquor.

"How . . . are you?" Scott said, gazing at Louis directly, so he'd know what he meant.

Smiling, Louis reached into his jacket pocket and pulled out a small burlap bag wound with twine. "Don't touch it. That's my bag of luck. I can help you get yours."

Scott hushed his voice. "Please tell me you're seeing a doctor by now."

"Time to time. I've been feeling good, though. See here?" Louis held up both palms above the table. His right hand still shook slightly, but no worse than before. "My hoodoo man's got this licked, Scotty. Come with me to see him."

"There's no need," Scott said, but he wasn't hungry anymore. He'd made himself forget about Louis's suspicions about Rose, and his fleeting fear of illness three years ago had been crushed by all of the losses in its wake. Everyone got headaches and muscle aches from time to time. That didn't mean he carried syphilis.

"The dog sleeps, Scotty," Louis said cryptically.

"So you've said."

"If you ain't got it, I'm glad for you. But hardly a nigger in here ain't carryin' the dog. I wouldn't feel no shame for it. Napoleon had it, too. Probably Shakespeare and all the rest. But that don't mean you shouldn't see after yourself."

"Follow your own advice."

"I *am* seeing after mine, Scotty. Believe it," Louis said, and put his bag of luck away.

Scott hoped Louis wasn't foolishly leading himself to a path of needless suffering, like poor Will's fight with consumption. Scott noticed a man across the dining room who looked like Will, except he was a few years his late brother's junior. The man was grinning, enjoying the company of the pretty dark-skinned woman who sat beside him, laughing at his every word. The woman had a more delicate face, but as Scott stared at her he realized that she bore a remarkable resemblance to Belle. Unless he was mad himself, seeing a pair of ghosts.

Scott felt such an acute sadness that it blocked his throat. He didn't miss Belle, exactly, but the thought of her and their first little apartment on Morgan filled Scott with grief. He wished he could reclaim the past three years and become that confident, energetic man again. Scott had eaten only half his plate of prime rib, and his stomach was already pinching.

"I see where you're looking, and you're better off without her," Louis said. "That woman wasn't no good for you, not from the start, and I told you as much to your face. Believe it or not, Leola still mentions your name from time to time. She'd be happy if you called on her."

Leola. Yes, the singer he had dallied with, whose eyes had shimmered into his. Last he'd heard, Leola had left the bar stages and was giving voice lessons, selling Poro hair tonic for extra money. Now that Belle had left him, what was to stop him from looking her up? *For what? So you can lie down with her and catch your morning train?*

"Maybe Belle was right," Scott said. "Musicians shouldn't marry."

"Marry?" Louis said, pretending to sway off-balance on his chair. "Man, what's wrong with you? I ain't said nothin' about getting married. Leola ain't the marryin' kind."

"What kind is she, then?"

Louis grinned. "The best kind, Scotty. The kind that treats you right and leaves you be."

The thought of a night in Leola's arms, in any woman's arms, seemed too great a gift for Scott to imagine. He remembered the time when he could have snapped his fingers and had any of a roomful of women who'd heard him give a private concert, when his rendition of "Sun Flower Slow Drag" had so stirred them that even John Stark had remarked upon their excitement—and those women were *white*. Music was a natural aphrodisiac, Louis liked to say.

But Scott didn't dare toy with Leola. She deserved to be courted, and he had neither the time nor inclination for courting tonight. If he had the money to spare, he might have ventured upstairs to one of the hotel rooms instead, slipping onto a canopied bed while a perfumed stranger whispered lies and made his forsaken skin tremble to her touch. Yes, he might have. My God, he was too broke for a night with a whore.

He had to go home. Or *find* home, if such a place existed for him.

Much of what Scott loved about St. Louis, he suspected, might be dying before his eyes.

CHAPTER SIX

*I*t takes a village to make a video, Phoenix thought. A sea of bodies lay before her.

The line for the dance audition wound around the building just after 9:00 A.M., when Phoenix arrived at Millennium Studios on Lankershim with Arturo and Sarge. The lithe, wiry hopefuls were male and female, mostly teenagers or in their early twenties, their skin tones reflecting every shade of God's rainbow. Olympia had advertised for a funky, jazzy look, so there were no leotards in this audition line, only baggy streetwear on the men, bare midriffs and colorful hairstyles on the women. Some dancers leaned against the building's wall, some sat cross-legged on the sidewalk, some were stretching; they looked like they had been lined up for hours. It was an amazing sight. Phoenix's heart raced with an adrenaline blast. All of this was for *her*.

Walking past the waiting dancers while she kept her face hidden behind her oversized Fendi Suns shades, Phoenix felt the crowd stir and glow in her wake. She heard whispered voices: *That's her. See her over there? She's in G-Ronn's video. That's Phoenix.* Arturo and Sarge matched her breezy pace on either side as if they were her bodyguards, and Phoenix realized they were. If she hadn't known it before, she knew it now: This was real.

"Damn, there's three hundred people here, yo," Arturo muttered as a Three Strikes intern in a black *TSR* T-shirt moved aside to let them slip into the side door where the line began. Olympia loved Arturo, so he had been spared an audition even though she was sure Sarge would be happy to have him bake in the sun with everyone else.

"Five hundred," the intern corrected. "The first group's already inside."

"How many are we hiring?" Phoenix asked Sarge.

"Twelve," Sarge said. "Including swing. Ten principals."

"All these people for ten spots?" Phoenix whispered, surveying the waiting crowd from the doorway. Word must have gotten out that G-Ronn would make a cameo in the video and help her with final casting, Phoenix thought. Ronn's name was a lightning bolt.

Four girls who looked sixteen stood at the front of the line watching Phoenix with eager eyes, documenting her every word and movement. They were small-breasted and thin, with spray-on gold and burgundy in their funked-up hair. Phoenix saw their dreams shining in their eyes. She wondered how far they had come, and how much they had sacrificed to get here. Phoenix hadn't known how to answer those hungry gazes in the line, but she gave the girls a smile. "Good luck," she said, meeting their eyes before she disappeared inside.

She's so pretty, so down-to-earth, she heard the girls marveling before the door fell shut.

Inside, more dancers wound in the hall leading to the dance studio. These were too preoccupied with preparations to notice her, checking their costumes and makeup, doing more serious stretches and splits, limbering themselves with popping moves to music in their heads. The closer Phoenix got to the studio doors, the more fevered the excitement burning from the dancers. One girl sat on the carpeted floor with her eyes closed, mouth moving in silent prayer.

"Go on in and watch, see if anybody catches your eye while you have time," Sarge told Phoenix quietly, handing her a thin sheaf of papers she recognized as her day's interview schedule. The first of four interviews was in an hour, with a man named Keith O'Hara from an L.A.-based magazine called *Basslines*. She had never heard of the man or the magazine. "It's good color for the reporters to see you here at the audition, build excitement for the video. You can do your interviews in the lobby when it's time. Those phoners from New York later will come to the reception desk. Anybody asks about your personal life, tell them it's off limits. Mystery is good."

"I'm on it," Phoenix said, nodding. Between the Starbucks grande iced latte she'd nearly finished and Sarge's pep talk yesterday, the malaise that had led her to Kendrick's arms in St. Louis had lifted. Phoenix didn't have time to stress about a tabloid story or her love life. She had blown her romance with Ronn, but she wasn't going to blow this chance. *Maybe it's best Gloria's still pissed and won't be around. I need to be about my work right now.*

The studio was large, with a shiny finish on the floors and mirrors stretching the length of the front and rear walls. Olympia already had six rows of ten dancers in place as she ran them through some of the steps Phoenix recognized from the St. Louis show, which Sarge thought had gone fine despite all the drama the night before. A video camera was set up in front, taping the auditions so Ronn and the director could see the footage later. Phoenix and Arturo tried to slip in without interrupting, walking close to the wall as they made their way to a semicircle of folding chairs set up in a back corner, but Phoenix could *feel* the dancers noticing her. She caught eyes gazing at her reflection in the mirror, watching. She would have to get used to people staring.

Shit. I'm paying for this, Phoenix realized suddenly. Sarge had explained that the cost for her music video would come out of her royalties, a depressing thought. The dancers they hired would make $250 a day for the week of rehearsals, and $475 a day during the shoot, which would last at least another week. And that didn't count sets, costumes, locations. Even though the director was giving her a break because of his friendship with Ronn, this video was going to cost a fortune, probably $50,000 or more, and that was *cheap.*

"You all got it? From the top," Olympia said.

The chorus from "Party Patrol" suddenly blasted from the sound system. A room of sixty dancers sprang into motion, and dozens of soles mewled against the floor. The dancers couldn't have been working long, but most of them mimicked Olympia's motion with surprising confidence. To Phoenix's eyes, they looked like she could hire any random dozen of the dancers in this group alone. After running through the routine twice, Olympia asked them to switch rows so the dancers near the back could move forward.

Watching, Arturo never ran out of criticisms: "OK, now girlfriend with the bald head better take some classes, and she needs to start with ballet," he whispered as part of his running commentary. "People always think they can come audition because they've seen some videos on MTV. I've been in classes since I was *eight*. Oh Lord, do you see Snoop Dogg up here hogging the line? He needs to move back and let somebody else show off. Olympia hates divas."

"Really?" Phoenix said, grinning. "Then why does she like you so much?"

"Why do you think? 'Cuz I'm the best, *chica*."

Phoenix studied Olympia's gentle, friendly manner with the dancers as she tutored them through the routine, and suddenly felt bad that she hadn't shed her reserve around her. She would do better, she decided, even though her band's shows had never needed a choreographer. All they'd needed was the music.

"You think Olympia's good?" she asked Arturo.

"Oh, yeah. She's smart. She's not afraid to push the edge, but she knows her roots. She loves Bob Fosse and Alvin Ailey and Katherine Dunham, like me. We can *talk*, see? And she likes my ideas. That's another reason we get along. She's gonna work your ass off."

"I know that's right. This looks like an audition for a Broadway show."

"That's what it is," Arturo said, nodding. "Remember how Roy Scheider said it in *All That Jazz*? 'It's *showtime*, folks.' We're gonna take videos to a whole new level with 'Party Patrol.'" Arturo sounded like Ronn, a convert. Maybe after all these years of storming off the stage, Arturo was growing up. If she could keep her own shit straight, she could take a village with her to Ronn's moon, sun and stars.

"Ya'll remember there's supposed to be some singing somewhere in this video, too, right?" Phoenix said, teasing.

Arturo feigned confusion. "What's your name again? Did you say something, Britney?"

"All right, now," Phoenix said, warning.

"Oh, I'm sorry—is it Monica? Imani? I get you all mixed up."

They tried to smother their laughter, like being back in their high school auditorium with Jay, and Phoenix suddenly missed their friend fiercely. It still didn't seem right that they had grown up without him.

Some of the dancers in the row nearest them glanced nervously over their shoulders, afraid they were being laughed at. Phoenix covered her mouth, but she couldn't stop giggling. It felt good to laugh, after the past few days.

"You need to turn back around and get your steps down," Arturo told the gawkers, and Phoenix pinched his muscle-bound arm to shush him.

"We're not laughing at you," Phoenix said.

"Speak for yourself," Arturo muttered, and she pinched him again.

The door opened, and one of the interns came into the studio accompanying a man with a reporter's notebook. Phoenix glanced at the watch Ronn had given her: It was already after ten, time for her first interview! Her days flew past. Glancing at the reporter again, Phoenix mistrusted her eyes. "You have *got* to be shitting me . . ."

"What?" Arturo said.

Now, she was sure of it. She recognized the reporter's ambling walk. "It's Carlos."

"Carlos who?"

"*The* Carlos, from high school," Phoenix whispered, and Arturo's eyes widened. No one in her circle at New World had been spared the story.

"Miss Smalls?" the intern said, leaning close. "The reporter is here. His name is—"

"I know his name," Phoenix said. He loomed so large in her memory, he seemed smaller now even though he'd gained weight in eight years, filling out his cheeks, giving more heft to his chest. But everything else was the same: His liquid brown eyes, baby-smooth Hershey's Kiss skin, and two front teeth that angled ever-so-slightly toward each other, a defect that made him attractive in her eyes. He still had a thin moustache groomed to perfection, and hair sprang from his head in short, tight twists she'd always called his *dreadlets*. His hair had once fascinated her. Everything about him had once fascinated her. Her toes twitched at the sight of him, and especially at the familiar scent of his cologne. No one wore Kenzo like Carlos.

It took Phoenix a long time to think of what to say.

"You don't look like a Keith O'Hara."

He shrugged, grinning, and his smile brought back her twitching toes. "I told Keith I'd take this interview. He's still writing your CD review, though. No conflict of interest. I hope this is all right." His clipped sentences told Phoenix he was nervous, an idea that amused her. *She* was the one who used to feel nervous around *him,* in their seventy-two-hour courtship.

Phoenix saw Arturo giving Carlos a careful examination, and he glanced at Phoenix with an approving smile. "I think you two need to be alone," Arturo said.

He stole the thought from her mind.

*P*hoenix and Carlos went to a small room beyond the lobby that had vending machines offering water, sports drinks and snack foods. At least they were out of Sarge's sight. Phoenix didn't know where her father had vanished to, but she hoped he wouldn't be back soon. Sarge would not be in the mood to see Carlos Harris, and Phoenix was tired of melodrama.

Carlos sat at the opposite end of a large black leather sofa, crossing his legs. His style was a blend of tropical and urban, his trademark; a peach Caribbean-style shirt, fashionably baggy jeans and unmarred white sneakers. His cologne filled the room, a scent that made Phoenix think of palm trees, seawater, *Calle Ocho,* and his apartment overlooking Biscayne Bay. She had once bought a bottle of Kenzo to smell in the privacy of her bedroom.

"So . . ." He began, folding his hands as he gazed at her. "This is awkward, no?"

Carlos didn't have any accent beyond a well-spoken brother, but she remembered how he'd sometimes spoken with a Spanish syntax, the mark of his early childhood in Puerto Rico. She'd loved how he could lapse into Spanish, remaking himself with everything from his rapidity of speech to his gestures, his accent lovely as rainfall. His Spanish was light-years better than her Hebrew. Maybe she'd been so drawn to him because, like her, he danced between two cultures. Carlos's mother was from San Juan, and his father was a black American photographer who'd lived there for years. She remembered that, too. She remembered details about Carlos as if they'd known each other for years.

First love sank deep. Phoenix was as tongue-tied now as she'd been at sixteen.

"I won't stay if you don't want me to," Carlos said.

"You can stay."

He looked visibly relieved, his clasped hands loosening. He nodded. "Good. I'd like to stay, Phoenix. Not just for the interview. I wanted to catch up."

Catch up. Phoenix was surprised to feel angry, suddenly. She thought she'd left the anger to Sarge. "I'm a legal adult now, one thing."

His eyes darted away from hers. "I see that." He was silent so long after that, she was almost sorry she'd said it. His eyes came back to hers only reluctantly. He combed his fingers through his hair, a habit she remembered. "I guess we need to talk about that first."

"Or you can just get started with the interview. Either way is cool with me." Her voice sounded more distant than she'd intended.

"I haven't contacted you before now because . . . I was embarrassed." He still looked embarrassed, but her anger wasn't yet sated, so she waited for him to go on. "I was an asshole. What I did was selfish and thoughtless. I was in a position to be a mentor, and instead . . . I tried to go somewhere else. That was wrong."

"I just thought you had a thing for high school girls," Phoenix said.

He blinked hard, a wince. "That was the first and last time, Phee. I'm not proud of it."

"You still didn't have to leave me hanging like that. I was all heartbroken and shit."

At sixteen, being heartbroken was a wing of Hell: Obsessively checking her e-mail a dozen times a day, calling Carlos's cell phone every other day like a religious ritual, struggling not to sound as angry, hurt and desperate as she felt. *So, how you doin'? I've just been thinking about you, and I was wondering if you had time to give me a call, if you're not too busy.* Each time a call had gone unreturned, she felt incinerated. Still, she'd saved every review and story he wrote in the newspaper just because the words were his. She'd made a list of everything she knew about him—his height (five-ten), his favorite music (Latin jazz), where he'd gone to college (Stanford)—just to feel like she was a part of his life. She replayed every moment of their interactions in her mind each night while she touched herself, trying to escape back into time. Billie Holiday's *Lady in Satin* sounded exactly like she felt, dressing her wound just right.

"Maybe I didn't trust myself, kiddo," Carlos said. "Besides, your father made it real clear he would kill me if I tried to contact you."

That was indisputable. When Carlos had pulled up in front of her hotel with Phoenix in the passenger seat of his silver Acura at 5:00 A.M., Sarge had been waiting for them at the curb. Sarge hadn't had the patience for *Mr. Smalls, I can explain* and all that jazz. Sarge had pulled Carlos out of the car by his hair and punched him so hard his mouth had spilled with blood, a back tooth knocked loose. Watching, Phoenix had screamed. Suddenly, it was *Romeo and Juliet,* the version she'd seen in her tenth-grade English class with Olivia Hussey and the stirring, unforgettable theme by Nina Rota. A timeless, doomed love.

And all in front of a Saturday-night crowd on Ocean Drive.

"So you punked out," Phoenix said.

Carlos smiled sadly. "Yeah. I punked out. Your dad is a convincing man. I saw him outside when I got here, and I made damn sure to stay out of his sight."

"He *definitely* would not be happy to see you."

"What about you?" Carlos said. His eyes hung on hers, waiting. "Apology accepted?"

"It's a little late. That girl's long gone."

"What if we start over?" He held out his hand to her. "Hello, Miss Smalls, my name is Carlos Harris. I'm a reporter for *Basslines* magazine, and we're writing a story about you."

The girl wasn't long gone, apparently. The girl thrilled to hear him say his name.

*E*xcept for its horrific ending and flawed core, Phoenix's romance with Carlos Harris could have been from a movie, complete with its own soundtrack. *Scene: South Beach.*

She and Gloria had convinced Sarge to let them have their own hotel room for the annual urban music conference on South Beach, an achievement without par. She was pulling a 3.8 GPA, and she and the band had been practicing almost nightly in the garage (one of the songs they wrote during that period had been good enough to end up on *Trial by Fire* a few years later), so her parents thought she was mature enough.

Sarge had a room at a different hotel, but it was only two buildings away—so he decided to trust her. *Cue laugh-track.*

The conference was Disney World. It was the nation's premier urban music networking session (*"Oh, shit! That's Russell Simmons across the street!"*), and Phoenix and Gloria were so psyched to be there that they vowed to be good. Back then, Gloria wanted to be Phoenix's manager, so she took the business side seriously for half a minute. Instead of using the fake ID's Gloria had scored during a family vacation in New Orleans earlier that year, they limited their activities to the daytime programming on making it in the music world, with their minds on their money and their money on their minds. The first day, instead of trying to sneak out to the clubs for one of the nighttime shows, they came back to their room early and were satisfied to sift through the bags of demos they'd grabbed from artists clawing their way up, guessing who would make it and who wouldn't. Gloria didn't even bring any weed with her, which was miraculous for Gloria when she was sixteen. They were going to be angels. When Sarge called at nine to check on them, they were in their room. When he knocked on their door for a surprise visit at midnight, he woke them up. Angels.

Enter Carlos Harris.

Phoenix first noticed him at a morning panel on marketing and promotion; or, rather, she noticed him checking *her*. He was easily the finest man in the room—which, granted, wasn't saying much, since she and Gloria had decided that rappers weren't going to win any beauty contests unless the judges were blind. (The term they coined was *thugly*). But Carlos was *fine*. And Carlos was older, which made his attention flattering. She guessed he was about thirty, and she was right. She liked his roguish smile, the way he kept looking away when she caught him staring. Usually any guys checking them out were really after Gloria, but Carlos's eyes were on *her*. He was wearing a mustard-colored pullover and slacks, a press pass dangling around his neck. Later, when he surprised her and Gloria with an offer to buy them Cuban sandwiches for lunch, she learned that he was a music writer for the *Miami Sun-News*.

"I'm going to the Lauryn Hill concert later," he said. "You coming?"

They hadn't even heard there was going to *be* a Lauryn Hill concert.

It was on the down-low, in an intimate setting on Fifth Street. In a bar. Phoenix felt her angel's wings wilt.

In that instant, Gloria did something so wonderful that it almost brought tears to Phoenix's eyes: "I'm gonna crash in the room," Gloria said. "You go on, Phee. Have fun." And she reached into her purse and handed Phoenix a fake ID.

Gloria was going to cover for her. It opened up a universe of possibilities. First, Gloria would answer the phone in the room if Sarge called. Second, Gloria could do a damn convincing imitation of her voice that had fooled her friends more than once—and if Gloria had to, she could try it on Sarge. He *might* not spring another midnight surprise visit to their room, since he knew they were expecting one. It was the most daring plot they had ever hatched.

"Get laid," Gloria whispered with her good-bye hug.

No one checked Phoenix's ID while she was with Carlos over the next three days, stealing time with him when she dared. His press pass was a veil of invisibility, diplomatic immunity. All the bouncers knew Carlos. All the club owners knew Carlos. Phoenix felt like she was in *Goodfellas,* whisked in through the back doors to all the best tables. Lauryn Hill did a single set at the Stephen Talkhouse Bar at eight o'clock, alone on the stage with an acoustic guitar. She sang like an prophet. Midway through her set, the singer saw Carlos and nodded out at him, a silent, sisterly *whassup, Carlos.* Phoenix's jaw dropped. This brother was *hooked up.* That was when Carlos first held Phoenix's hand, and fever scorched her slippery palm. When he scooted his chair closer so that their shoulders were touching, she felt her body tremble. *Get laid.* Gloria's advice flurried in her head.

Carlos took her to a restaurant on Ocean Drive owned by Gloria Estefan, Lario's on the Beach, the best Cuban food she'd ever tasted. He let her sip from his tart *mojito* ("This was supposedly Ernest Hemingway's favorite drink," he said), all the while ordering her nothing but refills for her Coke. The restaurant manager spoke to him in a hurricane of Spanish, and he answered with his own hurricane, and Carlos's throaty laugh sounded like it was from a man who had seen the world. His rolled R's made her squirm in her seat. She stared at the strands of black hair growing above his halfway-buttoned shirt, wondering how he would taste.

His first kiss in his car was divine. She'd been kissed one or two times before—and she thought she'd been kissed *well* by Craig Roman in the back row of the movie theater at The Falls shopping mall—but Carlos's grown-man kiss was a revelation. He cupped the back of her head between his palms and kissed her gently at first, then he pulled her tongue into his mouth and sucked it with such practiced vigor that she couldn't imagine how lovemaking could feel any better. He sank his fingers into her hair, savoring its kinks, his fingertips rubbing small circles in her scalp. Each sensation was new, blotting her busy mind as her body took its place at her helm. When his hand brushed her breast outside of her blouse, Phoenix yelped.

Those precious days, she was his and he was hers. Whenever they ran into Sarge at the conference, Carlos disappeared into the background and she did not look at him. The secret made it all the more exciting. Phoenix, of course, was in love with Carlos right away.

Carlos must have kept a hundred CDs in his car, organized alphabetically in cases under his seat. He never started his car until a CD was loaded and ready to blast with the first turn of the key, as if music powered his engine. To help her learn, he dragged her away from South Beach to hear Tony Bennett at the ornate Gusman Theater in downtown Miami despite her protests that his music was too old ("Don't talk crazy. Good music is never old. Notice how he doesn't just sing it—he SELLS it."), and Phoenix finally understood why her mother had left her heart in San Francisco. Afterward, Carlos drove her to a restaurant called Centro Vasco in Little Havana, where Tony Bennett's black drummer, Clayton Cameron, took off his black jacket and slipped into a private jam session with older Cuban musicians in white *guayaberas,* shedding his perfect regimentation for something freer and completely perfect in its own way. He was one drummer in two worlds, at home in both.

Music was Carlos's aphrodisiac, and Phoenix was under its spell.

The last night of the conference, after treating her to dinner at a Haitian restaurant called Tap-Tap painted with bright murals that made her heart sing, Carlos took her to his apartment. It was neat and spare, a music shrine. The walls were ornamented with framed concert posters—Bob Marley, B. B. King, Mario Bauzá, Tito Puente—and two of his living room's walls were stacked to the ceiling with CDs, a collection of thousands. It was a tour through a wonderland.

Carlos played her a CD by an Egyptian orchestra leader named Hossam Ramzy, then he let her hear the same orchestra backing up Robert Plant and Jimmy Page on a mind-blowing version of "Friends." He played her African salsa she hadn't known existed by Pape Fall and Africando. He whispered the English translation to Rubén Blades's "Patria" in her ear, making her ache to love her homeland as much as Blades. He played Miles Davis's version of "My Funny Valentine," then Coltrane's "Someday My Prince Will Come," and by then she was light-headed with desire.

Phoenix wanted to marry Carlos Harris, move into his apartment, and dust his CDs all day to keep them clean. But Carlos was slow, so slow. Carlos seemed to forget she was in the room with him. He'd closed his eyes, enraptured by the music. Al Jarreau's "Teach Me Tonight" made Phoenix bold, so she kissed him, and he opened his eyes. She felt aware of her puny body, the curse of adolescence. She hoped he saw the woman ripe inside her.

"How old are you?" Carlos asked.

The question hurt, a violation of their silence. "You know how old I am."

"I know you're a student at New World. That's not the same thing."

She didn't answer, kissing him again. Kissing seemed like a good way to avert an argument. She wanted to shut him up so he would pull off her clothes. She couldn't imagine how she would find her dignity again if he pulled away from her.

But he didn't kiss back, this time. "Phee?" Carlos said, quiet. His index finger traced her hipbone when he slid his hand there, warm fingers tickling the fringes of her hair hidden just inside her jeans. Her stomach fluttered against his wrist. "For real, no playing. How old are you?"

She blinked, surprised at how close she was to tears. "Sixteen."

Carlos answered with a long, slow sigh. His breath swallowed her. But his hand didn't move. He was still deciding. "Have you . . . been intimate with anyone before?"

Damn. She'd been afraid he was going to ask that.

"How intimate?" she said. Craig Roman had squeezed her right breast once.

"You know what I mean."

"What's that got to do with it?" She tried to sound annoyed, but she only sounded miserable. Like a child. His point exactly.

"A lot, *linda*. A lot."

Linda was the most beautiful word she had ever heard. *Leeeeeenda*.

"Is it so bad if my first time's with you?" she said.

He massaged her scalp the way he had inside his car. Fingers had never felt so good on her scalp, even her mother's. "If I were a god at the top of Mount Olympus, no one could make me an offering more precious than that one," he said. He kissed her hair, then her forehead, then her lips, but only lightly. "But I haven't earned it. I'm not the one, Phee. Find someone to learn with you. I can wait."

Their beginning had been a splendid one. But when he drove her back to her hotel that night, the ending was waiting.

Dancers peeked into the lounge and tiptoed to the vending machines, keeping their eyes away, trying not to disturb them. Carlos's tape recorder was running, but after a half hour of reminiscing, the official interview had yet to begin.

Finally, Phoenix couldn't avoid the question. "Have you heard *Rising*?"

He nodded. She couldn't read his expression.

"Well?" she said.

Carlos cocked his head left, then right, weighing the matter. "Where's the band?"

"All over the place. La'Keitha was touring with Lenny Kravitz, last I heard. Jabari's doing jazz in New York, I think. Andres went to Berklee. You didn't answer my question."

This time, Carlos did smile. "I like a good steak, and I like a good cheeseburger. *Rising* is a good cheeseburger. Your last CD, *Trial by Fire*, was a steak."

Phoenix wanted to both slap him and hug him, just like old times.

"I like 'Party Patrol,' " he went on "Great violin intro, solid beat. And you did a nice cover of 'Love the One You're With,' very soulful, great gospel vibe. Are you still composing music? We're on the record now." He nudged his cassette player closer to her thigh on the sofa.

"I'm learning and growing with D'Real," she said. "He's great to work with."

"Will you go back to your emphasis on musicianship in the future?"

Phoenix felt irritated. Was he toying with her? "I'm grooving with the Three Strikes family right now. We know *Rising*'s gonna blow up, then we'll see what the future holds."

"Tell me about your rough childhood, Phoenix."

Now, Phoenix was sure of it: He was toying with her. "You have my bio," she said.

He reached into his back pocket and pulled out a folded press release with the TSR logo. "Yeah, I sure do . . ." he said, reading. "Grew up in the Miami projects . . . Father in prison until you were eighteen . . . And you're only twenty-one years old? God help me if *that's* not another lie. I'm afraid to do the math."

Phoenix felt her face coloring. She clicked off his recorder. "What's your game, Carlos?"

"I don't know, Phee," he said, winking. "What's yours?"

Phoenix sat closer to Carlos, lowering her voice as a bare-chested male dancer with his dance bag over his shoulder crept into the room and headed for the vending machines. "Just remember, this is show business," she said.

"Yes, but even in show business you can't forget where the lies end and the truth begins."

"Did you come out here to fuck with me? If so, I have a busy schedule."

His face softened. "No. I came to tell you I'm happy for you, and to make sure you're OK. That's the truth. No harm intended. I see you're defensive, so I'll stop."

Still, Phoenix saw too much smugness in Carlos's eyes, and her temper flared. "My sister and brothers grew up in the projects, and my dad *was* in prison when they were kids. It's not like I can't relate, OK? It's hype, and lots of performers do it. So don't sit over there judging me. You're in no damn position to judge anybody."

Carlos sighed, not speaking for a while. When he did, his voice was careful, measured. "I'm not judging. I just wondered why somebody as talented as you is afraid to say she grew up in the suburbs with an involved dad and went to a high school for the arts. Sorry if I hit a nerve."

Phoenix realized Carlos must be close to forty now, at least thirty-eight, and their age gap did not seem nearly as alluring as it had when she was sixteen. The potency of his apology had worn off, and she was mad at him again. She wished Sarge had broken his jaw that day.

There was a whir from the vending machine as the dancer's water bottle fell. She'd forgotten anyone else was in the room. The dancer sidled back outside with a story to tell.

"Like I said, I want to make sure you're OK," Carlos said.

"What are you now, my shrink?"

"Someone who'd like to be a friend, that's all."

"You're not a friend. I don't even know you."

"I said I'd *like* to be."

"Fine. I'll tell you about my life, but not the publicity bullshit. This isn't for print."

Carlos nodded, his hand over his heart. "If that's what you want. Off-the-record."

Phoenix began counting off on her fingers. "I just got dumped by my boyfriend. A tabloid is talking shit about me. I had a huge fight with my cousin Gloria, my best friend."

"I remember Gloria," he said.

Phoenix counted her fourth finger, her pinky. "There was a *stalker* in my hotel room in St. Louis, and we had to call the cops. I'm hearing voices of people who aren't there, and I think I saw a *ghost*. My world is messed up right now, so excuse me if I don't have a sense of humor when you try to get up in my business."

Carlos nodded, not blinking. His concerned expression looked almost paternal, which made her wonder why she'd never noticed how much Carlos reminded her of her father. Sarge had probably pulled that same music mack on Mom, whipping out his Al Green, Otis Redding and Charlie Parker while he tried to get into her pants.

"Tell me about this ghost," Carlos said.

"Why are you humoring me?"

"I'm not. I'll believe you."

Phoenix raised her eyebrow, chuckling. "Somehow, I don't think so."

"My grandmother's ghost visited me the day she died. I was ten," he said, and he wasn't joking. She could see it in his face, in his unblinking eyes. "She'd had a stroke, and we flew to San Juan so my mother could be at her bedside. I stayed with my aunt and uncle in Toa Alta while my parents were at the hospital. I fell asleep on the sofa, and when I woke up, *Abuela* was standing over me in her favorite Easter dress, a pink one. The smell of her perfume was what woke me up. I said, 'I thought you were sick at the hospital,' and she smiled and patted me on the head. She was swaying her hips to meréngue coming through the open windows, from a neighbor's house. She was *dancing*, you see. In Puerto Rico, you don't stop dancing when you're old. Then, she walked into the kitchen. When I tried to follow her, there was no one there. That was when the phone rang. It was my mother calling to tell us *Abuela* had died."

"Are you sure it wasn't a dream?" Phoenix said, her voice hushed. She was chilled, not charmed, by the image of the dead old woman's shaking hips.

"Even my aunt said she could smell *Abuela*'s perfume."

"You felt her *touch* you?" Phoenix broke out in gooseflesh.

Carlos nodded. "I was happy she touched me. She was *Abuela*. Tell me your story."

Phoenix glanced at her watch. Their hour was almost up. A reporter from New York would be calling her soon.

"I was at the Scott Joplin House . . ." she began, and she told Carlos about the black man standing at the window, and Milton's ghost story. Then, she told him about the man in her closet at the hotel, and the voice she thought she'd heard in her ear yesterday. As an afterthought, she told him about the strange piano incident when she was ten. She'd never woven the stories together as one, but they suddenly seemed as linked as her past with Carlos.

"Do you want to hear what I think?" Carlos said.

She very much did *not* want to hear what he thought, in fact.

He didn't wait for her answer. "That spirit feels a connection to you."

"Bullshit," she said, but her heartbeat accelerated.

"And the man in your room vanished into thin air? What about the voice in your ear?"

"The hotel thing, I don't know. But the voice was a dream."

"I don't think so," Carlos said. "I think you know better, too."

Phoenix's palms felt clammy, so she wiped them on her jeans. "Ghosts don't follow you."

"How do you know?"

"Stop trying to scare me."

"I'm not. I'm just wondering if Scott Joplin knew someone named Freddy."

Phoenix didn't have a clue. At that instant, the door opened again, but it wasn't a thirsty dancer this time. It was Sarge. Phoenix might as well have not been in the room, the way Sarge's eyes flamed past her to Carlos, torches.

"What the hell are you doing here?" Sarge said. His voice was quiet, not the way he shouted when he was angry for show. Sarge was seething to his core. So much for wondering if Sarge would recognize Carlos after eight years.

"We're just finishing an interview," Phoenix said.

"I asked *him*."

Carlos curled his lips, an expression that wasn't anything like a smile. He stared at the floor, sighing, then he reached into his shirt pocket for a business card he laid beside Phoenix's thigh. "I was on my way out, Mr. Smalls," he said. "Congratulations on your daughter's success. I've been following her career."

Sarge didn't answer. His eyes stared, combusting coals.

"Is he going to jump me on the way out?" Carlos muttered to her under his breath as he stood, gathering his things.

"Probably not," Phoenix said softly. "I can't say for sure, though."

Carlos shrugged, resigned. He tapped his business card. *"Llamame,"* he told her.

"I understand Spanish, motherfucker," Sarge said. "Move your punk ass on."

It was amazing, Phoenix thought, how history never quite died.

CHAPTER SEVEN

*P*hoenix didn't ask Sarge to come into her apartment to give it an inspection before he drove off for the night, but her fidgeting must have told him she didn't want to be dropped off at the curb. It was long after dark, almost ten o'clock, and after Carlos's ghost story Phoenix wasn't ready to be alone. Sarge peeked into her bathroom while Phoenix waited in the kitchen, anxious. *If I tell him he's looking for a ghost instead of a stalker, he'll think I've been partying with Whitney and Bobby.*

It didn't take Sarge long to finish his inspection. There wasn't much to the eight-hundred-square-foot apartment except Nia's bedroom, Phoenix's futon in the living room, and her silver Korg Trinity Pro keyboard hooked up to her Mac in the corner she'd turned into her home studio. Gloria bugged her about getting a nicer apartment, or a house, but Phoenix only cared about her image as far as her front door. Where she lived was nobody's business. Most new artists wanted to bling out right away, maxing out credit cards and leasing whatever they couldn't afford to buy, but bankruptcy wasn't in Phoenix's plan. Besides, why spend the money on a fancy crib when she was hardly home?

And there weren't any walk-in closets here. *Poverty has its perks,* she thought.

"Peanut, if you don't feel safe, you can come with me," Sarge said, searching for food in her refrigerator. The shelves were bare except for an old take-out container, a carton of milk that had been there a month, and the box of baking soda. "Shoot. Don't ya'll eat?" He opened the take-out carton and frowned, throwing it into the kitchen garbage can. "Ya'll are nasty."

"Where are you crashing, Dad?"

"I'm staying with my friend in Baldwin Hills. Her daughter's at Spelman, and she'd be happy to lend you the room."

Her father almost never talked about his girlfriend, and Phoenix liked it better that way. She would never understand how Sarge could have a girlfriend and be married, and she had to let it go. She didn't even want to know the woman's name. "Uh . . . no thanks."

"You know what's what. Don't make that face."

"Whatever," Phoenix sighed. "At least I know why Mom won't come out here."

He raised a finger. "Don't start." He'd stolen her favorite phrase.

"You two should just get a divorce, dang."

"Are you staying here or not?"

Phoenix's answering machine was blinking. Three messages, the red display said. If she heard a strange man's voice asking for Freddy, she might have to stay with Sarge tonight, or else at a hotel. "Hold on," she said, and pushed the button.

"Hiya, Buttercup, sorry I missed you. I'll be stuck at the county commission meeting tonight, and you know how those crooks like to kibbitz, so feel free to call late—" Mom. *"Heyyyy, girrrrrl . . . I couldn't find nobody to keep Trey, but I'm still comin' out Friday. Hope you don't mind a lil' shorty hangin' with us. Now I KNOW you're gonna take me to some of those parties with G-Ronn, right?—"* Serena.

The third message was a hang-up. Probably Gloria, she thought. Maybe Gloria.

"I'll be fine," Phoenix said, not sure she believed it. She watched her blinds, expecting them to flutter the way the bathrobe in her hotel closet had. A moving shadow in the living room caught her eye, but it was only Sarge closing the refrigerator door, dimming the light from the kitchen in a floating shaft across the wall.

"You don't seem fine. You're real jumpy."

"I just need sleep," Phoenix said. "There's a whole lot going on."

"Not with that SOB who disrespected our family, I hope."

"Daddy . . . I told you he's a writer. That was just an interview."

Now it was Sarge's turn to raise his hands. "I'm trying to keep my pressure down, so let's not get into it." He gave her a tight hug. "Love you, sweetheart."

"Love you, too, Daddy. Thanks for putting up with my silliness."

"Nothing silly about it. These niggers are so paranoid, I feel like I'm back running with the Panthers. Music sure has changed, Phee." His shoulders drooped as he exhaled, and suddenly Sarge looked much closer to his age. Her father was almost old enough for social security, she realized, an impossible thought. "I'll pick you up at eight for call-backs at the dance studio. Ronn said he might drop in. Tell your mom and Reenie I say hey."

Sarge's absence loomed in her empty apartment. How could she be surrounded by throngs of people all day and still feel quarantined? It was after 1:00 A.M. on the East Coast, way too late to call her mother no matter how long the commission meeting had gone, and she didn't want to wake up her twelve-year-old nephew at Serena's house. She also couldn't handle trying to fumble through apologies with Gloria. She'd talk to Gloria tomorrow, she promised herself the second night in a row. Tomorrow.

Tonight, she decided, the only companion she needed was music.

Phoenix heated up a package of frozen microwave spaghetti and sat at her Korg, powering it up. She hadn't touched the keyboard in ages, but Carlos had inspired her with his nosy-ass questions. It *had* been too long since she'd done any composing, or even playing for fun. Back when she was with the band, she used to practice an hour a day on her technique and programming, not counting rehearsals. She used to write two songs a week. She used to warm up with Mozart and Ellington. She used to. Now, her muse had curled up and gone to sleep. Did she need the band that much? Or had she run out of things to say?

Songs always came to Phoenix in chords first, the way she imagined Prince birthed his first droplets of "Purple Rain." Melody came next, and lyrics last, her weakness. Her hands struck a sultry C-major seventh chord, like a mellow Jobin bossa nova. She flowed with that awhile to see where that would take her, improvising an aching melody while her left hand lazed up and down from one major seventh chord to the next. She played a few stanzas in a bouncy South African township style, morphed that into reggae, then went back to the Jobin. In her mind, she saw Carlos's smile and the gorgeous mustard-colored shirt he'd been wearing the first time she saw him, so beautiful against his brown-red skin. Her toes twitched. *Damn.*

"Do not, do not, do *not,* let that man get under your skin again," she said to herself, saying it aloud to make sure she heard. "He's bad news, Phee. Always has been, always will be. Even if his ghost story was true, he just told you to try to get past your defenses. He's smooth even when he isn't trying. Move on."

That sounded similar to her mantra when she was sixteen, in the awful eight months it took her to stop mourning the loss of him. If Carlos could be that careless with a schoolgirl's heart, there was no telling what else he was capable of. *Never* again.

The music sounded good, like there might be something lurking in her subconscious, so Phoenix clicked on her Finale music notation program. *Who knows? Maybe some of this will be on my next CD,* she thought. An empty page appeared on the twenty-one-inch computer monitor. When she played the keys now, the screen captured the notes on rows of staffs as if she'd committed them with her own pen, a record she could save as a file, burn to a CD, or print if she chose. She might make corrections with her mouse later, but she was glad she didn't have to write the shit out by hand like they did back in the day. That must have taken forever.

A loud knock resounded. Phoenix stopped playing and listened in the silence, just to make sure it wasn't a neighbor's door. The knock at her door came again, three clear bangs.

Sarge never rested, she thought. There was always one last thing to tell her to do.

"Daddy, you better start taking care of yourself," she said, opening her door.

But no one was there. Not Sarge, not anybody. She peeked out of her doorway to look left, then right along the ground floor, which faced the open courtyard and pool area, but no one was in sight. Her neighbors' doors on either side of her were closed. No one was sitting in any of the poolside chairs. The pool's water reflected against the apartment wall, shimmering in the light from the solar lamp that made everything the color of fire.

Phoenix's breath felt thin in her throat. *Some kid playing a prank. Very effing funny.*

She closed her door, locking both the push-pin and dead bolt. She wrapped her arms around herself inside her doorway, not sure if she was nervous or cold. Maybe both. Before Phoenix could check the thermostat, she heard knocking again—this time, the thumps were against the wall, and they were coming from *inside.* They sprang from two or three places at once. From two inches in front of her face. The sound made her jump.

Phoenix noticed a dim light in the kitchen, which was otherwise dark. Breathing faster, she took a step closer, rounding the corner to see better.

The refrigerator door was now wide-open against the kitchen cabinets, its near-empty shelves exposed, as if it the door had been propped. The take-out carton Sarge had thrown away a few minutes ago sat on the kitchen counter next to her answering machine, in plain view. Phoenix felt her face crack, brittle ice. Her lower jaw lost its strength, and her mouth sagged open.

Something was here in her apartment. Something *was* here.

"Please leave me alone," she whispered, tears stinging her eyes. She had never been more terrified, not even when that piano began barreling down those stairs. A falling piano obeyed the laws of gravity, and she understood gravity. This was something else. This was a rupture to her roots. Fear erased the memory of how to control her shaky limbs.

"*Please?* Will you please leave me alone?"

Her answer came when the refrigerator door slammed itself shut.

By the time Carlos arrived, Phoenix had been sitting at the edge of a plastic lounging chair next to the swimming pool for nearly forty minutes, waiting. She wasn't wearing a jacket—she'd run out of her apartment with nothing but the cell phone in her pocket—so her teeth were clacking softly in the sixty-five-degree nighttime air. She had wet herself a little. She could feel a slight dampness between her legs, not enough to soak through her jeans, but enough to notice. She didn't remember when that had happened, but it had.

Carlos knelt in front of her, taking her hands. When he felt how cold they were, he rubbed her skin to warm her. His features were more severe in the lamplight, making him look like the stranger he was. But she hadn't known who else to call. Carlos was the only person she knew who believed in ghosts, and she didn't want to waste time trying to convince anyone else she wasn't crazy. She'd slipped Carlos's card into her back pocket that morning, and she was so relieved he'd written his home telephone number on back, she'd almost cried with joy.

"Are you OK?" Carlos said.

Phoenix shook her head. "My heart was beating so fast, I thought it would pop."

"Whatever's going on, it probably doesn't want to hurt you. That's a movie stereotype."

"Man, *fuck* that. I just want it to leave me alone."

She glanced toward her closed apartment door, which she'd been watching steadily, hoping it wouldn't come flying open. So far, it hadn't.

"I Googled Scott Joplin after we talked today," Carlos said quietly. "Do you want to hear what I found out?"

"What?" Phoenix said. "Did he know somebody named Freddy?"

"Yes. His wife."

Phoenix's heart jumped, but she shook her head. "That's not true. That guy at the museum told me his wife had another name. Belle, I think."

"Freddie was his second wife, after Belle," Carlos said.

That news was no comfort at all, only a confirmation that her life was as bizarre as she'd feared. Phoenix was mortified to feel tears spill from her eyes. She'd been a baby the last time she knew Carlos, and she was acting like one now.

Carlos clucked, wiping her tears gently with the soft pad of his thumb. "Don't do that, *linda*. I didn't tell you to scare you."

"Well, what does that mean? Why is it following me? I don't get it."

"Neither do I," Carlos said. "But I do think our instincts were right. We know *whose* spirit it probably is, based on your sighting at the Joplin House. And the voice you heard."

"How do I get rid of it? Why does it go wherever I go?"

"I don't know. I'm not a psychic. I think you should call one."

"Ghostbusters," Phoenix said ruefully, midway between a chuckle and a whimper.

"Something like that."

"I don't even believe in this shit," Phoenix said. "Next thing, I'll be seeing UFOs. This is crazy. Maybe I'm just cracking up with all this pressure." Gloria had always thought she was pushing herself too hard, and this was her first evidence that her cousin might be right.

"But you knew about Freddie, no?"

Phoenix only sighed, allowing her head to dangle forward.

After a pause, Carlos squeezed her hand and tugged. "Come on," he said.

"Where?"

"Back inside your apartment."

Phoenix yanked her hand away. "For *what*?"

He shrugged. "I'm not an expert, but I've heard people say that sometimes you only have to ask spirits very politely, and they'll leave you alone."

"I already tried that, and I just pissed it off."

He took her hand again. "We'll see. *Vamos.* I won't let anything happen to you."

"D-Don't we need some holy water or a cross or something?"

"You've been watching too many movies, Phee. It's not a vampire. It's a ghost."

His logic calmed her. For some reason, Carlos made her feel safe.

"OK, we can go in," she said. "But just for a minute. I'm not kidding."

Once inside, Phoenix couldn't identify anything inside her apartment that had changed. The refrigerator door was still closed, and the take-out container hadn't moved from the counter. The light from her overhead fan was still on the way she'd left it. Her half-eaten spaghetti still sat on the computer table, her computer screensaver showed a galaxy of passing stars on the monitor, and her electronic keyboard display panel glowed in spring green, waiting.

Two steps inside, however, the temperature dropped. Phoenix's bare arms pricked as if they were immersed in ice. "Carlos . . ." she said, ready to flee again. Her hand clamped his.

"I feel it." He looked up for a vent, but there was none above them. He stepped forward, then back, holding one hand up as if testing the direction of the wind. "I think it's right here where we're standing. A cold spot. That's common with ghosts. Amazing." He sounded awed.

He was right. When she walked farther into the living room, closer to her futon, the temperature rose to normal again. She felt her limbs relaxing, although her heartbeat didn't slow. She didn't know what the cold spot meant, or what its function was, but she felt better now that she wasn't standing in the heart of it. "I thought you weren't an expert."

"Since my experience with *Abuela,* I've been curious. I've seen a couple documentaries," he said, and Phoenix couldn't believe how casual his voice was. How could he be so composed when there might be a dead person walking around the room with them?

"Let's do this and go," Phoenix said.

"Shhhhh," Carlos said, listening. He stared around as if he were walking inside a painting at the Louvre, fascinated by all of its details.

"You can stay here all night and get to know each other if you want, but not me. I thought we came in here to send it away."

"All right, all right," he said. He sounded impatient. He gestured toward the futon, and she followed him there. Together, they sat. "Talk to him. But politely."

"Will you do it?" she whispered, curling close to him. Something about Carlos made her feel like a teenager again. "I don't think he likes me."

"Of course he does," Carlos said quietly. After some thought, he looked toward the ceiling, as if addressing the sky. "Mr. Joplin? I know you don't want to hurt this young lady, but your presence frightens her. We wish you peace, but we're asking you to please return to wherever you've come from. You are not welcome in Phoenix's presence."

Well, damn, that *was harsh.* Phoenix braced for the spirit's angry reprisal.

Nothing. She expected her keyboard to erupt into a cacophony the way pianos did in haunted houses, but the apartment was as silent as a crypt. She could barely hear the refrigerator's hum. "Maybe it worked," she whispered.

"I don't know. Like I said, you should find a psychic. The only problem is finding one who's legitimate. I know someone, though."

"What do I do right *now?*"

He squeezed her hand, winking at her over his shoulder. "Now, you have to decide where you're sleeping tonight."

Since Phoenix hadn't seen any ghostly manifestations in nearly an hour, she felt her life slowly settling back to normalcy. "It's always about the mack with you, isn't it?" she said.

"Not at all. I only meant that—"

Carlos didn't finish his sentence, because her computer screen suddenly flared white as the screensaver vanished. Her notation program reappeared on the screen, and she could see the blur of staffs and notes from across the room. Her screensaver never went off by itself. It always stayed in place unless someone touched her mouse or the computer keys.

"Is your computer supposed to do that?" Carlos said, hushed.

Phoenix shook her head, pulling Carlos's hand up to her chin. As she gazed at her computer, her lips went dry. She'd been capturing her composition when she was interrupted by the knock on her door, but even from here, the appearance was wrong.

"Holy effing shit," Phoenix whispered. She rose to her feet.

"What?" Carlos said.

Phoenix didn't answer, dropping Carlos's hand. She walked to her Mac so she could see the screen. All of her joints seemed to be slipping

out of place, each step wobbly. But it wasn't *fear* Phoenix felt, not anymore. Her entire body glowed.

"Th-this isn't mine," she said. "This isn't what I was playing."

Seeing the screen, she could hear the heartbreaking waltzing
melody in her imagination.

"It's really him," she said, realizing she hadn't truly believed it before. "It's Scott Joplin."

The piece on her computer screen was "Bethena."

Part Two

But One ordained when we were born,

In spite of love's insistence,

That night might only view the Morn

Adoring at a distance.

Paul Laurence Dunbar

CHAPTER EIGHT

Little Rock, Arkansas
February 1904

Here's Freddie now. Scott, this here's my youngest girl. Freddie, meet Scott Joplin."

Scott rose from his seat with a start. Until this instant, he'd hoped to escape the Alexanders' dinner invitation, but now he was elated by his luck. He had not expected to meet a creature like Freddie Alexander today.

When his host had mentioned a child named Freddie who was out finishing errands, Scott assumed it was his *son* who'd taken his motorcar to town, not a daughter. And what a girl she was! Freddie wore a simple outing coat, and her raven hair was windswept from her ride, her winter hat askew, but she carried herself with a bearing Scott had seen in few women besides Eleanor Stark, like an energetic royal. Her endless smile made her ravishing. Freddie's grandfather had been sired by his mother's slave master, or so the family gossip went, and Freddie's lineage was apparent in her pale buttermilk complexion. Still, her soft face reminded him of how Belle might have looked when she was a young girl, before her youth had been leeched by losses. How old was this girl? Twenty? Perhaps not even that old.

"You're the Scott Joplin of 'Maple Leaf Rag' fame?" Freddie said. Her eyes, the color of maple syrup, shimmered from her face.

Scott suppressed a grin for fear he would seem immodest, but he had never been more delighted to be known. "Fame or infamy, miss. Depending on the circles, I think."

"There can't be anyone alive who doesn't enjoy the 'Maple Leaf Rag,' " Freddie said, and Scott wondered if her words were making him blush. "Even Papa doesn't mind it. Do you?"

"Of course I don't," her father said. "Stop trying to vex me."

"We argue, you see, Mr. Joplin. He won't keep step with the times. Yours is the only ragtime he'll let me play. Or *try* to play, I should say. I wish I had the facility, but I have to accept the fact that I have a better mind for books than music."

Scott had known few colored women to speak in such a way. Her *voice* was music.

"Go tell your mama we're ready to eat," her father said, waving Freddie away. "I won't bother to ask you to go help her in the kitchen. We're all better off if you don't. Go on, now."

"Yes, sir," Freddie said, and Scott smiled at the ironic gleam in her eye. He was mesmerized by Freddie's motion, a glide that might harbor a gallop underneath. Then, he caught himself staring and turned back to his host, who was cutting himself a cigar in his parlor chair.

Scott might have met the Alexanders once or twice when he was a boy, or so his father kept saying, but he had no memory of it. If not for his father's insistence, Scott wouldn't have borrowed his friend Charles's market wagon to drive fifteen miles across Little Rock to the home of Lincoln Alexander, coating his clothes with dust on the dry winter roads. Scott lacked the gift for spontaneous gaiety with people he did not know; but his father hadn't been well since Will's death, understandably, and Scott's promise that he would call on Lincoln Alexander and his family had brought a rare spark to his father's eyes. Giles Joplin had known Mr. Alexander's father since before the War. They had both been plantation musicians, vowing to look after each other's families when they went their separate ways. Now that the elder Alexander had died, Scott's father was anxious to fulfill the vow but hadn't felt up to the ride.

The day's conversation had nearly exhausted Scott. Lincoln Alexander had discussed to death the demands of his city clerking job and then moved on to politics, a worse topic. Nodding in polite agreement was a taxing exercise. The daughter made the day's loss worthwhile.

"Smoke?" Alexander said, offering him a cigar.

Scott demurred with a raised palm. Tobacco coarsened his singing voice. "You trust your daughter to drive?" he said. Scott had yet to drive a motorcar himself.

"She handles that thing better than I do. But she thinks she's a man, and I'm 'fraid we've spoilt her for any normal life now. All her schooling's brought me is headaches," Alexander said. "She runs off any boy who walks through the door. I've tried to put her in the schooled circles to meet young people she'd shine to, but Pa used to say the monied coloreds in Little Rock are worse than white folks. It ain't good enough I've got a little money put away and worship in the same church if I've got the wrong name and didn't go to Yale. My white neighbors are more cordial." He scooted forward, eager. "*You* got any sons, Scott?"

Scott shook his head.

Disappointed, Alexander scooted back. "Odetta and me just had Freddie and her sister Lovie. Thank goodness the older one is more sensible. She's been married a year already. You just had the girls, too?"

Scott remembered his baby, the struggling cherub with his mother's face he and Belle had prayed over night after night. Then, he made himself forget. "I don't have any children."

"You're a lucky man and don't even know it. The *mouth* on this one! Talks gracious to goodness faster than Henry Ford can drive. Whoever takes her won't get a word in edgewise. You think I'm telling tales, just wait 'til we're at the table."

I can't imagine where she picked up that *trait,* Scott thought. He'd felt trapped all afternoon by the man's long-winded attempts to remember when last they might have met, or which people their fathers had known in common, but now the wait was interminable. Scott's stomach growled, but he wasn't impatient because of hunger. Scott's eye roamed again and again to the dining room, in hopes that Mrs. Alexander would call them to the table. Occasionally, he saw Freddie through the doorway with a steaming serving dish or an empty plate, and her eyes flitted to him, too. Each time, Scott looked away from her, his face warm.

He thought he was daydreaming when he heard music from the dining room. A tenor was singing in Italian, with an orchestra behind him. He knew the opera: *Il Trovatore.*

"Freddie, you turn that off! Mr. Joplin's here for dinner, not all your racket!" Alexander shouted. He sighed, gazing apologetically at Scott. "She's wild for that Talking Machine. She sits at dinner waving her fork to those marches and what-not."

"No, no, it's all right," Scott said, delighted by the image of Freddie conducting Sousa with her fork. "I don't mind. Dinner digests better with music."

"*See*, Papa?" Freddie called back.

"Nobody's talking to you. Mind what's your business, girl. I won't tell you again."

The call to the table came at last. The dining room was as graceful as the rest of the well-kept house, with a table and china cabinet that looked nearly new. The gramophone in the corner, a wooden box with an unsightly brass horn, marred the room's elegant effect as much as parking the motorcar there, but the music was pleasant enough. As the music played, Mrs. Alexander piled Scott's plate with stewed chicken, okra, corn on the cob and corn bread. It *was* good to be back down South. Mrs. Alexander led a short grace, her soft voice competing with a tenor's.

Freddie's chair sat directly across from Scott's. He was so nervous that his stares would be obvious to her parents, Scott kept his eyes on his plate, barely looking up when he answered Mrs. Alexander's questions about his work. Was composing difficult? *Sometimes, yes.* How did he find his ideas? *The people and events in my life.* Was he bothered by the controversy about ragtime? *Not all ragtime is created equal.* Mrs. Alexander was her daughter's twin, but without her refinement of speech. It was clear to Scott that the Alexanders had sacrificed to educate Freddie beyond their own opportunities, as most Negro families did. He longed to know where Freddie had studied, but dared not appear too interested in her. He guessed she had attended either Arkansas Baptist or Philander Smith, the two Negro colleges in Little Rock.

Finally, her father's promise came to pass, and Freddie spoke. "Have you recorded a disc for the gramophone yet, Mr. Joplin?"

"No," he said with an amused smile, finally free to glance up at her. She seemed more lovely than he remembered, and he quickly looked away so his thoughts wouldn't be plain. "As long as we have sheet music and music halls, I'm content."

"But not everyone can play your music or go to a concert. Enrico Caruso from Europe recorded his voice for Victor, and to think I'd never have heard him! With a gramophone, everyone can have you in their homes. And won't that make you more profits?"

Mrs. Alexander sucked her teeth, and her husband glared at their daughter. Scott couldn't help smiling more widely at the girl's boldness, and her naïveté. "I don't think Mr. Joplin wants to discuss his profits with you, or needs your business advice," her father said. "Hush."

"Edison's cylinder records tear, and these new discs wear out or break," Scott explained. "Piano rolls sound like circus music, the way the tempo's sped up. It's all fine for novelty, but I can do without the help of machines. They're no substitute for sheet music."

"That's what blacksmiths said about motorcars," Freddie said.

Freddie's quick tongue was a joy, even if she was misguided. "Indeed. Some still do," Scott said, smiling. "I'm not ready to send all the horses to the glue factory yet."

"That's what I told her, too," her father said.

Freddie's lips curled. "Which styles of music do you enjoy, Mr. Joplin? I like Sousa very much, and the latest waltzes. Papa thinks dancing is sinful, but . . ." Her father sighed heavily, stirring his food with such vigor that his fork clanked his plate. She went on: ". . . but I do love to listen to the waltzes. I think you're probably a very good dancer. Are you?"

Of all the dance programs Scott had staged and performed, none could compare to taking Freddie Alexander into his arms for a solitary waltz, he thought. "I rarely have the chance."

"Do you enjoy opera?" Freddie said. "My very favorite, I think, is *Carmen.* I have the new recording by Madame Calvé, and it's magnificent. Would you like to hear it?"

"I've written an opera," Scott blurted, a surprise. He'd had no thought of saying it.

"*Really?*" Freddie said, her voice rising high enough to rival the soprano on the gramophone. She grasped the edge of the table with both knuckles tight. "You see, Papa? He doesn't write only ragtime. He writes opera!"

"Yes, I heard you, and I'm sure the neighbors did, too. I said *hush,* girl."

"If she's a botherment, she can eat in the kitchen," Mrs. Alexander told Scott, flustered.

"No, not at all. In fact, Miss Alexander . . . once dinner's done, if it's all right with your parents, I'd be happy to play some of my opera for you. If you think you would enjoy it."

Freddie Alexander's eyes were wide O's. The lovely girl was speechless.

The Alexanders listened politely to Scott's playing for the first ten minutes, but then Mrs. Alexander excused herself to tidy the kitchen and Mr. Alexander said he had to feed and bed his horses. It was dark by then, and Scott dreaded the ride back to his friend Charles's house on darkened roads—Little Rock felt so backward compared to St. Louis, without enough evening lighting—but he could not pull himself from Freddie Alexander's company. He played her *A Guest of Honor* almost from beginning to end, singing some of the numbers softly, and he was surprised at how much he remembered: *Through work and faith there is no goal / Our hardy hearts can't sway. / For all my days I shan't forget / This White House feast today.*

The lyrics sounded flimsier than Scott remembered. John Stark might have been right when he said his lyrics needed work, he thought, chagrined.

But Freddie was captivated.

"A ragtime opera! How delightful. And you sing so nicely," Freddie said, when he'd finished. She sat beside him on the piano bench like one of his students and tinkled the keys, sounding out the melody of "Patriotic Patrol" with two fingers. She had a good ear, especially given that she'd only heard it once. "It was never published?"

"I had a thief in my company. He stole our proceeds, and I soon lost it."

"You should write it all again! Especially this song."

"I will . . . one day," he said, although the idea wearied him. The opera had been such a labor, and by now it was inextricable from its awful web of memories. "Old ground is tiresome. Maybe I'll write a new one."

"You see? If you had a gramophone recording . . ."

"Don't expect to find many operas by Negroes in your catalog."

"Not *yet*, but surely soon. We can't be kept chained back forever."

Kept chained back. Scott almost chuckled at her language. Perhaps she had been reading W. E. B. DuBois and his ilk. Scott had found that Negroes with very fair skin either distanced themselves from other Negroes entirely or were quicker to outrage, as if to compensate for their diluted blood. Anyone unfamiliar with the myriad shades of Negroes easily might mistake Freddie for white. Other women in her position might consider passing, or claim to be Mexican, as was common among octoroons. That would bring her an easier life!

Freddie laughed suddenly. "Papa will have a fit there's been so much ragtime in the house. You should hear him fret! A group at our church wants to ban it, and Papa's so eager to earn their respect, he shouts louder than the rest. But what can he say to Scott Joplin?"

Scott longed for any topic other than himself. He looked at Freddie beside him, and he saw her with fresh eyes. This young lady was a marvel, not merely a beauty. She played piano and knew opera, yet didn't disdain ragtime? He felt robbed that he had lived so many days, weeks and years without meeting her, nor even knowing of her existence.

Scott searched the room for clues about her and noticed the tightly packed bookshelves against the wall on the other side of the room, home to dozens of books with gold-gilded spines.

"Are those books yours, Miss Alexander?" he said.

"How did you guess? Oh, I told you how much I love books! I've read most of them more than once. I only wish I belonged to a proper book club so I could discuss the stories. Do you like reading, Mr. Joplin?"

"I haven't read as much as I should," he said. "If you like, Miss Alexander, you can suggest a book to me, and I'll read it to discuss with you on some future date."

Boldness! Scott regretted the words as soon as he spoke, but Freddie did not recoil from him. Instead, her face came aglow.

"That means you would have to come back to see us!" she said, leaping to her feet to hurry across the room. At the bookcase, Freddie pulled books out one by one, flipping through the pages, then changing her mind and pulling out the next. "I suppose you've read Dr. Washington's *Up from Slavery.* Fiction might be the best treat for you. Do you like tragic romance stories? There's *Wuthering Heights.* Or Thomas Hardy, if you have a stomach for misery—but you must be strong, I warn you. Hardy's characters never end well."

"There's enough tragedy in life," Scott said. "Choose a happy book where everything works out for the best."

"A fairy tale, then," she said, looking at him askance with a wry smile.

He clucked his tongue. "Like I told a friend of mine, you're too young to be a cynic."

"I don't believe it's possible to be too young," she said, tossing her head in a defiant manner that made him think she must argue with her parents almost constantly. Freddie let out an excited gasp, pulling a thin volume from the shelf. "This is the one! *Alice's Adventures in Wonderland.* I've read it a dozen times, and it's perfect for you. In fact, you can keep it."

"I couldn't do that. It's poor manners not to return a book."

"But worse manners to refuse a gift," she said, bringing the book to him. True to Freddie's claim, the Lewis A. Carroll book was scarred as if it had lived both indoors and outdoors over the years. Its pages were dog-eared, many of them folded at the corners. Scott flipped through, noticing a series of odd, clever illustrations. This was a children's book, obviously. He smiled, amused. Was Freddie more a woman or a child?

"I hope you don't mind reading a book about a girl," Freddie said.

"Why should I?"

"Some men would find it silly."

Scott tucked the book snugly beneath his armpit. "I don't mind being silly in private."

"I think you're humoring me," she said, her face pensive, suddenly. When she scowled, her unhappy eyebrows added years to her features, a chronicle of disappointments. "Are you?"

"I couldn't. Not when you're parting with such a dear possession. You have my word."

That put her at ease. Freddie's expression softened again, a sun's ray across her eyes.

"Your father is eager to marry you off," Scott said, shocked at his insubordinate tongue. Freddie, apparently, had instilled a fearlessness in him.

"I'm sure he's already asked if you have marriageable sons," Freddie said, taking the seat beside him on the piano bench again. She sat with such haste, her flared skirt nearly brushed against him, and he smelled the sweet dampness on her skin, from her neck. Scott glanced in the direction of the kitchen, wondering what her mother would think of their familiarity if she spied them—or worse, her father. "You can set your pocket watch by my dear papa. What was your answer? Am I soon to be a Joplin?"

Her words froze him, before he remembered her meaning. "I don't have any children."

She smiled, shrugging. "It's just as well. It would cause a scandal."

Scott's soaring heart tumbled. Did the shame of ragtime reach so deeply that she would hesitate even to marry into his family? "It grieves me if you believe that."

"It would be a *terrible* scandal, wouldn't it? That I should marry the son and have eyes only for the father?" As Freddie spoke those words, she dipped her chin and magnified her gaze in such a way that Scott rose to his feet, alarmed by their proximity.

"You flatter me, miss," was all he could say. His collar felt too tight against his throat.

Freddie moved to her father's parlor chair, folding her hands delicately across her lap in an imitation of her father's sober pose. "Mr. Joplin, from this moment on, I consider us engaged. We'll appoint a guarantor and make it official. Finally, Papa's search for my husband is finished."

She had no idea of the power of her beauty, he was certain, to make such sport with him. Again, Scott glanced behind him to make sure her mother had not overheard such careless words, which could be easily misconstrued, as if he had toyed with this girl. Mrs. Alexander was not in sight. "You . . . embarrass me with your jest, Miss Alexander."

"I'm nineteen, I know my mind, and I think convention is idiotic. Why should the man always woo and propose?" She clasped her hands beneath her chin, preparing for an ardent recitation: " 'Then Love the Master-Player came / With heaving breast and eyes aflame; / The harp he took all undismayed, / Smote on its strings, still strange to song, / And brought forth music sweet and strong.' "

Scott felt stunned. "You're a poet, too?" he said, nearly breathless. All she lacked were the wings, and she could be a genuine seraph.

"Do you like my poem?" She grinned, her eyes sparkling with mischief. "No, it's Paul Laurence Dunbar—a *Negro,* you know. He's my favorite poet. I think that love poem is about you, Mr. Joplin. Love, the Master-Player."

She was cruel, to use the word *love* so casually. And her boldness! Freddie's fine rearing was obvious, yet she enjoyed a freedom from custom he'd usually only seen of women in brothels without ties or prospects. Girls like Freddie were a new breed, he thought, like the finely dressed women he'd seen smoking cigarettes on public streets without a care. The heavier-than-air flying machine wasn't the only enthralling innovation of this new century, the twentieth.

"Any love poem about me would be a great surprise," Scott said, too low to be heard.

Freddie ignored his mumbling. "How old are you, my future husband?"

"I'll join your joke to be a good sport, miss," he said. "I'm nearly thirty-six."

Her smile faded, and she tapped her chin with mock seriousness. "Oh, no. That won't do. Papa is thirty-nine, so you see the problem. We'll have to agree on a fib. You can't be thirty, so we'll say you're twenty-seven. That's only eight years older. Or should we say twenty-five?"

"To be credible, say forty," Scott said.

Her eyebrows furrowed. "Hardly! You must see yourself with very queer eyes, Mr. Joplin. Or is it really so awful to think of marrying me?" Her voice, for the first time, made him wonder if he'd misjudged her intent. She sounded hurt.

"My eyes . . ." he began, but couldn't finish the sentence. Louis wove magic with his words to young women, wooing two and three at a time, but Scott lacked his friend's verbal dexterity. How could he tell her what was in his heart without sounding mad? *I know I've only met you, Miss Alexander, but you are the woman I was dreaming about even when I didn't know I was dreaming. My very soul knows you on sight. You are now, always have been, and ever shall be, my intended wife.*

"What's your favorite flower, Miss Alexander?" Scott said instead.

"What a *very* hard question. There are so many! I'm very eager for spring. Let me think . . ." she said, excited to have a challenge. Her talk of engagement seemed to leave her mind the way an infant forgot tears, proving to him that it had, indeed, been a game. Why had he allowed her fanciful talk to speed his heart? "I would choose roses for their heavenly scent . . . sunflowers for their audacity . . . orchids for their preciousness. But you know, of all of them, I think I like the fall chrysanthemums best, because they're beautiful *and* hardy. And they have a bold scent, sweet to some, offensive to others. Do you like them, too?"

Scott dampened his dry lips with the tip of his tongue. He slid his hands into his pockets so she would not see how her company made his fingers tremble like a smitten boy's. "I like chrysanthemums very much," he said. "My eyes are gazing on a beautiful one now."

Even Louis, he thought, could not have chosen his words better. He would always have the memory of this creature's bewildered, flaming face in the wake of his compliment. From the look of her, he might have been the first man to tell Freddie Alexander she was beautiful!

Tonight, she had heard it in words.

Soon, she would hear it in song.

CHAPTER NINE

Sarge's knock on her door came as usual. Phoenix had asked him not to come today, but she'd still been expecting him. "What's going on? You OK?" Sarge said, peering over Phoenix's shoulder, inside her apartment. The midmorning sun behind him blazed into her eyes. "I thought I heard voices."

Phoenix shrugged, trying to erase anxiousness from her face. "I'm just trying to get some rest, Daddy. I'll be fine."

Carlos and the two strangers had been good enough to duck into the bedroom to hide, but Phoenix knew there were enough telltale signs of company to stir Sarge's interest if he took a better look. The video camera mounted on a tripod in a corner, for one thing. At least Phoenix had remembered to throw her covers on top of the futon to make it look like she'd been sick in bed, the excuse she'd given Sarge when he called her that morning.

Sarge gave her a bag of food from El Pollo Loco, an early lunch. The scent of Mexican grilled chicken reminded Phoenix that she hadn't eaten yet. "I've rescheduled a couple interviews, but you don't want to come to the dance audition for a while? You should try to show while Ronn is there. He's trying to bring the buzz for *you*."

That would have seemed very important yesterday morning, but Phoenix's perspective had changed overnight. "I'm sorry. I really need to take the day off."

Sarge felt her forehead; his broad palm still felt large enough to cover

her face, as it had when she was a girl. "This doesn't have anything to do
with you and Ronn, does it? You'll have to get over that, Phee. This is
business."

"Sarge, you know me better than that. I just don't feel right."

Again, Sarge peeked behind her, and she saw his eyes wander past her
kitchen toward the bedroom and its closed door. He didn't quite believe
her, but he didn't push it. As her manager, it was his job to get her there
no matter what; as her father, his job was different. "OK, Peanut, you
better take care of yourself," he said. Suddenly, Sarge grinned, and his
worry lines dissolved. "I wanted to wait until it was a hundred percent,
but I think we've got you booked to do one song on *Live at Night*. If that
pans out, it'll happen next week, maybe Tuesday. So you rest up."

Live at Night was a late-night cable talk show hosted by comedian
Alex Campton, whom Phoenix thought of as a cross between Chris
Rock and Martin Lawrence, at turns both razor-smart and silly as hell.
Campton had co-starred in *Paid in Full* as the comic relief to Ronn's
hard-ass. He was a funny guy. His show wasn't MTV's *TRL,* but it was
her best venue yet.

"That's great," Phoenix said, but she and Sarge both knew that on
any other day, she would be shrieking.

"Phoenix, you *must* be sick, if that's all you've got to say. Two million
people might see that show, or more. Do I need to take you to the emergency room?"

"I'll be screaming tomorrow, Sarge, for real." Phoenix held him
tightly, resting her head on Sarge's shoulder. She hated lying to him, but
the truth brought too many complications.

Once Sarge was gone, Phoenix went to the bedroom and waved her
visitors out, apologizing for the interruption. "He wouldn't understand," she explained.

"Many people don't," the psychic said.

Heather Larrabee didn't look the way Phoenix had expected a psychic to look. She wasn't the diminutive near dwarf of *Poltergeist* or the
eccentric in *Ghost*. She was probably Carlos's age, in her mid- to late-
thirties, a businesslike woman with an athletic build, sun-browned skin
and hair that was more strawberry blond than golden like Gloria's, tied
in a youthful ponytail. Her nose was long and aquiline, like Phoenix's

mother's. Instead of a flowing dress and exotic jewelry, she wore black capri slacks and a sleeveless lilac turtleneck. In her "real life," she'd told Phoenix when she first arrived, she worked as an insurance claims adjuster. (*Talking to the dead is a big advantage in my line of work,* she'd said with a straight face.)

Her assistant, Finn, looked like the wannabe actor he was: strong-featured good looks, a flawless complexion, dark hair subdued by generous hair gel. He was wearing tattered denim shorts and a black *Matrix Revolutions* T-shirt. He looked like any one of thousands of guys in L.A.—except that Finn was a ghost-hunter. He'd come with two suitcases full of equipment.

"It's awesome you're working with your dad," Finn said, loading a tape into the camera, a plastic wrapper bobbing in his mouth while he spoke. "If my dad was my manager, that would last, like, sixty seconds. What's your secret?"

"Respect, I guess," she said. She'd answered that question a hundred times.

Heather smiled at her, squeezing her hand. "It'll be a wonderful memory."

"I hear you hang with G-Ronn," Finn said. "What's he like? Is he a real gangbanger?"

"He's rich," Phoenix said curtly, and shot a look toward Carlos. *Check your friend, man.* She hadn't invited this guy here to discuss Ronn. Carlos, leaning against the bedroom door frame, curled his lips ruefully, a silent apology.

This psychic thing wasn't going to work. This was the wrong way. In daylight, Phoenix's apartment looked painfully mundane; her only reminders of last night's adventure were the take-out carton on the counter and the sheet music to "Bethena" she'd printed out, which Heather now had in her hand. Finn's video camera was aimed toward her kitchen, but the refrigerator door wasn't going to do any theatrics again. Not today. The man at the Joplin House, Mr. Milton, had said the ghost only came out when it was quiet.

Heather clapped her hands together, a coach motivating her team. "Let's pick up where we left off," Heather said, taking a seat on the futon. "Can you come sit next to me, Phoenix?"

Phoenix sat, despite her skepticism. Carlos had told her he'd known Heather for six years, as long as he'd been in L.A., and he believed she had a true psychic calling. *Either that, or she's found a true cash flow telling people what they want to hear,* Phoenix thought.

"What Finn and I do is a hobby," Heather said, as if she were a mind reader. "I don't charge for my services because I've always been a little superstitious that I might lose my gifts if I did that. Carlos told me you experienced some extraordinary phenomena here last night, and we wanted to move quickly. We've never seen anything like what happened to you, so I'm going to admit we're a little envious. We've been doing this a long time."

"Friggin' right," Finn said, satisfied his camera was ready. His legs folded beneath him until he sat cross-legged on the floor, rifling through his suitcase.

"What *have* you seen?" Phoenix said.

"We saw a child's face in an attic window in a haunted bed and breakfast in Santa Barbara, and captured it on film," Heather said. "That was a good day."

"It was *awesome,*" Finn said.

"Other than that, we've heard a lot of unusual noises, seen a few flashes of light on our video camera, and recorded some temperature abnormalities, hot or cold spots like the one you described. No ghost has ever composed a piece of music for us, though. That's what makes this so special. We've also never worked with a spirit of Scott Joplin's notoriety." As Heather spoke, she lowered her voice in deference. "I'm going to try to channel him. Sometimes it works, sometimes it doesn't. So don't get discouraged if we don't get a repeat performance."

"Tell her about you equipment," Carlos spoke up.

"Right. Thanks, hon," Heather said, glancing back at Carlos with a fondness that made Phoenix wonder if they were more than friends. It might have been a harmless *hon,* or Heather might be staking her territory. Phoenix didn't want to care, but she did.

Finn took over. "Basically, I've got the video camera, a digital camera with zoom, a motion detector, some aluminum chimes and a temperature monitor, otherwise known as a thermometer. We'll see what happens. Hope you don't mind if we hang out awhile."

"What's awhile?" Phoenix said.

"*Definitely* overnight. We don't get our best data in daylight. Heather's gotta jet back over to her kiddies in Canyon Country later, but I can camp out here, if that's OK."

Again, Phoenix glanced at Carlos, questioning. She hadn't counted on a stranger spending the night in her apartment. Last night, Carlos had slept here on the futon while she slept on the bed in Nia's room, but that was different. She knew him, at least. "I'm not sure if . . ."

"Maybe we should play it by ear," Carlos said. "Pardon the pun."

Finn shrugged, his jaw flexing with irritation or disappointment, or both. He didn't answer, unpacking a boxed motion detector from Radio Shack.

"Whatever makes you comfortable, Phoenix," Heather said. "This is your place."

While she waited for Finn to set up his surveillance—*Gloria would be cracking up if she could see this,* she thought—Phoenix shared the food Sarge had brought with Carlos. Like her, Carlos hadn't had breakfast. They stood beside each other over the kitchen counter, awaiting turns while each stabbed at the chunks of spicy chicken and rice in the bowl. Neither of them spoke, but they both glanced occasionally at the styrofoam take-out container that had mysteriously appeared on the counter last night, which sat unmoving less than a foot from them. Their meal felt like the most normal thing in the world, but there was nothing normal about it.

"We're ready to rock, ladies and gentlemen," Finn said finally. He was standing near the front door with a long thermometer, where she and Carlos had felt the cold spot. "Everybody go where they're going and stay still, OK? We don't want anyone setting off the motion detector except Mr. You-Know-Who."

This guy definitely was *not* going to spend the night here, she decided. Carlos, once again, took his place in the bedroom doorway, sitting on the floor. Phoenix sat beside Heather.

"Wow. I'm actually a little nervous," Heather said, taking a deep breath. She closed her eyes, trying to calm herself the way Phoenix often did right before even her smallest concerts, when the nest of butterflies converged in her stomach.

Heather clasped Phoenix's hand between hers, and for an eternity, she said nothing. Phoenix heard their combined breathing in the room, a far-off siren and a closer ice-cream truck playing a manic circus tune through her closed door. Phoenix was sorry she hadn't gone to the bathroom first, because her bladder was pressing against her jeans. With her luck, she would wet herself again if the motion detector sounded, or if the chimes Finn had hung in the kitchen tinkled.

But for the longest time, the room was silent.

The longer she waited, the more Phoenix remembered the other things she could be doing right now, a list that was endless and panic-inducing. She still hadn't chosen a fashion stylist, and she had no idea what to do with her hair. Beyond that, she hadn't visited her voice coach in weeks. She'd better get in gear if she was going to be singing on national television next Tuesday. Ronn had told her to feel free to lip-synch when she needed to—plenty of other performers did—but Hell would get a cold spot before Phoenix Smalls would do anything as fake-ass as that.

"You got hurt when you were young . . . maybe nine or ten?" Heather said softly, jolting her.

Had Carlos told her that? Adrenaline streamed through Phoenix's arms. "Yes."

"What I'm feeling is . . . this was an accident."

"Yes," she said again.

"I'm feeling *he* wants you to know this was an accident," Heather clarified. "There was something of his . . . an item he once owned, or used, at an important time in his life. A bitter, angry time. He didn't mean for it to happen. He's sorry you got hurt."

The piano! Remembering her joy at finding that old piano as a child, Phoenix's breath went frosty in her throat. Had that piano her parents sold once belonged to Scott Joplin?

"I got hurt by an antique piano when it fell down the stairs," she whispered. She saw Carlos squirming where he sat with wide eyes.

Heather shook her head as if to clear it, her thin lips tightening, then she frowned. "There was a lot of pain," she said after a pause, but Phoenix didn't know if she meant there had been pain for Joplin or for her. Both of them, maybe.

Phoenix felt her heartbeat gather speed. Did she want the ghost to come back? It was the chance of a lifetime, something she'd regret forever if she didn't pursue it—but she was far from comfortable with communing with the dead.

Heather's eyes remained closed. Her brow knit itself, and for a long time she concentrated so hard that her face turned ruddy, almost glowing. She squeezed Phoenix's hand gently and rhythmically, as if she was trying to pump something out of her. A minute passed. More. "Damn, damn, *damn* . . ." Heather muttered finally, obviously upset. It was like hearing a doctor say *Oops* in the middle of an exam.

"What?" Phoenix said, anxious.

Heather's hazel eyes opened. She smiled, releasing Phoenix's hand, which was slippery from their combined perspiration. "Sorry to scare you. I'm just frustrated. I felt like he was . . . *sooooo* close. Finn?"

Finn shook his head, examining his thermometer. "Nothing yet."

"I don't think he'll come for us," Heather said, her smile turning sad. "I got that message for you, Phoenix, but . . . I think that's all he has for me."

"We can wait and keep trying," Carlos said.

"No," Heather said. "The best way I can put it, Phoenix, is that he wants to be with you."

Maybe I remind him of his wife, Phoenix thought, the theory she and Carlos had conceived in their long conversation last night, before she decided she was nervous enough to ask him to stay despite her vows not to. "I can't see anything else from him," Heather said, her envy obvious in her face. "But he has a beautiful spirit, I'll say that. You would have liked him very much."

Phoenix didn't doubt a bit that she would have liked Scott Joplin. She just wasn't sure how much she liked Scott Joplin now that he was dead.

"We should pack up, Finn." Heather sighed.

"Are you *kidding* me?" Finn said, walking toward them. The motion detector chimed loudly, and Phoenix jumped. "I blew off an open call for this."

Despite the way Finn grated Phoenix's nerves, she had to agree, considering she'd skipped an appearance with Ronn. "I don't mind if you stay," she said.

"I know you don't," Heather said. "But he does."

Heather's eyes didn't blink. She wasn't kidding. Phoenix felt her limbs tense. *Yeah, and I bet nobody likes to piss off ghosts. I bet that's a pretty bad idea.*

"Let me at least leave the camera. Will you let it run tonight?" Finn asked Phoenix.

"I guess so. If you show me how."

While Finn coached her and Carlos on the operation of the video camera—and the wireless monitor he'd set up in the bedroom—Heather packed his other things in his suitcase and gathered her knapsack, ready to go. She didn't look frightened, but she moved quickly, eager to leave. When Finn and Carlos retreated to the bedroom for one last gadget-oriented detail Phoenix wanted nothing to do with, she walked up behind Heather, who was in the kitchen gazing at the refrigerator door, touching it lightly with one finger, the way her mother tested furniture for dust.

"Bet you wish you'd been here last night, huh?" Phoenix said.

Heather turned, startled. "Yes," she said. "You're a lucky girl."

"It didn't feel so damn lucky. I wish it had been you here instead, believe me."

"Me, too," Heather said, and Phoenix wondered if they were still talking about the ghost. Heather sighed, wiping a strand of hair from her forehead. "I've been wrestling with something, Phoenix, and I've decided to break one of my rules."

"What rule?"

"Well . . . every once in a while, in the course of my spirit work, I come across messages, or knowledge, that might be unsettling. Warnings, you could call them. Usually it's my policy not to scare people over vague messages I can't help them interpret. When I was in college, one poor friend of mine hardly left her room for three months after I told her she might have an accident. As far as I know, she never did, so I scared her for nothing, maybe. I just don't know. This isn't a science, unfortunately. And I never like to share that kind of thing with clients unless it's something like, 'Stop smoking or you'll get lung cancer.' Not that you need a psychic for that." She laughed, but the sound was more nervous than mirthful.

"What is it?" Phoenix said, her voice tight. She'd better ask now, or she wouldn't want to hear it at all. "Something about the ghost?"

"I don't . . . *think* so . . ." Heather said. "Please remember that most ghost encounters are positive, in my experience, or at least neutral. I've never come across a spirit I thought wanted to hurt someone, even when they had a good reason to. And this spirit specifically said he was *sorry* you'd been hurt, and he was adamant about it." She sighed again, searching for words, blinking rapidly. She looked pained. "But there is something, Phoenix. How can I put this?"

Put it in English, and fast. Phoenix was nearly as frightened as she'd been when her refrigerator slammed itself shut in the dark. Her taut bladder complained, throbbing.

"You're not safe," Heather said finally. "That comes across very strongly, and it did from the minute I saw you, especially when your father was here. This is a dangerous time. I won't pretend I know it isn't the ghost, but it's probably something else, maybe something with your career. That *might* explain the father connection. Whatever it is, your life is at risk."

There was loud laughter from the living room, Carlos and Finn sharing a joke, and their jocularity shook Phoenix from a leaden stupor that had crawled over her as the psychic spoke. Finn was saying he'd nicknamed the camera his *piece-o-shitcam*.

"What am I supposed to do?" Phoenix said, trying to keep calm.

Heather gave Phoenix a helpless look, her eyes motherly. "That's the thing. I don't know. I don't even know what kind of danger it is. That's why I almost didn't tell you."

Their conversation caught Carlos's ear, and Phoenix saw him gazing over at them while Finn talked on. "In that case," Phoenix said, "I wish you hadn't told me."

Heather wrapped her arm across Phoenix's shoulder, resting their heads together. "I'm sorry. If anything else comes to me, I'll contact you right away, through Carlos."

"I'll give you my cell number, too, just in case," Phoenix said. Then, as an afterthought, she added, "Thanks for trying, anyway."

She gave Heather a hug for good measure, in case that might give her a flash of insight like on *The Dead Zone,* but the psychic only told Finn she was ready to leave. Phoenix watched as Heather called Carlos *hon* again, and he gave her a Miami-style kiss on each cheek.

Then, they were gone.

"She left in a hurry," Carlos observed.

"Yeah. Didn't she?" What Heather had told her about the piano might have been information she learned from Carlos, or just a lucky guess. Most psychics were bullshit artists. Even Carlos had said that. "How well do you know her?"

"Very well," Carlos said.

"Are you going out?"

That was the most polite term Phoenix knew for sleeping together. The question didn't faze Carlos. He reclined across the futon, propping one leg on the pale wooden arm as he popped a nacho chip into his mouth. "We did. We're not anymore."

"And she's probably not too happy about that. Right?"

Carlos smiled thinly. "Now who's the psychic?" His smile irritated her. She hoped she would remember never to fall into bed with him, no matter how comforting his presence when their clothes were on.

"Well, she said I'm in danger, and I wonder if she just said that to freak me out. Jealous women are nothing to play with."

At that, Carlos's smile vanished, and he sat up straight. "Heather's not that way. She would never say something like that to be spiteful. What kind of danger?"

"She didn't know. Maybe the ghost, maybe my career. Something to do with my dad."

"Maybe your father'll kill you when he finds out you're sneaking around with me."

"Don't flatter yourself," Phoenix said, with her own icy smile. "He'd kill you."

"Ah. Good point. But I wouldn't take Heather's message lightly. Considering those shootings implicating G-Ronn right now, it's not a big stretch. You told me about that panic in St. Louis. Remember? You had two thugs packing heat outside your door all night?"

Phoenix hated having her words parroted at her, especially when they were exaggerated. "They were guards. I didn't say they were thugs. And Ronn's not like people think."

"None of us is like anyone thinks we are. But I've made my point about the current company you're keeping, I hope. *Cuidado,* that's all." *Watch out.*

"To tell you the truth, I'm more worried about the company in this room."

"The ghost?"

"No," she said. "You."

He half smiled again. "I'm not dangerous."

"Is that what Heather would say?"

Carlos's eyes flitted away from hers. "I used to make the mistake of sleeping with my female friends, and when we weren't friends anymore, I was baffled," he said, returning her gaze. "Luckily, Heather is still a friend. She helped me grow up. She's a wonderful lady, and I respect her. But she has two kids, and I wasn't ready for that. Does that answer your questions?"

"But didn't you know she had two kids before you hooked up?" Phoenix said, angry for Heather's sake. She understood how much it hurt to lose Carlos Harris.

"She knew who I was," he said. "I told her all along. She made the choice to go there."

The angry feeling didn't dissipate. It was her own anger, she realized. It had nothing to do with Heather Larrabee, a woman she didn't know. Carlos was still too careless, showing glimpses of his marvelousness to women he had no intention of sharing it with. She could see that about him as clearly as she could smell his luxuriant cologne, which was now the strongest scent in her apartment, an old memory in her every breath. It was hard to be with him.

"Listen, Carlos . . ." Phoenix said, sighing. "I would appreciate it if you would stay here again tonight, just to make sure nothing else weird happens. I know you want to have more contact with this spirit, if that's what it is, and that's cool with me. But after that . . ."

He held up his hand before she could finish. "I understand," he said. "You're at an important crossroads in your career. You don't have time for dating. It wouldn't be fair to me."

"Good. You're a psychic, too."

"Not at all," he said, his voice as flat as glass. "That used to be my favorite speech."

*I*t didn't take Phoenix long to understand that she had fallen into a dream.

She knew as soon as she saw she was sitting in her parents' living room in Miami, on the walnut bench of the spinet piano from Grandpa Bud and Grandma Oprah. Mom was reading the Sunday *New York Times* at her reading table, while Sarge polished his trumpet on the leather sofa. The trumpet's finish gleamed like precious ore beneath his loving hand. An old-fashioned clock with two trumpet-playing angels, a clock she had never noticed, ticked from the piano.

They were waiting.

"Whatever you do, Phoenix, remember to make the smart play," Mom said, one of her favorite phrases. Mom peered at her over her purple reading glasses, the ones she only wore at home. Her hair was cut short in a way that made its silvery strands seem playful instead of tired. "This is the best thing for you. Think of how much you'll learn from him, how much more you'll understand the world outside these walls. What's more important than that?"

Sarge grunted. "He's so old," he said. "She'll be nursing him before long."

"Stop exaggerating, Daddy. He's not that old." But maybe he was, she thought. Maybe.

Sarge didn't argue further, glancing at the clock. When there was finally a knock at the door, three confident bangs, Sarge said, "Well, it's about damn time."

"Land sakes, mind your language," Mom said, a series of words that had never emerged from her mother's mouth. A reminder that Phoenix was dreaming.

Phoenix leaped to her feet, almost tripping over the many-layered white chiffon dress she hadn't realized she was wearing. Sarge called her back and told her to sit down, setting his trumpet aside with unhurried care. "Don't act so excited. It's unseemly. I'll answer it."

The man they were waiting for stood on the doorstep, standing five or six inches shorter than Sarge. Phoenix heard his voice greeting Sarge in a polite, masculine rumble as soft as a kitten's purr. Her heart quickened when she heard him. Leaning over to peek through the doorway, Phoenix saw a spotted horse tied to a magnificent canopied black surrey that shone in front of their house like the moonlight on the midnight ocean's plane. The surrey was a few years out of date, but lovely nonetheless. He'd chosen it special to come see her.

Her suitor was wearing a black suit, high collared white shirt, and neatly knotted black tie, as perfect as a photograph. He walked inside with Sarge, holding a single red rose. After he had greeted Mom by kissing her hand, he finally stood before Phoenix. He smiled with a shyness that proved contagious, making her glance toward her folded hands. He held the rose to her, and she met his eyes again as its scent enthralled her senses.

"I hope you don't mind a rose," he said. "It's too early for chrysanthemums."

"Anyone would be crazy not to love a rose," Phoenix said. "It's perfect."

Mom cleared her throat, gathering her newspaper. For the first time, Phoenix noticed that Mom was wearing a twilled sateen shirt waist with puff top sleeves and a high collar, one of the nicest spring outfights she owned, although Phoenix couldn't remember ever seeing her in it. Mom had dressed for this visit, too. "Let them visit awhile, Marcus," Mom said, lowering her chin until small folds of skin appeared at her tight collar.

Sarge gave them a long, lingering look over his shoulder before he disappeared from sight. "I'm so embarrassed about the way I acted before," Phoenix told her suitor. "I can't believe how childish I was. I can only imagine what you think about me."

"I thought you were charming," he said, laughing. "Don't be embarrassed."

"I'm surprised you would come back, after that."

"I had to," he said, smiling. "How else could I perform the song I wrote for you?"

"Did you really write something for me?" she said, rising from the piano bench. She checked his expression, and he seemed earnest.

"Listen for yourself," he said, and sat at the piano.

While her suitor played, she heard springtime in his fingertips. Honeybees, blooming flowers, and rain-showers filled the living room. The piece became more somber and thoughtful for a time, pondering possibilities as far as Old World Europe, before winding into a home-style celebration again, ending like the perfect kiss.

Phoenix couldn't speak, blinking. No one had ever given her anything like it.

"Since it was for you, I didn't call it a rag," he said. "It's an Afro-American Intermezzo."

"It's priceless," Phoenix whispered.

"I named it 'The Chrysanthemum,' after my beautiful young flower bud."

"If you keep saying I'm beautiful, I'll believe it soon. Then I'll be intolerable."

"That day will never come. And you *are* beautiful. To me, there is no one more beautiful. Not Maxine Elliott, not Ethel Barrymore, not the Queen of Egypt. You are womanhood perfected." With that, he took her hand. She could feel the shudder of his heartbeat in his warm, soft palm. "Do you know why I'm here tonight?"

She shook her head, although they all had their suspicions. She had to hear the words.

"I wanted to ask you a question," he said, his voice faltering.

"Oh? What kind of question?" she said innocently.

"Are you brave enough to leave your home behind?"

Phoenix stared around her at the living room, which looked changed in the dream. Her piano was here, and the same cream-colored leather sofa set she'd grown up with, but there was also furniture she didn't recognize, namely an elaborate parlor suit with elegantly engraved wood frames and burgundy satin upholstery—a sofa, a divan, a rocking chair and two parlor chairs. The walls were also crammed with framed photographs, almost like the Gallery of Greats. Her parents were in the portrait-sized photo above the piano, heads close in a loving pose, ebony and ivory. And Gloria in another beside them. And Serena. There was even a photo of Kai, Ronn's bodyguard, and she barely knew him. The photographs made her feel sad.

"If I left, where would I go?" Phoenix said.

He squeezed her hand, very gently. "With me."

"We'll have to ask my parents," she said, uncertain. Sarge wouldn't like that at all.

Her suitor began to play the piano again, his fingers dancing on the keys. "Of course," he said. "But as long as you say yes, that's all that matters to me. I'll be the happiest man dead."

"Don't you mean the happiest man *alive?*" Phoenix said, sure he'd made a joke.

Not looking up at her, her suitor shook his head. "I'll be the happiest man dead."

Suddenly, Phoenix wasn't sure she liked this dream. A shard of ice prodded her stomach.

"I have to think about it awhile," she said.

"Yes, but please don't think too long. I love you, Freddie."

What had he called her? "My name isn't Freddie," she said.

Her suitor didn't answer, playing on. Phoenix felt unsure for a moment, but then she looked at the photographs on the wall, and she remembered. "My name isn't Freddie," she said again. "My name is Phoenix."

He only gazed at her sidelong as he played, one eye and half a grin.

*P*hoenix, *wake up.*"

A man's voice. Phoenix gasped, and her eyes popped open because she didn't recognize the voice as her lover's. Where was Sarge? Where was Mom?

Carlos stood over her, bare-chested in faded surfer shorts, his night-clothes, and the weakened scent of his cologne swept her true memories back into place, washing the dream away. She was in her apartment in Los Angeles, not at the Miami house with her parents. And she was with Carlos Harris, not with anyone else.

Phoenix looked down at herself and realized she was sitting at her computer chair in a long T-shirt, which surprised her because she'd thought she was wearing a dress. Her face and shirt were soaked with freezing water, her nipples poking against the thin, sheen fabric across her chest, stunted tent poles. She hugged herself, her teeth chattering. "What the *fuck* . . ."

Carlos grabbed his blanket from the futon and gently draped it across her shoulders, wrapping her tightly, bundling the blanket beneath her arms to trap her body heat. "I'm sorry. You were yelling your name, and I threw some water on you. You wouldn't wake up when I shook you. I could have tried to wake you up sooner, but I didn't want to interrupt."

"Interrupt wh-what?" she said, still shivering and confused.

Carlos pointed to her Mac screen, which was brimming with merry, syncopated notes.

"Your playing," he said. "You've been playing the keyboard more than an hour."

Phoenix stared at the music she'd heard in her dream.

CHAPTER TEN

*N*one of them noticed the older-model gray Chevy Impala parked at the corner. It was a car meant to be invisible.

The Impala was there when Phoenix and Sarge left Three Strikes Records at 10:35 A.M., after finishing their publicity meeting with Manny. *Live at Night* was officially a go: The show's bookers wanted Phoenix to sing "Party Patrol." Sarge had hired two backup singers Phoenix had worked with before, and Phoenix fantasized that Serena could make her national television debut singing with her, too. She'd talked to her sister in Atlanta that morning, and Serena said she would *think* about it, Serena's typical delaying tactics. She'd been thinking for a year.

As Sarge drove his rented Grand Prix out of the TSR lot behind the building, past the waving guard at the gate, Ronn's black Lexus SUV pulled beside them and sounded its horn, the four-toned hook from Ronn's first hit, "Playa Dayz." Kai let his window down, signaling from the driver's seat. Phoenix didn't recognize the young man in the passenger seat, but he gave her a pleasant smile. He looked like Taye Diggs, except younger. He seemed small to be a bodyguard.

"Hey, Krispy Kreme, whassup?" Phoenix said.

Kai's thumb gestured toward the backseat. "Boss-man wants to holla at ya."

"Good," Sarge murmured. He'd been worried when Ronn was too busy to see her. Sometimes Sarge worried more than Mom, and that was a lot of worrying.

"I *told* you we're cool," Phoenix whispered to Sarge, and climbed out of the car.

As she walked to the back door of the Lexus, Phoenix fashioned a smile several watts brighter than the one she would have given Ronn if he wasn't her label's CEO. She felt wrecked. She hadn't done any sleepwalking since she was ten, and she had outgrown her childlike willingness to accept the bizarreness as an adventure. She was tired and freaked out, and Ronn had just broken up with her. This was not a good day.

"Hey, Ronn," Phoenix said, leaning inside once Ronn opened the door for her. The vehicle was built so high that she took Ronn's hand so he could lift her to the running board.

Ronn was wearing a skintight black shirt that molded to his weight-room physique. The scent of his morning joint wafted out, and he offered her a toke, which she didn't refuse. What the hell? Phoenix had to admit that she had missed Gloria and her stash the past few days. Phoenix didn't smoke nearly as much as Gloria and Ronn, but alcohol only knocked her out, and sometimes she wanted to escape the world and visit her head for a while. Ronn's productivity was all the more amazing when she considered how often he was high.

After she inhaled, she coughed. She'd forgotten that Ronn mixed tobacco in his joints, and tobacco seared her throat. "Ooh, that shit's nasty," she said, handing it back.

"Sorry, baby girl. I forgot you like your herb straight. Come sit down a minute."

While Phoenix settled against the leather seat beside him, Sarge walked to talk to Kai in the front seat, hovering close as usual. Stevie Wonder was playing, Ronn's favorite morning music. The bass player in "Superstition" was just getting busy. The television monitors built into the headrests facing Ronn played CNN in mute mode. More problems in Iraq.

Ronn took off his red-hued Kenneth Coles, and his eyes shone with fondness. He rubbed her knee. "How you doin', Superstar? Manny told me about *Live at Night*. That's gonna be off the chain. Your dancers look good for the video, huh?" Typically, Ronn's question was rhetorical, and he didn't give her time to answer. "You need anything else from me?"

Phoenix's mind stalled. All she could think about was the pile of sheet music she and Carlos had printed out from her computer that morning and mailed overnight to Van Milton at the Scott Joplin House, awaiting his judgment. She wished they could have faxed all 180 pages, but they did fax thirty so he could see them right away. All she really needed today was a musicologist who specialized in ragtime, and Ronn couldn't help her with that.

"Can't think of anything," she said.

"Well, if you do, just say it. You feelin' better today?"

"Yeah, sorry I got sick yesterday."

"Ain't nothin, ain't nothin," Ronn said, nodding. "You gotta take care of you first. We're gonna sit down with the tapes and get those dancers hired by Friday so they'll have time to rehearse for the video shoot, a'ight? You'll meet Jamal in a couple days, 'cuz he's flying in from London. Then you and me can hit a dinner spot this weekend. Saturday good for you?"

"Works for me," she said. "My sister Serena's coming to town. Do you mind if she comes with us? And her son?"

Ronn's face soured slightly, the first hint of his emotions beneath his businessman's mask, but he shrugged. "It's cool if they eat with us, but we gotta' walk in alone and walk out alone. It's all for the cameras, baby girl."

"Right. That's cool," she said. She was sorry she'd asked. It was an imposition. Or had he wanted to be alone with her?

"Remind Manny about that designer, whatchacallum. He has something he wants you to wear. It looks real good. Not too much, but nice for dinner."

"I will."

"What you gonna do with your hair for TV?"

Phoenix's Afro was particularly free-spirited today, since she'd hardly had time to breathe between the time Carlos woke her at her keyboard and when Sarge knocked on her door. Self-consciously, she patted the woolly fringes on the back of her head. "My sister's gonna hook me up with some extensions. She's a pro. I told her what you want."

"Lemme see a preview Saturday night, a'ight?"

"No problem." *Yes, sir,* she almost said. Damn. She and Serena would have to spend the whole day on her hair, and on her sister's first day in town.

At that, Ronn leaned over to peck her lips. "You're my girl, Phee." The peck, small as it was, inspired arousal in her, then regret. The magnitude of how badly she had fucked up her relationship with Ronn still dazzled her when she allowed herself to consider it.

The song playing switched abruptly from "Superstition" to "All in Love Is Fair," with Stevie's silken voice oozing through the rear speakers. Phoenix had heard this CD a dozen times in Ronn's car, and this ballad wasn't next on the playlist. She glanced up at the rear-view mirror, and saw Kai's eyes gazing back, watching. Kai was messing with them.

Ronn noticed, too, shifting beside her uncomfortably. For a few seconds, neither Phoenix nor Ronn knew what to say. In their uneasy quiet, Phoenix heard her father's booming laughter as he leaned into the front-seat window. "I *told* you the Dolphins was gonna go after that boy on the Ravens, that big-ass nigger from Alabama State. They better go after somebody."

"They could hire an army, and they'll still be sorry," Taye's twin said, dangling his cigarette out of his window. "You're livin' in the past, O. G. Marino's *been* gone." That ignited a good-natured debate, the three of them trying to talk over one another, Sarge loudest of all. The men's easy fellowship brightened the car.

Ronn offered Phoenix another toke, and this time she inhaled only a sip so she wouldn't cough. She already felt fuzzy-headed. She couldn't take her eyes away from Ronn's manicured nails, remembering how his broad hands had slipped inside her clothes, cupping her breasts while he pressed his primed solidness against her from behind. Stevie was singing about how he never should have left his lady's side, and Phoenix's stomach churned with acid.

"You a'ight?" Ronn said finally.

"Except for feeling like shit," she said, choosing honesty. "You?"

He nodded. "Been better, but I'm surviving." He clasped her hand, holding it a few seconds while the yearning music submerged them. Kai turned the rear speakers' volume up, exactly what Gloria would do, but whatever else was in Ronn's mind, he toyed with it in silence. "OK, I gotta roll. Don't forget my digits, baby girl," he said finally. He kissed her cheek a quarter inch from her lips, moist and lingering, midway between a friend's kiss and a lover's.

"Thanks for everything, Ronn." She felt like she should be asking him for a second chance, even while she wasn't sure what she would do with one.

As Phoenix climbed out of the car, and the door closed behind her, she heard Ronn ask Kai, "Man, what the fuck's wrong with you? Don't be puttin' Stevie in my business." Kai laughed, and they argued like two junior-high schoolboys as the SUV drove off.

"I *know* I didn't just see you smoking grass back there," Sarge scolded as they walked toward his rental. He was probably more concerned about Ronn's kiss, if he had seen it.

"It's just schmoozing, Sarge," she said. "And they don't call weed *grass* anymore, by the way. Don't act like you never smoked it. I know what was going on in the sixties."

"I was running with Muslims. I didn't smoke, period. Don't mess with that shit, Phee." Ever since his struggle to get Malcolm off crack, Sarge preached as if smoking weed was as bad as doing crack, all facts and statistics aside. *Legalize weed and ban beer and cigarettes, and we'll see which drugs are the worst ones then,* she thought, smiling.

Phoenix noticed the gray Impala down the street just as she was about to open her car door. The car was half a block away, but it moved with a lurch that caught her eye. Its windows were darker than Ronn's, pure jet, with rims glaring in the sunlight.

When Ronn's SUV slowed at the stop sign, the waiting car lunged, catlike. Phoenix caught her breath. That car was going to *hit* them!

Kai swerved with a scream of brakes. A man's voice shouted from the Impala.

"Is that guy drunk?" Phoenix said.

"Down," Sarge said, a single word. Sarge tugged on her arm so hard that she felt her shoulder snap. She was losing her balance when she heard the *pop pop pop,* then a frenzied whine as a car sped away. Dual explosions followed—*BOOM BOOM*—echoing across the row of buildings on the street, rattling windowpanes. The ringing sound of breaking glass mingled with onlookers' screams.

"Ronn!" Phoenix called out, forgetting he was too far to hear.

As she fell to the ground, Phoenix's right knee hit the pavement hard, sending a wave of pain through her leg. Her heart was bloated with adrenaline, pumping in a fury as Sarge snatched her close, crouching with her beside the front tire closest to the passenger door. Phoenix realized she was thirty yards from a drive-by shooting, one of Ronn's gangsta films come to life.

Oh shit. Oh shit. Oh shit. Phoenix's mind raced, matching her speeding heart. She trembled as though she were naked. Running footsteps came from everywhere, witnesses fleeing for cover. With the shouting and running, the street became chaos. A terrorist zone.

The third *BOOM* thundered. Phoenix clamped her hands over her ears. It sounded like a river of blood. "Oh, God," Phoenix whispered, praying as tears flooded her face. "Please, please, please . . ." *Please let them be all right. Please make it stop.*

"That's Kai, Phee. That's his .357," Sarge said. He knew without raising his head.

"You hit?" the guard from the TSR gate said, kneeling beside them, his black gun ready.

Sarge waved him away. "We're fine. Go see about Ronn." He was hoarse.

Now, Phoenix smelled acrid smoke and burned rubber in the breeze. An engine revved, more whining tires. The vehicle sounded as if it was coming *toward* them. Phoenix peered over Sarge to look beyond the hood of their car, expecting to see the Impala coming to ram them. Instead, the Lexus had turned around speeding back. Through the unbroken windshield, Phoenix saw Kai hunched forward, both hands clinging to the steering wheel. Ronn leaned over the front seat, in excited conversation with the young brother who looked like Taye.

They're okay, she thought, relieved. *Ronn's bulletproof, you stupid motherfuckers.*

The TSR guard waved the SUV on, his gun in the air. "Go, go, GO!" he yelled with a sweeping motion, as if he directed traffic at shootings every day.

When the SUV roared past, not slowing even when it nearly clipped Sarge's car, Phoenix saw an ugly dent in the Lexus's passenger door, beneath jagged, broken glass in the window. She also saw what she'd dreaded most: an unmistakable patch of blood on clothing, gone in a blur.

The window was down, she remembered, her heart freezing. Ronn wasn't talking to the Taye look-alike. He was propping him upright.

Phoenix gasped, watching the gleaming black tank make its retreat, her heart surging behind it. She mouthed a silent prayer for the man by the window, wishing she had taken the time to give him a happier smile and ask him his real name. Phoenix remembered laughing the day Ronn told her his Lexus SUV was bulletproof. She had thought he was fronting, taking his lyrics about street life too seriously. Now, Phoenix could only moan; a strained, half-crazed pant of air.

She owed that psychic, she realized. She owed Heather Larrabee an eight-thousand-dollar Rolex, just like the one Ronn had given her.

Ronn Jenkins owned four or five homes, but in Los Angeles he lived in a twenty-room mansion on an outcropping in Hollywood Hills, overlooking his winding street on one side and a fabulous northward view of the San Fernando Valley on the other, showcased through multistory picture windows. The sand-colored manse had a Mediterranean-style tile rooftop barely visible over the snarl of palms, spiny-trunked floss-silk trees and magnolias that shaded Ronn's security gate. The house had cost many millions; Ronn's neighbors were Leonardo DiCaprio and Cameron Diaz on one side, Heather Graham and Denzel on the other.

Phoenix hadn't expected to see Ronn's house again so soon.

In the furor after the shooting, the tide had swept them all here. Ronn wanted to avoid the crush of news vans outside of TSR headquarters, so he'd asked his staff to convene at his house, behaving as though it was a normal workday. The doorbell rang in endless succession: D'Real, Manny, Katrice, Lil' Mo and several large men Phoenix didn't know, who didn't work at the label. Nearly buried inside their baggy clothes, they sauntered into the house with heavy-lidded, watchful eyes. The phone trilled so constantly that Ronn's housekeeper had stopped answering it.

Kai wasn't here. He was still with the police. Just as Sarge had said, the second and third rounds of gunfire had been from Kai's gun as he fired back at the Impala. He'd blown out a portion of the car's rear window, but Phoenix didn't know if he'd hit anyone. So far, the Impala had vanished. Kai had acted in self-defense—all the witnesses said so—but apparently the police didn't look kindly on gunplay on a street where people wore suits to work. Phoenix hoped Ronn's lawyers would take care of it. She didn't want Kai to be in trouble.

The second man, Taye's double, was in the hospital with a .38-caliber bullet wound to his upper shoulder, so close to his neck that if it had hit him an inch higher, the doctors said he would be dead. His name, she'd learned, was Lamar Jenkins. He was Ronn's nephew from St. Louis, and he wasn't a bodyguard; he'd been visiting Ronn for a week. Lamar was the only child of Ronn's dead brother, twenty-two years old.

It was a bad day.

Ronn's Rottweiler, Max, remembered Phoenix. The dense-bodied black dog hadn't stopped trotting behind her since she'd been back here. Phoenix had no idea how Rottweilers had gotten such a bad rap, since Max was the sweetest dog she'd ever met. But maybe Max was sweet like Kai, she remembered. Sweet until it was time.

Ronn, Sarge and the label staff were in the front study he called his War Room—aptly named, she realized now—but she'd already been to the bathroom twice with dry heaves that made her stomach ache, and she didn't feel like sitting at a conference table. Ronn's house was an easy place to disappear.

Phoenix gazed at the midafternoon haze outside through the picture window in the sunroom on the far end of the house, a room that was a festival of white tiles and white walls with colorful framed prints by painter Jacob Lawrence, a Harlem Renaissance artist she had suggested to Ronn. He had bought six large prints to enliven the room. Her favorite was *Dreams I,* full of red and gold, a dark man and woman in bed at arm's length behind golden bedposts that looked to her like prison bars, with charms hanging over them while they slept. The grimace on the man's face was the portrait of a nightmare. Sometimes, the couple seemed to be sleeping, but when she blinked, they were dancing instead. The painting mesmerized her, always alive.

A piece of her lived in this room, Phoenix realized.

The flatscreen plasma TV mounted on the wall was tuned to the afternoon news, and the chatter captured her ear. "—erupted in the quiet

Leimert Park district of Los Angeles today in what police say is part of the ongoing feud between rapper and actor G-Ronn and rival rapper DJ Train. One unidentified man is in the hospital today after at least five gunshots were fired. A gunman ambushed . . ."

She could be listening to a story about someone she'd never met.

"You have to make the smart play, Phoenix," her mother's voice said from the cell phone pressed to Phoenix's ear, and déjà vu mingled with Phoenix's sense of shock. Hadn't they just had this conversation yesterday? Mom had called her as soon as she'd seen G-Ronn's name streaming across the bottom of her television screen while she was watching a congressional hearing on CNN. "I know you've invested a lot in this relationship, but—"

"We're not dating anymore," Phoenix said, the sixth time she'd reminded her today.

"I'm happy to hear it, but that's not the relationship I'm talking about. Is this CD worth risking your life? Are you blind to this insanity?"

Phoenix wanted to say *Of course not, I was there,* but she didn't. She and Sarge had decided it was best if Mom didn't know how close she'd been to the shooting, another lie. Ronn had kept her name out of the police report. There was no need to mention her, since eight other witnesses had seen what happened up close. Like Carlos said, if she repeated the lie often enough, she might forget the truth.

"What kind of world is this you're moving into? I hardly know you anymore, Phoenix."

Phoenix sighed. "You do know me, Mom, and it's not my world. I'm just a singer."

"That's *not* all you are," Mom said, her angry voice shaking. "You're brimming with creative spirit, and I'll never understand why you're taking the easy way out. Is money so important to you?"

"You think this is *easy?*" Phoenix said, her face flashing hot. Phoenix stroked Max between his ears, and the dog nuzzled her calf, her sole comfort.

"Yes, Phoenix, hiding behind someone else's music and name is easy. What's harder is being brave enough to fail. What's harder is taking the time to find out who you are. *That's* how you share your gift with the world, not like this. I don't know what this is."

Phoenix set her jaw, waiting for her throat to unseal itself as her stomach tumbled. "I have to go, Mom. I have a lot to do. I'm singing on national television Tuesday night."

"Make sure your father calls me, please. Right away."

Would it kill you to congratulate me? "Thanks for the support, Mom. Bye," she said, and clicked off. If she felt like a teenager in Carlos's presence, she felt like she was ten with her mother. She was so angry, her skin was burning.

Her phone didn't ring again, so her mother wasn't going to call back, and Phoenix didn't want to either. Phoenix felt orphaned and dwarfed sitting alone in the expansive room, which was bigger than her entire apartment. Max whimpered and rested his chin on her foot. She petted him again, feeling tears gathering. All she did was cry these days.

". . . dates back to the early nineties, when both rappers achieved prominence in the midst of the East Coast–West Coast rap wars . . ." the newscaster's voice said. "But unlike the old vendettas—which most famously ended the lives of rival rappers Tupac Shakur and Notorious B.I.G.—this one refuses to die, dramatically illustrated by the drive-by shooting today—"

Phoenix fumbled with the complicated remote control, pushing buttons until she found the one to make the television go dead. Ronn was right: The media was eager to resurrect the East Coast–West Coast bullshit, ignoring the fact that Ronn had grown up in St. Louis and DJ Train was from Dallas. Phoenix didn't know the reasons behind their beef, but it had nothing to do with the old blood feud between the Los Angeles and New York rappers.

"There they go, tearing me down like they do every other brother out here tryin' to make it." Ronn appeared from behind the sofa, mopping his face with a hand towel. Max stirred, hearing his master's voice, but didn't leave his place beneath Phoenix's stroking fingers. Ronn sat beside Phoenix, leaving several inches between them.

"Your meeting's done?" For a moment, Phoenix could think only of small talk.

Ronn grunted. "Yeah, it's done. Sarge is lookin' for you."

This was their first time alone since the shooting. Phoenix reached to Ronn and pulled his head to her breast, like a mother, and he didn't resist. She wrapped her arms around his taut neck. There, she could feel arteries pounding the flood of fear Ronn's face refused to betray. "I'm so sorry, baby. I'm so sorry. Lamar's gonna be fine."

"Yeah, that's what the doctor said. I gotta head back over there, though. Felicha's still with him, but Aunt Rita wants . . ." Ronn stopped, suddenly. He raised his head to gaze at Phoenix's face, almost as if to remind himself who she was. Then he sat up straight and took his original position away from her, leaning his elbow against the armrest. He wasn't going to allow himself to confide in her, she realized. That made her sadder.

"Sarge said you hurt your knee, Phee. That true?"

"No, it's fine. I just bumped it. It's not even swelling."

Ronn looked relieved. "Listen, I'm sorry 'bout the way that went down, all that madness. Kai had to get us out of there in case somebody else rode up on us. Lamar was hurt, and I knew my boys would look after you. They're off-duty LAPD—"

"Don't even say it. I understand." Right after Ronn's SUV sped off, four TSR guards had circled Phoenix as if she were the president's wife, ushering her and Sarge inside.

"That shit will never happen near you again," Ronn said. Whatever tenderness she'd seen in his eyes earlier today was gone, replaced by something she didn't recognize. "We're gonna have to forget that dinner Saturday, a'ight?"

"OK," she said. Damn. Serena and Trey had missed their chance to eat with G-Ronn. She'd been looking forward to it, too, even if it was only for show.

"Everything's gonna be a'ight, baby girl. This shit's about to get handled."

She nodded, feeling nausea butt the base of her throat again. "You can rise above this, Ronn," she said. The words sounded empty and simplistic, even to her.

Naked annoyance flashed in Ronn's eyes, then melted away.

"Ronn . . . we've known each other a long time, right?"

"A year and two months," he said. She was surprised he'd memorized it.

"And I've never tried to worry about your business, have I?"

"No, because you respect me," he said. "It's a mutual thing."

"So I've earned the right to ask questions, right? Tell me what happened when Kai shot back at that car. Did he hit somebody?"

Ronn shrugged, dispassionate. "Kai don't miss. One of them niggers is dead, no doubt."

So, there it was. She had been present at a shooting scene where somebody probably had died. Phoenix blinked back her tears so she wouldn't show Ronn how fragile she felt, just as he didn't want to show her. "So why don't you just walk away from this now?" she whispered.

Ronn's beautiful lips pursed tight. "Can't do that."

"You'll lose *everything* over this, Ronn."

"If it's lost, it's already gone. I've got a bullet coming to me, Phee," Ronn said. His voice cracked slightly when he said her name. "I've been some places you never had to go, baby girl. Things went too far a long time ago, before we started rapping. I tried to move past it, but old history comes back to haunt you. I know what happened, and Train knows, and his beef is real. But I can't have crazy motherfuckers shooting down my nephew. I can't sit still for that. And even if I could, Train don't know when to quit."

"Maybe there's a way to have a meeting, to—"

"We both got friends tryin' to squash it. Shit, you don't think the whole *industry* don't want this squashed? But there's too much blood, Phee. Too much blood." Ronn sighed, resigned. He let his eyelids fall closed, weighted with worries she could only imagine.

Phoenix couldn't think of another word. Even during her unruliest days, Gloria had never brought her a problem this big. This was a problem she had no idea how to fix.

Suddenly, Ronn's eyes were open again, and he stood up. "Show everybody who you are on TV Tuesday, Phee," he said.

"I will." Phoenix could hardly force out words.

Ronn backed away. *"Come,"* he said, one word, and Max snapped to Ronn's heels, following his master. For an instant, Phoenix had thought he'd called her.

Phoenix walked behind Ronn and his dog the length of his house, past his tile, marble and stainless steel, beyond his weight room, his game room, and his living room with the white concert grand piano he kept for decoration, the one he said she'd been the first to play. The War

Room was closest to the front door, a traditional office and library. As they arrived, the Three Strikes crew was streaming out.

D'Real grabbed Phoenix and swung her in a warm embrace, as if they had never exchanged a sharp word in the studio. "Sorry 'bout today, Phee," her producer said, kissing her cheek. Manny hugged her next, then Katrice. They patted her, stroked her, fussed over her. Was she all right? Did she need anything? Phoenix said she was fine, and in that moment, she was. Safe in the bosom of her new family.

Sarge was waiting for her by the front double doors. Sarge's eyes were as red as the lenses in Ronn's shades. At first, she wondered if her father had been crying, a thought as alarming as the gunshots, but she decided he was only weary. "I'll go get the car," Sarge said, and slipped out without meeting Ronn's eyes, which seemed deliberate to her.

Phoenix knelt and hugged Max close to her face, allowing the dog to lick her with his warm, velvety tongue. She didn't know when she would see Max again, and she missed him already. "You keep your daddy safe," she whispered, hugging the dog's sturdy neck.

Ronn didn't offer Phoenix a good-bye, nor even a gaze.

Phoenix watched Ronn walk into his War Room, greeting the four near-silent men now huddled inside its doorway with handshakes and quick, one-armed embraces. Ronn's first meeting was over, and a new one was underway. The four strangers spoke so low she couldn't hear them, but their faces and eyes were armor. Ronn and these men were a marshal and his counsel.

Phoenix remembered the last scene of *The Godfather*—Michael Corleone accepting the destiny he'd fought so hard against, gathering his capos around him—as Ronn followed his friends into the War Room and pushed the door closed.

Carlos's apartment wasn't the same one she'd seen in Miami, but his decor was unchanged in so many ways that she felt she'd been there before. Even the framed concert posters on the walls and potted palm trees looked the same. The living room walls were an imaginative golden color, but to her glutted eyes his rooms looked cramped, and there were none of the fine touches and detailing she had seen at Ronn's. The only view through the glass sliding door leading to his small balcony was the apartment building across the street. But Carlos had his walls of CDs in his living room, his own riches on display.

"Where did you tell your father he was dropping you off?" Carlos said. He offered her a glass of white wine he'd poured in the kitchen, but she shook her head. He sipped it himself, taking a seat across from her at the Rooms To Go pinewood table in his dining area, a table that might be from a dollhouse, built only for two.

"I told him it was you. I'm sick of acting like I'm still in high school."

"What did he say?"

What had been more unnerving was what he *hadn't* said. Sarge had barely blinked when she told him, and his silence worried her more. "I guess he's just happy you're not Ronn," she said. In retrospect, it was obvious Sarge had told Ronn to keep away from her, and Ronn had agreed. She couldn't be mad at either one of them, but her nausea from Ronn's house had not entirely left. "I think he's just glad I had somewhere to go. He didn't want me to be alone."

"Today has been crazy for you," Carlos said, his eyes mournful. "What can I do?"

Phoenix smiled. "You're doing it. I didn't want to go back to my haunted apartment."

"I can do more," he said, rising from his seat. He stood behind her, and his palms found her shoulders, kneading. She instinctively tensed, pulling forward.

"Relax," Carlos said. "I'm good at this."

I'm sure you are, Phoenix thought, but she surrendered her muscles to Carlos's plying. Her bones melted beneath his touch, a fluidness that streamed from her shoulders and traveled the length of her body. She slouched, closing her eyes, her head dangling backward. Her head sank against his taut stomach, but she didn't move. From this position, so close, Carlos's cologne was a feather bed she could sink into and sleep.

"I just got out of a relationship," she said quietly. "I'm having ghost issues, and I could have been shot today. You're not going to get the wrong idea about me being here, are you?"

His magical fingers plied on. "You need a friend. That's the idea, no?"

"Thank you," she said, her eyes still closed. The truth was, wine or no wine, if Carlos slid his hands to her breasts and pinched her nipples with just the right pressure, she would be helpless. Her body felt starved for touch, her nerve endings chafing inside her clothes. But she'd tried sex as an antidepressant before, and it didn't work for her. "I'm just worried that . . ."

"*Shhhhh,*" he said.

"I'm not gonna lie, Carlos, I'm stressed out. I'm singing on *Live at Night* Tuesday, and I'm not ready. My voice sounded like shit at my lesson today. I need to start singing on a treadmill again and get in shape. And I have to figure out my hair. I look like I'm supposed to be the opening act in a coffeehouse, and this is *television.*"

"Your hair is beautiful. Don't be ridiculous," he said, sifting a few strands through his fingers, like gold dust. "You're talking too much. Relax, I said."

While Carlos massaged her, Phoenix felt her consciousness drifting. She imagined a man's dark hand giving her a rose, and she snapped to alertness, her eyes open. Away from the shooting and its aftermath, last night's dream disconcerted her again. She didn't remember all of it, but she could remember images. A rose. A black man in a formal black suit.

She noticed a stack of sheet music and books about Joplin and ragtime on Carlos's table. Phoenix hadn't recognized the pieces she'd played in her sleep when she'd studied them that morning, and none of the pieces had been "Weeping Willow" or "Bethena" again. They certainly hadn't sprung from *her* mind, that much she knew.

"Did you tell that curator guy to look out for our package?"

"He said he'll keep his eyes open for it. I mailed it to the Joplin House."

"That dream was the ghost's way of visiting me last night. I'm sure of it," Phoenix said.

"I agree," Carlos said, as if it were nothing, a discussion of the weather. "By the way, Heather says she sends you a hug. She heard what happened today. I hope you don't mind, but I told her about your dream and the music. She just laughed. She said Scott Joplin definitely wasn't interested in talking to anyone but you."

"What's going on, Carlos?" Phoenix felt a shudder wind its way across her shoulders, coiling down her spine to her tailbone. "Why did he pick me?"

"I don't know."

"Do you think it'll happen again? Do you think he'll follow me here?"

"If you're worried, I'll sleep beside you. If anything happens, I'll be there. If you start acting weird, I'll wake you."

His offer seemed magnanimous. Phoenix never would have asked a grown man who was attracted to her to sleep beside her with no expectation of sex. "You would do that?"

"Of course, Phoenix. Anything you want. Come—I'll show you."

Phoenix hesitated, wary, then she took his extended hand. They moved from his dining area to his living room, where he reclined on the sofa and pulled her against him after putting on a safe CD, Ladysmith Black Mambazo. He had told her once that he thought South African harmonies were the most beautiful on the planet, and hearing the tenderly blended voices, she had to agree. Under the music's massage, Phoenix fell in and out of wakefulness. True to his word, Carlos only hooked one arm around her waist and let her lean across his chest. He did not press his lower torso against her, keeping a pillow between them. Each time she opened her eyes, the sky was darker outside, but Carlos didn't move to turn on the lights, not wanting to disturb her. The room began to turn gray, as if a new morning was already beginning.

She would be able to sleep if she could get that gunfire sound out of her head, the crackles that had sounded like a string of fireworks and the explosions that had shaken the windows. She couldn't stop thinking about Ronn, worrying for him.

"What do you think of G-Ronn?" Phoenix asked Carlos finally.

"I've never met him."

"His music, I mean."

Carlos sighed, shifting his position beneath her. "I *loved* rap when it first came on the scene. I memorized The Sugar Hill Gang's 'Rapper's Delight,' and Run-DMC blew my mind with 'The Jungle,' then 'Walk This Way,' since I liked Aerosmith, too. And Ra-Kim laid it out with those great rhymes. Tupac's 'Keep Ya Head Up' is still one of my favorite rap songs. And I've got nothing but respect for Public Enemy."

"Hell, yeah," Phoenix said, smiling. " 'Fight the Power' is *the* song. I love that cut."

"Dancing is in my blood on both sides of my family, and I used to love the message in rap, too. The rawness. But something's happened. To tell you the truth, I was reading through those books on ragtime today, and you know what I thought? A lot of the stuff G-Ronn does isn't so different from a kind of music they called coon songs."

Phoenix sat up, gazing back at him incredulously. She expected him to be smiling, messing with her, but even in the dim light, she could see he wasn't. "OK, that's way too harsh. You sound like my mother now."

"But you *did* ask," he said gently. "Just hear me out. Spike Lee talked about that in *Bamboozled*, how so much rap has become a minstrel show. I don't blame the young brothers trying to get by. If there's a choice between rapping about selling rocks and selling rocks for real, I choose the rapping, I guess. But in Joplin's time, the country was crazy for these songs about blacks acting foolish and violent, slicing each other up. Songwriters got rich churning out that crap. G-Ronn's doing the same thing, Phee."

Carlos sighed. "Listen, I know he's close to you, and I *hate* what happened today. It's tragic, and I pray for his nephew. But I've been listening to G-Ronn's music since 'Playa Dayz,' and it hasn't changed. He's still slinging, fighting, and fucking up his enemies. Now it's 'Don't Fuck With What's Mine' and 'Funeral Party.' Come *on*. You can't tell me there's no relationship between that and someone trying to blow his head off. He shouldn't be surprised someone got hurt, and that someone could have been *you*. That makes me mad."

The gunshots came back, the memory so visceral that Phoenix flinched. She touched the arm Carlos had wrapped around her. "Ronn told me whatever happened with DJ Train goes back before his music," she said. "The music doesn't make it happen."

"But his music *celebrates* it, Phee. I cried all night when Tupac died. I'd met him, back when he was doing publicity for that first movie he was in, *Juice*. We talked for an hour about shit that had nothing to do with the movie, the state of the world and black America. I walked away thinking, 'Damn, that kid is going to set the world on fire.' And instead, the world set him on fire. As bright as he was, he'd been through too much to break free. So, yeah, I understand these guys enjoying their power, expressing their anger. I *get* that black men here haven't had the chance to say whatever the hell they want before. But in

South Africa, the superstars are rapping about AIDS prevention. I'm waiting for G-Ronn to stop lining his pockets playing dress-up for America's wildest fantasies. They're *coon* songs, Phoenix, and he should know better by now."

Phoenix felt a flare of pain in her chest. The man had been shot at today, and Carlos didn't have an ounce of compassion. "You're one cold-sounding SOB, Carlos."

"Maybe so. I know I love our music, or I used to. Mostly, my heart is broken."

While they weren't paying attention, the room had gone dark, with only the cool blue display from the stereo to show them their shadows. The South African singers in Ladysmith Black Mambazo were praising the rain in harmonies so pure they were fierce. Phoenix understood why Carlos was heartbroken. Too many kids in the ghetto heard G-Ronn's rap persona as a beacon, not a warning. Where was *their* beautiful music?

"He's not rapping anymore after this CD, he says," she said, a TSR secret. "And the label is experimenting with new stuff. That's why he's doing R&B. It's going to be different."

"Good. I hope so."

Across the room, Phoenix's cell phone rang inside her purse. She jumped up to grab it, thinking the curator might be calling about the faxed music. She moved so quickly that she dizzied herself. But Gloria's number, not Van Milton's, was on her green-lighted Caller ID. Damn. She should have called Gloria a long time ago.

Phoenix's cousin didn't return her cheerful greeting, speaking in a no-nonsense tone: "I only want you to say seven words, Phee."

" 'I'm sorry' is only two words," Phoenix said softly. "But I'm sorry."

"Not good enough. I want you to say you were wrong, and I was right."

Phoenix smiled. "You were wrong, and I was right."

"Very funny, but I'm not kidding. I bought myself a plane ticket today—yes, with my own money, since I've been mooching—but before I come, I want you to say those words. Some freakazoid was stalking you in your hotel room, and I was right to speak up about that kid Kendrick, even if it turned out he wasn't the one. You know I was. I'm

sorry about the fallout with G-Ronn, I really am, but we knew something like what went down today could happen. I was trying to protect
you, cuz. I was just doing my effing job."

Phoenix couldn't remember all of the things she'd shouted at Gloria
that night in St. Louis, but it had been bad. *Fuck off and go home,* maybe.
"I know you were, Gloria."

"Great. Now, say those seven magic words. And speak up so I can
hear, because your cell phone signal still bites."

Instead, for the first time, Phoenix told her cousin about her visits
from Joplin's ghost.

CHAPTER ELEVEN

Missouri
July 1904

*T*he train's shriek shredded Scott's veil of sleep, waking him as the giant string of cars careened around a turn. In the miles since Webb City, the *chunk-chunk-chunk* of the train's march across the tracks had been a lullaby. He'd spent an exhausting afternoon singing and playing at a picnic in the Jasper County town at the foot of the Ozarks; the dancing townspeople's energy had been endless, with calls for encores past dark. Webb City had virtually ignored *A Guest of Honor* when he'd toured there last year, but its citizens couldn't get enough dancing.

Where am I? Scott glanced through his window and saw darkness through the grime, save an occasional distant light flickering like a downed star. A cramp forced him to sit forward, and he stretched his back muscles, which were taut and sore from the hard wooden seat. He checked beneath the seat to be certain his black traveling satchel hadn't been stolen from its nook. The satchel was where he'd left it. Next, Scott slipped his hand inside his shirt to feel the thirty dollars he'd clipped there, safe from a pickpocket's reach. The lump was intact. He tried to read his pocket watch, but he couldn't make out the face in the weak moonlight that was overrun by the car's shadows. *You'd think the porters could light a lamp, at the least!*

For a full blurry minute, Scott forgot that Freddie Alexander occupied the seat beside him. His eyes, learning to see in the darkness, made out her head dangling forward, vulnerable to the train's swaying and grinding on the tracks. *My wife is sleeping beside me,* he thought, and the words caught themselves in his head, erasing every concern, every frustration. His wife was sleeping beside him. Freddie Alexander was his wife.

He had married this girl in the very living room where they had first sat together and she gave him *Alice's Adventures in Wonderland,* a book that had delighted him so much that he'd dreamed of it. He'd heard strains of "The Chrysanthemum" in his sleep, dreaming about the lost girl and the Cheshire cat, although of course Alice had looked like Freddie in his dream. Scott felt an unlikely kinship to little Alice himself these days, blinking his eyes at his strange new life in the rabbit hole. His wife—yes, Freddie Alexander was his *bride*—had danced at the picnic today, turning over her shoulder to look at him with such tender admiration while he played that he could not imagine what he could do in his lifetime to earn that gaze. (Small wonder Louis had criticized Belle so mercilessly! Scott hadn't realized a wife's eyes were capable of such esteem.)

The blanket he'd draped across Freddie's shoulders before he'd succumbed to sleep was now at her feet. Retrieving it, he found that dampness and muck had ruined it for her.

"Not that she needs a blanket," he muttered. The railcar was a sweltering cookpot simmering with a sour, awful odor.

The colored car was behind the locomotive, as always, so an ever-present spectral haze hung in the car, smoky sheen from the train's engine. Still, Scott and Freddie had sat closer to the locomotive to avoid the bucket behind a tattered curtain at the car's other end. The ammonia smell from the pisspot had grown stronger, the waste steeping in the heat trapped in the car. Scott's bladder called for relief, but he would rather deny nature's call. Freddie's bladder was more constant, poor girl. She'd pinched her nose and asked Scott to stand over her so the curtain wouldn't part and expose her to the crowded car. Even Freddie, who claimed to be fearless, had looked mortified that her husband of only a month was so close during such a private moment, never mind the strangers within easy view. But what choice had she had?

Scott was grateful Freddie was asleep. At least she might be spared any further indignity before they arrived in Sedalia. If the train was on time, they would arrive before midnight.

Freddie deserved more than a rock-hard seat in a stinking segregated railcar. She deserved more than the paltry thirty dollars he'd pocketed in

his half dozen performances between Little Rock and Sedalia since she
had been traveling with him from town to town. He was already tired,
between the World's Fair in St. Louis and his tour since their wedding,
but he would work day and night in Sedalia until he could rent Freddie
a proper house. He didn't want to rely long on the Dixons and their
boardinghouse, no matter how much his friends insisted it was their
pleasure to host them. Emmett Cook and Otis Saunders had already
written to him about how primed white folks were for dances and concerts, and his friends at the *Sedalia Conservator* would keep his name in
print. He would do right by this girl. He had promised her parents: *I'm
not one of those musicians who lives hand to mouth, playing all night and
never stopping to call anywhere home. I'll have a house and go home to it,
and my wife, every night.*

By God, he hoped he hadn't married this girl on the basis of a lie, no
matter how innocent his intention. What if he'd only confused his
dreams and this waking toil? Should he warn Freddie she might be trailing after him and sleeping in train cars forever?

Scott saw Freddie's smile before he realized her eyes were open.

"I've become an honorary show person!" she said. "Never the same
town in two nights. I'm going to hate myself for neglecting my diary.
Where are we now?"

"Close to Sedalia, I pray. I wish you'd gone to the white car like I asked,
my love." His voice was gentle, but he felt annoyed. Freddie had seemed
shocked when he suggested she walk onto the whites-only car as if she belonged there, but he wished she had trusted his judgment. Freddie's stubbornness had been no illusion, and how he'd inherited it. Imagining
Freddie in a sleeper car, or even a dignified third-class seat where she might
eat a meal, would have brought him so much more peace. In Freddie's
company, his frustrations were threefold. He couldn't remember ever feeling this agitated on a train, as if he might cuss out a porter because the car
had no light and smelled like an outhouse. He cracked his knuckles,
kneading restless hands. His friend Otis Saunders was happy to change
from Negro to white at any opportunity, vanishing in midconversation
with a quick tip of his hat and a smile: *See ya later, boy.* Freddie could have
made it a game like Otis and put his worries to rest.

Freddie rested her hand over his. "I don't pass," she said. "My mother's the same. It's a political choice. I hold that higher than personal comfort."

The childish girl he'd met was already gone, replaced by the woman he'd married. Scott didn't know either of them well, but each day with Freddie surprised him in ways big and small.

"I respect that," Scott said, relieved to know she wasn't simply contrary.

"It's the same reason you won't cork your face," she said.

"Blackface is becoming unfashionable nowadays. I wouldn't call it political."

"Others still do it. If you're like most people, you're more political than you think."

Scott tried to gaze through the folds of night to see his wife's shining eyes. "Lean against me," Scott said, putting his arm around her, and she sank against him, soft and pliant. After glancing around the empty car to see that the three other passengers were sleeping, Scott ventured a kiss to her cheek. Her skin felt hot to his lips. "You're burning up, Freddie."

"This heat," she said. "I'm all right."

"I bet you're sorry now you didn't wait in Little Rock for me to send for you from Sedalia. I told you that would have been easier for you."

"And wait all that time to meet the man I married? A whole month?" she said.

"There's letters, like while I was at the Fair." As magnificent as the World's Fair was, Scott's correspondences with Freddie had surpassed all of its offerings. He had walked through the fairgrounds with Freddie in his eyes, seeing her doubles everywhere he looked.

"Letters aren't the same. We were courting then. I'm your wife now."

"Yes, my wife who won't listen to what's good for her. So . . . my *wife*," he said, giving her a private squeeze. "What do you think of what you've married? Dances and picnics and parties?"

"And concert halls," she reminded him.

He smiled. Her imagination was vivid! That would be extraordinary, indeed. "Yes, and concert halls."

"And boardinghouses," she said, and he saw the bleached gleam of her grinning teeth.

Scott's trousers, clinging with perspiration, felt heavy against his groin, suddenly. "Yes, and boardinghouses," he said. He'd first seen Freddie without her clothes in a boardinghouse, on a brass bed with a red blanket and four white goosefeather pillows. She had boldly posed herself like a photograph across the pillows for him, but she'd been a virgin. The spots of blood on the bedsheets told him that.

"I can't imagine having more fun, or loving my husband more, that's what I think." Freddie's voice became hoarse, a whisper. "I feel guilty for it, like I'll be scolded."

"You'll never be scolded by me," he said, and this time his kiss met her lips. For all her talk about freedom from convention, Freddie only allowed his brazen kiss to linger a second or two before she pulled her mouth away, shy about the public display even on a darkened train. But she had no shyness behind closed doors, only unself-conscious curiosity. She'd known next to nothing of lovemaking, and wanted to know everything.

A moving bulk told Scott one of the other passengers was waking. He couldn't make out any features, but it was a large man. The man stood and started toward them in a way that made Scott sit up straight, tightening his grip across his young wife's shoulder. He hoped he wouldn't need the razor in his pocket, but he never traveled without one.

"You looking for someone?" Scott said. If not for Freddie's presence, he might have stayed quiet until the man announced his motives. Now that the stranger was closer, Scott saw the snowy white of his long beard and smelled strong spirits on his breath. This stranger might have bathed in the past week, but not in the interval. He was holding some kind of sack in front of him, and the scent of food made Scott's stomach rumble.

"I got fried chicken. Two pieces and a biscuit, twenty-five cent," the man said.

"That's highway robbery. It's worth a dime, if that," Freddie whispered to him.

"We'll take four pieces, two biscuits," Scott said. He reached into his pocket for two quarters, glad he wouldn't have to bother his money clip. Usually he would have a sack of food for the train, but there hadn't been any left for him to take after the picnic. Freddie had been polite enough not to mention it, but he knew she was hungry. Scott lapsed into a folksier tone to compensate for his sharpness. "Don't make 'em all wings and drumsticks, neither. One of 'em better be a big ol' hunk of white meat. Who cooked this bird?"

"My grandmama cooked it," the old man mumbled, and Scott appreciated the lie, at least.

Scott hadn't seen the man on the train earlier, so he might have gotten on at the last stop. As his eyes sharpened further still, he saw that the man was wearing a large necklace of shells and chicken feathers that looked like a conjurer's costume over his stained shirt. *I know what to expect now,* he thought. Conjurers were the worst con artists, preying on hope and ignorance.

"I'll tell yo' fortune," the man said. "Twenty-five cent."

"I already got all the fortune I need right here," Scott said. "Good night, now."

"I got John the Conqueror root and bags o' luck. Twenty-five cent."

"No, thank you."

"Ain't nobody can't use a bag o' luck. Ten cent, then."

The man was only trying to earn extra money, Scott knew, but his persistence, coupled with his imposing size, made Scott uneasy. He was nearly as big as Tom Turpin. Scott guessed this con artist was accustomed to forcing sales just so his customers could be free of him. But he'd already spent half a dollar, and that was more than enough. Remembering Louis's gullibility only fed his irritation. Bag of luck! Even Scott's father had turned superstitious since Will's death, blaming curses and lighting candles.

"I said thank you and good night," Scott said evenly. "You're finished here."

The man laughed. "Oh, I'm *finished?*" he said, mocking him. "Nigga, where you from, tryin' to talk so white? You too biggity for a bag o' luck?"

"Maybe one bag?" Freddie whispered, close to Scott's ear. The man made her nervous.

"You've already heard my answer," Scott said, and rose to his feet to make his point. With a certain kind of man—men who were drunk, particularly—he'd learned to show he couldn't be pushed. Softheartedness was a weakness to some men, an opportunity, and he didn't know if this self-proclaimed conjurer was that kind.

"Oh, I see how you gonna be," said the man as he stepped back, reaching upward for the car's safety bar to keep his balance. "You got yo'self a high-yella woman and you think you white, huh? Got you a suit, so you ain't a nigga no' mo'?"

"I said good night, sir."

"Yeah, well, don't choke on none o' them bones . . . *suh*," he said, and whistled a tune that might have been merry except for his morbid tone. He tipped an imaginary hat at Scott, a gesture as perfect as any hotel porter's. "That's right, don't you choke."

Although the man was retreating toward his end of the car, his words remained rooted in Scott's memory, more potent than his physical presence. His warning about choking had sounded like a threat, as if he could will harm upon them. Scott cursed the quickening he felt of his heart. He might as well be an old woman clutching her *gris-gris* to ward off evil.

"The chicken's good," Freddie said, already at work on her first piece, which she held unself-consciously with bare hands. Nothing stood between this girl and her appetite. "I'm glad he came by. I was famished."

Scott sat again. The man had returned to his own his seat, although Scott couldn't make out his eyes. "I'm sorry I couldn't get you a proper supper."

"We would've missed the train! We ate a very late lunch, anyway." As always, Freddie refused to find any conclusions except the happiest ones. He should expect that trait to wear off after a time, but he would enjoy it while it lasted.

Freddie coughed. The hacking sound alarmed Scott, as if somehow that conjurer *had* visited a curse on her through his chicken bones, but when Freddie took a breath and kept eating, he realized she wasn't choking. He remembered hearing her cough once or twice before, but the sound hadn't been so harsh, from her lungs. "Are you ill, Freddie?" he said, pressing his palm to her hot forehead. "I think you have a fever."

"I'll be glad to sleep in a bed tonight," Freddie said softly. "I'm sorry, colds have always been drawn to me, since I was a girl. But nothing cures them like rest."

"How long have you been sick? Why didn't you tell me?"

"Tuesday, my throat started tickling. What could I say? Colds run their course."

"Not in drafty train cars. And on so little sleep, from town to town."

"Am I with my husband or my father?" Freddie said, annoyed.

"Always tell me if you're ill," Scott said. "Don't be an actress with me, Freddie."

Don't sound so cross when you're only angry with yourself, he thought. Belle had always said the house could burn down around him, and he wouldn't notice, he was so lost inside his music. When he was at his piano and Belle was out, their baby might have cried thirty minutes before he heard a thing. He should have guessed much sooner that Freddie wasn't well.

"I've been feeling poorly, Scott," Freddie said softly. "But you had your concerts. I didn't want to slow you down."

He pulled her close to him again, nuzzling cheeks. "I should have noticed. But I saw you dancing today . . ."

Freddie giggled, which drew another cough she politely hid behind her palm. "I couldn't help *that*. I've been denied dancing so long, I forgot my cold."

"Olivia Dixon will pamper you to death, I'm afraid. She won't let you out of bed."

"Yes, that sounds wonderful," Freddie said. "A bed."

The conjurer got off at the next stop, in Windsor, twenty-seven miles outside Sedalia. In the lamplight from the tiny depot, Scott saw the man look toward him and Freddie before he lumbered down the train's steps. Scott was relieved the man didn't speak to them again.

A white-coated colored porter poked his head into the car and announced they would reach Sedalia soon. "I sho' am sorry they ain't no light back here, Mr. Joplin," the young porter said, darting inside their car with a hushed voice. "This colored car's gone all to hell. Sorry to cuss, ma'am."

"I've been thinking that and worse," Freddie said.

"The conditions aren't your fault," Scott told him. "How do you know me?"

"Because you're a famous man, silly," Freddie whispered.

"Who don't know Scott Joplin? I seed you play lots of times in Sedalia. That's where I live. I heard you was ridin'." He came and stood directly before them, bending down to eye-level. "Ain't nobody left in third-class, if you wanna move. It's cooler down there, and better seats. Anybody tries to say nothin', blame it on me. This ain't my only job. I play piano, too."

The porter's offer for better seats could hardly have been more tempting, at that hour. But Scott glanced around the car, and two other colored passengers remained. He couldn't tell if they were sleeping or awake, but he felt confident that he knew his wife's mind on the question.

"What's your name?" Scott said.

"George."

"I mean your *real* name," Scott said. White passengers called every Negro porter George, so it was no wonder they forgot who they were.

The young man grinned. "George is the name my mama give me. I'm Lessie Mae's nephew, from 'round by the depot. Lessie Mae's brother Ben is my stepdaddy."

Lessie Mae was East Main Street's most successful colored madam, but so well-liked that she joined political groups and social clubs with no fear of exclusion. Her brother, Ben, was a respected minister—and one of their clan, Lionel, was a good singer and dancer Scott had hired alongside his brother Will for *The Ragtime Dance* at the Wood's Opera House. Scott could only imagine the far-ranging conversations at their family Christmas dinners. Scott hadn't seen Lessie Mae in years, but she had given him work when he needed it.

"Be sure to tell Lessie Mae I'll be dropping by to see if she's well," Scott said. "Thanks for your offer, George, but if this is the car for coloreds, this is where we'd better ride. Next time I come through, maybe I can afford a car of my own."

"I heard your Scott Joplin minstrel troupe was fifty folks strong. Musta been a sight!"

Maybe last year's tour *hadn't* been forgotten, Scott thought. "Well, we weren't that big, but we were an opera troupe. Started out that way, anyway." By the time most of the troupe's members had deserted, even before the final theft, they had to call themselves a minstrel company to get bookings.

Scott didn't know what the word *opera* meant to a boy who might never have heard one, but the porter's grin widened. "Yes, *sir,* an opera!"

The boy shook his hand, then studied his own palm as if he were trying to see his lines. "I just shook hands with Mr. *Scott Joplin,* who wrote the 'Maple Leaf Rag.' I better go pinch myself and make sure I ain't 'sleep."

Then the whistle sounded, and the porter vanished like a jackrabbit through the door.

"You have such a gift, Scott," Freddie said, as the train lurched forward.

"Music? Yes, it's quite a blessing." Without music, Scott imagined he might be a porter like George, or picking cotton, or else a railroad worker like his father, brother and so many Sedalia residents, braving terrible conditions. That work would have made him miserable, and he was damned lucky to have avoided it. He never forgot that, not a single day.

"Your real gift is for making Negroes feel proud," Freddie said. "I'm not as fond of Booker T. Washington as you—he doesn't make enough demands!—but if you think he's one kind of Moses, then you can be another. Those were *your* words, not his, you wrote in that opera. Your music can help free our people from their binds, so no one can make slaves of us again."

Scott couldn't discard Freddie's talk of Negroes as slaves again. He might have laughed a few years ago, but not anymore. True, the number of colored doctors, lawyers, ministers and clerks was growing all the time, and their race now bore writers and poets, including Freddie's beloved Dunbar, whose love poems she now recited to him nightly. But Scott had traveled enough to see the fear and despair. The growth of segregated facilities after the ominous *Plessy* ruling in '96 was the first wind of it. A violent storm was spreading, and closer to home.

He'd heard about a young trombone player, Louis Wright, who'd been lynched in New Madrid a couple years ago, near Missouri's Kentucky and Tennessee borders. The way Scott had heard it, the young man had cursed at whites throwing snowballs at him, and one thing had led to another until there was a riot at a theater. The entire troupe had been jailed, and Wright had died at the end of the rope. Scott's father had told him he couldn't remember a time he'd heard about more lynchings, even before Emancipation. And anyone who wasn't a blind fool could see that Reconstruction had failed, with little hope of resurrection. Times *were* dire.

But what could a musician do?

"I'm well liked in Sedalia among Negroes and whites both, and I aim to get my feet under me," Scott said, eager to change the subject. Freddie's admiration felt burdensome. He'd be satisfied with a reliable bank account these days. "I don't give speeches. I write music. I'm lucky to be in demand for picnics and dances."

"What you see in yourself doesn't matter," Freddie said. "It's what *they* see. You're a Negro, and you've reached a high station. President Roosevelt probably knows your name."

Scott covered his face, shaking his head. "Come now, Freddie. I doubt that." He had dreamed of seeing *A Guest of Honor* performed at the White House one day, but that notion had been another casualty of the tour. How had he expected to make it to the White House when he couldn't survive a handful of performances? Or overcome the treachery of low character in the theft by another Negro?

"You can help us *all* get better seats on the trains, and equal treatment everywhere. Your music gives you a platform, Scott. You'll be heard." Freddie spoke so emphatically that her words triggered a coughing fit, and Scott was ready to leap up to find a tin of water for her when Freddie waved with both hands to tell him she was all right. Her gray gloves swooped like doves in the dark. "The smoke excites me, I think. I'll have to stop talking so much."

"All I want," Scott said, "is to get my wife out of this smoky car. And safely to bed."

"I'm sorry I got sick. I should have stayed in Little Rock," Freddie said, sounding tired; her new bride's facade cracking at last. "Don't come too close to me, or you'll be sick, too. *That* would be a catastrophe. You have to be well to play."

Belle had thought his concerts were a bore at best, a nuisance at worst, but Freddie was still charmed by them, protective. Scott prayed that would last awhile. If so, he was married for certain! He kissed his wife's feverish forehead and held her to his side, feeling her heartbeat against his breast. "I would rather have you with me, sick or well," he said. "And you'll be well soon, dancing to make up for all the time you've missed. I'll teach you how to cakewalk, so no one will guess how behind the times you are. I'll teach you all the dances I know."

"And you'll bare your soul like Paul Laurence Dunbar? You'll go back to your opera?"

Truly, she was relentless. "One day, I suppose, Freddie. Of course I will, by and by."

Satisfied with his promise, Freddie closed her eyes and slept.

Marching music accompanied the train's moans and hisses as it came to a rocking stop inside Sedalia's stately Katy Depot. Scott wiped dark dust from his window with his handkerchief to see the ruckus: A dozen members of the Negro Queen City Band were assembled on the platform, playing a rousing rendition of the "Washington Post March," the cornets, clarinets and trombones bobbing to the tempo. The soaring structure amplified their music, making it all the grander. The band members were even wearing snappy uniforms in blue and red, and matching caps, no longer a bedraggled group. Emmett Cook, as usual, played the bass drum, and Scott was glad to see his friend wasn't in jail, which had been the rumor. Scott didn't know most of the other young men's faces. He had been gone too long.

Emmett saluted Scott with his drum mallet raised high, then spun it, grinning, before he found the beat again. At that hour, they'd be lucky if they weren't locked up for disturbing the peace! At least there was little fear of lynching here. Scott had been reared in Texarkana—and he would always love St. Louis—but Sedalia might have been his home all along.

"I've married a prince," Freddie said, leaning over him to take in the sight of the band.

"No," he said, smiling. "They're good folks, and I'm missed here."

The night Scott Joplin arrived with his new bride in the town where he had composed his most beloved song, he couldn't imagine needing any luck beyond that.

CHAPTER TWELVE

Los Angeles

Phoenix was congratulating herself on a night of normal sleep when she saw the piano.

Since she was not in her own bed, first she had to remind herself where she was: *This is Carlos Harris's bedroom. I agreed to sleep in here last night.* Carlos's queen-sized bed was big enough to give them space without touching, as he'd promised. First question answered. But although Phoenix had been dead tired when he dragged her to bed at midnight, she was sure she would have remembered seeing a shiny piano with a tall, old-fashioned wood cabinet blocking his closet door, so big and misplaced that it jutted almost as far as the bedroom doorway. This piano didn't belong in Carlos Harris's bedroom. ROSENKRANZ, said the label painted in gold across the upraised key cover, above the keys.

This piano *especially* didn't belong here, she realized, examining the instrument in the silvery morning light. The piano's appearance was all wrong, dramatically altered—but she *knew* this piano. She knew its height, its width, its decoratively carved legs, its engraved flowers on the pale rosewood cabinet, and especially its two candelabra spaced above the keys to give light in the time before electricity. She knew its stare. This piano was a ghost, its youth restored. This piano had chased her down the stairs.

Phoenix heard Carlos breathing slowly behind her turned back. Carlos was here, asleep, and that simple knowledge was Phoenix's anchor to sanity. There was nothing to panic about. All she would do, she decided, was roll very slowly onto her back, reach over to shake Carlos, and ask him if he could see the piano, too. Maybe the piano wasn't really here. Or, maybe she *was* dreaming. Carlos could tell her one way or the other. She would have launched her plan if she hadn't noticed the foot of the bed and forgotten her plan altogether.

There, a black man was sitting at the edge of the mattress, not three inches from where her feet were entwined. He sat with his legs wide apart, hands clasped between his knees, staring at the carpeted floor. If she twitched, she would kick him.

So this IS a dream, Phoenix thought, her heart slamming her chest. But in truth, her heart was sending out an alarm because she did not feel like she was dreaming. Last night's dream had seemed real at the time, but Phoenix understood the difference now. Last night, she hadn't felt the stabbing awareness that she was awake, the constant on-slaught of reminders. The satin bedsheets against her skin, the lumpy mound in the center of her pillow, or her skin itching all over, starting at her feet. The smell of Carlos's aftershave, the thin cobweb billowing beneath the air-conditioning vent, and the words *Calle del Cristo* painted on the artwork shaped like a miniature country storefront hanging on Carlos's wall.

Irrefutable clues that she was wide-awake were everywhere.

Phoenix dug her nails into her palm so hard that she carved raw crescents into her skin. She would rather hurt herself than risk a movement that might make the man sitting on the bed look toward her, or chase him away.

That is not a real person. That is Scott Joplin's ghost, and he's not going to hurt you, Phoenix thought, trying to soothe herself, but she couldn't forget she was lying: She didn't *know* he wasn't going to hurt her, she only hoped he wasn't. She was pinning her hopes on a psychic's conjecture and movies about sad, yearning ghosts. The hard truth was, she didn't know anything about this realm that kept brushing against her shoulder. She had not known this man in life, and she knew him less in death. *Please, please go away. Shit shit shit, please leave me alone.*

Phoenix's feet trembled. Her efforts to lie still turned her muscles against her, shooting conflicting impulses across her rigid, restless body. Her eyes kept trying to look away from the man who wasn't there, as if she hoped he would vanish if she blinked, but Phoenix forced herself to stare. The veins in her neck bulged from the effort, but she was going to look at him the way she would stare directly at an eclipse, even if there were consequences.

The man's profile didn't look like the stoic photograph she had studied these past days; his jowl seemed looser, and his lips were almost Ronn's, with that plump velvet cushion on the bottom. He was darker than Ronn, maybe half Ronn's size. His skin was onyx against his downy white dress shirt. His hair was wiry, tiny black coils. Agony had hollowed out the exposed side of his face. He might be praying or crying, or both. He was the portrait of misery. On her bed. And he was dead.

Phoenix's mouth shook as words tried to bring themselves out for air: *What do you want from me? What can I do to help you?* But the words never came. Phoenix borrowed more oxygen from her lungs, trying to speak, but her voice had shut itself down, useless. She had never been more sorry to be afraid. But if he looked at her, she might faint. And if he *touched* her . . .

On her nightstand, Phoenix's cell phone rang, and her fear set itself free as a scream. Her eyes went to the phone for a half second as she remembered where the ringing had come from. A second at most. But when she looked back, the man at the edge of the bed was gone. The piano, too. Phoenix felt like she was a part of a slideshow clicked to the next image, this one not quite identical to the last.

"C-Carlos," she said. Her arm flailed for him.

Carlos's eyes were already open, slits nearly hidden in the shadows across his face. He lay stock-still as a corpse, his eyes trained on the spot where the ghost had been. "I saw," he whispered, not moving, as if he still expected the visage to come back. "He was there . . . ten, fifteen minutes." Carlos didn't sound blasé anymore. He was a man who had seen a ghost.

"Why didn't you wake me up?" Phoenix felt a flash of irritation.

"I couldn't. Anytime I moved, he seemed to fade. I pretended to be asleep."

"Did you see a piano, too?"

"No. I saw a man sitting on the bed."

"In a white shirt?"

"Yes. And he was posed like Rodin's *The Thinker,* but his hands were folded. Every few minutes, I heard him sigh. Most of the time, he was looking right at you."

By the time Phoenix noticed her phone again, it was on its fourth ring. The 314 area code told her who it was, and she thanked God for his timing. Her hands were so unsteady, she dropped the phone and had to slide from his bed to retrieve it from the floor.

"Mr. Milton?" she said, afraid she'd missed him.

"Yes, it's me," Van Milton said, sounding as relieved as she felt. "I—"

"The ghost was just here. In my bedroom. He was sitting at the edge of my bed, I swear. He was right *here.* Can you please tell me what's going on?"

A blast of static on the line made Milton's voice hard to hear. Puffs of her hair fell across Phoenix's earlobe, and she brushed them aside while she strained to listen. "I was hoping you'd tell *me,*" Van Milton said. "I need to see you, Miss Smalls. Right away. How can I find you?"

"I'm in L.A.," she said.

"So am I. I just landed, so I'm using my cell phone. After I saw the faxes you sent me, I took the first flight I could find."

*V*an Milton looked like he might be in his bedclothes when he met Phoenix and Carlos in the TSR lobby at eight-thirty in battered gray sweats and a faded T-shirt from a Sedalia ragtime festival. His eyes were overanxious and rest-broken, so he probably hadn't slept on the overnight flight. By the way he lurched to his feet, he might have dozed off waiting for her.

Phoenix hadn't wanted to meet the curator in such a public place, but there was no way around it. He'd refused to discuss more on the telephone, and she had an appointment in Ronn's office at nine with Katrice, Manny and Jamal Lewis, the director of her music video. Sarge had been surprised when she said she didn't need a ride to the studio—*So you're still with him,* he said, the *him* being Carlos—but he'd kept his criticisms to himself. She'd see her father at the meeting. Felicha told Phoenix that The Mothership was free, so she and Carlos met privately with the curator in Ronn's most prized studio, which Phoenix thought befitted the occasion.

Phoenix told Van Milton about the ghost they'd seen on her bed. While he listened—or half listened, she thought—the curator spread the pages of sheet music she'd faxed him across the control boards until paper blanketed the machinery, a makeshift exhibition.

When she was finished, Milton tapped the silent keyboard of the gray Yamaha MOTIF ES. "How do I get this to work?"

Since that was one of the few questions about Ronn's studio Phoenix *could* answer—and despite the violation of The Mothership's number one rule, *Nobody better fuck with the equipment*—she was happy to turn on the synthesizer and test a key. Her touch set off a blast from a techno-happy brass section, which made them all jump. "Let's try a piano," she said.

Milton nodded. "Please."

That done, the curator's practiced fingers launched into a ragtime melody on the MOTIF's convincing imitation of a piano. Despite its cheer, the music filled Phoenix with dread even before Milton spoke. She didn't know this song, yet she did. "This is 'The Chrysanthemum.' When I pulled your fax out of our machine, it jumped out at me in the first measure. Joplin dedicated it to Freddie Alexander, who was soon to be his wife," he said.

Freddie again. It might be a melody Phoenix had heard in her sleep, but she couldn't be sure. Phoenix wrapped her arms around herself, rubbing her skin for warmth. The Mothership always got cold overnight, so it was frigid, ghost or no ghost.

"Joplin's publisher claimed it was inspired by a dream about *Alice's Adventures in Wonderland*. It's good work, from 1904, available in any full collection of Joplin's rags. So when 'The Chrysanthemum' was at the top of your stack of so-called ghost music, I asked myself, 'Why is this girl trying to make me out like some fool?' I almost didn't bother with the rest. I'd had an aggravating day . . ." Milton's hands tinkled out a rapid melody in a different key.

"But *this* one caught my attention. I didn't recognize it right away because I've never known how it begins. I called it 'Page Two,' the second page of an unpublished Joplin manuscript. One day in 1947, Joplin's widow invited a photographer to the house, and he captured one of Scott Joplin's unfinished manuscripts in a photograph. An enterprising

young man in Chicago, Reginald R. Robinson—he's a friend of mine—
was researching Joplin a few years ago when he found that photograph
of handwritten sheet music. Well, Reginald—now, he's a bright young
man who also happens to be a self-taught musician from the projects—
had the brilliant idea that if he *enlarged* the photo, he could see the
music clearly enough to transcribe it, which is what he did. He recorded
it for the first time on his last CD, all thirty-one seconds of it. It was a
rescue, because that original sheet music in the photo has been lost, like
everything else Mrs. Joplin had in the 1940s. Or, we'd *thought* the music
was lost."

At that, Milton gazed at Phoenix above his glasses, a significant look
that made her realize he had not made up his mind about whether to
trust her. "But now, thanks to you, I also have Page One. And pages
three and four, which make it complete, so I was able to play the whole
thing last night. If it's what you say it is, I'm the first to play the entire
piece since the man who composed it. Except for *you*, that is. In your
sleep." His tone was skeptical.

"I'm just telling you the way it happened, Mr. Milton," Phoenix said,
defensive.

"Yes, so you've claimed," he said with that same undecided, blank
look again. "I should tell you, Reginald said he had a similar experience
at the Joplin House, in the parlor. He sat at our piano for two hours and
composed something he called 'The Ventriloquist.' He told me he felt
like he was channeling Joplin's spirit. The piece is good, and it sounds
like Joplin, but Reginald is an excellent composer. My guess is, there's a
thin line between revelation and imitation."

"Not with me," Phoenix said.

"We have it on video," Carlos said, speaking for the first time. He
stood apart from them beside one of the video games near the door. "It
may not prove she was sleeping, but if you saw the tape . . ."

Milton half shrugged, shuffling through his pages of scores. "If it
were done cleverly enough, how would I know? Any good composer
could imitate Joplin's style." He sighed, gathering several pages in his
hand and slowly pulled off his glasses to pocket them. "I have a sense of
humor, so when I came across 'Page Two,' you got my attention. It's
pretty obscure. But I could have called you from St. Louis about that. I

didn't need to use my sister's discount flight pass to get here overnight."
Milton's eyes shimmered as he gazed at her, probing as if he hoped to see
past her mask. "Then I got to the next pages. These. And I had a different feeling."

He showed her a longer score, which began with a florid introduction
over a two-step tempo. He had at least fifteen pages of it, continuous.

"Yeah, that one's different," Phoenix said. "Some of it looks like ragtime, some doesn't."

"It's an opera," Milton said quietly. The hum of the equipment almost swallowed him.

"Didn't Joplin's opera go to Broadway in the seventies?" Carlos said.
"*Treemonisha?*"

"This isn't *Treemonisha,*" Milton said. He hesitated, begging Phoenix
with his eyes to confess it now if she was trying to scam him.

"I didn't even know he wrote operas," Phoenix said. "All I know
about Scott Joplin is what you told me on the tour. I heard about his
wife named Freddie, and that's it."

Milton sighed, going on reluctantly. "Volumes of Joplin's manuscripts have been lost. Before she died, his widow said he had more songs
unpublished than published, but it's all vanished over the years, the kind
of thing that drives music historians crazy. One loss is especially sad,
given its significance. In fact, one time we found a trunk in the attic of
the Joplin House and we got excited, thinking maybe it was *the* trunk.
But it wasn't."

"What trunk?" Phoenix said.

"Joplin lost a trunk in 1903. Supposedly, every copy of his first opera,
A Guest of Honor, was in that trunk, and it was never retrieved, so it's
lost. No one has laid eyes on it in more than a century, yet I might have
a copy of the first pages in my hand."

"Is there a recording of it?" Phoenix said, her heart skipping.

"No, unfortunately," Milton said.

"Then what makes you think this is it?" Carlos said.

"I don't know how I know it, but I do. It's vintage Joplin, start to finish. If it's not *A Guest of Honor,* what's the point of all this? *A Guest of
Honor* is the one scholars have been bedeviled by, and I assume that's
why you've just given it to me." Milton waited, watching their faces.

Phoenix thought her eyes must be blank, because her thoughts were a cacophony.

Carlos came closer, staring at the music in Milton's hand. *"Dios mio,"* Carlos said. "If you're so sure it's Joplin, why don't you believe what we've told you?"

"Why? Why *would* I?" Milton said with a sarcastic chuckle. "All these years, there's been a storm of speculation about Joplin's missing music, especially his lost opera. And here you come sending it to me over a fax machine? If it's authentic, you got this music somehow. Maybe you're brokers. That I understand. But why tell me it came to you in a dream? That you were sleepwalking? You must think I'm a special kind of fool."

"You're the one who told me about the ghost," Phoenix said.

Milton's eyes spilled a hidden pool of anger. "Yes, and I've worked there for *ten years,* and I've played the piano in that building night and day, and nothing like you described has ever happened to me." He sounded as envious as Heather Larrabee, and Phoenix felt sorry for him.

"He didn't choose you," Carlos said evenly. "He chose Phoenix."

There was a knock at the studio door. Felicha stuck her head in, apologetic, saying something about Jamal Lewis being there early, and how he wanted to know if Phoenix could go with him for coffee down the street so they could talk about the video.

At that instant, it was excruciating to think of sitting at the cafe to discuss the finer points of the "Party Patrol" music video, or whatever else might be on her director's mind. Phoenix didn't look over her shoulder at Felicha, keeping her eyes on Milton. "I can't," she said. "Tell him I'm sorry. Tell him I'll be out as soon as I can."

As soon as the door closed again, Milton spoke rapidly, knowing their time was almost finished: "Please tell me you have the originals of the pages you faxed to me?"

Carlos held up his satchel. "As original as they can be, from a Mac. It's 188 pages in all. Your copy is probably sitting on your desk back at the Joplin House."

Milton looked alarmed, reaching into his back pocket for his cell phone. "I'll want to see those you have, of course. But I'll call my office and tell them to guard that package like gold. I've already faxed my pages to a ragtime scholar in New York named Edward A. Berlin. He's likely to have a different idea about it—he'll assume it's a fraud, since he's seen others—but I want his opinion. And I didn't want it lost again, no matter what our outcome here today."

"What kind of outcome?" Phoenix said.

"You tell me," Milton said. "What are your plans for this music?"

"I don't have any plans," Phoenix said. "You can't seem to get that straight."

"What did you hope to gain by faxing this music to me?"

"I just want to know what's happening to me!"

Phoenix wondered who was shouting so early in the morning, shrieking like a nut in the presence of an elder. Her body trembled, and she realized she was leaning against the console for support. She had an end-of-the-day headache already. Carlos guided her to a swivel chair, and she'd never been happier to surrender her legs and feet.

"This has been hard for Phoenix," Carlos said. "I need you to lighten up, Mr. Milton."

As Van Milton looked at Phoenix trembling in her chair, still clinging to herself for warmth, the gentle lines and creases in his dark face began to reshape themselves. His head tilted forward, and his eyes dimmed, then sparked.

"This music came to you in your *sleep*?" the curator said.

As if he was hearing it for the first time.

Sarge, what's up with your girl?"

"Good morning to you, too, Katrice," Marcus Smalls said, scanning the headlines of the *Final Call* newspaper he still sometimes bought by his barbershop on Crenshaw, just to see what Farrakhan's boys were talking about these days. Marcus could have used a few minutes' reflection before he ran into Katrice Daniels, since the intense, willowy woman reminded him of his ex-wife, a similarity that wasn't going to do their working relationship any good. TSR's vice president for marketing and promotion was six feet tall and hard to take in large doses, but he couldn't afford to piss her off. Katrice would be running her own label in a year. Besides, Katrice told you what she thought, a trait worth the price of the aggravation.

"Look, Sarge, you know how much I love Phoenix's vision, so I'm an advocate, okay? But she doesn't have her head wrapped around this process. She's not engaged. Between you and me, she got jacked in the studio with D'Real, and she's walking that same road again. Jamal Lewis is here to find out what she's thinking—which is so rare for Jamal that we should declare today a holiday—but where's Phoenix? She's got her own little meeting going on in The Mothership she can't pull herself away from, Felicha says. Can you please give your client a gentle 4-1-1 that if she wants to have a voice in her career, she better start using it now?"

Katrice had a clear-eyed way of seeing things that always made her sound like an oracle in a designer pantsuit and a bad mood. Phoenix had already complicated his day, and days were getting too short for complication. "Katrice, drink some tea and chill out, little sister," Marcus said. "Don't you think she might be a little distracted because she almost got shot yesterday?"

It was a cheat to bring that up, but sometimes Marcus couldn't pull his claws back.

Katrice pointed her pencil at him. *Touché.* "You hear me," she said and pivoted away.

Mentioning the shooting was the quickest way to be left alone. Even yesterday, at Ronn's, they'd all talked around the thing uppermost on their minds, with Ronn sitting there at his conference table like the emperor wearing no clothes. Marcus had let Ronn know he wasn't going to play the hear-no-evil-see-no-evil game when his daughter was involved. The first time Ronn had laid eyes on Phoenix—when Marcus had seen the light across his face—he'd told Ronn he believed in business being business and only business. *But if it's ever more than that, young blood, do me a favor and back off if there ever comes a time you can't be good for Phoenix.* Well, the time had come and left footprints. End of story. Marcus would not pretend that shit away, whether it was Ronn Jenkins or whoever-the-hell-else with a few million dollars.

He had brought his daughter here, and he was going to see her through.

"Stardom equals influence equals power," Marcus whispered, closing his eyes. On days like this, his mantra kept him from forgetting why he was here. Ronn Jenkins and Katrice Daniels could groom Phoenix and make her a star. Three Strikes knew how to move units, and sales were what Phoenix had always been missing. Stardoms equals influence equals power.

If she was going to work her ass off regardless, Phoenix deserved some money, not the thirty-thousand-dollar contracts she'd had to split with her band while they slept five to a hotel room so they could afford to go on the road. She'd be better off in law school, but if music was her calling, she'd better get on her feet so she wouldn't go out like Marvin, Bird and Billie, always broke. Even if she only recorded one CD with Three Strikes, she could save a chunk of cash. Inherited wealth was still the biggest disparity between blacks and whites, and he and Leah wouldn't have much to leave her. The cash they'd invested in Phoenix's career aside, Leah had drained them holding on to her father's club for all those years out of misplaced sentiment.

Marcus had no room for misplaced sentiment. Phoenix might be strong enough to stomach either poverty or obscurity, but he doubted his daughter could stand both. If an artist could find a way to make some money, hallelujah. And at least Three Strikes was black-owned, even if it wasn't Motown. (Hell, Motown wasn't Motown anymore either, he reminded himself). Ronn was a sharp kid. He reminded Marcus of his son Malcolm, as bright and hungry as his namesake, except his son had burned so much of his life energy trying to throw off the yoke of crack that he would be lucky to make a good living and have a family, much less excel. Unlike Malcolm, Ronn was one of the moths who'd gotten out of the jar.

But Ronn's money didn't come for free. Phoenix must not have been paying attention when Katrice told her Three Strikes expected her to do six months of advance publicity for *Rising,* and up to six months after that if the singles caught fire, like "Party Patrol" was already. Phoenix was lucky as hell to have the tour support, but Katrice was right: Phoenix was still idling at the starting line, and the race had already begun. That had been true before yesterday's shooting. That had been true for a long time.

Without knocking, Marcus opened the door of The Mothership and walked in.

The person closest to him, standing two strides from the door with his back turned, was Carlos Harris. Beyond Carlos, Marcus saw Phoenix sitting at the console, her head bent over a pile of papers while a man Marcus didn't know—a man who might be in his sixties, also shaved bald—spoke urgently to her. Katrice hadn't been exaggerating; Phoenix was in a damn *meeting* while Jamal Lewis was waiting to see her.

Carlos was closest to the door, so Marcus took Carlos by the crook of his arm and invited him outside with a tug that nearly pulled him off his feet. "Let's talk a minute," Marcus said with more civility than he'd believed he had in him. He was so quick, it was possible Phoenix hadn't seen him snatch Carlos before the door closed behind them.

Llamame, Carlos had said to Phoenix the other day, like a pimp snapping his fingers, but the smug smirk on Carlos's face was gone now. Instead of trying to yank his arm away, Carlos went limp against the wall. Few men forgot a good ass-kicking, and the empty early-morning hallway must have looked ominous. Sarge leaned on top of Carlos the way he had in the pen when he needed to make a point, his chest pressed to Carlos's, his face two inches away. This pretty boy was lucky he'd never done time, because he wouldn't have lasted long behind the wall.

"Mr. Harris." Marcus breathed down the bridge of Carlos's nose.

"I think you should calm down, sir." Carlos's head lolled, a guilty man's eye contact.

"You've been having a good time hanging with Phee these past couple days, huh? I've been meaning to ask you something: Do you have a good memory? I have a *great* goddamned memory. Ask me about something you think I should remember, and I'll tell you if I do."

"I'm not trying to fight you, Mr. Smalls," Carlos said, his hands shoulder high.

"I thought about you a lot back in the day, son. I had a catalog of ugly fantasies with your face attached, but I had to settle for the shit I wouldn't go to jail for. I sent a long complaint to your editor at the paper, and I spelled it all out. Did you ever hear about that?" Leah had signed the letter, too. Marcus had figured a letter from a white School Board member would get more attention than a black ex-con.

"Actually, you sent it to the publisher," Carlos said. "That letter almost got me fired."

"What I *really* wanted was send your ass to jail—and I've been locked up, so I know of which I speak. For me to want another nigga in lockup is really saying something, you dig? I never did know if Phoenix told me the truth, but I wish you could have gone to jail *just in case*."

Carlos's face looked sickly, and Marcus had to admit it felt good to have another conversation with Carlos Harris. Marcus was masterful at scaring people, but his skill was mostly wasted in polite society, aside from brushes with drunken clubgoers or hardheaded fans. This felt good, but it also felt *right,* a combination that was hard to come by.

"I didn't have sex with her," Carlos said softly, contrite. "We never did that, and we're not now. I really am sorry about everything. I wish I could go back and fix it. We're—"

"What the fuck good does an apology do me now?"

"Let go of me," Carlos said, not blinking. With his apology spent, his options must seem thin, Marcus knew. Marcus tightened his grip on Carlos's forearm, grinding muscle against bone. Carlos tolerated the pain, hiding it except in his squinting eyes.

"You disrespected me, Mr. Harris," Marcus said. "You disrespected my family. You disrespected my daughter, playing doctor with a school-girl because it made you feel like you had a bigger dick. There's no com-ing back from that, son. Phoenix is grown now, and I can't give her the eyes to see through you, but you better know right now that you will *never* earn trust or respect from me or my wife. That door is locked, and you don't have the key."

"I understand," Carlos said, his voice dull.

"Try, 'Yes, sir.'"

"Yes, sir," Carlos said.

Marcus finally let him go. "Now, what the *fuck* is so important that Phoenix is back here bullshitting with you instead of doing her damn job?"

And so Carlos told him.

*P*hoenix heard her father licking his fingers as he ate from the order of tandoori chicken he'd brought in from Punjab House down the street. He sat at a barstool at Phoenix's kitchen counter with his *Billboard* and a can of Red Bull. "So, what's your plan, Peanut?" he said.

Everybody wanted to know her plan. Milton, Carlos, now Sarge. Her only plan was to try to find the sense in her life again. Phoenix was sprawled across her futon with a cold, damp washcloth over her eyes while her Mac played back its recording of the music she'd composed in her sleep, glibly showing her the face of a new world. The music was vivacious and wonderful—priceless, Milton had said—and she had rescued it. But from where? And how?

"I keep thinking about this poem by John Keats," Phoenix said. She was so tired, she could only mumble. "He's my favorite poet we studied in my AP English class. He was really young, but he was sick, always afraid of dying."

"Marvin used to read Keats. Marvin was deep." When Sarge mentioned Marvin or Diana or Smokey in his stories, no last names were needed. Like Huey and Malcolm and Stokely.

"He has this poem called 'When I Have Fears,' and there's this great line: *When I have fears that I will cease to be / Before my pen has glean'd my teeming brain*. I've never been able to forget that line. It freaked me out when I read it. Like, damn, this guy knew he was gonna die, and he'd never have the chance to write all the poems he had in him. Scott Joplin must have felt that way, too. He didn't want his music to die with him."

"Yeah, welcome to the club," Sarge said. "Phee, you're adding a whole lot of chaos to your life you do not need right now. You need to let this Joplin shit go."

Phoenix pulled the washcloth away her eyes, stunned. Sarge cracked a chicken bone between his molars, gazing back at her. *Yeah, you heard me,* his eyes said.

"This is from the same man who sent me to the Joplin House?"

"I wanted you to pay homage. You've taken this to a whole new tier."

"I see what this is about," Phoenix said, disappearing behind the washcloth again even though her skin had leached away the coolness. "Carlos is involved, so you think it's bullshit. You don't believe me about the ghost."

After reading the full score, Van Milton had trailed behind Phoenix all day, asking questions when he could. He'd wanted to spend the night at her apartment, hoping for a musical encounter, but she'd sent him home with Carlos instead. Maybe the phantom piano would show up for him, at least. She'd noticed Carlos hadn't invited her back to his place, but she didn't mind. She didn't need to sleep anywhere she didn't have a toothbrush, because she didn't belong.

"What if I do believe it?" Sarge said. "What if I believe you saw this ghost and he sent you all this music? Hell, I saw what happened when you were ten. I was there. I've been in the world long enough that you can't surprise me. But it's done now. You gave the music to the experts, and you can let it go."

"Sarge, if you really believed me, you wouldn't say that."

"I'm not here to argue metaphysics, Phee. I'm living in *this* world. You missed an interview last night. Jamal Lewis felt dissed today. You're messing up. If you want to break your contract with Three Strikes and go hunting for Scott Joplin, more power to you. Just let me know, so I can start spending what's left of your advance on lawyers."

Sarge had a gift for bringing the vitals into focus. Phoenix had committed a year of her life to this CD, maybe more, and now it felt like millennia. She was trapped and hadn't noticed.

"What did you say to Carlos?" she said.

"Don't change the subject. If you have a question for Carlos, you need to ask Carlos."

"He's been a big help through this, Daddy."

"I didn't say anything he shouldn't have heard from you first."

"He heard it, believe me."

"He's heard it now," Sarge said, and licked his fingers again. "Katrice said something that blew my mind today, by the way. Thought you'd like to know."

"Don't change the subject."

"Katrice said you got jacked by D'Real in the studio. Those were her exact words."

"She said what?" Phoenix said. She sat up, grateful when no cannon-ball rolled between her temples. Her headache from this morning had erupted to a migraine, but she was feeling better.

"That's right," Sarge said. "Katrice said she wanted more of your vision in *Rising*."

"She didn't act like it." Besides D'Real, Katrice had been the main one always pushing her to sound more commercial, more R&B, more urban—in other words, more like everybody else.

Phoenix heard Sarge walking toward her, heavy soles on her tiles. He sat beside her. "Appearances are deceiving."

"Remember that about Carlos," Phoenix said.

"You remember that about Carlos, too." Sarge leaned over her as if he were telling her a bedtime story. "Next time you're in the studio, fight harder. Hold your ground. Marvin started doing his best-selling stuff, like 'Grapevine' and 'What's Going On,' when it was from the heart. People had to know him first, though. He didn't just come from nowhere. After *Rising,* people will know you—but you have to take it from there."

Sarge had done it. For nearly a minute, Phoenix had forgotten about her ghost and remembered her music. Sarge was a wizard, but his wizardry wouldn't be enough tonight. She wasn't going to be like Ronn, pretending her life was still in her control. Something had changed this morning, maybe when she'd seen the nape of Scott Joplin's neck. Something had changed when Van Milton told her the magnitude of the gift Joplin had given her in her sleep. Sarge might not be able to see it yet, but she didn't have a choice. Something had changed.

"I think I'm gonna get some rest, Daddy," Phoenix said. Her yawn began for effect, but it became real once it was in motion, mined from deep in her lungs.

"If you want, I'll stay here with you, Peanut."

"No," Phoenix said. "I'm fine by myself tonight."

For the first time, Phoenix wanted to be alone with her ghost.

Part Three

Goin' around.

Swing, swing, goin' around,

Keep on a-goin' around . . .

Scott Joplin
Treemonisha
Act I, Scene IV

CHAPTER THIRTEEN

*P*hoenix barely recognized herself in the mirror beyond the circus of bright lights. With a mortician's care, the makeup artist for *Live at Night* dabbed Phoenix's face with shine-resistant powder while Phoenix sat and stared, transfixed by her hair. Her forehead was bordered by tight rows of narrow, zigzagging cornrows, with her golden scalp glistening and radiant between them. Braids bound the front of her head, but the rest of Phoenix's hair was liberated in an explosion of puffing hair like a halo around her. In this bright light, Phoenix could see the tinges of red hiding in her dark brown Afro, nearly the color of her eyes. Serena was a genius.

"Are you sure you want to go with the Macy Gray look?" Gloria said behind her.

In the mirror, Phoenix saw her cousin puff on a Newport and pass it to Serena. Serena had quit smoking two years ago, gaining twenty pounds in the process, so she must be nervous today. Serena was forty-eight, and despite her expertly dyed hair, this was the first time Phoenix thought her sister looked her age, more like she could be her brown-skinned mother. Serena looked so much like Sarge, they were often mistaken for brother and sister.

"Snow White's got a point, Phee," Serena said. "I've got you looking fly, don't get me wrong, but you said G-Ronn wanted extensions. We should'a gone with that Italian weave I brought, and I could've had hair halfway to your behind. That's how all the big stars do."

Phoenix smiled. "This is the way I want it, Reenie. It's perfect."

"Yeah, that's right, Aunt Phee," Phoenix's nephew Trey said from the back table, where he'd been popping potato chips and cheese squares into his mouth. "Aunt Phee's keepin' it real. She wants to look *black*."

The makeup artist gave Trey a surprised glance over her shoulder, and Serena rolled her eyes. "Lord have mercy. Marcus made this child read *The Autobiography of Malcolm X,* and now he thinks he's Huey from *Boondocks*. Stop trying to talk like you're grown," Serena said.

It had been two years since Phoenix had seen Trey, and she'd been startled to discover that her little nephew was already half a man. If Trey were Jewish, he'd be studying for his bar mitzvah the way Mom had forced Phoenix to go to shabbat school for her bat mitzvah. Mom had said she wanted to pass on her heritage, even though she ate bacon regularly and let Phoenix go to church with Sarge. *Baruch atah adonai elohaynu malech ha'olam.* The prayers she'd learned still came back to Phoenix, mementos of somewhere ancient and far away. Sarge was teaching Trey his own version of his people's story.

"You look beautiful, Aunt Phee," Trey said. "Like a queen in Africa."

"Oh, she's a little princess for sure, but not the African kind," Gloria smirked in her best Long Island accent, and Phoenix gave her cousin the finger.

"Daddy? What do you think?" Phoenix said.

Sarge had been quiet today, sitting on the love seat in the back of the green room while he watched her prepare for the performance, occasionally snapping pictures for Mom with his digital camera. She was still the bridge between her parents, at least. "Trey's right. You look beautiful, Peanut. Whether or not the label will like that look for you, I don't know. I guess we'll see."

Serena made a quiet *humphing* sound, gently shaping the edges of Phoenix's hair. "Yeah, you figured out it ain't all about 'Black Is Beautiful' no more, huh, Marcus?" Serena said. Her voice was teasing, yet it wasn't. Serena had always called her father by his first name, maybe because he had been only seventeen when she was born, and it seemed to grant her license to say things Phoenix never would, like a scolding old friend instead of his daughter.

"Right now, it's about legacy and surviving the marketplace, Reenie,"

Sarge said. He stood and walked behind Phoenix's chair, wrapping both arms around her neck so he wouldn't muss her makeup or her hair. Phoenix felt self-conscious, since she never saw Sarge hug her sister this way. "You're beautiful, you've worked hard, and this is your moment. *Rising* is your *Rhythm Nation,* Phee. Two million people will see you tonight. After this, the charts are gonna be yours to take. Enjoy yourself out there. *Own* that stage." He kissed the top of her earlobe, and the rough stubble on his cheek brushed against her, tickling.

Gazing at their faces framed together in the mirror, Phoenix remembered seeing her parents' portrait on the wall in her dream, when she'd been preparing to leave home. An unnameable sadness welled in her. "Thanks for getting me here, Daddy. I love you."

"Love you, too. I'm gonna go check my messages."

That was Sarge's all-purpose escape from any room, and Phoenix wasn't surprised. Sarge always found ways to avoid being near Serena too long, even if he couldn't admit it. Serena was the only person with that power over him, because Sarge never backed away from anyone else. Sarge had told Phoenix he and Serena had been very close before he went to prison—she was fourteen when he was sentenced—and Serena had told Phoenix that she refused to visit him in prison, so she didn't see Sarge again until she was twenty-two. When Sarge and Serena were together, their missing eight years yawned between them, unspoken, even when they smiled.

Phoenix couldn't understand how Serena didn't hate her for getting everything from Sarge she hadn't. Her half brothers were happy to pretend Phoenix didn't exist, although Serena had told her that when she was famous, she'd see enough of Malcolm and Junior to last a lifetime. But Phoenix didn't miss her brothers today. All the people she cared about most were here, except for Mom, but Mom was everywhere in spirit.

He was here, too. But no one knew it except her.

Phoenix could see him. He was in the upper corner of the makeup mirror, where the lights converged to create a blazing, glowing ball too bright to stare into. That was him. Phoenix was tempted to point him out, but it had taken a lot of concentration to learn how to see him, and she'd learned after frustrating moments with Gloria that not everybody could. (*"What? So the light burned out. Big deal, Phee."*) He was every-where. A piece of paper had floated to her feet as she passed the recep-tionist's desk when she arrived for the taping, and that had been him again, invisible. Maybe he had always been following her, and she had just learned how to notice.

Serena hummed a few bars of "Party Patrol" under her breath, and Phoenix smiled.

"Sing it with me, Serena," Phoenix said. She'd been asking Serena for three days, but this was her last chance. "You'd tear it up out there on TV."

When she heard the word *sing,* Serena's head shook violently back and forth. Phoenix remembered when she'd felt that nervous about per-forming, when Sarge used to coax her onto the stage the way he'd coaxed her through physical therapy after she almost died. But Phoenix didn't feel nervous today, of all days.

"You're *such* a chickenshit, Serena," Gloria said. "You're the best singer in this room."

The makeup artist looked taken aback, but Phoenix only smiled. "She is," Phoenix told the woman. "You should hear her."

"How would I look, almost a fifty-year-old woman out there tryin' to be an R&B singer? And fat as hell, too? Please. Ya'll are trippin'."

"Who's fat? You ain't fat. Big is beautiful," the makeup artist said. She was bigger than Serena, but not as tall. Serena had height from Sarge's side of the family, so she was five-ten and solid, hiding her weight evenly across her frame. She looked good, except that Phoenix could remember how she had looked before her marriage to Trey's father broke up. To Phoenix, Serena's fifty extra pounds looked like a coat of sadness.

"Hey, listen here, ya'll," Serena said, "I don't know if *big* is beautiful, but Mickey D's fries and Dunkin' Donuts are damn masterpieces. They're straight-up works of art. O-*kayyy*?"

As they laughed, Phoenix saw that her ghost in the mirror was flick-ering instead of blazing. Was he laughing, too? Phoenix would like to think so, but it didn't seem likely. She hadn't seen him in the form of a man since the night she slept in Carlos's bed, but she imagined he was sighing near her even when she couldn't hear him. Otherwise, why would he still be here?

What do you want? What do you want me to do? The questions came to her again and again. She never forgot him long, even when she tried.

The door opened, and a passing woman stuck her head in. "Big man's comin'," she said, a warning, and walked on. Was Ronn coming to see her, or was he still in hiding?

The makeup artist stubbed out her cigarette and leaned close to Phoenix's ear, her voice low. Her breath smelled like tobacco and mint gum. "He don't come back here unless he thinks the guest is fine," she told Phoenix, and Phoenix knew then she wasn't talking about Ronn. "Remember, he's got two babies and a girlfriend."

"Uh-oh. Cockblock," Gloria whispered, and she and the stylist snickered.

When Alex Compton walked into the green room, the space suddenly seemed smaller because his presence was so large. He had a smooth face and a cleft in his chin, more like an actor than a comedian, and his snappy silver-gray suit was camera-ready. Phoenix felt currents shooting between Trey, Gloria and Serena when he appeared. There *was* something hypnotic about spying a familiar face on a stranger, Phoenix thought. She felt mesmerized herself.

Compton knocked on the open door even though he was already inside, just to make sure everyone saw him. "So, *this* is where the party's at! Just thought I'd pop in and holla, ladies. We're amped to have you with us, Phoenix. I'm Alex." He gave her a smile that looked dazzling in the mirror's reflection, nearly as bright as her ghost's light.

"Mr. Compton, can I have your autograph?" Trey said, bounding to him. Sarge had already asked G-Ronn and D'Real to sign Trey's book. "You are *so* funny, man."

"Thanks, little homey. Gotta laugh to keep from crying," Compton said. As he signed, his eyes never left Phoenix's in the mirror.

A bottle of crimson nail polish on the makeup table fell to the floor, unnoticed by everyone except Phoenix. The bottle rolled until it lay directly beneath her feet, tinkling against the metal base of her chair. To her, the sound was deafening, snapping her from her bedazzlement.

"Phoenix, if there's anything you need, say the word," Compton said. "I'll—"

"I need a piano," Phoenix said, spinning her chair to face him. It took her several seconds to wonder why she suddenly felt resolved about it, but she wanted a piano. Badly.

Compton froze in place, one arm akimbo, the other outstretched as if he'd planned to shake her hand. He glanced behind him at the empty doorway, then back at her. "Oh. Okay. I'll have to figure out . . . how to do that. We're right at showtime." Panic crept into his face.

"Can I have it center stage, please? Any piano is fine," Phoenix said.

Gloria made a face at Phoenix. *Piano?* Gloria mouthed.

"Someone will talk to Patti. Patti will take care of it right now," the makeup artist told Compton in an assuring, parental voice, and Compton's muscles relaxed, the smile back.

"OK. It's all good, then," he said, happy to go while the problem was solved.

"Shit. I gotta tell Patti," the makeup artist muttered, leaving on his tail.

All she'd done was ask for a piano, but she'd huffed and puffed and blown them all away.

"Man, did you see that?" Trey laughed. "Aunt Phee snaps her fingers, and they *jump*!"

Gloria stood in front of Phoenix, arms crossed against her chest. "Excuse me, diva girl, but why do you need a piano for a prerecorded track? Sarge won't want you changing the set."

It was one more thing Phoenix couldn't explain. She wasn't sure she knew.

Carlos was sitting in the front row. Phoenix saw him right away, a spotlight's ray singling him out of the gray faces in the audience hidden behind the glare. She smiled and gave him a *Whassup, Carlos* incline, just like Lauryn Hill at the Stephen Talkhouse Bar, and Carlos blew her a kiss. Phoenix talked to Carlos on the phone every day, but she hadn't seen him since the day Milton came and went, so she was glad he had accepted her invitation. Phoenix felt unusually happy; maybe the happiest she'd ever been. She hadn't expected to find the happiest moment of her life on the stage of *Live at Night* in Studio B in Burbank, but here it was.

Phoenix looked for Sarge next, shielding her eyes from the lights.

There he was. Sarge was standing offstage beside the camera monitor, next to a woman with a clipboard. Phoenix couldn't make out the subtle details of his face, although the tilt of his head and the rise of his chest told her he was proud of her. Phoenix assumed that the woman standing next to Sarge was Patti, the producer who had found her a piano. The piano wasn't center stage as she'd requested, but it was on hand and ready, a satin black Steinway she wouldn't mind owning if she had room for a piano.

Phoenix glanced behind her at Danielle and Monisha, the backup singers, who stood in matching black spandex with smiles pasted, waiting for the cameras to come on. She wished Arturo were here instead. They were decent singers—and they were model-thin—but Phoenix knew Serena would have chewed them up if she had been brave enough to show herself.

An APPLAUSE sign lit up, and a disembodied man's voice barked: "And five . . . four . . . three . . . two . . ." The audience came to life, clapping and hooting while red lights popped on atop the video cameras to widen the view by a couple million people.

Alex Compton stood on his mark, before a mammoth screen showing Phoenix's publicity shot from her promo packet—sultry eyes gazing from beyond a mask of mascara, a hip thrust seductively to one side—the photo she thought made her look like her twin sister, the pretty and daring one. "Her joint *Rising* is about to drop, and her first single, 'Party Patrol,' is blowing up. Everybody's talkin' about it, and I've got her *first*. From Three Strikes Records and executive producers G-Ronn and D'Real . . . *Pheeeeeeee-niiiiixxxxx* . . ."

The audience applauded as if they loved her already and had worshipped her for years. The air was as thick as the wind before a storm. Phoenix's ears popped.

Egyptian strings blared around Phoenix, her orchestra of one playing on the speakers from the song's intro. Then came the rhythmic burr of the Egyptian tabla, and the funkilicious Marshall Jones bass line D'Real copped from that old Ohio Players cut, "Skin Tight." The song exploded to life, compelling motion. Behind her, Phoenix's dancers swayed and bobbed. Phoenix had rehearsed so long, her hips rolled right, then left, without direction from her.

So, THIS is what this feels like, Phoenix thought. It was a perfect memory.

Then, as suddenly as it had come, the moment's significance passed. Phoenix took a deep breath, listening in silence as her cue to sing sailed by on the recording. The girls behind her waited a confused millisecond, but they hit their cues, singing backup to her silence. The music pounded on without Phoenix, with only her faint vocal underneath the music track to help her remember where she was supposed to be. *I think I'm losin' control . . . out on this Party Patrol . . .*

Sing, sing, SING, the aware part of her shrieked, but Phoenix felt so detached from herself, she might be sitting next to Carlos in the audience, watching as this fool stood frozen on the stage. Finally, tired of watching herself, Phoenix raised her arms until they were above her head, and she waved with long, slow swoops. The black sleeves of her costume fanned around her, as if she thought she could fly.

The music stopped abruptly. Uncomfortable confusion jittered through the audience, but the APPLAUSE sign came on and everyone forgave her, calling out encouragement. Maybe they thought she was afraid, and they were right. But not for the reasons they thought.

Phoenix brought her microphone to her lips as she stared out at the abyss behind the lights. "Ladies and gentlemen, I'm sorry for the change in the program, but bear with me," she said, and her voice was sure of itself. Didn't she owe her audience the truth?

"I've been in communication with the ghost of Scott Joplin, a black composer who died in 1917, and I'm going to play an excerpt from an opera that hasn't been heard in a hundred years. You're about to witnesses a piece of history sent to us from whatever's on the other side of the curtain. If you still want to hear 'Party Patrol,' tune in to your radio. Peace."

Did I just say that? It was hard to remember, even as she sat at the piano bench. The audience was so silent, she wondered if they'd left while her back was turned. The cameras were still on, red lights staring. In the corner of her eye, Phoenix saw the producer waving her clipboard at someone across the stage. Sarge was nowhere in sight.

Thinking of Sarge startled her. *What the hell am I doing?* But she didn't wonder long.

Phoenix's eyes closed, and she played. Key of F. Jaunty bass notes and
a trilling high F to start, then a folksy introduction in a flowery ragtime
style. As she played, words came to Phoenix's mind that slipped easily
across the melody, a perfect fit. At first she thought she was improvising
to match the piece, but then she realized she was *remembering*, somehow.

Phoenix leaned to her mike stand and sang the first act of her ghost's
lost opera:

> Hear me speak, my brethren here,
> And my comely sisters too.
> We've toiled so hard for many a year,
> And our future many rue.
> Our old way of life will never be
> Since 'Mancipation's set us free.
>
> To cuss and curse your brother's fate
> Is not the way to seal our bond,
> If we are to improve our state
> For tomorrow and beyond.
> Our old way of life will never be
> Since Mr. Lincoln's set us free.
>
> I am a man with many plans
> To lift us from starvation
> I will build a school, so all our clans
> Can leave this lowly station.
> Our old way of life will never be
> Since 'Mancipation's set us free.

She sang as she never had, until perspiration sprang to her forehead,
and her throat felt raw, until her mouth was parched. Phoenix's hands
capered across the piano keys with eerie precision, drawn to the chords
and elegant melody flourishes, always at perfect harmony with her
soaring voice. She sang with ease, and not a single note wavered.

Phoenix sang for six minutes solid, nearly twice her allotted time, before Sarge walked to the piano and rested his palms across her shoulders, which was how she knew it was time to stop.

Phoenix heard three sets of enthusiastic, clapping hands. But the APPLAUSE sign was nowhere to be found.

*H*ere, cuz, drink this," Gloria said. The liquid in the styrofoam cup was tepid, some kind of tea. Phoenix couldn't taste it. She wanted to spit it out.

"I'm not thirsty." Phoenix's voice was a whisper. She'd shorn her throat, or it felt like she had. Every piercing note on the stage had left tatters. Her heart was a drill in her chest, as it had been since Sarge led her offstage and she understood what she had done. No, it wasn't what *she* had done—it was what her ghost had done to her. He had taken her sleepwalking again, only this time she'd been awake.

"Drink it anyway. And take some deep breaths. Inhale for five seconds, exhale for five." It was easy to forget that Gloria was trained as a lifesaver, until Phoenix needed her.

Tremors came in violent waves, from her toes to her scalp. She huddled on a corner of the leather love seat in the green room, her limbs drawn up tightly around her. Her teeth chattered, but she didn't feel cold this time, only weak. None of her muscles remembered how to support her. Her fingers were trembling so badly, she had to sit on them to keep them still.

"Th-that wasn't me out there," Phoenix said.

Serena sat at her feet, rubbing Phoenix's knee. "It's all right, girl. God was just workin' through you. That was the Spirit in you. It's all right." Serena bowed her head and whispered *Yes, Lord. We heard you, Lord,* squeezing her knee so hard it hurt. Phoenix craved the way Serena's faith was so uncomplicated, without competing versions of God in her head. Phoenix wanted to call for God today, and she wasn't sure how.

"I want to see Carlos."

"You know Sarge won't let him back here," Gloria said.

"Gloria . . . I *need* to see him." She wished she could raise her voice above a whisper. Carlos had always understood, so maybe he would understand now, too. She needed to hear him say she had nothing to worry about, that her ghost would not hurt her. Carlos was always so confident about that, but she didn't know. This was different. This was scary.

Gloria sighed. "I'll see what I can do about Carlos, but drink this first. And breathe."

"I fucked up," Phoenix whispered to Gloria after another sip. "Huh?"

Gloria smiled a sour smile and nodded. She pulled Phoenix's head close, kissing her forehead. "Yeah, you fucked up, cuz. We all do it. Life goes on."

"That was the Holy Spirit in you, Phee," Serena said, gazing up at her with bright eyes. "Did you hear yourself? That wasn't you alone. That was the Spirit, girl."

Phoenix hadn't told Serena and Trey about her ghost. Gloria already knew, so that was different, but Serena had been so excited about getting her ready for *Live at Night,* there were long hours when Phoenix had forgotten her ghost altogether, and she hadn't minded the respite. Otherwise, if she wasn't careful, she was watching for him all the time. Waiting for him, just as she was now. He wasn't in the mirror anymore. Was that her ghost in the microwave door popping itself open no matter how many times Trey pushed it shut again, as if they were playing a game? Was he in the starbursts of static floating across the muted television screen? He might be the sheen on the fresh-mopped black floor. Sometimes, most times, it was hard to tell.

When the door opened, Phoenix hoped Carlos would walk in, but it was Sarge. Sarge's eyes sat with hers only an instant before they went to Gloria. "How's she doing?"

"A little better."

"Good, because we need to bust ass out of here. We've overstayed our welcome."

"What about the show?" Phoenix whispered, but she didn't look up at him. Her father had not returned any of her gazes since he'd taken her offstage, shaken her shoulders, and begged her to perform "Party Patrol." She'd flatly told him no, but only because she could hardly stand, not because she didn't want to. Looking at Sarge hurt.

"You ran live on the East Coast, but they're editing you out of Central and Pacific. Any other questions?"

"I'd better talk to Ronn," Phoenix said, remembering.

Sarge backed away and laughed, a sound soaked in anger. "Ronn's already called me, since apparently Alex called him. I don't think Ronn wants to talk to you this minute. Not right this minute." When Sarge left, the door closed gently behind him on a hissing hinge, but he would have slammed it if the door had been the slamming kind. He had slammed it in his mind.

"Come on, Trey," Serena said, standing up. "Let's go. You've got the right touch for putting Grandaddy in a better mood."

Her sister and nephew might be the only ones with the power to reach Sarge today. Strangers might not have seen it, but the rage in his eyes had left a bloodstain on Phoenix. She didn't think she had ever seen her father so angry. When she was sixteen, he'd bound his anger into a fist, but now it didn't have anywhere to go.

"You sang real pretty, Aunt Phee," Trey said, smiling down at her.

"Thanks, lil' bit." Phoenix's voice was hoarse and thin.

Phoenix was glad when Serena took Trey away. She didn't like her nephew seeing her like this. Even if she told him her ghost story, he would probably think she was just strung out, because that was exactly how she looked. Sarge must think she was Malcolm all over again.

"Sarge thinks I was effing around," Phoenix told Gloria.

"He'll get over it."

"You don't think that, do you?"

"Nah, you sounded too good to be effing around," Gloria said. "That was genuine. The cameras were on you, and you wanted to say something, not just shake your ass. That took guts, Phee. No kidding. I admire what you did."

"Don't admire me," Phoenix said. "It wasn't me." The tremors came over her again.

"Who was it, then? The ghost again?" Gloria didn't hide her incredulity.

"Who else could it have been? I don't know that song. I couldn't do it again now."

Gloria sighed. Despite hearing the stories and seeing the music, Gloria was no more impressed with her ghost than she'd been that first day at the Joplin House. "The mind is a funny thing, Phee. I learned that in psych.

Don't stress about it now. It happened, and it's done," Gloria said. "Can you make it outside to the car?"

Phoenix nodded. "I just want to go home, cuz."

With the exception of Sarge, who must have left ahead of them, Phoenix's family flanked her as she made her way through the endless hallways of the studio. She tried not to feel the burning eyes on her as Serena held her steady by one arm, Gloria by the other. *Yeah, she was wildin' out in the green room, too,* she heard her makeup artist say, already embellishing the tale.

Outside the television studio's rear entrance, the uniformed driver opened the black stretch limousine's door for her. The chauffeur looked like he should be driving a hearse instead. *He must be baking to death in that black suit and cap,* Phoenix thought. Still, he was the only one who smiled at her, so his smile meant all the more. Gloria and Serena guided her into the cavern of the limousine.

"Phoenix!" a girl's voice yelled.

Phoenix turned and saw two college-age girls, one white, one black, standing at a respectful distance with a handwritten placard over their heads: PHOENIX ROCKS!!!!!! "We *love* you!" the girls shouted in unison. One of the girls waved a gold-colored CD that flashed in the sun, *Trial by Fire,* the last one Phoenix had recorded with her band—the CD all of them, Sarge included, had believed would be The One. Seeing that CD was like seeing her child exhumed from its grave. Phoenix's eyes fogged as she waved back to them.

Silence waited inside the car. Sarge was already sitting far across the vehicle's U-shaped expanse of leather seats, staring outside his tinted window at anything but her. Phoenix didn't have the strength to sit anywhere except by her door, so Trey, Serena and Gloria climbed over her. A whiff of cologne filled Phoenix with hope, made her look outside again.

Carlos leaned toward the car's open doorway, a bidden mirage. Carlos was winded, his face solemn with concern. Phoenix wanted to climb out and let him hug her, but she couldn't move again, even to touch his offered hand.

"Llamame," Carlos said, the last thing she heard before her chauffeur closed the door.

CHAPTER FOURTEEN

Sedalia, Missouri
July 1904

*H*ow in Heaven did this happen?"

Scott peered out from behind the brocaded curtain backstage, assessing the audience as it streamed into Liberty Park Hall, filling the large room with a din of conversation. He'd worked hard to plan this event, so he'd expected to be thrilled by the assemblage of ladies in summer wraps and ostrich-plumed hats, and men in their linen suits, white straw boaters and canes. There must be close to two hundred here already, and more arriving, but there wasn't a single Negro face among them. Not one. *We can get everyone to come but our own,* he thought.

"What you expect, Scotty?" said Hortense Cook, the barrel-chested tenor sharing the program with him. Like Scott, Cook was dressed in a smart black suit and tie, his shoes at a high shine for the show. Cook cleared his throat, spitting into his handkerchief. "Your ad said *whites only,* and seems like the correction you put in the paper ain't out in time. You know how folks is. Nobody wants to fly hot and get bumptious just to get in the door. White folks' twenty-five cent is as good as anybody else's."

Attendance was improving, thank goodness, but he hadn't ignited the excitement among Negro concertgoers he'd hoped for since he'd been back to Sedalia. For tonight's show, he'd tried to encourage a larger audience by specifying in his advertising that "white friends" were welcome, but maybe that had been foolish. He wouldn't be surprised if the newspaper's mistake wasn't a mistake at all. Mixed crowds had been decried in St. Louis, mostly relegated to the sporting district, and there were plenty in Sedalia who would rather keep their pleasures separate, too. But what a shame! Here they were at the fringes of Liberty Park, where Sedalia's Negroes would celebrate Emancipation Day in only weeks. Emancipation wasn't enough, by far.

"You wanna see more colored folks, make the concerts free," Cook joked.

"If I could afford that, we'd all be happy."

"Ain't *that* the truth?" Cook patted Scott between his shoulder blades. "I think there's one niglet in the woodpile you'll be happy to see, Scotty. Take a look." He pointed, grinning.

At first, Scott thought his wife must have a twin. He had left Freddie at home in their bed this afternoon, where she spent more and more of her days with a new book in her hands. Her cold had steadily worsened. Each time he and the Dixons were sure Freddie was improving, her illness took a new turn, and she'd been all but bedridden for weeks. Hortense Cook was one of his few friends who had met his wife since he'd been back.

Freddie *couldn't* be here, yet she was front row center in her gay Sunday best, fanning herself with a lace fan that matched her soft pink summer gown, her hair wound atop her head in a style more becoming than any she had worn since their wedding day. Nothing in her appearance betrayed his wife's frailty.

"What in blazes does she thinks she's doing?" Scott said. "She's too ill to be here."

"Scotty, if that was my woman, I'd be happy to see her any time she showed her face, sunup to sundown. Now wave to your wife."

Even if he went down to order Freddie back to bed, she would only laugh at him, or else sulk like the child she almost was. This girl had her own mind, and she considered Scott's demands only suggestions at best. She purposely hadn't told him she planned to come so she wouldn't hear his arguments against it. There was no time to caution her about the danger of an unexpected night chill. Perhaps he worried too much, but Freddie should have recovered three times over, yet she had not. Dr. Walden had no good advice for them, except bed rest and a cure to prevent consumption Freddie claimed tasted like rotten eggs and apparently had little effect to boot. *God in Heaven, what if I lose her, too?* Scott tried to shutter that thought away, but it sent stony dread through his veins.

Scott stepped from behind the curtain, revealing himself, and Freddie's searching eyes found him. She grinned, waving her fan, and he sternly shook his finger at her in return. Predictably, Freddie laughed. It *was* good to see her laugh. A girl so full of life would surely be well one day soon. He had to believe that, or else he had nothing to believe in.

He was glad she had come. Freddie hadn't seen a single Sedalia concert yet, and he would make sure this was one to remember.

"Showtime," Cook said, and Scott saw Artie taking center stage.

No one could ask for a better master of ceremonies than Artie Barnes, who was a ship captain at his helm whenever he set foot on a stage. His hair was greased back in stylish waves, glistening in the electric stage lights like his gold pocket-watch chain. Artie didn't play or sing, but he loved performers, and his basso voice made audiences squirm with anticipation.

Scott felt his heartbeat speeding, and he wiped his damp palms on his trousers. No matter how many times he prepared to face an audience, he was still beset by the nerves he'd felt when he and his brother Robert asked their neighbors to join them in a quartet to sing at the First Baptist Church social in Texarkana when he was sixteen. If he could make enough of a living from composing and royalties, he thought, he might never visit a stage again. He didn't live for the stage like Louis, who lived for nothing else.

"Fair Sedalians, as we all know, there is one performer here tonight of national repute. He's been away in the big city making his name and fortune, and now he has come back to join us with his lovely wife, where our ears can delight again and again to the splendiferous artistry that is unique to his talented fingertips. This is no mere performer, ladies and gentlemen, but a composer of a national order. Back in the Queen City for your own personal enjoyment, please welcome first to our stage . . . the composer of the song that is the biggest hit of the St. Louis World's Fair, 'The Cascades' . . . the composer of such classic rags as 'Elite Syncopations' and 'The Entertainer' . . . the composer of 'The Augustan Club Waltz' in honor of the social club to which many of you fine gentlemen in attendance tonight can boast membership . . ."

"Is this my introduction or my eulogy?" Scott muttered, and Cook chuckled beside him.

". . . and, of course, ladies and gentlemen, immortalizing our very own Maple Leaf Club, none other than the *one and only* composer of 'The Maple Leaf Rag' . . . *Mister . . . Scott . . . Joplin!*"

The amplitude of the audience's reaction nearly halted Scott in midstep as he strode toward the grand piano at the center of the stage. A legion of two hundred people clapped and shouted. It was not the unrestrained love of the Rosebud Bar among those who saw their own futures reflected in his face, but it was a hero's homecoming nonetheless. These people did not see a Negro, he realized. They saw a *man*.

Standing beside the piano, Scott bent his elbow across his stomach in a gentleman's posture, met his wife's smiling eyes, and bowed low. His bow elicited more applause, nearly a frenzy. And he had yet to take the piano bench!

When Scott sat at his piano, a blanket of silence fell across the hall, save a single man's coughing near the back, muffled behind his hand. The audience must have believed Artie's hyperbole, and they expected to hear greatness tonight. Scott glanced at Freddie again, and his dear wife was clutching her fan to her chin, her mouth slightly agape as if he were illusionist and had transformed himself into a giant twenty feet high.

He would be a giant for her, Scott vowed as he played the gentle opening of "The Cascades," his homage to the World Fair's display of fountains that had looked like a creation from Freddie's beloved Wonderland itself. He would play the ambitious bass runs in the C section so well that his fingers would ache. He would play himself to exhaustion.

Every note from his piano tonight would be for Freddie, his audience of one.

*F*reddie had coughed for an hour before she finally quieted. She lay on her customary side of their brass bed against a bank of pillows, her eyes and face red from her ordeal.

"Promise me," Scott said, "you'll never do that again."

"I just promised God the same thing, if only He'd let me have rest," she wheezed, taking the glass of water he offered her. When her first two sips eased her coughing, she emptied her glass as if she had been thirsty all day.

All playfulness and merriment were gone from Freddie. Her hair was still beautifully styled from her evening out, but Freddie looked weary and broken. The sight of his wife alarmed Scott anew each morning, when sunlight showed him the gray craters beneath her pretty eyes and her cracked lips that were no longer ruby but a fading pink. He couldn't see all of her illnesses's ravages in the gentle kerosene lamp on her night-stand, but morning would come soon enough.

"What were you thinking, to sneak out that way? The Dixons are mortified. They think I've married Harry Houdini."

"Stop, Scott. My poor lungs have scolded me enough. I wanted to see you play."

This had become their most common meeting place: Freddie in the bed, and Scott beside her in the rattan window chair he'd arranged within arm's reach. In his lap, Scott balanced the Dixons' sterling silver serving tray he used when he fed Freddie her breakfast, and sometimes her lunch and dinner, too. He was a musician in his spare time, but his new occupation was Freddie's caretaker. *If I could only serve her better,* he thought, *Freddie might become well.*

"Now you know you're not missing anything," he said.

She smiled, touching his cheek. "Just the opposite. You were wonderful, and now I'm more frustrated than before. I broke my rule for you tonight. No one guessed I was a Negro, except maybe the biddy next to me who kept staring. And I was so angry, thinking of all the colored ladies who could have enjoyed your concert, too."

"You didn't break your rule. Any other Negro could have come."

"They love you, Scott, but they can claim Dvořák and Wagner and all the rest. They don't need you the way our people do. You see?" A pitiable urgency came to her face.

"Darling, of course," he laughed. "Do you think I plan to bar Negroes from my concerts? Don't worry, I'll still have plenty of opportunities to save our race. They'll dance themselves senseless on Emancipation Day."

She folded her arms, angling away from him. "You're teasing me."

"Yes I am, but I also love you. And of course I was upset about the mistake at the hall tonight. I promise it won't happen again, not by my doing." He stroked her forehead, which was never cool enough to satisfy him. "Artie mentioned the waltz I composed for the Augustain Club, remember? It's a very exclusive club, and I was honored to be asked, so I labored on it a month, trying to perfect every note. But when it was time for the performance, they wouldn't let me play because I'm a Negro. They hired white musicians instead. I was good enough to compose it, but not good enough to set foot in the door. I have a hundred stories like it, Freddie. You think I don't despise this, too? My publisher's daughter plays ragtime as well as any Negro. Music doesn't have a skin color! But I have to confess, I was much more upset tonight when I saw my ailing wife out alone at night, away from her bed. That I won't tolerate, Freddie."

"Yes, sir," she said, without sarcasm or irony. He almost hated to hear her so yielding, because it made her seem weaker than she should be.

"I wouldn't be surprised if you've set yourself back."

"How can I, when I've never gone forward? Sometimes I think I'll never be well."

Neither of them had dared say it aloud, until now. Scott held her clammy hand. "You will. You have to learn patience. That's what my friends always tell me."

"This room is a prison."

It was hard to admit to himself, but Scott had come to look forward to his gigs if only for liberation from their room. Upon their arrival, the room had suited their needs perfectly. It was one of the largest rooms in the house, easily the size of two bedrooms, with smoothly finished wooden floors and a decor to match that of a fine hotel: a fireplace with an attractive clock on the mantel depicting angels blowing their heavenly trumpets; Irish Point lace curtains in the windows; bookshelves brimming with books; an oak bureau and mirror; attractive woodland prints on the walls; and a tea table and rattan rocker by the large window, facing Olivia Dixon's flower garden.

Scott had expected his wife to spend many happy hours reading by that window, but most often she was in bed. It was a heartless irony: When they were still courting, Freddie's father had warned his daughter that she would spend her best years nursing her *husband*! If Freddie was this frail, how could they hope to have a child? He was afraid to think of the consequences of having relations with her, if she was ever well enough again. He had touched Freddie like a husband only three times, in boardinghouses between gigs in their earliest days of marriage. Those memories followed when he soaped himself in the warm water of his bathtub, and when he tossed in search of sleep at night.

"I'm going to ask Father to send Lovie," Freddie said. "You're too busy to be a nurse, and I won't put out the Dixons this way."

"We pay for boarding, so we're a help, not a burden. There's no need to bring Lovie, Freddie. Your sister has a family of her own. I can care for my wife."

Freddie sighed, not sounding convinced. "Are you sorry you married me yet?"

"Never."

"Maybe you should have married Lovie instead. You were only a year too late. She's never sick, and her name is so much prettier than mine."

"Your name is unique for a woman, and it suits you. I've never known another like you."

"Father wanted a boy. He wouldn't give up even when he saw my sex."

Scott was glad Freddie had moved her thoughts from her illness, since it wasn't like her to be so morose. Her mood was a contagion, and it was hard enough to fight low spirits while Freddie was sick. "What would you rather be named?"

"Something refined and feminine, like a name from one of my English novels," Freddie said, brightening the way he remembered when he'd asked her favorite type of flower. She propped herself up higher on her pillows, a sign that she was regaining her stamina. "I'm married to a prince, so my name should suit a princess, not a boy."

"Gwendolyn? Juliana?"

Freddie made a face, laughing. The sound of her laugh cleansed his heart. "No, I gave myself my own secret name when I was little."

"Tell me, then."

"It might sound silly to you. I've only told Lovie."

He kissed her hand and rubbed it to his cheek. Touching her always stirred desire in him, but he'd learned to quell it. It was not yet time to lie with her again, no matter how much he wished it. Sharing a bed with a woman he hesitated to touch was torture, but it was a torture he could withstand as long as he must. "Tell me, or I won't bring you any of Olivia's pound cake."

Freddie paused so long, he thought she'd decided to keep her secret. Then, she said it so gently, he almost didn't hear. "Bethena." He heard a girl's wonder as she spoke it. He could imagine her in pigtails, christening herself while she gazed in a mirror beneath a crown of flowers.

Scott had never heard the name before, but it *did* suit her face. "Bethena is a pretty name," he said. "But not nearly pretty enough for the woman who dreamed it."

"It sounds perfect when you say it," Freddie said, her eyes bubbling with pleasure. Then, she began coughing, that horrible sound that originated far too deep in her lungs, raking her chest. Something so stark and shadowed veiled Freddie's face that Scott squeezed her hand, alarmed until she quieted. Freddie let out a small gasp as she found her breath.

"Will you remember me that way, Scott? Will you remember me as Bethena, too?" She sounded as if she'd dunked her head beneath a pond's surface and was coming up for air.

"Shhhh. Nonsense, dear heart," he said. "You'll be the one left remembering me."

Scott held his wife's head to his breast, gently caressing her hair, as silken as an Indian squaw's. He prayed Freddie couldn't hear his resounding heart, still excited from her coughing fit that had filled him with foreboding. He prayed she wouldn't heed the tiresome ticking of the clock on the mantel marking her long imprisonment, and, most of all, that she would ignore the angels' clarion call if they ever tried to hasten her Home.

The next night found Scott in Windsor, where he'd been engaged to play for a private party at the home of a white family celebrating their eldest son's admission to an Eastern college. At seven o'clock, Scott stood at the wood-frame depot with four newly earned dollars, waiting for his train home in the waning daylight. He was glad it was early, so he'd be back at home before Freddie fell asleep. As he'd feared, her night out to the concert had set her back, and she'd barely eaten today. He wanted to be sure to kiss his wife's lips before she drifted into her dreams. Whenever he got home too late to bid her good night, he dreaded that something might steal her from him while she slept.

Windsor seemed a ghost town, with no one else in sight as the setting sun lit up the rooftops in gold paint. Six crows lingered near Scott at the empty depot, fighting over an ear of corn near the tracks, and Scott remembered how upset Olivia Dixon had been when she'd discovered a crow on the kitchen table that morning, making tracks in spilled flour. The bird must have flown through the open kitchen window.

Now that's a sure sign of death, Olivia had said after a startled scream, then she'd noticed Scott in the doorway and given him an embarrassed smile. Scott's mother would have been equally upset about the event, God rest her soul, and her mother before that. Scott had chided Olivia for such old-timey superstitions, but he couldn't deny feeling uneasy at the sight of the crows. His mother had counted crows, assigning significance to their number: One was bad luck, two was good. Three was health, or was it wealth? He couldn't remember the portent of six, but it probably wasn't promising. Sickness or death, no doubt. Remembering that, the terrible sound of Freddie's coughs followed him here, even miles from where she lay.

The train arrived at the near-deserted station with a gush of smoke, the churning brakes screaming in a racket. Only one man climbed out of the colored car, and Scott was surprised to recognize him: It was the same bearded conjurer he'd seen when he was riding with Freddie. Yes, this had been the man's stop, Scott recalled. The man wore the same filthy clothes and strange, ritualistic necklace that had caught Scott's eye before. On closer look, the conjurer looked about sixty. The conjurer mumbled to himself, not looking in Scott's direction as he debarked the train, and Scott meant to wait for him to pass and board the car unseen. But he didn't.

Instead, Scott watched as the man walked away, carrying himself with a slight limp Scott hadn't noticed before. The sight of him was strangely fascinating, taking Scott away from the train's waiting doorway. Before Scott realized it, he was following a few steps behind the stranger, away from the depot and toward the dirt road to town. Windowpanes flared in the dusk light as he walked past. A dirty yellow mongrel with pronounced ribs sleeping outside a closed hardware store came to its feet and shook itself, watching their approach.

"Got any chicken today?" Scott called after the man.

The man hardly slowed, and didn't turn. "Chicken's sold," he said, and walked on.

Scott's next words shocked him. "How 'bout you tell my fortune, then?"

The man stopped walking. Scott regretted his words when the conjurer turned to look at him, his chin turning first, slumped shoulder following. He had struck up a conversation that would likely make him miss his train. What had possessed him?

Guilt, perhaps. He had been sharp with this man before, and maybe he hoped to make amends. Or, perhaps the conjurer's accusations had stung him deeper than he thought. But why? He wasn't the first to accuse Scott of abandoning his race, especially when careful diction alone could invite the insult. Not an hour ago, the man who'd hired him—a retired banker who traveled frequently to Sedalia—had shaken his hand heartily with parting words he'd intended as a compliment: *You don't seem like a nigger at all!*

The conjurer walked toward Scott in his half-lurching gait, resting more weight on one leg than the other. He fumbled inside a cloth sack slung across his chest and pulled out a pair of spectacles, which he fitted across his nose. He peered at Scott with curiosity while a handful of white passengers walked between them as if they were not there.

The eyeglasses made the conjurer look almost scholarly, and Scott's guilt surged. He'd treated him more rudely than he deserved.

"I know you," the conjurer said. "I know that suit. You the biggity nigger from the train, few weeks back." It wasn't a question. He pronounced his *th* sounds more like *d's*, akin to Scott's father's dialect. Scott guessed he'd been born a slave and never had a day of schooling.

"I wanted to apologize," Scott said. "I had no call to act that way."

"Folks gon' act how they gon' act," the conjurer said. "Call or no call."

A ramshackle wagon turned toward them, creaking under its own weight, driven by a boy who might have been fourteen. The wagon was harnessed to a gray nag that walked nearly as gingerly as the conjurer.

The nag's eye visible to Scott was filmed over, white. By the look of it, the wagon was ready to collapse into kindling and the nag was half-blind. *It would be faster to walk,* Scott thought. He felt pity for them. To people like these, the inventions of the new day—speeding motorcars, "snapshot" cameras, radios, and electric trains—might as well be a fairy tale. They had been left to wallow in ignorance and poverty not unlike their fathers and grandfathers, free or not. And how many generations of Negroes would follow?

The train's whistle sounded. Windsor was a small stop with no line of passengers waiting, and the train would not linger. Yet, Scott did not turn away. "I wondered if—"

"How yo' pretty wife?" the conjurer said.

Scott's spine was an iron rod in his back. "She's not well," Scott said, stopping short of demanding why he had asked, as if he knew she was sick. "How much to have my fortune told?"

The conjurer regarded him with what might be a sneer. "A dollar," he said.

Scott remembered why he had first disliked the man: He was a swindler. Twenty-five cents for a fortune was bad enough, but a dollar was outrageous. A dollar could buy two or three records for Freddie's Talking Machine, if he could spare it. As the train's wheels geared up for departure, Scott felt foolish in a dozen ways. If he missed this train, another wouldn't come for hours. "Never mind," Scott said, trying not to show his irritation. "There's no time."

The conjurer tossed his sack into the back of the wagon, unconcerned. He shrugged. "Don't make me no diff'rence," he said. "My wife ain't the one in a bad way."

Scott could not walk away, and he felt the boy's eyes on him, impatient. Scott couldn't believe he was considering squandering a full quarter of his day's earnings on nonsense, but he felt himself reaching into his pocket, as if he no longer had control of his own hand. He wanted reassurance, he realized. He wanted to hear the man say *Freddie's going to be fine,* even if this conjurer had no more knowledge of the future than the pitiful nag who pulled his wagon.

Scott pulled out a folded bill. "A dollar, then."

The conjurer showed no change in his face, but he took the money and gave it to his son. That elicited a smile from the youngster, whose teeth were already gray from lack of care.

With a grunt, the conjurer tugged down the wagon's loading door, which whimpered on its hinge. Taking his time, the man pulled his sack toward him and rifled through it. The train's second whistle sounded, and Scott fidgeted with a sigh. *You've missed the train, so accept it and stop fretting,* he told himself, but he still felt sullied, the way he had on the rare occasions he'd accepted a whore's invitation upstairs after a night of entertaining at a bawdy house. Now, as then, he was determined to see his desire through despite his displeasure with himself. Sure enough, he heard the train pulling away behind him.

Now he had lost a dollar and Freddie's good-night kiss, with no one to blame but himself.

The conjurer pulled out a handful of small bones that might be from chicken, beef or pork; Scott couldn't tell because their distinguishing features were worn away. The conjurer held ten or twelve pale bones with jagged edges. These bones were smaller than the beef ribs his father and uncle had cleaned and played to accompany fiddles at family dances when he was young.

The boy was curious, and he hopped down to the empty bed of the wagon to watch. He was barefoot, the soles of his feet nearly black. "Those bones don't never lie," the boy said.

The conjurer shook the bones in his loosely closed palm like a pair of die in a sidewalk craps game. "What you gon' axe? A dollar'll buy three questions."

Scott hesitated, feeling both ridiculous and strangely troubled. Was he *afraid*? He couldn't make himself ask the question most plain in his thoughts, so he chose another. "How long will my wife and I be together?" Scott said.

The conjurer tossed the bones, and they landed on a heap on the flat wagon door, crisscrossed among the swirling patterns of the wood. The conjurer peered at the bones a long time, and Scott's breath was thin as he waited. He watched the conjurer's face as carefully as he watched the face of Freddie's doctor when he visited, looking for news in his expression.

"A hunnert years," the conjurer said. "Prob'ly mo'."

"Excuse me?" Scott said, thinking he'd misunderstood his dialect. "A *hundred* years?"

The conjurer nodded, his face vacant. "Ya'll's souls is stuck like cold sap to a tree."

"Then she'll be well soon?" Scott said, feeling more foolish than ever for his relief.

The conjurer gathered his bones, and tossed them again. This time, gazing at whatever messages were supposedly hidden in their random positioning, the conjurer's face slackened. He chewed his bottom lip, shaking his head. "She ain't gon' be well," he said at last.

Turn and go on your way. Don't listen to another word of this, Scott told himself, but he couldn't walk away. He hadn't realized how unburdened he'd felt by the prediction that he and Freddie would live together for a hundred years until it had been wrested away.

"What do you mean?" Scott said. There was anger in his voice.

"Her lungs ain't right," the conjurer said, and shrugged.

Scott forced himself to laugh, although a laugh was the furthest thing from his heart. "You tell me in one breath we'll live together a hundred years, and that she'll never be well in the next? I deserve more clever lies for my dollar. You can do better than that."

"I ain't said a hunnert years in *this* world," the conjurer said. "I ain't said nothin' 'bout *livin'*." He was gazing at Scott head-on, challenging him. One corner of his lip turned upward, the beginnings of what would be a vicious smile if he loosed it.

Scott stood rooted, his heart crashing in his chest, stanching his breath. This stranger was playing a cruel game with him, yet it was nothing like a game, at least not any Scott knew. Suddenly, he felt as if he were bargaining for his soul. "*Living* is the only damn thing I care about," Scott said. "Tell me what you see for me in *this* world."

The conjurer picked up his bones again, and threw them for the third time. They fell across the wooden plank with a scrabbling clatter.

Scott's hands trembled, and he took a single step away, but not so far that he couldn't see every weathered line in the conjurer's face as he leaned over to peer closely at the bones, or couldn't smell the sharp scent of the conjurer's sun-broiled skin and old chicken grease on his fingertips. Scott had led himself into a trap. He didn't know how he knew, but the realization made him want to run the entire twenty-seven miles home.

The conjurer looked up at him, this time with a grin. Several of his teeth were missing, making his smile hideous. "This world ain't got no luck fo' you. All yo' luck's waitin' in the next," the conjurer said. "So I guess you ain't so biggity now, is you?"

"I apologized for that," Scott said, his voice unsteady. "There's no reason to—"

"Any bad turn you can think up, that's what's gonna pass yo' way in this life. That's what the bones say."

Scott shuddered. "You're a trickster," he whispered.

"Your wife won't never git well. She won't live to harvesttime. You sick an' don't know it, and you won't never git well neither. You gonna lose them fingers, too. Time comes, you won't be able to hold yo' own dick to take a piss. You been bit by the dog, ain't you?"

Scott's blood had drained from his face at the reference to his fingers, but he felt faint when the conjurer said *the dog*. Impossible! He took two more steps backward, nearly stumbling over a block of wood half-buried in the dust. The boy's eyes watched him, doleful.

"Don't t-try to make me think you're putting a curse on me," Scott said, pointing a shaky finger at the conjurer. If he'd been wearing a cross the way his mother had always advised, he would be clutching it now. It was as if the devil himself had stepped off the train and crossed his path. "I'm a Christian man, and I don't believe in hoodoo."

"I ain't one to throw curses, but if I *had* underworlded you, you'd know it," the conjurer said. "You axe me fo' the future, an' that's what the bones say. The future ain't nothin' to be skeered of, boy. The future's already came an' went. Yo' wife'll be lost from you fo' a time, but we all gits lost. You'll see her agin by and by."

"The bones don't *never* lie," the boy said, shaking his head, and climbed back to his berth.

Scott felt his stomach heave, and it took all of his body's restraint to keep from spilling his last meal on the ground. He pressed his hand to his mouth, hardly daring to move. He watched in silence while the conjurer climbed up into the wagon's bed and pulled the door up behind him. The half-starved mongrel sniffed near Scott, lured by the lingering chicken scent, and Scott didn't move to shoo the dog away. He stood in a fog of fright.

"I don't believe you," Scott said, desperate to break the man's strange hold on him.

"I ain't axe you to b'lieve me. You the one axed *me*," the conjurer said. His smile was gone, and he looked at Scott as impassively as if they'd been chatting about the train schedule and last night's rain. "I ain't the one skeered o' what's gon' come."

The boy clucked to the nag and snapped the reins, and Scott watched the sorry wagon jounce away. The conjurer gazed back at Scott from where he sat with neither malice nor pity, a man untroubled to deal out death every day.

CHAPTER FIFTEEN

N o, sorry, this isn't Marcus Smalls. My name is Gloria Katz, and I'm
Phoenix's personal assistant, so I'm taking her manager's calls this
week . . . Yes, Phoenix *is* available for interviews, if you'll let me check
my book. . . . Who are you with again?"

Phoenix heard her cousin's voice through the cracked bedroom doorway, so professional that she fooled her again for a split-second, making
Phoenix wonder when she'd hired an assistant, or how she could afford
it. Sarge had kept most of his phone work away from Phoenix's hearing,
so she hadn't realized how intrusive his telephone was, like a child in
constant need of feeding. Phoenix would have preferred to shut the
thing off after Sarge relinquished his phone to Gloria in the limousine—
saying he'd had enough, that he'd put up with as much as he could
stand—but Gloria, true to her spirit as a lifesaver, insisted on answering
its constant ringing.

Career CPR, Phoenix thought. *Good luck with that, cuz.*

Phoenix couldn't keep her own attention anymore, so she didn't
blame Sarge for quitting. Creative differences, that was all. Sarge was
stubbornly trying to live in the present, and suddenly Phoenix was more
fascinated by the past. Sarge was playing family man today, sightseeing
with Serena and Trey, and Phoenix couldn't be mad at that. *That's what
he should have been doing all along.*

Phoenix raised her head from the pile of books in her lap long
enough to gaze at the gathering of strangers in her living room; not one,

not two, but *six* psychics watching the videotaped image of her playing her keyboard the night she had sleepwalked. The music on the tape preserved another era while they craned to see her on the tiny black-and-white video monitor Finn had left, since she and Nia didn't own a television set. All of them sipped peppermint tea from styrofoam cups someone had brought, nibbling from a plate of homemade brownies, as if Phoenix were hosting the monthly meeting of the City of Angels Psychics Club.

Heather and Finn were here, and so were a white-haired Mexican man with tortoiseshell glasses who cleared his throat a lot; the guy with the flowing mane of dark hair and a moustache who reminded her of a famous magician she'd liked as a child, but whose name escaped her now; a woman in her late twenties with crew-cut red hair and bright freckles across every inch of her visible skin; and a middle-aged black woman they all deferred to, Johnita Somebody, who had written a best-selling book about being a psychic and flown in from Seattle because she was Heather's mentor. *What do you call a meeting of psychics? A gaggle, like geese? A murder, like crows?* A passel of psychics, Phoenix decided. That sounded right.

The passel had been here since early morning, walking through her apartment the way she'd walked through the Joplin House, trying to catch his vibes in the walls.

Phoenix was doing a good job of ignoring the psychics, just as she'd mostly been ignoring Gloria. Phoenix had reading to do. The five books about Scott Joplin Carlos had brought her after yesterday's television performance were plenty to keep her occupied, and she sat on a corner of her futon marking passages with a neon green Hi-Liter dangling from her mouth. Words and phrases jumped out at her: Syphilis. Teacher. Sedalia. *Treemonisha.*

But she always came back to Freddie, the stern photograph of the appealing, pale-skinned woman Scott Joplin had pictured on the cover sheet of his original publication of "Bethena" in 1905, the photograph that might be the only remains of Joplin's second wife.

The wife, incidentally, who had died while they were married.

Carlos had neglected to mention Freddie's death when he first told Phoenix whose name she had heard in her ear, but Phoenix understood why he'd hesitated. That night by the pool, she had already been freaked out, peeing on herself, so she wouldn't have been ready for that knowledge then. But things had changed. She was ready to understand, or at least to try. Phoenix felt as if she were preparing for an arranged marriage, trying to learn everything about her betrothed the way she'd studied Ronn, hoping to glimpse the breathing man hidden in the pages of facts and dates.

Freddie had almost been erased from history, Phoenix had learned. Historians had known about Belle and a third woman Scott Joplin married late in life, but apparently none of the people who'd known Joplin best mentioned Freddie in later interviews, not even the widow who had survived him. It was as if Freddie had never existed.

When Phoenix had called Van Milton yesterday to tell him about her television appearance and the first lyrics to *A Guest of Honor*, their conversation turned to Freddie after his excited speculations about Joplin's link to Phoenix. The curator mentioned that Freddie might not have been unearthed at all if not for his friend Edward A. Berlin, the Joplin biographer who had discovered her existence in the late 1980s. Phoenix recognized Berlin's name: He'd written one of the books in her stack, *King of Ragtime: Scott Joplin and His Era*. Phoenix convinced Milton to give her Berlin's number, so she and Carlos had called him at his home in New York last night, late for the East Coast. The gracious musicologist had been too polite to offer any opinion on the scores Milton had sent him—*Yes, this isn't the first time* A Guest of Honor *has mysteriously shown up on my doorstep,* he'd said dryly—but Edward Berlin had been happy to talk to her about Scott Joplin and Freddie.

Such an unhappy, sad, depressed man, and he wrote this joyful music, Berlin had sighed, as if Joplin was a friend. Berlin told her about how he and his research assistants had combed historical cemeteries without any luck while he was researching Joplin's biography, hoping to find a second wife he suspected existed. He'd pieced the second marriage together from vague references in interviews with people like the granddaughter of a man named Solomon Dixon, where Joplin had boarded for a time in Sedalia. Berlin had finally found Freddie's death notice in several old Sedalia newspapers—the *Conservator, Democrat, Sentinel* and *Capitol*—rescuing her memory from oblivion.

Freddie had been a kid when she died, twenty years old, and she had been married to Scott Joplin only ten weeks, not even three months. They'd hardly known each other when they got married, and their marriage had lasted the blink of an eye. But Berlin said Scott Joplin had obviously based the young lead character in his beautiful opera, *Treemonisha,* on Freddie: strong-willed, educated, a leader. His perfect woman. *And he's still mourning her now,* Phoenix had thought while she listened. *Either that, or he thinks he's found her again.*

"Freeze it right there," Johnita said suddenly, and Finn paused the tape. Johnita was wearing a loose, African-inspired dress and large hoop earrings dangling near her shoulders. Her dark hair was short enough for West Point, dotted with silver strands like paint specks. "*There.* Do you see that streak of light in the upper-left-hand corner? He's behind her."

The passel scooted forward to look more closely at the monitor, and a round of *ahhhhhhs* made its way from person to person, along with breathless smiles. The Mexican man began scribbling notes. Phoenix glanced up, too, but she couldn't see anything on the screen worth noticing. It was hard to get excited about a blip on a videotape when she'd seen him sitting on her bed, and he'd sung the words to *A Guest of Honor* through her mouth just yesterday.

But her ghost wasn't going to come while they were here.

Her ghost had hidden himself the first time Heather was here, and she understood why after listening to the Houston Grand Opera recording of his opera, *Treemonisha.* The evil villains in *Treemonisha* were conjurers. A band of old conjurers kidnapped the heroine and conspired to keep the freed slaves ignorant and superstitious, trying to sell them bags of luck and rabbits' feet while Treemonisha preached education. Conjurers must have really pissed Scott Joplin off, Phoenix thought. Her ghost wouldn't visit while the passel was here.

She knew him, at last. A little, anyway.

"Phoenix?" Johnita's voice said gently. Phoenix looked up again. She hadn't realized the video had stopped playing, and now the passel's eyes were on her. "Heather mentioned something about an accident with a piano when you were a child. Where's that piano now?" She folded her hands, bright eyes waiting.

Phoenix felt possessive, suddenly. Van Milton had asked about that piano, too. "I don't know. My parents sold it to a collector a few months after the accident."

"That piano could be very significant, the root of your connection to Joplin."

"Yet, it hurt her," the Mexican man said.

"But that was an accident. Joplin came through to make sure I knew that," Heather said, and the other psychics nodded, gazing at Heather like a sage. "He's her spirit guide."

"Oh yeah, totally," said Freckle-Girl.

"But that piano . . ." Johnita pursed her lips, sighing. Phoenix thought she could see plans for her next book in the woman's eyes. "It's a loss. It must have had significance to him."

Instinctively, Phoenix looked around for Carlos, before she remembered he'd gone out to get her groceries. She was tired of the passel now. She didn't like the way they talked about her like a science project, and she was ready for them to go away and leave her to her reading. Scott Joplin was the only one who could teach her what she needed to know.

"Sugar?" Johnita said, and for the first time, Phoenix heard a pinch of the South in the woman's accent. Sarge had told her his mother used to call him *sugar,* and Phoenix liked the word's cozy warmth. She'd never had the chance to meet Sarge's mother, who had been long dead when she was born. "You look like a rabbit caught in a trap. Hon, we're not here to hurt you or exploit you. I know it's unnerving to have a room full of psychics. I'm grateful you've invited us here into your sacred space. If I'm pushing too hard, just say so. My feelings don't get hurt that easy. Heather is a gifted lady, she told me there was something special here, and she was right. But this is *your* journey. Now . . . I know you've had some fear through this . . ."

Phoenix nodded. "I'm starting to get past that."

"Well, that's excellent, sugar. Sometimes it takes people years to get over their fear of the dead. Right?" She turned to the passel, and they agreed.

"My twin sister died when we were three," Freckle-Girl said matter-of-factly, "and I *still* wig out when I turn around and see her behind me."

"I drive a mile out of my way every night to avoid the cemetery," said the man with long hair. "I'm not proud of that, but it's true."

"And this is all happening to *you* in a matter of days," Johnita told Phoenix. "You didn't believe in ghosts, and now you're working to embrace one in your life. You thought all psychics were frauds, and now you know some of us are the real thing."

That was true. Heather had been all the proof Phoenix needed.

"So I'm sorry if you thought I was trying to claim your experiences, that I want to book myself on Oprah with Scott Joplin's haunted piano. That's not the case, I promise you." At that, Johnita smiled. "All right, I have to tell you something: There's a presence in this room, and I'm being scolded. She's reminding me there's more than one Oprah. Does that ring a bell?"

Phoenix blinked, and her nostrils stung. "My mom's mother was named Oprah. She died when I was fifteen. She bought me my first piano." Phoenix didn't tell Johnita that she thought about Grandma Oprah a little every time she played a keyboard, and that her death was the worst thing that had ever happened to her. Those things were private. Phoenix wasn't sure if she was glad to hear her grandmother's name or annoyed at the psychic's casual intrusion in her loss.

Johnita nodded as if she'd quizzed her, and Phoenix had passed. "This room is full of people who love you. I know you haven't asked me for a reading, but you should think about it, sugar. I'm booked nine months in advance, and there are people willing to pay crazy money for what I'm offering you for free."

"I don't know. My last reading was a downer." Phoenix avoided looking at Heather.

"I promise not to tell you anything I think might upset you."

Which means there's something bad, and she knows it, Phoenix thought. "OK," she said, although she wasn't sure it was.

"Would you rather do this privately?"

Phoenix shook her head. "Nah. I'm good."

The Queen Psychic didn't hold her hand or hesitate. "A name starting with J is coming through, or maybe Jay *is* the name. He's a friend."

When Phoenix blinked, a tear shook loose. "Yeah. My friend Jay, from high school."

"Jay wants you to know he's fine, and he's proud of you. He says he misses writing songs with you." Phoenix suddenly remembered her

notebook from fifth period Spanish in high school, which she and Jay
had passed back and forth as they wrote lyrics; most of them bad, but
some of them very good. When she'd had her band—when she'd been
actually collaborating instead of only giving in—Phoenix used to ask
herself, *How would Jay write this?* and the words would come. Johnita
went on: "I can't linger with anyone too long, because there's a lot of
crowding. Sorry about that. Now I'm feeling a very powerful spirit, a
matriarch. Not Oprah this time, but another grandmother, an L name."

"Lulu," Phoenix said. Lulu Mae Watson, whom she'd never met. "My
father's mother."

Something brushed Phoenix's arm, and she jumped. Her heart tried
to leap out of her mouth until she realized it was only Gloria, who had
left the bedroom and sidled beside her, sitting on top of the futon's armrest. Gloria's hair smelled damp and sweet from Nia's apricot shampoo.

"Your Gramma Lulu loves you very much, and she wants you to
know she's always been here. She was a professional singer as a young
girl. Did you know that?" Johnita said.

Phoenix shook her head. Sarge had never told her that.

"She says you sing fine, but your gift is something else. The two
grandmothers are in agreement on that. They see you writing, composing. Maybe that's part of what Joplin sees in you, too. You've been
frozen, something like stage-fright, and you need to get over it. But they
want you to go to school first. The school message is very strong, for
both of you girls."

The truth in the psychic's words felt as real as everyone in the room.

"Yeah, that sounds like Grandma Oprah," Gloria muttered. She
tapped Phoenix's shoulder with her red appointment book, trying to get
her attention, but Phoenix waved her off.

"You're going to . . . go through some changes," Johnita said, and the
halting way she spoke told Phoenix she was choosing her words very
carefully. "But greatness is waiting on the other side. I see a gold-colored
piano wrapped in a ribbon of light, and to me that symbolizes greatness.
Innovation. Like that guitar player . . . what's his name?"

Phoenix shrugged. "Hendrix?" she said, a wild guess. Wishful thinking.

Johnita's face softened into a smile. "Yes," she said. "Jimi Hendrix.
Something unique."

Phoenix's heart, frightened before, sped with exhilaration. If not for Johnita's knowledge of Jay and her dead grandmothers, Phoenix would have thought she was telling her what any musician would want to hear. *Greatness* was a powerful word.

"But you have to be strong," Johnita went on. "And you have to make the right choices."

There's always a catch, Phoenix thought. "Like what? What kind of choices?"

Johnita shook her head. "We don't see everything, sugar. I wish we did."

"Is the ghost going to help me?"

"It's possible," Johnita said. "But if he's here now, he's not coming forward to say."

But Phoenix didn't need a psychic's confirmation. It was so obvious, she wondered why she hadn't realized it before. *That's why he came to me. His music is going to help me.*

"Like they say, it's all who you know," Gloria said, so offhandedly that Phoenix knew the psychic hadn't convinced her cousin. "Hey, this Joplin guy's helping you already, if it's OK for me to interrupt here. Phee, I don't think Three Strikes is pissed at you anymore. I just heard from their publicity guy. What's his name again? Mikey?"

"Manny," Phoenix told her.

Gloria grinned, leaning close to her face. "*Rolling Stone* wants to interview you. Oh yeah, and so does *MTV News*. That opera stunt you pulled is paying off, cuz. *Ka*-ching."

Phoenix's mind went white. She didn't have time to find her thoughts again before the front door crashed open, and Trey ran in, his sneakers skidding against her tile floor. Trey was in trendy shades and a white Universal Studios T-shirt hanging to his knees. "Quick! Where's your radio, Aunt Phee?" he said. To him, there was no one else in the room.

Phoenix hardly heard his question, hoping Sarge would walk in behind him. Instead, Serena followed alone with an armload of shopping bags, closing the door. A grin filled Serena's face, as if she'd already heard Gloria's news.

"What?" Phoenix said.

Trey spied the boom box on her plywood stereo shelf and fumbled to turn it on. Static roared from the speakers, and the radio sputtered and popped as her nephew spun the dial. Then, a voice she almost recognized came on in full FM sharpness: *"I think I'm losin' control . . ."*

"Oh, shit!" Gloria said, just as Sarge's cell phone rang yet again.

"They said it's the debut on their request line!" Serena said, scooting her way past the knees and legs of the passel to join Phoenix on the futon. Serena's full weight landed on top of Phoenix, and she wrapped her arms around her so tightly, Phoenix felt her breath sucked back into her lungs. But she hardly noticed. How could she?

For the first time, Phoenix heard herself on the radio singing a song that bore her name.

Silence enveloped Phoenix when she plunged her head beneath the water of her complex's heated swimming pool, except for the sound of her escaping breath rising to the surface in a flurry of bubbles. The silence was fascinating, erasing everything in sweet peace. *Maybe this is what death is like,* she thought. That was what the psychics had said, that death was nothing to fear. The light from the solar lamps above her looked far away, refracting across the warm water.

When her burning lungs needed air, Phoenix's head broke the surface, and she gently paddled to tread water. She was no great swimmer, but she loved the pool, especially at night, when it was almost always empty. She ventured only midway across the pool when she swam, until she couldn't tap the floor with the tips of her toes. Phoenix could swim from one end to the other as long as she kept her head above water, but she preferred to stay where it was shallow enough to stand if she wanted to, floating more than swimming.

Marc Anthony's earnest voice and a celebration of salsa awaited her from the poolside boom box, which was playing low so they wouldn't disturb the neighbors. She'd listened to 100.3 The Beat to try to hear "Party Patrol" all day, and after it came on twice more, Carlos put on CDs instead, complaining that the repetition in pop radio drove him crazy. Salsa was good. Salsa made Phoenix remember Miami.

"Party Patrol" had played on St. Louis radio, and probably other places, too, but Phoenix had never heard it herself, until now. She hadn't expected an event so simple to amaze her so much, but it did. Sarge hadn't come to see her, but he had called to congratulate her, so that was progress. Phoenix felt as wired as someone who'd been drinking coffee all day, with cocaine chasers. Only the silent water calmed her back to normal, the warmth inseparable from her skin.

Gloria and Carlos sat at the edge of the deep end of the pool with their bare feet dangling in the water, discreetly passing a joint between them while they engaged in the most civil argument Phoenix had ever heard, keeping their voices pleasant, almost playful. They were negotiating Phoenix's future in the full moon's light while she pretended not to hear.

". . . I didn't say you're *actually* Satan, but I think you have the guy on speed dial, dude," Gloria said with a flip of her crimped hair, massaging the back of her long neck. "Every time you show up, stuff goes wrong for my cousin. Don't fuck things up for her. If she blows the concert in New York next week, her label is going to shit. Let her have a chance."

Carlos laughed, shaking his head. The joint pressed between his lips flickered as he chuckled. He didn't answer right away, hoarding the smoke. "You're not hearing me, *rubia*. What's going on with Phoenix has nothing to do with me. Come on, now." Phoenix saw the smoke from his nostrils diffuse against the lamplight. "Don't talk like her father."

"Look, Sarge's controlling bullshit gives me hives, for real, but I think he's right this time, Carlos. Today I'm trying to get Phoenix on the phone with MTV, and she's sitting with a roomful of pscyhos—oh, I'm sorry, *psychics*. Those were your friends, right?"

"Only one was my friend. But they're experts at what they do, and they say what's happening to her is revolutionary. She's communing with one of our country's greatest composers, our Chopin," Carlos said, like a teacher talking to a remedial student. "MTV didn't call her because of 'Party Patrol.' They called because of what she said about a ghost, and because she dared to sing opera on late-night TV. Who knows where else this collaboration might lead? She can bridge the past and the present. Phoenix can create history."

"Phoenix doesn't need help to create history. She'll do fine on her own."

Phoenix had sworn she would never be like the fragile, pampered artists who couldn't operate a Coke machine without a handler, and yet here she was, listening to Carlos and Gloria talk about her as if she wasn't there. And maybe she wasn't. Phoenix dunked her head beneath the water again, and their argument disappeared as water clogged her ears. She kept her eyes wide open, staring at their blurry calves and feet; one pair pale and smooth, one thick, hairy and dark. Gloria was kicking the water gently, creating ripples across the length of the pool.

Their legs were close together. Carlos and Gloria were probably attracted to each other, Phoenix realized. She wondered if she minded that, and she wasn't sure she did. She couldn't claim Carlos for herself, even if she wanted to. Carlos only belonged to Carlos. Besides, she felt spoken for now in a way she had not with Ronn, adjoined to her ghost instead.

As Phoenix held her breath beneath the water, her future became clear to her. She would do the concert in New York. She owed her label money, and she would make good on her contract. And she would perform whatever songs Three Strikes asked her to, even if she had to fight for control of her own vocal cords. Ronn deserved that, at least.

But she wouldn't run away from her ghost. Van Milton was already trying to plan a conference to study her music, and he thought she should record it right away. Phoenix hoped more music would come, that her ghost would come back to her tonight now that the passel of psychics was gone. The idea that he might not come again panicked her.

Phoenix ran out of air, gasping as her face broke free of the water.

"You liked me once, Gloria," she heard Carlos say as he rested an arm across Gloria's shoulder. "I have Satan on speed dial? Ouch. What makes you think I'm that bad?"

"I did like you, as a kid. But being fine isn't everything, dude. This is my cousin."

Yes, they're flirting, Phoenix thought. Or Carlos was, at least, even if he wasn't trying.

"You two shut up and come get in the pool," Phoenix said.

Obediently, Carlos pulled his feet out of the water and yanked open his rolled-up jeans, hiking them down and pulling his woolly legs free as if he undressed in front of them every day. He was wearing black bikini briefs, pulled snugly across his ample lump. Carlos flung off his T-shirt, and Phoenix enjoyed her first glimpse of his bared chest, the subtle rises that surfaced as he stood at the edge of the pool and raised his arms. Carlos dove, hardly splashing as he commanded the water to part for him. He swam toward her, a quick brown eel under the water. She hadn't known he was such a good swimmer.

"This time zone's killing me, so I'm gonna crash early," Gloria said, standing up. She shook her legs dry. "Working for you is hard damn work, cuz. You better get rich, because you owe me. You can have the room tonight. I'll sleep on the futon."

Gloria didn't ask if she would be going to bed alone, and Phoenix didn't know. Maybe Carlos would want to be here in case the ghost came back, or just because he wanted to be with her. And maybe she would decide she wanted him to stay. Phoenix felt her pores tingling as she wondered what would happen tonight. Sometimes, not knowing was most of the fun.

Carlos's head appeared beside her, and he rose, taller, as his feet found the pool floor. "Where's she going?" he said, watching Gloria retreat. Gloria was wearing white shorts, and her calves were twice the size of Phoenix's, like a surfer's. Carlos watched Gloria a long time.

"Bed, she said."

Carlos didn't say anything for a while, not moving.

"Float on your back," he said finally. "I'll hold you."

And so she did. Phoenix allowed her body to float free, her arms outstretched, while Carlos's palms braced her from below. The lapping warm water caressed her ears and cheeks. She closed her eyes, remembering the sound of her voice on the radio. Phoenix felt her body floating as if she could drift up into the sky.

Through half-open eyelids, Phoenix watched Carlos staring down at her, and she recognized the look he tried to hide deep in his eyes; Kendrick had looked at her this way in her hotel in St. Louis, as if a deity had landed in his arms.

so close to her that she hadn't seen it before: Her Rosenkranz piano. The piano wasn't old and neglected the way it had looked that day on the stairs; this was the Rosenkranz with elegantly shining rosewood and a gleaming candelabra she had seen in Carlos's room. *It belongs here. It lived here once.*

The only thing Phoenix couldn't find in her dream was evidence of herself: She felt no body mass, no hint of whether she was sitting or standing, or floating. She was nowhere and everywhere in this room, surrounded by its stoic existence even while her own felt imaginary.

Solomon Dixon opened the front door, and Phoenix saw the deluge outside. Lightning lit the skies. A crack of thunder mirrored Phoenix's heart's leap when she saw a man's silhouette and realized who was standing at the door. *He's here, too.*

He stepped into the room, and she saw his face, which was softer than in his photographs. His face was round, Sarge's shade of brown, and wild-eyed, not reserved the way he'd been captured for posterity. His brown coat was nearly too big for him, making him look smaller than he was. "What happened?" he said, breathing harshly. "Where's Freddie?"

"Don't fret, Scotty. She's here."

"M-my hands are shaking so much, I couldn't use my key."

Solomon Dixon planted his hands on Scott Joplin's shoulders, leaning down to talk to him the way a father might. "Dr. Walden just left. He says it's turned to pneumonia."

"Dear God," Scott said. "I heard . . ."

"He got the fever down, but she's been talkin' out her head."

"She's *delirious*?" Scott said. He looked as if he'd been kicked in the stomach. He snatched his cap off his head and balled it his hand, nervous. He looked right at her, and his sudden gaze sawed into her. "Why isn't she in bed, Sol?"

"She won't sit still. I figger she'll be all right now you're here."

Scott walked past Solomon Dixon and knelt in front of Phoenix, grasping her hands. She hadn't been able to feel her hands until he touched her, then her entire body came alive, remembering all of its nerve endings. Scott held one of her hands up to his cheek, which was as smooth as the skin on her own. Her hand vibrated, white-hot.

"What did he say to do?" Scott said.

CHAPTER SIXTEEN

*P*hoenix didn't realize she'd been asleep until she woke up in Solomon Dixon's parlor.

At the same time she wondered *Who's Solomon Dixon?* another tendril of her psyche recognized the man on sight as he walked past her toward the door; his hollowed cheeks, large ears and a slight overbite that made him look vaguely displeased even when he wasn't. He was her host, a friend of Scott's, and he was worried about her.

Then her certainty she was dreaming broke through the stream of impossible knowledge. She couldn't be in Solomon Dixon's parlor because she was at home in her roommate's bed in Los Angeles. She was not in Sedalia, Mississippi, and Solomon Dixon had been dead for generations. So, she had to be dreaming. The things she knew about Solomon Dixon might be true, but they certainly weren't real.

Which meant that this room wasn't real either, she thought, gazing around her.

But it seemed very real, an assault of details, a new one with each beat of her heart: a gray cat sleeping on its back near the fireplace, tufts of white fur exposed on its belly. A newspaper called the *Sedalia Conservator* with a headline about Emancipation Day. A pale ring on a wooden table where someone had left a water glass. The blue-and-white woven rug that spanned one length of the room to the other. A black overcoat dripping onto the wooden floorboards from the coatrack near the door. The smell of a roasting sweet ham. The most startling detail came last,

"I got her some water," a woman's voice said, "if she'll take it. Doc said to be sure she don't go thirsty." That voice was Olivia Dixon, Phoenix remembered. Solomon Dixon's wife.

" 'Sides that, he says time will tell," Solomon Dixon said. "He says plenty of folks come through it, Scotty."

"Freddie?" Scott said, so close that the tip of his nose almost touched hers as he searched her eyes. His breath smelled like mint sprigs and coffee. "Do you hear me?"

Phoenix heard him perfectly fine, but she couldn't say so. She was captivated by feeling the deep ridges of his smooth, damp palm, and the soft pads of his fingers. No touch had ever soaked into her so deeply, seeping inside of her.

"Come on with me back to bed, dear heart," Scott said. "You have a fever."

Phoenix realized she was sitting at Rosenkranz's bench. She suddenly smelled the wood polish. The piano's rack was covered in pages of hand-written sheet music, one piece scrawled "The Favorite." The dream was intent on convincing her it was real.

Phoenix decided to say something, or at least to try. "Play for me."

Phoenix had never pulled language into a dream, so she was surprised to hear her voice at all. It was a whisper, but it was *her,* talking to him.

And he heard her. He looked as surprised as she was. "Please, Freddie, you have to be in bed. You're very, very sick." His love for her was un-conditional, but the weight of it showed everywhere in his helpless face.

"Play a lil' somethin' for her, Scotty. It's all right," Solomon Dixon said. "Give the girl some music. That's prob'ly the best thing for her."

They call him Scotty, she realized. She hadn't seen that in any of the history books.

"Play," she said again, a struggle. This whisper was weaker than her last.

"Only if you promise me you'll go back to bed. Do you promise?"

She tried to speak, but she couldn't hear anything this time. She hoped she was nodding.

Scott took her hand from his cheek and laid it across three black notes, F-sharp, G-sharp and B-flat. He rested his hand on top of hers, warm and damp, matching the web of her fingers. His broad fingers felt heavy on top of hers. He pressed her index finger, and the F-sharp sounded, so pure it dazzled her. The piano's terrible racket was gone, replaced by a fresh, beautiful exuberance. The Rosenkranz hadn't turned sour yet. Not the way it was *going* to.

"Freddie? I sent for Lovie. Your sister's on her way, so please fight to be better, sweet gal," he said, leaning into her ear. As he stroked her hair, Phoenix's scalp smarted, a sensation that raced the length of her body like a mild electric shock. No touch in her dreams, or her waking life, had ever matched it. She might have gasped. Only then did she realize how hard it was to breathe, nearly impossible. The air in the room was too thick to inhale without a struggle.

Scott squeezed her hand. "Yes, Freddie. *Fight.*"

"*Play,*" she said, the only word she could form in the mouth she had borrowed.

Scott Joplin played, a familiar trilling. High F. He was playing the introduction to *A Guest of Honor,* as she'd hoped he would. Thunder cracked so loudly outside that the parlor windows shook. The sound of the storm buried the music.

"I'd better go see that the barn door's latched," Solomon Dixon said.

"I hope the windows upstairs are closed," Olivia Dixon said, almost at the same time.

Scott sank his fingers harder and louder on the Rosenkranz's keys, and the room erupted into melody. Phoenix watched his fingers at work, transfixed by the way his left hand bounced between the bass notes and chords while his right hand carved out a melody, a practiced liberation dance. The music was so convincing that Phoenix looked up at Scott's face, expecting to see some evidence of joy there. How could he play such a triumphant piece without a smile?

Instead, Scott's face looked gutted of joy. The melancholy she had seen from a distance in his visage was fully realized now, more like terror etched into the bones of his face. His fingers played with joy that was missing in his eyes, as if he were erecting a wall, note by note, between the world and his breaking heart.

"Scott?" she said. "Sing it for me."

Scott's lips remained so tight, she didn't think he had heard her. A tear dripped from the tip of his nose onto the piano keys. She was mustering the strength to try again when his gentle tenor voice escaped, hardly a breath: *"I am a man with many plans . . . To lift us from starvation . . ."* His voice was a revelation. His singing was beautiful. Were his talents endless?

"Record your voice," she said, "or no one will hear it. No one will know."

She gasped again, and the cinching of her lungs made her heart falter with dread. The wall of mucus coating her throat threatened to choke her. This body she wore in her dream was so flimsy. It felt ready to collaspse on top of her.

Scott sang on, playing the piano's keys blind while he soothed her with his unbroken gaze.

Freddie is dying, and Scott knows it, Phoenix realized. *They sat at this piano together.* If not for the music, their sadness would have smothered her. Phoenix felt tears scald her new face, until they followed Scott's to the Rosenkranz's keys.

Their tears blended beneath his fingertips, inseparable.

*P*hoenix was in a bed when she opened her eyes, and she expected to be somewhere else—a place she couldn't quite remember—but her first sight was Scott sitting at the edge of her bed in an undershirt, and her chest rose with relief at the sight of him. A graying white towel was slung around Scott's neck. He had sloping shoulders, and his bare arms were lanky muscle, flexing as he brushed his fingers across his scalp.

"Where am I?" she said.

Her voice seemed to startle him, then he smiled at her from everywhere except his eyes. "*Shhhhh.* You're at home, in bed."

But she wasn't at home, or anything like it. She had never lived in a room that was wood from ceiling to floor. Or a room filled with the dark, heavy oak furniture of another era, with intricately carved patterns in the bed's headboard and its matching, mirrored dresser. And lace everywhere, from the curtains to the doily on her nightstand beneath a vase of half-wilted roses. And the scent of cedar and wildflowers, a way her bedroom had never smelled. The light was dimmer than she was used to; a brass oil lamp with a globe embossed with flower patterns glowed from the dresser, the single light in a large room.

The clock on the mantel with two angels in white robes blowing long horns looked familiar for a moment, but maybe she'd only seen it in another dream.

"What happened?" Phoenix said. Talking was much easier now.

"You fainted," Scott said. "How do you feel?"

Phoenix gazed at Scott's face as closely as she could, because sometimes she could see every eyelash above his eyes, and sometimes she couldn't focus on him at all, as if the room's light was dimming. He might be fading, she realized. He was leaving her again.

"Touch me," she said. He'd never been as real as when he'd touched her in the parlor.

"You need rest," Scott said. "I don't think . . ."

Phoenix reached for his hand, relieved when she felt warm, living fingers. The single brush of his fingertip against her wrist made Phoenix jump, her body rigid, thighs pressed tight. What was this new power he had over her? How had he taken control of her body, too?

"Touch me . . . here," she said, and laid Scott's hand across her breast. She could feel the hot glow of his palm even through her gown, a sheet and the quilt between them. Her body wanted to levitate toward the magnet of his skin. Scott kept his hand flat atop her at first; then, tentatively, he pressed with one fingertip, making a small circle. She hissed when her nipple popped awake against his finger, rolling a gush of warmth across her stomach that came to rest in the swell between her thighs.

"You know I want to . . ." His voice sounding clogged in his throat. "But this is the wrong time. After what just happened . . . your condition . . . I don't think . . ."

"Touch me," she said. "Everywhere. Please."

He leaned over her, and this time she saw him clearly, all of the deathly worry in his face. "You're sure?" he said.

Instead of answering, Phoenix sat up and pulled at her clothes, eager to be freed. He helped her, making her naked with a single yank over her head. Phoenix trembled in the sudden air. She hadn't realized she was so cold. Or was it just that her skin was so damn hot?

"What . . . do you want me to do?" Scott asked, rubbing one hand down her back, gently traversing every bump on her spine.

"Make me remember you." She was so hoarse, she was whispering.

Once Scott had his instructions—once he knew what she wanted—he was ready to give her everything. He nibbled her neck with an assured sensuality that astonished her, and her neck became a tangle of live wires. Phoenix whimpered, forgetting her ailments. Scott dampened his fingertips in his mouth, first his left hand, then the right, and hugged her from behind, massaging her nipples with his slick fingers while his lips chewed at her neck. Her first, gentle orgasm pulsed early, and she felt her body pushing itself outward, bloating and ready.

Scott's mouth found its way to her nipple, sometimes suckling, sometimes lapping, and a dam broke inside of Phoenix. Dampness soaked her upper thighs. How did he already know her body so well? How did he know exactly how much pressure and how long?

Scott's chest was bare when he climbed onto the bed, hooking her legs around his neck as if he were harnessing himself to her. He stooped to lap his tongue against her quivering right thigh. Then, the other. His tongue plunged into her navel like a harpoon trawling deep beneath her skin, and Phoenix felt her stomach quake. Next, warm wetness darted between the gaps in her thicket of pubic hair, until Scott's tongue slowly parted her with its delicious, sustained prodding. Phoenix's buttocks clenched tight, stone. Her next orgasm made her buck as her body tried to devour his tongue.

Phoenix grasped his swollen penis hard, committing the weight and width of him to her palm's memory. The pad of her thumb explored his peak, damp from his eager juices, and circled his ridge. She sat up so her tongue could test his flavor: clean perspiration, salt, candied skin. She created a soft bed with her tongue and swallowed him. She retreated slowly, then swallowed him again, locking her lips rigid. She felt tiny veins throbbing against her tongue. He sucked in air by her ear, whispering something as his fingers tightened across her scalp. A prayer?

They were both wet now, as if they'd been out in the rain. Perspiration glowed from their skin, one fire feeding another.

He turned her over until she was on her stomach, then she felt him slide his damp, naked weight across her back, a second covering, as if she were inside him. His rigid manhood plied against her, and he gently pulled one of her legs apart to help him burrow, seeking darkness and warmth. He used his hand to guide him, then he plunged, sure.

Phoenix's fingers tightened against the sheet beneath her, claws. She was filled to overflowing. The rainstorm had come indoors, because now rain was spilling out of her. The pleasure he forged in her was so large and sudden, she lost herself in its current, feeling his searing breath against her back. Phoenix raised her hips against him as far as his weight allowed above her, and felt him creep deeper inside her, to her core. Her slick body flopped against him. He slid his hands beneath her to cup her breasts, pinching her nipples until Phoenix felt tears of pleasure. With slow, even strokes, his pelvis cleaved behind her, prying her open. Setting her free.

Phoenix could barely catch her breath beneath him, but she wouldn't ask him to climb away even if it meant she would suffocate. Phoenix's third orgasm made her faint again, or something like it, her mind flickering. She blinked and woke up in time to feel turbulent pleasure gathering itself up to smother her again.

She craned her neck to find his mouth, sinking against his lips. Scott welcomed her kiss.

His mouth and breath were as cold as a refrigerator door.

The moment Phoenix dreaded had come: She didn't know if she was sleeping or awake.

Morning light warmed up outside the edges of the aluminum foil taped to the windows. The old Raggedy Ann and Andy alarm clock Nia had kept since childhood said it was six in the morning. If the alarm had been set, maniacal children's voices would have begun their daily harassing chorus: *"We were sent to wake you, so here we are to say . . . Please get up, brush your teeth, and start your happy day!"*

But this was the wrong clock. The last clock she'd seen had been of angels and trumpets. The wood furniture had been replaced by a double bed with no headboard, and the matched bureau and nightstands were plastic crates and U-build-it white bookshelves crammed with old scripts and books about films and filmmaking. There could be no doubt about it: She was in Nia's room, where she'd gone to bed last night; therefore, she could *not* be dreaming. She was where she belonged.

But something had changed. Something was different.

Phoenix gazed down at herself, peeking beneath the single sheet. She was naked, and she never slept naked. Even if it was only a T-shirt, Phoenix hated to sleep without clothes.

Phoenix's body suddenly quivered with the memory of lovemaking. Her clitoris throbbed, still aroused, and the pressure of her full bladder made the arousal feel urgent. Phoenix's fingers rested between her legs, comforting her body with the steady pressure. *He made love to me,* she thought, overwhelmed by the magnitude of the memory. Her body ached for him even as her mind spiraled, confused.

How could that have happened? How could she have made love to a ghost?

That was when Phoenix heard breathing behind her, nearly soundless in sleep. She wanted it to be him—prayed it would be him—even when she knew it wouldn't be. It *couldn't* be.

When she turned to look beside her, Carlos lay naked, asleep. The sheet covered one of his legs, but not the one bent at the knee. His genitals sat in her view, his half-flaccid penis pointing away from her, uncircumcised. She had never seen an uncircumcised penis before, she realized. Carlos's nakedness embarrassed her.

Phoenix fought for her memory, and found nothing. All she saw was a face that was not Carlos's, skin that was a shade darker than Carlos's, and a room that was not this room. This must have been how Gloria felt when she was a student at UM, on those mornings she'd called Phoenix in a panic after a night of drinking and frat parties: *Phee, I think I had sex with somebody last night.* Phoenix had told her cousin that having black-outs was a sign she had a problem, and Gloria hadn't touched alcohol since.

Now, it was Phoenix's problem. She felt sick to her stomach. She waited for the spell to pass, then she pulled her sheet up to cover her chest to cover herself. Finally, she nudged Carlos.

Carlos awoke with a squinting, sleepy smile. He propped himself on his elbows, gazing at her without reaching to touch her. "'Morning," he said.

"Did we have sex last night?"

He grinned, but his grin broke in half when he saw she wasn't joking. "What?"

"I don't remember, Carlos. Did we or didn't we?"

Carlos's eyebrows dropped with an expression she didn't know him well enough to recognize. Quickly, he sat up on the edge of the bed and found his jeans on the floor, which he hiked up in a flash, still scowling. For a moment, she thought he planned to leave without answering her question. "What do you remember?" he said, snapping his fly.

"Having sex with him," she said, because she had to tell someone. "With Scott."

Carlos sighed, combing his hands through his hair, one after the other. Scott had done that, too, she remembered. "I see," Carlos said. It was the most quiet she had ever seen him. He stared toward the foot of the bed, but occasionally he looked at her through the corner of one eye. "I'm sorry to hear that."

"What do *you* remember from last night?"

"A different version," he said. Talking seemed to cause him pain. "You sang in your sleep for a while. The opera. I brought the camera in here to capture it." He gestured, and for the first time she noticed the video camera on its tripod, aimed toward the bed. "That was for about an hour. Then, I think you fainted. But you woke right up. You said you were all right."

"And we had sex after that? After I fainted?" She hadn't meant to sound accusing, but accusation crept into her voice like a hatchet.

"Jesus, Phoenix, I said it wasn't the right time . . ."

Yes. She remembered that part, the conversation. But she didn't remember Carlos being there. Scott was the one who had thought the time wasn't right.

"I was somewhere else," she said. "I wasn't here. It was another bedroom, full of antiques. More pillows on the bed, and a kerosene lamp. And it was him, not you." Even as Phoenix remembered, she could feel the memory draining away. She would never remember it as well as she did at this moment, she realized.

"Turn the camera back on," she said, and Carlos jumped behind the camera to do as she'd asked. Phoenix closed her eyes, trying to rescue details. "His friend called him Scotty. It was raining. We were at some kind of boardinghouse, I think. Solomon and Olivia Dixon. Freddie had pneumonia. She was there. She was me, but she wasn't. He spoke softly, with an accent, like, from the South. Other than that, he talked like you or me. His touch was . . ." She stopped there. She couldn't think of the words to do his touch justice, and she wasn't sure Carlos would want to hear if she could. Phoenix suddenly felt alone, abandoned. "He sang, and it was beautiful. I told him to record his voice, or no one would know . . ."

Suddenly, Phoenix heard herself sob. The grief that engulfed her stole her words. She had *talked* to him, and he was gone. Scott Joplin had never recorded his voice, and he had been dead more than eighty years. Yet, she had heard him speak and sing, and he had touched her.

The memory of his touch, the part of him that was still living, helped her get past her tears even though she still trembled every few seconds, in waves. "I fainted, but I woke up in a bedroom with him. I told him to touch me."

"I heard you say that," Carlos said. "I thought you were talking to me."

"He said he wasn't sure it was the right time, but I didn't want to wait. We took off my clothes. He made love to me from behind. Lying on top of me."

"That wasn't me," Carlos said. "I would never do that the first time. How do you kiss?"

Phoenix remembered her ghost's cold, dead kiss. She couldn't say that part aloud. Already, she wanted to vomit again, and she fought to keep her stomach from lurching. She had never been so sad, but the kiss made her sick to her stomach. Phoenix didn't know how to feel.

"How did it happen with us?" she asked, so she could stop thinking about her ghost.

Carlos looked furtive as he clicked off the camera's red recording light. "Like I said, you fainted. Then you woke up, said you were OK, and we went to bed. A while later, you said you wanted me to touch you." He cleared his throat. "It went on from there. Maybe I'll tell you all about it sometime, but I don't feel like reminiscing right now. What do I say, *I'm sorry*? I thought you were talking to me."

"You used a condom, right?" Phoenix said, remembering. She'd fallen off the pill on tour, forgetting to get a refill in Memphis. The last thing she needed was to get pregnant—or, worse, to get AIDS. How much did she really know about Carlos?

Carlos searched the floor for his shirt, which he yanked on as if he had to hurry to get to work on time—even though he made his own schedule. "*You* woke *me* up, Phoenix. You put my hand on your breast and asked me to touch you. Yes, I used a condom." He sounded like he was giving testimony at a trial. Standing across the room instead of lying with her in the bed, he seemed as far from her as he could be.

"I'm not pressing charges, Carlos. I'm sorry, too. It's not like I forgot on purpose. I remember asking you to spend the night. Did you think that was all about the ghost?"

That slowed Carlos's dressing frenzy, even if his face still looked stricken. He stared at the floor. "OK, sorry. I thought you were imply-ing . . . I don't know . . ." Carlos's face changed, and he became the same man she'd known. He shook his head at himself, scooting across the bed until he was cradling her, careful not to expose her beneath the sheet, as if he had never seen her nude. "You're the one who should be freaked out, *linda*. Are you okay?"

"Sort of," she said. She sank against Carlos, and she didn't feel nearly as nauseated and abandoned with him holding her. Her heart slogged in her chest.

"Is he still here?" Carlos said.

Phoenix's eyes darted around the room, but she couldn't tell. There were no light patterns, no noises, no cold air. The air did not feel elec-tric, as it often did when he was near. Would she be glad if the closet door flew open and her ghost came striding toward her bed in a man's form, or would she scream? *Probably both.*

"I don't think so," she said.

"Do you want to tell me more? What happened?" Carlos said.

Phoenix *did* want to tell him more, she just wasn't sure she should. "It's like . . . when I'm there with him . . . I love him already. I don't know how to explain it. It's as if I really *know* him, Carlos. That's why, when he touches me, it's so . . . different. I st-still . . ." She blinked, squeezing her eyes closed. The grief was receding, but she could still cry for hours if she were alone, she thought. All the pleasure her ghost had brought her was pain now.

Carlos stroked her hair. "It's OK. There's a strong bond, something to do with his wife. We knew that. He scared both of us this time, Phee, but it's OK. You're just feeling it more deeply. So now we've learned again that ghosts don't always come the way we expect them to. I just want to be sure you didn't feel like he . . . forced you?"

"No," she said, plugging her damp nostril with her wrist. "I wanted him."

"Would you want it to happen again?"

Her body sang. Phoenix was too tired for lies. "Yes."

"But are you sorry about what happened with us? With me?"

"No," she said. "I'm only sorry I don't remember."

Carlos sighed, and she wondered if that seemed like a small consolation. He kissed her forehead. "I can live with that if you can," he said, in a sober voice.

"You can?"

He made a soft, thoughtful humming sound. "We'll see." That sounded less hopeful.

"Did I sing the whole opera, Carlos?"

"I think so. I might have missed a little at the beginning, but we got the first song on the *Live at Night* tape. I think you have it now, Phoenix. All of it. You've done it, kiddo."

"And? How is it?" she said. It had been beautiful to her, but she was biased.

Phoenix looked at Carlos's face in time to see his eyes soften from slighted lover to music enthusiast, someone who understood how miraculous Scott was. "It's masterful," Carlos said, squeezing her hand. "The lyrics, some are better than others—he's a little preachy—but it's breathtaking to hear it all the way through. A little folksier than *Treemonisha*, but maybe as good. Or better. You'd have to figure out the orchestrations . . ."

"Maybe he'll give me those next time," Phoenix said.

The mention of *next time* cut their conversation short.

Phoenix stared at Carlos's chest, noticing that he had more curly spirals of hair than the man who had made love to her last night, and his skin's brown retained a hint more of a Native American ancestor's, and his face was more angular than round. All of the differences between the men leaped at her.

"Did we talk about rules last night?" Phoenix said. "Before we had sex?"

"Since it turns out you were asleep at the time, there wasn't much conversation, if you know what I mean," Carlos said, and she was glad to hear him joke about it. When Carlos wasn't scared, it was much easier to believe she shouldn't be either. Otherwise, she might vomit and never leave her bed. Phoenix was fighting fear with everything in her.

"OK, well, that has to be the first rule," Phoenix said. "There are rules."

Carlos nodded tentatively, crossing his arms across his chest as he waited to hear them.

The student becomes the teacher, she thought. She'd heard that saying somewhere, and she remembered it now because Carlos had been there when she first realized she needed rules, during the eight months she'd mourned him. That was when her rules had been born, when she'd first made vows to herself about the sacredness of her heart and skin. Phoenix had never written down her rules in a diary or told anyone what they were, but two one-night stands and a few bad relationships later, Phoenix was ready to live by her rules.

"I'm not in the market for a fuckbuddy," she said. "We're not going to say yeah, let's keep in touch, stay out of each other's business and jump in bed every time I happen to be in town. I tried that with Ronn, and it didn't work. If that's what you're looking for, we can pretend last night never happened."

Carlos's expression didn't change, as if he were listening to a mission he might or might not choose to accept. No flinches so far.

She went on. "If I'm sleeping with you, you're my boyfriend, and I'm your girlfriend. When you're with me, you'll have to try not to fall over yourself when you see a woman with nice legs. Or blondes. And no flirting with my cousin. Period."

Carlos opened his mouth to object, but he reconsidered, granting the point. "Go on."

"And we're monogamous," she said. "No sex with anyone else."

Carlos raised his eyebrows, a challenge. He didn't have to say the words aloud.

"I know what you're thinking, and that doesn't count," Phoenix said. "Even if I knew a way to keep him from coming back, I don't want to."

"Of course not. I wouldn't ask you to."

"Anyway, that's different, Carlos. It's more like a dream with him. It isn't real."

Carlos touched her chin with his index finger. "What's real is what you remember, Phee."

What *did* she remember? She remembered climbing out of the pool with Carlos, asking him if he thought the ghost would visit, and how they'd stood squirming in the moonlight before she finally took his hand and said, *Come on in. Stay with me.* After that, there was only Scott, even if her memories of Scott had faded, as if she'd had last night's dream a year ago.

"I promise to remember next time," Phoenix said, stroking a dreadlet that had fallen near Carlos's eyes, tightly woven jet threads. She could be talking to Carlos or Scott, or both.

Carlos pursed his lips, turning away in mock sulkiness. "Isn't there some paperwork you need me to sign first? Some fine print I need to read?"

She shook her head, smiling. "No paperwork. Just rules."

"And meanwhile, you still get to play with your Backdoor Man?"

"You're right, Carlos. Fair is fair. You can have sex with all the dead people you want."

With a playful grunt, Carlos grabbed her tightly around her middle, rolling her closer to him. The bedsheet pulled free with her, until Phoenix and a mound of covers lay directly atop Carlos's chest. As he breathed, she rose and fell with his rib cage. Neither of them had brushed their teeth yet, and their breath smelled the same.

"You sure about that?" Carlos said. "Because I just got a very friendly visit from Dorothy Dandridge, and she was lookin' kinda fine. Halle didn't do her justice."

"She must be pretty damn fine."

"She's not the only one." His face was so close, they breathed the same air. Carlos's smile vanished as he gazed up at her. His eyes looked more like Scott's, suddenly. "*Cuidado,* Phee. Be careful. Make rules for him, too. You don't want to be in love with a dead man."

Phoenix's stomach tightened, more grief. She still missed him, she realized, a useless feeling with nowhere to go. A hard feeling. "I know. I'll be careful."

When Carlos Harris kissed Phoenix again for the first time in memory since she was sixteen, his mouth and tongue were a warm, welcome haven. A homecoming.

And alive, Phoenix reminded herself. *Alive.*

Part Four

"It's showtime, folks!"

JOE GIDEON,
All That Jazz

CHAPTER SEVENTEEN

St. Louis
1906

*W*hen I saw the name on my pad, I had to look twice," the physician said, beaming at Scott from behind round, gold-rimmed eyeglasses. He grasped Scott's hand, pumping hard. "This *is* a pleasure. Tom Turpin's mentioned your name, sure enough, but I didn't realize you were back. Do you know my wife and I played 'Maple Leaf Rag' on our wedding day?"

Dr. Otis Wiley was a dark young man with a broad smile and hulking shoulders nearly too large for his white physician's coat. He could be the Negro boxer Jack Johnson, except for his eyeglasses and the stethoscope around his neck. His moustache was trimmed stylishly thin, the ends disappearing as blacks wisps so tightly wound they looked braided. Scott would have preferred an older doctor, but he looked capable enough.

"The band played it so fast, we were about to trip over our feet," Dr. Wiley said, not discouraged by Scott's silence. "'Maple Leaf' is one of our favorites."

Scott heard new stories about "Maple Leaf" all the time, as if his piece were a child away prospecting for gold, and from time to time he caught wind of its adventures. Apparently musicians from far and wide used his piece to try to outshine each other, carving their own fame. The most outlandish story, to date, was that President Roosevelt had cake-walked to "Maple Leaf Rag" at an event at the White House. It seemed unlikely, but Scott didn't know. His song had its own life, and less and less of it had anything to do with him.

"You didn't have to come to my office," the doctor said. "I would've been happy to come see you at home, Mr. Joplin. You're out in Clayton? All you had to do was phone."

"I don't mind it," Scott said. "It's a chance to get out." Two sentences of chitchat had drained Scott, and the day was only getting started. Tom told him he should get out more, but the world beyond his parlor was a tiring exercise.

Everyone said he would get his feet under him again after Freddie, and he'd tried to believe that the first year despite every evidence that he would never have his footing again. In the beginning, every third woman he saw looked like her and he could cry half a day straight. After a year of that, he *needed* to believe there was another way to be. But his poor girl had been gone two years now, and Scott was still tired from the time he woke up each day. Grieving was the hardest work he'd ever done.

"What brings you to the doctor today?" Dr. Wiley said.

Finally. He could be out with it. He could have it done.

"My hair's been falling out in back," Scott said. He didn't touch the nape of his neck, where it itched. He'd learned how to ignore the itching during daylight, never scratching in public, but the nights were driving him mad. "Tom thinks it might be overwork. You know, tension and the like. I guess I'm all right with it, but his wife insisted, so here I am."

"I see," Dr. Wiley said. He walked behind Scott to gaze at his hairline. "So . . . are you working on any new compositions after 'Maple Leaf Rag'?"

Scott felt his back teeth tighten. "Always," he said, trying to smile. On another day, he might have explained that he'd published two dozen pieces since "Maple Leaf," and he would be happy to list the names. Most people thought "Maple Leaf" was his only composition, and he found some humor in that sometimes. But not today.

"How long's the itching been troubling you?" the doctor asked.

"Comes and goes," Scott said. "A couple weeks so far, this time."

The doctor tentatively touched the back of Scott's neck, parting the hair to show his scalp. "Where's the most exciting place you've ever performed, Mr. Joplin?"

Scott realized his fingers were tight around his wooden armrests, and he exhaled and forced his hands to go slack. His nervousness might be apparent, so this doctor was trying to take his mind from this visit. Already, the doctor pitied him.

But better to be here, he reminded himself. *Better to have it done.*

"I guess that would be the World's Fair," Scott said, swallowing the dry mound in his throat. Freddie had all but blotted the fair, since his giddiness after meeting her and his visions of Wonderland from the book she'd given him had inspired him to write the piece he'd been playing the night Tom Turpin told him he had a letter from Freddie, the night he learned her father had said yes, and they were engaged. All that had happened during the fair.

Scott raised his fist to clear his throat again. "You remember those fountains? What a display! I wrote a piece about them and played it. Colored musicians played, you know, in the breezeways, but a lot of people enjoyed it even so. There were people from everywhere. All over the *world*, really. That felt good." As Scott spoke, he opened his fist and stretched out his fingers. Sometimes he felt a razor's first kiss across his tendons when his fingers stretched, and sometimes he felt fine.

But he would bring that up later. One thing at a time.

"Your hand bothering you, too?" the doctor said, not letting him wait.

Scott shrugged, and his right shoulder twinged. He'd almost forgotten his shoulders, which complained more and more when he raised his arms too high, or even when he didn't. One more thing for his list. "Yeah, I've got some stiffness."

"For how long?"

"Some time now, I guess. Couple years, on and off. Maybe more."

While the doctor wrote that down, Scott's mind looked for diversions. Where was that fool Louis? One of the reasons Scott had looked forward to being back in St. Louis was to be near Louis, who, like him, had moved to Chicago and back. Louis never came to the Rosebud anymore, Tom said—but then again, neither did anyone else, since Tom was talking about shutting his place down. Scott hadn't been able to find Louis in a month. Louis wasn't at his last-known address, but Scott was determined to find him. A man needed his friends the most during the times he didn't want to be found.

The doctor walked around to face Scott. He folded his arms and leaned back against his desk, as if he didn't want to tower too high above him. "When's the last time you saw a doctor, Mr. Joplin?" Dr. Wiley said. His voice was as gentle as he would speak to a child.

"My wife took sick two years ago, suffered seven weeks. I'd seen enough doctors," Scott said. He made his heart go cold so he could get through the facts without dredging up the memory. The horrifying sound of Freddie's struggles to breathe was a burden he couldn't carry today, not in front of a stranger.

"I'm very sorry. What took her from you?"

"Pneumonia, the doc said. Consumption, I think. Her lungs." *Her lungs ain't right.* Scott had to stop talking about Freddie. He'd have to say so if the doctor asked about her again.

"God keep you. That's a dreadful loss," the doctor said, writing again. "But when did you last see a doctor for yourself?"

"Been a long time," Scott said. "I don't recall."

"Have you had any rashes?"

"Besides whatever's itching my head?" Scott said. "Not in a while. How far back?"

"Up to . . . ten years ago?"

The dog sleeps, Scotty.

Scott's hands clung to his armrests again. "Yeah, I have. I think so."

"Where did the rashes turn up?"

"My feet."

"Anywhere else?"

Scott made himself meet the young doctor's eyes, as much as he wanted to look away. "My privates. Well, my thigh, but . . . close to my privates," he said, trying to sound matter-of-fact. "I had a sore, maybe in '99. It healed."

Unless it was Scott's imagination, the doctor's face had become a mask over another expression, but pieces escaped in the man's eyes, a quiet alarm. Scott looked toward the windows, feeling a sudden certainty that none of them were open. The office felt like a hothouse, but all three rectangular windows were pushed up high. A plant on the sill trembled in the breeze.

"Did it leave a scar?" the doctor said.

"Yes. Not bad, though."

"Sorry I have to ask you this, Mr. Joplin, but may I see the scar? I have a screen and a gown. I'd like you to disrobe, sir."

"Why?" Scott said.

"Seeing the scar will help me get a fix on your symptoms."

"What do you think it is?" Scott said. Only five words, but few had ever weighed so heavily on his tongue. He'd been avoiding those words for six years.

Before today, the hardest words he'd uttered had been the night a stupid boy ran up to him at a gig in Sedalia and claimed Freddie had died. The news had sent Scott fleeing for home in a rainstorm, but it turned out the doc had come and pronounced she had pneumonia. How the news had gotten so confused, Scott never knew. Pneumonia would kill Freddie sure enough, but not *that* day. The boy's report had always sounded slapdash, so Scott had refused to believe his wife could be dead—he *couldn't* believe it—until Sol Dixon met him at the door, and he saw his friend's face. Then, suddenly, the worst was plausible. *What happened?* Scott had asked.

Those had been his hardest words, until today.

The night of the storm. The night he sang. The night he last made love to Freddie.

"There's any number of ailments to explain a rash," Dr. Wiley told Scott, not blinking, and Scott's heart skipped, hopeful. The young man had an honest face, so he might even be telling the truth. Good news would be worth undressing and the indignity of this whole awful affair.

The examination was careful, nearly twenty minutes. Scott stood behind an Oriental-styled screen while the doctor examined him head to foot, following with quiet questions. *Have you noticed bald patches on your head? How long do these outbreaks on your scalp usually last?* The doctor asked about his hands, his arms, even his moods. As Scott stood in the doctor's office naked except for his black socks—and even those came off for a time when the doctor turned over his feet to look at his soles—Scott didn't know how he'd mistaken the room for hot before. He felt cold. And ridiculous. And damned.

When Dr. Wiley left the room to let him dress himself in privacy, Scott thought about the story he'd have for his father when he saw him next. *Yeah, Pappy, I went to see a colored doctor with a hincty office on Olive*

Street, and the white patients waiting to see him called him "Doctor," not "boy." The degree on the wall says he graduated from Oberlin, but Tom says he's not ashamed to two-step like a fool. Freddie would have liked him.

Scott wasn't nervous by the time Dr. Wiley came back. In the doctor's absence, hearing the motorcars, barking dogs and newsboys carrying on three floors beneath them, Scott discovered the secret to keeping his nerve: He was ready to know. Knowing was its own salvation. Knowing was enough.

Dr. Wiley sat behind his desk this time, farther away than he'd been. His face's guise was gone now, so Scott knew what he was going to say. He'd known since Louis came to see him on Morgan Street, even if he'd lied to himself. The doctor had trouble choosing his first words.

"Well?" Scott said.

The doctor's eyes looked like glass. He twisted the end of his moustache, then folded his hands on his desk, disciplined. "Mr. Joplin . . . there's talk of a new blood test, but I'm not equipped for it. But to speak frankly, I've seen these cases before, and I feel a duty to share my mind."

"Yes. Tell me."

The doctor's jaw locked. He picked up his fountain pen and wrote something on a fresh page of his notebook. Then, he tore the page free and reached across his vast desktop to give it to Scott, past thick books, models of the human body and shiny instruments of healing.

S-y-p-h-i-l-i-s, the slanted script said.

So, there it was, in front of his nose. At last.

"Is my writing clear?" the doctor said.

Scott nodded, clasping the page with both hands. His heart was calmer now than before. All his concentration lay within the doctor's words. The world was this man's voice.

"Not all cases of this damnable disease come to this, but some do. You might have seen a doctor sooner, but I don't know if it would have mattered. I've never held much stock in the mercury cure. There's some promising talk about arsenic, but that's still talk, too. Either way you look at it, this disease is difficult. And where you are with it . . . I'm not hopeful your symptoms will improve."

Freddie.

"My wife?" Scott whispered. As he thought of Freddie, Scott became so rigid that his bones felt like they might crack. "Did I . . ."

"How long did you know her?"

"Three months before we married."

The doctor smiled, elated to have a glimmer of good news. "Then this disease posed no danger to your wife, Mr. Joplin, not for many years before you met. No matter what some doctors believe, it's my firm opinion that once a year had passed since your *first* experience in 1899, you were no danger to anyone. I promise you, whatever happened to your wife is not a cross for your conscience to bear. That was God's province, and God's alone."

The relief that swamped Scott exposed the maw in him he'd held at bay, and he doubled over in his chair, gasping. "Thank you, Doctor," he whispered, tears spilling from his eyes. "*Thank* you, dear Jesus, dear Lord."

He could not have lived knowing he had hurt Freddie. It was hard enough to think she might be alive if he had left her with her parents during that tour, if she had never been with him to catch her fatal cold. But to have cursed her through the act of making love, when he had only sought to give her bliss, to imprint his heart upon her soul? Precious reprieve! *Then I had no hand in killing either of my girls, my Freddie or my baby. Dear God, only by chance . . .*

Scott heard Dr. Wiley's chair slide across his wooden floor, and hurried footsteps as the doctor came to him. "Are you faint? Do you need salts?"

Scott shook his head. "I'm sorry. A moment," he said, and the doctor backed away to give Scott time to summon his masculinity and straighten himself in his seat.

"Anything I tell you today is with the highest discretion. No one will hear any hint of this visit from my lips," Dr. Wiley said. "You have my word."

Scott clenched his hands into fists, and the razors between his knuckles stabbed him. All this time, he'd lived under the foolish hope that grief alone had caused his body so much havoc. When he hadn't liked the sound of his piano, he'd given his hands rest for a day or two, and sometimes he sounded fine after that. He'd even begun using an arthritis tonic advertised in the *Palladium*. This doctor must think he was a fool! And wasn't he?

Scott stared down at the royal purple Persian rug beneath his feet, his black shoes lined up in a V at the heel, perfectly still.

"I'm a musician. I play piano," Scott said. "What about my hands?"

Dr. Wiley almost hid the wobble in his words. "I don't know, Mr. Joplin," he said.

Scott hoped it was his doctor's first and only lie.

*T*he man in a smart white Stetson exited the rear stage door with a swoop of his long coat, a sudden apparition beneath the lamplight. He was almost invisible as he swept past the congregation of young men and ladies sharing cigarettes in the alleyway against a brick wall, the women in heels so high they looked like they might topple. The man in the Stetson didn't slow when they called praises after him. His wide brim hid his profile, but Scott knew Louis by his height and his walk, even if he was missing his swagger as he rounded the corner into the lamplight.

Louis had billed himself at the theater as *The Black Paderewski,* after the Polish pianist and composer Ignace Paderewski, but the comparison hadn't held. Louis's fingers had fumbled at least twice during his rendition of Chopin's "Polonaise in A major—Military," and his crisp, extraordinary command of the keys was gone. The audience might not have noticed, but Scott had. Louis was still very good, but he did not play like Louis Chauvin. Scott feared otherwise, but he hoped Louis was only drunk. The performance had been hard to endure.

Louis paused beside a poorly dressed black man plucking his guitar where the alley met the sidewalk. The player coaxed whimpers from his strings, harmonic sounds of hope and misery he'd brought from somewhere else times were harder. His chords slid between C, F and G, a tale of woe. Louis tossed a coin in the man's hat and walked on.

As Louis departed against the tide of night revelers on Beaumont, Scott nearly let him go. There would be no such thing as easy conversation tonight. The sight of Louis's retreat in his Parisian-style coat and favorite hat was heartening, like a photograph from a Kodak box camera, one moment frozen the way it should be. This was how he wanted to remember the boy, not by his decline in the concert hall. *How will Louis want to remember me?*

Scott followed Louis half a block. "You can play, lil' man, but can you *fight?*" he called.

Scott was sorry for his miserable attempt at humor as soon as he spoke, watching Louis's body go to stone. In the old days, Louis would have whipped around with a razor ready if a stranger taunted him from behind. But Louis only stopped walking, his hands in his coat pockets, patiently awaiting his fate.

"It's just me, Louis," Scott said, trotting beside him.

Louis gave him a glare, but didn't stand still long enough for Scott to get a good look at his face. "Fuck you, old man."

"How 'bout dinner?"

"Ain't hungry." Louis kept walking.

Scott hurried to catch up to him. "Where you headed, youngster?"

"I got a yen," Louis said. "Come if you want. If not, I'll see you when I see you."

This was the same way Louis had been in Chicago last year, unrecognizable. Scott had moved to Chicago hoping to find other publishers so he wouldn't have to settle for John Stark's offers when he didn't like them; but also because Louis, Sam Patterson and Arthur Marshall had all moved to the Windy City, heeding Chicago's appetite for lively music and quality musicians. In Chicago, it had taken Scott a month to track Louis down. He and Sam Patterson had found their friend living in a small rented room in a South Side cathouse, clinging to his pipe. The madam who prepared Louis's meals and tolerated his moods told them he hadn't played a piano in two weeks. *He don't like the way his hands work,* she'd whispered. But someone had apparently been helping Louis capture some of his themes on paper, because there had been scraps of sheet music tossed around his room, amid the clutter and filth.

The themes were crudely drawn, but beautiful. One particular habañera had been so gently harmonic, full of Louis's essence, that Scott asked to take it with him, if only to salvage it from the trash. Louis had been surly, but he'd agreed. *Why don't we go on down to the piano, then?* Scott had said, practically leading him by the arm. They'd only spent an hour working out a few ideas, but they'd both seen the clear way to couple their music, a collaboration. And that had been the end of it. Louis was always hard to find, and he'd never sought Scott out since.

But at least he was performing again.

Today, Tom had tipped Scott off that Louis was in a high-class vaude-ville company playing at the Douglass Theatorium at the corner of Beaumont and Lawton. Watching him play, Scott had hoped his friend was free from his poisonous despair. Apparently not.

The sign in the darkened picture window of the multistory building where Louis stopped advertised *Cigars, Pipes and Tobacco!* But appar-ently tobacco wasn't the only substance sold within, Scott learned as he followed Louis to the alleyway entrance behind the sleeping storefront, beneath the building's spiraling metal fire stairs. Louis knocked only once, and the door cracked open. Scott smelled opium, rich and sweet.

A large white man's squarish face peered out.

"Curtain already, maestro?" the man said to Louis. "The show's get-ting shorter."

"Not short enough," Louis muttered. He gestured at Scott. "This here's Joe."

"Must be a dozen Joes here. You all can start your own social club." The man widened the doorway to allow them in, and Scott squeezed past his paunch.

Inside, Louis knew his way past the maze of stacked crates and boxes lining the dimly lighted hallways, his pace quickening. Louis took off his coat and loosened his collar at the neck, so Scott followed his exam-ple, removing his jacket. His shirt was damp with perspiration. Without the cool breeze off the river, it was nothing but August inside. The cloy-ing scent grew stronger, a thin haze above them.

"Is this where you live now?" Scott said.

"Would if they'd let me." Louis followed eight brick steps down half a floor and found a wooden door, his destination. He pushed the door open, and Scott followed him inside.

Scott knew plenty of men and women with a taste for opium or lau-danum, but he'd never visited an opium den. Based on stories he'd heard from San Francisco, he expected to see rows of Chinamen reclined on pallets and silk pillows with hookahs between their lips. But there were no Chinamen in sight.

The windowless room was long and narrow, the walls covered in an array of mismatched felt curtains in dark, meditative colors. The room suffered from uneven lighting, with candles burning on tables throughout. Parlor chairs, settees and pillows with colorful tassels stretched the length of the room. Nearest to the door, a middle-aged white man splayed across a settee whispered conversation with a younger woman nestled against him. Something in her demure bearing made Scott think she was his wife, not a mistress. As they passed, Scott heard their English accents.

The room was otherwise occupied by men in gentlemanly attire spaced to create their own private retreats. Passing their tables, Scott saw absinthe glasses, burned spoons and pipes of a half dozen varieties. Scott heard some languid conversation, but no one made eye contact or greeted them, cocooned in their pilgrimages as they sat with eyes closed, or staring beyond the walls. *A fraternity of escape,* Scott thought. Many of the men were young, closer to Louis's age, and they seemed undisturbed by the arrival of two Negroes. Laws separated the races by day, but by night people didn't seem to mind each other.

The winged chair farthest across the room, facing the door, was empty. Swathed by tall, potted plants, the empty chair reminded Scott of a throne, and sure enough, that was where Louis took his seat. A teenaged attendant came, and Louis wordlessly exchanged coins for a china dish with two small, tarry balls of opium. Louis wasted no time striking a match to light the water pipe on the table beside him. The ball of opium held the flame as it burned, almost a candle itself, and Scott heard water bubbling as Louis inhaled his favorite tonic from its hose. Scott's nose smarted at the scent, like burnt berries.

Satisfied, Louis lay back in his chair, eyes closed, hands folded across his stomach. Scott sat near Louis on the ottoman, his first chance to study his friend's face, and his heart plunged.

He had expected Louis to be thin, so that wasn't a surprise. Louis had been fifteen pounds thinner in Chicago last year, and the lost weight altered Louis's face most, honing his jaw, erasing his youth. Now, in addition, Louis's complexion was marred by splotches that resembled razor scars across his cheeks and chin, visible even through his stage powder. *Someone with Louis's vanity must loathe his shaving mirror,* Scott thought.

But there was no loathing in Louis's expression now. Only dreamy peace.

"Take a turn if you want," Louis said.

"Thanks all the same." The smell of opium gave Scott a headache. "I'm surprised you bother with all this ceremony and don't smoke at home like most people."

For the first time, Louis smiled, although his eyes stayed closed. "Some folks go to church . . ." He didn't finish, and didn't need to. Perhaps he'd skirted outright blasphemy.

The woman laughed from the other side of the room, but she quickly smothered it. Bars and cathouses were tumultuous, full of music and revelry, but this opium den felt more like a chapel. No wonder Louis imagined he was in a church, Scott thought. Everyone here had come to worship silence.

"She's a poet from London," Louis said, his voice low. "Lots of writers come through. Symphony players. Bankers. Politicians. This is the best circle I've been welcome in yet."

When Louis leaned over for another turn with his pipe, Scott saw his hands tremble violently. This time, Louis had to struggle to keep his fingers steady long enough to light the match. Scott looked away. He tensed his own fingers and felt the razor tease his knuckle.

"You all sure put on a show tonight," Scott said.

"We try."

Scott paused. "Your playing is still very good."

"Good enough."

"You heard the Rosebud's closing soon?" Scott said. "That's what Tom's saying."

"I heard." Louis's face was all tranquility.

"Sam's off touring with Bill Spiller and them on vaudeville."

Louis didn't respond to the news of Sam Patterson, a lifelong friend, except to grunt. Scott had so many things he'd planned to say to Louis, and now that they were talking, he couldn't think of how to say even one. *Good news, Louis. I saw my doctor today, and you're not alone in your journey to Hell, youngster. Do you mind if I come along for the ride?*

"John Stark's talking about moving to New York," Scott said. "I've been thinking about it, too. They talk about New York's like it's the Promised Land, with Broadway and whatnot. And all the biggest publishers are there now. If I could just get some fire under me . . ."

Louis remained in repose. He was more unreachable, and sinking.

Scott opened his satchel and flipped through his papers for the score he'd written. Scott wasn't sure if he should show Louis, if the music might provoke him somehow, but they would have to work out the business end if they were going to get it published.

The rustling of papers got Louis's attention. His eyes opened, unfocused.

Scott gave him the pages. "You remember those themes I got from you in Chicago? And we sat and I tacked on a couple of my own? Well, I cleaned it up, and the result's real good."

Louis pulled the pages close to his face. "Nigger, what the hell is a heliotrope?"

So much for wondering if Louis would like the title of their collaboration. But Louis sounded more animated now than he had since the day they'd worked on it. Scott was glad he'd brought the music. He wished the room had a piano.

"A heliotrope's a flower that always blooms toward the sun."

Louis scanned the pages quickly, but the music symbols didn't hold his interest long. Louis turned back to the title page, and Scott stood up to look at it over his friend's shoulder:

Heliotrope Banquet. By Scott Joplin and Louis Chauvin.

Louis stared at the title page a long time. Then, he gave the stack back in silence.

Scott flipped to the third page and bent lower to point out passages, following the music with the tip of his index finger: "Yeah, see, where you end the *da-da-da-daaaa-da-da* section in the key of G, here's where I go to C with *de-da-de-da-de-daaaa* . . ." Scott sang the melody line.

Slowly, Louis nodded, first in approval, then keeping rhythm. *He hears it,* Scott thought.

". . . So, we start it off with that elegant, newfangled sound you've got, a whole new direction, then it comes full circle. I think it blends us just right."

Finally, Louis smiled. "That's real good, Scotty. *Yeah.* I remember it now."

"I figure on sending it to Stark, see if he'll pay what it's worth for a change. If not, there's other fish in the sea. Especially in New York."

"Louis Chauvin and Scott Joplin . . ." Louis murmured, closing his eyes. "How 'bout that?"

Scott was so happy Louis liked the piece, he hated to ruin the mood with another word.

"I heard that waltz, 'Bethena,' " Louis said, his eyes still closed. "I never got around to sayin' so, but I thought it was the best thing you ever did. You were telling the *truth*. That's what I like about that man picking his guitar outside the Theatorium. Plain truth, that's all. Music ain't all about sitting up in a theater and clapping when it's done. Sometimes you want to dance. Sometimes you want to cry."

Scott blinked, staring down at his shoes. For a while, he had forgotten to miss Freddie.

"Sorry about that gal you married, old man," Louis said. "Wish I'd met her."

Scott nodded. "Me, too."

"Hear you've been keepin' busy, though. Not just in music."

Scott had courted indiscriminately since Freddie's death, trying to fill the hole she'd made. Women felt like Scott's tonic now, except their effects were temporary. None of them were like Freddie. No one was. "Leola wasn't the match you thought she'd be," Scott said. Leola was pleasant enough, and a very good singer, but she had wanted to marry him after only a few visits. He wasn't ready for a new wife, he'd told her. She'd finally turned him away in search of a more likely prospect. "Can't blame her, though," Scott said.

"Women ain't got no more hold on me, and I'm glad. Right here is all the lovin' I need."

Scott gazed around the room again, and he realized suddenly that it did not resemble a chapel at all: It felt more like a crypt, with its flickering light and still, silent bodies.

"How you doing, youngster?" Scott whispered finally, the words he'd avoided.

"You got ears, don't you? My sweet lady's leaving me. Looks like I can't trust her neither, in the end." To Louis, the piano was a living thing, an appendage, almost. Scott loved his pianos, too, but not like Louis. "But she won't get away that easy. They say Paderewski played until his keys were bloody, show after show. She ain't gonna buck me without a fight."

The memory of his doctor's face made Scott feel a boulder lodge in his stomach. *This is the time to tell him,* he thought. Until he told someone, his own ringing brain would never accept his doctor's words. He opened his mouth, waiting for the courage to face it.

"I'll tell you something I wouldn't say to nobody else in this world, Scotty," Louis said before Scott could speak. "I'm glad it was me got it instead of you. I mean it."

Scott's mouth closed. He didn't know if he could open it again.

Louis went on: "I got aches and pains and ailments, sores, headaches, seeing things that ain't there, but I wouldn't give a shit about all that if I had my *hands*. I wouldn't wish it on nobody. 'Specially you, 'cause you don't just play music, you write it for keeps," Louis said, and for the first time emotion climbed into his voice, parting the haze.

"You go on and sell our music to old man Stark, so maybe a person or two will realize there's a professor named Louis Chauvin, and he could play the shit out of a piano. You go on to New York and be the *real* Black Paderewski. Naw, hell—Paderewski's gonna wish he was *you*. When you're up there facing the sun, I figger I'll be there with you one way or another."

Scott thought he saw tears in Louis's eyes, but the dew was gone when Louis blinked. Scott's chin shook. He didn't know where his grief for Louis ended and his own began.

"We've had a good visit, old man, but I'm gonna have to ask you to find your own way out," Louis said. "I don't plan on doing much in the way of talking in a minute or so."

"I understand," Scott said.

Scott lingered, gazing at Louis the way a painter would: Beneath the slant of his Stetson, Louis's curls were limp with sweat, his hollowed face scarred, and he was barely propped in the oversized chair, as if he were boneless. He was a scarecrow in a radiant white dress shirt with a theatrical ruffled collar, black tuxedo trousers, and shoes shiny enough to talk back to the candles.

Louis would always be a showman. Always.

The last time Scott Joplin saw Louis Chauvin, he was a terrible and beautiful sight.

CHAPTER EIGHTEEN

*P*hoenix closed her eyes, feeling her seat vibrate as the 747 achieved takeoff speed, racing for flight. She reached beside her for Carlos's hand, and he clasped it tightly in his lap. In all her years on the road, she realized, she'd never had a lover travel beside her. She'd had band-mates, Gloria or Sarge, yes, but never a lover. Smelling the just-enough whisper of Carlos's cologne, Phoenix realized she had become one of the people she used to envy on airplanes. She and Ronn had never trav-eled alone as a couple, never side by side.

Carlos's hand felt so good, Phoenix forgot her fear of takeoffs. The loud shudders, groans and whines of machinery and wheels beneath her didn't make her heart race. *Besides, I have a friend in a high place now. Scott will keep me safe.*

Scott still came to her at night—not always with music, but with memories. Five times now, she'd relived the memory of Scott's last night of lovemaking with Freddie, when she'd been sick. Phoenix didn't feel the sensations as keenly as she had the first time, with Carlos's human hands doing a ghost's work, but each time she awoke, she had trouble catching her breath because Freddie's pneumonia touched her in her sleep. Two nights ago, Phoenix had awakened with tears drying across her face, whispering *I love you, Scott* until Carlos shook her awake. Freddie's love for Scott burned strongest when Phoenix's dreams were fresh, inseparable from her heart.

They might be only dreams, but to Phoenix love had never felt so real.

Phoenix expected to see Scott's face in her airplane window when she opened her eyes, but she only saw her own blurred features as the plane climbed through the spongy mountain of clouds. Scott could be in the clouds. Scott could be in the reading light above her. Scott could be in the shard of sunlight breaking its way through the cloud bank, a radiant blade.

Scott could be anywhere. Everywhere.

She would get this New York show behind her. Then, she would be free for him.

Carlos was with her in first class because he'd used all his frequent-flyer miles to upgrade, but Gloria, Serena, Arturo, two other dancers and the two backup singers were in coach. As Phoenix's manager, Sarge would have argued for his own first-class ticket, but Gloria didn't have Sarge's influence with Three Strikes, even if she was doing Sarge's job now. By sending three dancers and two singers, the label was giving Phoenix extra support—*unprecedented* support, Katrice had pointed out—so she couldn't complain about Gloria's coach ticket. Before her singers and dancers boarded the flight, they had looked at her as if they dared her to fuck up again. Even Arturo had given her a stern look, and she knew he wanted this, too, and badly.

I have an entourage, Phoenix reminded herself with disbelief, testing the word in her imagination. *This isn't just about me.*

Phoenix had been sure Sarge's anger would thaw after a week, but he still wasn't speaking to her. With Gloria's prodding, Phoenix had been doing interviews, meeting with her video director and rehearsing her dance steps despite the distraction of Scott, but Sarge was stubborn once he'd made up his mind, just like both of his daughters. Sarge had promised Gloria he would get to New York in his own time and way. She had lost Trey, too, since Serena stuck by her plan to send him home for the start of a Bible camp one of her girlfriends ran in Georgia.

She hoped Sarge would come. If he came, she wouldn't disappoint him again.

And one day soon, she would be Scott's.

Van Milton was already planning her next tour, trying to find backers for a full-scale production of *A Guest of Honor* at next year's Sedalia Ragtime Festival at least—or, better, on a New York stage. Phoenix would have a third incarnation as a performer, this time as a ragtime high priestess. And Scott would be back on the stage where he belonged.

"You OK, *linda*?" Carlos said. Carlos rarely maintained eye contact long, one of his traits she was still trying to get used to. His stare now was conspicuous.

"Yeah, why?"

"You looked tired all of a sudden."

"Nah, I'm good," she said. "Especially with you here." Carlos could use a few kind words. They hadn't talked about it since the first night Scott's ghost made love to her, but Carlos knew where she was in her dreams, whom she was with, and she was asking a lot of him. If Carlos had offered her the same arrangement, would she have accepted?

Carlos looked wistful, keeping his eyes away. "Can we make a deal?"

"What's that?"

"Let's not talk shop on this flight. Nothing about Joplin."

Phoenix smiled, resting her head on his shoulder. Gloria was worried about how obsessive she had become, resenting the way Carlos supported what Gloria saw as a dangerous delusion. "Great idea. What should we talk about?"

"Anything else. I dated a coworker at the *Sun-News,* and we brought work with us everywhere. We need to have more than one thing, or we won't last."

Or we won't last. Since the night Carlos accepted her rules, neither of them had talked about their relationship like a living, growing thing; it just *was.* Carlos was the first man who had told her he wanted to last with her. The honest simplicity of it made her heart billow.

"OK, so let's tell our favorite things," she said.

"Favorite book?" Carlos said.

Phoenix didn't have to think about that. "*Beloved,* by Toni Morrison."

He nodded. "I'd say Ellison's *Invisible Man,* but I like *Beloved,* too. Favorite song?"

Phoenix shook her head. "Are you joking? *Maybe* I could give you a top ten list."

Carlos grinned, nodding. "For me, maybe a top twenty or thirty."

"And even then, what about the different styles?" Phoenix said, matching his grin. It was hard to find people who loved the breadth of music the way she did. "Jazz. Blues. Soul. Rock. Classical. R&B. And what about reggae? What about salsa?"

"And music from which countries?" Carlos said, finishing her thought. "Brazil? South Africa? Mexico? Zaire? Madagascar? You're right. Silly question. You pick the next one."

The humming Phoenix felt was not from the plane's constant roar; this was the warm, electric hum she'd experienced lying beside Carlos on the carpet in his Miami Beach apartment, meeting a man who felt like the missing piece of her. Phoenix played with the curly hairs on Carlos's bare arm. Instead of a question, she chose a disclosure. "I've had sex with four other people."

Carlos laughed, startled. "Seriously?"

Phoenix wondered if he thought the number was too low or too high. She'd been a virgin until she was eighteen, and she felt too inexperienced around most people. But she felt like a tramp compared to her mother, who'd had only three lovers in all. "What about you?"

"I knew that was coming . . ." Carlos reclined his seat as far as it would go, which on this plane was nearly out of sight. Carlos's chair became a leather bed. "More than four, kiddo. Believe it or not, I'm not keeping count. I'll get a blood test, if you want to put your mind at ease about all the ghosts in my bed."

"Good. A friend of mine died from AIDS in high school." Phoenix had never had the nerve to ask Ronn to take a blood test, which should have been her first warning sign, she thought. How could she be in a relationship with someone she couldn't speak her mind with?

"I admit I haven't always used the best discretion," Carlos said.

"Don Juan Jones out in the clubs?"

"No, that's not my style. But I've lost a lot of friends."

"Serial heartbreaker."

Carlos looked reflective, staring up toward his light panel. "There are things I would change because people felt hurt, but didn't I have to be that person to become who I am now? That's how I look at it, anyway."

"What about me?" Phoenix said, and her heart sped. The Phoenix Smalls she'd been at sixteen had never had the chance to ask Carlos any questions. Even now, she'd hesitated to bring it up in case her anger was only in hiding.

Carlos's eyes came back to hers, tender. "That was different. That was something else."

"How was it different?"

Carlos didn't answer for a long time, then raised his seat to speak close to her ear so she would hear him over the airplane's engine. "I saw an ambitious young sister with some talent, so I thought I could be a big brother. I didn't understand how I could feel anything else. Kids have never been a turn-on for me. Even in high school, I liked older women. I argued myself to sleep every night, but I couldn't keep away. I vowed I wouldn't touch you, then I did. Nothing like that had ever happened to me. It scared the shit out of me."

Phoenix realized she was holding her breath. Had he felt something special, too?

Carlos squeezed her hand. "I was giving you these expectations, doing somersaults trying to impress you, but where could it go? To this day, I wish I'd never kissed you then. I felt like such a jerk, I didn't tell any of my friends about it. When that letter from your parents came to my paper, *Dios mio*. I couldn't believe it. My *publisher* was asking if I'd taken a minor to bars, if we'd spent the night in my apartment. And so was my managing editor, my section editor, the people I'd worked hard to win respect from. The more I tried to tell the truth, the more everyone thought I was lying. There I was, the paper's first black music writer, the first Latino, too, and some shit like that came down the grapevine. My father's a freelance photographer in Miami, and even *he* asked me about it. I discovered I'm old-fashioned about name and reputation, because I'd never felt so embarrassed. No—*dishonored*." Carlos's voice shook.

"After that, thinking about you was hard. I tried to talk myself out of coming to see you when I heard you were in L.A. The memory alone was a problem for me. But now that I'm with you again, the whole thing seems simple to me now: For whatever reason, I loved you from the beginning, Phee, almost on sight, and I never stopped. So, there it is. *Punto*." Carlos made a gentle gesture, his fingers like tissue fluttering in a breeze.

He loved me the way Scott loved Freddie, Phoenix thought, stunned. All this time, she'd thought she agonized over Carlos alone. Carlos had recited his confession as if loving her was a condition he'd learned to tolerate, with no expectations. She wasn't ready to say *I love you, too,* but nothing else seemed right, so she didn't say anything.

Carlos's eyes left hers again. "What happened in Miami was still bull-shit, Phee. Do you accept my apology?" The raw regret in Carlos's voice was another surprise.

Phoenix rubbed his knee. "Carlos, I wouldn't be with you if I was still carrying that. And remember: *I* wanted to have sex with *you.*" Carlos had been her masturbation fantasy throughout her adolescence, the reason she'd discovered how to create magic from hand lotion when she was sixteen. She hadn't known her body's longings were so strong, waiting for somewhere to go.

"You were a kid, and I should have known better," Carlos said. "If I loved you, so what? People fall in love every day. A patient falls in love with her doctor, a teacher with her student, a married mother with a great guy at work. Sometimes you're free to pursue it, sometimes you aren't. Love needs your *permission,* and that's what no one will admit. I gave myself permission. Now you're stuck with the consequences."

"What consequences?" Phoenix said.

"Your father might have come with you on this flight if I hadn't been here. Part of the reason he avoids you is me. That's my fault, and I hate that."

Phoenix hadn't thought about it that way. Sarge might have come without Carlos, but probably not. Probably. "That's not on you. That's Sarge. He had no right to harass you at TSR like that, either." The idea of her father cornering Carlos in the hall gave her an angry pang. Carlos had been sheepish about bringing it up, but Phoenix was glad he'd told her. Once she and Sarge were talking again, that would be one of the first things they would talk about.

"Life's hard enough without complications, Phee," Carlos said. "You'll see."

It was then, only seconds after Carlos declared his love, that the plane shook suddenly, or Phoenix *thought* it had. Phoenix's body felt so jarred that her head flipped forward and she clung to both armrests, looking for balance. The lights grew brighter, as if the plane had taken a sudden turn into the sun. But Phoenix's skin felt taut and cold, frostbitten.

"Phee?" Carlos said.

Music exploded in Phoenix's head, a cacophony of overlapping glissandos. She gasped.

He was here, like he'd come to her at the TV taping. As always, Scott was going to talk to her in his own way. Phoenix remembered relinquishing her body at the television studio, trying not to fight. She didn't want to fight.

Yes, Scott. I hear you. I hear you, Scott. I'm ready.

"I need paper," she said.

A notebook appeared in front of Phoenix, graph paper. Carlos had pulled her tray table down for her, and he slipped a pen in her hand. "A message from him?" he said.

Phoenix barely heard Carlos, because her hand was no longer hers. Her fingers were growing numb, as if she were dipping her fingertips into a cold gel, one joint at a time. Phoenix watched her hand grasp the pen tightly and carve out five horizontal lines nearly perfectly spaced an eighth of an inch apart on the page. Startled, she tried to make herself stop. When she curled her fingers, the numbness flushed away, replaced by warm blood. Her pen stilled in midstroke.

NO. You've been waiting for this. Don't be afraid of him. Don't be afraid.

When Phoenix relaxed her hand, her pen flew again. This time, she drew a skillful treble clef with its rounded belly, and dots, dashes and numbers—6/8 time, it read. Then, Phoenix watched herself draw the first string of lively quarter-note chords, like clusters of grapes. As she drew, the music played itself in her head, much faster than her hand could capture it, but her hand was racing to try. Phoenix was skydiving, a cold wind rushing against her face.

"I didn't know you could write music by hand," Carlos said, across an impossible gulf.

"I can't," Phoenix said, and made herself forget Carlos, everything except her hand.

I'm doing it. I'm really doing it.

Phoenix Smalls and Scott Joplin flew together.

New York was always a homecoming for Carlos Harris.

He'd lived in the city his junior year at Stanford when he interned at the *New York Times,* and even with his fortieth birthday looming in six hundred days, Carlos was convinced he might still move to New York one day. It was never too late. He'd almost fled here after the nightmare in Miami, when his bosses practically branded him a child molester. (Some reporters at the *Sun-News* still believed the lie that he'd gotten a sixteen-year-old girl pregnant). Los Angeles had won him because his business partner was there, but New York was Carlos's first choice, always.

Carlos had enough work and family to bring him back at least four times a year, and that was enough for now. He had relatives in New York on both sides, and he'd helped his parents make their calls after the planes hit on September 11—Tia and Tio had still been asleep in the Bronx; his cousin Pilar had been riding on the N/R line to meet a friend for breakfast in SoHo; Aunt Josephine had been on her way to work at Hue-Man Bookstore uptown in Harlem; and his cousin Darnell had been late to his early meeting at One World Trade Center because of a parent-teacher conference at his daughter's school. Darnell had collapsed in tears when he heard Carlos's voice. Over the next few days, two dozen of Carlos's friends had shared their chorus of wonderment and grief. New York lived in Carlos, and he lived in New York. Just not yet.

This time, it felt strange to be back, surreal. Carlos felt like he was walking through an absurd dream crammed with fascinating elements: Life. Death. Music. Love. All the essentials. Phoenix was at the center of Carlos's dream, creating miracles at will, shattering and rebuilding him in alternating breaths. He hadn't had time to regain his balance since the first night he heard her voice on the phone, when she called to tell him she had just run into a ghost.

Me, too, he'd wanted to say. And now he was sharing her hotel room, her bed—and something bigger than anything he knew how to manage. But he didn't have to wonder, because for once, he *knew:* He loved Phoenix, and she was only the second woman to hear those words from him since he was nineteen.

Today, Carlos barely recognized the woman he loved.

Phoenix's modernist suite at the Bon Maison Hotel on Forty-Seventh and Broadway was being transformed into a miniature television studio. A technician from the cable show *New York View* switched on two bright floodlights, erasing the color from Phoenix's face except for her makeup, which Carlos thought looked like a clownish veil over the beautiful woman underneath. Phoenix sat waiting on the love seat with her eyes half-lidded, her lips moving to silent music in her head. *She looks like a drug fiend,* Carlos thought. Carlos had seen enough young performers implode under the weight of sudden celebrity to make him wish fame came with an antidote. Too much work, privilege and bullshit were a predictable combination.

No wonder Phoenix's label had sent both its publicity director and a bodyguard to practically camp in Phoenix's room. Manny—who was a *boriqua* from a family of musicians in San Juan, it turned out—and the huge man named Kai sat across from Phoenix, sharing Krispy Kreme doughnuts and coffee, just out of the camera's range. The room was so crowded that Gloria and Phoenix's sister had retreated to the bedroom, but Carlos wanted to keep Phoenix in his sight. He was worried about her, too, but in a different way. Different, and deeper.

Carlos wasn't sure Phoenix had slept. Their flight had arrived at JFK late, he had helped her find a pad of blank white paper and a ruler (no easy feat at midnight, but God bless CVS), then she'd sat up drawing staffs and writing scores until Gloria's 6:00 A.M. wake-up call. He'd fallen asleep without her, and he was sure Phoenix had never joined him in the bed.

Whatever had happened to Phoenix on the television stage had reappeared with more power and clarity, creating a waking channel between Phoenix and Joplin for hours on end.

This was what they had hoped for, of course. Phoenix's union with this ghost reaffirmed Carlos's faith in God every day. Sometimes when he was alone, he found he was crossing himself like his mother, thanking the Virgin and saints for choosing him to witness it. Last night, Phoenix had channeled at least twenty full-length Scott Joplin scores. He'd counted the pieces while she was in the shower, and he'd felt his joints shudder while he marveled at the heavy, purposeful writing that was not Phoenix's, that had plowed its way through time and death to come to his hands. God's work. God's hand. *Precious Lord, Take My Hand. El mano de Dios.*

But hoping for it and watching it unfold, as it turned out, were very different. Watching it frightened Carlos more all the time. This morning, Phoenix had made an effort at sleepy conversation as she dressed and Serena labored over her makeup and hair, but Carlos hadn't seen Phoenix eat anything since they'd left L.A. It was all there in her eyes: She was an ecstatic still in the throes of her rapture. Carlos didn't mind Phoenix going away with Joplin, as long as Joplin let her come back.

"And we're ready," the reporter announced with a megawatt smile.

Phoenix opened her eyes, alertness seeping in. Manny and Kai were leaning toward Phoenix like lifeguards waiting to rescue a swimmer.

Carlos didn't know the reporter, a tall, sharp-jawed sister with memorable lips, dressed in a white jogging suit and a B-boy style baseball cap. She was too attractive and talented for this job and she knew it, her eyes said—someone should be interviewing *her*—but her voice quivered with cheer: "I'm here with Phoenix Smalls, an R&B newcomer who's already burning up the airwaves with her first single, 'Party Patrol.' She's here for Friday's Hip-Hop R&B MegaJam, which promises to be the H-O-T, *hottest* party of the summer, if ya'll ain't heard."

Phoenix wasn't smiling for the camera yet, listening impassively. Carlos knew what was in her mind, the only thing that had been on her mind since the plane landed: She wanted to go back to her notepad. She wanted to go back to Joplin.

"So, Phoenix, we gotta cut to the chase—your relationship with G-Ronn. First we hear you hooked up, then there's a tabloid story about you and another man on the down-low, and now rumors say you're through. What's the 4-1-1?"

That question had come up in every interview Carlos had heard all week, but usually the reporters were savvy enough to save it until last. At the mention of G-Ronn's name, Kai shot Carlos a look, hot disapproval. It was just a shift of his eyes, but it hit Carlos like a blow. Carlos fidgeted in the entryway, wondering what he'd done to piss off G-Ronn's personal bodyguard, except maybe sleeping with his boss's ex. Was *that* it? Life with Phoenix was a gauntlet. Carlos had never been so self-conscious in a woman's presence, bracing for disapproval everywhere. God, he hoped Phoenix wouldn't mention him in her interview.

Phoenix didn't blink, gazing at the reporter. "Next question," she said in a monotone.

"Is that a 'No comment'?" the reporter said.

"G-Ronn is one of the best people there is, but my personal life is my own business. So, like I said, next question," Phoenix said. That was good. If Phoenix could manage this much diplomacy, maybe she had been plucked away from the ghost music in her head. Carlos hoped so.

"Phoenix, tell me: Are any of the Three Strikes artists like you, Bing Boyz or Kamikaze worried about getting caught in the vendetta between G-Ronn and DJ Train? Since DJ Train is based right outta Brooklyn, some people might say you're in enemy territory."

"Those people would be ignorant," Phoenix said. "I'm here for a concert. I leave all that hype to the media."

Carlos glanced at Kai from the corner of his eye. The man's face was vacant, and Carlos didn't dare let himself get caught looking. Carlos's friends in the Brooklyn club scene thought Kai *positively* had killed DJ Train's cousin and bodyguard last month, a man named Gerard Houston. There were allegedly at least six witnesses, even though none had come forward to police. *Come on, Carlito, he's hard to miss,* his ex-girlfriend, who tended bar at Clubhouse, said. Just like in the Tupac and Jam Master Jay shootings, the people who knew weren't talking. Carlos did not feel safer with Kai near Phoenix. The rumors could be wrong, but they could be right.

"I see you're a tough cookie," the reporter said, her smile turning icy.

"I'm just keepin' it real," Phoenix said.

"Were you keeping it real on 'Live at Night'?" the reporter said. "You got cut from a recent show after you sang a song you said you channeled from Janis Joplin."

Phoenix's eyes flashed. "*Scott* Joplin. The Pulitzer Prize–winning composer."

The reporter pursed her lips, unfazed. "O-kay, then . . . Scott Joplin. What was *that* about? Were you looking for a little extra publicity for your single?"

Phoenix hesitated, and Carlos saw her glance toward Manny before she answered. "That was just a onetime thing. At the concert, I'm singing 'Party Patrol.' " She couldn't have sounded more rehearsed if she'd been reading from cue cards.

"You believe in ghosts?"

"Yes," Phoenix said, just when Carlos was hoping she would lie.

"And . . . you believe a ghost is sending you music?"

"Yes, as we speak," Phoenix said. "I've been meeting with a musicologist who specializes in Scott's music. We're salvaging the music I channel, and I'm going to record an instrumental CD so I can share Scott with the world. Death is not the end. My real hope is that Scott Joplin can have another day, through me. I'd love to create something like the Scott Joplin revival in the seventies, after *The Sting*." For the first time, she sounded wide-awake.

The reporter looked confused, her plastic smile fading. "You mean . . . *as we speak,* you can hear Scott Joplin music? In your mind, you mean?"

"Yes," Phoenix said, and Carlos groaned inwardly. Gloria was right; Phoenix sounded like a nut. Until now, Phoenix had trained herself to avoid the question of her *Live at Night* performance as well as she dodged questions about G-Ronn, but she was talkative today. *That's enough, Phee. Let it go.*

"And will you record that Scott Joplin CD for Three Strikes Records?" the reporter said, wheedling. Manny mouthed the words *FUCK no,* mostly to himself.

"I'll record Scott's CD myself, on my own," Phoenix said. "After *Rising.*"

The reporter leaned forward, forgetting the camera. "Wait . . . For real, you think a ghost—"

Manny clapped his hands. "We're out of time," he said. "Phoenix has a busy schedule."

As if Manny had flipped an on-off switch, Phoenix's eyes glazed again, half closed.

The reporter pursed her lips. "But I wasn't . . ."

"Sorry," Kai said, his voice an octave lower than Manny's. "No time, yo."

That was the end of the conversation.

While the video crew packed up, Kai gave Carlos an unmistakable look again—*WHAT, nigga?* Carlos remembered that look from black boys on the basketball court when his family moved from San Juan to Atlanta when he was ten. Carlos had always been fluent in English because of Dad, but his accent must not have been quite right, and the sound of his voice provoked the kids he'd hoped to befriend. *What you lookin' at, nigga?* In San Juan, Carlos had never heard that word, except in music. Carlos's mother was as brown as a Zulu princess, but she said she'd never thought about her skin color until her parents filled out U.S. Census forms and no one knew which boxes to check for race. *We just thought we were Puerto Ricans,* Mami said. Things were different on the mainland, with its categories, so Carlos had fucked up on sight.

Kai hovered over Phoenix, so big that he blocked the light from the lamp on the end table. "Lil' mama, you did great. You a'ight? You need anything? If you do, you know I'm here to drop the philosophy on you," Kai said, his eyes unarmed. He offered a meaty, thoroughly tattooed arm so Phoenix could shake his hand. He must genuinely like her, Carlos thought. Kai didn't look like anybody's kiss-ass flunkie.

Phoenix nodded, grasping Kai's hand. "Yeah, I know that, Krispy Kreme. It's all good. I'll lay off the ghost stuff. I'm sorry."

Phoenix sounded more like herself than ever, suddenly. For the sake of Phoenix's friendship with Kai, Carlos hoped the rumors about this man were wrong. If the rumors were right, Kai was a hit man, and he'd killed for G-Ronn before. According to lore, back when G-Ronn was a rising entrepreneur in the crack cocaine business, G-Ronn had told Kai to gun down a courier who'd cheated him, and that courier had turned out to be DJ Train's brother. Or something like that. Carlos felt torn about what to say to Phoenix, since Kai was her friend.

And we know rumors are never wrong, are they, Carlos? Of course not.

The room's gentle doorbell sounded. Since Carlos was closest to the door, he turned to answer it. Probably another reporter, he thought.

"Yo, hold up, fool," Kai said, and brushed past him, deliberate contact. "I'll get that."

"Who are you, the Secret Service?" Carlos said before he could stop himself. Kai turned to give him a slow gaze that shot ice into Carlos's spine. Carlos mustered a smile to show he was kidding—*ha ha, get it, dawg?*—and Kai walked on. Silently, Carlos cursed his own stupidity. He had to remember who the hell he might be talking to.

After the door opened, Kai bellowed, "What *WHAT?* Hey, O. G., where you been?"

Sarge's voice came next. "Here and there, man. Everywhere but in trouble. Listen, this is my wife, Leah Rosen-Smalls . . ."

There was a party outside Phoenix's door. Sarge entered hand in hand with a thickset white woman with active eyes and silver-streaked dark hair. She was carrying a bouquet of shiny helium balloons. Phoenix had her mother's nose and jawline, Carlos realized. Leah Smalls wore a purple batik tunic, loose matching pants and earthy, open-toed sandals. An artistic soul, Carlos could see. Behind her came a lanky black man who looked vaguely familiar, and a white couple with a man who was Carlos's height but portly, his hair windblown, and a blond woman with an athlete's build she had preserved into middle age. *Gloria's mother.*

Sarge saw Carlos, but shifted his gaze and walked right past him, and Leah Rosen-Smalls nodded cordially, not knowing who he was. The tall black guy, whose slightly receding hairline made him look a little older than Carlos, was dressed in a bright cobalt suit, black T-shirt and a large gold medallion. He gave Carlos a soul shake as he passed. "Hey, man, how you doin'? I'm Malcolm Smalls." He said his name like he knew it meant something, and didn't wait for Carlos to respond before he moved on, introducing himself to Kai the same way as if he had a deadline to meet everyone. One of Phoenix's brothers, Carlos figured. *That* was why he looked familiar: He was a less bulky, smoother-faced version of Sarge.

When the group reached the living room, Phoenix shrieked and laughed in a way he had never heard. "Oh my *Goooooodddddddd,* I didn't know you guys were coming today! Mommm*meeeeeeeee.*" She sounded more like a child at that moment than she had when he'd met her.

Serena and Gloria came out to join them, and the room was laughter and exclamations, surprise and delight, love and history. Voices babbled as they exchanged stories, commented on endless details of personal appearance—hair, clothes, and physique—and then agreed on how happy they were to see each other. They reminded Carlos of his family on *Mami's* side, all abandon.

"Phoenix, do you *eat* on the road? This size doesn't look healthy for you," Leah Smalls said after their dancing hug. She and Phoenix draped their arms across each other's shoulders, touching noses.

"Oh, Mom, please," Phoenix said, although Carlos thought she *did* look too thin.

". . . This is *sooooo* perfect," Gloria's mother told Gloria, "because we stopped by the box-office on the way, and we lucked into orchestra seats for *Avenue Q* for eight *tonight* . . ."

Malcolm Smalls hung near the edge of the circle, talking to Manny: "Yeah, my dad's been sayin' we need to put our heads together . . ."

Manny nodded, reaching for a business card. "Yeah, man, yeah. Sarge has told me you've got great contacts, and we need promotion help in the Southeast. Maybe you, me and my boss Katrice can sit down . . ."

A family reunion and networking session all in one, Carlos thought.

Everyone belonged here but him.

Carlos tried to catch Phoenix's eye, but she was at the center of the circle, and as soon as one person was finished with her, someone else wanted to give her a hug. He would leave her to her family, he decided. He could use some lunch. He would write a note and slip out.

Carlos was just returning from the bedroom, where he'd gone to re-trieve the leather satchel with his Palm Pilot and notebooks when he almost walked into Sarge, just beyond the bedroom doorway. Sarge had been waiting for him. Sarge nodded back toward the bedroom. "Talk to you?" Sarge said.

Carlos couldn't think of anything good that would be waiting for him behind a closed door with Sarge. "I'm just on my way out."

"Then don't let me stop you."

Carlos walked past Sarge, careful not to violate his personal space. He hoped to catch Phoenix's eye as he passed her, but she was in the middle of what seemed like a tentative embrace with her brother, almost at arm's length, both of them eager to separate.

Carlos sensed Sarge following him by two paces.

"Can I help you?" Carlos said, not looking back.

"Wouldn't want you to get lost," Sarge said, still trailing.

"I know my way, Mr. Smalls. I live in this room."

In the long foyer, when Carlos tried to open the front door, he couldn't. Sarge had reached above him to brace it closed, and the space between them was now very narrow. Carlos wished he had kept his mouth shut instead of announcing to a man who didn't like him that he was screwing his daughter, but Carlos had passed his tolerance for harassment today. In the living room, a round of laughter made Carlos feel unalterably lonesome.

"Young man," Sarge said quietly, "you must want to get hurt."

"No, sir, I don't," Carlos said, turning to face Sarge's gaze. Carlos was the giant of his family at five-ten, but Sarge made him feel short. "Mr. Smalls, I get where you're coming from. I made a mistake. I've apologized to you for the past, from my heart. But Phoenix and I are two adults. If you put your hands on me, don't expect me to let it go again."

"Did it feel good to get that out, son?" Sarge said. "I got one for you, too: My daughter is gonna pee in a cup for me today, and if I find out she's been acting funny because she's doing coke or H, and you're somehow involved in that, you *better* have me arrested. You should call the cops right now."

Sarge still expected him to be a monster, Carlos thought sadly. But what else was the man supposed to believe? "Phoenix isn't doped up. I think you know that."

"I don't know shit," Sarge said, and backed away.

Carlos took his chance to escape. When the door slammed behind him, his loneliness sharpened. Phoenix's suite was at the end of the hall, and the paisley carpeting of the empty hallway seemed to stretch halfway to Harlem.

What had happened to him? Here he was amid the thumping heart of his beautiful city, and he wasn't eager to go outside to vanish into the streams of humanity on Broadway; into the army of Yellow cabs, or to feel grand beneath towering billboards fit for ancient gods in their spectacle of lights and movement. He wasn't eager to see acrobatic boys casually defying gravity for tips, Senegalese street vendors with third-rate trinkets from the Motherland and knockoff designer sunglasses, struggling musicians forced to play in daylight, Puerto Rican women selling *pasteles* fresh from their steamy kitchens, or black Muslims pushing bean pies and earnestness. His nostrils weren't hungry for dank gutter steam, exhaust, sauerkraut and gyros.

Instead, Carlos wanted to go back into his room to be with Phoenix. *Life is hard enough without complications.* Which wise man had said that?

Carlos had walked within fifteen yards of the elevators when one made its polite *ding,* and he heard the doors slide open. A black man in a white suit stepped out, walking toward him. His heels snapped hard on the marble floor, but went silent where the floor met the carpeting. The man's diamond necklace flickered in Carlos's eyes.

Carlos wouldn't have noticed another thing about the man if he hadn't been striding directly in Carlos's path. The way the man's shoulders leaned forward, if he'd been running instead of walking Carlos would have thought the man was charging him. Carlos would move aside to make room for an old man, or someone with a cane, but this man's dogged pace irked Carlos. Why was everybody fucking with him today?

"Hey, man, what—" Carlos began, and in that instant the man's face was upon him.

The dark-skinned man was two inches shorter, his shoulders slight, his face a series of round features: round cheeks, round lips, round nose, round ears. *He was Scott Joplin.*

Carlos realized who he was as the man reached him, and he felt his mind drain clean. Instinct made Carlos brace, expecting a collision, but there was none.

Instead, he looked down wide-eyed as the back of the man's leg and his white coattail faded to nothing, passing *through* him, beyond his shining belt buckle. The impossible sight froze Carlos in place, until he felt his body quiver, gelatin. Carlos rocked with dizziness, his knees buckling. His breath was gone, as if he'd been punched in the stomach.

Carlos fell against the wall, hard, and his shoulder roared with pain, the only thing he could feel across the length of his body for three seconds. Carlos gasped, and his lungs labored. Had the walking phantom somehow been swallowed *inside of him*? As sensation crept back to his limbs, Carlos untangled himself and turned to see if the man had emerged on the other side.

To his relief, Carlos saw the figure walking away. The visage in the white suit hadn't slowed, hadn't changed his bearing, as if Carlos hadn't been there. Three steps, four steps, five steps. The man reached the door at the end of the hall on the sixth step and did not pause.

Scott Joplin passed straight through Phoenix's closed hotel room door.

CHAPTER NINETEEN

*Y*ou know this is completely pointless, right?" Phoenix said, flushing the toilet behind her bathroom's partition of marble and smoky beveled glass while Sarge stood in the doorway, her sentry. Phoenix had half filled the plastic cup from Sarge's drugstore testing kit, a ritual he had insisted was the only thing that could make him stay.

"We'll see, Peanut. Give me the sample."

"Don't stand there in the doorway like she's a criminal, Marcus," Mom called, from where she lay across Phoenix's hotel bed. "Why are you hovering? Give her some privacy."

Where had the day gone wrong? First, Carlos had vanished without saying anything, leaving a one-line note about getting lunch—*Gee, thanks*. Now, this. Phoenix ground her teeth, gazing at her specimen cup, which she'd accidentally spattered in her stream. *Too bad. Let Sarge wipe it off.* She couldn't believe she was putting up with this. Through the bedroom door, Phoenix heard George Clinton's "Atomic Dog" playing on the hotel room's sound system at party volume. She was missing her own celebration.

"Urine test results can be faked," Sarge said. "You can buy clean piss on the internet."

"Marcus, you sound like a lunatic. She's doing what we said. Give her some dignity."

Mom and Sarge were arguing, their natural state, but Phoenix hadn't seen her parents this unified in a long time. Worrying about her had brought them into the same bedroom again, at least. Phoenix smiled about that, washing her hands with the hotel's kiwi-lime exfoliating soap, or whatever exclusive blend it was.

Phoenix left Sarge to the test strips on the bathroom counter, joining her mother on the king-sized bed. Lying down, she realized how exhausted she felt, and she fought to keep her eyes open. Leah Smalls was lying on her side, her head propped on one elbow, and Phoenix mirrored her mother's pose. Mom looked radiant to the tips of her silvery hair, which she had stopped coloring last year. Instead of making Mom look old, the streaks made her seem exotic. She looked better than Aunt Livvy, and that wasn't easy. Aunt Livvy had always been the showier of the sisters, more preoccupied with her looks, but seeing her mother and aunt together today, Phoenix noticed that her aunt must spend too much time in the sun. The skin on her face seemed leathery, like a Halloween mask of a gorgeous woman. Mom's body wasn't perfect, but her face was still hers. Retiring from the School Board last year had been good for her, Phoenix decided. Her mother finally had her own life.

Mom reached across the bed to gently hold Phoenix's hand, and her array of copper bracelets chimed. Mom's blue-green eyes didn't blink. "Hon . . . if you've gotten in trouble, please don't underestimate it. Drugs are pandemic in music, and it's not the road you want to take. Remember Charlie Parker? Bill Evans? Billie Holiday? Jimi Hendrix, who wasn't much older than you when he died? It would kill Marcus and me both if we had to watch that happen to you."

Phoenix might have laughed except for the earnestness in her mother's eyes. Mom should know her better. Phoenix didn't like the fuzziness of alcohol and had never been curious about Ecstasy, much less had she tried coke, heroin or meth. She liked weed fine on her downtime, but she'd learned with her band that her playing was sloppier than it seemed when she was high, so she'd never trusted weed as a habit. Phoenix had spent too many hours lost in melodies in her head—both before and after her ghost—to understand why so many musicians had forgotten that music didn't need help.

"That's not me, Mom," Phoenix said, stroking her mother's rough knuckle. Mom had never taken good enough care of her hands, always running to meetings to take care of other people, and some of her cracks had grown deep.

"Marcus says you've been acting strange, saying strange things. And we've never seen Glo this upset about you."

That's her own fault for being so stubborn, Phoenix thought. Last week, Gloria had wasted a dozen opportunities to accept Scott's presence. He had tripped her on the same spot on the rug three times in the same afternoon, but she refused to see him. The sheet music scores Phoenix had written in her frenzy last night were on the bed where her mother had been thumbing through them, and Mom *had* to know the music hadn't come from her, even if Gloria wouldn't. One piece didn't look like ragtime at all; it might be a movement from a symphony.

"Drugs wouldn't make me write that music."

"You really wrote these last night, Phoenix?"

She nodded. "My new boyfriend watched me do it."

"A new boyfriend already? What does he do?" Mom said. When Phoenix had turned eighteen, her mother had marched her to a doctor's office to get her a prescription for the pill, no questions asked, her approach to sex education. Since then—with the exception of Ronn, who had scared her—Mom had savored details about Phoenix's meager love life. Phoenix could feel her mother's heart traveling vicariously with hers.

"You'll meet him." Phoenix couldn't bring herself to say Carlos's name yet.

From the bathroom, Sarge made a surly noise. Sarge probably had something to do with Carlos vanishing today, and how could she blame Carlos for leaving? *Awkward* didn't do this mess justice. Besides, this wasn't a family reunion, it was an intervention.

"Daddy, you know I had some weed with Ronn the other day, but that's it," Phoenix said toward the bathroom doorway. "If anything else shows up on those tests, it's a lie." From the bathroom, Sarge only grunted, so Phoenix went on. "I'm not the one you need to be testing, anyway. Malcolm's the one acting like he's bugging out."

Phoenix was sorry as soon as she'd said it.

Phoenix's mother swatted Phoenix's hand, clucking. "Shame on you."

Phoenix heard her father's measured footsteps across the bathroom's marble floor, and he poked his head out of the doorway to look at her. A thunderstorm was brewing on her father's face. Malcolm was Sarge's youngest son—he'd been ten when Sarge went to prison—and Malcolm had gone through rehab three times for crack addiction since he was twenty. Malcolm was the biggest open wound of her father's life, and she'd jabbed it just to have something to say.

"I'm sorry," Phoenix said before Sarge could open his mouth.

"Bugging out?" Sarge said, ignoring her apology. "In case you're interested in someone else's life for a change, Phoenix, Malcolm has been clean two years. You want to know why he's *bugging out*? He doesn't have any reason to have confidence in himself, and he's shaking hands with people from a major label for the first time in his life, people who can help him believe in a dream. It may be tough for you to remember that most people don't take these blessings for granted and piss all over them. Your brother is *nervous*. Cut him some fucking slack."

Phoenix blinked, her face hot. "Daddy, seriously, I'm sorry. When I saw Malcolm with you, I was really happy for both of you. For real. I don't know why I said that."

Sarge didn't answer, returning to the bathroom. She could almost hear his thoughts: *What else do you expect from a junkie?*

The door to the bedroom clicked and swung open toward them, allowing the music from the living room to fly in at full volume. "Atomic Dog" had become Sly & the Family Stone's "Dance to the Music." Phoenix heard Serena and Malcolm laughing, telling loud stories on each other. But no one walked into her room.

"Hello?" Phoenix called.

No answer. Phoenix got up and glanced into the living room to make sure no one was nearby. Kai and Manny were closest, but they were bent over the minibar, not looking at her.

Phoenix closed the door again, shaking it to make sure it stuck, then she smiled.

You're here, Scott. I know.

She hadn't thought about Scott with her family around, and maybe he got restless when he was ignored. Maybe he'd expected her to fax the new pieces to Van Milton right away, and to pay his biographer, Berlin, a home visit. But Scott would have to wait.

"I suppose that's your ghost?" Mom said, eyeing the door with suspicion.

"It's possible. He shows up in different ways."

"You sound very cavalier about it."

"I've learned you can get used to anything."

Right, Mom? Phoenix wondered how much her mother knew about Sarge's lady friend in Baldwin Hills with a daughter at Spelman. Did she pretend she didn't exist? Was she relieved? Mom never talked about her relationship with Sarge, and Phoenix longed for more days like today, with her parents acting as a team. Unless she'd imagined it, they'd been holding hands when they first came. It was too bad the current crisis would be over so soon.

Sarge came out of the bathroom, holding a test strip in each hand. Phoenix had no idea how many drugs he was testing her for, but Sarge was grinning. "Well, you're clean," he said.

"I know I am."

"I really thought you were strung out, Phee, and that scared me. You know what I've been through with that. I apologize."

Phoenix hugged her father, their first real hug since the television taping. His arms were a cradle. "If you accept my apology about Malcolm, I'll accept yours."

Sarge kissed her forehead. "Deal." He took Phoenix's hands and stared at her, probing. "Phee, if it's not about drugs, what is it? Where's all the Joplin coming from? Help me understand. You've never been interested in ragtime. Just that one night."

Phoenix's heart thundered. Maybe today was her chance, she thought. Phoenix squeezed her father's hands as hard as she could to keep his attention.

"Daddy . . . what if you woke up in the middle of the night and found out you'd filled up a notebook with fifty pages of somebody else's handwriting? And a historian told you the writing looked like Malcolm X's, and a psychic told you Malcolm had chosen you to write the book he *would* have written if he hadn't been shot? What would you do?" Phoenix thought she saw something in her father's eyes, a shard of understanding. "Would you keep up your life as usual, or would you try to help Malcolm be heard?"

"Or Anne Frank," Mom murmured, trying to imagine it. Anne Frank was her heroine.

"*Right,*" Phoenix said. "That's what happened to me. I didn't ask for it. I don't know how or why, but I think it started with that piano that hurt me. From the Silver Slipper."

"Oh, my God," Mom said, a sudden realization.

"What?" Phoenix said.

"That piano was haunted. Remember, what I told you, Marcus? From when we were kids. Something happened. Ask your aunt Livvy, Phee. Livvy knows." But just that quickly, the ghost dropped from Mom's mind as she studied Phoenix from head to toe. "Darling, don't fall into the same trap I did when I was dancing. You're skinny as a rail. Even people who make their living on the stage have to *eat*."

Kai and Manny were gone by the time Phoenix and her parents came back to the living room (*Jay-Z's got a better party uptown,* Gloria explained), so everyone left was family. After declaring he was tired of funk, Sarge switched the music to Charlie Parker playing on WBGO. Phoenix saw him whisper to Gloria while her cousin's eyes tracked her, and Gloria grinned with relief. Sarge not only patted Gloria's shoulder, but kissed her cousin's cheek, a rare sight.

Three large pizzas from Broadway Pizza arrived, and they sat in a loose circle eating together, passing Coke cans and napkins and shredded mozzarella back and forth, no big deal. But it *was* a big deal. Serena and Malcolm had never been in the same room with Aunt Livvy and Uncle Dave. Even she, Sarge and Mom hadn't shared a meal in forever. The sight of her family warmed a part of Phoenix she hadn't realized was craving warmth. Phoenix was so happy, she felt like Scott, floating invisible in the room. *I wish Carlos could have stayed, too,* she thought, but his absence didn't dull her contentment. He would come back.

"I gotta give it up to you, sis," Malcolm said, raising his pizza slice in a toast. Phoenix expected him to turn toward Serena, until she realized he was addressing *her*. "You're not at all like I thought. I guess I always figgered you'd be stuck-up. Huh, Reenie?"

"I told you," Serena said, smiling. "Phee's good folks."

"Why'd you think I was stuck-up?" Phoenix asked.

Malcolm shrugged. "Hey, no reason, I guess. That just shows what I didn't know. But you've got it goin' *on,* I'm blessed to be your brother, and I pray to God for your success."

Everyone mumbled their agreement, raising their glasses. Phoenix got up to kiss Malcolm's cheek, and she meant it this time, not like the brushing kiss she'd given him when he first hugged her, a virtual stranger who'd appeared from nowhere. She wished she could take back the awful, thoughtless thing she'd said about him to Sarge.

"Welcome to the party, Malcolm," she whispered.

"I'm just glad to be upright, sis. Praise God."

"Amen," Serena murmured.

Gazing at her sister, Phoenix felt a sudden inspiration, pointing at her. "Sing with me Friday night!" she said. "You'll rehearse with me and my crew, and it'll be great. *Please?*"

Serena looked startled, and her automatic headshaking began. When Serena opened her mouth to decline, she was drowned out. Finally, Serena stood up and surveyed the room as if she were already taking the stage. "OK, ya'll know what? Last week Trey was riding me, and Gloria's been riding me, and Phoenix has *never* let up. If ya'll want me to get up and make a fool of myself in front of two thousand people . . . *I'll do it.*"

"Reenie, for real?" Phoenix said. Her heart, like the room, had gone silent.

Serena grinned from molar to molar, raising her arms in surrender. "How am I gonna teach Trey to go for what he wants in the world if his own mama won't do it?"

Phoenix shrieked and leaped from her seat, giving Serena a hug. Phoenix could feel her sister's heart galloping in her chest, genuine terror.

"*Mazel tov,* ladies!" Aunt Livvy said, and everyone applauded. By the time their hug ended, both Serena and Phoenix were blinking away tears.

The radio suddenly went silent, the sound system's panel losing its light. Phoenix saw Sarge fiddle with the knobs and dials, even checking the plug, but the components refused to come back on. In Phoenix's old life, an occurrence like that meant nothing. Now, nothing slipped her notice. Scott's hand was everywhere.

"Forget it, Daddy," Phoenix said.

Sarge gave her a puzzled look.

"Oh, here we go," Gloria said, rolling her eyes. "Phoenix and her ghost again."

"*Please* don't try to freak us out with your ghost stories," Serena said.

Aunt Livvy's eyes came to Phoenix's, pale lasers. "What ghost stories?"

"You tell me yours first, Aunt Livvy," Phoenix said. "What happened with you and that piano at the Silver Slipper?"

Aunt Livvy gasped, and her half-empty can of Heineken dropped to the coffee table, nearly falling over. She and Uncle Dave steadied it. No one else was drinking beer at midday. Mom thought her sister drank too much. "I can't believe you brought that up!" she said. "I was just thinking about that. Dave and I saw a piano being moved on the street today, and it gave me *shivers*. To this day, I won't have a piano in the house. Tell her, Dave."

"Oh, she won't." Uncle Dave looked annoyed, flipping the page of his *Time Out New York* while a string of his thinning hair fell across his glasses. He had always reminded Phoenix of a mad professor. "My wife is insane."

"He's still livid. Last year, the father of one of our partners died, and Mitch wanted to *give* us this beautiful cranberry concert grand piano. I said we couldn't take it because we don't have room, but I *cannot* have a piano in my house, not after that other one."

Mom shrugged. "I never knew what scared you so much that day. I was—"

"In school," Aunt Livvy finished, shaking her finger with the excitement of a rediscovered memory. "That's right, because I was four and you were seven. And while you're at school, Mom and Dad are schlepping me around the Slipper all day. I *hated* that place."

"Really? Phee and I loved it there," Gloria said, gnawing on her crust. "Beer on tap."

Mom gave Phoenix an unhappy look, and Phoenix passed it on to Gloria. *Good going, loudmouth.* Phoenix had hated the taste of beer at twelve, but Gloria loved sneaking sips.

"Thanks for reminding me what a lying terror you were, Glo," Aunt Livvy said. "Anyway, I'm four years old,. and it's a Friday afternoon. On

Fridays, I'm alone with Pop because Mom is with her mother at the home from noon to three every week. And Pop's going nuts trying to keep the place running, racing up and down the stairs, taking meetings, futzing with mikes and shit on the stage. And he'd sit me in his office in this big, cracked, leather chair, and say, 'Olivia, you stay right here,' and then I don't see him again in God-knows-how-long. There was always something going on at this place. Everybody came through the Slipper in those days, I'm talking about 1960. Jackie Gleason, Frank Sinatra, Nat King Cole. And let's not forget Sam Giancana in the audience, and sometimes he'd bring friends. I had no idea at the time, of course—all grown-ups are equally boring when I'm four—but Pop loved to brag about meeting famous people. Pop's killing himself to make everything go right, the perfect this and that so nobody goes away unimpressed. Pop thought the sun rose and set on the place, you have no idea."

"God, yes," Mom murmured sadly, nodding. Grandpa Bud had lied about his income for years to pay his debts and try to keep his supper club's doors open, and one day his lies had caught up to him. Unlike Serena and Malcolm, Mom and Aunt Livvy had been fully grown when their father went to prison. He died soon after serving two years for tax evasion, and Mom said he'd never been the same. In elementary school, Phoenix had loved telling her friends that both her father *and* grandfather had been to prison, before she'd learned to feel embarrassed by it.

"So this particular Friday, I'm sick to death of sitting in Pop's chair, which is annoying anyway because it squeaks when it spins. I wander to the next room, which is this storeroom upstairs. The door to this room is always closed, but that day it's wide-open. I'm a kid, I'm bored, so naturally I want to know what's in this room."

Phoenix felt goose bumps race up her arms. She glanced toward Gloria, who was already looking at her.

"I can just barely reach the light switch to turn it on. It takes me three tries. The room is full of all kinds of crap, but the only thing I remember is this *piano* sitting there, like it's waiting for something. I'm only four, but I can tell this thing is ancient. This is an ugly piano, like it's been in there a million years without any light. Like it's mad because it's forgotten how to make music. The minute I see this piano, I'm sorry I left Pop's office. I close my eyes and start to back away from it the way I used to back away from that maniac dog our neighbor had, the one that was always biting little kids. And then I bump the back of my head on something in the doorway."

"The door had closed?" Phoenix said.

"The *door* had *closed*?" Aunt Livvy said, snorting. "Please. Sweetie, I *wish* it was just the door had closed. No, when I turn around . . ."

"I remember you telling this part," Mom said, nodding. "You were hysterical."

". . . *The piano has moved*. One second this ugly piano is in front of me, and the next second it's behind me. How do I know it wasn't there before? Because I can't get around this damn thing, it's so big. This piano is *blocking* the doorway. I can't even see over it. I scream for Pop, but he doesn't come. I am desperate to get out of this room. As scared as I am of this mean piano, I try to push it, but the thing weighs a ton. I climb on the keys, making a racket, but then I'm scared to try to jump off the top, it's so tall. In my memory, this piano is fifty feet high. And I distinctly remember feeling like this piano would be *glad* if it hurt me."

Phoenix had only taken one bite of her pizza, mostly to please Mom, but what little appetite she had fled. Serena sucked in her breath, and Malcolm was leaning closer so he could hear each word. Phoenix felt sure she knew what Aunt Livvy was going to say before she spoke.

"Leah, you talk about hysterical? I had a nervous breakdown. I climbed down off that piano and had a tantrum like never before, crying, my nose plugged, I can't breathe. But then—and here's the blessing of being four years old—I just curled there on the concrete floor and went to sleep. The next thing I know, I hear Pop calling for me from down the hall, and that piano was back where it was in the beginning. Like nothing had happened. And when I got home, none of the geniuses in my family would believe a word I said."

"Livvy, you were *four*," Mom said, as if she still was. "That's such a wild story. How can you trust a memory from when you were that young?"

"Damn right I was four. And it's *because* I was four that I'll never forget it."

"So, wait . . ." Serena said. "Is that the same piano that fell on Phee down the stairs? Because *that's* what I remember. That was in 1991."

Serena had spent two weeks with her family the year Phoenix was in the hospital. That was when Phoenix and her sister had become friends, as Serena read her Bible verses and tried to make sure her soul was saved.

"It's the same piano," Phoenix said. She knew that now, if she hadn't before.

Aunt Livvy shook her head. "When I think you had it in your *home,* Leah! I have no idea what was going through your mind."

"Don't blame me," Mom said. "After that accident, I wanted nothing to do with it. Marcus is the one who brought it to our house."

"Hey, now—hold up," Sarge said. He was fully reclined in the room's office chair, his sock feet propped on the desk near the window, where he had a panoramic view of midtown. He hadn't said anything in so long, Phoenix had almost forgotten he was in the room. But that was Sarge. He chose his moments. "Wasn't me. The thing was waiting for me on the porch."

Mom turned to him, wide-eyed. "What are you saying? *You* didn't bring it?"

"I figured you'd hired somebody yourself. It surprised me, but . . ."

"That isn't funny, Marcus," Mom said, her voice a warning. "I mean it."

Sarge shrugged, refusing to retract his story. Phoenix's goose bumps flared. She'd played a piano that had brought itself to her doorstep. That piano had bewitched her somehow.

"All of ya'll need to stop fooling," Serena said. "For real."

"What happened that day the piano fell, Phoenix?" Sarge said. "Tell me the truth."

"We *told* you the truth," Gloria said. "We left the piano in the storeroom. When we came back, it was at the top of the stairs."

"She's right, Sarge," Phoenix said. "We thought maybe Mr. Bell's sons had moved it. But maybe not. Maybe it moved itself. Like . . . the way it got to our house."

That idea would have blown her mind two weeks ago, Phoenix realized. Not today.

A long silence followed. Uncle Dave shook his head, disbelieving. Serena shivered, rubbing her elbows. Malcolm let out a whistle while he sat back and crossed his long legs, his ankle to his kneecap. His dress socks were bright white. "*Dag.* I would have chopped that piano up for firewood after all that," Malcolm said.

"Shoot, I thought about it," Sarge said. "But Phoenix was attached to it."

"I still refuse to believe you didn't bring it home, Marcus. You just don't remember," Mom said. "Believe me, it was the biggest eyesore you ever saw."

"It was that, all right," Sarge said. "But my memory is fine. Three in the afternoon, I show up at home, and there's the piano. I wanted to cuss out the movers for leaving it outside."

Everyone else could remember that piano better than she could, Phoenix thought. When she tried to visualize it, she could only see the ghostly piano that had appeared in Carlos's bedroom, the one in her dream, not the real one she'd seen as a child. She remembered taking Gloria to the storeroom, the accident, having the piano at the house, everything except how it had looked, exactly, or why she'd wanted anything to do with it. The Queen Psychic was right: That piano had something to do with her connection to Joplin. If she found it again, she might be able to make their connection stronger.

"Mom, do you remember who bought that piano from you?" Phoenix said.

Mom sighed, planting her palm on her forehead. "Oh, wow, that's been forever. Not off the top of my head. Marcus?" Sarge was already shaking his head. "Well, I'm my mother's daughter, so I bet I have it in a file at home somewhere."

Serena suddenly stood up. "Can we change the subject? I can't stand scary stories. Phee, where's the thermostat? This room is cold as hell."

Serena was right, Phoenix realized. The room was so cold, the tips of her fingers were smarting, which she'd assumed before now was from the cold soda can. The others exchanged glances, realizing how suddenly the cold had come. Phoenix expelled a strong breath of air and saw the faintest trace of mist. Serena tried, too, puffing air into her palm. Then she looked at Phoenix, her eyes wild with questions.

"Nobody panic," Phoenix said. "But I don't think it's the thermostat."

As soon as she spoke, the lights in the room flared, then switched off abruptly. If not for the sunshine through the picture window, the living room would have gone dark.

"Phee, I don't know who's paying for this room, but somebody's gettin' played," Malcolm said, just before her bedroom door behind them slammed shut. The sharp sound made Serena and Livvy scream. Gloria looked startled, her eyes casing the room. Even Uncle Dave's face had gone gray. He yanked off his glasses, staring over his shoulder at the door.

"Who's in there?" Gloria said.

"Nobody," Phoenix and her mother said in unison. Mom stared at the door, but she also stared at the air around her, wondering if the source of the cold was something she could see. It was a winter's day in the room, and they were dressed for summer.

Malcolm rubbed his hands together for heat. "What the hell's goin' on?"

"Cold spots and hot spots are evidence of ghost encounters," Phoenix said. "I've had the same thing in my apartment. I know some of you have been thinking I'm out of my mind, but I'm not. These things are happening because of a ghost. It's the ghost of Scott Joplin."

"Oh, *hell,* no," Serena said, reaching for her purse on the floor.

"*Shhhhhhhh,*" Phoenix said. "He's not going to hurt anyone."

"Cuz?" Gloria said, nearly a whimper, and Gloria was not one to whimper.

"Yeah, cuz?"

"I was wrong, and you were right."

"This is so amazing," Aunt Livvy said in a hushed voice, clutching her husband's hand to her breast. "That's the part I didn't tell about that day with the piano. When Pop found me in the storeroom and took me out by the hand, something made me look over my shoulder, and there's this black man standing at the other end of the hall." She spoke more quickly, and Phoenix knew she was only filling the room with chatter so she wouldn't be afraid.

"He's dressed up in a suit like a man would wear to temple, very nice. And this is during segregation, so you didn't just see black people out of the blue. They had to have passes to work on Miami Beach, white and colored water fountains, everything. Disgusting. I'm four years old, so if I see a black man, I automatically think, *Oh, he's a musician.* So I call out to him, 'Are you going to play tonight?' And I'll never forget: He turns to look at me, and his *face*. Such sadness! 'One day,' he says to me. Now, Pop is already worried about me because I must have looked like I'd been crying for days. He kneels, and says, 'Olivia, who are you talking to?' And when I point, there's nobody there, I swear. I'm talking to nobody. Just like the piano—there one second, gone the next. My God, do you think that's who it was? Was it Scott Joplin?" She looked around as if she thought she might glimpse on old friend again.

And Scott *was* close to Aunt Livvy, Phoenix realized. The light glimmering on the wall behind the sofa looked like a reflection from chrome, but it was him. *Be careful, Scott. You're scaring them.* Could he hear what she was thinking the way he knew her dreams?

Serena crouched with her purse, ready to get out of the room once she dared to move. "A *ghost* is in this room, Phee? Ya'll are crazy, sitting in here like this!" she said.

Sarge was suddenly on his feet. He put his hands on his hips as he gazed toward the ceiling. "Well, I know *one* thing . . ." Sarge's voice boomed, and he was not addressing the living. "I extend my deepest respect to Scott Joplin, because he was a great man, a very influential man, and I'm honored to be in his presence. But Scott Joplin has had his time. And if there's a ghost in this room, that ghost better show Phoenix some respect, too. That ghost better not interfere with Phoenix's concert Friday night, because both my girls are singing on that stage. Phoenix Smalls is living *now,* and she has her own work to do."

Whatever spell Scott had woven was broken when Sarge spoke, as if Sarge were a shaman from an ancient culture who only now was revealing his power. Sarge's words shot around the room.

A piercing shriek made them jump and gasp, but it was only a trumpet solo from the radio, suddenly back on at full volume. The lights came next, every single one; even the banker's lamp on Sarge's desk, a black torchiere lamp behind Phoenix and overhead spotlights that had not been on before. The temperature rose abruptly back to normal, killing the cold. The glimmering light behind the sofa was gone, too.

Phoenix hadn't realized her ghost could be commanded. Even the psychics hadn't been able to tell Scott what to do. Phoenix felt envious that Scott was so willing to heed Sarge's spoken words, but what if Sarge had banished him somehow? Phoenix joined her family in staring at her father, speechless.

Sarge calmly straightened his shirt, then he rubbed the last of the cold out of his hands as he prepared to take his seat. After reclining again, Sarge picked up a half-eaten slice of pizza and took a bite. He took his time chewing.

Sarge gave a shrug. "Look, ya'll, I've spent eight years in lockup and sixty-odd years as a black man," Sarge said. "I guarantee you, like the song says, I ain't scared of no damn ghost."

*I*t was after eight when Carlos got back, past dinnertime.

Phoenix had declined at least four invitations while she waited for him: Dinner at B. Smith's with her parents, a pilgrimage to Radio City Music Hall with Arturo and the dancers, dancing at an Indian hip-hop club with Gloria, Serena and Malcolm, and drinks with an East Coast TSR rep who'd called Sarge's cell phone only minutes ago, and Sarge had told her she should go. Carlos had been in such a hurry, he'd left his cell phone on the nightstand, so Phoenix hadn't even had the satisfaction of calling him to tell him how pissed she was. Aside from two taped telephone interviews with local radio stations promoting the concert, Phoenix hadn't done anything but wait since Scott chased her family away, and the wait was lonely.

Scott hadn't come back since Sarge's talk with him, either. Not yet.

Phoenix was half-asleep when she heard the door open. As soon as Carlos appeared with his satchel and two shopping bags, Phoenix knew they were going to have their first fight.

He sat beside her at the far end of the sofa, rubbing her bare feet. "Hey," he said.

Hey? Groggy, Phoenix sat up and looked at her watch. Eight-fifteen. He'd been gone at least nine hours. "That's it?"

"Sorry. I couldn't stay, for the obvious reasons." Despite Carlos's apology, he didn't seem apologetic. He was barely looking at her.

"I have a phone," she said. She hated to sound like a cliché, but wasn't she?

"I know. Sorry I didn't call. I hooked up with some friends in Park Slope. Sorry."

It was possible, Phoenix thought, that she'd never felt a ball of rage like the one that rolled across her chest as she stared at Carlos staring away from her. She could hear one of Mom's old scripts with Sarge about to fly from her lips: *So how hard would it be to tell me your plans? Do you always have to be gone so long?*

"You're good at apologizing," she said.

"I've had a lot of practice."

"So I better take it or leave it?"

"I didn't say that."

"What *are* you saying?"

He sighed, raising his arms in a resigned gesture. *That's all I've got for you.*

Phoenix's anger couldn't possibly grow, so she felt it receding instead. Carlos was baiting her, even if he didn't realize it. He had probably pulled the same crap with Heather. Carlos was used to running away, and who was *she* to judge? She had shamed Ronn in grand style, and Ronn had treated her with nothing but grace. Carlos deserved grace, too.

"Let me guess . . ." she said softly. "When you start sleeping with someone new, this is the time you start feeling like it's not worth the risk. Cut your losses. Let's be friends. Right?"

The stoniness melted from Carlos's face, and he blinked. Her insight surprised him. "Sometimes now. Sometimes a little later." He cleared his throat, ready to talk to her like a real person again. "Phoenix . . . this thing with your father is a problem, no?"

"I didn't know my parents were coming like that today."

"That's not your fault. But it's also not the issue. This won't go away."

"I'm going to talk to him," she said.

"If I were him, a talk wouldn't matter."

"But it might. If it doesn't, we'll figure it out. Do you think I'm that easy to cut loose?"

A sad smile appeared on his face. "You'd have legions of others to choose from."

"I don't want them. I want you."

The fight was already over. Carlos leaned over and kissed her, and his lips tasted like sweet rum. *He really does love me,* she thought, her heart thumping, and she wondered if she already loved him back.

Carlos pulled up one of the shopping bags. "I didn't have it wrapped, but I got you something to say congratulations on *Rising* and the Osiris gig. This is a big deal, Phee."

Phoenix crossed her arms. If he'd presented his gift and a better apology to start, she never would have felt that ball of anger. "You just want me to feel bad for getting pissed."

He gave her the large bag, plain white plastic. "Go on. Look inside."

Phoenix didn't know Carlos well enough to guess what kind of gift he might buy her, except that it wouldn't be trite. She hoped he hadn't spent too much money. When she pulled out a thick black woolen bomber jacket with shiny leather sleeves and trim, her eyes went out of focus.

"It's genuine, from the Rhythm Nation tour," Carlos said. "It's not signed or anything, but she probably wore it a few times. The guy who sold it was a roadie on a couple of her tours."

Janet Jackson's RHYTHM NATION 1990 World Tour was elaborately stitched in silver on back, but Phoenix had been unable to comprehend the words until Carlos said them aloud. This was a like-new jacket from Janet's tour, the one after *Control* that sealed her escape from Michael's long shadow. Phoenix had seen Janet at the Miami Arena when she was nine, the reason she was singing, the reason she was here. How had Carlos seen through her to her memories? "But you don't even like Janet Jackson," she said. Carlos was biased toward musicians, not pop stars, so how could he understand what that concert had meant to her?

"I like her fine, but so what? *You* are a true fan. You talked about her long ago, and now here you are. Being a fan is something special, whenever and however it happens. Congratulations, Phee."

While Carlos hugged her, Phoenix was still staring at her jacket, seeing it anew each time she blinked. The jacket made her remember swords of light stabbing the air from the stage below, the smoke bowing to Janet's electrifying, mechanized movements with her corps of dancers. The jacket was alive, almost.

Suddenly, Phoenix felt like a fraud. "I'm so far from being Janet," she said.

"You're not supposed to be Janet. You're Phoenix. You're something else."

Phoenix remembered to hug Carlos, wrapping both arms around him hard, pinning him in place. "This is the best gift anyone has ever given me. In my life. *Ever.*"

"You're welcome." While Carlos held her, she felt the heat from his neck tickle her cheek. He kissed her again, and her exhausted body tried to rouse itself.

Then, she remembered.

"The ghost was here." They had both said it at once.

By the time they had exchanged their sighting stories, Phoenix and Carlos were stripped to their underwear and under the covers although it was only nine o'clock. Phoenix wanted to make love to Carlos tonight, but she was so tired, she could barely talk. So far, he had only wrapped himself around her, as if he sensed he would have to wait. Didn't he always?

Carlos laughed when he heard how Sarge had sent Scott away, warning the ghost not to mess up her gig. "Sarge is a hell of a manager, all right," Carlos said.

"It's the thing he does best," Phoenix said, but they wouldn't talk about Sarge. She wanted to talk about Scott. She envied Carlos for his sighting in the hallway. Scott had never appeared to her face on when she was awake, not once. He hid himself from her, only revealing his face when she slept. "What did it feel like, Carlos? When he walked through you?"

"I guess it felt . . ." Carlos paused, looking for the word. He chose one that was nothing like what she had expected Carlos to say: "Unnerving."

"Really?" Phoenix's voice went hoarse, but she cleared her throat and propped herself up to stare at him more closely. "Do you think he was trying to scare you?"

"No . . . not exactly," he said, although he didn't sound sure.

Phoenix felt bad for Carlos, who looked like he had met one of his idols and discovered he was an asshole. Carlos had known more about Scott than she did in the beginning, and probably still did. Carlos and Van Milton were truer peers, even if Carlos couldn't play the piano.

Piano. Phoenix remembered Aunt Livvy and the piano, a thunderbolt.

"Did he hurt you?" She couldn't say it louder than a whisper.

Carlos sighed, not exactly a *no*. "I was in a sensitive mood, so maybe it was me. But I was standing there watching this ghost go somewhere I wasn't free to go myself. It wasn't fun."

She smiled, relieved. "So, basically, you were just jealous."

"Ghosts make whatever impression they choose to make. Maybe I should be jealous, Phee." She couldn't tell if he was joking, but she hoped so. Carlos pulled himself away from her, gently guiding her head to her own pillow instead of the softness of his upper arm. "You need tea for your voice, so I'll make you some. Then I want you to sleep."

Phoenix closed her eyes and mumbled thanks. Carlos was right. Missing any more sleep would destroy her thin-ass voice by Friday; she'd be lucky to sound decent during tomorrow's rehearsal. At least having Serena on the stage would inspire her to give her vocal cords a workout. As Carlos walked toward the bathroom for the coffeemaker, Phoenix stared again at the tour jacket she'd hung on back of the desk chair. Seeing it, her toes tingled. She vowed to wear it at least once every day.

Thirty seconds later, Phoenix realized her toes weren't tingling because of the jacket.

Her skin felt a lash of electricity, and she wriggled, startled. The room seemed to career to one side, then the other, as if she were being rocked in a giant, slow-moving hammock. Phoenix found herself grasping at the headboard, trying to keep her balance.

Next, music crashed inside of her. Thumping, insistent, discordant piano music, a collision of notes, dozens of pianos at war. The noise in her head hurt.

Finally, noise became a single frolicsome melody, inviting her to come play.

I'm tired, Scott. I'm glad you're back, but can we do this tomorrow?

As if in response, the crashing noise came again, and this time Phoenix clapped her hands over her ears. That had been more like a true pain in her head, not just her ears feeling offended. A pinprick, maybe, but pain all the same. Scott wouldn't take no for an answer.

By the time Carlos brought her a mug of tea, Phoenix had taken last night's place at her desk, drawing new sets of lines. She'd forgotten to buy blank sheet music, but that was okay. She'd gotten very good at drawing the lines straight.

"What are you doing, hon?" Carlos said. "I thought you were going to sleep."

"I hear music," she said. "He's back."

"He can wait, Phoenix. You didn't sleep last night. You need to go to bed."

He already sounded far away again. Phoenix shook her head, finishing one line, then the next. Five lines, beautiful and straight, the perfect canvas. Carlos was wrong; she didn't need sleep. She'd been sleeping all day, waiting. Scott and his music were back, and she was more awake than she had ever been.

"He's here," she heard herself say.

She forgot she was talking to Carlos as soon as the words were out of her mouth.

CHAPTER TWENTY

New York
September 1911

A stack of scored pages landed on the table an inch from Scott's nose,
making him flinch, the most he had moved in a half hour. Scott was
bent over the table with his face resting against the bony pillow of his
folded arms. His eyes were open, but he hadn't seen anyone walk in.

"You ain't the only one tired," Sam Patterson said. "I was up at dawn
working on these, Scotty. There's a devil of a long way to go with the
orchestrations, but at least—"

"Show's canceled," Scott said. He barely heard himself speak. His
voice was dust.

"What?"

Scott raised his head and looked up at his friend from St. Louis, satisfied that the tears he held at bay would not appear. Disappointment cut
deeper when he wasn't feeling well, which was true too much of the
time. His moods were as volatile as an expectant mother's, but *wasn't* he?

"It's always about money, Sam," he said. "Tom Johnson left here just
before you came. Turns out the theater in Atlantic City won't go for an
opera. We can't do *Treemonisha*."

Sam pulled off his derby, as if he'd just heard news of a death, and
took the seat across from Scott at the lone table in the empty basement
that served as his rehearsal hall. "Can't he find another stage for you?
What about one in the city?" Sam was never willing to take his bad news
straight. He was chubby-cheeked and only five-foot-three, his build so

slight that he was often mistaken for a boy although he was twenty-eight. His optimism was boyish, to be sure.

"Tom's backing out. I got hot, and so did he." Scott hadn't thought of himself as a man with a temper, but one had surfaced when Tom Johnson brought him the news. Scott might only be forty-four, but he knew why old men became so brittle: They had lost too much, especially time, and patience was a luxury reserved for people with time. His relationship with the Negro producer and former theater owner might be soured for good, and he didn't have a friend to spare.

When John Stark had refused to publish *Treemonisha*—history repeating itself, and the last rupture in a relationship that was already strained—Scott had published the score himself, all 230 pages. It had cost him more than he could afford, but he thought the sacrifice had paid off when his opera's review was published in the *American Musician and Art Journal*. He still could hardly believe the words from a white man's pen: *It is in no sense ragtime, but of that peculiar quality of rhythm which Dvořák used so successfully in the* New World Symphony, the reviewer had said. *Although this work completed by one of the Ethiopian race will hardly be accepted as a typical American opera for obvious reasons, nevertheless none can deny that it serves as an opening wedge, for it is in every sense indigenous. Its composer has . . . hewn an entirely new form of operatic art.*

To compare his work to Dvořák! To assert that he, a Negro—who could be turned away from white-only theater seating in New York—was the only American composer truly creating an American operatic form! Further, the reviewer had claimed he was the equivalent of Booker T. Washington and Paul Laurence Dunbar, his dear Freddie's poet hero.

Scott lay awake at night with images flurrying in his mind that had seemed within his grasp for the first time: A proper orchestra. Colorful costumes. Set pieces painted with care—a detailed re-creation of Arkansas in 1884, with cornfields, dense forest and a peek of the Red River.

Could it be? he'd asked the darkness. *Will we have our opera at last, Freddie?*

Now, he had his answer. Scott felt the weight of his new grief across his aching muscles. In a few minutes, by six o'clock, the cast would begin filing in, forsaking their families for the dinnertime rehearsal. Since Atlantic City was too far for regular rehearsals, Scott met with them in the basement of a building where one of the cast members lived, a hotel porter named Courtney. The space was dank and windowless, but it had been their sanctuary.

And what a cast! These young people were so dedicated, they made his traveling company for *A Guest of Honor* look like a band of school-boys. There were no thieves in this group, nor drunks, nor gamblers. And what would he have done without Sam to help him write the end-less pages of orchestrations? He'd had only a piano score when he was promised the theater in Atlantic City, and without Sam he wouldn't have believed *Treemonisha* could be staged in time. None of them had taken a day of rest in three weeks, even on Sundays, and for what?

Sam patted Scott's hand twice, firmly. "Well, don't lose heart, Scotty. This way, you'll have a chance to keep working on it. I say it needs more action to hold the music together. Maybe this is a blessing in disguise."

Scott was too sad to be angry, but he wished Sam had chosen his tim-ing better. "If I were Louis, I'd sock you for saying that to me now, Sam."

Sam smiled grimly. "Sorry, Scotty. If you were Louis, I'd have known better." He chuckled, until it faded to a sigh. "And I'd sure as hell be glad to see you."

Louis's name came up at least once whenever he and Sam were to-gether, a presence even in his absence. Had it already been three years since Louis died? Scott was the one who'd written to Sam with the news of their friend's death, since Sam had been touring with the Musical Spillers when word came. Neither of them had been with Louis when he succumbed, so maybe distance made it harder for the truth to settle. Some nights, visiting a dance-hall where a skillful professor was at work, Scott caught himself wondering what Louis was up to, or where he was playing, until he remembered all over again.

"Sam, if we don't do it now, we never will." *Or I won't live to see it.*

"That's nothin' but boohooing. Not after the way that reviewer licked your boots."

"You know as well as I do the Negro theaters want variety shows, and the opera houses will laugh me out the door. It takes more than a good review."

"Just takes time, is all."

Yes, youngster, but like Louis, time is the one thing I cannot afford.

A few were home sick with flu, but thirty people assembled within twenty minutes, filling the hall with laughter, warm greetings and playful grousing. Most of them were Sam's age, many of them younger, although Scott had found a few older performers willing to play the conjurers. The cast sat in circles eating dinner from the sacks they often brought, and a few stood off by themselves, warming up their voices the way Scott had taught them. Many of his players had never had professional training—and although it was evident in their performances, it was less so each day. Scott had no doubt they would have been ready for that stage in Atlantic City, a minor miracle. All companies became a family after a time, but this one had been one from the start. Staring at their ready faces, he almost showed his hidden tears.

Why did they believe in him when so few others did? Or did they believe in *themselves*?

Scott remembered how he'd felt at sixteen, leaving Texarkana for gigs with his brother Robert and their vocal quartet, marching into the mysterious and frightening world before them. Today's players had much more to dream for, perhaps. Negro music was reaching every corner of the nation nowadays, even if most people would rather discard its origins. In the scads of dreadful so-called ragtime being published today, Scott couldn't remember the last time he'd seen a Negro face on a cover sheet, as if their music had materialized from thin air.

Now it was Irving Berlin and "Alexander's Ragtime Band," a song that made Scott's teeth grind every time he heard mention of it. Maybe it was only coincidence that Berlin's piece sounded so much like the original finale of *Treemonisha,* but Scott didn't believe it. He would never again be fool enough to share pages of an unpublished score with a composer who might not be trustworthy. Scott had been forced to rewrite a portion of his own opera so no one would think the theft was the other way around! If Negroes weren't careful, history would never show their footprints on the music and dance fads that had sprung from the misery of Southern plantations everyone was so eager to forget. *Treemonisha* would have helped them remember, Negro and white alike.

Reluctantly, Scott got up to face his company.

"I have an announcement you all need to hear," Scott said, and the room's merry din quieted. If Scott lacked the respect of the Negroes storming New York music and theater—not to mention the white elite who disdained Negroes—he was still a king in the eyes of his company.

Scott felt stung by the large, eager eyes of his young lead performer, a tireless girl named Sally whose family had moved to New York from a small town in Florida to escape the terror of lynching. At seventeen, she was a year younger than the heroine, Treemonisha, but after losing her brother to a mob and a rope, she sang with a lifetime of wisdom. Sally's skin and features were not far removed from whichever ancestors Africa had sacrificed to bring her here, but she embodied Freddie's spirit more than any girl her age he had met since his dead wife. In Sally, Scott saw his beloved girl's twin. With Sally singing Treemonisha's pleas for education and uplift, sweet Freddie would have lived again.

"I'd give my soul not to have to say this, since you've worked so hard, but the show is canceled," Scott said. "We won't be performing in Atlantic City. I'm sorry."

There weren't any gasps or exclamations, only a deathly silence from one end of the room to the other. Scott swallowed, and for a time he couldn't find his tongue. "You're the best company I've ever known. I mean that. You're rich in spirit even where your talent is raw. If I could change it for your sakes, I would," he said. "I suppose it's my fault. I needed a bag of luck and didn't have sense enough to get one."

A few people took his last words to be a joke and chuckled, although Scott had not spoken in jest. *Treemonisha* ridiculed conjurers, but he could never forget the conjurer who had told him the horrors to await him, and the old man had not yet been wrong. Sometimes, Scott felt certain the conjurer on the train *had* struck him with a curse, and the thought gave him a chill. *The boy said the bones don't lie. Have I only been railing against my future?*

"Mr. Joplin?" Sally said, raising her hand as if she were a pupil in school. Her cheekbones were marvelous, hewn from obsidian. "I don't care if the show's in Atlantic City or at the subway stop. We know the parts, and we should put it on like we set out. Colored folks *need* to hear it. Just like you wrote in the opera, we've got to keep marching onward."

When the company agreed, applauding, Scott brushed an escaping tear from his eye. That was precisely what Freddie would have said. He had cast his Treemonisha well.

"Sally, I'm touched by your enthusiasm, dear heart," he said, "but I've lost my producer, which means I have no backing. I have no way to pay you." With his fame for "Maple Leaf Rag," most people expected him to be wealthy, but Scott had lost the shame he'd once felt about admitting the truth. By now, he was masterful at the art of polite begging.

"Ain't no way you *could* pay us enough for all this work," said Jeb, who was a fright as the white-haired conjurer who kidnapped Treemonisha and tried to throw her in a wasps' nest. Jeb was growing his beard un-groomed since Scott had asked him to, and he looked more like the con-jurer on the train at each rehearsal. By day, Jeb worked on the docks, but by night he sang with an amateur quartet and played his banjo wherever he could find an audience. Jeb was a scrappy baritone who had told Scott he might have tried to make his living as a singer if he hadn't needed more steady work to feed his family of six. "I don't know 'bout nobody else, but I didn't learn all this hee-hoo and goofer dust talk for nothin'. I play on the street when I got to. I sing for anybody who'll put up with the noise. You find me a stage, Mr. Joplin, and I'll be there."

This time, the company agreed with stirring shouts.

Scott was unable to speak another word.

New York had seduced Scott, at first.

Scott didn't have the common vocabulary to describe New York in letters to his father, who had never seen a city bigger than Little Rock. How could he describe trains speeding under the ground to a man who had spent his early life shucking corn and driving mules for his master? All other cities were puny beside this tempestuous jeweled queen, whose ambitious architecture still inspired Scott to walk with his eyes raised high, like a child's, even four years after his arrival. He was lucky he'd never walked into a lamppost or crossed the path of a taxi. The city was more bedazzling at night, with Broadway's white electric lights, a glimpse of Heaven's glory.

Scott had never heard a city so full of music, and not just from the countless supper clubs, dance halls and cabarets showcasing young tick-lers like James P. Johnson and one-legged Willie Joseph, whose hands struck the piano keys with precision that would have shocked even Louis. Scott also heard music in the chorus of motorcar horns, vendors' dueling cries in Yiddish, Italian, Spanish and Chinese to accompany exotic scents, the stampeding footsteps of natty Wall Street businessmen on their way to make their fortunes, and tinkling piano keys from music publishers' open windows like a musical rainstorm on a vast tin rooftop. Even when the music was bad—and so much of it was, and worse all the time—the sheer volume was breathtaking.

Today, walking with Sam past the exuberant tiers of billboards and notices for plays and follies posted at Forty-second Street in Times Square, Scott felt a stirring of belief that his luck *might* lie right around the corner. Signs of success lay everywhere, lighthouses for weary sojourners. *Which would be more tragic? To be deaf here, or blind?*

To be cursed, Scott thought. That would be worst. No sooner had he passed the billboards then he came upon a row of crowded brick tenements with alleys stinking of human waste. For the unfortunate who lived inside these hovels, tuberculosis ran unchecked, and the weak fell victim to summer heat and winter cold alike. *Perhaps my true home is among this city's accursed, not its blessed,* Scott thought.

Scott had taken heart when he heard about Paul Laurence Dunbar's Broadway triumph as the librettist for *Clorindy* in 1898, a year before the publication of "Maple Leaf Rag." While Scott was conquering a small town in Missouri, Dunbar and Negro composer Will Marion Cook had already collaborated to conquer Broadway, following with six other shows. But what had Dunbar's innovation and brilliance won him? Dunbar had died penniless two years after Freddie, a young man of thirty-four.

Why did Negroes court such early death? Or did Death stalk young Negroes for sport?

"Slow down, Scotty. My stomach's growling," Sam said, stopping beside a dusky-haired sweet-potato vendor with a metal cart on the corner. *Slow down.* That was almost funny. Scott's disease had forced a gingerly walk upon him, so Sam was the one forced to slow down.

The familiar scent of warming sweet potatoes wafted from the cart's spout, the smell of his mother's oven. The vendor's Irish brogue was so thick that Scott couldn't understand his answer when Sam asked him his price, but Sam bought two, handing Scott a potato without asking him if he was hungry. Scott took the food, grateful. The warm sweet potato felt good in his hand, since the fall air was cooling. His joints bothered him when the air got cold.

"Thanks, Sam. It'll be nice to bring Lottie something for a change," Scott said.

"That's a good woman, all right. Best thing to happen to you."

"Any woman who'd take up with an artist is either a saint or a fool."

"Lord knows Lottie's neither, but you're lucky to have her," Sam said.

Two months ago, Scott had moved into a comfortable three-room apartment on Forty-seventh Street with a sharp-minded woman named Lottie Stokes, and she'd begun calling herself *Lottie Joplin* although neither of them had seen the need to see a preacher. Two weddings were enough for any man's lifetime. He and Lottie shared her bed, but touching wasn't uppermost in their minds. Lottie knew like no one else how little of his manhood remained. But Lottie loved music, and she believed in his potential like no one since Freddie. She was also much smarter with her pocketbook than he could ever hope to be, so she might save him from utter destitution. Sometimes Scott wasn't sure what Lottie got from him in return.

"Isn't that Jim Europe?" Sam said, nodding toward the intersection.

Sure enough, James Reese Europe himself was crossing the street toward them, in animated conversation with a tall, wispy white man who looked like that young dancer from England named Castle. The sight of the celebrated Negro bandleader in a tweed suit and spectacles gave Scott dual pulses of excitement and frustration. Luck around the corner, indeed.

With a single word, James Reese Europe could help him gain backers for *Treemonisha* all over New York. His Chef Club Orchestra was extraordinary: Playing for the highest echelons of New York society, the Chef Club was more than a hundred musicians strong, each man more solemn than the one beside him, and none with a strand of hair, shirt button or shoelace out of place. An orchestra like that for *Treemonisha* would never be forgotten.

"Now's my chance to ask him to look at the score," Scott said, rushing to pull a few pages out of his briefcase as he watched the approach of the commanding, dark-skinned young man.

"Go easy, Scotty," Sam muttered. "You've gotta pick your time with Jim."

Six months ago, the only time Scott had cornered Europe to mention his opera, the orchestra leader's eyes had flitted away. *We're trying to get away from the plantation, not move back to it*, he'd said with a dismissive laugh, and Scott had guessed Europe didn't know any more about the hardscrabble lives of Negroes in the South than he knew about the sands of the moon.

Scott felt hopeful when Europe smiled and raised his index finger to his hat, like a salute.

But the bandleader's eyes were only on Sam. "Hiya, Sam," Europe said with a nod, and Sam barely had time to answer his greeting before Europe and his companion breezed past them. If Europe had recognized Scott, his face hadn't shown it. He was gone before Scott could open his mouth. If Scott hadn't felt so tired, he would have chased after him.

"He didn't see you," Sam said.

"Maybe he did, maybe he didn't." Scott turned around to watch Europe's retreat until the broad shoulders of the man's impeccable suit were blocked from his sight by a passing two-level bus. The gaggle of women riding atop the bus held tight to their fall hats, barreling toward their own futures. Scott pocketed his sweet potato, walking on.

"You're swimming upstream with opera, Scotty."

"Now you sound like Stark."

"Stark didn't get where he is being nobody's fool."

"Sissieretta Jones sings opera. Negroes have performed operatic pieces on Broadway."

"Not like *Treemonisha*. Don't take it so personal. Joe Jordan told me he'd be glad if you'd compose something more popular, and maybe he could put together a show like *The Shoo Fly Regiment* he directed at the Bijou. *That's* how you'll get to Broadway. You got to give folks what they want, or else make your peace and quit asking for what you can't have. You want it both ways, Scotty."

"Seems like I can't have it any kind of way. I'm damned if I do and damned if I don't."

"You're *damned*?" Sam said, chuckling. "Listen to you. If Scott Joplin is damned, the rest of us don't got a chance, do we? You hear music in your head other folks don't hear, *Treemonisha* and all the rags to boot. That music ain't yours, Scotty. It came from God, and God don't promise you nothing else. Like my mama used to say, don't look a gift horse in the mouth. If it ain't *Treemonisha's* time, so be it. Just be glad God let you hear it."

Scott blinked rapidly. "Then I'd rather not hear it, Sam. God can leave me be."

"You don't mean that."

"I mean it today. Ask me again tomorrow."

They rounded the corner toward Scott's apartment building on West Forty-seventh, amid a cluster of apartment buildings and brownstones, some of which Scott knew served as covert silk-tie brothels. From his bedroom window at night, Scott watched gentlemen embark on their adventures from carriages and taxis, hardly visible before they dashed inside. The flesh trade on this street was more quiet than it had been in Chestnut Valley, but it generated steady traffic, never wanting for business. Lottie was advertising for a female boarder to share their apartment, and she'd told Scott she could charge more rent from a woman who received male visitors for pay. *I'm not a madam, Scotty,* she'd told him, *but folks will say so because the girls trust me, and that doesn't bother me worth a damn so long as it doesn't bother you.*

Who was he to make demands of Lottie on moral grounds? They knew each other's secrets, another of the comforts Lottie gave him. He could never have faced telling Freddie about his affliction, and the secret would have burned a hole in his soul. Lottie knew more about his ailment than Sam, unless Louis had confided their shared fate. But Scott didn't think so. Sam had never mentioned the word *syphilis* in the time he'd known him. Sam told anyone who asked that Louis had smoked and drunk himself to an early grave.

What will Sam say about me, then? Will he say it was my opera that killed me?

"What's all the fuss?" Sam said, gazing toward the alleyway separating Scott's building from the identical narrow structure beside it.

That was when Scott first saw the piano.

An upright piano with a candelabra sat beneath the last rung of the ladder from the fire escape. The piano looked so odd among the crates and soap-boxes in the alley that it had drawn a crowd. Scott had seen pianos neglected, abused and untuned for years, but never a piano deserted.

The piano looked new. The pale rosewood reflected the day's last light with a burnish that told Scott it had been polished and well cared for, until now. He made his way past two newsboys and four adult onlookers, and he immediately saw the reason for its banishment: The piano's keys were streaked with blood. A bright, wet smear gaped at the exact center. When Scott saw the blood, his stomach kicked his throat.

He knew this piano, or one identical to it. Solomon Dixon had a Rosenkranz in his parlor. He and Freddie had sat together at those keys and cried together a heartbeat before she died.

"What happened?" Scott said, his mouth dry.

"White man and a nigger fought it out," the orange-haired white newsboy said. "They fought over a nigger gal, see, and the white fella took his knife and carved open the nigger's belly like a hog to slaughter."

"That ain't it," the second boy said, eating from a sack of roasted peanuts. "It was the other way around. A nigger carved out a white fella's heart and laid it on the keys."

"Two men brung the piano on a truck. They said they brung it on account of the cops," the first boy said.

"Evidence," the companion clarified wisely.

When a new passerby joined the crowd, the boys told their story again: This time, they argued over whether a white man or a Negro had pulled out a derringer and shot out the other's eye. Obviously, neither boy knew anything about the piano's origin.

The newcomer, a middle-aged Negro man in a neat brown suit and tie, sighed and shook his head. "Whatever it is, I know bad juju when I see it," the man said, meeting Scott's gaze, and walked on his way in a hurry. The comment startled Scott, who had been fooled by the man's professional attire. Was *everyone* full of ignorant superstition?

"Scotty boy?" a voice sang from above him.

Scott looked up to the second-story window, where the fading lace curtains had been pulled back so Lottie could lean outside. She'd straightened her hair with her metal hot comb since he'd seen her this morning, and limp jet strands draped her shoulders girlishly, framing an oval-shaped ginger face. Lottie's bosom rested across the windowsill. "I've been waitin' on you to come back, baby. You see that piano?"

"I see it," Scott said, embarrassed to have to raise his voice in front of strangers. Lottie had no such reservations, often calling to him from the window.

She grinned down at him. Lottie's vivacious grin was big enough to bring light back to the dusk sky. "Well . . . What you think?"

He and Lottie had no piano. The all-male boardinghouse Scott had moved out of on West Twenty-seventh Street had a piano in the parlor, but Scott had suspended his lessons for two months because the only piano in Lottie's building belonged to the couple downstairs, and he didn't like to play it except when a new composition demanded it. He knew the exact piano he wanted: A black Steinway cabinet grand piano, one worthy of Paderewski. He had seen the piano in a music-store window, and he was saving for it, a little week by week.

"What do I think? I think the keys are sticky with blood," Scott called up to her.

"Shoot, I know how to get rid of blood," Lottie said. "What you *think*?"

Blood aside, Scott still didn't care for the piano. Rosewood was attractive, and it was ornate enough to be called art in its own right, especially with the old-fashioned candelabra to betray its age. But it wasn't his Steinway. His Steinway had a sound elegant enough to accompany Sam and the other singers he and Lottie entertained at home, because in Lottie, thank God, he had found a woman who had created the musician's haven he'd craved since he married Belle more than a decade ago. *This is not the piano I wanted.* That thought railed in his mind, a child's tantrum.

But that wasn't all. He sensed it, but couldn't put a voice to it. There was something else about the piano he did not like, something beneath its polished wood and bloody keys. It looked too much like the one in Sedalia—as if this piano, like his grief, had followed him all the way to New York. He understood why the man in the brown suit had walked away so quickly. Scott touched one of the piano's keys, the high G, and the single note rang in the alleyway as the hammer met the string, a strident sound. The note sounded as lonely as any Scott had ever heard. The rash on his feet, one of his illness's more annoying reminders, suddenly itched terribly. He'd been in a bad mood before he laid eyes on the piano, but his mood felt worse now.

"What did I just tell you about looking a gift horse in the mouth?" Sam said. "Take this damn piano inside before somebody else does. It's probably worth sixty dollars outright, or more. You oughta clean it up and sell it, if nothing else. You got no mind for business, Scotty."

"You tell him, Sam. All he's talked about is needing a piano. What am I gonna *do* with this man?" Lottie's voice drifted down.

A white man with wide-set eyes scowled at Scott. "Say, what gives you claim to it?"

"He's Scott Joplin, that's what," Sam said.

"Yeah, sure he is, and I'm President Taft," the man said, and mounted his bicycle to ride off. The piano's allure diminished when the question of its future seemed settled, so the other onlookers began to drift. Even the two newsboys scampered away, as if they'd heard their mothers calling from the distance. If he wanted this piano, Scott thought, it was his. *This won't replace my Steinway,* Scott vowed to himself.

"All right, Sam. You take one end, I'll take the other." Scott hoped he wouldn't kill himself trying to get the desecrated instrument up the stairs.

As it turned out, he and Sam had to solicit the help of two Negro men leaving his building after their day's last ice delivery to haul the piano up the ten steps, with Lottie calling out advice from the landing. For every step they climbed, the piano tried to lurch back two, as if a lead weight were rolling inside the cabinet. The piano made Scott think of a wild horse defying its trainers. But the more difficult the effort to move the piano, the more determined Scott felt to have it. Excited, even. How could he have nearly walked away from such a godsend?

Upstairs, the piano made their parlor look tiny. There was no clear spot big enough for it with the way their furniture was arranged—a six-octave boudoir piano might have fit, but this one was too large—so the piano sat squarely in the center of the room, with Lottie walking around it to offer Sam and the two deliverymen cool glasses of water and fresh-baked dinner rolls for their help. Scott could only sit in a straight-backed chair to catch his breath after the ordeal, perspiration streaming off his cheeks, forehead and chin. His arms and legs trembled slightly;

not enough for anyone else to notice, but enough to alarm him. He was too young to be so taxed. This exhaustion was his illness at work, not his age. He didn't need a doctor to know that.

The deliverymen left with grateful thanks for the rolls, and Sam put on his hat and jacket as soon as he'd drained his glass. "I need to get in my hour of practice on my saxophone before my show," Sam said. "It's got a hell of a sweet sound, but I'm a cornet man, so my mouth don't know what to do with a reed yet. The sax is where we're going, though."

"You'll get it. You can play any instrument you touch, Sam," Lottie told him.

"Knock on wood. Congrats on your new piano, Scotty."

Scotty was too tired to respond verbally, so he only waved good-bye.

Once they were alone, Lottie leaned over Scott and kissed the top of his head, the spot above his temple where his forehead encroached upon his scalp. Scott smiled up at her, although he was almost too tired to smile. "What's Lottie Joplin's secret to getting blood off piano keys?"

Lottie winked at him. "Two parts salt, one part lemon juice—and don't ask how I know. But come on to dinner first. Don't you want to eat?"

Scott shook his head, taking a deep breath as he stood up. His joints had calmed, thank goodness, and he didn't know how long his second wind would last. "Let me get her cleaned up. I can't stand to see a piano so ruined. It would keep me awake to leave it overnight."

"Aw, that piano's not ruined. Sometimes things just *look* ruined, 'til somebody comes along to fix 'em up. You'll see," Lottie said, and left him with his new acquisition.

After lighting candles in the piano's candelabra to give him the best light, Scott took the rags Lottie had brought him and pulled up his chair to begin. A closer look at the stained keys turned his stomach, and he doubted if he'd have an appetite later. Some droplets were already so dried they looked like powder, but the keys from middle C to high C were bloodiest, and Scott wondered if the soupy crimson would ever wash completely away.

Scott used damp rags to mop up whatever blood he could without scrubbing. He rinsed his rags in a bucket while he worked, and the water slowly went from clear to pink to muddy red, murkier with each wringing. The piano might as well be wounded and bleeding, a mirror of his own soul.

"What happened to you, poor girl?" Scott said. He doubted that anyone had been blinded, gutted or had his heart cut out, but whatever had happened over this piano had spilled a lot of blood. As he worked, gummy blood crept beneath Scott's short fingernails, staining them, too. Scott thought about Louis and his razor fights, and every skirmish and scuffle he'd been witness to in dance halls, brothels and on street corners. Would Negroes and whites ever be at peace? *Or will Negroes kill each other first and save the lynch mobs the trouble?*

The piano looked better after his preliminary wiping, but the ivory was still stained red across at least ten keys, and he could only guess how much blood was still trapped between them. Lottie's salt and lemon juice mixture came next. Scott's steady buffing motion triggered a bath of perspiration, until his shirt clung to his skin. He bit his bottom lip from his effort, but he hardly blinked as he worked, his concentration fixed as dissonant keys sounded again and again beneath his strokes. *The neighbors must be in misery,* he thought.

The job took Scott two hours. He hadn't noticed while he was working, but the sharp, coppery scent of blood filled the entire parlor and coated his skin and clothes. He'd splattered runny blood across his shirt, which he figured was ruined—unless Lottie knew a secret to removing blood from clothes. She probably did. Scott didn't discard any clothes lightly anymore. He had a spiffy white suit he wore when he wanted to high-prime in crowds of diamonds and furs—Negroes never ceased to amaze him in their crusade to dress like they had more than they did—but that suit felt more like a costume. Most of his clothes were modest and worn.

Scott heard Lottie humming passages from "A Real Slow Drag" in *Treemonisha* as she walked toward the parlor, and his heart felt stung. He hadn't dwelled on his setback while he worked on cleaning the piano.

Quickly, Scott got up to open the parlor windows so the room could air out. Lottie shouldn't have to tolerate the smell of a stranger's blood in her home. But Lottie didn't complain.

"Well, my, my, my," Lottie said. She had changed into her flannel gown, her slippers flapping on the wooden floor. "This could be another line of income for you, Scotty boy. You're a mess in that blood, but your piano's pretty as a new bride."

Lottie was right. The piano that had seemed so ominous to him in the alley looked nothing less than splendid now, with its engraved wreath across the cabinet's breast and the ornamentation carved up and down both legs. It wasn't his Steinway, but it would do until he could afford it. The freshly scrubbed ivory keys shone like precious stones in the lamplight.

"What are you waiting on?" Lottie said. "Let me hear how it sounds."

Scott rested his foot on the sustaining pedal, testing its spring. The pedal was responsive, like new. "What should I play?"

"That one you just wrote. It sure gets my foot to tapping."

Despite its ordeal, impossibly, the piano was reasonably tuned. But Scott expected that, because there was nothing ordinary about this Rosenkranz.

Scott played the delicate introduction of the piece he'd been working on, one Lottie said he should call simply "Scott Joplin's New Rag." It was a fitting name, since he'd been so busy with *Treemonisha* that he hadn't written many others. He didn't know where he would sell it, except that it wouldn't go to John Stark. John wasn't offering royalties for new pieces, and Scott's patience with him was done anyway. Just because Stark had published "Maple Leaf Rag" a lifetime ago didn't mean Scott owed him his life that remained.

But Scott had barely begun his piece's merrily circus-styled A section when a sharp cramp shot from his knuckles to his elbow, nearly taking his breath. The pain startled Scott so much, he stopped playing. The room went silent.

You gonna lose them fingers, too. Time comes, you won't be able to hold yo' own dick to take a piss. The memory of the conjurer's words raked Scott's spine.

"What is it, baby?" Lottie said, her hands on his shoulders. Her skin smelled like rosewater, a welcome departure from the smell of blood, but then the irony struck him: Lottie smelled like Rose, the octoroon from St. Louis whose company he and Louis had shared.

"I don't feel much like playing," Scott said, realizing how rarely he'd uttered those words. Any other time, he could play even when he could do nothing else.

"You don't have to. Play it tomorrow."

"The show's off in Atlantic City." He hated to tell Lottie more than the cast, even.

"I know, baby. Sam told me. It'll all be fine. Come on to bed, Scotty."

Scott blinked, thinking of Freddie's slim, youthful nakedness with a pang. He almost never thought about Freddie when he was with Lottie, something he was proud of. He wanted to do right by Lottie. She knew he'd been married twice before, but the first night she invited him to dinner at her apartment, she'd told him plainly that she didn't want to know about the women in his past, and he wasn't to ask about the men in hers. That agreement between them might be the cornerstone of their tranquility. He only wished he were still man enough to please her the way she deserved. Like Freddie, Lottie was not the kind of woman who would consider relations with her husband a duty. When he was able, Lottie cherished relations with him.

"You go on. I think I'll stay up for a while," Scott said.

As always, Lottie's kiss to his lips was soft and loving. Lottie's kisses sustained him. She had given him his life again when he'd wondered if he had any left. Scott knew he would cherish her the rest of his days. "I sho' 'nuff loves ya, Scott," Lottie said, imitating Bert Williams's vaudevillian minstrel style.

"I sho' 'nuff loves ya back, Lottie."

With Lottie gone, Scott sat rubbing his cramped knuckle. All that labor, and he'd barely been able to play a note. "You owe me better than that," Scott said to the piano. Louis had addressed his pianos frequently, but Scott had never taken up the habit, until now. "You can see what I did for you. You're mine now, so what will you do for me?"

It was an inspiring idea, like the tale from *Arabian Nights*. What *would* he ask for, if Aladdin's fabled Jinni appeared to grant a wish? Scott knew the answer in a heartbeat.

"Immortality." He spoke the word aloud, a confession to no one but himself.

That was the truth of it. He wanted to spread the gospel of education in *Treemonisha,* but didn't he also want to be recognized? Didn't he want to prove that Negroes were artists, not just showmen? Didn't he crave assurance that the music God gave him would not be ignored? Sam was fooling himself if he didn't think all artists wanted to be remembered.

Maybe Sam was too young to think of such things, unchained by thoughts of death. What a blissful luxury! Scott could think of hardly anything *except* death. When Freddie died, Scott's hopes for progeny had died with her—and with no children to bequeath his memory to, only his music would remain. Lottie kept every scrap of paper he sketched a tune on, but that was not enough. Just as Jim Europe and Will Marion Cook were ignoring him, so might the world, and forever. How could Sam claim that Music itself didn't starve without an audience to hear it? Scott had sacrificed poor Freddie on the altar of his music, dragging her with him from town to town to scrape a few pennies together—and for what?

He might never have immortality without *Treemonisha*. With the flood of awful music and bawdy lyrics to poison the name of ragtime, Scott felt more certain every day that the public would not take wider notice of his rags. No one except Lottie, perhaps, and a handful of artists like James Scott and white composer Joseph Lamb, who had both sought him out—men who understood that lasting art was born of fine composition and thoughtful execution. Ragtime was treated like a greater scourge each year, and he'd been called its king.

And what would you render for immortality, Scott?

The question came to his head as if it had flown in through the open window, whispered in a voice that was not his, that was not the voice of anyone he knew—a voice, in fact, that wasn't from anyone or anything in particular as much as it was a rustle nearly shrouded in the silence.

"Anything," Scott whispered, a tear rolling from his chin to further wash the keys he had scrubbed lovingly with his failing hand. "I would render everything."

That night, for the first time in years, Scott dreamed about Freddie.

*H*aving a piano in the apartment renewed Scott's spirit.

The next morning, he set out right away to plan a performance of *Treemonisha* on his own, without backers. He found his luck at last when he turned a corner and ran into a friend from Harlem who offered to try and convince a theater owner to rent Scott his stage on West 135th Street at a lower price on Sunday afternoon, when the doors were usually closed. By the next day, Scott had his answer: *The stage is yours.*

But the offer was for Sunday and that Sunday only, which meant Scott had only two days to prepare. He would have no time to post notices or place an ad in *New York Age,* even if he could have afforded the expense. He and Sam wouldn't have time to finish the orchestrations, much less cobble together an orchestra. Two days meant no sets and no costumes, since the cast would have enough work bringing their voices up to the opera's demands.

Still, it was something, and they all knew it.

The cast members were excited, letting out such a cheer at his announcement that they might have thought they were singing in full costume at the Metropolitan Opera instead of in their own clothes at the Lincoln Theatre near Lenox Avenue in Harlem. They improvised dance steps in their basement rehearsals, but agreed to save their most ambitious dances for the scottische, dude walk and slow drag at the finale.

During those two days, the air was crisper and Scott felt a snap to his step. He had his stage, and that was enough. Sally would be his Treemonisha, and he would invite as many influential people as he could to the two-hundred-seat theater, so his opera could fly free into the world. Freddie *would* live again. He would see to it.

But Sunday arrived with all the promise of storm clouds. First, the performance was delayed a half hour because the employee who was supposed to come with the keys to the theater was nowhere to be found. He finally ambled up to their waiting huddle with a flask of whiskey, claiming he'd just come back from services at Abyssinian Baptist Church.

The electricity wasn't working properly, flowing to a few lamps but no footlights, so the theater was nearly dark except for whatever light could force its way past the screened windows. The theater's piano was also alarmingly out of tune, something Scott had forgotten to check beforehand. He would *never* have made such an oversight if he'd been at his best! After his warm-up scales, the cast assured him that the piano sounded fine, but they were lying to themselves. Still, the piano hardly mattered, in the end.

"Ladies and gentlemen—*Treemonisha*," Scott said with all the heart he could command.

At the piano, Scott's hands ached during the overture and never stopped. Sally sang like a warrior, but just when Scott was telling himself it might turn out fine after all, confusion reigned at the beginning of the second act, when an epidemic of forgetfulness ran through the cast. Without costumes, the "Frolic of the Bears" was nonsensical, even embarrassing. The finale was the saving grace: The dance numbers looked as well as they might have in Atlantic City, with everyone remembering their steps and lyrics, but by then Scott was nearly in tears because his unsteady hands were in mutiny and he missed note after note.

Scott was relieved when a lukewarm dribbling of applause signaled that he had survived the ordeal. The cast was happy with itself, each of them silently noting their personal triumphs as they took their bows, but there were more than twice the number of people crowding the stage than there were sitting in the audience. Only seventeen people had witnessed the opera's performance, and Scott was glad there hadn't been more.

It's only a start, he told himself, but he didn't believe it. That doubt made him a prophet.

It was the only production of *Treemonisha* Scott Joplin would live to see.

CHAPTER TWENTY-ONE

*B*e quiet Be quiet Be quiet

One hour to rest—only sixty minutes—and someone was playing piano music so loudly through her hotel room wall that Phoenix couldn't sleep. *For FUCK'S sake, SHUT UP.*

The day had been torture from the time she'd opened her eyes. She wished she had listened to Carlos's warning not to stay up writing two nights straight, or that she *could* have listened. Last night, after a day of interviews and rehearsals, Phoenix had dropped into bed nearly unconscious by ten, and she'd still felt like a rag doll all day, her eyes only painted open.

And the Osiris show was today.

At the theater early with Serena, Arturo and the others for a three-hour rehearsal they were lucky to get, Phoenix had liberated herself by wearing her Moog Liberation shoulder synth. She'd brought it with her to New York, for once, so Arturo had to help her modify her dance steps so she could keep up with the choreography of "Party Patrol." No small feat wearing a fourteen-pound synth, but she had done it, and behind Arturo's lead, they finally looked like a unit. And since she'd complained about the canned sound of the background vocal tracks on "Love the One You're With," yesterday, Sarge had rounded up a dozen kids from a teen choir in Harlem willing to sing for a small contribution to their church. The extra singers were a logistical nightmare (and the groggy sound man had glared at Phoenix for the last-hour change), but the kids sounded great, especially with Serena belting the more aggressive power notes. Manny had nearly wet himself when he heard their last take at sound check. *Damn, Phoenix, what do you think this is, the Grammys?* Her crew was ready.

But Phoenix wasn't. She'd sung in a whisper at most of the rehearsal, trying to save her voice, and she hoped that would be enough to get her through the show. *One hour.* That was all the time she had for a nap. In one hour, she had to get up so Serena could fix her hair and makeup. The concert started at seven, and she was the opener, so Sarge said she had to arrive at the Osiris no later than six. *One hour.*

Majestic, self-important piano music thumped through her wall, relentless. Who the fuck was playing a piano on this floor? The music was so loud, it sounded like it was in her ear.

BE QUIET

"Babe, can you please call the front desk and complain about this effing noise?" Phoenix mumbled to Carlos, who had curled beside her to guard her from interruptions.

Carlos didn't answer, and his silence set off a domino effect of enlightenment in Phoenix's mind. *Shit.* Why would there be a piano on this floor? There wasn't, of course. She must be dreaming the music, then. Phoenix refused to open her eyes, trying to wish the dream away.

I can't do this now, Scott. Please let me rest. Come back tomorrow, after the show.

This piano music sounded like *Treemonisha*—she'd listened to the opera's CD enough to recognize it—but some of the passages sounded different, veering out of place. Van Milton had told her Scott was revising his opera at the end of this life, but those pages had been lost with so many others. Phoenix felt herself sob inside. She had never been this tired, not ever. She couldn't let Scott rob her of her last nap before her show. Too many people were counting on her, including twelve kids from Harlem.

I can't fix everything, Scott. It's not my fault it's gone. Please let me rest, just once.

The music grew louder, willful. A growling run in the lowest octave shook her teeth.

When Phoenix gave up and opened her eyes, she saw that she wasn't in her king-sized bed in a midtown–New York hotel room. No panoramic view of the city waited for her now. Carlos, the bed and her room were gone. Yes, this was a dream, like the others.

Except that she also wasn't in Solomon Dixon's boardinghouse lying in Freddie Alexander's deathbed. Instead, she was outside in a field, curled on the ground, penned in by green stalks. Sitting up, Phoenix realized she was surrounded by ripening plants in an endless cornfield. The sky was dark except for a stifled glow, pinks and grays. Sunrise or dusk.

Phoenix was relieved she had learned how to tell the difference between her waking and dreaming lives. Her dreams had very few *smells,* for one thing. When she grabbed a clump of damp, moist soil and raised it to her nose, she didn't smell a thing. Images shifted very quickly in her dreams, too. She saw a scarecrow not too far from her, and she was almost sure it hadn't been there when she first opened her eyes. The scarecrow was erected on a pole, its straw arms outstretched, Christlike, while six black crows sat across its arms in a row, one atop the scarecrow's dangling head. The way the figure hung, listing to one side, it looked more like a man than clothes stuffed with straw. Phoenix was afraid it would move, but it didn't. She looked away from it quickly.

The music played on, sounding very close to her, hidden beyond the stalks of corn. *Scott is here,* she remembered. Scott hadn't invited himself into her sleep in a long time, and now that he was here, she was excited to see him.

What was I so worried about? What could be more important than seeing Scott?

Following the stirring strains from "A Real Slow Drag," Phoenix walked until the forest of corn thinned, and she saw a clearing ahead where ten or twelve men and women sat over straw baskets, shucking the corn with disciplined snatches. They worked diligently, and Phoenix thought their arms might be moving in synchronization to the music.

A horn pealed from somewhere. The sound reminded Phoenix of the *shofar* the rabbi blew at her mother's temple on Yom Kippur, one of two High Holy Days her mother observed. The corn-shuckers stopped working when they heard the horn, standing up to stretch their legs and backs, groaning and arching toward the sky. One by one, they took their baskets and disappeared into the cornstalks. The clearing was now empty except for a man in a white shirt playing a piano, his back facing her. Somehow, she hadn't seen him before. His arms stretched from one end of the keyboard to the other as he played in a frenzy.

Phoenix's heart swelled, and light brightened the sky. "Scott?" she said.

Scott stopped playing and turned around. His face, usually so somber, gave way to a joyous grin that seemed more heartbreaking, somehow. *"Freddie?"* he said. He looked like he couldn't believe he was seeing her, as if he were the one waking inside a dream.

The instant she thought about moving closer, she was standing beside him, moving in a way only dreams allowed. She dropped her hand to his shoulder, gently kneading his muscles. Touching him broke her heart. "I've missed you," she said.

"No, dear heart, *I've* missed *you*," he said, his eyes brimming. "Where have you been?"

"Where I've always been," she said.

He stood up to face her, bringing his chest against hers, and she noticed for the first time that they were almost the exact height, although her hair made her taller. Her hair was wrapped in a tall mound atop her head, the way she'd worn it when she went to Liberty Park Hall to hear him—the way she'd worn her hair in the photograph Scott used on the cover sheet of "Bethena," the song he wrote for her. *Was that really me in Sedalia? Was it me in Scott's arms all along?*

Scott suddenly clamped his palms to her cheeks, holding her so tightly that she felt her face pucker. Her cheeks vibrated, as if they could absorb his flesh into hers. "Don't leave me again, Freddie," Scott whispered. "You promised."

"I . . ." *Had* she promised him? "I . . . didn't want to leave."

"Then *why?*" Scott said. "I looked away a minute, and you were gone."

She didn't know why she had left him, or how anyone could. She couldn't speak.

Scott smiled again. "I wrote another opera. The girl in it, Treemonisha, has your soul."

"I know. I heard you playing." But confusion came again. *How* had she heard him playing here when she had been somewhere else, somewhere far away?

Suddenly, she knew: the piano. Phoenix didn't want to look at the piano again—this was a piano that could be provoked, and curious things happened to her when she gazed on it, she remembered—but she felt as compelled by the piano as she did by Scott's touch.

The piano sat waiting for her, patient. It had looked new when she first saw Scott playing it in this clearing, but now it had aged by centuries, a scarred relic. It wore a dusty lizard's skin, like before. This was the piano she knew and did not know, the one she had once touched. She couldn't read the manufacturer's proud label, because it had long ago faded away. The keys were stained dark brown, not white. The rest were covered in blood.

Startled, Phoenix pulled Scott's hands from her face to look at them. His palms, too, were caked in blood. Watery blood spattered his white shirt. She pulled his palm to her nose and sniffed it, and the barbed scent tore its way into her nostrils, as real as her own. She raised her fingers to her cheeks, where Scott had touched her, and her fingertips slid against the sticky dampness of it. Blood was everywhere.

"I'm sorry, Freddie," Scott said more loudly, his voice urgent. "I didn't know."

Why does he keep calling me that? What's my name? She combed her memory, seeking herself, and could find only a void.

A monstrous racket made her look at the piano again, and the wood of its cabinet splintered along its scars, shards cracking, breaking apart. As she watched, the piano crumbled to dust; a silent mound, unrecognizable. The stoic low echo its last low C-sharp rumbled, resounding against Phoenix's bones until they shook.

"What have you done?" she said to Scott.

"Stay with me," he said, and leaned closer, his lips entreating hers. "Sing for me."

Her lips quivered, fervid for his lifeless touch.

*P*hoenix? Are you listening to me? *You don't have to do this concert.*"

Carlos could be at the other end of the Holland Tunnel, he sounded so far from her, but Phoenix felt steady pressure as he squeezed her hand.

She had to answer him, she remembered. Her long silence had wrought panic in his voice.

"Yes. I do," she said. It was mumbling, but she was almost sure she'd said it aloud.

"She's not hearing me," Carlos's apparition said again. Phoenix tried to see Carlos, but couldn't quite make him out; everything was jellied and unfocused, shades of light and dark.

"Yes, I hear you, Carlos. I *have* to." She was still mumbling, but louder this time.

Carlos cursed and muttered in Spanish, something he'd never done while talking to her. She must be remembering herself, she thought, because it pissed her off not to understand what Carlos was saying about her, even if she could comprehend his panic just fine. She didn't blame him. If her head were more clear, she would be panicked, too.

"Maybe she's all right now," Serena said.

"Bullshit. She fainted. She never faints." That was Gloria, who would know.

"Maybe she's just nervous. Shit, ya'll, I know *I* am."

"She just gets diarrhea when she's nervous," Gloria said. "Something's wrong with her."

Please stop talking about me like I'm not here, Phoenix thought, but since she couldn't speak aloud without tiring herself, what if she *wasn't* here? That thought triggered her mantra: *I have a show at the Osiris. I'm going to sing "Party Patrol" and "Love the One You're With." I am not Freddie Alexander. I am Phoenix Smalls, and I am still alive. I am not dead.*

Her memory rebelled even as she spoke the words, making her forget their meaning. She might be awake, but she hadn't escaped Scott. He had his own plans for her today.

Sing for me.

Phoenix's nostrils and throat clogged with a harsh, piercing scent, and her head popped back hard against her headrest as she cried out. Was Scott stealing her away?

"Calm down, cuz. It's just smelling salts," Gloria said.

When Phoenix opened her eyes, she saw her cousin's tanned, manicured hand in front of her face, holding a small vial. The late-afternoon light was bright, almost blinding, but suddenly she could see clearly, without the viscous, ethereal film. She was in the backseat of a Town Car with gray seats and tinted windows. She was in the middle, Carlos sat to her left, Gloria to her right. Serena was up front with the uniformed driver, her arm propped on the seat as she stared back at them. Phoenix saw a street sign marking Seventh Avenue. When she blinked, she saw the stately row of refurbished Victorian town houses on Strivers Row. What year was this?

"Convince me you're all right, or I'm calling Sarge at the theater to tell him we're canceling," Gloria said. "I'll take you to a hospital, I swear."

"Eat me," Phoenix said. "How's that?"

Gloria didn't smile. "That's not good enough. Tell me what you've been doing the last hour. Prove to me you're not zoned out."

"The last *two* hours," Carlos said. "She fainted in the bathroom once, too."

Much to Phoenix's relief—and a little surprise—it was suddenly there, all of it, so she recited it for them: Carlos had thrown a cup of water in her face to wake her from her nap, explaining that she'd been talking in her sleep and wouldn't open her eyes. She had taken a shower and fainted on the bathroom floor, which explained the throbbing knot on the side of her head. Then, while Serena was fixing her hair, she'd fainted again on the living room's sofa. Both times, she'd come back to consciousness on her own. Now, they were on their way to the seven o'clock show at the Osiris Theater on Lenox Avenue and 138th Street. She threw in the address to impress them. "I haven't fainted in an hour," she finished. "I'm fine now. For real."

Three faces gazed at her in intent silence. Phoenix glanced at the rearview mirror, and the driver was watching her, too, his eyes smug with whatever he thought he knew. "Why don't you watch where the fuck you're going?" Phoenix said to the driver, and his eyes went back to the road. Phoenix never snapped at strangers, but she enjoyed it more than she wanted to. It had felt good to say what she was thinking. *No wonder there are so many assholes.*

Gloria sighed, Carlos next. In the front seat, Serena looked uncertain, twirling her index finger in the curly, rust-colored weave she'd picked for herself. Phoenix wasn't sure the hair's shade worked for her sister's skin tone, but Serena looked beautiful. Yesterday, Serena had bought a black formfitting dress on sale at Le Chateau that was forgiving in all the right places.

"Carlos?" Gloria said, looking at him for his opinion.

Carlos shook his head. "I'm not happy."

"Well, too damn bad—it's not your decision. I have a show to do, and I'm doing it."

That brought silence. Carlos dropped his head against the seat, lips pursed, and Phoenix was glad he was quiet. If he said anything else, her next words would be dangerous. She suddenly resented Carlos's presence. He wasn't the one who should be with her. He wasn't . . .

He wasn't *who*? Phoenix didn't bring the name to consciousness, but she didn't have to. Suddenly, the ache of missing Scott was the only thing about the day that didn't feel dreamlike.

My God, I'm really losing my fucking mind. Phoenix closed her eyes. *I have a show at the Osiris. I'm going to sing "Party Patrol" and "Love the One You're With." I am not Freddie Alexander. I am Phoenix Smalls, and I am still alive. I am not dead.*

Carlos's spicy cologne intensified as he brought his mouth against her ear, and the scent moored her to the car again. Carlos hadn't had time to shave, and his day's stubble brushed her earlobe, reminding her only of how much she preferred the smoothness of Scott's face. "This stops now, Phee," Carlos said, only loud enough for her. "I'm scared for you. I called Heather, and she's asking her psychic friend in Seattle what we should do. It's gone too far. *Punto.*"

Punto. Who did he think he was talking to, telling her what to do? Phoenix felt resentment stir again, but she had no choice but to nod. She gripped Carlos's hand hard, and she didn't stop clinging until the Town Car lurched to a stop.

OSIRIS THEATER. The sky wasn't yet dark, but the theater's ageless neon sign was lit up in a magical white-gold that had glittered on Lenox Avenue for decades. Phoenix stared up at the marquee, mesmerized. The large red block letters posted against the lighted marquee were reserved for the biggest names, of course: Tyrese, Imani, Kamikaze and Bing Boyz. AND OTHER SPECIAL GUESTS, the sign promised. But in smaller letters that were still large enough to read for blocks, a new name blared out: PHOENIX.

Someone had added her name as an afterthought, and Phoenix smiled, grateful. *Yes, I am Phoenix Smalls, and I am alive. I am not dead.*

Phoenix noticed four security guards in the doorway of the grand white brick and limestone building, busily waving black wands up and down the arms, legs, backs and chests of every prospective attendee, searching for hidden weapons. They might have to spend all night out here, Phoenix thought. The line already stretched down the street as far as she could see.

It's showtime, folks, Phoenix thought.

She wouldn't let Scott take her time away from her.

What's this I hear about you fainting twice today?" Sarge said, handing her a water bottle.

Phoenix could barely hear her father over the backstage bedlam, which felt like the fabled Grammy party Gloria had been fantasizing about since they were in high school. The rap music playing for the audience was loud back here, too, so muffled that the beats and vocals crashed into each other, incoherent against the sound of backstage laughter, conversation and inevitable arguing. Phoenix had never met most of the artists she shared the program with, so she was startled to see Tyrese stroll past her in a matching oversized denim jacket and jeans, trailed by a bodyguard. Tyrese's casual dark chocolate majesty stalled her brain. How could this man look even *better* in person?

"I'm *talking* to you, Phoenix," Sarge said. "Did you faint today?"

Phoenix took the bottle and swigged the frigid water. "Who told you that?" She had sworn Serena and Gloria to secrecy.

"Your friend," Sarge said, and swung his head toward Carlos, who lingered a few feet away, behind a stack of huge amplifiers. Carlos's red backstage pass dangled from his neck, and in that instant, Phoenix wanted to revoke it.

"I'm fine."

"Hold up. Let me look," Sarge said, stooping. He studied her eyes the way an astronomer might look at an anomaly through his telescope, careful and lingering. Still, the worry lines in his forehead were softer than she remembered. The days off had been good for Sarge, she thought. Hopefully, his time with Mom in New York had been good, too.

"I'm *fine,* Sarge. I'm ready to do this."

"Don't do this to prove anything to me, Phoenix," Sarge said. "I was wrong about the drugs, and that's all I care about. I'm not pushing you, hear? If you're sick, say so."

"I'm not sick."

That was another lie, one of too many she'd told her father. She *was* sick, or something worse than sick. Sarge's concerned gaze made Phoenix long to cling to him. The longer she was alert, the more she felt convinced she needed protection—not Ronn's kind of protection, with his armored car and army of guards, but *something* to stand between her and her own impulse to consort with the domain of the dead. Something inside of *her* kept dragging her back to Scott, even as she fought to stay away.

Seventeen hundred people could hear me sing Treemonisha *tonight. I have a platform.*

That thought pounded through her with every flush of blood from her heart, which was beating faster all the time. Where was the thought coming from? She'd believed she was obeying her own thoughts at *Live at Night,* but she knew better now. Had she really lost her own will? How had she let it come to that?

Sarge hesitated, his lips parting. "I know you're . . . bearing a burden, Phoenix." Despite the bravery he'd shown in the hotel room, Sarge didn't bring up Scott's name.

"I can handle two songs. I'm singing 'Party Patrol' and 'Love the One You're With,' and I'm doing it because that's what *I* want to do," Phoenix said, speaking more to herself than to Sarge. "After that, I'll take a break, see a doctor, whatever you want. I promise."

Sarge's face yielded, venturing a smile. He was convinced. "That's my girl," he said, and kissed her forehead. "This stage has history. Billie Holiday, Jackie Wilson and James Brown have all been on this stage. Come with me to your dressing room. Someone wants to see you."

Phoenix waved good-bye to Carlos before she followed Sarge, and he blew a kiss in return, still watching her as if he expected her to break. One day, she vowed, she would find a way to make all the pieces of her world fit together, and she wouldn't have to leave Carlos behind.

As she and Sarge walked in the narrow white hallway, Phoenix saw her crew gathered like a tribe, and they reached out to hug her one by one; Arturo and the other two dancers, Rochelle and Monique, and her backup singers, Monisha and Danielle. She could smell their anxiety and excitement in their perspiration. Arturo's hug was so enthusiastic that he lifted her from her feet with iron arms and swung her from side to side. "This is it, *chica*," Arturo said. "The Osiris tonight, then the video next week. Let's do this one for Jay."

"For Jay," she said, and pecked his lips, her throat stinging.

When Sarge opened her dressing room door, the strobe effect from flashing cameras dizzied Phoenix. The teenagers in bright purple choir robes were taking a flurry of pictures with their disposable cameras, but the cameras weren't pointed toward her. Their frenzy stemmed from the center of their circle, so Phoenix guessed maybe Tyrese or one of the rappers from Kamikaze had stopped in to say hello to her kids. The room was crowded to capacity, between the kids, Serena, Gloria, Kai and another bodyguard Phoenix remembered from TSR. She looked for her mother, until she remembered Mom and Aunt Livvy wanted to get their seats early and watch the show from the audience, not from backstage.

"I said *one* picture each. None of ya'll can't count to one?" Kai said, clapping his hands. "You need to hustle your little asses on out of here. Don't make me mad. Go on, now."

The six boys and six girls obediently put their cameras away and began to scurry out of the room in a blur of shiny, newly pressed hair and cologne borrowed from their fathers' bureaus, murmuring *Hi, Phoenix* as they passed. She gave each of them a hug, too, wishing them luck.

As they cleared away, Phoenix recognized her visitor's Hugo Boss black slacks and matching nylon shirt, the portrait of subdued celebrity. Ronn Jenkins leaned against her far wall, signing a last autograph for a starstruck young fan. No one had told her Ronn would be here. No wonder her kids were losing their minds.

Phoenix felt a twinge from somewhere in her that wasn't yet at rest. "I heard you were staying in L.A." What she'd actually heard—what everybody knew—was that DJ Train had a price on Ronn's head in New York. Why was he taking chances?

"Couldn't miss my girl's big night," Ronn said. He smiled and pulled her against his solid frame, a hug nearly as tight as Arturo's. Phoenix knew Ronn was probably in New York for reasons that had nothing to do with her, but the words sounded nice.

As always, guilt doused her. "Ronn, about *Live at Night*—"

He shook his head, raising a finger to cut her off. "Manny says your set is off the *chain*."

"We're trying."

"Then it's all good. Go out there and do your thing."

"Why do you put up with me?" she said, resting her cheek against his shoulder. She heard Serena hiss, terrified that she was mussing her makeup.

A wink was Ronn's only answer, but she knew why he tolerated her: She was making him money. *Punto*. "Come hook up with me at the after-party at Anju, a'ight?"

Carlos wouldn't like her hooking up with Ronn anywhere tonight, but business was business. "Are you sure it's a good idea to be hanging out in the clubs?" she said quietly, trying to reach the rattled man she'd seen the day someone tried to kill him.

Ronn laughed at that, and his laugh would have sounded sincere if she were a stranger. Ronn ignored that question, too. "OK, I gotta move on, baby girl." He gave her a handshake, not a kiss like he had in his car. He knew about Carlos, she realized. Kai might have told him.

Ronn exchanged pleasantries with Serena and Gloria, kissing their cheeks. Next, he gave Sarge a warm embrace, and Phoenix watched the two men, transfixed. Her face lost all sensation as bleak intuition settled across her skin. Ronn would not make it to an after-party at Anju. Something would go wrong before.

"Ronn . . ." she began. But no one heard her in the clamor as the door opened.

Kai glanced outside of the dressing room, scoping the hallway, then he walked ahead of his boss, and the second bodyguard walked behind him. Then, Ronn was gone.

"Phee, sit your behind down. *Look* what you did to your face," Serena said.

Her sister's voice cut through her fears, setting Phoenix free.

• • •

New York, New York—*ARE YOU READY TO GET BUSY?"*

The MC's voice screamed over the theater speakers, buttressed with frenetic bursts and scratches from his turntable. The hyped-up crowd met his challenge in a wave of booming cheers. The audience was almost loud enough to silence the presence nesting in Phoenix's mind, the voice that was more restless with her every breath.

Sing for me. Scott's voice.

Phoenix stood posed with her crew for "Party Patrol" on the dark stage. Phoenix silently drummed the keys of her Liberation, which was strapped across her shoulder, ready. She was so happy to be holding her keyboard, her fingertips were pulsing. She should have known how much she had missed playing music on the stage. Who had she been trying to fool?

Sing, Freddie. Sing for me.

Phoenix's heart thundered as dizziness swayed the stage. She heard piano refrains, the Overture from *Treemonisha,* as if the opera blared from the theater's speakers. The sound of the music was a homecoming. Phoenix's heart ached when she felt Scott's cool breath dance across the back of her neck, his familiar caress.

Sing "The Bag of Luck," "The Corn Huskers" and "We're Goin' Around." There are seventeen hundred sets of ears to hear your tribute the way it was intended. Sing "Aunt Dinah Has Blowed the Horn" and "When Villains Ramble Far and Near." March onward for me, Freddie. Sing for me. An unseen hand guided her fingers to the keys of his choosing.

"I . . . can't," Phoenix whispered to the spirit, and wrested her hand away.

Phoenix's eyes desperately sought out a face to keep her rooted. Behind her, she could see only the silhouettes of Serena and the singers, and shadows of dancers splayed on the floor in their poses. Sarge wasn't in sight, and Phoenix couldn't remember if Carlos had decided to watch from backstage or in the audience. Protected in the stage's shadows, Phoenix scanned the seats to look for Carlos, hoping his face might keep Scott away.

Instead, she saw her mother. Mom, Gloria, Aunt Livvy and Uncle Dave were in the second row, not quite center, made conspicuous by their pale skin and formal dress, as if they were at a theater on Broadway. Malcolm sat beside them, grinning as he talked to a man who looked like industry, someone here to work instead of having a good time.

Phoenix waved out to her family, before she remembered she was invisible in the dark folds. Still, seeing them helped. Her family was here watching her. She had something to fight for. The next voice that filled her mind was hers alone. *I'm going to sing* "Party Patrol" *and* "Love the One You're With." *I am NOT Freddie Alexander. I am . . .*

I am . . .

The theater speakers gusted with a symphony of Egyptian strings. Just when she needed it most, Phoenix heard the MC shout her name.

*C*ome on, Phee. You can do it. You can do it, linda.

Carlos Harris felt sick to his stomach as he clung to the tattered black curtain backstage. He had an unobstructed view of Phoenix now that the stage lights were up, and he could see she wasn't well. By now, maybe everyone could see it.

In the carnival of colored lights sweeping the stage, Serena and the singers were swaying, and the dancers were on their feet, nearly synchronized in their vaults and landings. Phoenix, center stage, was the only one who wasn't in motion. Phoenix was a statue with a keytar across her shoulder, the instrument's neck pointed upward, still and mute, like a medieval sword.

Carlos tugged at his hair, distraught. He was to blame. He should have broken off Phoenix's union with the entity the first time he saw her at her keyboard in her apartment, playing Scott Joplin in her sleep. Where was his judgment? If he hadn't been so blinded by his vain desire to attach himself to something extraordinary, he would have known she was at risk.

Phoenix's father stood watching the stage near him, a pensive bear. Perhaps this man had been right about him all along, Carlos thought. Perhaps his blindness made him a monster.

"She shouldn't be on that stage," Carlos said.

Marcus Smalls looked back at him, startled. Carlos was amazed the man had heard him over the deafening music tracks, but a father's ears were sharp. For only the second time since Carlos had met this man, Marcus Smalls wore a neutral expression, devoid of loathing. His eyes were clear the way they'd been when warned about Phoenix's fainting spell. Phoenix's father opened his mouth to answer, but didn't have time before a voice drew them back to the stage.

"Me and my crew's gonna roll . . . we're on a Party Patrol . . ."

Phoenix was singing, her voice clear and strong. She snapped her body in line with her dancers, mirroring their cross-kicks. Still dancing, she made a swooping motion with her keytar like a marcher in a black college band, eliciting calls from the audience, and her sure-handed notes on her synthesizer blended with the prerecorded bass line from "Skin Tight." The biggest show of Phoenix's career was under way, and she was here to witness it this time.

Perhaps he *hadn't* destroyed this girl.

Carlos never would have believed he would be so happy to hear "Party Patrol," which had made him wince when the demo landed on his desk. *Phoenix, what have you done to yourself?* he'd muttered, shaking his head. It wasn't as bad as MC Hammer trying to thug himself out for his foray into gangsta rap, but the sound hadn't fit her. "Party Patrol" was a bland summertime paean, the kind of song that would be blaring from teenagers' open windows and boom boxes until school took them hostage again in the fall.

Carlos had known it would be a hit right away, and that made him hate it all the more. The sampling and lack of imagination in its bright, overproduced tracks hurt his ears. Where was *Phoenix*? Some of Phoenix's keyboard solos on her two other CDs had been lustrous, reminiscent of *Purple Rain*–era Prince. He'd recognized Phoenix's violin and her homage to Hossam Ramzy in the "Party Patrol" intro, a spark of hope, but then Phoenix had vanished altogether, a painfully lean voice singing over someone else's music.

In "Party Patrol," Carlos had heard what Phoenix traded away. Maybe that was why he hadn't been more worried about the ghost. If Phoenix's soul was already for sale, he'd figured, why not entrust it to more capable hands—even if they were dead?

"I think I'm losing control . . . out on this Party Patrol . . ."

But Phoenix was evolving on the stage tonight. Carlos felt it.

The woman who had been fainting in her hotel room only three hours ago was not only kicking ass with the choreography, but she was singing and playing with new life. Phoenix's voice charged above the chorus of backup singers with the coarseness in the higher register she'd used effectively on *Trial by Fire,* more rock than R&B, but better than pretending to have a church soloist's voice when she didn't. She was singing like she meant it.

Good girl, Phoenix. Make your voice work for you. Be yourself.

Phoenix's keyboard solo—a fat, funked-up synth voice that barged into the song and rearranged it—was breathtaking. Carlos had laughed at Phoenix's keytar, an instrument most musicians had abandoned in the 1980s and would always remind Carlos of bad music. Not tonight. Phoenix's synthesizer crossed the time barrier with relish. She played one-handed, but her fingers were as true as they were wild. Phoenix set the stage afire.

The crowd cheered, awakening from their stupor. Like almost two thousand others in the theater, Carlos could not take his eyes off of her. His ears were captive to the passion pouring from Phoenix's fingertips. Lauryn Hill. Marc Anthony. OutKast. Beyoncé. Juanes. The Black Eyed Peas. He'd known they were stars the first time he'd seen them perform. He knew what he was witnessing. This wasn't the coronation of a hit song—it was the birth of a star. The woman on the stage was not the one who shared his bed. This creature only appeared under bright lights, her own act of creation.

Carlos felt someone stir near him. G-Ronn had slid up to him, shoulder to shoulder. He was gazing at the stage with his arms folded across his broad chest, his face dispassionate, as if he were studying his portfolio. Carlos couldn't help the instant aversion that came from contrasting himself to a man who was bigger and wealthier. His eyes fell on the massive diamond stud in G-Ronn's ear, and he remembered the diamonds on the ghost that had passed him in the hall. *That earring cost him more than I could afford for an engagement ring.*

"God damn," G-Ronn said, his voice full of awe. "She's good."

"Yes," Carlos said, smiling. "She's here forever."

There were times, although not often, when Marcus Smalls was happy to be wrong.

A man who had made as many mistakes as Marcus learned how to spot them before the real damage was done. Marcus was through with mistakes. His cup had runneth over and flooded his soul. He was vigilant in his search for hidden motives, selfishness and foibles. Like Malcolm X said, *The price of freedom is death.* If he was to be free of blame, his assumptions about himself had to die a little more each day.

So when Leah told him over fried chicken and turnip greens at B. Smith's the other night that she didn't think Phoenix had the heart to be a pop star—that Phoenix had only pursued her high school dream this long to try to win his time and approval—Marcus couldn't be angry or surprised. Leah only confirmed a theory he had been entertaining late at night, when he meditated for a half hour before bed and cataloged his human flaws, the lifesaving technique a Buddhist brother had taught him at Raiford. Meditating last night, he'd decided he agreed with Leah. The longer he thought about it, the more he realized he had known it all along.

Phoenix was doing it for him. And maybe—just maybe—so was he.

It fit the dimensions of the puzzle exactly: Marcus hadn't been in prison when Phoenix was young, but he'd been on the road, which was no different to her. And the minute she said she wanted to be Janet Jackson, he had given her his full attention—because *that* was something he knew how to do. Phoenix had no interest in politics or philosophy—but music? Now, *there* was something they could both relate to. He'd failed Serena and his boys, but he could make his second-chance child larger than life.

Self-reflection was a bitch, Marcus thought. No *wonder* Phoenix had started fighting the minute she got within arm's length of what she'd claimed she wanted.

And then there was the ghost.

Marcus hadn't seen anything like the events in Phoenix's hotel room since he spent the summer at Grandmama's house when he was seven. She and Big Papa had bought a colonial house that had once been a plantation, complete with ramshackle slave quarters in the overgrown yard. The ghosts in that house made Marcus's life a living hell, between the slamming doors and profane messages written in lipstick on Grandmama's mirror, which brought her running to his room with a switch every other night. He never spoke of that time, but he would take

Phoenix to that old house one day and tell her about his adventures. He'd lost a few hours' sleep after Leah told him she never brought that piano to the house, but in retrospect he could accept that, too. Apparently, ghosts were a part of the family. It was time Phoenix knew how far back it went.

But as a man of ideas, Marcus had to look beyond Joplin's ghost itself to what the ghost *meant*. He didn't understand why the piano had chosen her, but there was a reason Phoenix had invited Joplin into her life, even if she didn't know what it was. This ghost was one more obstacle to prevent her stardom.

Some artists needed to be famous, and others were happy to play for regular crowds on weekend gigs. Maybe Phoenix was the latter. Let Phoenix go to school and have a stable life like Leah wanted her to, then. If Phoenix didn't need to be famous, God bless her. She was one of the lucky ones. Maybe she was shelving her old dream the way she'd put away her toys when she was ten.

Would her voice fail her? Would she trip over her feet and blow out a knee? Would she relinquish herself to the ghost and get booed off the stage trying to sing a damn opera?

Marcus didn't know how it would happen, but he had steeled himself to watch the demise of his daughter's pop career. He had already rehearsed his speech for after the show: *Sometimes, Peanut, the hardest thing is knowing when it's time to let go.*

Marcus knew that better than most. He and Leah had been creeping around the edges of surrender for years, neither of them courageous enough to say the words. But all journeys end—and as Earth Wind & Fire would say, that's the way of the world. He and Leah might end up accidentally married forever, but now Marcus had accepted that Phoenix would never be a star.

There was only one hole in his theory: He was dead wrong. As wrong as he'd ever been. "Party Patrol" made him a liar.

Phoenix had turned "Party Patrol" into something he had never heard from her. The choreography, the vocals, the solo—all of it had fallen into place, better than the rehearsals. Marcus watched, stunned, while his daughter cast a spell over the Osiris Theater, communing with all the hall's ghosts of performances past. Most of this audience had never even heard of her, and she had seduced them with a single song.

One more song in the set, and Phoenix could leave the stage a triumph.

The silence between the songs felt too long, and Marcus held his breath backstage, waiting. His heart rarely got excited anymore—not since he'd stopped listening to speeches and believing in the revolution—but it was beating at a gallop for the first time in years.

He wished her next song wasn't "Love the One You're With." The addition of an amateur choir seemed like begging for trouble. And how could she match the freshness of "Party Patrol" with a cover of a Stephen Stills rock classic released before most of this hip-hop audience had been born? What could Phoenix do with "Love the One You're With" that Aretha hadn't already done?

Still, Marcus discovered he was a believer.

Do it, Peanut. Give them something they'll never forget.

Phoenix struck the first chord on her synthesizer, a full-bodied organ voice that filled the room. The recorded tracks joined her, gaining volume on the song's gospel-kissed, two-chord intro. But everyone else on the stage was frozen, stock-still. *Where are those damn kids?*

Suddenly, they were there. The kids filed onto the stage, marching double time, clapping on the beat as they swayed, their robes billowing. The sight of the kids excited the crowd, who erupted as if they'd fallen asleep and woken up on Sunday morning.

Phoenix tugged off her headset. There would be no more dancing for her. Instead, she tilted a microphone on a glistening mike stand to her mouth and sang, her Afro framed against the lights. As soon as Marcus heard the first weathered note from her lips, he realized his daughter *knew* this song. She knew it as well as he did. She knew about disappointment, distraction and impossible love, and her knowledge was stripped naked in her voice. When the choir joined Phoenix to sing about the rose and a fisted glove—exquisitely harmonized, perfectly timed—their music was revelatory.

Between verses, Phoenix motioned to someone on the stage to come forward, something she hadn't done in rehearsal. Serena glided beside Phoenix center stage, shining with confidence Marcus hadn't seen his eldest daughter since she was twelve, standing in front of the congregation at First AME Church before he went away. Serena had been some-where Marcus couldn't see her—hiding as always, even her voice—but this time Phoenix relinquished the microphone to her sister. Serena's God-given gift leaped octaves, pealing across the walls, up to the ceiling and probably through the theater door to Lenox Avenue itself.

Cheers rained inside the Osiris.

When the singers joined forces for the last set of *do do do*'s—his twelve young soldiers from the Harlem projects and his two daughters sharing a microphone, their cheeks pressed tight—Marcus felt a dike in-side himself break and carry him away to a place he had never been.

Marcus Smalls only stopped shouting when his throat was blocked by a sob.

*W*as it okay?"

Phoenix hooked her arm around Serena's slippery neck, trying to catch her breath. She didn't know why she was breathing only in short bursts, unless it was because of the adrenaline flooding her bloodstream, making her feel as if she were floating and falling simultaneously. Some-times Phoenix could hear the cascade of clapping hands, and sometimes she couldn't hear anything except her heartbeat. She no longer trusted her ears or her eyes. The cheering crowd looked like a dream she'd had when she first saw Janet Jackson at the Miami Arena.

"Was it *okay*?" Serena said, laughing as she clung to Phoenix. Serena was so excited, her breasts danced in her black dress and she nearly pulled Phoenix from her feet. "Phee, *listen*."

But listening was hard, because Phoenix's mind kept rejecting the pattering sound rolling across the theater like high tide, the camera strobes twinkling from the darkness. She had never performed before an audience this big, so she hadn't known how it would sound and look. What if Scott was trying to confuse her? What if she was only dreaming again?

"Was it okay?" she asked Arturo, stumbling past the bank of micro-phones. Instead of answering, Arturo let out a whoop and swung her in a circle in his strong, sure arms.

"Was it okay?" she tried to ask her teenagers, but the kids were too busy high-fiving, exchanging stories and tripping over cords.

Phoenix left the stage in a slow daze, sleepwalking again. She'd seen Beyoncé say in an interview that performing onstage was like having an alter ego, as if she became possessed by someone else, and Phoenix understood now. This was no different than "Live at Night." The set had been over so fast, and she'd been trying so hard to fight Scott away, she might not have been there at all. How had it *sounded*? Had her voice been in key? Had her keyboard solo worked?

When Phoenix saw her father silhouetted beyond a footlight, near the curtain, she was relieved. Sarge wouldn't lie to her. "Daddy . . . was it okay?"

Sarge's face emerged from the shadows, and Phoenix saw moisture in his eyes that made her heart catch in place. "What happened?" she whispered, prepared for tragedy. The set couldn't have been *that* bad. She had never seen her father cry, not even after she got hurt.

When Sarge grinned at her through his tears, Phoenix breathed.

Someone tackled Phoenix from behind, his arms locked around her waist. "Baby girl, you tore it *up*," Ronn said, kissing the side of her neck, and her skin shivered even though she wanted him to be Carlos instead. "Oh, *shit*. Imani says she wants you to open on her tour. That's my *girl*!" Phoenix had heard Imani was touring thirty cities later this summer, with her last shows in London and Munich. Maybe the set had been better than okay.

Sarge whispered four words in Phoenix's ear: "You did it, Peanut." When Serena joined them, still laughing, Sarge hugged her sister against him and rocked, his arms and elbows wound around Serena's head as if he meant to keep her from blowing away. His eyes were part joy, part pain. "Just like the old days, Reenie. Like the old days."

Activity flurried around them as the stomping bass of the background music came blaring back on and theater techs prepared the stage for the next act, either the Bing Boyz or Kamikaze. Backstage became a beehive intruding on their private party, and Phoenix's huddle drifted back to the white rear wall to make room, everyone in a babble of excitement. With Ronn still hugging her from behind, faces came toward Phoenix in a rush of exclamations and grins.

"Off the *chain*," Manny said.

"Sky's the limit now, lil' mama. Keep God close," Kai said, kissing her cheek.

"You got a vision, Phee," said D'Real. She hadn't even known her producer was here.

While Phoenix smiled and accepted their praises, her eyes roamed the darkened backstage space, beyond the giant amps, old card tables and stacked metal chairs. Where was Carlos? Why wasn't he here? Just when Phoenix felt something in her chest about to prick and deflate, she saw Carlos nudging his way past Kai to get closer to her, his hand reaching for hers.

Phoenix grabbed his warm palm and held tight. No one was going to keep Carlos away.

"Ronn, this is Carlos. I couldn't have made it today without him," Phoenix said, finding her breath. The hands hugging her waist fell away as Ronn leaned over to shake Carlos's hand.

"Hey, man. Ronn Jenkins." Ronn's smile had changed, plastic.

"Carlos Harris," Carlos said. "Congratulations on your success, man."

"Naw, congrats to *you*. Take good care of our girl," Ronn said, and stepped away so Carlos could take his place beside her. *Changing of the guard,* Phoenix thought.

"If he doesn't, you'll see him on the evening news," Sarge said, and people laughed because they thought Sarge was joking.

"Ooh, I gotta go get my camera out of the dressing room," Serena said, flustered, part of the new cacophony. Kai told Phoenix he'd be looking for her at the after-party. D'Real asked her when she would be ready to go back into the studio. If not for Carlos's hand in hers, squeezing periodically, Phoenix would have felt as lost backstage as she had when she had dreamed she was in Scott's cornfield.

"You done fucked up NOW, huh nigga? Ain't you?"

Phoenix heard the voice, and didn't. It was a lone, faraway voice in a symphony of voices, and she took faint notice of it only because its gruffness didn't match the others. It was the only voice that wasn't celebrating.

Phoenix didn't have long to wonder about the voice, because an explosion made her deaf.

Her ears ringing, Phoenix turned around, a primal instinct telling her where to look, and she saw a small-boned man in a black ski mask charging toward them from behind the amps where Carlos had been standing before the set, throwing fire at them. His hand was sparking.

Once. Twice. Three times.

The man was shooting at them from fifteen yards away, closer with every measured stride.

Phoenix was pinned to the wall as Kai fell against her in a wild embrace. He fell too hard, and it hurt, buckling her knees. When Phoenix blinked, she realized the three-hundred pound man had gone limp. Another blink, and she knew what was wrong with him: *Kai's been shot.*

Sarge shouted something Phoenix didn't hear, pushing against Kai with so much effort that the veins across his temples bulged like snakes, and the pressure lifted. Phoenix felt such a violent yank on her arm from the opposite direction that she thought it must be severed. Her feet left the floor, and she flew until her jaw crashed against the edge of a tabletop. Then, she was on concrete, her shoulder landing hard on the floor. Pain bolted through Phoenix's body, not knowing where to rest.

"You like Magnums, motherfucker?" a voice said.

Be still—cuidado, said another, one she barely heard through the noise. Carlos?

In her strange bubble of deafness beneath the table, Phoenix saw Serena running in one direction—*oh thank you God Reenie's safe*—and Ronn diving behind boxes in another. Purple choir gowns scattered everywhere, a tangle of panicked retreat. *My poor kids,* Phoenix thought, sorrowful. She couldn't move to try to see the man in the mask beyond the table. Her limbs were locked in place. Why couldn't she *move?*

"Phoenix?"

Phoenix's ears stopped ringing long enough for her to hear her father's voice.

"Daddy!" she called back.

She heard a gunshot clearly this time, a godless, colossal roar.

Phoenix met her father's eyes in time to see a patch of his shaved scalp above his left eyebrow snatched away like a divot of grass after a golfer's chip shot. As his blood sprayed, Sarge knelt to see after her with such care, she knew the gruesome injury must be an optical illusion. It *couldn't* be as bad as it looked, because it looked like gaping death.

"You OK, Reenie?" Sarge said with an urgent gaze, unblinking, still tall on his knees. Blood ran down his face in twin streams, one across the bridge of his nose and one between his left ear and eye, but he didn't seem to mind, just as Phoenix didn't mind being called Reenie.

I'm dreaming this right now I'm dreaming this right now I'm dreaming this right now

Phoenix smelled Carlos's cologne woven inside the terrible scent of blood—the scent she had smelled in her dream today—and the cologne, at last, told her why she couldn't move: Carlos was cradling her on the floor, wrapped around her in a vise. The man in the mask was gone, buried beneath a heap of shouting men, and Phoenix saw his smoking gun spin on the floor.

She would tell Sarge she was fine. She would tell him Carlos had saved her just like Sarge had saved Mom during the 1980 riot. But when Phoenix tried to tell him, she only felt a shock of pain from her injured jaw. Phoenix nodded *yes,* she was all right, so Sarge would know.

Sarge smiled a sickly smile—or what looked like one—but the smile left when his eyes emptied. Two full seconds passed before he toppled facedown to the floor, a foot from where Kai lay propped against the blood-spotted wall. Only then did Phoenix hear the screams and pleas with Jesus from the frantic people around her, sounds indistinguishable from her howling heart.

For the rest of her life, Phoenix would wish she hadn't nodded *yes.* She should have told Sarge she wasn't the least bit all right, that she needed him forever. Why hadn't she known what to say *that* night, the night she saw Sarge shot at the Osiris?

Needing to see her safe was the only thing that had kept her father alive.

CHAPTER TWENTY-TWO

Harlem
1916

*S*inging.

The undulating voice sounded like Lottie's, although Scott wondered if his ears were trustworthy. He thought he heard singing most nights now, although Lottie said it wasn't her, and neither of Lottie's girls would confess to it either. If he was doomed to hear imaginary noises, Scott thought, he could do worse than singing.

Scott's knees were sore and unsteady against the kitchen's wood floor, and he knew he couldn't expect his body to kneel much longer at the cool blue steel door of the stove. Glancing behind him to make sure no one would see, Scott grabbed another handful of papers from the fat stack under his armpit and shoved them beneath the grill. He had collected his scores for days now—from the Steinway's piano rack, from his drawers, from boxes, from forgotten notebooks. Some pieces were complete, start to finish, and some were ideas that had never found a home, but they were all going home now. Scott buried the ink-splotched pages in ash so Lottie wouldn't see them when she lit the coals for dinner. *Better to return you to God than see you made bastards, your composer's name forgotten.*

Scott heard Lottie's singing again, and the gentle voice of a piano as someone accompanied her on the Steinway grand, as perfect as any concert hall, just the way they wanted it. The singer *had* to be Lottie; he wouldn't tolerate such tone-deafness from an imaginary voice. But Lottie's sour notes suited "Memphis Blues," because Lottie sang blues tunes like she owned them. When Lottie got to the part about the sinner on revival day, Scott wondered if she had written those lyrics herself.

The singing made Scott sigh. He still had fifty pages under his arm, but Lottie only had to round the corner from the parlor, and she'd be standing in the kitchen doorway. She would throw her iron skillets at him if she saw what he was doing. Lottie had a temper, too, it turned out.

But this matter didn't concern Lottie. This was between Scott and God. Well, God or the Devil. Scott had warned both that he would send any new music back, but someone still sent more, even now that the handwriting was illegible even to Scott. And for what? To further torment him? Scott decided he would take his time disposing of the next piece, because his *Symphony No. 1* deserved a reverent cremation. He must mourn the pure scope of its undelivered promise; not only its singular virtues, but those of the pieces that would have followed, a dozen or more. *Symphony No. 1* would have elevated his name to Dvořák's. *But not by a Negro, no. Someone else would have claimed it as his, because surely no Negro is capable of composing such art.*

"Ashes to ashes, amen," Scott muttered, closing the stove door. He wanted to light the flames himself, but Lottie hid the matchbox from him. He would find it, by and by.

Scott groaned, reaching to the tabletop to try to pull himself back up to the kitchen chair. This trusted chair was one of his favorite resting spots, with sturdy wooden armrests to keep him propped upright. Scott could no longer sit at a piano bench comfortably, so he cherished the kitchen chair, the parlor settee and his bed. He was like poor Freddie now, shuttling between the few meager spaces he could master, the bed his last resort.

Lottie would send him away soon. She'd only mentioned it once, almost in passing—*One day I won't be able to look after you on my own, Scotty*—but Lottie revealed her thoughts only once they were set. Lottie said he should go to Chicago to be with his sister, but if he didn't hurry, Lottie might change her mind and send him to a hospital instead. Every day, Scott saw Lottie studying him, looking for his weaknesses.

Could he withstand a Chicago winter? Would he survive another winter anywhere?

"What you doin' hidin' back here?" Sam said from the doorway.

Scott was so startled, he nearly dropped his pages. "Minding my business," Scott said. Sam was one of the few people fluent in his mumble.

Sam grabbed half a slice of sweet potato pie from the counter and shoveled it into his mouth in a swoop, talking all the while. "Lottie sent me to fetch you, so come on." After slapping his hands clean, Sam grabbed Scott beneath his armpits, lifting without a grunt.

Instinct made Scott pull away, mortified. He clung to one armrest so he could reclaim his seat. No one except Lottie helped him walk. "What if I don't *want* to be fetched?"

"Lottie said to pay your mouth no mind, so hush up and let's go. If you don't like it in the parlor, you can come on back in here and hide." A swing, and Scott was on his feet. He leaned across Sam's shoulder, and they began to walk. "That new music you got, Scotty?"

Scott pinned the pages beneath his armpit more tightly. *"Treemonisha,"* he lied. As much as he wished he had the heart to destroy his opera, Scott could not. Too much of Freddie lived within its pages. How would she find him without it?

That lie only gained Scott a lecture. "What you still carryin' that around for? It ain't natural, Scotty. Louis always said you'd get fixed on something and wouldn't let it alone."

"Louis should have been worrying about his own damn problems," Scott mumbled.

"I didn't hear all of what you just said, but I'd speak kind of the dead if I was you."

By leaning most of his weight on Sam, Scott was able to imitate the motion of walking even with limbs that had no interest in obliging him. One foot in front of another. Sam could support more of his weight than Lottie, so Scott didn't have to stoop so badly. Scott walked into his parlor as a man, not a ward. Lottie was watching, and he smiled at her. *You see, baby? I'm fine after all. No need to consider me a bother.*

The parlor was crowded. Parties appeared on their own in Lottie's parlor, with a quick rap at the door, a call to the window, or a jangle of the telephone in the hall. Then, music and laughter followed without fail, often until after he was in bed. Lottie's boardinghouse was a gay home for dying.

A young tickler boarding with Lottie from New Orleans named Walter Powell was sitting in Scott's place at the Steinway, but he moved his hands to his lap when Scott entered the room. Scott saw arched eyebrows, bright eyes and thin smiles that told him all five of them had been talking about him and didn't want him to know it.

Lottie stood beside the Steinway in a bright blue dress Scott had never seen before. Unhappiness made Lottie visit shop windows, gazing at dresses she couldn't afford. Her dress of ruffles and taffeta might have cost twelve dollars or more, but how could he object? He hadn't earned any money since the piano rolls, except the royalties that dribbled in from "Maple Leaf." *What would I have done without my loyal child?* Their apartment on 138th Street in Harlem was only a block from a row of ornate brownstones that were architectural prizes well out of reach despite their proximity. Lottie planned to buy their entire building, which would be its own triumph, and some days the notion of wealth sitting so close by didn't bother Scott at all.

"Scotty, what were you doing in the kitchen?" Lottie said.

"He was sittin' right at the table, Lottie," Sam said. Sam often answered for him.

Lottie reached for Scott's music, but he pivoted away from her so quickly that he nearly lost his balance against Sam. While Sam lowered him onto the settee, Scott moved his scores from one underarm to the other, hunched like a crab.

Lottie's eyes sparked with anger and hurt. She wagged a finger at him. "Unh-hnh. I'll go see right now. If I find something in my stove shouldn't be there, it's gonna be me and you." Lottie swept past him toward the kitchen, and he almost confessed in case it might spare him some of her anger. It broke his heart to make her angry. He only couldn't get his mouth to work. Lottie's outburst had silenced the room, the singing mood gone.

Joseph Lamb, the sole white visitor, pulled the parlor window down in a whimper, since the room was getting cold in the fall chill. It was good to see Lamb. The composer kept to himself and hadn't been by to visit since he came to show off his girlfriend a while back. Lottie's new girl, Sadie, sat smoking a cigarette, leaning over the coffee table to look at the pictures in *Harper's* magazine with such little regard for the posi-

tion of her cleavage that Joe was red in the face. A drummer named Herbert Wright, an out-of-towner Sam had met at a gig, sat across from
Scott in the parlor chair, rattling a pair of dice together in his hand, like
bones.

"Lottie *really* don't want you messing with her stove, huh Joplin? My
girl in Boston don't like my cooking neither, but I see Lottie means business," Wright said. He pocketed the dice, pulled out his penknife, and
sliced away a neat section of the apple in his other hand.

Everyone except Scott laughed louder than the joke deserved, the
sound the room needed. "What happened to the music?" Scott said.

"Scotty's right. Where'd the music go?" Sam said, his translator.

"Somebody play somethin' we can *dance* to," Sadie said.

Scott didn't trust Sadie, who wore a bright red wig and constantly
watched her face in the mirror, chronicling time's insults with pursed,
painted lips. Sadie liked to stand over the Steinway reading his pages of
music, when he was careless enough to leave them in plain sight. Lottie
thought Sadie was only curious, but Scott knew a Tin Pan Alley spy
when he saw one.

"Where are those piano rolls you recorded?" Joe said. "Scott recorded
'Maple Leaf' for Uni-Record. And didn't you do some other songs for
another company? I forget the name."

Scott suddenly felt like the guest of honor at an early wake.

"You know better, Joe. Rolls don't sound good, the way they make
those changes," Scott said. He would have ranted longer if it weren't so
much effort to speak. The music was barely recognizable. Scott could
blame his hands, of course, but it was more than that. Mostly he'd done
it because he imagined how happy Freddie would be that he'd recorded
a piano roll. Her pleas with him to record his music still followed him in
his dreams.

Walter Powell tapped the piano keys. "Lemme play ya'll the blues rag
I just wrote."

"Man, first you wanted to call everything a rag. Now, everything's
blues," Sam said.

"You want to sell it, you *better* call it blues."

"That nigger Handy's makin' some money, ain't he?" Wright said.
"'Memphis Blues' sounds like the same old cakewalk to me. Don't it? He

don't even know blues, an' he's got everybody thinkin' he did it first. Shit, that nigger ain't dumb."

"He got it right in 'St. Louis Blues,' though. That's *blues*," Sam said.

"You should write a blues number, Mr. Joplin," Walter Powell said. "We'll make you the Blues King next." When the young man had first realized he had moved in with Scott Joplin, he'd been so shocked that he was mute for days. Now, Walter talked to Scott like he owned his own publishing company, like John Stark reborn.

"I wrote a little blues," Scott said. He had peppered "Magnetic Rag" with enough blues harmonics to make Lottie squeal the first time he played it for her. "Magnetic Rag" was already two years old, and it would be his last publication. He was certain of it.

Lottie's voice killed the party just as it was waking.

"Yeah, I see you been writing a *lot* of music," Lottie said, dabbing the ash-covered pages from the cookstove with a white kitchen towel. Lottie's eyes were accusing, but more weary than angry. "What's this, Scotty? 'Scott Joplin's Blues Rag'? 'Lenox Avenue Rag'?"

"They're *mine*," Scott said, his teeth clenched. He wasn't mumbling now. "*Not* yours."

Lottie blinked fast, the woman's trick of sudden tears. "These belong to the man who wrote them, not to this one who's half out his mind. When you get your good mind back, I'll give you Scott Joplin's music. You got *no right*."

"And you're a *fool*. They're illegible!" Scott said. He and Lottie argued all the time now.

Lottie raised her arms with pages fanned in each hand, a performance that embarrassed him. "See what he's doin'? I told you, I can't let my eyes off him a *minute*. This man is *burning* his music and sending it out with the trash every chance he gets. I'll feed him and wash him—I'll carry him from one end of this flat to the other—but I will be *goddamned* if I'm gonna watch him burn up what's left of Scott Joplin. You better talk to him, Sam."

"It's all right, Lottie," Sam murmured, patting her shoulder. He steered her gently from the room, speaking in her ear. "I'll talk to him. It's all right."

At least I don't have to wonder if my wife will be deprived of male company after I'm gone, Scott thought, watching his friend's tenderness toward his wife. Lottie might be running with any of his friends, or all of them. Was he still Lottie's husband, or only one of her boarders?

He wouldn't let Sam see his music either, he decided. Sam might steal it for Lottie.

Joe Lamb was the first to put on his hat and reach out his hand for a parting handshake. *The first mourner to reach the casket before he goes on his way,* Scott thought.

"Hiya, Scott."

Scott grunted. It had taken training to get Lamb to stop calling him *Mr. Joplin.* Lamb was a good rag composer and had been since the day Scott met him, but he treated Scott as if he'd been his teacher. "I'm working on a new rag for Stark," Lamb said. "When I'm finished, maybe I'll come by and play a few bars so you can tell me what you think. Like old times."

Scott grunted again, nodding this time. "How's John?" he said.

Lamb leaned closer, cupping his ear with a svelte hand. "Once again?"

"Stark," Scott said, trying to force a single clear word past his tongue.

"Back in St. Louis. He's not the same since his wife died. Nell's fine, though."

Scott nodded. He was glad to hear good news about John's daughter, anyway.

"You take care of yourself, Scott."

"I'll do my best," Scott said.

Watching Joe Lamb tip his hat to the others and leave the parlor, always a gentleman, Scott felt a gentle intuition about the man: Lamb, like Sam, was going to live a long life. Music had strengthened his spirit instead of poisoning it. Scott felt so much envy for a white man walking into his future on his own two legs that he had to look away.

"I better bookity-book on out of here, too," young Walter Powell said, reaching for Scott's hand. "There's hell to pay with Europe if you're late."

"You still playin' for Jim Reese Europe?" Herbert Wright said with another swift slice from his apple. "Everybody I talk to says I gotta see

Jim Europe. Put in a good word for me with that bossy SOB. I need some weekend work."

"You want to meet Jim, you better come on now, then. You might get lucky, but watch your mouth. Try not to sling sassy for half a minute. You're crazy, man."

Wright shook his head, standing. He reached behind him for his bass drum, which he carried in a case wherever he went. "Never did like bossy folks," he muttered. "But let's go."

"I thought you wanted a taste, baby," Sadie protested, sidling beside Wright. Sadie was the perfect actress, her face sagging from undue injury as she rubbed a slow, sensuous ring on Wright's back, beneath his shoulder blades. Despite himself, Scott wished she were touching him instead. He had almost forgotten touching.

"I gotta get somethin' in my pocket first, angel," Wright said. "Save me a lil' bit."

Sadie's smile was fit for a wedding chapel, although her eyes never smiled, day or night. "I'll save you more than that, sugar."

The faces changed, but the conversations were no different than the ones Scott had heard at the piano in Sedalia cathouses, with transactions competing to keep pace with the music. It was impossible to escape one's beginnings. Scott wished someone had told him from the start.

When Herbert Wright shook Scott's hand in parting, Wright's eyes darted around the room like a cat's, and those eyes gave Scott a shudder. He felt a sting of premonition strong enough to make him queasy. Herbert Wright didn't like rules, and he was the type to kill a bandleader like James Reese Europe one day. Herbert Wright, like Scott, was pure bad luck.

"You look better today, Joplin," Wright said with a wink, which made him a liar, too.

One by one, everyone escaped to their own lives, for good or for ill. Sadie gave Scott a long look—almost as if she hoped to invade his thoughts—and walked back to her room, humming the "St. Louis Blues." Or was it the second movement from his symphony he heard fluttering lazily from her nostrils? Why wasn't it obvious to Lottie that this girl was spying on him?

Sam came back to the parlor alone, without Lottie. He had been gone a long time. "Lottie's gonna keep herself company for a while. You need some help somewhere before I go?"

"My room," Scott said, little more than a sigh.

Sam pulled Scott's arm over his shoulder and hoisted him to his feet, so high that Scott's soles barely touched the floor. "She thinks you've gone crazy, Scotty," Sam said, carrying Scott to the hall. Without Lottie watching, Scott barely made the effort of moving his legs.

"Madness is the least of what ails me." Scott closed his eyes as they approached the long mirror on the buffet, refusing to look at himself as an invalid in Sam's arms.

Since Lottie had caught Scott burning his music, she had moved his things to the spare room down the hall. Instead of Lottie's decorative heirlooms and draperies, Scott had only his bed, a lamp, a night table, a wardrobe, and the silent, neglected Rosenkranz, where no one could touch his piano but him. *This room is a prison,* Freddie used to say. He had his own cell now.

"If you'd give me that music, it would make Lottie real happy," Sam said, turning so they could both fit through the narrow doorway. "That woman loves you, Scotty. But she's tired, see? Love don't fix everything."

"You're wrong," Scott said, as Sam lowered him to his bed. A chuckle came, a bad taste in his mouth. "Love doesn't fix *anything,* youngster."

He felt corrupt speaking those words to a man with a cherub's face and a long life ahead, but talking had become hard work. Scott had decided that if he was going to make the effort to speak anymore, he might as well tell the truth.

This time, when he tried to go to sleep, Scott didn't hear singing. He heard crying instead.

A lost girl, he thought, waking. The crying had made him dream about Alice and her adventures in Wonderland. He had seen a girl running past giant toadstools with a Cheshire cat grinning at her from the treetops, like the illustrations in Freddie's book. All along, Scott had thought the crying was part of his dream. But Scott's eyes were wide-open now, and the sound of a crying girl was more distinct, from somewhere in the dark.

"Who's there?" Scott said into the darkness. No light from the streetlamps could find this room, with his window shades pulled low. "Lottie?"

Another sob came, and it didn't sound like Lottie. This girl's voice was higher pitched, years younger than Lottie. Scott opened the drawer to his night table, fumbling for a match, until he remembered that the lamp on his night table was electric, not kerosene. Besides, Lottie had taken his matches away.

Scott almost expected the crying to stop when he switched on the lamp, but it didn't.

In the light, he saw the girl crouched on the floor beside the Rosenkranz in bare feet and a thin white gown that didn't reach her knees, much less hide her pale nakedness. Her face was buried in her arms as her thin shoulders shook with sobs. If he was only imagining the girl sitting beside the piano, he was more mad than anyone thought.

But her arms . . . her hair . . .

"F-Freddie?" Scott said, afraid to say her name for fear of being wrong.

The girl only cried on, a sound so pitiable that Scott's eyes melted. All these years, when he'd dreamed about Freddie, she'd always been smiling. He had never imagined her in tears.

The girl suddenly looked up, her eyes wide and expectant, as if she had just heard him call her. As if his words had traveled a great distance to reach her ears, riding the wind.

"My God . . ." Scott whispered, his heart lurching into a dance. The rush of blood through him made Scott's skin hot. "It *is* you. I *knew* you were there. I've felt you with me, even when I was only dreaming. Freddie! Oh, my dear girl!"

Freddie stood up, steadying herself against the piano. Wherever Freddie had come from, her trip had tired her, he thought. *The Rosenkranz brought her here, repaying its debt,* he thought, elated. Scott couldn't recall the details of his agreement with this piano, but Scott knew they had an agreement just the same.

Scott searched his wife's face, hoping to see her smile, and instead he saw the absence of a face beneath her dark hair. The closer he tried to look, the less he saw. There were impressions of faces from one instant to the next in the place where her face should be, but none were hers—and yet, all of them were Freddie. It was Freddie who was now taking quick steps toward him, and Freddie who curled beside him in his bed, weightless and angelic.

"Oh, my dear heart. My dear, sweet girl. What's wrong?"

Again, Freddie seemed not to hear him at first. Then, she only cried with more anguish, sobs that tore his skin. Was she sad only to see him so reduced?

"I can't bear to hear you like this," Scott said, stroking Freddie's hair, which was springier than he remembered and smelled of sweet fruit. He whispered to her, searching for her pale earlobe in her nest of hair. "You don't have to bring any pain with you here. I won't let any hurt touch you while I'm near. I promise you, dear heart. I promise."

Freddie clung to his neck, exactly like a child grasping for her father. Scott held her, and in his arms she was not weightless, only as light as a feather pillow, with flesh that seemed to meld to his rather than touching him. When he hugged her, Scott sank inside of her, and she into him. Scott's mouth opened as a shock of sensation traveled through him.

In his better days, Scott's toes had curled from pleasure at women's hands, but what Freddie gave him in that instant made the memory of fleshly union trivial. Scott felt the current of his love for her course through them both, and her love for him dazzled him in return. He had never needed to hold someone so much, and she had never needed so much to be held.

She had come back to him. She had found him.

"Stay with me, Freddie. Please. Stay with me," Scott Joplin said to his ghost.

Part Five

When I have fears that I may cease to be

Before my pen has glean'd my teeming brain,

Before high-piled books, in charactery,

Hold like rich garners the full ripen'd grain;

When I behold, upon the night's starr'd face,

Huge cloudy symbols of a high romance,

And think that I may never live to trace

Their shadows, with the magic hand of chance;

And when I feel, fair creature of an hour!

That I shall never look upon thee more,

Never have relish in the faery power

Of unreflecting love!—then on the shore

Of the wide world I stand alone, and think

Till love and fame to nothingness do sink.

—JOHN KEATS, "When I Have Fears"

CHAPTER TWENTY-THREE

On the third floor, the two bodyguards were the only people visible in the carpeted hall.

The bodyguard beside the elevator on Phoenix's floor tracked Carlos with his eyes for a moment, then ignored him. The firm-jawed brother's name was Terrell, but that was all Carlos had learned about him in seventy-two hours. The guard at the other end of the hall—who was friendlier and had the unforgettable name of John W. Gacy—hitched Carlos a nod.

The guards were dressed in business suits and ties like Wall Street executives, hired courtesy of Three Strikes Records—bling without the sparkle. The brothers had perfect posture, stood with their impeccably shined shoes in a V at the heels and called the medical staff "ma'am" and "sir"—so these guys were ex-military. If Ronn Jenkins could afford to hire an army for Phoenix, Carlos figured she deserved that and more. Ronn Jenkins had a lot to answer for.

Ronn's ongoing feud had inspired a twenty-one-year-old kid to camp out in the theater overnight to elude metal detectors and shoot two people dead, firing into a crowd of bystanders, including minors. The man in custody, Cecil Taylor, was a cousin of DJ Train's. He had admitted to police that he wanted to kill Kai and G-Ronn to avenge three killings in Los Angeles and Brooklyn; one a decade old, one a month old, and one a week old, on the street outside of Three Strikes Records. G-Ronn had once dined at the White House under President Clinton, so he had scaled great heights; but even if he had never killed anyone himself, Ronn Jenkins had blood on his hands.

Ronn didn't visit Phoenix, but he insisted on giving Phoenix a private, comfortable place to heal. The Harbor Recovery Center on the Upper West Side was only a slight downgrade from her hotel suite at Le Bon Maison midtown—and the private mental hospital was much pricier at $2,000 a day, Gloria said. *Even Ronn Jenkins doesn't have enough money to pay Phoenix what he owes her,* Carlos thought. Ronn hadn't gotten so much as a nick during the melee he had wrought, and Phoenix had lost her father.

The tremors Carlos felt in his psyche showed no sign of abating. Thinking about the Osiris made Carlos's cheek quiver involuntarily, so he thought about the shooting as little as possible. Carlos couldn't imagine anyone heartless enough to try to hurt Phoenix now—she was hurting enough—but the guards kept the reporters away. Phoenix Smalls was famous, at last, but not in the way any sane person would want.

Phoenix's official diagnosis was a mental collapse after witnessing her father's murder, and that might be part of it. But Carlos knew it was more than that, even if that was plenty.

Just as he reached Phoenix's door, Gloria slipped out of the suite. Synchronicity.

"Thank God you're back. I need nicotine," Gloria said. "The *real* loony bin is in that room, Carlos. I can't handle it."

"I know."

Carlos noticed the floral scent of her perfume even though he wasn't trying. Gloria was cute, and blondes were an old weakness. If once upon a time wasn't far behind, Carlos thought, he might be another bad thing about to happen to Phoenix. It would kill him to let that happen.

"Mom and Dad are trashed, so they're back at the hotel. Can you stay with Aunt Leah?"

"Of course. That's why I'm here."

"Thanks, dude." Gloria leaned into him for a hug.

"Take it easy, *rubia*. *Cuidado*. New York doesn't run out of bars," Carlos said. This morning, Gloria's breath had reeked of beer when she showed up for duty at her cousin's side. Gloria nodded. "That's what Phoenix would say, but I need to go somewhere, get shit-faced, and dance my ass off." Gloria noticed they were still hugging the instant he did, and pulled away quickly. *We could help each other forget for a while.* Carlos was disappointed when the thought appeared, but relieved he was able to push it away.

"Carlos, I have to say it again—I was so wrong about you. You're good people. If you weren't seeing my cousin . . ."

The unfinished sentence made Carlos's head swim with images of Gloria's sturdy legs, seeing them bared the night he almost gave up on Phoenix. "Same here," Carlos said.

The taboo dangled, a hot wire between them, and he knew they were two of a kind. Taboo was a tiresome, persistent fetish.

"I would never do anything to hurt Phee," he said, once it was time to stamp it out. He meant it, even if this conversation felt better than anything that had happened all day, or yesterday, or the day before. And probably tomorrow. Now, Carlos knew why Heather's grief had ignited her sexually when her aunt died a year ago, while they were still sleeping together: You wanted to feel something else. Anything else. Everything else.

"Good thing, or I'd kick your ass," Gloria said.

Carlos kissed Gloria's forehead, a brother. "No need. I love her, too."

Gloria nodded. Either she had applied her makeup wrong, or Gloria's eyes had sunken during the day. She slipped her pearl-colored lighter into her back pocket. "My Newports are calling. 'Night, Carlos. She'll be back."

She'll be back. That was the promise that kept them all going.

Room 315 was L-shaped and regal, with a caramel-and-brown pattern on the walls and a showpiece black sofa patterned after old Egypt, each armrest guarded by two golden pharaohs in head cloths. Lush potted trees in African-patterned clay pots were scattered in the corners. The room was nearly as big as Phoenix's apartment; a living room, dining area and separate bedroom. It would have been cozy, if not for the rest.

This time, Phoenix's room was hot.

As soon as Carlos opened the door, he unbuttoned his top three buttons. The heat wouldn't get better soon; the temperature changes lasted for hours. It had taken a day and a half of maintenance men to make them realize that Phoenix's room made its own decisions, no matter where she moved. Phoenix's room had its own mind.

The Venetian blinds, which were pulled to the side and clumped together at both ends of the picture window, swung slowly back and forth as if they were on a rocking ship. The swinging had started suddenly this morning.

The room's large picture window was fogged with runny condensation. The interaction between whatever was in Phoenix's room and the air conditioner was making steam, he realized. He thought he saw writing on the window between the lines of slowly running water, craggy paths on the pane. *CARLOS,* it said in cursive, a greeting that vanished when he blinked.

Carlos reached into his pocket, fumbling for the cross he kept in his wallet, the one he wore only time to time but carried everywhere because he'd promised Nana when he was ten. Phoenix's room made Carlos want to remember how firmly his mother and grandparents believed in a just, protective God and to forget that he had ever doubted. Carlos was relieved to find his cross was where he had left it. He rubbed it, walking farther into the room.

Finn, as always, stood beside the door, the silent observer behind his video camera. Finn slept in a sleeping bag beside his tripod each night and hadn't shaved in three days. Finn nodded at Carlos, his camera trained toward the swinging blinds.

"What's the temp?" Carlos said.

Finn sneezed. "One-oh-two and climbing," Finn said, pulling off his T-shirt. "Unreal."

Finn didn't have to say that the air conditioner was on full blast, or that there was no mechanical explanation for the rise in the room's temperature, which was ten degrees hotter than it had been outside all day. Carlos knew without asking.

The staff at The Harbor hadn't made many demands of them, but one rule was firm: The video camera must be out of Phoenix's view. The rule was easy to comply with. The L-shaped suite was so spacious that Phoenix's bed was not visible from the doorway; it was hidden past a large bamboo partition closer to the window, behind a thicket of potted palms.

Malcolm and Gloria's parents were gone, so the room was less crowded. Malcolm Smalls had flown to Atlanta yesterday to help his brother make funeral arrangements, since Phoenix's collapse was only one of the tragedies facing the Smalls family this week. Phoenix's father had always said he wanted to be buried in the cemetery of his grandmother's little Georgia church, so they were following his wishes. After an explosion of family politics, the funeral had been set for Sunday. Carlos had already agreed to stay with Phoenix once her family flew south for the services. As much as Carlos wanted Phoenix to be herself again, he hoped he wouldn't have to be the one to tell her she had missed her father's funeral.

Serena rocked in the rattan rocker at the foot of Phoenix's bed, pushing from the balls of her feet. Serena's sure, beautiful humming gave the room its spirit while she fanned herself with an *Essence* magazine. Sometimes Serena's voice thinned to nothing. From some angles, Serena seemed to have aged twenty years, which made Carlos think she might be the most frightened of any of them, except for Phoenix's mother. Humming must be one way Serena prayed, he thought.

Heather and her psychic friend, Johnita, hadn't moved from the small dining table, which was also out of Phoenix's view—doctor's orders. The psychics sat in a meditative silence, occasionally writing notes on their pads. The sound of their scribbling filled Carlos with dread.

As soon as Johnita had met Phoenix, she had known three things, according to Heather: Phoenix's music would be remembered. She was in love. Her father was going to die very soon. Heather said her mentor had sat up with her that night and told her what she'd gleaned, and they debated whether or not to say anything about her father. Would telling Phoenix prevent his death? Johnita Poston hadn't thought so. Deep down, Phoenix already knows, she had said.

Maybe the psychic is here to do penance, Carlos thought.

"Any news?" Carlos said quietly. He'd been gone for three hours, and a lot might have happened since then. Room 315 was a lively place.

"It's hot as Hades," Johnita said. Even in a black tank top, the psychic's skin glimmered with sweat. Heather was in her Occidental College sweatshirt because the room had never been warmer than forty degrees yesterday, so now her face was pink and flushed. She must be miserable in the heat. Heather rarely glanced at him when she was here; maybe out of deference to Phoenix, or maybe because she was working.

"I noticed that," Carlos said.

"You missed a neat trick about an hour ago," Finn said. "The TV kept coming on and off. Very *Poltergeist.*"

"It's busy." Johnita swatted a fly from her purple reading glasses. "A lot of chatter."

"Is that good or bad for Phoenix?"

The psychic shook her head. "Just busy, sugar." Which meant she didn't know.

Johnita and Heather called it *chatter* or *traffic,* mundane terms from everyday life, but they were at Phoenix's dinner table transcribing the words of the dead. Carlos sidled beside Heather and tried to make out the words of her hurried scribble. *Forgive me,* one phrase said. *I think it's the gas this time, Mother,* said another. *Come jump with me,* a third. Snippets of lives.

But these were the wrong lives, so far. As Johnita had put it, Phoenix's room was like an old-time telephone switching station, so as far as the psychics could tell, they were writing messages from industrialists, influenza victims, soldiers, slaves, schoolteachers and children from as far, it seemed, as Port-au-Prince, Haiti. But none of the messages seemed to be from Joplin, or had anything to do with Phoenix. Johnita and Heather had no idea how to rescue Phoenix, or what was wrong with her. Phoenix and Scott Joplin were in a place the psychics couldn't see, right under their noses.

Carlos ventured a glance over Johnita's shoulder, too, and saw a single word: *Rosenkranz.* A dead German hoping to be remembered?

"A little air, please," the psychic said, and Carlos knew his cue to leave her alone.

And he had put off seeing Phoenix long enough.

When Carlos had gotten the message that his editor back in L.A. needed extra help, he had been happy to go work in Phoenix's hotel room midtown, as far away as he dared to go. Back at Le Bon Maison, it had taken some work to get over the misery of Phoenix's open drawer in the bedroom, a pair of her black panties crumpled on the bathroom counter and her Janet Jackson jacket hanging where she'd left it on the desk chair. But he'd done it.

After that, the hotel room was an amazing release, the way he'd felt after Hurricane Andrew when he left the crushed South Dade neighborhood where his father lived to flee back to his air-conditioning on Miami Beach, a quick drive worlds away. In Phoenix's hotel room, Carlos had been truly alone for the first time since the shooting, and when the sound of gunfire on a rerun of *Law & Order* reduced him to sobs, he realized he had his own emotional issues to deal with. He'd slogged his way through the edit, then he wanted to do nothing but go to bed and sleep for three days to make up for the ones he'd lost. No argument could have sent him back to The Harbor to be with Phoenix's tragedy-ridden family, except one: *They need you.*

Carlos rubbed Serena's shoulder as he passed her on the way to Phoenix's bed, and Phoenix's sister, still humming, squeezed his hand hard.

Three fly strips were hanging in the room—two near the window, one next to Phoenix's bed. All of them swung gently in invisible breezes, like the swaying blinds. An upscale facility like The Harbor wasn't accustomed to having a fly problem, but they had one in Phoenix's room. The brown fly strips were dotted with black flies, more all the time. Before he'd left, Carlos had counted sixty flies on the strip hanging above Phoenix's night table, at her bedside. Now he was sure there were more flies caught on the tacky paper, angrily buzzing their wings before they exhausted themselves and died.

Flies followed Phoenix from room to room, too.

Leah Rosen-Smalls sat in the reclining leather chair beside the bed, her head facing Phoenix. Her eyes were half-lidded, but watchful. She must be exhausted. Over the past three days, Leah Rosen-Smalls had become one of Carlos's favorite people. She had to be in the greatest agony of her life, or close to it, but no detail got past her in that chair.

Carlos rested his hands on Phoenix's mother's shoulders, his chin on top of her head. "You need dinner, Mom?" he said. He didn't know why he had started calling her *Mom*, but she didn't mind. If she had figured out Carlos's history with Phoenix, his past offenses were irrelevant.

Everyone said Ronn had dived for cover while Carlos saved Phoenix's life.

"Serena brought sandwiches from that place the concierge suggested, but I'm not hungry." A crumbling tissue was always clenched inside her fist, and she rubbed it against her nose while she watched the nurse, Lydia, administer eyedrops to her daughter.

When Carlos saw Phoenix, his chest tightened as always. She looked like a corpse. Phoenix lay propped with the same wide-eyed gaze, staring at nothing and everything. Her jaw was black with the bruise he had given her when he pulled her beneath the table, but the bruise was easier to face than her eyes. As far as Carlos knew, Phoenix hadn't blinked her eyes in three days.

Lydia was leaning over her with a dropper to hydrate Phoenix's eyes, her routine. Lydia wasn't bothered by the flies, the temperature variations or the spirit traffic in Phoenix's room, but she was nervous around Leah Rosen-Smalls. She worked with a nervous laugh, constantly glancing toward the judgment chair behind her. *Tranquilo,* Carlos had murmured to the nurse on her way out once, and Lydia had smiled like he was flirting.

"How's Phee?" Carlos asked Lydia.

"No change. She's still trying to talk, so I guess that's good."

Yes, but to whom?

"Lydia, would you be sure to dry her face where it's getting wet, please?" Leah said. She might be powerless to rescue her daughter from wherever she was, but she would not abide any form of carelessness in her sight.

"I will, Mrs. Smalls," Lydia said. The girl had epic patience.

"Did she eat dinner?" Carlos said.

This time, Phoenix's mother answered. "Not a bite," she said, sighing. Phoenix had always been willing to chew and swallow her food as long as someone fed her, even if she wasn't responsive. When she was admitted, Phoenix's doctor told them that if Phoenix stopped eating longer than forty-eight hours, they would transfer her to a hospital with an intensive care unit. "And she would have loved it. Her chef fixed a wonderful jerk chicken soup, or bisque. When I was in the hospital having Phoenix, all I got was dry sandwiches and soupy mashed potatoes."

She was trying to make a joke. Good woman. "Bling bling," Carlos said, smiling. But not eating was a serious matter. *Please start eating again tomorrow, Phee. Stay with us.*

Lydia pocketed her eye-dropper. She glanced at the dangling fly strip for an instant, then quickly away. In this heat, the strip had a faint smell that promised to turn putrid in time. *"Mañana,"* Lydia said, ready to leave. "Her color looks better, Mrs. Smalls."

"I think so, too," Leah said, although Phoenix's face looked waxen to Carlos.

As Lydia was leaving, Carlos heard Johnita call out to her. "Let Dr. Romanowski know I can't do that reading tonight. I can't pull away right now."

"Oh, my God," Lydia said, as if she might cry. "We're all looking forward—"

"Eight o'clock tomorrow, first thing," Johnita said. She held up a finger. "One hour."

Johnita Poston was the true celebrity in Phoenix's room.

The psychic's book was apparently a perennial best seller, which helped, but prophecy was her calling card. After she performed a single private reading for Phoenix's psychiatrist, Dr. Young, no one on The Harbor's staff objected to the unorthodox practices and virtually unlimited visiting hours in Room 315. The staff respected Johnita Poston's wishes. No wonder Phoenix called her the Queen Psychic.

Lydia nodded eagerly. "Yes, we'll be there. There's ten of us. Is that OK?"

"That's a lot, so no more. And don't look so nervous: Your father will come through his bypass surgery fine, if that's what you wanted to ask me."

Apparently, it was. Lydia's face bloomed into a smile. *"Gracias, señora.* Yemayá talks to you. You are blessed from God." She picked up Johnita's left hand and pressed it between her palms, as if to kiss it.

"I'm only a messenger," Johnita said, something she said often. Politely, she pulled her hand away. She wasn't interested in worship.

Carlos could understand the impulse to revere the Queen Psychic. Heather had exposed him to some strange circles, so he had met a lot of people who seemed to know the future, the past, and the thoughts of the dead. Not all of them had the discipline or desire for books and television shows, but they knew what they knew. Of all of them, Carlos had never seen a psychic as good as Johnita Poston, who could pluck knowledge out of the air. The unseen spoke to Johnita in crisp, clean sentences.

"Does Phoenix look better to you, too?" Phoenix's mother asked him, after Lydia was gone. She wanted a second opinion.

Carlos stared at Phoenix's open eyes, the color of pale rosewood. He missed her so much that his stomach hurt. Seeing her eyes now, he remembered what it had felt like to roll off her at the Osiris and see those eyes, and the blood and saliva dribbling from her mouth. For a terrible, unchangeable moment, he had been certain she was shot, too.

"I don't know, Mom," Carlos said, the best he could do without lying.

Phoenix's head dipped slightly, giving the illusion that she had angled herself to look at him, steering her all-seeing eyes. Phoenix's mouth trembled, working up and down. Carlos smiled, stroking her forehead. "Yes, it's me, Phee." *Why don't you sit up and chat with me for a while? Why don't you tell me where you've been? Why don't you come back home?*

"She's glad to see you," Leah said, sounding happy.

"Yes, she's definitely still in there," Carlos said, and he kissed Phoenix's nose. "I know you love me, Phee. I love you, too."

They kept their voices hushed because sometimes fragments of words came from Phoenix's mouth. Most of the sounds she made were gurgles and grunts, but sometimes there was more. They wrote everything she said down on the notepad beneath the fly strip on the night table. In three days, she had said twelve words: *Daddy. No. Awake. Reenie. Mommy. Hold. Here*—or *hear. See*—or *sea. Carlos.* And *Scott* three times, maybe more. He wondered whose name she was calling during the times her lips moved without any sound.

Phoenix's lips shuddered, then fell still.

"I'm right here, *linda*," Carlos said. "I'm ready to hear anything you want to say."

This time, there was no motion, no sound from her. Nothing but a heartbreaking stare.

"She started moving her fingers once," Leah told him. "Like she was playing a piano."

"When did that happen?" Johnita called. Her ears picked up the words of the living, too.

"Two or three this morning. I think she was sleeping. She did it with both hands. It wasn't ten seconds, but I saw it. I happened to be awake." *Not that she sleeps,* Carlos thought.

"That's important, Leah. Write that down, if you haven't," the psychic said.

"I didn't even think of it, until now." Leah sat up, energized by the thought of doing something. She grabbed her notepad.

"Significant movements. Changes in her eyes. Auras. Write all of that down." The psychic sounded like a commanding officer in wartime.

Carlos leaned closer to Phoenix, gazing at her unblinking pupils. Sometimes, when he stared long enough, Carlos felt as if he could fall into her. "You sure you don't want to tell me something, Phee?" he whispered. "We're getting worried about you."

Phoenix's throat rumbled softly. Her lips fell open again, bobbing once.

"I promise to listen very carefully," Carlos said. "I promise to try to understand."

Phoenix blew a puff of air against his earlobe. A *puhhhhhhh* sound.

He lay his hand on her blanket, the spot where he knew her stomach was. He pressed with weight, a silent encouragement. *Yes, Phee, please go on.*

Suddenly, a gurgle popped out as a word. "Piano," Phoenix said, more than a breath.

"Oh my God. I heard that," Leah said, writing faster. "Thank you, sweet God. She said piano. Is that what you heard, Carlos?"

"I heard it."

"Finn?" Heather said.

"Got it over here," he heard Finn say from the doorway. "Pi-a-no."

That was the clearest-sounding word yet. Leah came to her feet, joining Carlos over Phoenix's bed. "That's it, Buttercup. Don't push too hard. You can rest now. Talk to us again when you've rested." She grasped Carlos's hand. "Two hours. She said her last word only two hours ago. This is the fastest she's spoken again."

"What did she say two hours ago?" Carlos said. No one had mentioned that.

Leah blinked. "Scott," she said. "Four or five times now. She's with him. I know it."

"Maybe a piano will help us contact her," the psychic said. Johnita claimed she was mostly guessing when it came to Phoenix, but that hadn't sounded like a guess.

"Marcus said when Phoenix was in the hospital, he used to play music for her when he visited. That's why we play the CDs," Leah said. Phoenix heard CDs several hours a day, but so far none had the impact they'd hoped for. Not even Joplin.

"She was in a coma, no?" Carlos said. "Maybe this is like that. Maybe they're related."

Serena stopped humming. "Marcus told me how Phoenix played that piano after her accident. He would know . . ." She'd spoken of him in present-tense, until she remembered.

"I was there, too," Leah said, filling Serena's silence. "I saw it. She played in her sleep."

"Maybe she could do that again," the psychic said. "I told Phoenix at her reading that it was very important to find the piano from the accident." Her tone sounded almost scolding.

"Yes, she asked me about it," Phoenix's mother said. "Two days before." No one said what had happened within Phoenix's earshot. They never said *shooting,* or *murder,* or *dead.*

"We need to find it and bring it to her," Carlos said. He felt hopeful, suddenly.

"It was so long ago!" Leah said, raising her hand to her forehead. "I can't remember the name of the collector we sold it to. Do I have to go all the way home to dig it out?"

The pause was only two seconds at most. "Burnside?" the Queen Psychic said.

Leah gasped. "*Yes*. From Cutler Ridge. How in the world could you know that?"

"It wasn't me, it was you. You knew. I just helped you wipe off a little dust."

Goose bumps tickled the back of Carlos's neck. Johnita Poston was spooky. *Her Highness could have been a dangerous woman in another life,* he thought, peeking around the corner at her. A fly landed on the end of the psychic's pen, and she held the pen up to her face so she could examine the fly more closely. The insect stayed in place while she stared.

"It's almost as if they're bringing the messages on their wings," the psychic said, murmuring mostly to herself. Then she went back to writing, intercepting another of the buried whispers. As soon as her pen touched the paper, the fly was gone.

It had flown away, Carlos was sure. But it had looked like it vanished instead. *Poof.*

Carlos went back to Phoenix's bed and gazed at her eyes, and pain stabbed his stomach again. Phoenix's face was paralyzed in her life's greatest instant of horror. He wished he could leap inside her pain and pull her to safety. *Come back to us, Phee. We miss you. We need you here on this side.*

"I'm going to get that piano, Ms. Poston," Carlos said to the psychic. "If we bring Phoenix that piano, will Joplin let her go?" The blunt question made Phoenix's mother's face turn ashen. None of them liked to call it what it was, but somebody had to.

"All I know is that I don't know," the psychic said, and he heard the scribble as she kept writing. "Let's try some faith. Once we have the piano, Phoenix will show us what to do."

It was the closest thing to prophecy Carlos had heard since the gunfire at the Osiris that took Phoenix away.

CHAPTER TWENTY-FOUR

Was it okay?

Phoenix heard her own voice in the darkness, endless repetition. *Was it okay?*

Reenie's throaty voice joined the chorus, laughing from a tunnel. *Was it OKAY?*

Daddy . . . was it okay?

"You did it, Peanut." Her father's voice was in her ear.

Sarge's voice brought a flash of light, and Phoenix could finally see again. Sparks flared in the distance like fireflies (*but these sparks are from cameras, not the other kind*), and a wave of sound grew louder until it snatched her beneath an ocean, deaf in its vast noise. It took Phoenix a long time—maybe minutes, maybe hours—to realize she was hearing applause.

When the sound of whistling, clapping and shouting became distinct to her, no longer a mystery, her sight sharpened. She knew exactly where she was, suddenly—she was center stage at the Silver Slipper, sitting on the bench of a breathtaking white concert grand piano with its lid raised high, performance-ready. She had dreamed about this piano, long ago, and she had missed it without remembering it was gone.

Then he must be here, too, she thought, and she peered through the open lid so she could see an identical piano facing hers. Sarge was there, in place at his bench. Sarge wore a black tuxedo and bowtie, and white gloves—but also his mud-cloth skullcap, or it wouldn't be Sarge.

Sarge grinned. No stream of blood ran alongside his left eye, or down his nose.

"Where you been, Peanut?" Sarge said.

I don't know, Phoenix tried to say, but speaking was difficult now.

The audience went deathly quiet. Sarge removed his white gloves one after the other, shaking out his hands to limber them up. "You ready?" he said, winking. "It's showtime."

Phoenix glanced down at her piano's ivory keys. No blood. *Thank you, God.*

A conductor stood before them, silhouetted against the footlights. The conductor raised his baton, and Phoenix's hands went to the keys in the pose Mrs. Abramowicz had drilled into her head—fingers loose, wrists high. There shouldn't be a conductor, since there was no orchestra, she remembered. But a conductor was here all the same.

The conductor's baton swooped, and Phoenix and her father played. Phoenix didn't recognize the piece, but she knew it by heart. It wasn't ragtime, jazz, blues, soul, rock or R&B, but it was descended from all of them, syncopated and improvised and ordered all at once. Sarge added his own flourishes—phrases from old music never mined that he had passed on to his daughter without his knowledge—but the music was Phoenix's. Together, Phoenix and her father brought her unborn music to life on their twin pianos.

The conductor's baton had gone still while she wasn't paying attention. They were not playing the piece the conductor expected of them, she realized. But they didn't need the conductor. Phoenix and her father raced and slowed, called and responded, crescendoed and whispered. Sarge began phrases and she finished them, flawless musical discourse. "Just like Pops and King Oliver! Like Dizzy and Bird!" Sarge shouted, laughing, although Phoenix thought they sounded more like Lauryn Hill and Wyclef Jean, or Big Boi and Andre 3000, or Jimmy Page and Robert Plant. Or Nat King Cole and his girl Natalie singing "Unforgettable," their duet from beyond death.

The piece ended as it was supposed to, with their combined pianos clapping like thunder on the final note. Phoenix felt her body fill with air, that feeling like floating that came after a good show. *You done fucked up NOW, huh nigger?* someone far back in the audience shouted, but his lone voice was smothered by applause.

When they stood up—her at her piano and Sarge at his—the audience exploded.

"You did it, Peanut. I love you," Sarge said, with his *Daddy* stare.

Sarge walked around his piano with steady strides to the front of the stage, and the conductor stepped aside to make room. Sarge's features vanished in the stage lights, but Phoenix saw his shadow waving to the audience, as if he spotted friends.

Elegantly, Sarge took his final bow.

You like Magnums motherfucker?
*nononononononononononononononono*NONONONONONONO

"Daddy?" Phoenix called to him, falling back to her bench as feeling seeped from her legs.

Sarge heard her, and turned around. When he stepped toward her, from beyond the light, Phoenix saw the hole in his head above his eye, and the streams of blood carrying him away.

"You've got to see about the revolution, Phee," he said.

Sarge turned and gave the Panther salute, and the audience roared its appreciation. Then, he began his walk toward the backstage curtain, head and shoulders high. *Every round goes higher, higher, soldiers of the cross.* Sarge was a soldier, and not the least bit afraid.

Not yet, Daddy, Phoenix tried to say, but her voice failed her again. She tried to stand to go after him, but her arms yanked her back, her hands glued fast to the piano's keys.

The white concert grand was gone. Phoenix's fingers were anchored to the sticky keys of the Rosenkranz. Four stunted, crimson-colored candles burned in its matching candelabra, and hot wax dripped onto the piano's keys like blood.

Come back to us, Phee. We miss you. We need you here on our side.

Phoenix felt a sudden, startling stillness as everything around her dimmed again. The voice puzzled her, intrigued her. She knew that voice. She knew that place. *Carlos?* she said, or tried to. The name was strange in her mouth even as she uttered it, already forgotten, but its sound strengthened her resolve. She would go to him, even if she had to wade through the river of her father's blood. All revolutions had blood.

Phoenix pulled at her fingers again, but the piano's keys held her in place, unrelenting. Phoenix felt a wail about to break itself free in her, a tide of grief and terror.

"Freddie?" a voice said behind her.

The tide receded, stilled. The voice made her heart leap. The stage disappeared.

She still sat the Rosenkranz, her hands wed to its keys, but the candles were gone. *There are no matches in here. Matches would cause an accident.* A hand grazed her shoulder, someone's lips brushed her ear. For an instant, she forgot her lover's name.

"Where do you keep vanishing to?" Scott said. "It worries me when you're gone."

Her heart celebrated when she saw Scott standing behind her, listing terribly, but at least on his feet. He must have made a tremendous effort to come to her, since he was confined to his bed. Now he was standing by himself, and she was the one who was trapped.

"Why won't it let me go?" she said.

"Every musician has an instrument that never forgets him, dear heart."

Trembling from either his anticipation or the effort, Scott leaned down to nuzzle her neck. At first, his cool skin made her flinch, but when their flesh rubbed together, she remembered him. Scott raised an unsteady index finger to her chin. His hand was a block of ice, but his touch jolted through her core, making her toes pinch.

"Let me live, Freddie. Live with me."

Suddenly, her hands came free from the piano, and warm light appeared, brightening everything until her vision was as crisp as it had been since before she died. It was like having a new pair of eyes—new *everything*, really, because her senses shed their sleep. The piano was so beautiful that she stared at it a long time, and the piano's beauty helped her see the refinement hidden around her. The room's walnut bureau was plain but well dusted, without a single scratch. The brass globes on the bed likewise gleamed. The light through the curtain was dying but still deep and fiery, dusk light. Her favorite time of day.

She saw Scott with fresh eyes, too. Scott's illnesses had aged him, so the man who stood over her might be sixty except for his jet-black hair.

If he had lived, Scott wouldn't have had a gray hair on his head until he was an old man. He was meant to have lived a long time. Scott hadn't seen a barber in a long while. His hair was springy, a fledgling Afro.

She smelled baking chicken from the kitchen. From the smell, Lottie must be quite a cook, and that made her jealous.

"Is Lottie good to you?" she said.

"When I let her be," Scott said.

She smiled at that. Scott was the definition of tenacity, she remembered. Like her.

"She'll make sure you're remembered," she said.

"Can't ask for more than that," he said, but that was a lie. He knew who he was, and he wanted to see more, that was all. Like everybody else.

"Stop burning your music, Scott," she said.

"Burning is the only way to send it away for good," he said. "Ashes to ashes, amen."

"Stop burning your music. The time will come when you'll regret it."

"There are *thieves,* Freddie. They t-take—"

She silenced Scott by taking his face into her hands, bumping their noses gently. His skin still didn't feel quite right to her, but it was warmer all the time. "What did I say?"

Their eyes were so close, they might be sharing the same pair. Scott's eyes began smiling at her. Then, dancing. "I won't burn my music," he said. "But promise me something back."

"I won't promise until you say what it is."

Scott smiled. "Allow your husband to carry you to our bed."

When she nodded, Scott gathered her into his arms like a bundle of bed linens. He pressed his mouth to hers, and the singular taste of him made her eyes fill with tears. His taste was such a comfort, she felt her limbs sag, releasing the coiled fear she had forgotten was there. She would let Scott carry her wherever he wanted her to go. *Ashes to ashes, amen.*

He twirled her around, away from the piano, and the drab room suddenly seemed lovely. She didn't need riches to be happy! The waiting bed and its brown blanket were plain but quaint, and made her recall the pillows on the bed where she had given her virginity to him. Somehow, she had lost that memory before.

But if Scott had been her first lover, had Scott come *after* she met Carlos?

The question was so immense that it rocked her mind. Who *was* she? Was this her home, or was there another home beyond her memory? Who was the man she remembered with his fist in the air, and why did his memory make her so sad?

Scott had questions, too. He lay beside her on the bed, his arms locked around her waist, pulling her so tightly against him that she felt his ragged breathing. His eyes shimmered, fearful. "Am I mad, Freddie?" he whispered. "Or are you really here?"

"Yes, Scott, you're mad," she said. "And yes, I'm really here."

When they kissed again, their questions dissolved.

CHAPTER TWENTY-FIVE

*T*he salmon-colored door to the ranch-style house at the end of the street opened after only one knock, and Carlos took a step back, his breath diving into his lungs. Four days and counting since the Osiris, and sudden movements still startled him. *Dios mio.*

The balding man at the door had an ample beer gut and sideburns fashioned after 1970s-era Elvis, wiry bottle brushes alongside his ears. While he gulped iced tea from a glass with a Miami Dolphins logo, the smell of pizza inside tantalized Carlos. All he'd had on the plane was stale pretzels. Hunger, combined with the startling Miami humidity he'd somehow forgotten, made Carlos feel queasy. His cousins in San Juan would laugh.

"You the guy who called this morning?" The man had a leftover Brooklyn accent, a transplant like most of his neighbors. Los Angeles was full of transplants, too.

"Carlos Harris." Carlos almost shook his hand, but a formal gesture felt awkward, given the insanity that lay beneath this facade of business. *Yes, I'm the nut who called, the one who wants to buy your haunted piano.* Calls to random Burnsides throughout the Miami telephone directory had led Carlos to Rich Burnside in Perrine, the only one who tuned and restored pianos.

Burnside rubbed his moustache, which was mostly brown with sprays of gray. The moustache drooped dramatically, almost a style from another era. "You flew from New York just like that? Same day?" Burnside said. "That's a lot of trouble for a worthless piano."

"It's not worthless to me," Carlos said. His hands were in his pockets, curled fists. His knuckles chafed against the denim. The odds that Burnside actually remembered the piano Leah had sold him more than a decade ago were slim, but he'd claimed he did. "Can I see it?"

"Why don't you come in first, grab a glass of tea and a slice? My wife and I just—"

"If you don't mind," Carlos said, "I'm hoping to catch a flight to JFK in three hours."

The man looked at his watch, eyebrows jumping. "Good luck, this time of day. Traffic's a bitch on 826, and the Don Shula's a parking lot after four." He sighed, pondering something, then he turned to look over his shoulder. "Susie?" he called. "I'm running over to Old Cutler. Wrap up my pizza."

"You *sure*?" came the surprised voice of a woman in house.

"It'll keep." Burnside looked forlorn, though. Apparently, Carlos had arrived on the heels of a late lunch. "Let's vamoose," Burnside said, fishing his keys from his front pocket. "Fact is, I'm glad to get rid of the piano."

Carlos's heart squirmed. "Why?" he said. He'd delayed the questions that would make him sound like a headcase, but Burnside had brought it up.

Burnside shrugged instead of answering. He pulled the front door closed while it chimed behind him, a delicate tinkling of shells. Burnside nodded toward his half-circle driveway of crushed stones, where a white van painted with *A-1 South Dade Piano Tuning and Repair* in red script was parked beside a silver PT Cruiser.

"Too much aggravation," Burnside said finally, unlocking the van's driver's side door.

"Like?"

Instead of elaborating, Burnside waved Carlos into the van. He pulled a cigarette from the pack of Salems in the glove compartment and lit up before starting the engine. While Carlos strapped on his seat belt, Burnside pulled out of the driveway and navigated through the neighborhood of L-shaped homes, which Leah said was close to where Phoenix had grown up. Many of the houses sat on the bank of a winding canal as wide as a small river, beneath eucalyptus and palm trees that made portions of the street feel like the tropics. Burnside slowed the car to let a trail of ducks meander across the street, all of them ignoring approaching traffic as if they were blind.

Burnside's van was an older model, with a cassette player instead of a CD. Burnside punched on the music, and Peter Tosh's "Legalize It" filled the van with a serene reggae vibe that didn't match Carlos's mood. He didn't want to be nervous, but he was. Gloria had changed her mind about coming with him to retrieve the old piano, and he could understand why. *I'm in no hurry to see that piano, dude,* she'd admitted, and Carlos wasn't either, except that he had to be.

A sharp fear that Phoenix was going to die—a fear so rooted that it reared as a certainty—coursed through Carlos until it was a hot boulder on his chest. The idea that he would never again be able to talk to her, or hear her soul's laughter through her music, paralyzed him. In his mind, he had already cleaned up their history to tell their grandchildren: *I met her the day she graduated from high school, on her eighteenth birthday. When I first heard her demo, I knew she was a star already.*

"The good ones always go young," Burnside said suddenly, and blood drained from Carlos's face. Burnside went on. "Tosh. Marley. The greats always kick before their time."

The term *kick* made Carlos feel sick to his stomach, forcing him to imagine Phoenix's IV feeding tube and the flies hovering near her bed. "Not all of them do," Carlos said in her defense, but there was no arguing the point. Aaliyah had just started to get his attention when she died. "I'd like to hear what happened with this piano, if you don't mind. You never told me."

Again, Burnside went quiet. Old Cutler Road appeared at the end of a lonely roadway, and Burnside turned left, keeping his eyes trained on the road like an old man. Old Cutler Road had once been a cool haven from the sun, but the foliage in South Dade hadn't grown back the same since Hurricane Andrew in '92. Some spots were still dead.

"Brace yourself for something that'll sound crazy," Burnside said, his voice husky.

"Try me."

"That piano's been trouble since the day I bought it. This one gets herself lost. What I mean to say, the damn thing *moves*. You get me?" His profile was rigid.

"I get you." *And I'm way ahead of you,* Carlos thought.

This was the right piano.

Old Cutler Self-Storage (AIR-CONDITIONED! FIRST MONTH FREE!) was a collection of drab warehouses with bright orange doors, hidden on the roadway behind eucalyptus trees with dangling roots. The facility's asphalt was black, new. Burnside drove to the unmanned arm blocking the entrance and punched in a code, and the arm lifted to let him in. He coasted to a stop beside the rear line of warehouses, a stone's throw from the green water of the Saga Bay lake.

Carlos watched the circles of ripples that appeared on the water's surface, invisible fish looking for food. The life beneath the water was like the unseen world in Phoenix's room.

"You saw the piano move?" Carlos said. His tongue felt sticky.

"Didn't need to," Burnside said, leading Carlos on a gravel path toward a large storage room. "When I bought her, I carted her straight to my garage, figuring I'd look her over closely the next day. I wanted this one on sight, for some reason, but I had a feeling the soundboard was shot to hell, and if that was gone, I'd wasted my money. I wanted to put off the bad news. But the next morning, when I went out to the garage, she was gone."

Burnside mashed out his cigarette on the path before jangling through his keys to find the one for the lock on the storage door at 8A. "I called the police, filed a report. That same day, my son Danny goes into the workshop behind our store on South Dixie, and the missing piano's sitting against the wall like it's always been there. But I didn't move it there, and neither did Danny. I'm saying it moved *itself*. And that wasn't the only time. It showed up here on its own, too. If you don't believe me, Danny and Susie will tell you."

Burnside hesitated, his key poised beside the lock. He overcame his sheepishness and stared Carlos in the eye. "You get me?" he said again, his head tipping forward. Burnside's eyes were a friend's, not a businessman's.

Carlos nodded, his palms wet. "Yes," Carlos said, trying to sound sure of himself. He nodded to Burnside. *Go on. Let's go in.*

The storage bin's aluminum door rolled up with a rusty *tick-tick-tick* while Burnside grunted, pushing with one arm. The cool, dank space huffed out the smell of old wood, mildew and a strong cleanser, maybe turpentine. Carlos couldn't see anything except the shadows of what might be a dozen pianos. They stood in a dark collection of silence.

"I call this my Graveyard," Burnside said. "Special projects I don't have time for. About the time I bought this one, I had a bad piano habit. Susie made me stop going to estate sales, so now I only refurbish to customer request. I should get rid of most of these, I guess, but I keep thinking I'll get to them one day." He surveyed the dark room, which apparently didn't have any lighting beyond the open door panel. "Shit. She's done it again."

Carlos knew, then: The piano was not there. The piano was not *anywhere*. He had flown to Miami for nothing, and something awful had happened to Phoenix while he was gone.

Burnside pointed. "This morning she was in back, but there she is, misbehaving as usual."

As light poured into the room from the open door, Carlos's vision improved. Most of the pianos were lined up neatly along the sides of the storage bin, but one shadow stood in the path of the doorway, ten yards back. When Carlos stepped forward, the shadow became a dark, aged piano with two adorning candelabra, room for two candles on each end. Clear as day. He hadn't seen the piano when the door first opened. How had he missed it?

Carlos opened his wallet and felt for his cross. This time, he kept it in his balled hand.

"Not exactly what you'd call ideal storage conditions," Burnside said. "Even with A.C., this room's too humid. I'd never bring a client's piano here. I keep promising I'll clear the place and save the money on storage. That and a decent round of golf, and I could die a happy man."

When Carlos took three strides toward the piano, his feet burned as if he'd stepped into an anthill. Carlos stopped walking, stamping his feet on the bare concrete floor. Phoenix's mother had told him something about itching feet.

"That goes away," Burnside said matter-of-factly, but Carlos noticed that Burnside walked no closer to the piano himself. Instead, he stood in the light, keys still jingling. "Go on, take a closer look if you want. I've got a flashlight in the van, if you need it."

Carlos didn't want to examine this piano any more than he would want to lean over a table at a morgue and study a fresh corpse. The discarded instrument glowered, and the thought of bringing this piano to Phoenix's room felt worse than foolish. It felt spiteful. The piano's presence was larger than the space it occupied; it filled the room, an unsettled energy that reminded Carlos of what it would feel like if three or four people were hiding inside here, lying in wait. How could this piano do Phoenix any good?

The Queen Psychic's intuition felt more fragile in the piano's presence. This piano was more powerful than Johnita Poston, and he was sure the Queen Psychic had never encountered anything like it. He should have sent her here instead, a translator for whatever the piano was whispering beyond his hearing. He should have stayed with Phoenix.

Carlos steeled himself and took two more steps toward it. The piano shuddered as some kind of shadow passed behind him, maybe a bird, making the light into the storage space blink. Carlos raised his arm, unconsciously tilting his body sideways as he drew closer to it. The piano felt like an animal, as if it might spring. And it *had* sprung at Phoenix, he reminded himself.

Holding his breath, Carlos took in the piano's details: Dingy, piss-colored keys, a cabinet so weatherworn it was like a skeleton, and two candelabra that looked mocking instead of stately. The piano's ugliness offended him more because of how majestic it once must have been. It put a bad taste in his mouth. Finally, Carlos looked away. He didn't intend to look at it again, not soon. He wished he never had to see it again.

Carlos craved *evidence* that the piano was the answer, the same standoff he had reached with God when he was thirteen and decided he was agnostic. Did he truly believe he needed the piano, or did he only want to believe because there was nothing left?

"Can the movers pick it up in the morning?" Carlos said after a deep breath.

"Danny can wait here awhile, but not all day. Pin them down on a time."

"How much do you want for it?" Carlos said. He and Leah had decided to get the piano at any cost. Neither of them wanted to, but they would ask Ronn to help, if it came to that.

"Well, she's worse off now than when I bought her, and whatever I paid was too much," Burnside said. "You'll be paying more than she's worth to haul her to New York, so I don't have the heart to charge you. She never belonged to me, anyway. I'm just a caretaker."

The gesture was so appropriate, Carlos forgot to thank Burnside for his generosity. Burnside should be paying *him* to take this piano away.

"Why do you want it?" Burnside said. "If it's not too bold to poke my nose in."

"This piano once belonged to Scott Joplin," Carlos said. It was a silly thing to say before the piano changed hands, but it popped out before he could think. He had to tell someone.

"No shit? Who says? I read Joplin had a Steinway." Carlos knew he shouldn't be surprised Burnside knew that, given his job, but he was. True music lovers were sages.

"It's just a theory. A hunch," Carlos said, and left it at that. "How would I know if this one's a Steinway? I didn't see a label."

"The label's faded with the wood finish, but you'll see all the manufacturing details if you open the cabinet up top," Burnside said, although he made no move to do so, and the idea of touching it made Carlos feel sick. "It's a German company. She's a Rosenkranz."

Rosenkranz.

The torrent of relief that broke loose in Carlos's chest killed his fear cold.

M̲ost often, she traveled as light. A speck was all she needed.

She had learned that it took time and energy to appear as a person, to claim so much space; and every time she did, Scott said he did not see her for several days afterward. Skin and hair had its advantages, because nothing seemed to make Scott happier than to lie beside her in his bed, to embrace the substance of her, to explore her with his hands. The touching was nice, if only because it awakened memories, but the skin she wore here was only a covering. Skin didn't feel the way she remembered; sometimes when he touched her, she felt nothing at all.

Mostly, she was happy just to be in the room with him, flitting from place to place without thought or effort. In one instant, she was in his lamp; in another, she was floating across his ceiling, or gliding up and down his walls. In the process, sometimes she knocked his lampshade askew, or bumped the wardrobe so hard that the door fell open. The piano was easiest to visit, a lure, so often she appeared inside the gleam of its rosewood case, even when it made her feel trapped. Sometimes, she bounced on the high-G key while everyone in the boardinghouse was sleeping, laughing herself silly.

Scott's room was her favorite place—probably because the piano was there—but she ventured to the hall, parlor and kitchen to prove her independence. She got in trouble this way. Once, she was amusing herself with the current of water from the kitchen faucet when Lottie walked in, and it was too late by the time she shut the water off. Secretiveness was instinct to her—she was only a guest, after all—but if Lottie Joplin hadn't seen her that day, it was only because she refused to.

Lottie knew someone else was in her house.

For one thing, Lottie heard Scott talking to her. Scott didn't try to hide her from Lottie, no matter how sick Lottie looked when Scott got to talking with his ghost and stubbornly refused to glance Lottie's way. He didn't talk to Lottie nearly as much as he talked to her, or with the same tenderness. She was mostly a memory, after all; Lottie wasn't at the same safe distance.

But she understood Lottie, even if Scott didn't. She didn't blame Lottie for being in Scott's room today, slowly packing his clothes into an old brown suitcase that seemed too small to hold the remnants of a man's life.

"I knew you'd never come to nothin', Lottie Stokes. That's your name, you know. *Stokes,* not Joplin," Scott said, slumped on his bed as she packed his things. Scott chose cruel things to say at random, trying to escape his fear. He was afraid all the time.

Lottie didn't glance at him, intent on her task. Lottie pulled out the spotless white suit hanging in the wardrobe, but she didn't fold that one to pack. Lottie ran her fingers across the shiny fabric, a small smile surfacing on her lips as she remembered how dandy and successful he'd looked when he wore it. In Lottie's mind, this was the one suit proclaiming that this man was Scott Joplin, the Ragtime King. When Lottie replaced the suit and closed the wardrobe door, her smile had become a tear in her eye.

"Yessir, you've always been Lottie Stokes," Scott said again, one last attempt to hurt her.

"I know my name," Lottie said, giving him a wan smile. Most people had trouble understanding Scott's slur, but Lottie understood better than she wanted to. "I know who I am. So do you." Lottie's smile was so brave it was heartbreaking.

You stop that, Scott, she whispered. *Try to see past your own pain. Lottie's hurting nearly as much as you, as much as anybody outside your skin. She's been wanting to come in here and pack your things for two weeks, and she couldn't bring herself to do it. She lets the music play late in the parlor, but she cries herself to sleep. You call her by her true name.*

"I won't," Scott said, a stubborn child. "She's casting me out."

She can't keep you by herself.

"Well, she ought to try. This is *my* room. *My* house. This is *my* piano."

"Bellevue has a piano, Scotty," Lottie said. "Don't worry."

"Nobody's talking to you," Scott said. "This piano's *mine,* you hear? Nobody better touch it. Not Sadie, not Sam, not none of them. It better be right here when I come back."

"It'll be here," Lottie said. She chuckled. "Thought you weren't talking to me, Scotty."

Music came through the wall from a neighbor's flat, a thumping piano bass line that sounded like a boogie-woogie, even though nobody called it by that name yet. The piano was probably old, because it was badly out of tune, but the player had found a few good notes to bring joy to it. People always made music with whatever they had. The happy, rousing sound erased the cruel lines from Scott's forehead, but fear shrouded him again. When Lottie stood closer to his bed, Scott reached for her hand.

But Lottie didn't offer her hand right away, withholding. "Say my name," Lottie said.

"Lottie Joplin," Scott said. He'd even made the effort to speak slowly and say it clear.

"I sure as hell won't never forget that, and I'll make sure nobody else does neither," Lottie said, clasping his trembling hand between both of hers. "It's all right, Scotty. Now tell me where you went and hid that symphony. I won't get mad."

Instead of answering her, Scott began to sing through an exaggerated grimace. *"Oh, I wish I was in the land of cot-ton . . ."* His voice was ruined, bitter, as he sang "Dixie."

Lottie ignored his singing, speaking over it. "That symphony could make you a great man, Scotty. And that 'Lenox Avenue Rag,' I bet that's good, too. Tell me where they're at."

She decided to try to help Lottie, to enlist Lottie as a partner. Weren't they both wedded to Scott? It was hard to make yourself known to people who didn't want to see you, but she tried. Riding the wings of a horsefly, she threw herself against the bedroom's windowpane, tapping hard. If Lottie went to the window and stared straight down, she might see a page or two of music in the alley below. As soon as the snow started yesterday, Scott had taken an hour to pull himself out of bed, open the window, and toss out the pages of *Symphony No. 1,* hoping to bury it in ice, not ashes.

But Lottie wouldn't look at her even when a corner of the window flared. Lottie must have thought the light was from a streetlamp; either that, or Lottie was determined to pay her no mind. Some women couldn't stand knowing that their man had loved before.

Sam Patterson came to the doorway. Louis's spirit stood behind Sam, except more quiet, at a distance. Louis preferred to visit Scott in dreams, although he rarely made time for visits. Not everyone liked to visit. Sometimes they waited. The wait was never long.

"We got a car downstairs, Lottie," Sam said. "When you're ready."

Lottie did the things for Scott a spirit couldn't: She found a pair of socks and slipped them over Scott's cracked, dry feet. Next, she fit his feet into his shiny black shoes and tied the laces, making sure they were even at the ends. Lottie brought in a spiffy overcoat, and while Sam held Scott up, she put the coat on over Scott's sleeping clothes, buttoning it to the top. Last, she combed through his hair, patting it until he was neat. The sight of Scott looking so good nearly made Lottie change her mind. She had turned him into Scott Joplin again.

"Please come with me, Freddie," Scott said. "Stay with me."

My name isn't Freddie, she thought. When she was here with Scott, she had no name.

"You know that ain't my name," Lottie muttered, weary. "I'd rather be called Stokes."

"You don't need the piano to follow me," Scott said. "The piano brought you, but now that you're here, you can stay with me forever. The Rosenkranz will keep us together."

Lottie lifted Scott under one arm, and Sam the other as they slowly made their way out of his room. They all knew it was the last time Scott would see the room, but they didn't linger.

"He talks on about that piano," Lottie said, shaking her head. "Wish we could take it."

"He don't even play it no more," Sam said.

"I think he does, late at night. I hear it sometimes."

Panic rose in Scott as they drew farther from his bedroom, closer to the door to the hall and the cold waiting outside. His legs scrabbled weakly against the floor as he turned around, looking for her. "Freddie? Are you coming?"

She knew Scott wasn't only inviting her with him to Bellevue, or to the one last place Lottie would send him after that. He wanted her to be with him when he made his Leap, because Leaping alone was terrifying. She had told him it only took an instant, and he would think his fear was silly as soon as his Leap was done. She had told him she couldn't hold his hand at the end, because she didn't belong with him yet. The part of her that *wasn't* Freddie had a bit more to do somewhere else, and the longer she was gone, the harder it would be to find her way back.

"Please, Freddie?" Scott called, his voice nearly shorn by a sob.

She landed on his nose and made him itch, so he would know she was there. She couldn't stand to see him so broken and afraid. *I'm here, Scott*, she said. *I'll go with you.*

Scott has a powerful but famished spirit, she thought. He was like the drowning swimmer who would pull his rescuer to her own death.

CHAPTER TWENTY-SIX

*N*ever thought I'd see *this* thing again." Gloria stood over the newly arrived piano with her arms folded tight, bracing against a blast of cold. "This is an ugly effing piano. I got it right when I saw it the first time."

Es verdad, chica, Carlos thought. But it was worse than ugly. The hair on his arms stiffened as Carlos gazed at the Rosenkranz against the wall, replacing the psychics' dining table.

The piano looked worse in the gentle lamplight of the room, without shadows to hide it. The piano's key cover was down, concealing the keys, so it was easy to forget that it was a piano instead of an oversized, mis-shapen piece of furniture with no natural use. The twin candelabra, which were probably brass, were black with age. The cracks in the cabi-net's finish were magnified in the light, making it look more like a reptile than an object made of wood.

Carlos had almost given up on the Saturday delivery he'd been promised when the movers called at six, saying they were on the way. They complained incessantly while Carlos signed the paperwork: They'd gotten lost three times. The piano had slipped off the ramp and almost crushed their feet. Their elevator stalled while they were bring-ing it up. Ordinarily, it would have sounded like excuses or stumping for tips. Ordinarily.

"I don't like having it here," Carlos said, his voice low.

"Hey, I don't like it either." Gloria sighed. "But what can I say? My instincts have been wrong about this whole thing since day one, so I want to trust the psychic, you know? She said to bring it here. She wouldn't leave unless I promised."

Phoenix's room had exhausted the team of psychics. Johnita Poston and Heather had left for much-needed rest right before the movers called. Even Finn was gone, since his cold had worsened and he'd decided to get a hotel room for the night. As always, his camera remained behind, watchful. When Carlos realized the piano would be arriving tonight after all, he'd called every number he had for Heather, Finn and Johnita Poston, but he got voice mail everywhere.

He wasn't going to reach them, he knew. That, apparently, already had been decided.

Everyone else was gone tonight, too. Leah, Serena and Gloria's parents had caught an afternoon flight for Atlanta for Marcus Smalls's funeral tomorrow, waiting as long as they dared before leaving in case Phoenix's condition changed.

"You can still try to fly out tonight, Gloria," Carlos said, although the last thing he wanted was to be alone with Phoenix and the piano.

Gloria murmured, nodding. "Yeah, I just got a message from my travel agent, and she said she can get me on a flight from Newark at ten. Last-second opening." While Gloria talked to him, her eyes never left the piano. "I'd just feel bad leaving you."

And believe me, I'd feel bad getting left. "Go on with your family, kiddo. Phoenix would want you with her mother and Serena. Somebody needs to help them manage, especially if there's press. Tabloids will be there looking for Phoenix and G-Ronn. Bet on it."

Gloria nodded, half-shrugging. Her lips thinned. "I know the shooting happened, and I know Sarge died, but . . . it's not real yet. The background music was so loud, we couldn't tell what was going on from the audience. A guy behind me said he heard gunshots, but I was like, 'Yeah, right.' The next thing we know, cops are everywhere. *Bam,* just like that. That's why Phoenix won't wake up, Carlos. She doesn't want to see Sarge put in the ground, so it'll never be real."

"That's part of it," Carlos said, but now that the Rosenkranz was here, he was certain the piano *was* responsible for Phoenix's condition, somehow. That knowledge filled him with dread, but there was hope nestled there, too.

"I can imagine the stories people will tell at the funeral," Gloria said. "Everybody has a Sarge story. You don't know the half of it. But he loved Phee more than life, he kept me in line when nobody else could, and I'm so mad about how he died, I feel like I need to kill somebody. You ever felt like that, Carlos?" Her voice was husky.

Carlos shook his head. He'd lost his grandparents to old age, a twenty-year-old roommate at Stanford to an unexplained cardiac arrest and three musician friends to AIDS, but he had never felt angry about death. Baffled sometimes. Sad, always. But never angry.

Gloria's eyes burned with fury as she gazed at the piano, as if she blamed it for Sarge's murder. "I hope you never do. I hope you never lose somebody to something as sick as this, because nothing will make this go away. No wonder Phee is so fucked up." Suddenly, Gloria was crying with clumsy, silent sobs, her face red. Gloria did not cry often. He could see that.

Carlos held her, but he didn't urge her not to cry. He would never understand why people told mourners to stop crying when crying was exactly what they needed. "She'll be back," Carlos whispered, but their mantra sounded like an empty phrase, an outright lie like the ones people always told when death left them with nothing else to say.

"What's that word in Spanish you always say to me? Be careful?" Gloria said, sniffling.

"*Cuidado.*"

"That's the one. *Extra* careful, Carlos. I'd keep my eye on this piano, if I were you."

Gloria sounded just like Phoenix then, the way sisters mirrored each other's cadences. It made him miss Phoenix more. "I will. Go catch your plane."

Carlos escorted Gloria out of the room, standing halfway through Phoenix's doorway while he watched her walk to the elevator. Carlos realized the hallway was empty. Where were the bodyguards? The guards switched off at night, but there was usually someone on watch. He didn't remember seeing the bodyguards when the movers finally arrived. He didn't see any staff, either. There were only closed doors on either side of the dignified hallway. Carlos fought off the idea that if he went from door to door, he would discover that no one was here except him and Phoenix. That idea cut too close to a reality he didn't want to know about.

When the elevator door hissed closed, Gloria was gone, too.

As soon as he was back inside Phoenix's room, Carlos's eyes went to the Rosenkranz, which was still where he'd left it, a relief. But he stared longer than he'd planned, because something was wrong already. The piano hadn't moved an inch from the wall, but . . .

Something *was* different, as soon as he'd turned his back. What?

Then, seeing the discolored piano keys, he knew: The piano's key cover was raised! The piano's stained, dirty keys were bared at him like teeth.

Carlos's cross fell to the carpeted floor without a sound. "Phee?" Carlos called, his heart prepared for either terror or jubilance. Could Phoenix be awake? Had she found it already?

Holding his breath, Carlos ran around the corner to the bedroom. There, Phoenix was still in bed where he'd last seen her, fully reclined. With a sheet pulled up to her chin, she looked like she could be sleeping. Except for those wide-open eyes.

"Shit," Carlos whispered. He turned back to the piano, a quick *gotcha* pivot. The key cover was still open, the horrible keys still visible.

Carlos tried to remember if he or Gloria had opened the key cover. Every time he concluded that neither of them had touched the piano— why *would* they?—his mind faltered. Had the cover always been open, then? Memory was tricky. An open key cover wasn't like Burnside's claims that the piano hopped from building to building, but the idea of the piano moving behind his back made Carlos's heart barrel. *This is going to be a long night if you're already having a meltdown, Carlito,* he thought.

The red recording light atop Finn's video camera near the door gave Carlos an inspiration. Still watching the piano from the corner of his eye, Carlos went to the video camera and checked the viewfinder. He saw a tiny black-and-white image of the Egyptian sofa, the love seat, the suite's window, shades pulled closed—and the piano, key cover up.

Carlos rewound, his heart drilling his breastbone, and he stopped when he saw himself hugging Gloria beside the piano. This time, he couldn't see the cover because they were blocking the camera's view.

Carlos fumbled for the headphones dangling from the camera so he could hear the sound. ". . . I'd keep my eye on this piano if I were you," Gloria's voice said.

"I will." Carlos repeated the words in unison with his videotaped image.

He and Gloria loomed huge as they walked toward the camera, and suddenly the room was empty. Finally, he could see it: The piano cover was *down,* just as he'd remembered. The piano keys were hidden from sight. Carlos paused the tape, startled, and looked up at the Rosenkranz a few yards across the room. The cover was still up.

"Finn's got you on tape, you sonofabitch," Carlos whispered, pressing his eye back to the rubber viewfinder to watch the tape play. After days of psychic phenomena that yielded maddeningly little videotaped evidence, he felt starved for something indisputable. Preserved.

So far, nothing. An empty room, a closed piano. The image remained fixed. Carlos waited, his heart pounding. This *couldn't* be right! He was only in the doorway for a few seconds, and he'd come right back. Watching the tape, he counted off: *Fifteen . . . sixteen . . . seventeen . . . eighteen . . .* He felt agitated as he watched, his feet squirming in his shoes. *Twenty-nine . . . thirty . . . thirty-one . . .*

Was it *impossible* to capture supernatural activity on tape? If so, no wonder—

Motion sprang from the tape as the piano's cover flew up. It opened with a *BAM* so loud in the headphones that Carlos cried out, tugging them off. His ears rang.

Mierda. Carlos sucked in his next breath, forcing his lungs open again. He had been standing right in the doorway when the cover flew up, and he couldn't have missed that racket. How could something have happened on the tape that hadn't happened in life?

Carlos gazed at the Rosenkranz again, and its keys leered at him. The optical illusion refused to go away when he blinked. The piano was *grinning.*

"J-Jesus help me," Carlos whispered, unaware he had made a sound. Carlos's eyes swept the carpet in search of the cross he'd dropped. When he didn't see it at first, he fell to all fours.

A noise came from deep inside the piano, like a scurrying mole, gone as soon as Carlos noticed it. Still, the unmistakable sound of long, scrabbling nails resonated across his clammy skin. Instinct made his frame tighten, ready to spring for the door. But he didn't. He kept his eyes on the floor and looked for his cross, sure it must be close.

It was. The cross was at his feet, an inch from his soles. *Any closer and you'd trip over it, boy,* Nana would say. Hardly blinking, his eyes trained on the piano, Carlos snatched up the small, simple gold cross and tightened his palm around it. He wished the cross had been blessed by a holy man. He aimed his cross at the piano, a shield.

"What do you want?" Carlos said to the Rosenkranz. *"Let Phoenix go."* The seven bravest words of his life. His mouth was so dry it hurt.

The piano clicked from somewhere low, near the pedals. The sound was barely audible, but it made Carlos scoot backward. *"Shit . . .* motherfu . . ." he whispered, before his breath left him.

Carlos Harris prided himself on knowing the rules for situations across cultures, but he had exhausted his knowledge of diplomacy with the Unseen. Seeing gentle, deceased *Abuela*'s dance in his aunt's living room had not prepared him for this piano. Breathing in heaves, Carlos fought for power over his thoughts to decide what to do. Should he try to call the psychics again? Press the emergency buzzer and bring a doctor to Phoenix's room?

Once we have the piano, Phoenix will show us what to do, the Queen Psychic had said.

He would go to Phoenix, he decided. Phoenix had no use for psychics or doctors now, but she might have a use for him.

In the bedroom, Carlos said a prayer of thanks when he saw that Phoenix was still breathing and didn't look worse even if she didn't look better. He didn't see any new flies, just the old ones that hadn't escaped the flypaper.

But he didn't feel thankful long. Standing closer to Phoenix, Carlos realized that her lips were as purple as her bruised jaw. When he touched her hand, her thin fingers and palm were cool. Too cool. He pressed his hand across her forehead, and her skin felt bloodless. Only then did Carlos notice that a cold spot had settled over Phoenix's bed, precisely where she lay and nowhere else. This one spot was a meat locker.

Phoenix was fading before his eyes.

"Phoenix?" Carlos said, shaking her. She didn't answer, not even a bob of her lips.

Carlos jabbed the red button above the bed marked CALL, because every instinct in him clamored that Phoenix was dying, and *right now*. Death was close.

No buzzer sounded, and no red light went on to comfort him that help was on the way.

Carlos picked up the telephone at Phoenix's bedside, which was so cold that he felt the warm pads of his fingertips cleaving to it. He didn't hear a sound, no matter which buttons he pushed on the keypad. He knew his cell phone would be useless before he pulled it from his back pocket, but he checked anyway: *Searching for signal,* it said.

"*Fuck.*" Carlos rubbed Phoenix's hand, then her frigid cheeks. It *had* been a mistake to bring the piano here! Something had happened. Something *was* happening. "Oh, *Dios*. Don't do this, Phee. Come back. I *know* you can come back."

Carlos disentangled Phoenix from her IV tube, ignoring the droplets of blood that spattered her pale arm when he pulled the needle from her skin. Then, he bundled her into his arms, surprised that she weighed so little, almost a ghost already. The lyrics to Nana's favorite gospel song beat through his veins with his rushing blood: *I was standing by the bedside of a neighbor / Who was just about to cross the swelling tide, / And I asked him if he would do me a favor; / Kindly take this message to the other side.*

He scrambled around the corner and through Phoenix's room, every fiber in him leading him toward her door. Yet, Carlos stopped himself midway across the room, glancing over his shoulder because he felt someone watching him from behind.

The Rosenkranz, of course. The piano was the first thing he saw when he turned his head.

The piano's cover was down again, but Carlos wasn't interested in the cover anymore. He was so steeped in fear that he no longer felt it, a calm he welcomed as he held the woman he loved and tried to decide how best to save her. Carlos closed his eyes. What now?

Phoenix had to be near the piano, or she would never be free. *Punto.*

That was what the psychic had said, in her own way, and that was what he had known when he asked Burnside if the movers could bring it to Phoenix right away. He could not take Phoenix away from the piano. Maybe a psychic's heart was buried in him, but Carlos knew that one thing like nothing else.

As Carlos's adrenaline burned off, he realized his arms were tired from carrying her. She was heavier than he thought. Two steps took him to the Egyptian-style sofa, and he rested her gently there, easing himself onto the space beside her. He touched her cheek again, and the lifelessness of her skin brought tears to his eyes.

"Phee, listen to me. Come back," he said, leaning closer to her. He kissed her forehead, her nose, then her lips, very lightly. "Stay with me, sweetheart. Stay."

Carlos's forehead brushed Phoenix's lips as he nuzzled her, and he froze. Her lips already seemed warmer than they had been when he kissed her the moment before. Startled, he tested her lips with his index finger.

Yes. There was warmth. Phoenix's soft bottom lip was hoarding warmth at its core, and Carlos felt the warmth strengthen when he nudged his finger against her lip. There was life in his touch. "Phee?" he said. "I know you're there. Come back."

Carlos kissed her lips again, pressing harder now, with a mission. The warm core of her bottom lip answered him, flaring. When he nibbled her top lip, he felt heat flush that one, too.

Suddenly, Phoenix's staring eyes seemed intent on him alone. Carlos beseeched her with his own eyes: *Come back, Phee. I'll help you through. You know I'm not going to leave you.*

Phoenix's newly dampened lips pulled apart, slowly. Willfully.

"Phee?" Carlos said. "Talk to me. I'll hear you, hon."

"Tuhh . . ." she whispered, a cool draft from her lungs.

He lowered his ear until her lips brushed his skin. "What, hon? Please tell me, *linda.*"

Then, he *did* hear, two words meant only for him.

"Touch me," Phoenix said.

*S*cott was dying.

Dying was much worse than its outcome, but how could she expect him to know that? No one should have to die in a madhouse, she thought, even if there were ways in which a madhouse was the perfect place to watch the world unravel before your eyes.

Manhattan State Hospital would be recited by biographers forever as the place where Scott Joplin drew his last breath. Considering that, she thought the hospital ought to be better up to the task. The Graphophone in the dayroom had no needle, the first of many flaws. The young man crying on the floor looked filthy, as if he hadn't been washed in days, and his gown smelled of urine. The sanitarium attendant was patronizing, which annoyed her because she could remember a time to come when *Uncle* was no longer an acceptable name for a man not related to you.

But to her, the worst injustice was that Scott was suffering so close to spring, knowing it was too early for one last sight of the peonies, irises and roses in bloom. This hospital on Ward's Island had lovely grounds—right along the East River, where excursion boats would be passing soon—but Scott had never been well enough to enjoy the view.

In the end, Scott caught her in a moment of confusion and pity. He was a scarecrow sitting at his Rosenkranz in an asylum, and she felt sorry for him. She loved him, which was reason enough. Her heart was multitudes. She had loved his soul before, and she would when they met again. She loved him now as much as she would when he took a new name, a future face. They belonged.

She could not resist him in the moment he needed her most. She never could.

As soon as her image appeared, his eyes clawed for her. He had prayed to see her.

"F-Freddie . . ." Scott begged from his chair, struggling to speak as he looked up at her, his longing not yet dead in his eyes even if his body was frail. "Take me."

She was glad Lottie had sent the piano. The piano would have come to him whether Lottie sent it or not, but the gesture meant more this way. It didn't matter that Scott couldn't play; Lottie wanted to know something was there to remind Scott of what his life had looked like.

She shimmered for him, showing him a glimpse of his light to come, but she could not escort him. Leaping was always done alone. That was the way of it. The *alone* part was the reason no one wanted to go.

She wished he could use her memories to help him know what the Leap was, afterward. He would laugh at himself. Most people knew to laugh, at the very end, even if they had never believed there was laughter where they were going, but Scott was too mad at life to let go an inch of it. He should have left weeks ago.

The beautiful piano had brought him the joy Lottie intended, but it aroused his anger, too. He might live two or three weeks on his new anger. His dying would be all the longer.

"Do you want me to help you play?" she said.

She spoke the words of her own accord. She knew she shouldn't, but she did. If he played, he would be laughing sooner, and she wanted to see her beloved laugh. That was all.

And the *look* in Scott's eyes! Rapture. He might have looked this way when his mother pressed her rough palms over his eyes on the porch and said she had a surprise waiting for him in the house. A *special* surprise, she said, which had made Scott dream as big as licorice or a new pair of shoes. When you were poor, a new pair of shoes was Christmas Day. Their family had been poor as far back as anyone could remember.

Head bent down, Scott had peeked beyond his mothers' fingers and seen tracks across the packed-dirt floor. Even then, he couldn't let himself imagine it. Mama had bought him a *piano*. A part of Scott Joplin would always be stuck in that day, because his mother had changed his life. The old Scotty had died, and a new one was born. His mother had resurrected him.

She would be Scott's mother today, she decided. She would change his life, at the end.

"Yes. Yes, I w-want to play." Scott's desire to play baked from him.

The sanitarium attendant, a not-unpleasant man named Garth Mobley, wanted to move Scott back to his room and hush all the racket near so many insane and dying. Why torment an old cripple with an instrument he can't play?

But she wouldn't let him interfere. She was tired of Garth Mobley's interruptions, well-intentioned or not, so she dashed to him on a dust mote and whispered just enough to preoccupy his mind with worries about his father's worsening cough. She made Garth Mobley remember how much his father had given him, and Mobley was so overwhelmed by his love for the old man that he vowed to be a better son. For a precious moment or two, the attendant forgot about the man sitting at the piano and wandered away to mop up the pool of urine on the floor.

She and Scott were alone, for a moment.

She leaned over Scott, her gentle warmth draping his shoulder. She took one of his gnarled hands into hers, then the other, and raised them back to their berth on the piano keys. Scott knew, then. She felt the dribble of awareness come to him. He understood that the Rosenkranz had no heart of its own, only blind devotion. If he played this piano with her as one, she might not be able to untangle herself in time. The Rosenkranz would do its best to pull her down with him when Scott took his Leap.

But she was not afraid to be bound to another's soul at his Leap. Love in death was the truest form, and death was nothing new to her. She had been visiting Scott here so long, she had forgotten their other names, their other times. A gnawing sense of duty and propriety had kept her from entangling herself with Scott, but one must always question the concept of duty. Or propriety. Or order. What did those concepts have to do with her? Had they ever?

She was *here* now. That was enough.

"Freddie . . . wait," Scott said.

His unselfishness only made her more determined.

"*Shhhh,*" she said. Her flesh form melted as her hands slipped inside of his, a feeling like wading into lukewarm water. No, not water—*jelly.* The feeling was not entirely pleasant, because it was not natural. She would not be able to stay long. She felt his body trying to expel her, instinct. His body choked her. "Play, Scott. Use my hands to play."

Scott was infatuated with his fingers, wiggling them before his face like an infant. "Dear heart . . . how . . . ?"

Phee, I know you're there. Come back.

"Play, Scott. *Play.*" She hurt, suddenly, and she hadn't felt pain in a long time. She couldn't tell if the pain was from being crowded inside

Scott, or from somewhere else. Without skin, it was hard to judge where pain came from. The pain *might* have come when she heard the phantom's voice calling for someone named Phee.

Finally, Scott played. He played more crisply than she did, more slowly. He held his hands higher, more rigid in his adherence to form and technique. Even now, when he was engaged only with himself and his dying, he played with an audience in mind.

And the music! Music was the only language the living and the dead shared in common. Scott played one note for every joy that had escaped him in life, and the sound of his joy became hers. His playing made her remember hearing "Maple Leaf Rag" for the first time, riding her bicycle past Mr. Garrison's farm in Little Rock, and how it had made her skid to a stop to listen through his open parlor window. *Those rags are the devil's music,* Papa tried to tell her, the first time she knew with certainty that her father didn't always know the truth.

Scott should have Lottie play this at his funeral. He should make Lottie promise.

"That's *old*. I'm tired of that one, Uncle," the attendant said.

The attendant had escaped her notice because of the music, but the sound of his voice so jarred her concentration that Scott's hands nearly cast her out. Scott raced on to *Treemonisha,* and her effort to follow him that far was heroic. She was slipping away from him.

She was weak, she remembered. This was the price for appearing to him in a woman's form, manipulating the lights and shadows to create the effect before his eyes. She had to leave him now. In a blink of his eyes, his Leap would be done.

"I'll be back soon, Scott," she said.

And she was. *Soon* arrived immediately.

She felt the passage of time, but not in minutes and hours and days. She felt her *absence* dragging behind her, and it unsettled her. Two weeks or more of Scott's time may have passed, and she had never been freed. She was still tethered to Scott and his waiting.

She should not be here. She had another place to go.

This time, when she saw Scott, he was lying in his bed in the hospital room he shared with a man continuously reliving the Battle of Gettysburg, the journey he'd made as a young man to the true gates of Hell.

Today, the second bed was empty. Scott was mostly unconscious, muttering occasionally, but otherwise still.

Scott had not made his Leap. His dying was horrible in its endlessness.

Lottie sat at Scott's side, primly dressed, reading her *Harper's*. She was already wearing her gloves, because the doctors had phoned to tell her Scott wouldn't make it to morning, but the doctors had been wrong again. Scott had a stallion's spirit.

But Lottie knew this was the day. She and Lottie both knew.

The duet on the Rosenkranz had tired her too much to show herself to Scott in a flesh form—and that wouldn't be polite, not with Lottie here in her place as the grieving wife—but she brushed herself across Scott's hand so he would feel her. Touching was its own language. The visit was easier now than it had been at the piano. Scott was so much closer to where he was going, she reached him with barely a thought.

Because he was so close to his Leaping, Scott's spirit spoke to her while his eyes and lips remained closed. They were more alike than different, now.

I'm sorry, Freddie. The piano won't let you go. You'll have to burn it.

A bold idea, but it was impossible, of course. She could no more burn up his Rosenkranz than she could make the roof of his dying place fly away, or make Lottie walk across the ceiling. Hands with skin were needed to burn a piano.

But that wasn't all of it. As long as Scott's soul was restless, the Rosenkranz was his. The Rosenkranz would remember Scott's sorrows long after his flesh was gone. *She* had made the decision to play the piano with him, to tangle their souls. She had known the risks.

"It might let me go if you weren't afraid," she said.

I'm sorry. I don't know how to stop being afraid, Freddie.

"I've told you about the laughter? And the light?"

They've forgotten me already, and I'm not even gone.

No matter how much she tried, she couldn't force him to dwell on the next place, only the last. That was sad, but she tried to indulge him.

"Didn't I tell you about Broadway and the Pulitzer? The biographers?"

Why couldn't I have seen more? Why did I have so little?

"This was your ride, Scott. Everybody's is different."

But Freddie . . . does it matter? Will we matter?

The source of Scott's desperation became so obvious to her that she was angry with herself for taking so long to think of it. How could she call herself a gardener and not remember?

"I can let you hear," she said, elated.

She knew exactly how to do it. Someone else, not Scott, had given her the same elixir when it was the only language that could reach her. She remembered a rolling voice, a shining scalp. She remembered the loving and healing. Part of her remembered Sarge very well.

Where in the world would she begin? How should she season her stew?

She didn't use Scott's ears, because his ears were failing him. She gave Scott *her* ears, *her* future memories, searching in lightning speed. The soul could hear so much better anyway. Especially music. The soul heard music best.

She gave him Miles Davis and Duke Ellington. She gave him B. B. King, Otis Redding and Marvin Gaye. She gave him Mahalia Jackson and Shirley Caesar, Miriam Makeba and Jelly Roll Morton, Sly & the Family Stone, Gil Scott-Heron and Louis Armstrong. She gave him Dizzy Gillespie and James Brown. She let him hear Paul Robeson singing "Ol' Man River," and Billie Holiday singing "Strange Fruit." She let him hear "Respect" sung the way only Aretha could. She gave him Earth Wind & Fire and Arturo Sandoval, Al Green and Eric Clapton, Ray Charles, George Gershwin and Ella Fitzgerald.

She added a few Sarge hadn't thought about, because she had her own tastes: She spiced her elixir with Gonzalo Rubalcaba, Nina Simone and Lauryn Hill. She let him hear Tito Puente, Mario Bauzá and Celia Cruz. She gave him Hossam Ramzy, Ladysmith Black Mambazo, Carlos Santana and the Black-Eyed Peas. She gave him Bob Marley, Baaba Maal, Wynton Marsalis, Led Zeppelin and the Mississippi Mass Choir. Because he loved opera, she gave him Roland Hayes, Marian Anderson, Leontyne Price and Kathleen Battle. For fun, she threw in Run-DMC, Alicia Keys, OutKast and Robert Randolph & the Family Band.

It grieved her to neglect so many others, but there wasn't time for everyone. The rest could wait. He would know all of it soon enough.

Last, she let him hear Phoenix. That music came from a different place in her memory, because most of it had yet to be written. But she heard it, and so did he.

Scott Joplin's face didn't change, but she felt his soul's glow.

"You matter, Scott," she said, a whisper.

Five days from now, the United States would enter the Great War, and James Reese Europe's Harlem Hellfighters would spread their orchestrated ragtime marching style like apple seeds, showcasing Negro music to the world. Jim Europe would survive the bullets and gas of the war front, but Herbert Wright would stab him to death with his penknife a few years later, in a dressing room back home. Such things happened sometimes; buds were cut down before they fully bloomed. But a bright, scrappy fifteen-year-old boy in New Orleans who loved Scott's rags even if he would never meet him was already gaining a reputation with a cornet he'd learned to play after he was sent to a home for wayward boys for shooting a pistol in the air to celebrate the New Year.

Scott knew things about the boy's future the boy could not, so when Scott heard that trumpet about to be loosed on the world, Louis Armstrong clarified everything. The living world wouldn't hear the song for more than a decade, but to Scott, Armstrong's feisty horn on "West End Blues" was Gideon's clarion call.

Suddenly, Scott could make out laughter down the way, where he couldn't see past all the light. He was close, and he was ready. At last. Hallelujah.

She was ready, too. She could Leap with him to his light and sacrifice some of her own. Didn't people in love do that every day?

Do you feel me where you are, Phee? I love you. Come back to me.

Somewhere, she still had skin. Somewhere, her lips were afire. And her neck. Someone was calling her. A voice was calling her name. Music was calling her.

Do you feel this, Phee? Or this?

"Find the kerosene, Lottie," Scott said, as best he could. "Burn that piano to Hell."

With one last gasp of sweet oxygen, Scott Joplin made his Leap.

All of the terrain Carlos's fingers and lips grazed on Phoenix's body grew warm, her blood surging to her skin's surface to meet him. He watched color return, creamy brown chasing the trail of his fingers across the pale snow of her neck, her collarbone, her chest. Digging her out. He hadn't realized how pale she was until he began repainting her with his hands.

"I'm here, Phee. I hear," he said, propping her upright. He unzipped her gown and let it fall across her shoulders while she dangled in his arms. Her eyes were no longer open, her eyelids resting in a different kind of sleep. Her eyes had thawed, too.

Phoenix tasted freshly bathed, new. Carlos suckled her neck, then her shoulder, and her skin flared beneath him. With one eye on the Rosenkranz, Carlos laid his palm on her cool breast as her gown slipped to her waist. Her nipple nudged against his palm, swollen. Warm again.

Carlos didn't like the piano watching as he touched her, nor the camera, but he would not risk her life because of discomfort. He lay Phoenix to rest, his mouth sliding over her breast as his head fell against her. He moistened her with his tongue, then he sucked as if he were nursing, gathering as much of her skin into his mouth as he could. Her breast nearly vanished inside of him. He warmed her other breast with his hand, gently kneading, his thumb pondering the solid ridge at its peak.

"Do you feel this, Phoenix?" he whispered in her ear.

Phoenix's mouth didn't respond, but her nipples spoke for her. He turned her on her stomach, massaging her graceful tracts of skin, feeling the spots across her ribs where her bones were extruding more than they should, her pliant thighs, the dense mound of her buttocks. Every part of Phoenix that Carlos could see, he touched and tasted. He took his time.

He didn't think about his own arousal until his jeans pinched, painful. His arousal felt urgent in a way it never had. She needed him, and he needed her.

"Phoenix?" he said.

Phoenix moaned, from far away. She still wasn't back. Not quite.

Easing his hand between her thighs, Carlos tested Phoenix gently with his index finger, only halfway inside her, and found her damp and ready. She also felt too cool, because he had missed a spot. Knowing she was waiting for him, Carlos felt his crotch tighten into a knot.

"God help me, Phoenix, tell me what to do," he said. "Tell me." He was unsnapping his fly, relishing the relief of easing pressure his zipper gave as it fell, tooth by tooth. Freeing him.

"Tell me what to do," Carlos said, but there was no sound from her. Phoenix's sleeping face made him doubt. He saw a naked girl unconscious in his arms, forbidden again.

But Carlos's body commanded him, even if Phoenix could not.

Carlos knew, body and soul.

*H*e was making love to her. She felt his heat inside of her; exploring, sowing.

Each time she forgot him, the tide of sensation rolled back over her, rocking her. Each time he touched somewhere new, she remembered. When his heat draped her from her head to her thighs, reminding her of how precious her skin was, she almost remembered his name and gasped it aloud. She almost opened her eyes again; to see, this time, not just to stare. Almost.

The wall was the only thing keeping her from him. The wall appeared with the sound of her own voice, from forever ago: *Was it okay?*

She didn't want any knowledge beyond those three words, so she retreated.

Until she felt him inside her again, tilling and plowing. He wouldn't let her run away. Now, his fingertips were kneading her scalp, pulling her closer still. Closer.

He stretched her to her capacities, forced her body to meld itself to him, hugging tight. He flooded her, drained her and flooded her again. Her nipples and clitoris dueled for her attention beneath his touch, then they joined forces to take her deeper into her skin, a maelstrom.

Was it okay?

She had not Leaped with Scott. She was expanding, floating nowhere near the laughter and light of his transformation. What was her name this time? Why was she so afraid?

"I love you, Phee. Can you hear me?"

Carlos. She knew his name, then, unalterably. She missed him. She nudged the wall to see how much it would yield without crushing her.

You like Magnums, motherfucker? The words jolted her, made her try to flee again.

But this time, Phoenix's body would not allow her to escape for even a blink. She soared, her body piloting her, afire in too many places to count.

The truth came when she heard her own voice in a whispered roar.

Daddy's gone.

The truth kicked her senseless, and there was no respite now. No solace.

Daddy's gone.

While Carlos's weight bucked and quivered on top of her, the truth made Phoenix's eyes fly open while she wailed to raise the dead.

CHAPTER TWENTY-SEVEN

Something was pinching Phoenix's lungs, forcing her to gasp for air, and every breath was a sob. It was the worst feeling she had ever known.

"It's all right, Phee. It's all right, hon. I'm here. I'm here, *linda*. I'm here."

Carlos's nakedness was hot on top of her. Seeing Carlos erased her confusion and pain for an instant, and she was so grateful that she hugged his neck hard enough to nearly fling them to the floor. His striking crown of dreadlets rested across her chest as he held her.

He pulled his flesh out of hers, very slowly, and she smelled a potent blend of cologne, perspiration and their bodies' shared juices. Despite everything else, her stomach flipped. Just as she had promised him, she remembered every glancing touch. Phoenix kissed Carlos's hair, clinging to it. She kissed his neck. Her skin sang with his memory, soothed. Her skin's pleasure dulled her grief enough so she could catch her breath.

"How long?" she whispered.

"Five days. We've been worried." Carlos looked older, with lines by his eyes. He looked more like Scott now, the way she remembered him.

"He's dead?" A sob nearly overcame her last word, because she knew.

"Yes, Phee. I'm sorry. Kai, too. I'm so sorry."

Phoenix succumbed to her sobs. By the time she remembered Carlos again, he had said nothing but *I'm sorry* for twenty minutes, sometimes in English, sometimes in Spanish. *Lo siento, Phoenix.* Sometimes he sobbed, too. Carlos's face was shiny with his tears as he reminded her of the things she should be grateful for. Serena and Ronn were fine. The kids from the choir were fine. She might have lost more of her family that day. Sarge died knowing she was safe.

When she nearly threw up, he forced her to take sips from a protein drink. The bitter chocolate taste made her feel sick, but she drank it because Carlos wanted her to. He didn't know she didn't like chocolate yet, but he would learn. Besides, she needed the protein, because she felt too weak to stand. She had nearly died, after all.

"Where were you?" Carlos said. "With Scott?"

"He's gone now," she said. But she couldn't mourn Scott, because his leaving was long overdue. Not like Sarge. Her father was gone early, ripped away.

"Will you stay here, Phee? Is it over?"

Phoenix was about to say *I hope so* when she saw the Rosenkranz. The blighted piano had been mauled by its journey, trailing her. It had never given up.

Tremors took control of her limbs.

"The psychic, Johnita, told us to bring the piano to you," Carlos said, wrapping his arms around her more tightly. "I'm sorry to scare you. She said you would know what to do."

Phoenix almost laughed, but it came out as a sob. She was so tired, the idea of *doing* anything made her cry. How gracious of the Queen Pychic to make that decree! Phoenix knew what to do, all right. She just doubted that she had the strength, or that the piano would allow it.

"If it scares you, I'll take you where you can't see it," Carlos said.

"My bed, please." That would be enough, for now. All she wanted was rest.

"I don't think we should go back there, Phee. It was so cold—"

"That doesn't matter. I'm here now." She should have died in that bed, but she hadn't. She could die anywhere. The bed wasn't to blame. She needed to lie down beneath her sheets.

Without further argument, Carlos lifted her until her bare feet dangled over his arm. He took her closer to the piano at first, and she closed her eyes when they walked past because the sight of it exhausted her. She didn't open her eyes until she felt Carlos take her around a corner.

This was a bedroom, and except for the flypaper, it was lovely. The Rosenkranz was safely out of her sight.

After Carlos helped her put on her gown to keep her warm, he picked up the telephone and pushed her buzzer, trying to reach someone. Phoenix held Carlos's hand so he wouldn't consider leaving her room. He wouldn't like what he would find if he went searching for her doctor, or for her nurse.

"This is bullshit. I haven't been able to reach anybody since that piano got here," he said, frustrated. "I'm trying to catch Gloria. She's on her way to the airport."

"Where's Gloria going?" Phoenix said. She missed her cousin. She remembered things from where she'd been, but the here and now was beyond her. Every small detail was a mystery.

"Atlanta." Carlos held her face. "Your father's funeral is tomorrow, Phee."

Phoenix didn't know how much time she lost to sobbing after that. The word *funeral* made it impossible to think of conversation, even about the piano. Especially about the piano.

Sleeping was the only way to stop crying, so she slept between her questions to Carlos and his gentle answers as he lay beside her in the tiny twin-sized bed, holding her. While Carlos stroked her, she sipped at the knowledge, then slept to forget. This went on for hours, but the time passed as minutes to her.

When Phoenix woke up again, she was shivering.

Her fingers flew to her forearms, where she pinched her biceps and skin, clinging to them.

You like Magnums, motherfucker? The memory of an explosion rang in her ears, fresh as new, and old tears she hadn't shed before falling asleep reemerged, still warm. Phoenix wiped her face with her tears and held her cheeks a long time, stifling a sob. Her throat hurt. Crying made its own pain, and she was tired of hurting. She was too weak to hurt like this.

She saw Carlos's sleeping face across from her, at the edge of her pillow. In sleep, his assuring mask was gone.

Phoenix leaned over, lightly kissing his lips. "Rest, baby," she whispered.

She didn't want to wake Carlos. Bless him for being here, but she needed time free of his stroking and coddling. As hard as it was to return to her skin and the memory of the Osiris, she had other things to remember. More pressing things.

You've got to be about the revolution, Phee.

It was 4:00 A.M., the digital clock on her night table said. Six hours since Carlos had woken her up the first time. Six hours wasted.

Moving gently, Phoenix slipped from beneath Carlos's arm and climbed from the bed, her bare feet sinking into the carpet. She felt all of her blood rush to her legs, and they tingled, nearly buckling at the knees because she hadn't walked for days. When dizziness made her sway, she steadied herself with her hand against the mattress, her eyes squeezed shut.

Please let me go. Not now. Please let it be over.

Carlos had forced down that protein drink, but she was still unaccustomed to her skin, she realized. Doubt and hurt tried to force Phoenix back into bed with Carlos, but she made herself keep standing. She might already have slept through her chance to be free.

Once Phoenix took her first unsteady step, the others came more easily as her legs remembered how to walk. She made her way lightly across the floor, soundless, batting away the hanging flypaper that brushed the side of her face. Flies always came where Death was near.

All of the pieces were in place: The New York asylum. The Rosenkranz. Her beloved alone at her bedside. Her death would follow Scott's, a coda. If she didn't change the last of her destiny the way she had changed Scott's on his deathbed, today was her dying day.

Carlos had interrupted the momentum of her dying, but today was the day. Her obituary was already written somewhere: *Eccentric rocker-turned–R&B singer Phoenix Smalls, dead from shock at twenty four after seeing her father gunned down, clipped before she could fly.* Such things happened with musicians, since their music took them so close to the laughter and light.

Not that she was afraid to die. She'd been places she didn't have words for that made all that drama silly, even if knowing that couldn't keep her from hurting over Sarge. The dying part wouldn't bother her the way her death would bother Carlos. And Mom. And Gloria and Serena.

She had to keep on living to spare them the pain. Her family had enough tears.

And mostly, her dying felt *wrong*. Scott didn't need the piano anymore. Scott's ghost was gone. She'd felt Scott Leap, and the Leap was clean, not halfway. He was free, like Sarge. Scott had breathed out his anger at the end—she'd felt it expel in a hot wind—so whatever anger was still locked in his Rosenkranz didn't belong here. It was a relic that didn't know its curse was gone. Like all antiques, the piano had outlived its owner.

Her escape should be clean, too. It was only right.

Holding the wall for support, Phoenix peeked around the corner to the other side of her suite. The piano hadn't moved, a dark spot against the wall. Even moonlight didn't reach it.

Without the spell of its novelty to draw her to it, Phoenix felt repelled. The piano didn't give off any odor she could detect, but it *should*. This piano was rotting in a way other pianos didn't, and it wasn't just the wood going sour. The Rosenkranz was rotting because of what lived inside of it. The Rosenkranz had been born angry, before Scott ever crossed its path.

No wonder she had recognized it when she was so young! It had been sent to find her, still trying to wed her to Scott, in death. Still hunting the glimmer of Freddie that lived in her.

But not after tonight. *Ashes to ashes, amen.*

Phoenix saw Gloria's pearl-colored lighter on the coffee table and snatched it up. *You've always got my back, cuz,* she thought. But she would need more than a lighter.

Dropping the lighter into the large pocket of her gown, Phoenix fumbled with the doors in her suite, opening a closet, then the door to the empty hallway before she found the bathroom hidden in an alcove. When she flipped on the light switch, the makeup mirror's brightness dazed her. Slowly, the room unveiled its marble floor, modernist sculptures and well-maintained plants, Ronn's gift to her. Sanctuary.

Phoenix glanced at herself in the mirror, but only once. She was so glad she remembered, she didn't mind that her hair hadn't been combed in days and that she could hardly see Sarge in her face because the lights made her so pallid. She was here, and she remembered.

I'm Phoenix Smalls. The knowledge was electrifying.

The cabinet under the sink was empty, but her family members had left things on the counter she thought she could use: Nail polish remover. A small bottle of alcohol. A brown bottle of hydrogen peroxide. *Something* would work. She had options now.

When Phoenix went back to the dark living room, she was glad the piano was waiting. Disappearing was the least of what it could do.

"If you'd been gone, I would have found you again," Phoenix whispered. "Believe it."

Something scuttled inside the piano, barely plucking one of the strings. The high G.

Plaintive, almost simpering.

Phoenix stood over the piano, gazing at the gaps where keytops were missing on the keys, brown as coffee. In the light from the bathroom, the piano's case looked flaky to her, like it could rub off on her hands. She would have to touch it, to move it. She couldn't burn it here.

Pushing the piano was an ordeal. Phoenix was so enamored of her newly restored muscle and skin that she'd forgotten she was five-foot-seven and 130 pounds, so the piano outweighed her. People her size did not move pianos alone, she remembered.

Not that she would let that stop her.

Phoenix leaned her back and tailbone against the end of the piano, pushing off the wall with her bare feet. The piano ignored her. It *couldn't* be this heavy, could it? Could it treat her like she wasn't here, like the spirit she'd been in Scott's world? Phoenix gave another push, throwing herself back hard against the piano.

The piano inched forward. The carpeting in the living room wasn't as plush as the carpeting in her bedroom area, or she would have failed before she began, but she felt it move. Apparently, there were wheels hidden down there, and she'd given them some momentum.

Already panting, Phoenix gazed across the length of the suite, which seemed to have grown. The expanse between where she stood and the door to the hallway—the *carpeted* hallway, she remembered—looked like an odyssey. Not to mention the journey to the elevator, which could take twice as long. At this rate, she would be moving this piano until daylight.

So you'd better get effing started, she thought, and pushed against the piano again.

Phoenix's crawl across the suite with the piano took twenty minutes. Her body had felt weak before, but there were times now she nearly fell. Her wet skin clung to her gown's Egyptian cotton. She was breathing as hard as she would be if she were running. But the piano was moving. She wasn't supposed to be able to move it, but she could.

"Phee, what are you doing?"

Carlos sounded breathless too. He had bounded from bed, still naked. His eyes were so wide, he must have been afraid she had vanished into the air. And it was almost true. Almost.

"I'm getting rid of this," she said.

"Why?"

"Because I don't want to set the building on fire. People might get hurt. The piano would like that."

For a moment, Carlos's face stayed frozen, as if he hadn't heard her. Then he understood, shaking his head as if he was trying to clear his ears. "You want to *burn* it? Wait. Stop." He disappeared into her bedroom, and when he came back he was climbing into his jeans. He sounded groggier than she did, gently taking her arm to pull her toward him. "Hon, wait . . . You're hurting yourself, Phee."

"I have to burn it, Carlos. *Tonight.*"

This was another reason she had left him sleeping, she remembered. Carlos had a convincing way about him. Already, his soothing voice was plying her, making her want to rest. "*Shhhhh.* Yes, *linda, si,* I agree with you, the piano should be burned. Fine. We'll get movers to take it to a dump somewhere and—"

"It has to be tonight. It has to be me."

"Why?"

"Because *this* is the day, Carlos. *This* is the day I die. I should be dead already."

Carlos's face moved closer to hers, fully illuminated by the light from the bathroom. His eyes were so tired they were red, but they were alert on her. "What do you mean?"

"You know what I mean."

Carlos's jaw clenched, hardening. He did know.

"Why do *you* have to do burn it? Let me do it," Carlos said quietly.

"Because Scott told me to. He gave me permission, and I'm the one who has to do it. He asked Lottie to, but she couldn't understand him. Anyway, you know Lottie—she didn't have the heart. She donated it to the hospital and kept the Steinway—she'd never liked the Rosenkranz in her house, even if she never said so—but she could never destroy anything of Scott's. It wasn't in her. Everything was lost *after* Lottie died."

Phoenix realized she was babbling when she saw the look on Carlos's face. There was a lot more she wanted to tell him about Scott and Lottie, but she could rescue the present, not the past. Carlos's eyes were retreating, she realized. He was pulling away. He didn't want to know.

"We should take the piano to the alley, so no one will get hurt," Phoenix said. "Scott found it in an alley. Remember? That's where it belongs."

"Why would I remember that? Hon, let me find your doctor. If you'll just stay right here, I can go look—"

"There isn't anyone here tonight, Carlos. You already know that, and you know what it means. Don't pretend you're anyplace you've ever been."

Carlos's face grew stony. "What I *really* know is that you've suffered a trauma. You have to appreciate that, Phee. A trauma like this can trigger strange ideas. Strange thoughts."

"You, of all people, know I'm not crazy." She pitied Carlos for his fear.

Carlos raised his palm. "I'm not using that word—that's an ugly word. But you might be confused. I'm willing to listen to you if you're willing to listen to me."

She closed her eyes, praying for patience. It was bothersome to have to explain things. "If *you're* right and I'm just confused, then worst-case scenario is, we drag this piano out to an alley and I light it on fire and burn it to Hell. If *I'm* right, worst-case scenario is, I go back to sleep like nothing is up and I never open my eyes again. If you were me, which one would you choose?"

Carlos blinked. He didn't have to answer.

"That's what I thought," Phoenix said. "So are you going to help me move this or not? If we don't hurry, it'll be gone. We might not find it again."

Carlos stared down at the piano, and his repulsion was naked on his face. He didn't move.

"It scares you," she said. "Even if you don't know what to call it."

Carlos nodded. Slowly, his fingers became fists. "It scares the *shit* out of me, Phee."

How could she explain? Scott was very bitter, at the end, and bitterness had a long life. All curses began with bitterness, with fear just underneath. She might be able to capture it in music if she wrote a song about it, but for now she didn't have the language, either.

"You don't have to do this," she said. His face told her he loved her enough to stay with her although he was afraid. He was steadfast in his devotion, like always.

"*Shhhhh*. Grab your end," Carlos said. He surveyed the piano, then squeezed past it to the other side of the doorway, to the hall. "You push, I'll pull."

His plan sounded like a miracle in the making.

*W*hen Carlos touched the piano, he felt something slither beneath his palm, an aberration the size of a goldfish scurrying inside the wood that made his hand jerk away. Carlos somehow stifled his cry, plugging his throat just as he was about to vomit.

Phoenix was right. He knew what the piano was. He was the Catholic-slash-Baptist boy who'd stopped believing in God only because he wanted to stop believing in Hell, and tonight some shard of Hell was at his fingertips, beyond recantation. *You're both already dead, so what's the rush? Somewhere, two or three centuries have passed. No one remembers you ever were.*

Carlos's heart beat a flood through his veins as he grasped the piano hard—one hand hooked around its jutting back corner, the other behind its trunklike, carved leg.

"On three," he said to Phoenix. "One . . . two . . ."

Before he reached three, the piano bucked up half an inch, scooting toward him with enough force to land on the tips of his shoes, pinching his toes. Carlos pulled free, shutting off valves in his brain to ward off the panic looking for a way to escape in him. Phoenix wasn't strong enough to lift the piano that high from the floor! Perspiration drenched his palms.

"That wasn't me," Phoenix said. "But keep pulling. At least it's going the right way."

Carlos envied Phoenix for wherever she'd been, because the peace she had brought back with her was astonishing. He no longer knew her, because she had outgrown him already. He couldn't pretend he wasn't afraid. On the plane with Phoenix to New York, he'd remembered the Musicians' Plane Crash Club, wondering if he would spend his last moment of life staring out of an oval airplane window while the world came crashing in, a victim of Phoenix's providence. The *idea* had flipped his stomach. He'd landed safely, but her tragedy had been waiting all the same.

"Ready?" Phoenix said. He realized she had waited to give him time to steel himself.

Wood flaked off the piano against Carlos's palms, damp and scaly, but he held on. "Yes," he said, tightening his hands, a chokehold. "On three again. One . . . two . . . *three* . . ."

Carlos pulled. This time, with coordinated effort, the piano slid forward, compelled. Carlos thought he heard a fleshy slapping sound as something writhed beneath his hands again, but his mind locked, never wavering: *One . . . two . . . three*. His world collapsed into numbers. *One, two, three*. The order never changed. Numbers were his prayer.

Carlos and Phoenix repeated their exercise twenty-four times without resting, until they reached the elevators at the end of the hall. The piano plowed a wide wake on the carpet, but on the marble floor near the elevator, the piano moved as if it were weightless before coasting still. The chandelier in the hall cast delicate, dancing sparks on the piano's leathery case.

Phoenix pushed the DOWN button for the cargo elevator, and the button filled with promising light. *I hope these elevators are working now,* Carlos thought. The maintenance men who had helped the movers were long gone like everyone else. He didn't want to know that, but he did. Gloria's last-minute flight, the psychics' exhaustion, the movers' hurry to leave. Everyone had a reason for not being here tonight. Tonight was Phoenix's alone, and his.

"What's your plan?" Carlos said, wiping perspiration from his face with his arm. His arms and back burned from the strain. He wished the movers had left their hand truck.

Phoenix spoke through heaving breaths. "We get it into an elevator. We t-take it out of the building to the alley. I light it up."

"What are you planning to burn it with?"

Phoenix reached into her pocket and brought out a lighter, then gave him three bottles. Nail polish remover, alcohol and hydrogen peroxide. Carlos frowned. "This isn't enough, not to destroy it the way you want. This'll only put it in a bad mood."

"What, then?"

"Let me find a storeroom. Some kind of cleanser might work."

"OK, but hurry," Phoenix said, and he saw her hug herself tight, swaddling herself.

"What's wrong?" Carlos said, but he knew when he touched her shoulder. Her skin was ice again, so cold that it had cooled the fabric of her gown. "*Shit*, Phoenix. When did this start?" He hugged her, wrapping his body against her in every place they could touch.

"As s-soon as we got out of my room. This must be how it happened before, when I was d-dying." Her voice was matter-of-fact, so her chattering teeth were from the cold, not fear. If she had to die, she wouldn't mind. But *he* did. *He* minded.

"Why didn't you tell me?" he said.

She shrugged. "We're already going as fast as we can. Get what you need."

"Forget it. We'll use what we have," he said, taking his place at the piano's helm again, ready to help steer it onto the elevator when it arrived. "Always tell me when you're sick, Phee."

Only the elevator's *ding* made him realize he had almost called her Freddie.

*T*he elevator lurched down, in fits and starts. When Phoenix felt her mind drifting, the elevator slowed, then stopped, swinging from its cables. When she snapped to alertness again, reminding herself of her mission—*We have to take this piano outside so I can burn it*—the elevator whirred its descent. She might be weak, but the Rosenkranz was weaker, exiled. She hoped so, anyway. For her family's sake. For Carlos's sake.

Second floor. First floor. Finally, the basement. The doors opened an inch and stopped.

Carlos cursed and went to the doors, prying. He pulled at the doors with all his strength, groaning loudly, as if the building was burning above them. The Rosenkranz would love to take the building with it, where prized possessions were strewn everywhere; and the building next door, where families were sleeping. The Rosenkranz wanted blood on its keys again.

We have to take this piano outside so I can burn it.

Suddenly, the elevator doors gave, nearly stealing Carlos's balance when they fell open. He shoved the piano forward to hold the doors open on one end, then he slipped out of the elevator. Phoenix wanted to leave the elevator, too, but she was too enamored of the feeling of the wall behind her, a support. She needed to rest. Maybe she could curl on the floor for a minute. No more than two.

"*Dios mio,* you're kidding me," Carlos said, as soon as he stepped out and surveyed the basement. She hoped his voice was glad, but she couldn't tell. All she could see was the stained concrete of the basement floor. They didn't have time to start again or go somewhere else. Next time, the elevator would not obey her.

"A fucking hand truck," Carlos said. He vanished for a moment, then he produced a red dolly with working wheels that rattled across the floor while he pulled it. "Our lives just got easier, Phee. Hold on. We're almost there."

The dolly helped, but not as much as she had hoped. Even with the hand truck, the piano's weight still needed two sets of arms. Phoenix's bare feet were so cold, she could no longer feel them. Her fingers were nearly useless, claws like Scott's. She was forgetting her skin.

"Do you see that bay door over there? That's where we're going," Carlos said. "I'll figure out how to open it once we get there."

Phoenix didn't see the bay door, in truth—the lights Carlos had turned on were too bright—but she heaved her shoulder against the piano, her head lolling with exhaustion. She didn't need to see where she was going. She would get there, by and by.

What's your name? She couldn't remember how to answer the question, until the scent of gasoline woke her up.

"Carlos . . ." she began.

"I smell it," he said, grunting. "There are oil spots on the floor, so people park down here. There may not be any gas cans, but I'll find something. Don't worry. Let's get to the alley. Hold on, Phee. We're almost there."

While Carlos flipped on more lights and tried to find a way to control the aluminum bay door, Phoenix leaned against the piano, craving support. A splinter pierced her skin right above her elbow, but she barely felt it. Most of her body felt numb, and the rest was already in pain.

Was that the sound of *Sarge* laughing, somewhere close to here?

A clang and a loud whirring chased Sarge's laughter away. Phoenix smelled humid air as the bay door slid open, letting in the night sky. Phoenix looked outside, and a large ramp was already in place, affixed to the wide doorway. She had known she was supposed to bring the piano here, but the affirmation felt good. A streetlamp made the alley golden.

"Step back," Carlos said.

Carlos rearranged the hand truck so that he was behind the piano, and he pushed. The piano's weight forced the Rosenkranz to slide down the ramp, ancient wheels growling across the surface. In an instant, the piano was at the center of the narrow alleyway, beneath the last rung of the fire escape. The closest thing to it was a Dumpster.

Someone squeezed her shoulders from behind, saying something close to her ear, but she couldn't make out his voice anymore. Her ears were failing her. Her lungs, too. When she breathed, sand sifted through her lungs and tried to climb into her throat. The pain was dazzling.

Clipped before she could fly. Stories untold, sent back to the sky.

She turned around to ask who she was, but he was gone. He had told her where he was going, but she had forgotten. Looking for gasoline? That might be it.

But she couldn't wait. She grabbed the first bottle she found in her pocket. It took her an eternity to unscrew the pink cap with such numb fingers, but she finally got it open, tossing liquid across the piano keys until the bottle was empty. Then, she shook the last droplets out on the piano as if she were seasoning a meal.

Her hand trembling, she searched her pocket for the lighter next. She found it, using both hands to try to coax out a flame.

"Wait," a voice said, startling her. She expected to see Scott, but she didn't quite recognize the face he was wearing. "If you want to burn it right, use this."

The scent from the unmarked clear jug was strong enough to make his point. With a wild swing, she emptied the jug's contents across the piano's case, dragging herself from one corner to the next, making it glisten. She drenched the two candelabra last, filling their cups until they overflowed.

You don't even know your name. You've died a dozen times already. Somewhere, you were never born. A voice mocked her; not quite a whisper, and not quite human.

And the voice was right: She *didn't* know. She *didn't* remember. But she didn't have to.

Her hands couldn't negotiate the lighter—its operation baffled her, suddenly—so it fell while she grappled with it. She saw the glow of the pearl case as it skittered toward a sewer grill, but she was too tired to chase it. The man beside her swiped, rescuing it before the sewer swallowed it. The man created fire, it seemed, with a snap of his fingers.

The tiny flame fascinated her. He gave it to her, careful to press her numb finger where it needed to be so the flame wouldn't die.

"Ashes to ashes," he said.

"Amen," she finished, and lowered the flame to the middle C.

The Rosenkranz became a ball of angry fire, its keys blackened and consumed by flames. The piano's outrage shot fire into the sky, clawing for food, but there was nothing within its reach but asphalt and bricks. Even the Dumpster beside it refused to burn, protecting its trash.

Watching the spectacle of shooting flames, the veil across her memories faded. She couldn't pin down her name yet, but she remembered what she must do. Tonight, she would rest in the arms of the man her soul had loved since before she was born, reunited.

In a few hours, she would bury her father.

Tomorrow, she had music to write.

Don't wanna die for a while—

I think I'll fly for a while.

PHOENIX
"Gotta Fly"

FINALE

Soon

"Test, test, test—one two, one two."

The microphone was hot, so it squealed under Phoenix's breath. La'Keitha strummed a charging minor-seventh chord on her Fender, and her impatient feedback fed the screeching. Jabari and Devon covered their ears. When the sound guy went red in the face, racing to adjust the levels as if Phoenix would have him beheaded, she smiled at him: *No big deal, man.* Andres scraped his gourd-shaped *guido*, working out rhythms in his head, burning off his nerves. Andres rarely spoke a word before a show, keeping his head bowed, hiding his face behind his sheet of limp brown hair. Phoenix wondered how a man so shy could make his living on the stage.

With two hours before showtime, the tables were still empty, but there were already two dozen people at the Scott Joplin House, clumped inconspicuously in the back, against the wood-paneled wall of the recreated Rosebud Bar. Every time Phoenix looked up, another person or two had appeared, silent arrivals. Gloria hadn't wanted to open the doors yet, but Phoenix didn't care who sat in on the sound check. Besides, the people inside were either press or had friends who worked here, so what could she do? It didn't cost her anything to let them watch.

Gloria came behind her to give her a gloom report. "Some of them have cameras, Phee."

"It's just music," Phoenix said. "It belongs to them already."

"Hey, not *my* part, sister," Jabari muttered. "My part belongs to my landlord."

"I don't care if it's a phone, a pencil eraser, a shoelace, whatever—if I see anyone shooting video with *anything*, they're out." Gloria sounded more like Sarge all the time. That helped, some days. Other days, nothing helped except knowing where he was. Laughter and light.

"Do what you gotta do, cuz. Make yourself happy." The chords to "Gotta Fly," the first song on the set list, were playing in Phoenix's head. She was far away from her cousin's turmoil.

"Don't kick out any fine ones, Glo," Jabari said.

Instead of answering, Gloria gave Jabari the finger before she left the stage, a heartfelt stab. Gloria was a fool if she couldn't see how much Jabari liked her, Phoenix thought, and he was a fool if he didn't tell her soon. Their stubbornness wasn't cute anymore. Philadelphia had been insufferable, with the games those two kept playing.

"Good luck at the Grammys, Phoenix!" a man called from the back, and the watchers erupted into unrestrained applause. They weren't press, then; they were fans. Or, maybe both.

Phoenix felt a ripple through the band. They had just gotten their heads together since last week's nomination announcement, and she hoped their minds wouldn't scatter again. The band had endured oblivion, but she wasn't sure they could weather what was coming now. Jabari gave a cocky grin, flinging his long dreadlocks over his shoulder while he fingered a quick bass line to "For the Love of Money" by the O'Jays, and Devon revved up his turntables, scratching a lead-in to a bomb bass-and-cowbell beat that had the younger watchers swaying before Devon pulled his white fedora over his eyes and stepped away from his instrument, always a tease.

"We won't need luck. We're the *soon-to-be* Grammy-winning Phoenix & Fire," La'Keitha said, one arm raised in a fist that reminded Phoenix of Sarges. "Luck is for posers. I just feel bad for the lip-synch posse about to get shamed."

"Everybody needs luck, so thanks," Phoenix said into her mike, loud enough to talk over La'Keitha. The last thing they needed was a self-worship service before a show, even if La'Keitha's guitar was as good as its hype. "It's good to be playing together again, and we're humbled someone hears us."

Phoenix & Fire. The *New* Fire didn't sound right anymore, although T.'s raps and Devon's turntable wizardry as MC Matrix made them sound newer than ever. The planet's most powerful element needed no qualifier. Besides, you couldn't go back. Nothing stayed the same.

A woman's voice called out. "You seen any ghosts lately, Phoenix?"

Phoenix couldn't miss Gloria's I-told-you-so gaze from the bar counter. Maybe it *wasn't* a great idea to have a crowd at sound-check, if they were bold enough to start asking questions.

"No ghosts," Phoenix said, trying not to sound weary. Ghost questions had been unavoidable on her solo tour, but this was an old conversation. She wasn't interested in being the poster girl for every ghostbuster and psychic wannabe. That wasn't her fight. Everyone would learn what they needed to know before long.

"There are no ghosts here," Van Milton spoke up, "but there *is* a fine museum next door."

Phoenix hadn't seen Milton come in, and the sight of him made her smile. She unhooked her Liberation and left it on the stand so she could walk up to Milton and give him a hug. Milton reminded her of her father, if Sarge's life had been more gentle. "See? You didn't believe me. Told you we'd come," Phoenix said, rubbing his bald scalp.

"Seeing is believing. Phoenix, we're honored. It's a wonderful thing you're doing." The curator waved to a white man across the room, beckoning. "You remember Ed Berlin."

Edward A. Berlin was a pleasant-featured man with glasses and a full head of graying hair that always looked slightly windswept. Phoenix hadn't seen Scott Joplin's biographer in at least a year, maybe more. His last contact had been an impassioned e-mail begging her not to use Scott Joplin's name on her *Joplin's Ghost* CD if the pieces were not authentic Joplin. Phoenix had given up on convincing her most vocal skeptic, so she was surprised to see him now.

"Hell must be frozen over somewhere," Phoenix said, shaking Berlin's hand.

The scholar looked sheepish. "We've had disagreements, but I can appreciate a wonderful composer. I'm on a research trip, and Van said your band was here. I didn't want to miss it."

"No ragtime today, though," she warned him. "This is Phoenix & Fire."

Berlin looked offended. "I hope you don't think rags are all I listen to. I'm a little more well rounded than that."

"My fault," Phoenix said. "Seriously, thanks for coming. It means a lot."

"No, *you* mean a lot, Phoenix," Berlin said, his reserve melting. "I'm very impressed with your Scott Joplin Adopt-a-Piano program. What a brilliant way to keep Scott Joplin alive."

"That's not just me. You can thank G-Ronn for that."

Phoenix and Ronn didn't see each other much nowadays—hardly at all since Sarge's funeral, except for occasional brushes backstage when their paths crossed—but when she'd called to ask if Ronn would donate money to help her launch a program to put pianos and electric key-boards in the homes of inner-city schoolchildren who wanted to learn how to play, he donated a million dollars. Between Ronn's involvement and the proceeds from *Rising* and the off-Broadway and CD versions of *Joplin's Ghost,* the program was a pet charity, always in the news. Her mother was promising to step in as head of the board of directors, so Phoenix figured any kid under the sun who wanted a piano would be able to have one soon.

"Don't let her be modest," Van said. "Phoenix is the spirit behind it."

Berlin put his hand on Milton's shoulder. "Van, what were you telling me about those schoolchildren here in St. Louis?"

"Cutting contests," Milton said, grinning. "Little seventh graders competing after school, playing Joplin. I'm trying to put together a regional contest here this spring. We're finding some talented young people, and they take to the piano like ducks to water."

"They've always been there," Phoenix said.

Berlin chuckled. "It shouldn't surprise me, because I know ragtime's roots, but I never thought I'd see this interest in the music again. I thought times were too different," Berlin said, then he sighed, studying her eyes. An argument was on the way, she thought. Berlin lowered his voice. "Now Phoenix, as much as I admire 'Lenox Avenue Rag' and *Symphony No. 1,* you'll never convince me that's authentic Scott Joplin music on your CD. Sorry."

Phoenix shrugged. "Can't convince everybody," she said. She knew, and her family knew, and that was plenty. That was enough.

"But it's top-flight ragtime, and I congratulate you," Berlin said.

"Even if I don't think you channeled him, I do think Scott Joplin is watching all this and smiling somewhere."

"Hope so," Phoenix said, but that wasn't true. She knew Scott wasn't sweating about who was paying attention to him and who wasn't anymore, a lesson she hoped she had learned from him. Scott had left those worries far behind.

La'Keitha sounded her Fender again, challenging her with the intro to "Gotta Fly."

"Hey, Phee, is this a sound check or a press conference?" La'Keitha called.

Phoenix shot her a look and turned back to the scholars. "Sorry for my friend's manners."

"What manners?" T. said, and the group snickered behind her.

"No, no, don't let us keep you," said Milton. "Go, Phoenix. Be a star."

The stage was too crowded. The Rosebud was intended for ragtime concerts with a single piano, not a full band. But this was a special event, a limited-seating fund-raiser for the Joplin House, so nobody would mind the way they looked as long as the music was good. Besides, they had more room here than they'd had in her parents' garage in Cutler Ridge.

As Phoenix strapped on her Liberation, she noticed that the audience of early arrivals had grown. By now, the more determined had claimed the tables in the front, and the growing crowd reminded Phoenix of the arena audiences that followed her from city to city: New Age ghost-lovers, young music fans and ragtime die-hards. Their dress ranged from tie-dye and sandals to suits and ties to hip-hop chic, but they had her music in common.

Phoenix was intrigued by a black couple sitting near the stage, especially the young man. Early- to mid-twenties, close-cropped hair. Tree-trunk shoulders. The name popped to her like a childhood memory: *Kendrick Allen Hart.* She had met him in another life.

Andres was already counting off with his drumsticks, so Phoenix didn't have time to walk over and say hello. But she found his eyes and smiled with a *Whassup, Kendrick* nod. Kendrick's grin filled the room.

People liked being remembered. Kendrick's date looked at him with new eyes, shocked and impressed. Phoenix knew that feeling well.

"... *Three ... four ...* "

The sound of Phoenix & Fire brought the Rosebud Bar back to life.

*H*ey, have you seen Carlos?" Phoenix asked, pulling Gloria away from her plate.

In the hour left before the show, the band had escaped to a meeting room upstairs to eat a catered meal of St.-Louis-style barbecue, Milton's thank-you. Downstairs, the audience was a throng already.

"Haven't seen Carlos in a while," Gloria said. She licked barbecue sauce from her pinky in a delicate way only she could master. "Not since he said he was taking a tour of the house."

Gloria said it casually, but there was nothing casual about that, and she knew it. *That* was a surprise, from Carlos. He almost hadn't come with her for this concert, since he had fallen out of the habit of trailing after her on tour. He had his life, too.

But this was different. This was Scott's house. She had thought it should matter.

Phoenix knew she had only convinced Carlos to come because it was a one-day gig, and she had promised him Sunday in St. Louis to themselves, a vacation. Her project was due in her electronic music class at USC's Thornton School of Music on Tuesday anyway, so her real life was still back in Los Angeles. She had to stay in the habit of spending time with him, or they were in trouble. They almost hadn't survived the two years she'd dedicated to *Joplin's Ghost,* and she understood why. Carlos had loved Joplin's music long before he met her, but their experiences had flavored Joplin with something he didn't like the taste of. Too much history, in every way.

"Where are you going?" Gloria said, when Phoenix turned to walk away.

"To find my man," Phoenix said. She nodded toward Jabari, who was laughing across the room with T. over a plastic cup of beer from the keg. "You should take the hint."

Gloria feigned disgust, shaking her head. "No way. Too effing immature. He's not ready." *She's in love, and she knows it,* Phoenix thought.

And Jabari *wasn't* ready. It was hard to grow up while you were getting famous, and love was scary. Love might be the scariest thing.

"Then trust yourself, Glo," Phoenix said. "I'll be back."

"Like hell. You're not walking over there by yourself."

"Excuse me? I'm not an invalid."

"No, you're not. You're *Phoenix,* which is worse. I'm walking you over."

Phoenix tried not to hear the steady hum of two hundred excited voices as she and Gloria got out of the elevator and slipped out of the Rosebud's side door. Milton was going to have crowd management problems, she thought. This wasn't the chaos at Staples Center, but small audiences jostled her stomach, too, at least until the set started. She had been surprised by the classical music Grammy nomination for *Joplin's Ghost*—she hadn't won, and hadn't expected to, given the controversy—but she hadn't performed that night. No pressure. This time, Gloria said the Grammy people had already scheduled them. *That* would be interesting.

You got me here, Daddy. I know you're still watching us.

Phoenix and Gloria crossed the wooden walkway from the Rosebud to the Joplin House, where a uniformed female employee was guarding the locked door. "Yeah, he's still up there," the woman said, standing aside. "I would remember seeing that fine-ass man come back down."

Phoenix blocked Gloria in the doorway. "I'm not playing, Glo. I'm fine. Nobody's gonna come snatch me with locked doors and a guard."

In Gloria's eyes, Phoenix saw the Osiris again, always at the edges. Time didn't erase it, and neither did the truce between Ronn and DJ Train. And, there was more than the Osiris at stake, Phoenix remembered: Her life had changed the last time she walked into the place where Scott Joplin lived. She couldn't expect it to be nothing.

"*Cuidado,* cuz," Gloria said, and hugged Phoenix at the door. "Love you."

"Love you, too, cuz."

Crossing through the museum lobby to the doorway to the adjoining town house, the one painted 2658-A MORGAN on the door, Phoenix's stomach bloated. It was the usual stage fright, and something new: She was nervous about being here. Funny how she'd hidden that from herself. How had she thought this would be easy?

The hall leading to Scott's home *was* brighter. Maybe it was only because the paint was a different color, a vibrant yellow, but the day's last light shone across Scott's floor in a way it didn't shine two steps before his threshold. When she touched the pipe banister to climb the stairs, the same thought came that had come the first time: *He touched this.*

It was the closest she would come to touching Scott again. In one way, the banister's solidity was soothing; in another, the distance felt cruel, unnecessary. Touching the banister was like remembering how Sarge's face looked at the Osiris after her set. Bittersweet. She wished she could have lived here with Scott, in the days before his promise became a burden.

It was a long climb up Scott Joplin's stairs.

Phoenix knew to go to the parlor first, because she was sure that was where he would be. She saw the room in her mind before reality came on her imagination's heels, everything in place: He was standing at the parlor window, staring outside, beside a chair and a small Victorian table with a globe-shaped lamp. This room was a portal, like before.

"Hey," she said, whispering.

Carlos turned around slowly. He smiled, but didn't answer. The light through the window was so brilliant, she couldn't make out all the features of his face.

"Well?" she said. "How is it?"

Carlos sighed, gazing at the ceiling, toward the fireplace, and, lastly, at the nondescript black upright piano against the wall, a random antique standing in for whichever one had been here for Scott, before the bitterness came. Carlos stared at the piano a long time.

"It's quiet," he said. "He's not here. Just like you said. Whatever you did, he's gone."

"He needed to be quiet," she said. "He deserved it."

Phoenix was glad Scott had escaped this room, and her gladness overcame the part of her that hated his absence. It wasn't as bad as missing Sarge, but the loss was magnified here. She was a hundred years too late, or Scott might have come around the corner with a smile and "Weeping Willow" in his hands, the ink not yet dry on the pages.

Carlos slid his arm around Phoenix's waist as she joined him at the window. Outside, there were cars parked everywhere, like the bustling city street it had been in Scott's time. But these cars were here for *her.*

"I thought you had a concert," Carlos said.

"Soon, but I always have time for you," she said. "Are you glad you came here?"

"I think so," Carlos said. "But . . . I wanted to feel something. Recognition. A glow."

Phoenix's heart jumped. "*You* have the glow, Carlos," she said.

Carlos sighed. Then, he grabbed her hand and walked her away from the window, across the parlor and through the entryway to the adjoining bedroom, which was darker, suddenly personal. The shaving mirror gleamed as if Scott's face could be hidden inside of it.

Carlos steered her toward the bed. "Let's lie down a second, Phoenix."

She resisted, laughing. "This is a museum. Van Milton would kill me."

"This is more than a museum to us," Carlos said, finding the spot behind her knees that made them collapse, so she slid on top of him, his hands bracing her buttocks. He had a gift for making her body do what he wanted, as if he'd mapped her. "Besides, Van Milton would love it. He'd post a sign over the bed: *Phoenix's ass was here*. And charge extra admission."

"You are a bad and evil man," Phoenix said. "That's not even a little bit nice." Milton was a true believer, mistaking her for something more than she was. Phoenix tolerated Milton's worship better than Carlos did. She couldn't have done *Joplin's Ghost* justice without Milton's help finding its audience.

But the thought of Milton's indignation couldn't keep Phoenix from enjoying her slow recline on top of Carlos as he lay down flat on the thin mattress. She couldn't resist the invitation of the brass bedposts. She welcomed the scent of the quilt, which was clean, but smelled its age.

The bed was tiny, and the room was too narrow for one much bigger. Maybe that had been the fashion then; she couldn't remember. Scott and his wife must have slept very close. You couldn't get lost through the night the way she and Carlos did in her king-sized bed.

"I'm about to disappoint you, Phee," Carlos said. "So, I'm sorry."

Phoenix prepared herself to grieve again. He was going to tell her that although he loved Phoenix Smalls, he couldn't share a life with *Phoenix*. "What do you mean?"

Carlos's face shimmered, sad. "What you believe about me isn't true."

"What do I believe about you?"

He waited a long time. "You think Scott Joplin is hiding inside me somewhere."

Put that way, it sounded silly. That was why she didn't say it often, because spoken words were so awkward. But after she and Carlos burned the piano in the alley outside The Harbor, after Sarge's burial day, she had tried to put it in words for him:

Think about it, Carlos. We loved each other as soon as we met, like Scott and Freddie. You're older than I am, just like Scott was older than Freddie. You don't play the piano, but music is in your soul. When I dreamed he was touching me, you were the one touching me instead. You helped me free him, and you helped me get free of him. I know I was Freddie once, because while I was gone, I felt what she felt. When I was gone, I knew Scott was you.

"I never said he's *hiding* in you, exactly," Phoenix said. "But, OK."

Carlos spoke very quietly, as if he were whipping her and wanted to apply his lashes as gently as possible. "I *want* to believe it, for your sake, because you went through this awful ordeal, a loss no one but you can understand, and I want to be there for you . . ."

"You *were* there for me," she reminded him, and wiped a quick tear from her eye. What he had done at The Harbor still touched her, given that they had been strangers then. Sort of.

"I want to believe what you believe about timeless love, two souls who find each other after a tragedy and get to live the life that was interrupted. But I feel like a fraud, Phee. I've been here in this house more than an hour, no interruptions, and it's just not there. Even at the piano—nothing. I don't feel him in me. I only feel me in here." His gaze didn't blink.

"We don't live their lives, Carlos. We live new lives."

An angry car horn sounded from outside, a new arrival anxious to hear her. Phoenix felt her nerves again, internal pressure squirming. High expectations were waiting on that stage.

"If we're going to do this," he said, bumping her nose, "Carlos Harris has to be enough."

"What?"

"You have to want *me,* not a fantasy. I'm a magazine writer who's won a couple of awards. I know a few things about music, and I'm good at what I do. I pay taxes and honor my parents. But I'm not Scott Joplin, Phoenix. I never was, and I never will be."

He never stopped searching for reasons she might get tired of him, she thought.

"Carlos, I never asked you to be Scott. I'm not Freddie either, not anymore. I just *was*. Of course it's enough if you're Carlos. You're the one I want."

"But you won't stop believing we've met before," Carlos said, not convinced.

She smiled. "No, I won't. I know it."

"Why do you think that?" he said, his face suddenly earnest. "*How* do you know?"

And there it was, of course: The question with no answer.

"I just do," she said. "I know where I was. I know you were there, too."

With the sound of the car's horn gone, the room sang in its silence. Carlos raised his head, no longer looking at her even as she stayed perched across his chest, riding his slow breathing. Neither of them spoke for a long time, enjoying the hush. This room was theirs now. This bed belonged only to them.

"Maybe I hear it," Carlos said. "I think so."

"What?" She was hoping he could put a name to it.

Carlos smiled, his eyes unfocused. "Music," he said.

Of course. That was the thing about Scott Joplin's house.

Music lived in the very walls.

Author's Note

In 1995, while I was on my first book tour promoting my first novel, *The Between,* a bespectacled man waited to talk to me when the modest crowd thinned at a now-defunct bookstore in St. Louis. This erudite, rational-seeming man told me he was the curator of the Scott Joplin House, then he fascinated me with tales about what he believed were encounters with the ghost of Scott Joplin. *A lampshade suddenly askew after being straightened the moment before. A man standing in the room, gone an instant later.* The curator's name was Jan Hamilton Douglas. (I recreated his claims within this book's text, when Phoenix visits the Joplin House and Van Milton tells her about the ghost.)

I was intrigued by his stories, but my schedule didn't permit a visit to the Joplin House. Instead, I scribbled some notes about the meeting in my journal, kept his business card, and wondered if a future story might bloom from our meeting.

I should say this: I do not write about the supernatural because of my own experiences. I often joke that I don't have a psychic bone in my body, so a ghost could be sitting on my lap and I would never know. My stories about the supernatural are shaped by conjecture and conversations with readers and sources who are insistent about the things that have happened to *them.* So, my interest in Joplin's ghost was purely in terms of what kind of story it might become. How might those encounters impact a character's life? What might a ghost encounter *really* be like, as opposed to what we see in movies? Something about those stories Jan Hamilton Douglas told me felt real, even if they were only his imagination.

I didn't think of the first real pieces of *Joplin's Ghost* until late in 2002, more than five years later—a story about a turn-of-the-century artist whose genius went largely unrecognized in an era of intense racism and a contemporary character suppressing her creative voice for fear of failure.

While I was planning the novel, I did a silly thing: Rather than calling Jan Hamilton Douglas right away to tell him I had a story idea for his ghost, I got it in my head to surprise him when I could make a research trip to St. Louis. When I finally made it to the Scott Joplin House in the spring of 2003, I learned that Jan Hamilton Douglas had passed away suddenly six months before. What a loss! Not only had I lost my primary souce, but everything I have learned about Jan Hamilton Douglas since tells me that he would have been an extraordinary person to know.

Still, the staff of the Joplin House was very welcoming. I visited the parlor Mr. Douglas had mentioned, and of course I experienced none of what he had described. No Scott Joplin. But there were two odd developments: In the Rosebud Cafe annex of the museum (a project Mr. Douglas oversaw and, ironically, the site where he died), the employees are displayed in a row of photographs. For two weeks after Mr. Douglas's passing, I was told, his photo fell to the floor and had to be hung again several times. Also, while I sat at a table in the Rosebud to begin my interviews, the door leading outside, which was beside me, swung open on its own.

Bad hinges? A strong wind? I can't say.

Research for this book also took me to ghost-hunter Lawana Holland-Moore and renowned psychic Jeffrey A. Wands, both of whom I interviewed by telephone. Jeffrey happens to share my publisher, and I'd heard stories of his visits to my publisher's office, where he amazed the employees with his readings. My main concern was to depict the psychics in my novel as accurately as possible, not to get a reading of any kind—but in the midst of the interview, Jeffrey told me a few noteworthy things about Freddie Alexander (Joplin's wife), as well as my own late grandmother.

He also made a suggestion for the story involving a music stand.

When I didn't respond to the idea right away, Jeffrey said, "That wasn't from me. That was from Joplin."

Did I use the suggestion? Ultimately, no. Whether or not Scott Joplin was being channeled that day, my attitude remains the same: *Thanks, dear sir, but I'll do it my way.*

Sorry, Scott. But I hope you like the story you inspired anyway, wherever you are.

Acknowledgments

Thanks to Edward A. Berlin, author of *King of Ragtime: Scott Joplin and His Era* (Oxford University Press, 1995), whose scholarship on Scott Joplin uncovered the existence of Freddie Alexander, Joplin's ill-fated young bride. Thank you for your tireless research on Joplin and ragtime, and for your indulgence in reading several early chapters of this book. Any mistakes herein are the author's responsibility, not yours. Read about more of his work at www.edwardaberlin.com.

Thanks to the staff at the Scott Joplin House at 2658 Delmar Boulevard in St. Louis, particularly Steve Hinson, Chantelle Moten and former site administrator William F. Hall, for your hospitality and knowledge. Also, thanks to the new site administrator, Victoria Love. The work you do is vital in keeping the memory of Scott Joplin alive. See the website at www.mostateparks.com/scottjoplin.htm. (No, as far as I know, there is no ghost there.) Also, thanks to Jason D. Stratman at the Missouri Historical Society.

Thanks to writer and pop culture guru Touré, for breaking it down. Thanks to Reginald R. Robinson, an extraordinary ragtime composer and performer—and winner of a 2004 MacArthur Foundation Genius Grant—for sharing your story and lovely compositions. Thanks to entertainment manager Jerome Martine. Thanks to Angelia Bibbs-Saunders at the Recording Academy. Thanks to psychic Jeffrey Wands, author of *The Psychic in You: Understand and Harness Your Natural Psychic Power* (Atria Books, 2004). And thanks to ghost-hunter Lawana Holland-Moore, at www.DCghosts.com.

Thanks to researcher Kenya Mosley and music writer and author Bill Campbell. Thanks to Chris Webber and Karen Wilson, for the time I spent with your lovely Rosenkranz piano. Thanks to Michael and Sally M. Snell of Shade of the Cottonwood, L.L.C., for searching for an interview with Jan Hamilton Douglas so I could hear his ghost stories again. See a lovely photo of Jan Hamilton Douglas at Snell's website at www.shadeofthecottonwood.com/Pages/a04.html.

To Darryl Miller, for making a significant contribution as an advance reader—and who could change my mind even when Joplin's ghost himself could not. And to Olympia Duhart, for her insights as an advance reader and her ongoing friendship.

To novelist Lewis Shiner, for writing *Glimpses* (William Murrow, 1993) and *Say Goodbye: The Laurie Moss Story* (St. Martins Press, 1999). To Kathi Kamen Goldmark and Dave Barry, for giving me so many unforgettable experiences singing and playing keyboard during concerts with the Rock Bottom Remainders. Under her "Don't Quit Your Day Job" Records label, Kathi also included me—along with Stephen King, Maya Angelou, Norman Mailer, and others—on the music CD *Stranger Than Fiction*. I sang Tina Turner's version of "Proud Mary," with the late Warren Zevon singing Ike Turner's part. Check out the label's site at www.dqydj.comprod15.htm.

Thanks to my amazing husband, Steven Barnes, who compels me to be my best self and, most of all, to explore the places I am afraid to go.

And to Mom, Dad, Johnita, Lydia, Nicki and Jason . . . always.

*E*xperience Joplin's music for yourself in the following CDs I recommend: *Scott Joplin: Piano Rags,* recorded by pianist Johsua Rifkin for Nonesuch Records; and the Original Cast Recording of the Houston Grand Opera's performance of Joplin's surviving opera, *Treemonisha*. There are many other recordings to choose from, but those will get you started. Enjoy.